EROTICA.

THE

ELEGIES OF PROPERTIUS,

THE

SATYRICON OF PETRONIUS ARBITER,

AND THE

KISSES OF JOHANNES SECUNDUS.

LITERALLY TRANSLATED, AND ACCOMPANIED BY POETICAL
VERSIONS FROM VARIOUS SOURCES.

TO WHICH ARE ADDED,

THE

LOVE EPISTLES OF ARISTÆNETUS.

TRANSLATED BY R. BRINSLEY SHERIDAN AND MR. HALHED.

EDITED

BY WALTER K. KELLY.

Fredonia Books
Amsterdam, The Netherlands

Erotica: The Elegies of Propertius, The Satyricon of Petronius Arbiter, The Kisses of Johannes Secundus, and The Love Epistles of Aristænetus

Edited by Walter K. Kelly

ISBN: 1-4101-0444-3

Copyright © 2004 by Fredonia Books

Reprinted from the 1854 edition

Fredonia Books
Amsterdam, The Netherlands
http://www.fredoniabooks.com

PREFACE.

THE prose translation of Propertius in the present
volume (from the pen of Mr. Gantillon, of St. John's
College, Cambridge) is based upon the text of the poet's
latest and best editor, Mr. Paley. Subjoined are some
metrical versions by Nott and Elton, being all those
which a careful search has discovered to us among the
writings of Englishmen. Dr. Nott is prone to the use
of strangely dissonant rhymes, such as *thee, delay ;
foretell, feel ; traduce, house,* &c. These blemishes it
has been attempted in several instances to remove by the
substitution of new lines enclosed between brackets.

The poems of Propertius seem to claim a sort of pre-
scriptive right to be associated with those of Catullus
and Tibullus ; but the latter already fill a volume in
this series, and of the other Latin poets not yet included in the Classical Library, the best would each
occupy a volume by itself. In giving a companion
therefore to Propertius, we have thought it better to
choose a work of substantial merit, like the Satyricon
of Petronius, than to sacrifice to a merely formal
arrangement considerations of more real importance.
The curious romance of Petronius has unfortunately
come down to us in a very mutilated state ; a circum-

stance which suggested to a certain Francis Nodot
the idea of publishing at Rotterdam what professed to
be the complete Satyricon, taken, it was said, from a
MS. found at the capture of Belgrade in 1688. Nodot's
additions are manifestly spurious; but as they serve in
a manner to fill up the breaks in the story, they are
usually printed in modern editions along with the genuine text, distinguished from it by a difference of type.
The same arrangement has been observed in this translation, for the whole of which the editor of the present
volume is responsible.

The remaining space has been devoted, not incon-
gruously, it is believed, to the Basia of Johannes Secundus, a work which, though written in the sixteenth
century, has attained the rank of a classic; and to the
lively and graceful Love Epistles of Aristænetus, which
belong to the Classical period, and are so agreeably
rendered by Sheridan and Halhed.

                                    W. K. K.

CONTENTS.

THE ELEGIES OF PROPERTIUS.

BOOK I.

THE SATYRICON OF TITUS PETRONIUS ARBITER.

THE KISSES OF JOHANNES SECUNDUS.

PIECES BY VARIOUS AUTHORS.

THE LOVE EPISTLES OF ARISTÆNETUS.

THE

ELEGIES OF PROPERTIUS.

BOOK I.[1]

ELEGY I.[2] TO TULLUS.

CYNTHIA'S eyes first took me, poor unfortunate, captive, previously affected by no passion: then did Love[3] cast down my resolute, disdainful eyes, and set foot on my neck : till in time he taught me, desperate power! to despise chaste maidens,[4] and to live recklessly. Even now, my present mad pursuit flags not after a whole year, though I am forced to have the gods opposed to me. Milanion, Tullus, by shrinking from no

[1] *Book I.*] The title of this used to be "Sex. Aurel. Propertii Cynthia, Monobiblos," the latter epithet being supported by Ovid, *Rem. Am.* 764, "Cujus opus *Cynthia, sola* fuit." It was written and published before the author's other works, A. U. C. 728, probably when he was about twenty years of age, and is quoted by the title of Cynthia in ii. 24, 2, Quum sit toto *Cynthia* lecta foro.

[2] *Elegy I.*] The poet laments the obduracy of Cynthia, who is worse, he says, than Atalanta, who was, in time, won by Meilanion : he desires the aid of witches, calls on his friends to extricate him, and concludes by warning such as are happy in love to be faithful, or they will repent it. This Elegy is addressed to Tullus, a friend and equal in age of Propertius, for whom see vi., xiv., xxii. ; IV. xxii.

[3] Cf. ii. 30, 9, *Tollere* nusquam Te patietur *humo* lumina capta.

[4] *To despise chaste maidens.*] *Castas odisse puellas :* that is, says Paley, to speak and think of female virtue as mere prudery and affectation, and to dislike it as presenting an obstacle to possession. Kuinoel understands by it, to hate all girls that were not as loose in conduct as Cynthia. According to others, the "chaste maids" are Minerva and the Muses.

B

toils, broke down the stubborn cruelty of the daughter of Iasus:[1] for once he roamed of yore crazed with love, amid the caves of Parthenius,[2] and tracked the steps of shaggy wild beasts: stricken too by the club of Hylæus,[3] he groaned, in pain, among Arcadian rocks. Therefore was he able to tame the swift-footed damsel. Such is the force of prayers and good deeds in love. In me slow-witted Love devises no plans, and forgets to travel, as before, in the beaten paths. Come ye, that are skilled in bringing the moon down from the sky, and whose dread work it is to solemnize sacred rites with magic fire, come and turn the heart of my mistress, and make her more pale than myself. Then I may believe you able to draw down the stars, and turn the course of rivers by Cytæan[4] spells. And you, my friends, who attempt too late to cry me back who am already fallen, find some help for my wounded heart. I will bear the knife and torturing cautery unflinchingly: let me but have liberty to speak what my anger wills. Carry me to the end of the world, or over the seas, whither no woman can know my track. Remain ye, to whom the god lends a willing ear, and may ye meet with kindred feelings, and your love fear no danger. Me my Venus torments with bitter nights, and Love at no time grants me a respite. Avoid, I warn you, this woe; let each hold to his own beloved one, and let no one abandon his wonted love. But, if any one shall be slow to heed my warnings, alas! with how great grief will he remember my words!

ELEGY II.[5] TO CYNTHIA.

WHY delight, my life, in walking delicately with hair elaborately decked, and in fluttering the transparent folds of a

---

[1] *The daughter of Iasus.*] Atalanta, who though *velox,* a swift-footed huntress, is not to be confounded with her namesake, the daughter of Schœnus king of Scyros.

[2] *Parthenius.*] A mountain of Arcadia, on which Atalanta had, in infancy, been exposed.

[3] *Hylæus,*] ὑλαῖος, (wood-man,) a centaur who attempted to violate Atalanta and was killed by him: see Ovid, *Ar. Am.* ii. 191, who makes him use a bow.

[4] *Cytæan.*] Cyta, in Colchis, was the birth-place of Medea, hence called (infr. ii. 4, 7) Cytæis: the epithet is equivalent to *magic.*

[5] *Elegy II.*] The poet begs Cynthia not to be so fond of dress, arguing from nature and the example of ancient heroines, and concludes

Coan[1] vesture ? Why drench your hair with Syrian[2] myrrh ?
Why set yourself off[3] by artificial means, to spoil the grace
of nature by purchased adornment, and not suffer your
limbs to shine in their own loveliness. Believe me, there
is no improving beauty like yours by adventitious aid : genuine Love likes not a disguised form. See what beauteous
hues the earth produces ; how ivy grows better at its own
free will ; how the arbutus springs more fairly in solitary clefts
of the rock ; how the stream runs in channels never formed
by art ; how the shore produces, of its own accord, pebbles of
varied hue, the growth of itself ; and how birds sing not the
more sweetly by any art. Not in that way did Phœbe,[4] the
daughter of Leucippus, set Castor's heart on fire ; nor did her
sister, Hilaira,[4] make Pollux in love with her by her dress.
Not so, in days of yore, did the daughter of Evenus,[5] on the
banks of her father's stream, become the subject of strife between Idas and the amorous Phœbus : nor did Hippodamia,[6]
that was carried off in the chariot of a stranger, attract her
Phrygian husband by artificial beauty ; but she had a face indebted to no gems, and a skin like that seen on the canvass of
Apelles. Their aim was not to get lovers from every quarter :
modesty, beauty enough in itself, was theirs. I fear not now

by assuring her that he will ever love her for her mental gifts, provided
that she will live more modestly.

[1] *Coan.*] Cos (*Stanco*), an island in the Ægean Sea, was celebrated for
its delicate silks. See Hor. *Od.* iv. 13, 13 ; Tibull. ii. 3, 57.

[2] *Syrian.*] *Oronteus*, from Orontes, the river on which was Antioch, the
capital of Syria.

[3] *Vendere.* Cf. Juv. vii. 136, Vendunt amethystina.

[4] *Phœbe—Hilaira.*] Phœbe was a priestess of Athena, and Hilaira of
Artemis : they were carried off and married by the Dioscuri, and bore
them children.

[5] *The daughter,* &c.] Marpesa, the daughter of Evenus, was carried
off by Idas, the son of Aphareus ; Phœbus Apollo, who was also her
suitor, chased and overtook them, whereupon Idas and he fought for the
maiden, till separated by Jupiter, who left the decision with Marpesa, and
she chose Idas. Her father had, at the first, pursued Idas and her, to the
banks of the Lycormas, and, on not being able to come up with them,
had thrown himself into the river, which was ever afterwards called by
his name.

[6] *Hippodamia.*] She was the daughter of Œnomaus, king of Pisa
in Elis, and was married by Pelops, after he had treacherously vanquished
her father in the chariot-race, and killed him. See Eur. Iph. T. ad
init.

lest you appear to me less worthy than these,—if she please one man a girl is sufficiently adorned,—since Phœbus favours you especially with his gift of song, and Calliope willingly adds the Aonian lyre;[1] a surpassing sweetness is not wanting in your language, and you have everything that Venus or Minerva loves. With these gifts you shall always be most pleasing to me, provided that you despise paltry gauds.

ELEGY III.[2] TO CYNTHIA.

LIKE to the Gnossian maid[3] as she lay, exhausted, on the solitary shore, whilst the ship of Theseus sped away; like to Andromeda,[4] the daughter of Cepheus, as she slept in her first sleep, released, at length, from the hard rocks; or like as when a Bacchante,[5] wearied with constant dancing, falls down on the banks of the grassy Apidanus:[6] like to these did Cynthia, with her head resting at ease on her hands, seem to me to breathe softly in her slumber, while I, drunk with much wine, walked with tottering gait, and the boys shook the torches at the midnight hour. I tried to lay myself gently on the couch by her side, having not yet lost all my senses; and although doubly fired, and urged on one side by Love, on the other by Bacchus, each a powerful god, to place my arm under her gently as she lay, and to put my hand to her lips

[1] *Aonian lyre.*] Aonia was a district in Bœotia, so called after Aon, the son of Poseidon: hence the Muses, from frequenting Mt. Helicon in Bœotia, are called Aoniæ sorores.

[2] *Elegy III.*] The poet, coming home elevated with wine, finds Cynthia asleep, but will not wake her: the moonlight at length arousing her, she reproaches him with leaving her so long.

[3] *Ariadne,* the daughter of Minos, king of Crete, whom Theseus deserted at Naxos.

[4] *Andromeda.*] The daughter of Cepheus, king of Æthiopia, and Cassiopeia: her mother boasted of her beauty, and said that she surpassed the Nereids: for this the country was inundated, and a sea-monster sent into the land. The giving of Andromeda to the monster stopped these two visitations. Perseus found her in that situation; slew the monster; and married her. See Ovid, *Met.* iv. 663 seq.

[5] *A Bacchante.*] The Edones were a people in Thrace, one of the principal seats of Bacchantic worship, whence Edonis signifies "*a Bacchante.*"

[6] *Apidanus,* was a river in Thessaly, tributary to the Peneus; now Sataldge.

and steal a kiss; yet I dared not disturb the rest of my mistress, fearing her stinging reproaches that I had before experienced: but I remained as I was, with my eyes fixed on her in ardent gaze, as Argus at the first sight of the horns of *Io*, the daughter of Inachus. At one time I loosened the chaplets from my forehead, and placed them on your temples, Cynthia: at another I amused myself by confining your truant tresses, or placing apples, stealthily, in the hollows of your hands: and I gave all my gifts to thankless sleep, gifts that often slipt from your slant bosom. And whenever at times your form moved and you heaved a sigh, my credulous soul was confounded by the idle presage, lest any unwonted vision was affrighting you; lest some one was forcing you against your will to be his. At length, piercing through the casement opposite her couch, the Moon, the officious Moon, with light that should have lingered, opened, by its gentle beams, her closed eyelids. Then resting on her elbow on the downy couch, "So, at last," she said, "another's contemptuous treatment has driven you from her closed doors, back to my bed. Where have you been spending the long hours of a night promised to me, and now come wearied to me, when the stars are gone? May you, wretch, endure the agony of such nights as you are constantly bidding me have, to my sorrow. At one time I tried to drive away sleep by my purple embroidery, and when tired of that, then with playing on my Orphean lyre. At one time, in my solitude, I kept quietly groaning over the long time spent by you in another's embrace: until, at last, slumber fanned me with his soft wings, and bade me yield; that was the last remedy for my tears.

ELEGY IV.[1] TO BASSUS.[2]

WHY do you try, Bassus, by praising so many maids, to make me change and leave my mistress? Why will you not suffer me to spend what life I have left in my present bondage, to

---

[1] *Elegy IV.*] He reproaches Bassus with attempting to wean him from Cynthia, who, he assures him, (vs. 21,) will take signal vengeance; and concludes by praising Cynthia's fidelity, and praying that it may last.

[2] *Bassus.*] This is, possibly, the poet mentioned by Ovid (Tristia iv. 10, 47) as "clarus Iambo:" we find another addressed by Persius in his sixth Satire.

which I am more accustomed. Though you talk of the beauty
of Antiope,[1] the daughter of Nycteus, and extol to the skies
the Spartan Hermione,[2] and all that an age famed for pro-
ducing fair women bore, Cynthia will not allow them to have
any name: much less, if she be compared with trivial beauties,
needs she fear the disgrace of being pronounced inferior even
by a fastidious judge. But this forms the slightest portion of
my passion for her; there are more weighty reasons, Bassus,
for which I am contented to perish with love: her native hue,
the grace in every limb, and the delights that her embraces
yield. Besides, the more you strive to part our loves, the more
will each of us continue to baffle you, as we have pledged our
faith. You shall not have the credit of this with impunity:
the girl, whose love for me approaches to madness, shall know
of it, and she will become your enemy, and no silent one.
Cynthia will no longer, after this, match me with you, nor will
she go to you herself; she will remember so heavy a scandal;
and, in anger, will go round to all the other girls, and inform
of you: alas, you will be welcome at no threshold. No altar
will she pass without shedding tears, and no hallowed stone,
what, and wherever it may be: no loss more heavy can befall Cynthia, than to have her guardian-goddess leave her,
and carry away her lover, myself especially. May she ever
continue in this mind, I pray, and may I never find anything
in her to complain of.

ELEGY V.[3] TO GALLUS.

O ENVIOUS one, restrain at last your tiresome tongue, and
suffer Cynthia and me to pursue our course hand in hand.
What would you have, madman? To feel my passion? Unhappy one! you are in haste to know the worst evils, to pass,
poor wretch, through hidden fires, and drink all the poisons of
Thessaly. She is not like to, or to be compared with, com-

---

[1] *Antiope.*] The daughter of Nycteus and Polyxo, and mother of Amphion and Zethus.

[2] *Hermione* was the daughter of Menelaus and Helen.

[3] *Elegy V.*] He declines introducing Gallus, a man of some family, to
Cynthia, assuring him that, even if she listen to him, she will lead him a
terrible life, and that he (Propertius) will not, in that case, be able to
help him.

mon streetwalkers: you will find[1] she is not one to be moder-
ately angry. But if, by chance, she turns not a deaf ear to
your prayers, how many thousand cares will she bring you!
she will leave you no sleep, no eyes; single-handed, she can subdue fierce-hearted men. Ah! how often, when rejected, will you
run to my threshold, when your brave words will die away in
sobs; a trembling chill with tears of sorrow will come over
you, and fear will set its unseemly mark on your countenance;
the words in which you would fain express your woe, will
escape you, and you will be unable, poor wretch, to know
who or where you are. Then you will be compelled to learn
the heavy bondage of my mistress, and what it is to go home
when shut out by her. Then you will not so often wonder at my
paleness, and at my having no strength left in all my body.
Your rank, besides, will not be able to help you in love: love
knows not how to yield to painted ancestral busts.[2] But if
you give the slightest token of your disgrace, how soon will
your great name sink into a by-word! I shall not, then, be
able to give you any comfort when you ask it, since I have
no cure for my own woe. But, luckless pair, suffering under
the same love-sorrow, we shall be compelled to weep upon
each other's bosom. Wherefore, Gallus, forbear to try my
Cynthia's powers: her favour is not asked with impunity.

ELEGY VI.[3] TO TULLUS.

I AM not afraid now, Tullus, of encountering the Adriatic
main with you, or of spreading a sail in the Ægean waves;
since with you I would fain climb the Riphæan mountains,[4]
and go beyond the abode of Memnon.[5] But I am kept back

[1] *You will find.*] Such is the force of the *tibi*, which must here be understood ἠθικῶς, i. e. acquisitively.

[2] *Ancestral busts.*] *i. e.* Love makes no account of illustrious descent.
The phrase is derived from the Roman custom of preserving waxen
images of ancestors in the atrium.

[3] *Elegy VI.*] Tullus, on being sent into Asia with his uncle, B. c. 29,
wished the poet to go with him. Propertius professes his full confidence
in Tullus, but declines the invitation, as he could not leave Cynthia,
and military service was not his vocation.

[4] *The Riphæan mountains.*] These were in the north of Scythia. Cf.
Georg. i. 240, Mundus ut ad Scythiam *Riphæasque . . . arces* Erigitur.
Ib. iv. 518, Arva *Riphæis* nunquam viduata *pruinis.*

[5] *Memnon.*] King of Æthiopia. The two regions are put indefinitely
for the extreme north and south.

by the words and embraces of my girl, and by the earnest
prayers she utters while her colour comes and goes. For
whole nights she keeps vehemently declaring her love for me,
and complaining in her desolation, that there are no gods.
She now taunts me with indifference towards her, denies herself to me, and uses such threats as a sorrowful mistress addresses to an unkind lover. Against such complaints I cannot
hold out an hour: may he perish that can love with moder-
ation. Can it be of such importance to me that I become acquainted with Athens, the seat of learning, and view the wealth
of time-honoured Asia, that on the ship being launched, Cynthia may upbraid me, and disfigure her face with passionate
hands, and say that kisses are due from her to the wind for
being contrary, and that nothing is harder to bear than a
faithless lover. Endeavour, you that may, to excel the well-
earned honours of your uncle,[1] and restore ancient privileges
to allies that have long forgotten them: for you have never
indulged in love, but your devotion has always been given to
your country in arms: may the boy, armed with fatal dart,
never bring on you troubles like mine, and all those distresses
that are made public by my tears. Suffer me, whom fortune
has always willed to lie low, to devote my soul to frowardness,
to the last. Many have willingly died after a long career of
love: in the list of them may the earth hide me also. I was
not born fit for campaigns nor for arms: the Fates will me to
undergo the service [2] in which I am. But you can go either
where soft Ionia stretches, or where the wave of Pactolus
dyes *with gold* the land of Lydia, whether to traverse the land
on foot, or cleave the sea with oars, and will form a part of
recognised authority. Then if there come any moment in
which you are not unmindful of me, be certain that I am living
under an unfortunate star.

[1] *Your uncle.*] This was L. Volcatius Tullus, consul in A. U. C. 271,
with M. Æmilius Lepidus.

[2] *The service.*] The analogy between love and warfare is frequently
noticed by the Roman poets. See Hor. *Od.* iii. 26, 2, *Militavi* non
sine gloria. Ovid, *Am.* i. 9, 1, *Militat* omnis *amans*, et habet sua castra
Cupido.

ELEGY VII.[1] TO PONTICUS.

WHILE you, Ponticus, sing of Cadmean Thebes and the fatal contest between the brothers, (and may I thrive as you are likely to rival Homer, chief *in Epic song*, if the Fates are gentle to your strains,) I, as is my wont, am pursuing my career of love, and trying to devise something for a stern mistress. I am forced to obey not so much my natural bent as my woe, and to complain of my hard fate in life. In this task my allotted span is consumed; this is my glory; it is from this that I hope my poetic fame will arise. Let me be celebrated as having been the sole favourite of an accomplished girl, and as having often endured her unjust reproaches. Let a despised lover, henceforth, read me constantly, and may the knowledge of my woes benefit him. If the boy Cupid shall have pierced you also with his unerring bow,—a disaster that I would fain wish the gods I obey may not have decreed,—you will weep, in sorrow, at your camp,[2] your seven bands of heroes lying neglected in lasting mildew: in vain, too, will you be desirous of composing a tender strain; for Love, if he comes late, will dictate no verses to you. Then will you often praise me as no mean poet: then shall I be preferred to the other wits of Rome: nor will the young men be able to refrain from saying over my tomb, "O great poet, *interpreter* of our pangs, thou art buried here." Beware then how you proudly despise my poetry. Love often comes late, and comes with a vengeance.[3]

ELEGY VIII.[4] TO CYNTHIA.

ARE you, then, mad? Has my affection no hold on you? Am I of less moment to you than cold Illyria? And does your friend, whoever he may be, appear of such consequence

---

[1] *Elegy VII.*] He recommends Ponticus not to despise love-poetry, because, if ever in love himself, he will feel the want of it. Ponticus, who is also addressed in the 9th Elegy of this book, was the author of a heroic poem on Thebes. He is mentioned by Ovid, *Trist.* iv. 10, 47.

[2] The description of the camp of either party in his "Thebaid:" *agmina septem* alludes to the Septem contra Thebas, or their antagonists.

[3] *With a vengeance.*] *Magno fœnore,* "with great interest."

[4] *Elegy VIII.*] The poet, on hearing that Cynthia purposed accompanying a certain Prætor to Illyria, tries to dissuade her, and ultimately succeeds.

to you that you are ready to go, without me, under any wind?
Can you brook to hear the roaring of the mad sea? Can you
lie with a stout heart on board a rough ship? Can you, with
your delicate feet, tread on the cold snow? Can you, Cynthia, bear snows to which you are not accustomed? Oh that
the winter season may be of double length, and may the mariner be forced to be idle by the tardy Vergiliæ.[1] May no ship
be launched for you from the Tuscan shore, and no unfriendly
breeze set my entreaties at nought; may I see no pause to
the gales that now are blowing, when the waves are about to
carry away your bark, and may they give me an opportunity,
as I stand on the lonely shore, to call to the cruel girl again
and again with angry gestures? But however you treat me,
perjured one, may Galatea[2] not be unfriendly to your passage;
in order that, after having safely passed the Ceraunian peaks,[3]
Oricus[4] may receive you into its quiet bay. No love[5] will
alter me, and prevent me from pouring out genuine grief on
your threshold: nor will I fail to stop sailors and say to them,
"Tell me, in what port is my mistress shut up?" I will say,
too, though she be fixed in Atracian or Elean[6] regions, she
will be mine once again.

* * * * * * *[7]

[1] *Vergiliæ.*] The Pleiads (πλεῖν, *to sail*) were called "Vergiliæ" from
their rising in the spring (*Ver*): they rose about the 16th of April, and
set about the 9th of November: their rising and setting were, respectively,
the signals to the mariner to commence and discontinue his voyages.

[2] *Galatea.*] A sea-nymph, the daughter of Doris and Nereus, the god,
of the sea.

[3] *Ceraunian peaks.*] These mountains, so called from the thunder-
storms (κεραυνοί) with which they were visited, were on the N. W. coast
of Epirus, and rendered the navigation very dangerous; hence we find,
Hor. Od. i. 3, 20, *Infames scopulos, Acroceraunia.* Cf. Lucan, v. 652.
Sil. Ital. viii. 632.

[4] Oricus (*Ericho*) was on the coast of Epirus, and celebrated for its
harbour, and the number of turpentine-trees that grew in the neighbourhood. See Æn. x. 136. Infr. iv. 7, 49.

[5] *Nullæ tædæ:* from torches being used in escorting a bride home.
The word came to be used for a marriage ceremony, (Ovid, *Met.* xv. 826,
Conjux Ægyptia, *tædæ* non bene fisa, cadet,) and hence for any amour.

[6] Atrax was a town in Thessaly; Elis, in the Peloponnesus.

[7] In some editions we find a new Elegy beginning here. The poet, having prevailed on Cynthia to stay, gives vent to his feelings in the remainder
of the piece. "The fact probably is," says Paley, "that the whole of
the Elegy was written after he had successfully dissuaded her, but in the
former portion he sets forth the arguments used by him, in the form of a
present appeal."

Here will she stay; here she has sworn to remain: let the envious burst with anger: we have prevailed: she could not withstand our constant entreaties: though greedy envy picture false delights, yet our Cynthia has ceased to dream of going to unknown regions. To her I am dear, and for my sake Rome is called most dear; and, apart from me, she refuses royal delights. She would rather share my humble couch, and be mine on any terms, than have for her own the ancient realm that was Hippodamia's dower, and all the wealth that Elis had previously gained by its mares. However much her friend might give her, and however much he might promise, yet she has not been covetous and fled from my embrace. I could not move her by gold, nor by India's shells, but by the gentle magic of my song. The Muses do, then, exist, and Apollo comes not slowly to a lover's aid: on these I rely, and continue to love. Cynthia, paragon of maids, is mine. Now may I tread the stars of heaven: whether it be day or night, she is mine. My rival cannot seduce my faithful darling: my old age will feel that honour.

ELEGY IX.[1] TO PONTICUS.

I USED to tell you, railer, that a love-fit would come upon you, and that you would not always be able to talk so big. See! you are prostrate, and submitting, as a suppliant, to the dictation of a girl; a purchased girl lords it over you as she pleases. Let not the Chaonian doves[2] pretend to surpass me in telling what young men each maid subdues. Grief and tears have made me deservedly skilled, and would that I might lay aside my love and call myself inexperienced! What boots it now to you, poor fellow, to be able to compose a heroic poem, or to tell in piteous strains of the walls built

---

[1] *Elegy IX.*] Propertius jests with Ponticus at his being in love at last, and that with a slave girl, in his own house, a kind of attachment which was considered peculiarly discreditable in a gentleman (ingenuus). He advises him to lay aside his heroics, and try love-poetry, assuring him that his present feelings are quite trifling compared with what some lovers experience.

[2] *Chaonian doves.*] The doves of Dodona in Epirus, a district of which was called Chaonia, by Helenus, from Chaon, a Trojan. See Æneid iii. 333. As to the epithet, cf. Ovid, *Ar. Am.* ii. 150, Quas . . . colat turres *Chaonis ales* habet.

by the lyre[1] of Amphion ? In love the lays of Mimnermus[2]
are of more use than Homer's : gentle love likes gentle strains.
Begone, I beg, and put away those melancholy effusions, and
sing something that every maid may wish to know. Suppose
your chance of winning your love was not easy, how *would
you fare?* now you are madly looking for water in the middle of a stream.[3] You are not yet pale, nor touched by a true
flame of love : this is but the first spark of the coming ill.
Then indeed you will be desirous of engaging with Armenian tigresses, and experiencing the torture of the infernal
wheel,[4] rather than feel young Love's shaft so often in your
vitals, and be able to deny your angry fair one nothing. To no
one has any love-affair been so facile[5] as not to have had its
checks occasionally. Moreover, be not deluded by the thought
that she is quite at your command : for if a woman is one's own,
Ponticus, she makes her way into our affections so much the
more deeply ; for in that case one may not turn away one's
eyes, and let them roam, nor does love allow one to keep
awake on any other account ? Love is not manifest, until one is brought into close contact with the beloved object.
Whoever thou art, shun constant blandishments. To them
flints and oaks must fain yield, much less canst thou resist, O
man inconstant as the breeze. Wherefore, if ashamed, confess
your errors as soon as possible. To confess one's pangs, is often
a relief in love.

[1] *Built by the lyre.*] The stones composing the walls of Thebes moved
of their own accord, so said tradition, to Amphion's music. See Hor.
Od. iii. 11, 1.

[2] *Mimnermus.*] An elegiac poet of Colophon, or perhaps Smyrna, in
Ionia, who lived about 600 B. C. From the words of Horace, (Ep. i. 6,
65,) Si, *Mimnermus* uti censet, sine amore jocisque Non est vivendum,
we may judge of his character and tastes.

[3] *Looking for water, &c.*] This expression is used of one who does not
know his own resources. The application here is that Ponticus' inamor-
ata was his slave, and so he had not much trouble in getting her affections.

[4] *The infernal wheel.*] This alludes to the wheel to which Ixion was
bound, for offering violence to Juno.

[5] *So facile.*] The expression, *faciles ita præbuit alas*, is derived from
an amusement, in vogue amongst boys, of holding a bird in one hand, by
a string tied to its leg, letting it fly, and then catching it with the other.
Cf. Aristoph. Nubes, 763, ἀποχάλα τὴν Φροντίδ᾽ ἐς τὸν ἀέρα, λινόδετον
ὥσπερ μηλολόνθην τοῦ ποδός, (like a cock-chafer with a thread tied to
its foot,) and Scholiast in loc.

ELEGY X.[1] TO GALLUS.

O HAPPY night, on which I shared your tears of joy, and
was witness to your first declaration of love! Oh the delight
that I have in recalling that night! how often is its remembrance to be appealed to in my prayers! It was then I saw
you, Gallus, dying in the embrace of a maid, and spending
long hours of converse with her. Though sleep was weighing
down my wearied eyes, and the moon was blushing in her
chariot from the middle of the sky; yet I could not withdraw
from witnessing your sport, so ardent was the affection expressed in your intercourse. But since you did not fear to
intrust me with your love, accept a token of the pleasure that
I received. Not only have I learnt to be silent on your love-
pains; there is something in me, my friend, more than mere
secrecy. I have the power of re-uniting parted lovers; I can
open the door of a coy mistress; and I can cure the fresh
anxieties of another,—there is no ordinary healing power in
my words. Cynthia has taught me what, on all occasions,
should be made sure of, and what guarded against. Love is
not entirely idle. Beware of desiring to resist a girl if angry,
or of talking big, or of being long silent: and, if she ask anything, put not on a stern brow and deny it, and let not her
gentle words of blandishment fall in vain on your ear. When
neglected, she becomes angry, and once offended, knows not
how to lay aside her just indignation. But the more humble
and yielding to love you are, the more will you, in many
cases, feel the good effect of it. He will be able to remain
happy with one maid, whose bosom never knows a respite
from love.

[1] *Elegy* X.] Gallus (see Elegy v.) had made Propertius his confidant in a love-affair: the poet expresses his gratitude for that proof of
friendship, and gives him some directions.

ELEGY XI.[1] TO CYNTHIA.

WHILE enjoying yourself, Cynthia, in central Baiæ,[2] where extends the path[3] made by Hercules to the shore, and while admiring, now, the bay at the foot of the realm of Thesprotus,[4] now that near noble Misenum,[5] does any thought of me prompt you to spend nights in remembrance ? Is there any room for me amid your love for another ? Has some fellow, some enemy of mine,[6] by pretended love, won you away from my strains ? Much rather would I that a little bark, guided by tiny oars, were bearing you on the Lucrine water, or that the Teuthrantis,[7] stream easily yielding to the swimmer's hand, were keeping you, in privacy, in its gentle waves, than that it should please you to be listening, while lying at ease on the quiet shore, to the soft whispers of another : for a treacherously disposed girl is wont to go astray when her guardian is removed, and to forget the gods of mutual love by which she is bound. I say not this as though you were not fully known to me, and of approved honour ; but in this point every love brings anxiety with it. Forgive me, therefore, if my words have caused you any anger : the

---

[1] *Elegy XI.*] The poet implores Cynthia, who had been staying some time at Baiæ, to return at once, lest she become corrupted by the demoralizing influence of the place. For descriptions of Baiæ, see Martial, xi. 80 ; Seneca, Ep. 51 ; Statius, *Silv.* iii. 5, 96.

[2] *Baiæ.*] This celebrated watering-place (*Baja*) was on the S. W. coast of Campania, between C. Misenum and Puteoli, whence the epithet *mediis.*

[3] *The path,* &c.] This road, (Herculeo structa labore via, iii. 18, 4,) between the Lucrine Lake and the sea, is said to have been made by Hercules when conveying away the oxen of Geryon. The road was afterwards enlarged by Agrippa.

[4] *Thesprotus.*] Campania was formerly peopled by some Thesprotians from Epirus, who derived their name from Thesprotus.

[5] *Misenum.*] A promontory to the S. of Baiæ, named after Misenus, the trumpeter and friend of Hector, and afterwards of Æneas, who was buried there. See Æn. vi. 162 seq. ; infra, iii. 18, 3.—The walk would command the view of the bay of Puteoli and the coast of Campania.

[6] *Some fellow, some enemy,* &c.] Ante *nescio quis* simulates ignibus hostis, &c. The *nescio quis* is said with marked contempt, as Kuinoel observes.

[7] *The Teuthrantis.*] A small river near Baiæ. The poet wishes Cynthia to bathe in private, not in the public baths of Baiæ.

blame shall be laid to fear. Could I take greater care of a dear
mother, or can I regard my own life at all, without you ?
You alone, Cynthia, are my family, you are my parents, to
you I owe all joyous moments. If I meet my friends in a
merry mood, or if, on the contrary, I am sad ; whatever I am,
or say, Cynthia has been the cause. Only leave corrupt
Baiæ as soon as possible : that shore has parted many lovers ;
that shore that has been ruinous to chaste maids. Oh ! ill be-
tide the waters of Baiæ, destroyers of love.

ELEGY XII.[1]

WHY do you ceaselessly charge me with indolence, as
though I lingered in Rome, the conscious scene of my passion ?
Cynthia is separated from my bed as many miles as the Hypanis[2] is from the Venetian Eridanus ; she no longer cherishes
my wonted love in her embrace, nor does her sweet voice
sound in my ear. Once I was dear to her : in those days
there was none whose lot it was to love with such true return.
Have I become the mark of envy ? Has some god crushed
me ? Or the herb, which, culled on the peaks of Caucasus,[3]
causes separation ? I am not what I once was : a long journey changes maidens : what an amount of love has fled away
in a short time ! Now for the first time am I compelled to
feel the misery of long lonely nights, and to weary my own ears
with my groans. Happy he, that can weep in presence of his
mistress ; Love takes no little joy in gushing tears.[4] If contempt can alter the warmth of love, there is also pleasure in
changing one's bondage. I can neither love another, nor quit
my present mistress : Cynthia was my first, Cynthia shall be
my last.

[1] *Elegy XII.*] Propertius had been invited by a friend, ignorant of
Cynthia's journey to Baiæ, to come and see him : on his excusing himself, he had been charged with indolence. He replies that it was Cynthia's absence that kept him at Rome, and the piece finishes with reflections on the unpleasant feelings produced by her being away.
[2] *The Hypanis.*] The Hypanis (*Bug*) was a river in Scythia : the Eridanus (*Po*) a river in Italy. The poet, of course, exaggerates, the distance
from Rome to Baiæ being about 100 miles.
[3] *The peaks of Caucasus.*] Prometheus is said to have been bound on
Mt. Caucasus, hence *Promethea juga.*
[4] *Love takes*, &c.] This line is imitated by Tasso in his *Aminta*,
though with a shade of variation in the meaning :

ELEGY XIII.[1] TO GALLUS.

You will rejoice as usual at my misfortune, Gallus, and at
my being forced, now that my love is taken away, to spend
my time alone. But I will not, traitor, imitate your cry:
may no girl ever wish to deceive you, Gallus. Whilst your
fame grows by deceiving girls, and, true to your principles,
you never care to form a long attachment, already lost in love
for a certain charmer, you are beginning to pine with cares
that have come upon you at last, and to own yourself beaten
at the first fall.[2] This will be welcome vengeance to the
girls for your scorn of their sorrow: one of their sex will
avenge the wrongs of many. She will put a check upon
those roving amours of yours; you will not always be an advocate for searching after novelties. I have not learned this
from spiteful gossip, or from divination: I have seen it myself; can you, I ask, deny what I testify ? I have seen you lan-
guishing, with your neck all encircled by her arms, and weeping, Gallus, in a long embrace, and eager to lay down your
very life upon the lips you crave for, and the rest, my friend,
which my modesty conceals. I could not part your embrace,
so frantic was your mutual passion. Not so hotly did the
god of Tænarus,[3] disguised[4] under the form of the Æmonian
Enipeus, embrace the willing daughter of Salmoneus.[5] Not
so hotly, after *the pile of* Œta's height, did the violent

> Pasce l'agna l'herbette, il lupo l'agne ;
> Ma il crudo amor di lagrime si pasce
> Nè se ne nostra mai satollo.   At. i. sc. 2.

[1] *Elegy XIII.*] The poet congratulates Gallus on his success with a
mistress of higher mark than those over whom he had been used to boast
his conquests. Propertius extols the lady in an enthusiastic strain, being
no doubt eager that his volatile friend should be fixed at last, and think
no more of Cynthia.

[2] *Beaten at the first fall.*] *Primo gradu:* this is a metaphor derived
from the wrestling-school, in which a man was not accounted fairly
beaten till he had been thrown three times. Hence, the phrases ἀτρί-
ακτος ἄτα, *irresistible woe,* and τριακτήρ, a *conqueror.* Æsch. Choeph.
339. Agam. 166.

[3] *The god of Tænarus.*] *Neptune,* so called from having a temple on
the promontory of Tænarus in Laconia.

[4] *Mixtus.* Cf. iii. 24, 5, *Mixtam* te variâ laudavi sæpe figurâ.

[5] *Tyro,* the daughter of Salmoneus; she was in love with the river-
god Enipeus : Neptune, τῷ ἐεισάμενος, embraced her, and became by
her father of Pelias and Neleus. See Odyss. xi. 235—259.

love of Hercules embrace, for the first time, the heavenly Hebe. One day was able to outrun all ordinary lovers : for she applied to your heart no luke-warm torches ;[1] nor did she suffer your old pride to revisit you, nor will she allow you to be led away : your own ardour will press you *to her service.* And no wonder, for she is worthy of Jove, and next in beauty to Leda, and Leda's offspring,[2] in her single self more pleasing than the three, and more bewitching even than Argive heroines, and would, by her words, force Jove to love. But you, since once for all you are doomed to perish with love, use your opportunity : you were not fitted for any other threshold. So let her be kind to you, since an unexpected delusion has come over you, and may she, in herself alone, be to you all the girls you can desire.

ELEGY XIV.[3] TO TULLUS.

THOUGH idly reclining by Tiber's wave, you may quaff Lesbian wines from vessels chased by Mentor's[4] hand, and admire now the boats that glide quickly along, and now the barges dragged so slowly by ropes ; and although every coppice present its growth of trees with nodding crests, as vast as that which loads Caucasus, yet cannot your opulence compare with my love : love knows not how to yield to great wealth. For if she court welcome sleep in my company, or wear away the whole day in gentle love, Pactolus' waves flow under my roof, and I gather pearls from the red main.[5] Then my delights assure me that kings must yield to me : may those joys last till the Fates doom me to death. For who takes pleasure in riches if Love be contrary ? Never come

---

[1] *Luke-warm torches.*] The metaphor is continued from the allusion (vs. 23) to the funeral pile of Hercules.

[2] *Leda's offspring.*] Helen and Clytæmnestra.

[3] *Elegy XIV.* This Elegy sets forth the happiness produced by love, which contains in itself all riches.

[4] *Mentor.*] A celebrated silver-chaser, who flourished before 365 B. C. His productions were highly prized. Cf. Juv. viii. 104, Raræ sine Mentore mensæ. Martial iii. 41 ; iv. 39 ; viii. 51 ; ix. 60 ; xiv. 93. In Lucian's *Lexiphanes*, § 7, (ed. Tauchnitz,) we find mention of a Μεντορουργης cup.

[5] *The red main.*] The *æquora rubra* are the Indian Ocean : the meaning is, that if he has Cynthia he has all the wealth in the world.

wealth to me with the frowns of Venus! She can lay low
the mighty strength of heroes, and wring even stern souls
with pain. She scruples not, Tullus, to enter a house furnished with Arabian luxury, nor fears to invade a couch of Tyrian dye, and make a man toss in disquiet all over his bed.
What relief do silken garments of varied tissue afford? As
long as she keeps me company in kindly mood, I will fear
no kings, and scruple not to look down upon the riches of
Alcinous.[1]

ELEGY XV.[2] TO CYNTHIA.

OFT have I feared many things hard to bear from your
levity, Cynthia, but never yet this perfidy. See with what
peril Fortune is whirling me, but you are indifferent during
my fear, and can deck your hair with your hands as yesterday, and, with lingering attention, set off your fair form, and
adorn your bosom with stones from Eastern climes just as
before, like a fair girl preparing to meet her new bridegroom.
How unlike all this Calypso, moved at the departure of the
Ithacan, wept to the desert waste of waters. Many days sat
she in sorrow, with hair unkempt, complaining deeply to the
cruel sea; and, though doomed never to see him again, yet
still she wept on from recollection of her long bliss. Alphesibœa[3] took vengeance on her own brothers for her husband's
sake, and love broke the ties of kindred blood. Hypsipyle,[4]
when the winds were bearing away the son of Aeson, stood
not like you, but lost in sorrow in her deserted chamber.
Hypsipyle, pining away with love for the Thessalian stranger,
felt no love again. Evadne,[5] perishing in the fatal flame

---

[1] *The riches of Alcinous.*] The luxury of the court of Alcinous, king
of the Phæacians, immortalized in Odyssey vi. seq., is proverbial.

[2] *Elegy XV.* The poet complains of the indifference and levity shown
by Cynthia, though he was about to leave her. With all her faults, however, he vows that he loves her still.

[3] *Alphesibœa.*] She was the daughter of Phegeus, and was married to
Alcmæon, the son of Amphiaraus and Eriphyle: he put her away and
married Callirhöe, for which her brothers killed him, and perished themselves by the vengeance of the wronged but faithful wife.

[4] *Hypsipyle.*] She was queen of Lemnos, where Jason landed on his
voyage to Colchis: Thoas was her son by him.

[5] *Evadne.*] The daughter of Iphis and wife of Capaneus, one of the
seven heroes who marched against Thebes: Jupiter struck him with a
flash of lightning, and while his body was burning, his wife leaped into

that burnt her husband, died the glory of Argive modesty.
None of these could change your behaviour, so that you also
might become a glorious memory.   Cease, in time, to reiterate
words of perjury, Cynthia, and rouse not the slumbering attention of the gods: O too audacious girl, and doomed to
sympathize with me in my peril, if haply something disastrous
befall yourself! Sooner will the rivers glide into the vast sea
without a sound, and the year bring round the seasons in an
inverted order, than regard for you be altered in my breast;
—be what you will, but never shall you be alien to me;—or
than those eyes, that have often beguiled me to believe your
false vows, seem odious to me. You swore by them, and
prayed that, if you played me false at all, they might be
plucked out by your own hands. Can you raise them to the
mighty sun? Do you not tremble, conscience-stricken, at
the wickedness you have committed? Who forced you to
grow pale, and change colour frequently, and to squeeze a tear
into your eyes against their will? It is by those eyes that I
am perishing, a warning to lovers like me, that safety lies,
alas, in believing no blandishments.

ELEGY XVI.[1] LAMENT OF THE TARPEIAN GATE.

I THAT once was opened for mighty triumphs, the celebrated gate of the virgin Tarpeia, whose threshold was en-
nobled by chariots decked with gold, and wet with the suppliant tears of captives, am now battered by nocturnal assaults
of revellers, and often complain of being knocked at by unworthy hands. Garlands too, signs of iniquity, never cease
to hang from me, nor torches, tokens of an excluded lover, to

---

the flames and destroyed herself. See Eur. Phœn. 1171 seq. Suppl.
980 seq. Ovid, A. A. iii. 20; Ep. ex. *P.* iii. 1, 52.

[1] *Elegy XVI.*] The house of Tarpeius, on the Capitoline hill, was the
scene of the treason and death of Tarpeia, daughter of Sp. Tarpeius,
commander of the fort. Attracted by the glitter of the bracelets worn by
the Sabine soldiery, she promised to betray the fort to them, if they
would give her what they wore on their left arms; whereupon, after having been admitted by her, they threw their shields on her, and crushed
her. For the story, see Livy i. 11: on the legend, Niebuhr, History of
Rome, i. 229 (ed. 1847); Arnold's Rome, i. 8. The house was inhabited
in the time of Propertius, by " puella quædam infamis et impudica."
The house-gate complains of the sad change that has taken place.

lie at my threshold : nor can I, made notorious, and the town's talk by obscene poems, ward off nights of debauchery from my mistress : [but she cannot be induced to spare her character, and desist from being more depraved than even this debauched age.][1] Amid these scenes I am forced to weep, in deeper sorrow *than an excluded lover*, and utter heavy complaints against the long, sleepless watch of a suppliant. He never suffers my posts to rest, pouring out strains of skilfully pointed compliment :

"O gate," says he, "more hard-hearted than even my mistress, why dost thou keep thy remorseless folds so mutely and firmly shut against me ? Why dost thou never open to admit my love, never open to convey my secret prayers ? Will no limit be vouchsafed to my pain ? Must I lie here warming this cold threshold in my sad sleep? The dead of night, the stars as they set, the cold breeze and morning hoar-frost, pity me as I lie. Thou alone, that hast never pitied human woe, returnest me no answer but by thy silent hinges. Oh that my ditty, conveyed through a hollow chink, may fall upon and reach my mistress' ears : though she be more impassive than Sicilian rock, harder than iron or steel, yet will not she be able to restrain her eyes, and a sigh will rise amid involuntary tears. Now she is lying, supported on the happy arm of another, while my words fall unheeded on the night wind. But thou, gate, chief and sole cause of my woe, art never overcome by my presents. I have never offended thee with any frowardness of tongue, such as the rabble utter in unseemly jest, that thou shouldst suffer me, hoarse with such long complaining, to linger out the anxious live-long night in the street: but I have often sung of thee in a new poem, and have often leaned against and kissed thy steps. How often, perfidious one, have I faced round before thy posts, and privily brought thee tributary presents ! "

Such are the strains, and others to the same purpose, such as you, unhappy lovers, know, in which he outbawls the birds that herald the morn. And thus through the dissoluteness of my mistress, and the endless laments of a lover, I am perpetually defamed and made odious.

---

[1] Lemaire considers vss. 11, 12 spurious.

ELEGY XVII.[1] TO CYNTHIA, ON THE STORMINESS OF THE SEA.

DESERVEDLY, since I have had the heart to leave my mistress, am I now addressing the solitary halcyons. Cassiope no longer, as is her wont, is going to look on my vessel, and all my vows fall unheeded on the thankless shore. Even when away from me, Cynthia, the winds favour thee. See how fierce and threatening is the chiding of the gale. Will not Fortune come and appease the storm? Is this small shore to cover my dead body? Do thou, however, change for the better thy angry complaints, let the darkness and the raging sea be vengeance enough for thee. Canst thou picture to thyself my disaster without shedding a tear? Canst thou endure to gather no bones of mine into thy bosom?[2] May he perish who was the first to introduce ships and sails, and to make a voyage over the unwilling sea. Was it not better to conquer the temper of a fickle mistress,—though hard, yet was she the paragon of maids,—than to be looking, as now, on a shore surrounded by unknown forests, and to be wishing and gazing for the Tyndaridæ.[3] Had any destiny buried my misery at Rome, and a stone, last tribute of affection, were standing over a lover's corpse, she would have sacrificed her hair, cherished as it is, to my grave, and would have fondly planted tender roses near my tomb: she would have exclaimed my name over the urn containing my dust, and would have prayed the earth to press lightly on me. But, O ye maidens, denizens of the ocean, children of the fair Doris, come in a protecting band, and speed us on our voyage. If ever Love has come down to your waters, spare me, a lover like yourselves, and make the shore kind.

[1] *Elegy XVII.*] Propertius, finding that his complaints had no effect on Cynthia, proposed to start on a voyage to Athens: he finds, however, that cure for love proposed by Theocritus (xiv. 52 seq.) did not always succeed, for he feels the pangs of Love as much as ever. This piece is supposed to be written at sea.

[2] *To gather no bones*, &c.] As a token of special affection, the urn containing the ashes of a deceased relative was carried in the folds of the toga, *sinus*, clasped to the breast. See Tibullus, i. 3, 5.

[3] *The Tyndaridæ.*] Castor and Pollux (*fratres Helenæ, lucida sidera*) were the guardian-angels of sailors. Cf. Hor. *Od.* i. 12, 27, and Macaulay, *Lay of the Lake Regillus*, Stanza xl.

ELEGY XVIII.[1]

OF a surety the Zephyr's gale rules alone in this desert spot, mute hearer of my wailings, and this forest, the abode of no human being. Here I may give vent, with impunity, to my secret pains, if only solitary rocks can keep faith. From what point shall I begin to recount your pride, my Cynthia? What first cause for tears did you give me? Whereas I used once to count myself among successful lovers now, when in love with you, I am forced to submit to disgrace.[2] How have I deserved so much? What offence changes you towards me. Is some fresh love of mine the cause of your anger? Restore yourself, and be kind, since no other than yourself has set her fair feet on my threshold. Although my sad heart is indebted to you for much suffering, yet will not my anger prove so implacable, as to give you real cause for continual rage, and for disfiguring your eyes with ceaseless floods of tears. Is it because I give but scanty proof of my affection, as far as change of colour goes, and no certain token of my love speaks on my countenance? Ye shall be my witnesses, if trees know what love is, O beech, and pine loved by the Arcadian god.[3] Ah! how often do my cries re-echo under your dulcet shades, and how often is Cynthia written on your bark! Alas! what cares has your injustice brought to me, cares known only to your silent door! I have been accustomed to bear patiently all behests of yours, cruel as you are, and never to complain of your treatment[4] of me, in piercing accents of grief. In return for which, O divine fountains,[5] the cold rock, and a hard bed

---

[1] *Elegy XVIII.*] That this Elegy was not written, as might be conjectured from its commencement, in a time of sickness and danger, appears from the concluding distich. It is full of deep feeling and tenderness to Cynthia, assuring her of his love even in the nether world.

[2] *Submit to disgrace.*] *Habere notam* is properly of those to whose names a mark was put in the censor's lists, and who were therefore degraded from their civic rights. Cf. Phædr. i. 3, 11, A quo repulsus tristem *sustinuit notam.*

[3] *The Arcadian god.*] Pan, whose mistress Pitys (Πίτυς a *pine-tree*) was changed into a pine by Boreas.

[4] *Treatment.*] *Facta*, the old reading is undoubtedly preferable to *ficta*, as read by Kuinoel, from being opposed to *jussa*.

[5] *Divine fountains.*] *Divini* fontes. Cf. Theocr. viii. 39, ἄγκεα καὶ ποταμοὶ, θεῖον γένος. Another reading is *devexi:* "sed ad fontes devexos,

upon a rugged path is allotted to me, and all that my sorrow can pour forth, I am forced to say, in solitude, to the shrilly-piping birds. But, be what may, let the woods re-echo " Cynthia " to me, and let the desert rocks not be unacquainted with your name.

ELEGY XIX.[1] TO CYNTHIA.

CYNTHIA, I fear not now the melancholy Manes, nor do I care for the fatal debt of death ; but lest, perchance, my death-bed be without thy love,—this fear is more grievous than death itself. The winged boy has not stuck to my eyes[2] so lightly as to allow my ashes to be oblivious of love. Down below, in the dismal region of the dead, the hero, the grand-son of Phylacus,[3] could not forget his beloved wife, but, de-sirous of folding his dear one within his phantom arms, he came, shade as he was, to his ancient Thessalian abode.[4] There, whatever I may be, I shall always be called your image : extraordinary attachments survive even beyond the fatal shore. There let fair heroines come, given, by victory over Dardans, to Argive heroes, yet none of them shall prove dearer to me than your beauty, O Cynthia : and may the Earth kindly allow this. Although a destiny of long old age delay you, yet your bones will be always dear to my tears :[5] and may you, on earth, feel the same, when my body has been burnt : then death, wherever it happen, will never be bitter to me. How I fear, lest, despising my tomb, merciless Love tear you away, alas, from my ashes, and force you, against

leniter in declive labentes, sedere non sanè triste est." *Lemaire.* The poet appeals to the fountains to witness his misery.

[1] *Elegy XIX.*] The poet declares his lasting affection for Cynthia.

[2] *Stuck to my eyes.*] The metaphor is derived, according to Hertzberg, from fowling : the lover, having smeared his eyes, and caught Cupid, cannot shake him off.

[3] *Phylacus.*] Protesilaus was the son of Iphiclus, the son of Phylacus (Il. ii. 705) : his wife was Laodamia, the daughter of Acastus. On his being slain by Hector, she prayed to be allowed to converse with him for three hours, for which space Hermes conducted him to the upper world : at the end of the time Laodamia died.

[4] Cf. Ovid, *Herr.* xiii. 2, Æmonis *Æmonio* Laodamia *viro.*

[5] *Dear to my tears.*] " The action of a survivor on earth clasping the bones of a deceased relative and bedewing them with tears, is poetically transferred to one who is previously deceased." See on iii. 4, (ii. 13,) 39. *Paley.*

your will, to dry your falling tears : even a true heart yields at last to importunity. Therefore, while we may, let us gladden each other with love : love is never long enough, last how long it may.

ELEGY XX.[1] TO GALLUS.

WE give you this advice, Gallus, from our long-lasting love: forget it not, nor let it slip from your recollection. "Often Fortune proves adverse to a thoughtless lover;" so we may learn from Ascanius,[2] that river so cruel to the Minyæ.[3] You have a dear youth most like Hylas, the son of Theiodamas, not inferior to him in beauty, nor different in name; him,—whether threading the windings of a river shaded by woods, or whether the wave of Anio laves your limbs, or whether you walk in the region of the giant-named district,[4] or wheresoever in your wanderings a river meets you,—him, always defend from the covetous grasp of the Nymphs: Ausonian Dryads are as capable of love as any others. May you, Gallus, not have the lot—'twas hard, indeed—of constantly searching mountains, and chill ranges of rock,[5] and rivers, after having experienced what Hercules did, in his wretched wanderings over unknown shores, and for which he wept near the pitiless Ascanius. For they say that the Argo, having left the docks of Pagase,[6] started on a long voyage to Phasis, and that, after having passed the waves of the daughter of Athamas,[7] they put in the ship, on her way to the rocky

---

[1] *Elegy XX.*] Gallus is warned, by the example of Hercules and Hylas, to be careful of a favourite boy on whom he had fixed his regard.

[2] *Ascanius.*] A river in Bithynia, (Georgic. iii. 269, Sonans Ascanius,) styled *crudelis* from its causing Hercules the loss of Hylas. See Theocr. xiii.

[3] *The Minyæ.*] The *Argonauts* are called Minyæ, from being descended from the Minyans, a nation in the north of Bœotia. See Pindar, *Pyth.* iv. 69. Ovid, *Met.* vii. 1.

[4] *The giant-named district.*] Cumæ in Campania, the district known as the Phlegræan plains, was the scene between the gods and rebel giants. The origin of the name (φλέγειν, *to blaze*) is undoubtedly to be sought in some volcanic eruption.

[5] *Chill ranges, &c.*] Compare Theocr. xiii. 66.

[6] *Pagase.*] The post in Thessaly whence the Argo started. See Ovid, *Met.* ut supr. cit., and *Fasti*, i. 491.

[7] *The daughter of Athamas.*] Helle, after whom the Hellespont ("Ελ-λης πόντος) was named.

abodes of the Mysians.[1] Thereupon the band of heroes, as soon as they had set foot on the hospitable shore, spread the level beach with a litter of leaves. But the companion of the unconquered youthful hero had gone farther to obtain water, of which there was but little there, from a retired fountain. Him followed two brothers, the offspring of Aquilo, Zetes and Calais,[2] and flew to snatch kisses as they hung on balanced wings, to carry off kisses from his upturned face, each flying away in turn. Now he is lifted from the ground, and hid beneath the wing of either; now he wards off, with a bough, the attack of the winged pair. Ere long the offspring of Orithyia,[3] descendant of Pandion, left him. O woe! forward went Hylas, went to the Hamadryads. There was in that place a spring, beneath the crest of Mount Arganthus, a liquid abode, loved by the Thynian Nymphs ; over it from the boughs of the trees in that wilderness hung dewy apples indebted to no care, and around, in the water-meadow, rose fair lilies, grouped with purple poppies. At one time, plucking the tops from these, with delicate hand, in boyish sport, he preferred the flowers to the task he had undertaken ; at another, bending, in guileless security, over the pretty ripples, he lingered in his wanderings to look play-fully at himself in the water. At length he prepares to dip in his hands and draw some of the water, leaning on his right arm that he might bring up a plentiful supply : immedi-ately the Dryad Nymphs, smitten with his beauty, left, in wonder, their accustomed dances, and gently drew him, as he leant forward, into the yielding stream. Then Hylas made a sound with his ravished body : Alcides responded[4] again and again from afar ; but the breeze carried the name *he shouted* back to him from the distant fount. Warned by this, Gallus, take care of your love ; whereas you have hitherto seemed to leave your Hylas to the mercy of the Nymphs.

---

[1] *The Mysians.*] Compare Apoll. Rhod. i. 1177.

[2] *Zetes and Calais.*] They were the sons of Boreas or Aquilo, and were among the Argonauts. Pind. *Pyth.* iv. 131.

[3] *Oreithyia.*] Boreas carried off from the banks of the Ilissus (Plat. Phædr. 229, B. Stallb.) Oreithyia, daughter of Erechtheus, son of Pandion.

[4] *Alcides responded.*] Compare Theocr. xiii. 58.

ELEGY XXI.[1]

SOLDIER, who art hastening to avoid the fate of thy comrades, having been wounded at the Etruscan lines,[2] why strain thy eyes, and make them swell with tears for me ? I am one closely connected with the war in which thou takest part. So may thy parents joy in thy safety, but let my sister learn these events from thy tears : that Gallus, saved from amidst the weapons of Cæsar, could not escape the hands of a barbarous spoiler, and that whatever bones she finds scattered over Etruscan mountains, she may know to be mine.

ELEGY XXII.[3]

TULLUS, from our friendship, you repeatedly ask me what is my rank, whence I derive my birth, and of what family I am. If you know Perusia, the grave of your countrymen, fatal to Italy when times were hard, when civil discord expelled her citizens from Rome,—let me be allowed, O Etrurian soil, to grieve above all others : thou hast suffered the limbs of my kinsman to be scattered abroad, thou hast not covered his ill-fated remains in thy soil. Umbria,[4] rich in fertile land, joining close to the champaign country beneath, gave me birth.

---

[1] Elegy XXI.] Gallus, a relative of the poet, was killed by bandits in the Perusine war : these are supposed to be his last words, which he desires a soldier to bear to his sister. This Gallus is not the person addressed in El. v., nor is he the poet mentioned in iii. 26, 91.

[2] The Etruscan lines.] The fortification of Perusia, now Perugia, in Etruria ; it was taken by Octavianus from Antony, B. C. 40. See Suet. Vit. Oct. § 14 ; infra, ii. 1, 29.

[3] Elegy XXII.] He informs Tullus as to his birth-place, paying a passing tribute of regret to Gallus.

[4] Umbria.] The poet was most likely born at Asisium, (Assisi,) about 12 miles E. of Perusia.

BOOK II.

ELEGY I.[1] TO MÆCENAS.

Do you ask whence it comes that I write of love so often?
Whence comes it that my book reads so softly? It is not
Calliope inspires my strains, nor Apollo; it is my girl herself
that gives me ability. If I see her walking in shining dress
of Coan dye, the whole of the present piece will be of the
Coan dress. If I see her hair flowing in disorder over her
brow, she walks proudly rejoicing in the praises of her
hair. If she has struck a tune on the lyre with fingers
ivory-white, we admire her skill in fingering the strings.
Or if she droop her lids in sleep, poet-like I find fresh
themes for song; or if she struggle with me, her vesture
snatched off, then indeed I compose a piece as long as the
Iliad. Has she done anything, has she said anything—no
matter what—whatever she says, a glorious long descant comes
forthwith out of a mere nothing. But if the fates, Mæcenas, had given me power enough to marshal heroic bands to
arms, I would not sing of the Titans, of Ossa piled on Olympus, to make Pelion the stepping-stone to heaven, nor of hoary
Thebes, nor of Pergamus, theme of Homer's song, nor that
by Xerxes' command two seas were united;[2] nor the old
kingdom of Remus, nor the spirit of proud Carthage, nor the
threats of the Cimbri,[3] and the gallant deeds of Marius: I would
tell of the wars and the exploits of your patron Cæsar, and
you next to the great Cæsar would be my care. For as often
as I sang of Mutina,[4] or of Philippi, grave of *so many*

[1] *Elegy I.*] Propertius assures Mæcenas that he cannot write heroic
poetry; and that he will ever continue faithful to Cynthia only.
[2] *Two seas were united.*] This alludes to the canal cut by Xerxes
through Mt. Athos, connecting the peninsula with Chalcidice. See Hdt.
vii. 22 seq.
[3] *The Cimbri.*] Probably inhabitants of the peninsula of *Jutland;*
they were defeated B. C. 101, by C. Marius, in the Campi Raudii near
Vercellæ, after having defeated six Roman armies in succession.
[4] Mutina (*Modena*) is noted for the siege sustained there by D. Brutus
(B. C. 43) against Antony, and for the battle against the latter, in which
the two consuls, Hirtius and Pansa, were slain.

citizens, or the sea-fight[1] and flight off Sicily, and the up-
rooted hearths of the ancient Etruscan people, or the taking
of the shore famed for the Pharos[2] of Ptolemy; or when I sang
of Cyprus and of the Nile, as, brought in triumph to the city,[3] it
flowed in a flagging stream with its seven captive waters, or
of the necks of kings surrounded with golden fetters, and
prows taken at Actium, travelling up the Sacred Way: my
Muse would always inweave with those exploits, you, a faithful subject both in peace and war. In the shades below,
Theseus, among men on earth, Achilles, call as witnesses to
their friendship, the one the son of Ixion, the other the son of
Menœtius.[4] But Callimachus has not lungs enough to thunder forth the Phlegrean contests of Jove and Enceladus; nor
have I the force to record the name of Cæsar among his
Phrygian ancestors in nervous verse. The sailor talks of
storms, the farmer of bulls, the soldier counts his wounds, the
shepherd his sheep. We, on the other hand, tell of those
whose field of battles is the narrow couch. Let each one
spend his time on the art in which he is skilled. There is
credit in dying for love: there is credit again in being privi-
leged to enjoy but one love. Oh may I enjoy my love without a rival. If I remember, she is wont to blame fickle girls,
and disapproves of the entire Iliad on account of Helen.
Whether I must drain potions like those of Phædra,[5] prepared by a step-mother for a step-son, but doomed not to
affect him, or whether I am to die by herbs of magic power,

---

[1] *The sea-fight.*] The defeat of Pompey by Octavius off the coast of
Sicily, B. C. 35, is here alluded to.

[2] *Pharos.*] The allusion is to the capture, by Augustus, B. C. 30, of
Alexandria. The Pharos was a lighthouse built on an island of the
same name (now *Pharillon*) by Ptolemy Philadelphus (B. C. 280). It
is described by Cæsar, *B. C.* iii. 112, *Pharus est in insulâ turris, magnâ
altitudine, mirificis operibus instructa, quæ nomen ab insulâ accepit.*
The word is used poetically for *Egypt*, as here. Cf. Lucan, viii. 442,
Petimus *Pharon* arvaque Lagi.

[3] *The Nile.*] Models of rivers formed part of the triumphal proces-
sions of victorious generals. Cf. Persius, vi. 47, *Ingentes* locat (*contracts
for*) Cæsonia *Rhenos.*

[4] *Peirithous* the son of Ixion, and *Patroclus* the son of Menœtius;
have obtained celebrity as the friends, respectively, of Theseus and
Achilles.

[5] *Phædra.*] Seized with an incestuous passion for *Hippolytus*, her step-
son, she tried to win him by a potion.

or whether a Colchian enchantress be kindling vessels[1] for me on Iolcian hearths:—one woman once stole my heart: in her embrace will I die. Medicine cures all human ills: love alone consents not to be tampered with. In time Machaon[2] healed the legs of Philoctetes, and Chiron[3] the son of Phillyra the eyes of Phœnix:[4] the Epidaurian god, too, restored by Cretan herbs dead Androgeos[5] to his father's halls: the Mysian[6] youth, too, was healed by the same Hæmonian spear that had wounded him. If any one can cure me of this failing, he alone will be able to put apples into the hand of Tantalus.[7] He is the man to fill casks from the urns of the maidens, *the daughters of Danaus,* and save their delicate necks from being constantly burdened by carrying water. Such a man might release the limbs of Prometheus from the rock of Caucasus, and drive away the vulture from his heart. Whensoever, therefore, fate demands back my life, and I become a short epitaph in a slender urn, O Mecænas, envied member of our youthful company of knights, if perchance you travel by the road near my tomb, stop your British chariot[8] with its ornamented yoke, and with tears pay to my silent dust this tribute: "An unrelenting mistress proved the death of this unfortunate."

[1] *A Colchian enchantress,* &c.] This alludes to the magic preparations made by *Medea* to restore Aeson.

[2] *Machaon,*] son of Æsculapius (the *deus Epidaurius* of vs. 61, so called from his having a temple at *Epidaurus* in Argolis). He and his brother Podalirius were eminent legendary physicians. Philoctetes was wounded in the foot, either by a snake or by the poisoned arrows of Hercules, a parting gift from that hero. He was left, in his wounded condition, at Lemnos, till, in the tenth year of the Trojan war, he was visited by Odysseus and Diomede, who told him that Troy could not be taken without him: this was the occasion on which Machaon cured him.

[3] *Chiron,*] son of Cronos and Phillyra, (Georg. iii. 550,) a celebrated centaur, and skilled in medicine and athletics.

[4] *Phœnix,*] the son of Amyntor, was blinded by his father for making improper overtures to his mistress. Cf. Ovid, *Ibis,* 259; *A. A.* i. 337.

[5] *Androgeos,*] the son of Minos, murdered by the Athenians, from jealousy at his excelling them in athletics. See Æn. vi. 14.

[6] *The Mysian youth.*] This was *Telephus,* afterwards king of Mysia, who was wounded and healed by the spear-point of Achilles.

[7] *Tantalus.*] Compare Odyss. xi. 582 seq.

[8] *British chariot.*] The *Esseda* were properly the Celtic war chariots. it was open in front, had a wide pole, and was always drawn by a pair of horses. See Cæsar, B. G. iv. 33; v. 16. Georg. iii. 204.

ELEGY II.[1]

I WAS free, and was resolving to live by myself, but Love,
though I had concluded a peace with him, deceived me.
Why does a form so fair as this linger on earth ? Jupiter, I
believe not those free amours of thine in olden time. Her
hair is flaxen, her hands tapering, and her whole form fully
developed, and she moves along worthy even of Jove as his
sister,[2] or like Pallas when she walks by Dulichian[3] altars,
with her breast covered with the snaky head of the Gorgon.
Like also to the heroine Ischomache,[4] daughter of Lapithes,
a delightful booty to the centaurs in their revels, and to Sais[5]
who is said to have yielded the embraces of her virgin form
to Mercury by the waves of Bœbe's[6] lake. Yield now, ye
goddesses, whom the shepherd once saw unrobe on Ida's
height. Oh that age may not spoil her beauty, though she live
as long as the Cumæan prophetess !

ELEGY III.[7]

THOU, that didst say no woman could hurt thee, now hast
been caught : that boasting spirit of thine is laid low. O unhappy one, thou canst scarcely rest a single month, and there
will soon be another disgraceful book about thee. I was expecting a fish could live on the dry shore, or a grim boar in
the sea, unaccustomed abode, or that I could waste the midnight oil in grave studies : a love may be interrupted, but never
extinguished. It was not so much her face, though fair it be,

---

[1] Elegy II.] In this beautiful piece Propertius declares his admiration of Cynthia's beauty.

[2] Jove as his sister.] Alluding to Juno's majestic gait. Cf. Æn. i. 46,
Ast ego quæ Divûm incedo regina Jovisque et soror et conjux.

[3] Dulichium,] one of the Echinades, was part of the kingdom of Ulysses.

[4] Ischomache,] otherwise called Hippodamia, wife of Peirithous, was
carried off by the Centaur Eurytus, and this act caused the celebrated
fight between the Centaurs and Lapithæ. See Ovid, Metam. xii. 210.

[5] Sais], the Egyptian name for Minerva: Kuinoel reads sanctis, and
in the next line Brimo, (βρέμειν, to be furious,) a name applied to
Proserpine from her resistance to the offers of Mercury.

[6] Bœbe.] A lake in Thessaly.

[7] Elegy III.] The poet again asserts his ardent love for Cynthia, whom
he describes as a second Helen.

that won me,—lilies cannot be whiter than my mistress : her
hue is like Scythian snow vying with Spanish vermilion,
like[1] rose-leaves floating in pure milk ;—nor her locks in fair
array, flowing over her dazzling neck, nor her eyes, twin
sparklers, lode-stars to me; nor that perchance she glistens
in Arabian silk,—I am not made a devoted lover by a mere
nothing :—*it was none of these things* so much as that she
dances beautifully, when the wine is removed, like Ariadne,
leader of the frantic crew; none of them so much as when
she strikes the vocal strings with the Æolian quill, and plays
with a skill worthy of the Muses' lyre ; and when she compares her verses with Corinna's,[2] and thinks that Erinna's[3] are
not equal to her own. In thy new-born days, my life, did
golden love sneeze,[4] loud and clear, a favouring omen ? It
was the gods that bestowed on thee these heavenly gifts :
think not, perchance, it was thy mother gave them to thee.
Gifts like those are no fruit of human birth: ten months
brought not forth those graces. Thou, above all others, art
born a credit to Roman girls ; thou art the first Roman girl
that Jupiter will take to his bed. Thou wilt not always be
my mistress on earth : thy form is the most beauteous, after
Helen, that the earth has seen. Can I now wonder at the
youth burning with love for thee ? It were more glorious for
thee, O Troy, to have perished through her. Once I used to
wonder at a girl having been the cause of bringing so many
warriors from Europe and Asia to Troy : now, O Paris, I
find that thou wast wise, and thou also, O Menelaus ; thou in
demanding her, thou in being slow to restore her. Her
beauty was worthy even of the death of Achilles : even Priam
must have approved of the cause of the war. Does any one
wish to outvie the ancient pictures, let him portray my mistress as an original. Whether he show her to Western or
Eastern men, she will inflame them both.—Let me, at least,[5]

[1] Cf. Anacreon, 28, 22, (Melhorn,) γράφε ῥῖνα καὶ παρειὰς ῥόδα τῷ
γάλακτι μίξας.
[2] *Corinna.*] A poetess of Tanagra in Bœotia, who flourished about
the beginning of the fifth century, B. C.
[3] *Erinna.*] She was born about 612 B. C., and was a friend of Sappho.
[4] *Sneeze.*] The omen of sneezing was considered lucky. Cf. Catullus
45, 17, *Amor*, sinistrum ut ante, Dextram *sternuit* approbationem. Theocr.
xviii. 16, and Dryden's version of the same.
[5] *Let me at least*, &c.] Some print the remainder of this Elegy as a

keep myself within the bounds of this affection: for what if another come upon me, to make my torments more bitter and deadly! Like as when a bull at first refuses the plough, and afterwards, having become used to the yoke, comes quietly to the field, so, at first, young men are intractable in love, and rage, but at length are tamed, and bear all things right and wrong. The seer Melampus,[1] detected in having stolen the oxen of Iphiclus, submitted to degrading bonds: it was not gain that urged him, but rather the fair Pero, doomed to be one day a bride in the house of Amythaon.

ELEGY IV.[2]

You must first complain of many wrongs in your mistress, often ask a favour, often meet with a repulse, often assault your guiltless nails with your teeth, and often, in anger and perplexity, stamp with your feet. In vain were unguents lavishly poured over my hair, in vain did I walk slowly and with measured step. In love no potion is of use, nor Medea-like[3] dealers in darkness, nor decoctions made by the hand of Perimede. For where we see neither the causes nor the manifest manner of attack whence all these evils arise, our way lies in darkness. This kind of patient wants no doctors, no soft beds: it is no season nor bad air that is affecting him. He continues to walk *as if in health*, and suddenly his friends are thunderstruck at his death: we see therefore, that love, whatever it is, is a thing against which there is no preservative. For to what lying necromancer have I not been a fortune? What sorceress has not discussed my dreams times out of number? May every enemy that I have fall in love with women: may every friend fix his regard on a youth. In that case, you go quietly

preface to the next, alleging the abruptness of *His ego*, &c., but if abrupt here, *a fortiori* will the words be abrupt at the beginning of a new poem. Propertius' poetry is the *beau-ideal* of abruptness.

[1] *Melampus*,] the son of Amythaon, (Georg. iii. 550) undertook to drive, from Othrys to Pylos, the herd of Iphiclus, that his brother Bias might so gain Pero, the daughter of Neleus, who refused her to any one who could not perform that feat, ὅς μὴ ἕλικας βοῦς εὐρυμετώπους ἐλάσειε. (Odyss. xi. 289.) Compare Theocr. iii. 43.

[2] *Elegy IV.*] Under the form of advice to a friend, Propertius recounts his own love-experience.

[3] *Medea.*] See note on i. 1, 24.

down the stream, without any danger of your boat upsetting: what harm can the wave of so narrow a sea do you ? The one is often softened by a single word: the other is scarcely appeased by your very life-blood.

ELEGY V.[1]

Is it true, Cynthia, that you are becoming the town's talk of all Rome, and that your disgraceful conduct is notorious ? Did I deserve this ? You shall pay me the penalty, treacherous one, and we will find a breeze, Cynthia, to waft us to some port.[2] Out of many treacherous girls, I shall yet find one who will consent to become celebrated in my poetry, one who will abstain from mocking me by conduct so notorious and cruel, and tear your character to pieces. Alas, though long loved, yet at length must you weep. Now my anger is fresh: now is the time to part: if the annoyance be wanting, of a surety will love return. The waters of the Carpathian Sea[3] change not colour so much beneath the north winds, nor is a darkling cloud so soon dispersed by a hazardous south wind, as angry lovers are easily changed by a word. *Propertius,* now that you can, withdraw your neck from the unmerited yoke. You will feel pain, but only for one night: every evil in love becomes light if borne. But you, my life, I adjure you by lady Juno's dulcet power, harm not yourself by your own waywardness. It is not the bull only that strikes a foe with his curved horn, but even a sheep, on being hurt, resists her assailants. I will not rend your dress from your false body, nor shall my anger break the doors that are closed in my face: nor will I venture, in my anger, to pull out by the root your clustering hair, nor mercilessly assault you with my fists. Let some rustic, whose head the ivy, poet's wreath, has never surrounded, stoop to a fray like that. I will write these words never to be forgotten while you live : Cynthia is beauteous in form, Cynthia is false in professions of fidelity. Believe me,

[1] *Elegy V.*] He reproaches Cynthia with her bad conduct, and threatens to leave her.

[2] *To some port.*] We read with Lachmann and Paley *aliquo* instead of *Aquilo.* The latter, as Hertzberg pleasantly remarks, "immanes tempestates interpretibus movit."

[3] *The Carpathian Sea.*] So called after Carpathus, (*Skarpanto,*) an island between Crete and Rhodes.

Cynthia, however much you set at nought the whispers of common report, this verse will blanch your cheeks.

ELEGY VI.[1]

Not thus did lovers throng the house of the Ephyrean[2] Lais, at whose doors all Greece bent, nor was the crowd so great in times of yore, at the house of Thais,[3] celebrated by Menander, with whom the people of Athens[4] disported itself, nor was Phryne,[5] who was rich enough to rebuild Thebes, made happy by so many admirers. Moreover you often say falsely that your lovers are your relations, and there are not wanting persons to kiss you by right of kinship. I am vexed by the pictures of young men, by the names you have ever on your lips, by the speechless infant boy in the cradle. I am annoyed if your mother gives you many kisses, if your sister, if she with whom your friend sleeps. I am annoyed by everything :—I am a coward,—pardon my cowardice,— and in my misery fear that under the woman's dress a man lies hid. These were faults, so says report, that brought men, in days of yore, to blows : from beginnings like these came

[1] *Elegy VI.*] This Elegy, in subject similar to the preceding, laments the degeneracy of the age, and ends with a commendation of chastity.

[2] *Ephyrean Lais.*] *Corinth* was called *Ephyra* after a daughter of Oceanus, (Virg. Georg. iv. 343,) the primitive inhabitant of the country. Lais was a celebrated courtesan of the place, who lived in the time of the Peloponnesian war ; she was notorious for her avarice and caprice. See Athenæus, 570, C.; 588, D. ; 585, D.; 582. The proverb, Non cuivis homini contingit adire Corinthum, "It is not every man that can venture on a visit to Corinth,"—arose from the enormous sums that she exacted from her admirers.

[3] *Thais.*] She was with Alexander the Great in his Persian expedition, and is best known from the story, somewhat doubtful though it be, of her having stimulated him, during a festival at Persepolis, to set fire to the palace of the Persian kings. See Dryden's *Alexander's Feast.* She is called *Menandrea*, (cf. v. 5, 43,) from Menander having inscribed a play with her name.

[4] *The people of Athens.*] The Athenians are called *populus Erichthonius* from an old king, Erectheus or Erichthonius.

[5] *Phryne.*] She was native of Thespiæ in Bœotia, and is said to have offered to rebuild Thebes, if Alexander would consent to having a tablet, commemorating the fact, set up on the walls. The *Venus Anadyomene* of Apelles, and the *Cnidian Venus* of Praxiteles, are said to have been painted from her figure. See Athenæus, xiii. 590, for anecdotes of her, more particularly that of Hyperides gaining her acquittal by causing her to bare her bosom before judges who were about to condemn her to death.

the fatal Trojan war. The same madness induced the Centaurs to hurl embossed vases at Peirithous.[1] Why need I recall Grecian instances? Thou wast the ringleader in an assault, O Romulus, nurtured by the milk of a wild she-wolf. Thou didst teach thy men to carry off with impunity Sabine[2] maids: owing to thee Love now dares anything at Rome. Happy was the wife of Admetus,[3] and the bed-partner of Ulysses, and every woman that is contented with her husband's house. What was the use of erecting temples to Chastity for maidens' use, when any married woman may be what she pleases? The hand that first traced indelicate figures, and placed in a chaste house objects disgraceful to see, corrupted the eyes, hitherto unsullied, of maidens, and would have them no longer ignorant of its own depravity. Evil be to him that produced on earth, by that art, quarrels latent in a mute object of pleasure. Walls were not, in former times, adorned with figures like those: houses, then, had no guilt exhibited on them. But it is not without reason that the spider has veiled the temple, and grass ignominiously overspread the place of the deserted gods. What guards, therefore, what abode, impassable by an enemy's foot, shall I assign thee? Rigorous custody, placed over a woman against her will, is of no avail. Cynthia, she that is ashamed of sinning[4] is safe enough. Neither wife nor mistress shall ever seduce me; thou shalt always be my mistress, and my wife.

ELEGY VII.[5] TO CYNTHIA.

CYNTHIA rejoiced indeed at the repeal of the law,[6] since the passing of which we have both of us long wept for fear it should divide us, though Jupiter himself cannot part

[1] See on ii. 2, 9.   [2] See Livy i. 9.   [3] Alcestis.
[4] *Ashamed of sinning.*] Compare Comus, 419 seq., *I mean that, too, but yet a hidden strength,* &c.
[5] *Elegy VII.*] He congratulates Cynthia on his being able to continue his connexion with her, which law had threatened to dissolve.
[6] *The repeal of the law.*] The law alluded to is *Lex Julia De Maritis Ordinandis.* It was enacted about B. C. 18; came into operation B. C. 13; modified A. D. 9. Had it continued in force Propertius must have married, and as Cynthia was a *meretrix,* a union with her was impossible. For the law see Tac. *Ann.* iii. 15. As this book was written B C. 25, there is a historical difficulty in the dates; some suppose that a previous attempt of Augustus is alluded to.

two lovers against their will. But Cæsar is mighty :—yes,
Cæsar is mighty in arms : but the conquering of nations avails
nothing in love. For sooner would I suffer this head to be
parted from my neck than submit to quench the fire of our
love by wedlock, or pass, as a husband, your shut up house,
and look back with swimming eyes on its forsaken door.
Alas, what sort of sleep, Cynthia, would the pipe play to you
in my wedding procession? sadder would it be than a funeral
trumpet. What care I for furnishing soldiers to aid my
country's triumphs? No soldier will ever spring from my
blood. But if I were to follow,[1] in earnest, my mistress to
the field, the mighty horse of Castor[2] could not go fast enough
for me. My fame, spread as far as the Scythians,[3] dwellers in
the snowy wild, has got me so great a name from my poet's
profession : so I fight not. You alone are pleasing to me :
may I alone, Cynthia, continue to please you : such love as
yours will be more precious to me even than family.

ELEGY VIII.[4]

A MAID long dear to me is taken from me, and yet, my
friend, you bid me not shed tears. No enmities but those of
love are implacable : stab myself and I shall be a more merciful foe. Can I imagine her locked in another's arms? Shall
she, that was once called mine, be mine no longer? All things
are turned upside down : of a surety it is so with love : yield,
or conquer : this is the wheel of Love.[5] Often have mighty
chiefs, often have mighty kings fallen : Thebes once stood :
once there was a lofty Troy. How many presents have I

[1] *If I were to follow,* &c.] "I read here, ' *Vera meæ comitarer castra
puellæ :*' Kuinoel has *Romanæ comitarent* by a conjecture most improba-
ble on any known principles of palæography." *Paley.* Jacob and Weber,
(Corp. Poet. Lat.,) *in verba meæ* comitarer, &c. The metaphor of *castra*
as applied to love-affairs is common enough, so Propertius adds *vera* to
imply going to war in earnest.

[2] *The horse of Castor.*] Cyllarus. See Geor. iii. 90. Val. Flace. i. 246.

[3] *The Scythians.*] They are called *Borysthenidæ*, from the Borysthenes,
(*Dneiper,*) their chief river.

[4] *Elegy VIII.*] He laments his desertion by Cynthia, and threatens
desperate things.

[5] *The wheel of Love.*] The picturing of Fortune with a wheel is an
old allegory : the poet gives one to Love here, from the changing nature
of that power as well as of Fortune.

given, what verses have I made! and yet the iron-hearted girl has never said, "I love." I have been thoughtless, then, for many, yea, too many years, in submitting to you, worthless one, and your house. Did I ever show myself free to you? will you be for ever casting disdainful words at me? So then, you will die in the prime of life, Propertius? Yes, die: let her exult in your death. Let her insult my spirit, vex my shade, dance on my funeral pile, and spurn my bones with her foot. Did not Bœotian Hæmon[1] fall on the tomb of Antigone, wounded in his side with his own sword, and mingle his bones with those of the maid, without whom he would not return to his Theban home? But you shall not escape; you must die with me: from this same dagger must the blood of either reek. Although a death of that sort will be dishonourable to me,—dishonourable it is,—you shall die with me. Even Achilles the great, when his bride was taken away from him, suffered, in his desolation, his arms to lie idle in his tent. He had seen the flight of the Greeks, and the scattered slaughter of them on the shore, and the Dorian camp[2] glowing with the fire kindled by Hector: he had seen Patroclus lying stretched out, in mighty bulk, on the sand, and his hair, reeking with blood, lying in disorder on the ground. He suffered all for fair Briseis' sake: so great and passionate was his grief on being parted from his love. But after that, by a late retribution, she, the captive of his spear, was restored, he dragged that brave Hector behind his Thracian car. As I am much inferior to him both in parentage[3] and arms, is it wonderful that Love fairly triumphs over me?

ELEGY IX.[4]

WHAT my rival is, I have often been; but, perchance, even in an hour, he will be turned off, and some one else be more

[1] *Hæmon.*] Son of Creon, king of Thebes in Bœotia. He was in love with Antigone, the daughter of Œdipus and Jocasta: when she was buried alive, by his father's orders, he committed suicide on her grave. See Soph. *Antig.* 1192 seq.

[2] *The Dorian camp.*] Allusion is here made to the firing of the Greek fleet by Hector. See Iliad xvi. 114, &c. He also slew Patroclus (xvi. 656, &c.; xvii. 192).

[3] *Parentage.*] Achilles was the son of Thetis, a sea-goddess.

[4] *Elegy IX.* He upbraids Cynthia with deserting him, and ends by

favoured. Penelope, woman worthy of so many suitors, was able to remain faithful for twice ten years. She was able to defer wedding any one by feigning to be engaged in spinning,[1] craftily undoing by night what she had woven by day; and though she never expected to see Ulysses again, yet she remained faithful to him till age came upon her. Briseis, too, embracing the dead Achilles, beat her fair face with phrensied hand, and, a sorrowful captive, washed *the body* of her blood-stained lord, having brought him to the Simoïs, and laid him by its yellow pools. Her hair, too, she disfigured, and bore *what the fire had left of* the corpse of the mighty Achilles, and his huge bones, in her little hand, when, O Achilles, neither Peleus nor thy mother, goddess of the azure main, came to thee, nor Scyrian Deïadamia[2] attended her widowed husband. Then was Greece blessed with true daughters: then virtue throve even in the camp. But you, unnatural one, could not be alone one night, nor remain one day in solitude; nay, you and your admirers quaffed the wine-cup with many a laugh: most likely abusive words were spoken of me. You even welcome him who formerly, of his own accord, left you: may the gods grant you enjoy him to your cost! Is this *the reward for* the vows made by me for your safety? When the Stygian wave had all but got you, and we, your friends, were standing, in tears, about your couch, where or what, in the name of heaven, was he, O treacherous one? If I were detained as a soldier in the distant Indies, or if my vessel were on the ocean, what would your feelings be? But it is easy for you to make up a story and frame excuses; in this accomplishment a woman is always a proficient. The Syrtes shift not so much with the changing breeze, nor are leaves so much shaken by the south wind in winter, as woman's anger comes and goes without any fixed law, be the reason important or of no consequence. Now, since such is your determination, I will yield. O ye Cupids, send out your arrows sharper, I pray you. Make them tell unerringly, and release me from this life: my blood will be to you the great-

declaring that his affection is still unchanged.—This stands as the tenth Elegy in some books, a break being made after vs. 16 of the foregoing.

[1] *Spinning.*] *Minerva*, as the patroness of spinning, is put for *telâ*.

[2] *Deïdamia*] was the daughter of Lycomedes, and mother of Neoptolemus.

est possible prize. The stars bear me witness,[1] and the morning hoar-frost, and the gate stealthily opened to me, poor wretch, that nothing in life has ever been dearer to me than you: now, too, you shall still be *dear*, although my enemy. No other mistress shall share my bed: I will be alone, since I may not be yours. And oh,—grant it, ye gods,— if perchance I have lived a guileless life, may my rival in the midst of his love become a stone. Not more fatally, while contending for the throne, did the Theban chiefs[2] fight and fall, despite their mother's efforts to part them, than I would fight *with you, my rival*, if my mistress were the prize, and I consent to meet death, so that I slay you at the same time.

BOOK III.[3]

ELEGY I.[4] [ii. 10, K.]

But[5] it is now time to traverse Helicon in other measures, and full time to give the field to my Thracian steed. It is now my pleasure to sing of troops of horse mighty in the fight, and to chronicle the Roman wars of my chief. But if my powers fail me, at all events my courage will be meritorious: in great attempts even to have had the will is enough. Let early youth sing of love, maturer age of war: I will sing of wars, since my mistress has been celebrated. Now I wish to proceed on my way with look more dignified and sober:

[1] *The stars*, &c.] Some suppose a lacuna here, but there is none really.
[2] *The Theban chiefs.*] The brothers, Eteocles and Polynices, who killed each other, their mother, Jocasta, having vainly tried to part them. See Eur. *Phœn.* 300—637.
[3] *Book III.*] Some say that the second book has been divided by Lachmann without any sufficient reason. We have followed Paley in adopting the division. To ordinary readers, however, the question whether there are four or five books of Elegies is of no great importance.
[4] *Elegy I.*] The poet declares his intention to sing of wars and heroic themes, but at the same time professes his inability to do so properly.
[5] *But*, &c.] Some suppose the commencement of this Elegy to be lost: the idea of the poet was, however, "Hitherto I have sung of love, but." &c.

my Muse now teaches me another kind of song. Arise, my soul: soar from a lowly strain, O Muses, and gather strength: my work must now be in a lofty tone. The Euphrates no longer boasts of the Parthian horsemen's[1] flying fight, and grieves that it sent not back the Crassi.[2] India, moreover, is submitting its neck to thy triumph, Augustus, the recesses of Arabia,[3] hitherto untouched, are trembling at thee; and every sequestered region of the earth will feel thy conquering hands. This campaign will I follow: by singing of thy military deeds I shall become a great poet: may the Fates grant me to survive to that day. As, when we cannot reach the head of great statues, a wreath is laid just at the feet, so I now, unable to reach the heights of Epic song, offer, in humble adoration, an ordinary offering of frankincense. Not yet are my strains acquainted with the founts of Ascra:[4] Love has only bathed in Permessus' wave.[5]

ELEGY II.[6] TO CYNTHIA. [ii. 11.]

OTHERS may write about thee, and yet thou mayest be unknown; let him who is for sowing seed in a barren soil praise thee. The dark day of thy funeral, last rite that can be paid thee, will carry off, believe me, all thy accomplishments in one bier, and the traveller will pass by thy bones in contempt, and will not say, This dust was once a learned maid.

[1] *Parthian horsemen.*] They were noted for their mode of warfare, which consisted in feigning flight, then turning on their saddles and sending a deadly shot at their pursuers. Cf. *Georg.* iii. 31. Hor. *Od.* ii. 13, 17.

[2] *The Crassi.*] M. Licinius Crassus, and his son, P. Licinius, fell in the well-known and disastrous expedition to Parthia, B. C. 54.

[3] *Arabia.*] The allusion to the disastrous expedition under Ælius Gallus to Arabia, marks the date of the poem, which must have been written about the time the expedition was contemplated, B. C. 25; and certainly not after its ignominious failure. Cf. Hor. *Od.* iii. 24, 1, *Intactis* opulentior *Thesauris Arabum.*

[4] *Ascra.*] In Bœotia, the birthplace of *Hesiod:* the poet means that he cannot rise to the majestic of Hesiod's song. His birthplace is described by Hesiod (*Opp.* 638) as οἰζυρὴ κώμη, χεῖμα κακὴ, ϑέρει ἀργαλέη, οὐδὲ ποτ' ἐσθλή.

[5] *Permessus.*] A fountain or river on Mount Helicon. Cf. Virg. *Eclog.* vi. 64.

[6] *Elegy II.*] A warning to Cynthia not to be too proud of her popularity, which she owes to his praises rather than to any qualities of her own, which will make her known to posterity.

ELEGY III.[1] [ii. 12.]

THINK you not that he had hands of marvellous skill whoever first painted Love as a boy?[2] He first saw that lovers
live careless of everything, and that great blessings are lost
with indifference. Not without a meaning did he add supple
pinions, and make the god flit in the human heart. For in
truth we lovers toss up and down on the waves, and the
breeze that wafts us remains settled nowhere. Rightly, too,
is his hand armed with barbed arrows, while his Gnossian
quiver hangs from his two shoulders.[3] For he strikes us
before we can see the foe and be on our guard, and from that
wound no one recovers. In me his darts are left; the image
of the boy is also present, but he has certainly lost his wings;
for he never flies from my breast, and is constantly warring
with my heart's blood. What pleasure canst thou find in
dwelling in marrowless bones? if thou hast any feelings of
shame, transfer thy darts elsewhere. It were more satisfactory
to try that poison of thine on the heart-whole: it is not I,
but my emaciated shadow, that is smarting: if you destroy it,
who will there be to sing of such subjects? This muse of
mine, low in degree though it is, is a great glory to thee, in
that it sings of the head, and the fingers, and the black eyes
of my mistress, and of her feet that touch the ground so
lightly as she goes.

[1] *Elegy III.*] An elegant little poem on the symbolism embodied in
the popular representations of Love.—*Paley.*
[2] *Think you not*, &c.] Compare Eubulus ap. Athen. xiii. 562, C.
"What man was he who first painted or moulded in wax the winged
form of Love?" A beautiful portraiture of a runaway Love will be found
in Moschus i.
[3] *Two shoulders.*] "Not that he had two quivers, as Hertzberg
remarks, but that the quiver with its strap (amentum) may be said to
hang from both shoulders. But I have some suspicion that the sense is
this: the quiver when not in use hung at the back from *both* shoulders;
when used it was pulled to one side, and so was suspended only from the
opposite shoulder. In this case Love holds the barbed arrow ready in
his hand, because (quoniam) he aims instantaneously, and does not wait
to draw the arrow from the quiver."—*Paley.*

ELEGY IV.[1] TO CYNTHIA. [ii. 13.]

ITURA[2] arms not itself with so many Persian arrows as
Love has planted darts in my breast. He forbade me to
despise the playful Muses so much, and bade me dwell in the
Ascræan grove with this object; not to have Pierian oaks
following me, or to be able to attract wild beasts in the
Ismarian valley,[3] but rather that Cynthia may be captivated
by my strains, and I then make myself more known by my
art than Inachian Linus.[4] I do not admire a fair form only,
nor a woman for being able to boast of illustrious ancestors.
Mine be the bliss to read my verses on the bosom of a girl of
talent, and to submit my writings to the approval of intellectual
ears. When this shall be my happy lot, farewell to the vague
and contradictory talk of the vulgar; I shall be safe if my
mistress be my judge; for if she turn a kindly ear to me,
and is disposed to friendship, I can then bear the enmity of
Jove. Whensoever, therefore, darkness shall have closed my
eyes, listen to the instructions you are to observe for my
funeral. Let not the procession display a long line of images,
and let not the trumpet pour forth a vain lament on my death:
let not a bier be laid for me with ivory supports, nor let my
body be placed on a couch luxuriously spread.[5] Let there be
no line of platters filled with perfumes: let me have but a
humble funeral in plebeian style. My procession will be
quite, quite large enough if it consists of my three books, which
I will give to Persephone as a most handsome present. Follow

---

[1] *Elegy IV.*]   He boasts that his Poems will prevent him from being
forgotten: this is followed by reflections on his death.

[2] *Itura.*] *Itura,* Paley; *Susa,* Kuinoel; *Scrauta,* Salmasius; (Brouckh.
in h. l.) Codices, *Etrusca.*   *Itura* is the correction of Pontanus:
Ituræa was to the N. E. of Palestine; its inhabitants were celebrated for
archery.   See Georg. ii. 448, *Ituræos* taxi torquentur in *arcus.*

[3] *Ismarian valley.*] Ismarus was in Thrace; *Orpheus* performed the
feat mentioned in the text.

[4] *Linus.*] Son of Apollo, and one of the Muses; there are various
traditions concerning his birth and death.

[5] *Luxuriously spread.*] Attalus was king of Pergamus, and left his
immense wealth to the Roman people: hence costly ornaments, furniture, &c. are described by the epithet Attalicus. Cf. iii. 24, 12, Aulæis
Attalicis.

me yourself, beating your bared breast, and cease not to call out my name, and imprint the last kisses on my cold lips when a box[1] filled with perfume from Syria shall be given you. Lastly, when the fire shall have consumed me, let a small urn receive my ashes, and let a laurel be placed on the top of my modest tomb, that its shade may cover the resting-place of the dead, and let two lines be written over me—" He who is now lying in unsightly dust was once the slave of Love only." My tomb will not, from this modest inscription, become less known than was the blood-stained grave of the chief of Phthia.[2] And whenever you come to die,—remember that you must travel that journey,[3]—come, at a ripe age, to my grave, where I shall be waiting for you. Meanwhile, beware of despising me in my tomb: the earth can sometimes feel keenly: and oh that any one of the three sisters had bidden me breathe my last in my cradle. For to what purpose is life to be preserved for so uncertain a period? Nestor was reduced to ashes after having lived through three generations.[4] Now if in the siege of Troy a Phrygian[5] soldier had cut short his life already far advanced, he would not have seen the corpse of Antilochus[6] buried, nor should we find him saying, O death, why art thou so late in coming to me? You, however, will ever grieve at the loss of your friend: it is allowable to love for ever those that are gone. Venus is witness to this, whose fair Adonis a cruel boar once slew when hunting on Idalium's crest: it is said that he lay, in all his beauty, among those marshes, and thither, Venus, it is said that thou didst go with dishevelled hair. But vainly, Cynthia, will you attempt to recall my dumb shade, for what answer will the scanty remains of my bones be able to make?

[1] It would appear that perfumes were burnt by the side of the dead body before it was placed on the pile. See Becker's *Gallus*, scene xii. The *onyx* was a sort of marble, *not* the precious stone of that name.

[2] *Phthia.*] *Achilles* came from Phthia: *Polyxena*, the daughter of Hecuba, was sacrificed over his tomb.

[3] This line is, probably, corrupt.

[4] See Iliad i. 247.

[5] *Gallicus* is the old reading, explained by some to be *Phrygian*, from *Gallus*, a river in Phrygia, mentioned in Ovid (*Fasti*, iv. 364); others read *Dardanus, Ilius*.

[6] *Antilochus.*] Nestor's son, who was killed by Memnon. Cf. Juv. x. 250.

ELEGY V.[1] [ii. 14. K.]

THE grandson of Atreus rejoiced not so much in triumph-
ing over Troy, on the fall of the great power of Laomedon ;
nor was Ulysses so delighted at having brought his wanderings to an end, and touched the dear shores of Ithaca ;[2] nor did
Orestes' sister Electra joy so much on seeing him safe, whose
bones she fancied that she had held, to her sorrow ; nor did
the daughter of Minos[3] see Theseus with so much delight,
after he had made his way safely out of the Labyrinth by
means of a clue : *the joys of all these* were not so great as what
I experienced last night : as happy as an immortal shall I be,
if I be blessed with another like it.   But whilst, in humble
guise, I walked with downcast head, I was called more worthless than a dry tank.[4]   No longer does she seek to answer me
by cold disdain, nor has she the heart to sit unmoved while I
am weeping. Oh that I had not known this treatment so late !
it is offering medicine to a man's ashes.—Before my feet, blind
that I was, a path was open as clear as day :—to be sure,
when mad with love no one can see.—This is what I have
found to answer best : Answer contempt with contempt,
lovers ; in this way any mistress that has refused yesterday
will come to-day. Others were knocking in vain at her door
and calling for my mistress ; the girl was kind to me, and
leaned her head on my bosom.   This victory is better in my
eyes than to conquer the Parthians : this shall be my spoils,
this my captive kings, this my triumphal car.   Rich gifts
will I place, Cytherea, on thy column : and under my name[5]

---

[1] *Elegy V.*] He expresses his delight at having won Cynthia's affections, and gives a specific (vs. 19) for lovers situated as he had been.

[2] *Dulichia.*] Here put for Ithaca, a part of Ulysses' kingdom for the
whole.

[3] *Daughter of Minos.*] Ariadne ; her connexion with Theseus is well
known. See Catullus, lxiv. 113.

[4] *A dry tank.*] In volcanic districts, such as the south of Italy, water,
being very bad and scarce, was preserved in tanks (λάκκοι) : the disgust
of a traveller on finding one of these dry originated the proverbial saying
in the text.—*Paley.*

[5] The gift would be accompanied by the words *Propertius posuit*, and
under the name the distich would be.—*Paley.*

shall be a verse like this: "These spoils[1] I, Propertius, place before thy temple, O goddess, for having been received as a lover for a whole night." Now it rests with you, my light, whether my ship is to come safe to shore, or is to be stranded, with its cargo, on the shoals. But if, by any fault of mine, you change to me, may I be found, in death, lying before your door.

ELEGY VI.[2] [ii. 15. K.]

OH happy I! Oh night, lovely in my eyes! and oh bed, made happy by my pleasures! How many soft words we interchanged when the light was by, how we strove together when it was removed! Now she wrestled with me with bare breasts: now she covered them with her dress and delayed me. She now opened with a kiss my eyes that were closed in slumber, and said, "Is this the way you mean to lie, sluggard?" How variously our embracing arms intertwined! how long did my kisses linger on your lips! I like not to have the joys of Venus spoiled by darkness. *Let me tell you*, if you know it not, the eyes are the leaders in Love's warfare.

Paris himself is said to have been smitten with love on seeing Helen naked, as she came from the chamber of Menelaus. Naked, too, Endymion is said to have captivated the sister of Phœbus, and to have slept with a naked goddess. So if you lie down with any clothing on, you shall feel my hands as I tear it from you. Nay, if my passion carry me any further, you will have bruised arms to show to your mother. Yours are not yet the flaccid breasts that forbid amorous dalliance; let any girl, who is ashamed of being a mother, look here.

While the Fates allow, let us feed our eyes with love: a long night is coming for you, and no returning day. Oh that you were willing we should be bound thus close: would that

---

[1] *Spoils.*] *Exuviæ* signify *the favours of Cynthia* wrested by Propertius from his rivals.—*Paley.*

[2] *Elegy VI.*] The subject is continued from the last Elegy. The poet recounts rather freely his amorous enjoyments, reiterates his profession of ardent affection and fidelity to Cynthia, and extols the pursuits of love as the best of all human occupations.

the Fates might bind us in such a chain[1] as never might be
loosed. Take example from a pair of doves, male and female
completely devoted to each other. He that wishes an end to
mad passion is wrong : true love can know no bounds. Sooner
will the land mock farmers by unnatural produce, and the
sun drive his black horses more quickly, the rivers begin
to roll their waters to their source, and the fish be stranded on the dry channel, than I consent to transfer my pains
elsewhere : hers will I be alive, hers will I be in death.
But if she consent to grant me such nights as the past, even a
year will be a long life for me : if she grant me many, I shall
become immortal by them : in a single night any one may become equal even to a god. Now if all were willing to live
such a life, and to lie overcome with much wine, we should
have no pitiless steel, nor ships of war ; the sea off Actium's[2]
coast would not toss our bones, nor would Rome, so often
beset all round by her own victories, be weary of dishevelling
her hair.[3] Posterity may certainly give me this deserved praise,
that I have provoked no god by my intemperance.[4] Only,
while it is yet day, do not you fail to grant me the joys of life :
if you give me all the kisses you can, you will give me too
few. Like leaves that drop from the withered garland, and
are seen floating every where in the cups, so, perhaps, to-
morrow will enclose in the tomb us who now love and hope
so much.

[1] *Such a chain.*]   An allusion to the legend of Mars and Venus
caught in a wire net by Vulcan.   See *Odyss.* viii. 275, seq.

[2] *Actium.*]   Now *La Punta*, a promontory in Acarnania at the entrance of the Ambraciot Gulf (*G. of Arta*) ; celebrated as the scene of
the victory gained by Augustus over Antony and Cleopatra, on September
2nd, B. C. 31.

[3] *Nor would Rome*, &c.]   " Rome beset all round by its own victories "
is a bold figure.   *Propriis triumphis* is interpreted by Kuinoel *civilibus
victoriis ;* and perhaps *propriis* may mean *de se ipsa* reportatis. The idea
however is, that its victories have been but so many defeats, and that it
has been wearied in weeping for its own citizens.   *Solvere crines* refers
to the dishevelled hair of captives. See v. 11, 38. " Africa tonsa," which
relates to the same custom, since either *cutting off* or *letting fall* the hair
implies the same disregard of personal adornment.—*Paley.*

[4] *Intemperance.*]   Possibly an allusion to Antony's well-known propensity.

ELEGY VII.[1] TO CYNTHIA. [ii. 16. K.]

THE prætor, Cynthia, a fine prey for you, a source of deepest vexation to me, is just come from the land of Illyria. Could he not have lost his life on the Ceraunian rocks! Oh Neptune, what gifts would I then offer to thee! Feasting is now going on, and tables are piled high, without me: the gate is now open all night without me. Wherefore, if you are wise, lose not the chance of the harvest, and pluck the dull brute while his fleece is thick. Then, when he has spent his substance and become poor, bid him sail to some other Illyrias. Cynthia looks not at rank, nor cares for honours: she always weighs a lover's purse.[2] Venus, help me in my woe, and make my rival kill himself by incessant indulgence. So then any one may buy love? Ye gods, it is for unworthy lucre that a girl loves to perdition. She is constantly sending me to the ocean to look for gems, and bidding me bring her presents from Tyre itself. Oh that no one were rich at Rome, and the emperor himself were content to live in a thatched hut! Mistresses then could not be bought for gold, and we should find a girl becoming grey-headed in her attachment to one man. It is not because you have been away from me for seven nights, with your fair arms encircling so revolting a lover, nor because of this *one* offence of yours, that I appeal to you, but because, as a general rule, fickleness has always been allied with beauty. A rude lout is now usurping my privileges, and, made happy on a sudden, is in possession of my kingdom. Consider the fatal effect of the present to Eriphyle,[3] and how great the torments with which Creusa[4]

[1] *Elegy VII.*] He tells Cynthia that the prætor (i. 8) has returned, and bids her make the most of him, reproaching her for her avaricious disposition.

[2] *Weighs a lover's purse.*] *Amatorum ponderat illa sinus.* The bosom of the robe (*sinus*) was used as a pocket. Covetous Cynthia poises in her hand the money-bag, hung from a lover's neck and concealed in his bosom, and computes its probable value before she accords her favours. Paley has, with a negligence unusual in him, overlooked the plain meaning of this passage, and given it this sense: "But no! my Cynthia cares not for honours, but only for affection."

[3] *Eriphyle.*] The wife of Amphiaraus, who, bribed with a necklace by Polynices, betrayed her husband, and was put to death in consequence by Alcmæon.

[4] *Creusa,*] or *Glauce,* the daughter of Creon, on her marriage with

burnt on her bridal-day. Will no wrongs make me cease my weeping? Knows not my grief how to part from you, false one? For so many days I have felt no pleasure in the theatre, no delight in the Campus, none in my poetry. But, certainly, I should be ashamed, yes, ashamed; unless, as they say, Love, when disgraceful, has generally deaf ears. Look at the leader,[1] who lately filled the Actian waters with empty noise, on his soldiers having been denounced. He was compelled, by infatuated love, to turn his ship about and fly, and seek a refuge at the end of the empire. This is the valiant exploit and gallant deed of Cæsar: with the hand that conquered he put an end to war. But all the dresses, emeralds, and chrysolites of gleaming yellow hue that he has given you, may I see fierce storms carry away, and, curses on them, would that they might become earth or water. Jupiter does not always smile placidly at lovers' treacheries, nor turn a deaf ear to prayers. Have you ever heard rumblings all over the sky, and seen deluges from their lofty abode? They are not caused by the Pleiads, nor by watery Orion, nor does the thunder's wrath fall in that way without a reason: the god then punishes deceitful girls, since even he has been deceived and wept. Prize not, then, a dress of Tyrian dye so much that for its sake you should be filled with fear whenever the south wind brings clouds.

ELEGY VIII.[2] TO CYNTHIA. [ii. 17. K.]

To cheat a lover of an appointed night, and to cajole him by promises, is as bad as to have one's hands stained with blood. Such an event I foretell, as often as, in my solitude, I pass bitter nights, tossing and bruising my limbs from side to side of the bed.[3] Though you may be moved at the lot of Tantalus, that he stands in the stream, and the water mocks his parched and thirsty throat, and recedes from his lips; or

Jason, received a dress from Medea, by which she was set on fire. See Eur. *Med.* 1136—1230.

[1] *The leader.*] Antony.

[2] *Elegy VIII.*] He complains that Cynthia has broken an assignation.

[3] *The bed.*] Beds that were destined for two persons had different names for the two sides: the side at which they entered was open and called *sponda*, or *torus exterior;* the other side was protected by a board, and called *pluteus*, or *t. interior.* See Martial, iii. 91.

you may wonder at the toil of Sisyphus, and at his rolling
his toilsome load all up the mountain; yet there is no living
thing on earth whose case is harder than a lover's, nor anything you would less wish to become, if wise. I whose felicity was the town's talk, Envy herself being lost in wonder
at it, am now scarcely admitted to your presence once every
ten days.—I would now fain throw myself, unnatural one,
down a precipice, or take a dose of poison into my hand.—
And I cannot sleep in the street under a waning moon, or
whisper through a chink in the door. Still, however things
may be, I will beware of leaving her for another: she will
weep when she knows that there is constancy in me.

ELEGY IX.[1] TO CYNTHIA. [ii. 18. K.]

WITH many women constant complaining produces dislike:
a woman is often bent by a silent man: if you have seen any
thing, always deny it; or if you have felt any pain, say that
you have felt none. What if I were now growing old, and
my hair waxing grey, and a wrinkle, slowly but surely traced,
were making a furrow in my cheek? Aurora did not despise
the old Tithonus, and suffer him to lie unheeded in her orient
abode. Often, in her watery home, she embraced him at starting, before briskly washing her yoked steeds.[2] Often when,
after having embraced him, she retired to the neighbouring
Indians to rest, she complained that the days came again too
soon, and called the gods unjust as she mounted her chariot,
and unwillingly discharged her duties on the earth. Her delight in the aged living Tithonus was greater than her grief
at the death of Memnon.[3] A damsel like her was not

[1] *Elegy IX.*] The poet continues to reproach Cynthia with her cruel
treatment of him, and ends by again urging her not to be so anxious about
personal appearance.
[2] Aurora's abode was feigned to lie in the sea, so that her horses would
have a plunge on their voyage from the submarine *stabulum* in which they
had passed the night. *Paley.*
[3] *Tithonus,* &c.] Tithonus was the son of Laomedon, and by the
prayers of Eos (Aurora) who loved him obtained immortality but not
eternal youth, in consequence of which he shrivelled away in his old age,
whence a decrepit man was called Tithonus, as in Ar. *Ach.* 688, ἄνδρα
Τίθωνον σπαράττων καὶ ταράττων καὶ κυκῶν, see Schol. in loc. Their
son Memnon was killed by Achilles and wept for night and morning
by his mother, whose tears are said to be the morning dew-drops.

ashamed to sleep with an old man, and to be kissed so often
by one with a hoary head. But you, perfidious one, hate me
though in my prime; and though at no distant day you will
become a bent old woman. I may console myself, however,
by remembering that Cupid is often wont to be cruel to him
to whom he has once been kind. Do you even now, in your
madness, imitate the woad-stained Britons, and pursue your
dalliance with your head dyed with shining juice of foreign
herbs? A form left as Nature made it, is always comely:
on a Roman face a Belgian cosmetic[1] is disgraceful. Under
the earth may great woe come to every girl that is silly enough
to put on false hair or dye her own. As regards me, you will
always have it in your power to seem fair; yes, fair enough
for me, if you come to me often enough. Suppose it were the
fashion to dye one's temples with indigo, would a blue complexion be therefore comely? You have no brother and no
son, and I, in myself, am son and brother to you. Let your own
bed *by which you are* pledged to me be your keeper, and do
not aim at appearing too highly dressed. I must believe the
character that report gives of you, so beware of going wrong:
report passes over both land and sea.

ELEGY X.[2] TO CYNTHIA. [ii. 19. K.]

ALTHOUGH, Cynthia, you are leaving Rome against my
will, yet I rejoice that you court the beauties of the sequestered fields without me. In the innocent country you will
have no young gallant to prevent you, by blandishments, from
continuing chaste; there will be no brawls before your windows, nor will your sleep be made uneasy by hearing your
name called out; you will be alone, Cynthia, and will behold
the lonely mountains, and the cattle, and the domain of a poor

Ov. *Met.* xiii. 622. In vs. 12, the Indians are called *vicini*, as living near
the *Eoa domus* of Aurora.

[1] *Belgian cosmetic.*] What this means is not exactly known: some
suppose it to be *Dutch soap*, as in Martial, viii. 33, 20, Mutat Latias
spuma Batava comas. Why not *rouge?*

[2] *Elegy X.*] Addressed to Cynthia on her contemplated excursion
into the country, and written in a cheerful and affectionate tone, which
presents a strong contrast with his anxiety at her absence at Baiæ, (i. 11.)
A very elegant poem, and displaying a fine sense of the beauties of nature.
to which Humboldt (*Cosmos*, vol. ii. p. 15) considers the Romans in
general to have been but little sensitive.—*Paley.*

farmer. There no games will be able to corrupt you, nor any temples, chief causes of your sins. There you will constantly look on the oxen as they plough, and at the vine shedding its leaves under the skilfully-plied pruning-knife; there, too, you will occasionally offer incense in a rude chapel, where a country-reared kid will fall before the altars; unrestrictedly shall you dance with bared leg, like the rustics, provided that all your beauties be safe from a rival's eye. I myself shall turn hunter; even now it delights me to enter Diana's service and quit that of Venus. I shall begin to snare the wild beasts, and hang their horns on the pine, and with my own voice to chide the unruly dogs; not that I shall go so far as to attack great lions, or swiftly pursue and grapple with wild boars. Let my bold attempts be confined, then, to lying in wait for timid hares, and piercing birds with ready arrow, where Clitumnus shrouds its stream between its wood-crowned banks, and where its waves wash the oxen white.[1] As often, my life, as you think of any mischief, recollect that I shall be coming to you in a few days. You see thus that neither the solitude of your woods, nor streams flowing at random over mossy heights, can turn me away from constantly having your name on my tongue: in my absence may no one think of wronging me.

ELEGY XI.[2] TO CYNTHIA. [ii. 20. K.]

WHY do you weep more bitterly than Briseis when she was taken away? Why do you weep more sadly than the woe-worn captive Andromache? Why, foolish one, weary the gods about the wrong that I have done you? Why complain that my faith has given way? The mournful Attic bird pours not forth her complaints so vehemently by night in Cecropian trees, nor does over-weening Niobe[3] shed tears so anxiously on Mount Sipylus over the tombs of her twelve children. Though they bind my arms with knots of brass,

[1] *Wash the oxen white.*] By drinking the water of the Clitumnus, cows were believed to produce white calves, so much required for sacrifices. This tradition was still current in the time of Boccaccio.

[2] *Elegy XI.*] A reply to Cynthia's expostulations on the poet's infidelities.

[3] *Niobe.*] She presumed to rival Latona, whereupon her children, and afterwards she herself, were turned into stone. Sipylus was in Phrygia: one of the sons of Niobe was also of this name.

and though my body be even hid in a prison like Danaë's,
yet, for you, my life, will burst even chains of brass, and
break out of Danaë's prison. Whatever is said about you
falls unheeded on my ears ; do you only doubt not of my constancy. I swear to you by the bones of my father and mother,
—if I am deceiving you, may the ashes of either lie heavily
on me !—that I will remain faithful to you, my life, till darkness finally come over my eyes ; the same day shall witness
the death of both of us, constant to the last. But if neither
you nor your beauty could keep me, the gentleness of your
bondage would suffice. The seventh full moon is now rapidly
approaching since all the streets have been ringing about you
and me ; meanwhile your door has been often kindly opened
to me, often have I been admitted to your embrace ; and I
have not bought a single night with rich gifts ; whatever I was
to you, I was through your fond affection. While so many were
wooing you, you alone wooed me : can I forget your kindness ?
Should I do so, may the tragic furies torment me ; may
Æacus condemn me in the shades below, and may I be preyed
on by vultures like Tityos, and roll stones with toil like
Sisyphus. Address me not beseechingly with suppliant letters ; my constancy to my last hour shall be what it was from
the first. This is my constant privilege to be the only lover
that does not soon tire, nor rashly become smitten.

ELEGY XII.[1] [ii. 21. K.]

AH ! may Venus be unfriendly to Panthus in the same
degree as he, in his letters to you, slandered me ! But do I
now seem to you a truer seer than Dodona? Your fine lover
has taken a wife. So many nights have been quite thrown
away ! Is he not ashamed? See, he sings in his freedom :
you, who believed him too easily, are lying alone. And now
you are a by-word for the pair ; he, in his mightiness, will say
that you were often at home for him against his will. May I
perish, if anything else than triumph over you is what he is
looking for : now that he is married, he prides himself on this.
It was thus that Jason, her guest, deceived the Colchian maid :
she was cast off, for Creusa became his wife. It was thus

---

[1] *Elegy XII.*] The poet plumes himself on having predicted the infidelity of one Panthus, who had won Cynthia's favours, and then left her.

that Calypso was forsaken by the Dulichian hero: she saw
her lover spread his sails. O maidens, too easy in lending
an ear, learn when you are deserted, not to be kind so readily.
This mistress of mine, *too*, left forlorn, has this long time been
looking for another lover,[1] that is left her. You may take
warning, foolish girl, from your experience of the first. In
every place, at all times, we are yours alike, whether you are
ill or well.

ELEGY XIII.[2] [ii. 22. K.]

DEMOPHOON, you know that, yesterday, many girls pleased
me equally, and you know that many woes are coming upon
me: I walk no streets without suffering: O theatres, too fatally
made for my destruction! If a girl spread her fair arms in
graceful motion, or trill forth varied notes of melody, or if a
fair damsel sit with bosom not entirely covered, or if there
stray over a snowy brow truant locks, confined on the crown
by an Indian gem, my eyes at once look for some object
to smite them fatally. If one of the damsels had looked at all
sternly and forbiddingly on me, a stream like cold water began
to trickle all over my face. Do you ask, Demophoon, why
I am so tenderly disposed to all? No love has a *why*[3]
in it. Why does many a votary gash his arms with hallowed
knives, and cut himself to the maddening music of a Phrygian flute.[4] Nature gives to every one some failing: my
destiny has given me the failing of always loving something; and though I be overtaken by the fate of the seer
Thamyras,[5] yet, to beauty, O envious one, I shall never be
blind. But if my limbs appear to you thin and emaciated,
you are mistaken: the service of Venus is not toilsome. Jest
as you please: often has my bed-fellow found me effective in

---

[1] *Another lover.*] Her friend the Prætor. Supr. El. 7.

[2] *Elegy XIII.*] In an address to an imaginary friend, the poet confesses his own weaknesses, and discourses on love-cares generally.

[3] *A why.*] Propertius here repeats, in another form, tho *our* of the
preceding line: cf. 17, 2, Excludit quoniam sors mea *Sæpe Veni.* Persius, v. 87, *Licet* illud et *ut volo tolle.*

[4] *A Phrygian flute.*] This alludes to the priests of Cybele. See the
Atys of Catullus.

[5] *Thamyras.*] A Thracian bard, struck blind for presuming, in his
conceit, that he could surpass the Muses in song. Milton (*P. L.* iii. 36)
mentions him as *blind Thamyris.*

my duty all night long.   Jupiter lay in bed two nights for
Alcmena's sake, and twice by night was the sky without a
king: yet he did not therefore resume his thunderbolts with
a feeble grasp: no love wastes its own strength.   What?
when Achilles had just left the embrace of Briseïs, were the
Phrygians less scared at the Thessalian darts?   What? when
the valiant Hector arose from the bed of Andromache, were
the Argive ships not afraid of the war?   The one could destroy a fleet, the other a city's wall: in love I am an Achilles
and a valiant Hector.   In the same way that we see the moon,
at one time, the sun at another, attendant on the sky, so one
damsel is not enough for me.   Let a second hold and cherish
me in her eager arms, if one ever refuses me her embrace;
or, if she have been, perchance, angered by my servant, let
her know that there is another ready to be mine.   For two
cables are surer protection to a ship than one; and a fond
mother looks more anxiously after twins.   If you are hard-
hearted, refuse me; if not, come to my arms!   What boots it
to regard promises as nothing?[1]   It is a vexation, above all
others painful to a lover, if a damsel he is expecting, suddenly
refuses to come.   How many are the sighs that rack him, as
he tosses over the bed, while thinking that some one, a total
stranger to her, is admitted to her embrace! and he wearies
his servant with asking him repeatedly questions already answered, and bidding him tell, in greater detail, what he fears
to learn.

ELEGY XIV.[2] [ii. 23. K.]

I, who once thought that this path, which I pursue in
common with the unlearned rabble, was to be shunned, now
find water drawn from the common tank to be sweet.   Is a
gentleman to bribe another's servant to carry to his mistress
the message that he promised?   And is he to ask times out
of number "what portico is sheltering her, I wonder?" and,
"In which Campus is she walking?" and then, after having
endured labours such as fame gives to Hercules, is he to have
her writing, "Have you any present for me?"   To be blessed
with the sight of a cross keeper, and, if observed, to lurk in a

[1] *What boots it*, &c.]   I would read *In* nullo ponere verba loco.
[2] *Elegy XIV.*] The pride of high-born woman is contrasted with the
facile compliance of the lower classes.

filthy hovel? How dearly does a night come round once a
year! Perish all they that are pleased with closed doors!
On the other hand, a woman that walks out boldly, without
muffling her face, and surrounded by no terrible guardians,
pleases: one who often paces the Sacred Way with dirty shoe,
and is coy to no admirer; she will never abuse you, nor
worry you, with many a word, for what your cross-grained
father will often weep that you have given her; nor will she
say "I am afraid; make haste, I beg; luckless one, my
husband comes home from the country to-day!" May the
women sent by the Euphrates[1] and the Orontes continue to
please me; I care not for a modest nuptial embrace. Since
a man, on falling in love, has no liberty left from that moment,
if a man chooses to love, he must give up all idea of freedom.

ELEGY XV.[2] [ii. 24. K.]

"Do you talk,[3] when, now that your book is known, you are
a by-word, and your Cynthia has been read all over the
forum?" Whose brow can fail to burst out with perspiration
at words like these?—Men of birth[4] must submit to shame,
or keep their love secret. Now if Cynthia were as favourable
to me as I could wish, I should not have the reputation of
being an arch-profligate; nor should I be scandalized and
become notorious all over the city, nor be annoyed,[5] though,
by concealing her name, I thought to deceive. Wonder not
then at my resorting to the common women; they abuse me
less: think you that a slight reason? At one time, besides,
she wants to have a fan made of a flaunting peacock's feathers,
and a ball[6] for cooling her hands, and wants to ask me,
though she sees me angry, to buy for her ivory dice, and the
cheap frippery displayed in the Sacred Way. May I perish

[1] *May the women*, &c.] The Syrian women were very debauched. Cf.
Juv. iii. 62 seq., *Syrus* in Tiberim defluxit *Orontes*. Et vexit . . . . ad
circum jussas prostare puellas.
[2] *Elegy XV.*] He excuses himself for his infidelity to Cynthia, on the
ground of her caprice.
[3] *Do you talk?*] Cogitandus est amicus, Propertio hæc objiciens. *Weber*.
[4] *Men of birth.*] Ingenuus: libri omnes: Paley, ingenuis.
[5] *Be annoyed.*] Paley reads *Urerer et quamvis nomine verba darem*:
Kuinoel, *ureret*. A comma at *et* seems to make the passage plainer.
[6] *A ball*, &c.] What this was does not appear to be known; perhaps
a piece of rock-crystal. See Paley.

if I care for those extravagances, but I am at last ashamed of being a jest to a deceitful mistress.

ELEGY XVI.[1] [ii. 24 cont. K.]

So this is what you bade me be particularly pleased at? Is not a woman so fair as you ashamed at being fickle? I have scarcely spent one or two nights with you, and you say that you are tired of me. You used to praise me once, and to read my poems; has that lover of yours changed your behaviour so soon? Let him rival me in ability; first of all let him learn to love one only; let him be ready, if it be your will, to go and engage with Lernæan hydras, and to bring you apples from the dragon of Hesperus; let him drain bitter poison readily, and shipwrecked gulp down the waves, and never deny that he is undergoing that misery for you. Oh that you would try the same toils on me, my life; soon will you find among the cowards that boaster who has now, by his arrogance, come into full-blown honour; next year will part you and him. But neither a period as long as the Sibyl's age, nor toil like Alcides', nor the great day of gloom, shall change me. You will lay my bones in the grave, and will say: "These are thy bones, Propertius: thou, alas, alas, wast faithful to me. Faithful thou wast, alas, alas, though neither of noble birth nor so very rich." I will endure anything; a wrong never changes me; I think the bearing with a fair maid no burden. I believe that no small number have pined with love for that form; but I also believe that many had no faith in them. For a short time Theseus loved the daughter of Minos, and Demophoon[2] Phyllis, each a treacherous guest. Long ago you have Medea carried away in Jason's vessel,[3] and left desolate by the man she had just saved. Hard-hearted is she that pretends love for many, and any woman that can

---

[1] *Elegy XVI.*] He desires Cynthia to try his fidelity against that of her present favourite.

[2] *Demophoon.*] The son of Theseus and Phædra: on his return from Troy, Phyllis, the daughter of Sithon, king of Thrace, fell in love with him. Before marriage he went to Attica, and Phyllis, thinking, from his prolonged absence, that she was forgotten, hanged herself and was changed into an almond-tree. With vs. 28, cf. Ovid, *Her.* ii. 1, *Hospita*, Demophoon, tua te, Rhodopeia Phyllis, Ultra promissum tempus abesse queror: and also *Ar. Am.* iii. 38.

[3] Paley reads Iasonia *amota* est.

array herself as a bride for many. Compare me not with the noble; compare me not with the rich; scarcely one of them comes to gather his mistress's bones at the last day. I will be to you instead of those; but I rather pray that you may bewail me with bared breasts and dishevelled hair.

ELEGY XVII.[1] [ii. 25. K.]

O THOU sole object of my care, fairest cause of my sorrow, since my lot shuts out *all hope of* "Come often;"[2] that form of thine shall become most celebrated by my writings, with thy consent, Calvus, and thy leave, Catullus.[3] The soldier, when full of years, lays down his arms and retires, the time-worn oxen refuse to drag the plough, the rotten ship rests on the desert shore, and the war-shield, when battered with age, hangs at ease in the temple; but from thy love no old age shall part me, live I as long as Tithonus or Nestor. Were it not better however to serve the stern tyrant, and to groan in the bull, made by thee, cruel Perillus?[4] it were better, too, to have been turned into stone by the Gorgon's look; nay, even to have endured vultures on Mount Caucasus. But still will I continue firm: an iron spear-point wears away with rust, and a flint-rock by repeated drops of water. But love is not worn away[5] by ever

---

[1] *Elegy XVII.*] The poet, after declaring that the love-pangs caused to him by Cynthia, have been most terrible, declares his constancy to her, and warns her present favourite not to plume himself on his victory; concluding with lashing male flirts.

[2] *Come often.*] "*Excludit quoniam sors mea Sæpe veni.* Jacob. *Sæpe veni* is used as a substantive here as *Quare* supr. 13, 14. Kuinoel has *excludi,* a comma at *sæpe,* and *venis.* Lemaire marks the passage as corrupt: the reading of Jacob, adopted by Weber, Paley, and Weise, (Tauchn. Classics,) is undoubtedly correct.

[3] He apologizes for using the word *notissima,* implying that Cynthia would be more known than Quintilia or Lesbia. Calvus was the celebrated lawyer, orator, and poet, alluded to in Catull. liv.; Ov. *Am.* iii. 9, 61.

[4] *Perillus.*] A cunning artificer in brass, who made for *Phalaris,* tyrant of Agrigentum in Sicily, a bull, to be used as a means of torture for criminals, a fire having been lighted under the figure after they had been put inside. As a reward Phalaris ordered the experiment to be first made on Perillus. Hence Ovid, *Ar. Am.* i. 653, Phalaris tauro violenti membra Perilli, Torruit: infelix imbuit auctor opus.

[5] *At nullo dominæ teritur sub limine amor qui.*—Paley.

so much sleeping near the threshold of a mistress : it remains
constant, and submits to unmerited threats. Though despised,
it makes overtures of forgiveness ; though hurt, confesses that
it was in the wrong ; and returns of itself, though its feet are
unwilling.[1]   Thou, too, credulous one, that, in the fulness
of thy amorous fortune, puttest on an air of pride, *remember
that* no woman has constancy in her long.   Does any one
pay vows in the middle of a storm, when even in port a ship is
often wrecked ?   Or does any one claim the prize before a race
is finished, before the wheel of his chariot has grazed the goal
for the seventh time ?[2]   Fallacious are the breezes that seem
to blow favourably in love : if a fall be late in coming, it is
great when it does come.   Do thou, meanwhile, though she
may love thee, yet keep thy joy shut up in the silence of thy
heart.   For in a love-affair it happens, I know not how,
that a man's proudest words always do him harm.   Though
she invite thee repeatedly, be careful to go only once : that
which excites envy does not generally last long.   But if the
times of old, and the girls who lived in them, were still in
vogue, I should be what thou art now : I am conquered by
the times.   They shall not however change my principles :
let each one know how to follow out his own path.   But as
for you that often transfer your attentions from one love to another, how much does the pain, so caused, torture your eyes !
You see a delicate maid exquisitely fair ; you see a brunette ;
either hue attracts you.   You see a maid of Grecian form ; you
see our own country-women ; the beauty of each captivates you.
Be a girl clad in purple, or in plebeian garb ; each of them,
individually, inflicts a smarting wound : since one maid brings
quite enough sleeplessness to your eyes, let one be sufficient
evil to every one.

[1] Cf. Ovid, *Rem. Am.* 217, Quanto minus ire voles, magis ire me-
mento : Perfice, et *invitos* currere coge *pedes*.
[2] *The seventh time.*]   In the Greek stadium and Roman circus the
racers took seven turns round the pillar (*meta*), the proximity to which
of the wheel is implied by *terere.* See Soph. *Ell.* 726. Sueton. *Domit.*
4, Missus singulos a *septenis* spatiis ad *quina corripuit.*

ELEGY XVIII.[1] [ii. 26. K.]

I SAW thee, my life, in a dream, wearily plying thy hands in the Ionian sea, after the wreck of thy ship; and confessing all the falsehoods that thou hadst told me; and no longer able to raise thy head, heavy with sea-water, and tossed on the purple waves of the sea like Helle,[2] who was carried on his downy back by the golden ram. How afraid I was lest the sea, perchance, should bear thy name, and the mariner weep, as he passed over water called after thee! How many were the vows that I made to Neptune, to Castor and his brother, and to thee, Leucothoë,[3] once a mortal, now a goddess! Thou, with difficulty raising the tops of thy fingers from the water, calledst, now at the point of death, continually on my name. If Glaucus had chanced to see thy eyes, thou wouldst have been made a Nymph of the Ionian main : and the Nereids, fair Nesæe,[4] azure Cymothoë,[5] would be carping at thee from jealousy. But I saw rushing to thy aid the dolphin, that, I suppose, had carried the harper Arion.[6] I was endeavouring to throw myself from the top of a rock, when fear awoke me and dispelled the vision.[7] Now let people admire the attachment to me of so fair a maid, and let me be styled powerful by all the town. If the wealth of Cambyses and Crœsus[8] were to be offered to her, she would not say, Begone, poet, from my couch. For when she repeats my lays, she says that she

[1] *Elegy XVIII.*] Propertius gives an account of a dream of his, in which Cynthia had been shipwrecked, and he had tried to save her: his object is to deter her from proceeding on a contemplated voyage, though at the same time he professes his willingness to accompany her.

[2] *Helle.*] She was the daughter of Athamas and Nephele, and was saved, with her brother Phryxus, by the ram with the golden fleece, from the sacrifice awaiting her brother, but fell into the sea between Sigeium and the Chersonese, which was afterwards called Ἕλλης ποντός. See Ovid, *Her.* xviii. 137.

[3] *Leucothoë.*] (*Matuta, Ino.*) She threw herself, to avoid the rage of her husband Athamas, into the sea, and was afterwards, with *Melicerta* or *Glaucus*, her son, worshipped as a sea-goddess.

[4] Cf. *Georg.* iv. 338. [5] *Æn.* i. 144.

[6] See Hdt. i. 23. Ovid, *Fast.* ii. 83—118.

[7] Cf. Ovid, *Her.* x. 13, *Excussere metus somnum: conterrita surgo.*

[8] *Crœsus.*] Crœsus, afterwards conquered by *Cyrus*, father of *Cambyses*, was king of Lydia, in which was the *Pactolus*, so celebrated for its golden sands.

hates wealthy lovers: no girl respects poetry so deeply. In
love constancy and fidelity avail much: he that can make
many presents, may love many maids. If my girl propose to
cross the wide ocean, I will go with her, and one breeze shall
waft us, faithful pair. One bed shall serve for us when
asleep, one tree for an abode; we will always drink from
the same cup, and a single plank shall form the couch for us
lovers, be the prow or the stern my bed-chamber. All hard-
ships will I go through: let the blustering east wind rage,
and the chilly south drive the ships before it, and all ye winds
may blow that troubled the unfortunate Ulysses, and a thousand Grecian ships on the Eubœan shore.[1] And ye that moved
two continents when a dove[2] was sent forward on the unknown sea to guide the inexperienced Argo: only let her
never be out of my sight, even though Jupiter strike the
vessel. Of a surety we will lie exposed, side by side, on the
shore: the wave may toss me, if but a little sand cover thee.
But Neptune is not unkind to love like ours: Neptune is as
great a lover as his brother Jupiter: witness the deflowering
of Amymone[3] in Argos while carrying water, and Lerne's
lake, made by the trident's stroke. The god granted her wish
at the price of her embraces, and her golden urn gushed with
water sent by a god. The rape of Orithyia[4] has shown that
Boreas is not cruel to lovers: Love is a god that lays low the
powers of earth and the mighty seas. Scylla, believe me,
will be gentle to us, and so will vast Charybdis,[5] and never
swallow up our ship with any alternate wave. The stars, too,

[1] At Aulis.
[2] *A dove.*] The *duo litora* are *Symplegades* or *closing islands*: they
used to unite and crush to pieces every ship that attempted to pass the
channel between them. The Argonauts, on coming to them, sent forward
a dove, by the advice of Juno, and by passing through immediately after
the rocks had parted, and before they could again close, escaped with
only the loss of their rudder.
[3] *Amymone.*] She was the daughter of Danaus, on whose arrival at
Argos the country was suffering from drought; Amymone was sent for
water by her father, and while so engaged, was met by Neptune, embraced, and directed to the well at Lerne, which, according to another
version of the tradition, he made to gush out of a rock which he had
pierced with his trident, after having hurled it at a Satyr who was mo-
lesting Amymone.
[4] *Orithyia.*] See note on i. 20, 31.
[5] *Charybdis.*] See Odyssey, xii. 105.

themselves, will be shrouded in no darkness: Orion and the Kids [1] will be clear. But if my life must be given up in trying to save you, I shall come to no inglorious end.

ELEGY XIX.[2] [ii. 27. K.]

You mortals are ever uncertain of the hour of your death, and of the way by which death is to come ; and you explore the sky's clear face for the Phœnician discovery :[3] what star is lucky for a man, and what unlucky, whether he is bound for the land of the Parthians on foot or of the Britons by sea, and has before him the uncertain perils of a journey by sea or land. You weep at turmoil again raging round your head, when Mars brings two hostile bands together. You are afraid of fire in your house, or of its falling, and lest poisoned cups reach your lips. The lover alone knows when, and by what death, he is to perish ; he fears neither the blasts of Boreas nor the battle-fray. Even though he be sitting, with oar in hand, under the Stygian reed-bed, and be looking upon the melancholy sails of the infernal bark, if but a flying glimpse of his mistress recall him, even though doomed to die, he will be allowed to return from a journey to which all are liable.

ELEGY XX.[4] [ii. 28. K.]

JUPITER, have pity, at length, on a suffering girl ; the death of one so fair will be a disgrace to thee. For the season

[1] *The Kids.*] The Kids heralded a storm on their rising, which was about the 6th of October. See *Georg.* i. 205 ; *Æneid*, ix. 658 ; Hor. *Od.* iii. 1, 27.

[2] *Elegy XIX.*] The lover alone knows that he is doomed to die with love for his mistress, a spell powerful enough to revive him even at death's door.

[3] *The Phœnicians.*] The Chaldeans generally had the reputation of being the discoverers of Astrology. Propertius attributes the origin of that art to the Phœnicians in consequence of their well-known skill in navigating by observation of the stars.

[4] *Elegy XX.*] This beautiful poem was written on an occasion of Cynthia's dangerous illness. Nothing can be more refined and tasteful than the mythological allusions by which he at once compliments and consoles her. At the same time he warns her that sickness is sent as a punishment for broken vows.—*Paley.* According to Hertzberg's chronological arrangement of the poems, the present one was written later than A. U. C. 729. and before 732.

is come[1] when the air is scorchingly hot, and the land is beginning to glow beneath the parching dog-star. But the fault lies not so much in the heat, or in the sky, as in the frequent contempt cast on the sanctity of the gods. This it is that destroys hapless maidens, this has destroyed them in times past ; all their vows are carried away by the wind and water. Has Venus herself been incensed that you have compared your beauty with hers ? She is a hostile goddess to those who surpass her in beauty. Have you despised the shrine of Pelasgic Juno, or ventured to deny that the eyes of Pallas are handsome ?[2] You fair ones never know how to govern your tongues ; this malady has been brought upon you by your talking and your beauty. But to you who are now suffering the vexations and the many perils of life, a gentler time will come with your last day. When Io's head was metamorphosed, she lowed in her youth ; now she is a goddess, whereas she once drank, as a cow, of the water of the Nile. Ino, too, was a wanderer on earth in her early years ; her now, as Leucothoë, the distressed mariner implores. Andromeda had been made the prey of sea-monsters ; she afterwards became the glorious wife of Perseus. Callisto[3] had wandered, as a bear, through Arcadian lands ; as a star she now directs the ships by night. But should the Fates bring you speedily to your last rest, happy will be your lot after burial ; you will be able to tell Semele[4] of the danger to which a fair woman is exposed ; she will believe you, being taught by her own misfortune ; and you will have with unanimous consent the first place among the Nymphs sung by Homer, and the Heroines. Now that you are stricken, bear with fate as well as you may ; the divine will, and even the day of doom, can be altered.

---

[1] *For the season is come.*] The unhealthiness of Rome in summer and autumn is well known. Hence *enim* (for) refers to *mortua* (the death, &c.), and implies that the hopes of Cynthia's recovery were but slight at that season.—*Paley.*

[2] *The eyes of Pallas.*] Paley thinks this alludes to some foolish discussion of the day as to whether γλαυκῶπις (having eyes of a grey or greenish grey colour) was a complimentary epithet, or the reverse.

[3] *Callisto.*] The daughter of *Lycaon.*

[4] *Semele.*] She was the daughter of Cadmus and Harmonia : Juno, from jealousy, induced her to ask Jupiter, who was in love with her, to visit her with the same majesty as he did the queen of heaven ; he came as the god of thunder, and Semele was consumed by lightning, the child, Dionysus, with whom she was pregnant, being saved by Jupiter.

Even Juno, goddess of marriage, will grant you this favour ;
Juno herself suffers when a damsel dies. The wheel, turned
with magic spells,[1] fails ; the smouldering laurel-leaf is lying
on the desolate hearth ; the moon refuses to come down so
often from the sky ; and the bird[2] of dusky hue is croaking
forth its ill-omened note. One dark boat, instrument of fate,
sailing on the waters below, will carry all my love. Have
pity, gods, I pray, if not on one, on two : I shall live if
she lives : if she falls, I shall fall. In return for the fulfil-
ment of my prayers, I engage[3] to offer verses in the temple :
I will write "THE DAMSEL SAVED THROUGH MIGHTY JOVE."
She, too, with covered head, shall sit at thy feet, and shall relate as she sits the dangers of her long illness. Let this thy
mercy continue, Persephone,[4] and be not thou, O husband of
Persephone, more cruel. There are, down below, so many
thousands of fair women : let there be one beautiful form, if
allowable, in the regions above. You have Iope,[5] and fair
Tyro[6] and Europe,[7] and impure Pasiphäe,[8] and all the beauties
produced by ancient Troy, and Achaia, and Thebes,[9] and the
plundered kingdom of old Priam ; every Roman maid, too, in
the number *of the beautiful*, has gone. All these the greedy
fire has taken. Neither beauty endures for ever, nor is any
one's prosperity lasting : either far or near, his death is awaiting every one. Since you, light of my eyes, have been res-

[1] *The wheel.*] The *rhombus* is the ἴυγξ of Theocr. 2.
[2] *The bird.*] The raven, whose croaking to this day is said to portend
death in a family.
[3] *I engage.*] *Damnatus* is used of one obliged to pay anything. Cf.
Hor. *Sat.* ii. 2, 85, Ni sic fecissent, gladiatorum dare centum *Damnati*
populo paria.
[4] *Persephone,* &c.] Some editors make this the beginning of another
Elegy, but without sufficient reason. Having spoken of what he will do
in the event of Cynthia's recovery, Propertius now goes on to speak of
it as realized, and begs of Proserpine and Pluto not to withdraw the boon
they have granted.
[5] Iope, or *Cassiopeia*, was the wife of Cepheus, and mother of Andromeda. Some read *Antiope*.
[6] *Tyro.*] The daughter of Salmoneus.
[7] *Europe.*] The daughter of Agenor, carried off to Crete by Jupiter
under the form of a bull. (Moschus ii.)
[8] *Pasiphäe.*] The wife of Minos, is called *nec proba*, from her suffering the embraces of a bull, and thereby becoming the mother of the
Minotaur.
[9] *Thebes.*] *Et Thebæ*, Scaliger, for *Phœbi*.

cued from imminent peril, pay to Diana her due tribute of a
chorus.   Pay also your tribute of watching to the goddess
that was once a heifer; pay also to me the proper tribute of
ten nights.[1]

ELEGY XXI.[2] TO CYNTHIA. [ii. 29. K.]

As I was tipsily wandering, light of my life, late at night,
without a slave's hand to lead me, I was met by a tiny crowd of
boys,—I know not how many, fear prevented me from counting
them:—some of them seemed to be keeping in store for me
little torches; others, arrows: some even seemed to be preparing bonds for me.   They were naked: one of the more mis-
chievous said, "Seize that man, you know him well. This was
the man: it was for him an angry woman engaged us."   He
spoke, and in a minute a rope was round my neck.   Thereupon
one bade them pull me into the middle of them: but another said,
"Hang the man for not taking us to be gods.   She has been
waiting for you,—more than you deserve,—for whole hours
together; but you, stupid man, are making for I know not
what door.   When she has unbound her Sidonian night-cap,
and opened her slumber-laden eyes, there will be wafted to
you odours from no Arabian herbs, but some that Love has
made with his own hands.   Spare him now, brothers: see, he
promises to be constant in love; and, we have now arrived at
the appointed house."   So they led me forwards, and put my
garment on me again, and said, "Go now, and learn to stop
at home at nights."   It was morning, and I wished to see
whether Cynthia was sleeping by herself: she was alone in bed.
I was thunderstruck: she had never appeared to me more beautiful, not even when in her purple dress, and when she was
going from her house to tell her dreams to chaste Vesta;
dreams that would hurt neither her nor me.   Thus she appeared when just awake: ah! how powerful, of itself, is a
fair form.   "Why act you the spy on your mistress in the
morning?" said she.   "Think you that I am like yourself?
I am not so easy: I am contented with one intimate friend,

---

[1] *Ten nights.*]   Part of the worship of Io, or Isis, was the abstinence
from conjugal rights for ten nights. See infra, 25, 2. Propertius plainly
hints that Cynthia had better devote those nights to him than to Isis.

[2] *Elegy XXI.*]   The poet playfully excuses himself for having played
the spy on Cynthia, assuring her that it was a drunken frolic.

either yourself, or some one more truthful than you. There are no signs of two having been lying in the bed. See, there is not in my whole body any panting or heaving to indicate a foregone amorous conflict." She spoke, and preventing me, with her right hand, from kissing her, bounded away with her feet in loose slippers. So for my prying work upon so faithful a mistress, I am turned out of doors. Ever since then I have not had a happy night.

ELEGY XXII.[1] [ii. 30. K.]

WHITHER for flying, madman ? flight is impossible : you may fly to Tanais, yet Love will ever follow you. Riding in air on the back of Pegasus [2] will not avail; nor though your feet be furnished with wings like Perseus,[3] nor though the breezes, cleft by your winged heels, waft you with a lofty flight like Mercury's,[4] will it be of any use. Love is always hovering over your head : he hovers over a lover, and alights with all his weight on free necks. A stern guardian he is, ever awake, and will never suffer you to raise your eyes from the ground when once caught. Besides, if you are in fault, he is a god that can be moved by prayer, if he only sees that your prayers follow close on the offence. Let surly old men find fault with our merry habits: let us, my life, continue to travel in the way that we have once set before us. Let their ears burden themselves with musty saws : this is the place for you to sound, O skilfully-tuned pipe, undeservedly tossed into Mæander's wave when the face of Pallas [5] was disfigured by

[1] *Elegy XXII.*] This somewhat obscure poem is a soliloquy of Propertius, to the purport that it is impossible to fly from love ; that therefore it is folly to attempt it ; and that Cynthia had better agree with him in that conclusion.

[2] *Pegasus.*] The celebrated winged horse was the fruit of the intercourse of Jupiter and Medusa, hence we find him called (*Juv.* iii. 118) *Gorgoneus caballus.* By his help Bellerophon was enabled to overcome the Chimæra.

[3] *Perseus.*] On going to fight the Gorgons, he was furnished with winged sandals by the Nymphs.

[4] Mercury is generally depicted with wings attached either to his hat. or sandals.

[5] *Pallas.*] She is said to have been the inventor of musical instruments, more particularly of wind instruments, and to have thrown away the pipe on seeing, by reflection in the water, that her face was disfigured by blowing it. See Ovid, *A. A.* iii. 505. *Fasti,* 700. Aristot. Polit. viii. 6.

the puffing of her cheeks. Are you now prepared, stern soul, to cross the Phrygian waves, and sail for the shores of the Hyrcanian sea ? to defile by mutual slaughter gods common [1] to two nations, and to bear to your country's altars honours bought too dear ? Am I to be ashamed of living contentedly with my mistress only ? If this be a crime, it is the crime of love. Let no one charge me with it. Make up your mind, Cynthia, to dwell with me in a cool grot on a mossy hill : there shall you see the tuneful Sisters cling to the rocks, and sing of the delightful thefts of ancient Jove : of how he was consumed with love for Semele,[2] how madly fond of Io, and how, in the form of a bird,[3] he flew to the halls of Troy. But if there is no one on earth able to resist the arms of the winged one, why am I alone arraigned for a universal fault ? Nor will you put the Virgin Muses to the blush : their company, too, knows what it is to love, if, at least, one of them submitted to be embraced by one in the form of Œagrus amid Bistonian rocks.[4] When they place you at the head of the dance, with Bacchus bearing his skilful[5] thyrsus in the midst, I will suffer holy crowns of ivy to hang from my forehead, for without you my genius is powerless.

ELEGY XXIII.[6] [ii. 31. K.]

Do you ask why I am late in coming to you ? A portico decked with gold has been opened to Phœbus by the great Cæsar. The whole was magnificently arranged with rows of columns of Carthaginian marble,[7] among which was the

[1] *Gods common.*] Allusion is to a treaty between Pontus and Rome against the Parthians.

[2] *Semele.*] *Semela* is the ablative : *combustus* alludes to Jupiter's ardent love, and to the violent death (supr. 20, 26) of Semele.

[3] *A bird.*] In the form of an eagle Jupiter carried off "the son of Tros, fair *Ganymede*," either from Troy or Mount Ida.

[4] *Bistonian rocks.*] The Bistoni were people of Thrace, for the whole of which country their name is often used. *Calliope* became, either by Œagrus or Apollo, the mother of Linus.

[5] *Skilful.*] The epithet *doctus* is applied by a common figure to the thyrsus with which Bacchus regulates the movements of the dance.

[6] *Elegy XXIII.*] A description of the temple dedicated to Apollo by Augustus, B. C. 27, in commemoration of the victory of Actium. The subject proves the poem to have been one of its author's earliest compositions.

[7] *Carthaginian marble.*] See Hor. *Od.* ii. 18, 4, Non trabes Hymettiæ

company of the daughters of old Danaus. There I saw Phœbus, in marble, more beautiful than life, reciting verses, though to his mute lyre. Around the altar stood four life-like oxen, carved by Myron's[1] hand. From between the porticos, the temple rose of polished marble, and dearer to Phœbus than his native Ortygia. Two chariots of the sun surmounted the highest point: the doors, too, nobly wrought of Libyan ivory, set forth, one, the hurling of the Gauls[2] from Parnassus' peak; the other, in mourning imagery, the deaths of the daughter of Tantalus[3] *and her children*. Lastly, the Pythian god, between his mother and sister, dressed in a long robe, sounds forth verses.

ELEGY XXIV.[4] TO CYNTHIA. [ii. 32. K.]

WHOSOEVER sees you goes wrong: he therefore that does not see you, will not desire *to sin:* your showing yourself must bear the blame. For why, Cynthia, do you constantly go to the doubtful oracles at Præneste,[5] or the fort of Æacan Telegonus?[6] Or why does a carriage constantly whirl you to Herculean Tibur?[7] Or why does the Appian Way[8] so often

premunt *columnas ultimâ recisas Africâ.* The marble came from Numidia, and was of the sort now called *giallo antico.* Fea in Hor. l. c.

[1] Myron was born in Bœotia B. C. 480, and was a great sculptor of animals: he is particularly famed for a *Cow* (Bucula, Auson. *Epig.* 58) and his figure of the *Discobulus.* He was an engraver on metals.

[2] The Gauls, under *Brennus* their leader, made an attack, B. C. 279, on the temple at Delphi, whence they were repulsed by the steady bravery of the inhabitants, aided, according to the common account, by Apollo. See *Justin.* xxiv. 8, and cf. iv. (iii.) 13, 51.

[3] *The daughter of Tantalus.*] Niobe.

[4] *Elegy XXIV.*] A jealous remonstrance to Cynthia for her frequent absence from Rome, upon false pretexts and for no good purpose. The poet concludes by saying that if she shelters herself on the plea of being like other women, and professes her approval of their profligacy, he will have nothing to do with her.

[5] *Præneste.*] Now *Palestrina,* a town in Latium, to the S. E. of Rome, was celebrated for a temple of *Fortune.* See Cic. *De Divin.* ii. 41, for an account of the *Sortes Prænestinæ,* and *Dict. of Antiq.* s. vv. *Sortes, Oraculum.*

[6] *Telegonus.*] Tusculum (*Frascati*) is said to have been built by Telegonus, the son of Ulysses and *Circe,* whence he is called *Ææus.* From a tradition that he murdered his father, Horace (*Od.* iii. 29, 8) calls the place *Telegoni juga parricidæ.*

[7] *Herculean Tibur.*] Tibur (*Tivoli*) was a seat of the worship of Hercules. See v. 7, 82.

[8] *The Appian Way.*] This road made, B. C. 312, by *Appius Claudius*

F 2

convey you, old woman as you are ? I wish you would walk here any leisure time that you have, Cynthia: but the crowd prevents me from believing you, when it sees you running, in devotional eagerness, with kindled torches, to the grove of the Trivian goddess,[1] and bearing lights in her honour. Pompey's portico, I suppose, with its shady columns, and magnificently ornamented with purple curtains, palls upon you, and the thickly-planted even line of plane-trees, and the waters that fall from a sleeping Maro,[2] and in streams lightly bubbling all over the city when a Triton at intervals spouts water from his mouth. You are deceiving yourself: those journeys of yours betoken a secret love. It is not from the city you are so madly eager to escape, but from my sight. Your efforts are useless: the snares that you are laying for me are in vain: you are idly spreading for me nets that I am aware of, experienced *in your tricks* as I am. But it is not for myself I care so much; it is you will suffer from a loss of your good name, proportioned to your deserts. A report of you that lately came to my ears grieved me: in the whole city there was not a good word about you. But, *you will say to me,* you ought not to believe an unfriendly report: beautiful women have always had to pay the penalty of scandal. Your character has not been damned by poison having been found on you: Phœbus, thou wilt bear witness that the hands on which thou lookest are pure: and if one or two nights have been spent in long dalliance, I am not one to be moved by slight offences. The daughter of Tyndarus left her home for a foreign lover, yet she was taken back alive and uncondemned. Venus herself, though she intrigued with Mars, was nevertheless always respected in heaven; and though Ida can say that the goddess loved the shepherd Paris, and lay with him[3] among the

---

Cæcus the Censor, led from Rome, through the *porta Capena*, in a S. E. direction, to Capua, and was afterwards extended to Brundusium. We find the following towns mentioned as on it by Horace, (*Sat.* i. 5,) Aricia (*La Ricina*), Appii Forum (*Bongo Longo*), Anxur (*Terracina*), Fundi, Sinuessa, Capua, Equotuticum, Beneventum, Canusium, Rubi. Lanuvium (v. 8) was also on it.

[1] *The Trivian goddess.*]   Diana, worshipped at Aricia.

[2] *Maro.*]   The son of Silenus. His figure, teeming water from a jar, was a very common device for fountains and conduits in Italy: hence Lucret. vi. 1264, Corpora *silanos* ad aquarum strata jacebant.

[3] *Lay with him.*]   This legend is not recorded by any other writer.

flocks of his fold. This was seen by the troops of Hamadryad sisters, and old Sileni, and the sire of the troop, with whom, Paris, you gathered apples in Ida's grot, catching in your hand gifts dropped into it by the Naiad *Œnone*. Among such a swarm of immodest women does any one ask, "Why is this girl so rich? who made her the presents? whence got she them?" Oh! too happy would Rome be in our time if one girl were to act contrary to custom! Before *Cynthia*, Lesbia did the same as she:[1] one that follows *a bad example* is, surely, less to be blamed. Any man that looks for men like the primitive Tatius,[2] and the hardy Sabines, has but lately set foot in our city. You would be able to drain the sea, and count the stars on high with mortal hand, sooner than make our girls dislike sinning: that was the custom in king Saturn's reign, and when Deucalion's flood was on the earth, and after the flood of Deucalion renowned in story. Tell me, who has been able to preserve the bed undefiled? What goddess has lived faithful to one god? The wife of mighty Minos in days gone by, so men say, was smitten by the handsome form of a grim bull. In like manner, Danaë,[3] when surrounded by a wall of brass, could not say no, though chaste, to the great Jupiter. But if you admire the profligate Greek and Roman women, live free, for ever, from my censure.

ELEGY XXV.[4] [ii. 33. K.]

THE dreary ceremony is now coming again, to my sorrow; Cynthia has by this time engaged to keep ten nights.[5] May the daughter of Inachus perish, for introducing ceremonies for Ausonian women from the warm Nile! The goddess, whoever she may have been, that has so often parted eager lovers, has always been odious to me. You, Io, when Jove

---

It is not impossible that the poet, who has elsewhere erred in his mythology (see vs. 4, 40,) has confounded Paris with Anchises.—*Paley.*

[1] *Lesbia.*] The mistress of Catullus.
[2] *Tatius.*] The king of the Sabines in the time of Romulus.
[3] *Danaë.*] Jupiter descended to her in a golden shower.
[4] *Elegy XXV.*] After abusing Isis, by ceremonies in whose honour he is debarred from Cynthia's company, the poet entreats his mistress to be kind to him, ridiculing, at the same time, her taste for debauchery and loose company.
[5] *Ten nights.*] See supr. 20, 61.

was secretly in love with you, felt what it was to wander
over many ways, when Juno forced you, maiden as you were,
to have horns, and to lose your human voice, and speak but
in the rude cry of an animal. How often have you hurt your
mouth with oak-leaves! how often, after feeding, have you
been shut up in solitude in your stall! Have you become
proud as a goddess because Jupiter stripped you of your
beast's look? Is not Egypt, with its swarthy denizens, enough
for you? Why did you come all the long way to Rome?
What good is it to you to see girls sleeping by themselves?
You will have horns again, mark my words; or else we will
drive you out of our city, cruel one; the Nile has never been
on friendly terms with the Tiber. Let me, however, with
you whom I have softened with great pain and grief to myself, when released from these nightly engagements, enjoy a
fill of love.

You hear me not, and suffer my words to be laughed at,
when the oxen of Icarus[1] are now slowly turning the stars to
the morning. You sit long at your wine; midnight moves you
not; is your hand not yet weary of throwing the dice?
Perish he who introduced neat wine, and he who was the first
to mix wholesome water with nectar! O Icarus, fitly slain
by Attic shepherds, thou knowest how fatal is the smell of
wine. Thou, too, O Centaur Eurytion,[2] didst perish by wine,
and thou, O Polyphemus,[3] by the juice of Thracian grapes.
By wine beauty is lost; by wine man's prime is spoilt;
through wine a mistress often forgets her protector. Ah me!
deep draughts of wine affect her not; well, go on drinking;
you are beautiful still; wine harms you not, when your garlands droop, and fall forward into your cup, and you read my
poems in a drawling tone. Let your table flow more liberally
with Falernian, and let it froth more delicately in your golden
chalice! But no one retires with good will to her solitary

---

[1] *Icarus.*] A king of Attica who received from Bacchus bags filled
with wine, which he distributed freely, giving it, amongst others, to some
shepherds, who killed him, thinking that they were poisoned. He was
placed in heaven by Bacchus, and is the same as Bootes or Arcturus,
commonly called *Charles's Wain.*

[2] *Eurytion.*] See note on ii. 2, 9.

[3] *Polyphemus.*] Ulysses made Polyphemus drunk, and then put out
his one eye, and slew him. See Hom. *Odyss.* ix. passim, and Eur. *Cycl.*
411 seq.

couch. There is something that Love forces you to miss. There is always a more favourable disposition towards absent lovers ; long possession lowers the value even of the devoted.

ELEGY XXVI.[1] TO LYNCEUS. [ii. 34. K.]

How is it that any one continues to intrust the person of his mistress to Love? In that way I have nearly had my girl snatched from me. I speak from experience ; no one is faithful in a love matter. Not seldom does every one look after a beautiful woman as his own prize. That god sets at defiance laws of kinship, parts friends, and drives to arms perfect friends. A guest came to the hospitable house of Menelaus, and proved an adulterer ; and did not the Colchian maid follow a stranger? Lynceus, traitor, could you meddle with my darling? did not your hands then fall powerless? Suppose she had not been as faithful and true as she was, could you have lived, and been so guilty? Stab me to the heart, or poison me if you please ; only keep off from my mistress. You shall be my most intimate friend, and closest companion ; I admit you, my friend, as a master over my property ; from my mistress, from my mistress only, I beg you keep away ; I cannot bear even Jupiter as a rival. When by myself, I am jealous of my own shadow, a thing of nought ; foolish am I, and foolish the fear with which I often tremble. The only reason for my pardoning so great a sin, is that your tongue erred from excess in wine. Never shall I be deceived by the wrinkle of an ascetic ; all know, now-a-days, how sweet it is to love. Even my friend Lynceus is madly in love in his old age : the only thing on which I hug myself is that you are becoming a votary of my gods.

What will your skill in Socratic philosophy avail you now, or your knowledge of the motion of the universe ? Of what fruit is the reading of the poetry of the Erechthean[2] sage ?

---

[1] *Elegy XXVI.*] Lynceus, a fellow poet, and old friend of Propertius, had attempted to win Cynthia's affections, for which he takes him to task, advises him, since he has at last fallen in love, to change the style of his writings : the piece ends with a eulogy on Virgil, and an exhortation to Lynceus to follow in the steps of other poets that have sung of their mistresses.

[2] *The Erechthean sage.*] Æschylus, born at Eleusis, hence called Erechthean, which is equivalent to Attic. From Ar. *Ran.* 1046, we see that he confessed to have no love in him, and never wanted any. Some read *Cretæi* of Epimenides.

Your aged authority is of no use in a violent love.   It would
be better for you to imitate Philetas,[1] the favourite of the
Muses, and the dreams[2] of the not turgid Callimachus.   For
though you treat of the streams of the Ætolian Achelous, and
how the river flowed when conquered in a severe love contest,[3]
and how the deceitful wave of Mæander strays over the Phrygian plains, and thwarts its own progress,[4] and how Arion,[5]
the speaking horse of Adrastus, was a melancholy conqueror
at the funeral games of Archemorus ;[6] the melancholy destruction of the chariot of Amphiaraus[7] is of no use to you,
nor the fall of Capaneus[8] that pleased the mighty Jove.
Cease also to write verses after the style of Æschylus,[9] cease,
and let your limbs indulge in the soft dance.   Begin now to
confine your strains within a narrower range, and come, grave
poet, to describe your own love-fires.   You will not live safer

  [1] *Philetas.*]   A poet of Cos, who lived about B. c. 272; his poetry was
chiefly elegiac, devoted to the praise of his mistress Bittis (or *Battis*,
Ovid, *Trist.* i. 6, 2, Nec tantum *Coo Battis* amata *suo*) ; he is mentioned
by Theocr. (vii. 39) as his model.—*Lachmann*, as the form *Batto* is
found in this line, reads Tu, *Battus*, &c., " Imitate in thy song Philetas
the chronicler of Batto :" compare *Argus* (supr. 18, 39).

  [2] *The dreams*, &c.]   By *somnia*, Barth and Paley understand the
Aίτία of Callimachus, (for which see Blomfield's Callim. p. 172,) so called because he pretended that the subject of it was suggested to him in a
dream.   Prop. calls Callim. *non inflati*, to acquit his favourite poet of
the common and not altogether unjust charge of being inclined to bom-
bast. See ii. 1, 40, Intonet *angusto pectore* Callimachus, which expresses
precisely the same idea.

  [3] *Love contest.*]   The river-god Achelous fought with Hercules for
Deïanira. See Soph. *Trach.* ad init.

  [4] *Thwarts its own progress.*]   By the excessively tortuous manner of
its course.

  [5] Arion was the offspring of Poseidon and Demeter. Adrastus received
him from Hercules. (Hes. *Scut. Herc.* 120.)   Statius (*Theb.* vi. 417) calls
him *præsagus*, and in the following lines a description of his conduct in
a race is given.   For another instance of a horse speaking, see *Iliad* xix.
404 seq.

  [6] *Archemorus.*]   Son of Lycurgus king of Nemea.   When the *Seven*
were on their way to Thebes, his nurse left him alone to show them the
road, on which he was killed by a dragon.   Amphiaraus, seeing an omen
boding death to himself and friends, called the child, whose name was
Opheltes, Archemorus.   The Nemean games (cf. the Epigram, Ζηνὸς
Αητοίδαο Παλαίμονος, ᾿Αρχεμόροιο) were in his honour.   The horse is
called *tristis* from the melancholy origin of the games.

  [7] The chariot of this hero, together with himself, was swallowed up
near the Ismenus.

  [8] See on i. 15, 15.   [9] Write Elegiac poetry.

than Antimachus or Homer:[1] a comely maid looks down even
on the mighty gods. But the bull yields not to the heavy
plough till he has his horns caught in the tough lasso, and
you will not of your own accord submit to so harsh a bondage
as love ; you are restive and will have to be first tamed by
me. No woman now-a-days cares about inquiring into the
system of the universe ; or why the moon is eclipsed by the
steeds of her brother ; or whether any judge awaits them
after the Stygian waves ; or whether lightnings flash and thun-
ders roll from any design. Look at me, who had but little
property left me by my father, and can boast of no triumph
of my ancestors in ancient warfare, how I am the chief guest
among a company of lasses through the same talent for which
I am now disparaged by you. Be it my delight whom a god
of unerring aim has pierced to the heart with a shaft, to lie
at ease with yesterday's garlands on my brow. Let Virgil,[2]
who is now reviving the arms of Trojan Æneas, and the
building of a city in Latin districts, find pleasure in describing
the shore of Actium, guarded by Phœbus, and the brave fleets
of Cæsar.

Yield, ye Roman writers, ye Grecian poets, yield ; something greater than the Iliad is arising. Thou, O Virgil,
singest of Thyrsis beneath the pinewood of shady Galœsus,
and of Daphnis with their well-worn reeds, and how the sending of ten apples, and a kid[3] of a goat that was never milked,
can bribe maidens. Happy man that buyest love cheap with
apples ! Tityrus himself may sing to such a maid, though
she thank him not. Happy Corydon who tries to enjoy the
young Alexis, the darling of his rustic master ! Though he
tire[4] of his oaten pipe, and desist from playing it, yet among
the Hamadryads he gains praise with equal ease. Thou de-

---

[1] See Catull. xcv. 9.
[2] He alludes to Virg. *Æn.* viii. 675 seq. *In medio* (of the shield of
Æneas) *classes æratas; Actia bella cernere erat.* There was a temple of
Apollo on the promontory, from which Apollo was called *Actius.* (See
Thuc. i. 29.)
[3] *Thyrsis, Daphnis, apples, and a kid,* &c.] Allusions to Virgil's Ec-
logues, more particularly v. vii. iii. 70, ii. 30, 2. The sense of v. 72 is,
" Though his mistress may not thank him, yet, as a tune on the pipe does
not cost much, it will not trouble him much to play to her.
[4] *Though he tire,* &c.] That is to say, Though he lays down the
bucolic reed, he gains equal reputation in singing of forest trees (the

liverest the precepts of the sage of Ascra, and of the best land for corn-crops, and the best mountain-land for vines. Thou, Virgil, composest such a strain as Apollo's skilful fingers deftly play on the harp. These strains will not fall unpleasantly on the ear of any reader, be he skilled in or ignorant of Love. But the tuneful swan[1] is not made inferior by strains of this stamp, nor, if inferior, has he been silenced by the insipid not eof Anser. Varro,[2] too, sported in this way, having finished his poem on Jason, Varro, a most ardent lover of his Leucadia. This theme has also been sung in the writings of the amorous Catullus, by which Lesbia has become more known even than Helen. The page of the learned[3] Calvus confessed this, when singing the death of the hapless Quintilia ; and how many wounds inflicted by the fair Lycoris[4] has Gallus, lately dead, washed in Lethe's stream ! Cynthia, too, *will become known*, from having been praised by the song of Propertius, if fame will place my name among these poets.

Georgics). He pleases the Nymphs, and therefore knows how to win woman's favour.

[1] *But the tuneful swan, &c.*] The meaning is, "If Virgil does write love-songs, he does not lower himself by it : nor, if they are worse than his Epics, will Anser prevent him from writing." Virgil (*Ecl.* ix. 35) has "Neque adhuc Vario videor nec dicere Cinnâ Digna, sed argutos inter strepere *anser* olores," implying that his poetry, as compared with that of Varius and Cinna, was like the cackling of a goose, (*anser*,) contrasted with the note of a swan, the bird of song. Propertius, accordingly, applying to these lines the name of a certain Anser, a Grub-steet bard of the day, and a detractor of Virgil, says that his abuse will not prevent him (v.) from writing. Anser is mentioned in Ovid, *Trist.* ii. 435.

[2] *Varro.*] Varro Atacinus, so called from being born B. c. 82, near the Atax, translated the *Argonautica* of Apoll. Rhod. and wrote, besides, love Elegies, with the title of *Leucadia*, perhaps from the name of his mistress. For *flamma* we find in some editions *cura*, or *fama*.

[3] See note on 17, 4.

[4] *Lycoris.*] Her real name was Cytheris, she was famous as the mistress of Corn. Gallus, poet and statesman, who killed himself, B. c. 25, on becoming suspected of high treason by Augustus.

BOOK IV.

ELEGY I.[1] [iii. 1. K.]

O SHADE of Callimachus, and sacred rites of Coan Philetas, suffer me, I pray you, to enter your grove. I am the first[2] priest who enter it to introduce among Greek strains Italian poetry drawn from a pure source. Tell me, in what cave was it that ye both composed your fine-spun verses ? In what way did ye enter there ? Or what water did ye drink ? Farewell to him that employs his Muse on warlike themes ! Finely polished[3] be that verse through which fame is to raise me on high from earth, and a Muse originating with me is to triumph with steeds bedecked, the tiny Loves are to ride with me in my car, and a crowd of writers is to follow my wheels. Why do ye vainly strive against me with slackened reins ? A broad road by which to reach the Muses is not to be had. There will be many writers, O Rome, to exalt thy glories, and to sing that Bactria[4] is doomed to be the limit of thy empire: but this production from the Sisters' mount, which thou mayest read in time of peace, our page has brought thee by a way hitherto untrodden. O Muses, give soft wreaths to your poet-votary ; a hard chaplet will not suit my brow. *I am not unattacked by envy*, but any merit that an envious crowd may have denied me when alive, honour will restore to me, after my death, with double interest. After

[1] *Elegy I.*] He again expresses his determination to write Elegiacs only, as best suited to his genius. This book consists of Elegies written A. U. C. 371-2.

[2] *I am the first*, &c.] The meaning is that his Elegiac poetry is the first that is written professedly in imitation of that of the Greeks of the Alexandrian school.

[3] *Finely polished.*] *Tenui pumice exactus*, properly applied to the parchment on which the poetry was written, (Catull. i. 2 ; xxii. 8,) is borrowed to express the careful composition of the verses. The expressions in 9—12 are borrowed from a triumphal procession.

[4] *Bactria.*] Bactria (Balkh), the chief town of the province of Bactriana, is put for the province itself. The expedition against the Parthians which took place A. U. C. 734, B. C. 20, was already in contemplation. See infr. El. 4.

a poet's death, antiquity enhances all he has done, a man's name is greater and more talked of after he is in his tomb. For who could know of the battering of the citadel by the wooden horse; or that a river fought with the Thracian hero;[1] that the Idæan Simois was the cradle of Jupiter in infancy; that Hector, dragged round the plain, thrice stained the chariot wheels of his foe; who could know of the prowess of Deiophobus, and Helenus, and men like Polydamas, *but for the poet?* Scarcely his own country would know Paris, under his different characters. Ilion, thou wouldst now be but little spoken of, and thou, also, O Troy, twice captured by the powers of the god of Œta.[2] Homer, too, the chronicler of thy fall, has found his work gaining in repute as time sped on: so Rome will praise me amongst its remote descendants: I, of myself, foretell that life after my death. That a mere stone point not out the spot where my bones lie in their disregarded tomb, is provided for by my vows which the Lycian god[3] approves. Let me, meanwhile, return to the usual subject of my song, that my mistress be touched by and pleased with the accustomed sound.

ELEGY II.[4] [iii. 2. K.]

THEY say that Orpheus, with his Thracian lyre, arrested wild beasts, and stopped the course of rapid streams: they say that the stones of Cithœron, brought to Thebes by musical art, united, of their own accord, to form the city-wall. Moreover, Galatea halted her steeds, wet with Ocean-spray, beneath wild Ætna, at the sound of thy strains, Polyphemus. Are we to wonder that the race of maidens delight in my strains, since Bacchus and Apollo are propitious to me? What though I have not a house supported by columns of Tænarian marble, nor ivory-like panels between the gilded

---

[1] *The Thracian hero.*] Achilles. The allusion is to his fight with the Xanthus or Scamander. See *Iliad* xxi. 210 seq.

[2] *The god of Œta.*] Hercules: Troy was taken (1) by Hercules himself in the time of Laomedon, (2) by help of his arrows, borne by Philoctetes, in Priam's time.

[3] *The Lycian god.*] Apollo, "qui *Lyciæ* tenet dumetæ, natalesque silvas." (Hor. *Od.* iii. 4, 62.)

[4] *Elegy II.*] The poet professes his contentment with his present condition, saying that Poetry supplies the place of riches and magnificence.

beams of my rooms; and though I have no orchards to rival
the Phæacian plantations,[1] nor water from the aqueduct of
Martius[2] supplying artificial grottoes; yet I have the Muses
as companions, and my verses are dear to the reader; and
Calliope wearies herself for me in choral efforts. A happy
damsel thou, who art celebrated in my book! My verses will
be so many monuments of thy beauty. For neither the costly
Pyramids that tower to the sky, nor the magnificent tomb of
Mausolus,[3] are exempt from death at last. Their grandeur
will be brought low either by fire or rain, or their solid mass
will be overcome by time and fall: but a name gained by
genius will never perish by time: the honours of genius are
deathless.

ELEGY III.[4] [iii. 3. K.]

METHOUGHT I was reclining in Helicon's soft shade, where
flows the fountain opened by Bellerophon's steed, and that I was
able to tell, on my harp-strings, of thy kings, Alba, and of
their exploits, a mighty theme; and I had put my humble
lips to those grand fountains whence thirsty father Ennius
drank before me, and sang of the brothers Curii,[5] and the javelins of the Horatii; and trophies won from kings and brought
home in the bark of Æmilius;[6] the successful delay of Fabius,
the fatal fight of Cannæ, and how the gods gave ear to holy

[1] *Phæacian plantations.*] See Hom. *Odyss.* vii. 112 seq.
[2] *Aqueduct of Martius.*] Q. *Martius Rex* was Prætor 144 B. C., and
commissioned by the senate to build an aqueduct, having his tenure of
office prolonged another year that he might be able to complete it. See
Pliny, xxxi. 24. The aqueduct commenced at a distance of 36 miles from
Rome, and the excellence of its water was proverbial. See Dict. of Antiq. v. *Aqueductus.*
[3] *Mausolus.*] The tomb erected at Halicarnassus, by Artemisia his
wife, to Mausolus, king of Caria, who died B. C. 353, was one of the seven
wonders of the world. Compare with vs. 17—22, Shakespeare, Sonnet 55,
"Not marble, not the gilded monuments," &c.
[4] *Elegy III.*] We have in this Elegy a description of a dream, in which
Propertius is urged by Apollo and Calliope to attend to Elegiac poetry
only.
[5] *The brothers Curii.*] See Livy, i. 24.
[6] *Trophies won,* &c.] Not the defeat of Perseus, king of Macedonia,
by Æmilius Paullus, which took place (167 B. C.) two years after Ennius
died, but that of *Demetrius,* governor of Pharos in the Adriatic, by Æm.
Paullus the consul. B. C. 219.

prayers ; Hannibal scared by the Lares from Rome ; and the safety of Jupiter caused by a goose's cackle :—when Phœbus, looking at me from Castalia's wood, spoke thus leaning against the grot, with his hand resting on his golden lyre :

"What have you to do, madman, with such a stream ? Who bade you enter upon the work of heroic song ? Propertius, you must hope for no fame here : your little wheels must roll gently along the smooth meads to have your book taken up and laid down often, for a maid to read it while waiting for her lover. Why has your page gone beyond the beaten track ? You must not overload the bark of your genius. Let one of your oars skim the waters, the other graze the sand : keep yourself safe : in the open sea there are very many whirlpools."

He spoke, and showed me, with his ivory quill, a seat, where a new path was cut through the moss-covered soil. There was here a green cave, with artificial stone-work, and tympana hung from the hollow rock. Accordingly I found images in earthenware of the Muses, and father Silenus, and thy reed, O Tegæean Pan : the winged doves, too, of my lady Venus, my favourites, I found dipping their purple bills in the Gorgon fountain :[1] nine maidens, too, each having her own province, employ their delicate hands on their respective gifts. One gathers ivy for thyrsi, another sets verses to music, another weaves wreaths of roses with both hands. One of these goddesses,—as I infer from her beauty, it was Calliope,—said to me,

"You shall always be content to be borne by snow-white swans, and the tramp of the war-horse shall not lead you forth to arms. Let it not be your concern to sound on the harsh horn the praises of naval daring, nor to surround the Aonian grove with Mars, or to tell of the camp in which the battle is going on under the standard of Marius,[2] and where Rome is crushing the Teutonic power ; or how the foreign Rhine,[3] reeking with blood of the slaughtered Suevi, bears wounded bodies on his sorrowing wave. Your care will be

---

[1] *The Gorgon fountain.*] It was made by the hoof of Pegasus, the offspring of Medusa, one of the Gorgons.

[2] *Marius.*] See on ii. 1, 24.

[3] *The foreign Rhine.*] This alludes to the defeat, B. C. 58, in Alsace, near the banks of the Rhine, of Ariovistus, the German chieftain. See Cæs. *Bell. Gall.* i. 53, and Long's note.

to sing of lovers, with wreaths on, standing before an unfriendly threshold, and of the tokens of a drunken rout by
night, so that he who wishes by his skill to deceive surly husbands may know how, by your help, to sing fair ladies out of
their locked apartments."

Thus said Calliope, and drawing water from the spring,
gave me a draught such as had inspired Philetas.

ELEGY IV.[1] [iii. 4. K.]

THE divine Cæsar is preparing an expedition as far as the
wealthy Indians, and to cleave with a fleet the waters of the
gem-bearing sea.[2] Great, O crews, will the reward be: the
end of the world is preparing triumphs: the Tigris and the
Euphrates will submit to and flow under thy commands, O
Cæsar. At last that region will become a province, subject
to the Roman fasces: Parthian trophies will accustom themselves to Latian Jove. Go, speed ye, give sail to the prow that
has been tried in war, and take with you the accustomed gift
of a horse[3] fit for bearing armed men. The omens that I
announce are propitious: avenge the murder of the Crassi;
speed on your way, and provide for the historical glory of
Rome. O father Mars, and O fire of Vesta that contains the
destiny of Rome, before my death, I pray, may that day be,
on which I may see the car of Cæsar laden with spoils, and
the horses often stopped amid the cheering of the people:
and, leaning on the bosom of my beloved girl, I may look on
and read the names of the taken cities, and see the captive
weapons of the flying horsemen, and the bows of trouser-
wearing soldiery, and the conquered chieftains sitting beneath
the armour. Venus, by thy presence preserve thy offspring:
long life to that head which thou seest surviving as a descendant of Æneas. Let the booty be given to those whose toils have
earned it. It will be enough for me to be able to applaud on
the Sacred Way.

---

[1] *Elegy IV.*] A prophetic Carmen Triumphale on the issue of the
expedition against the Parthians.
[2] *The gem-bearing sea.*] The Indian Ocean.
[3] *A horse.*] The Equites were each provided, at the public expense,
with a horse.

ELEGY V.[1] [iii. 5.]

LOVE is the god of peace: we lovers worship peace: *but* I have, constantly, hard battles with my mistress. My breast, however, is not racked by desire of unseen gold, nor do I quench my thirst in a richly-jewelled cup; nor is rich Campania, with its thousand hills, ploughed for me: nor do I sordidly hoard up brass,[2] obtained by thy destruction, O Corinth. O primeval earth, unlucky to the modeller Prometheus! he executed his work with but little forethought: when putting together the parts of the body, he looked not after reason in his skilfully-devised work: sound sense should have been the first thing he attended to. Now we suffer ourselves to be carried by the wind into the open sea, and must look for enemies *abroad*, and add war to war. Thou wilt carry no riches to the waves of Acheron: thou must be carried naked, O fool, in the infernal bark. Conqueror and conquered will be together in the shades below. Captive Jugurtha,[3] thou art side by side with Consul Marius. There is no difference between Lydian Crœsus and Dulichian Irus:[4] Death is most excellent when it conveniently comes during poverty. I am delighted with having courted Helicon in youth, and joined in the dances of the Muses. I love, too, to fortify my senses with deep draughts of wine, and always to have my head wreathed with the blooming rose. And when time shall have stopped my career of love, and hoary old age shall have scattered

[1] *Elegy V.*] In this poem, which alludes like the last to the intended expedition to the East, Propertius declares that war is not for him, except it be under the standard of Venus, and he announces his intention to devote his youth to love and wine, and his old age to scientific pursuits.

[2] *Brass.*] At the destruction of Corinth (B. c. 146) by L. Mummius, an alloy was accidentally made, so says the legend, of various metals, more particularly *gold* and *bronze:* this cannot be true, as many artists, whose compositions in this metal are celebrated, lived long before that date. Some suppose it to have been nothing more than highly refined bronze. See Dict. of Antiq. s. v. *Æs.*

[3] *Captive Jugurtha.*] Jugurtha, the grandson of Masinissa, was conquered by Marius, B. c. 106, and starved to death in prison, B. c. 104: the war with him lasted five years, and was conducted, successively, by L. Cassius, Spurius, and Aulus Postumius Albinus, Q. Cæcilius Metellus, and C. Marius.

[4] *Dulichian Irus.*] Irus was the beggar of Ithaca, who "boxed with Ulysses for some kid's-fry," (Byron,) and was ignominiously punished by him before the suitors. See *Odyss.* xviii.

my black hair, then may it be my pleasure to search deeply
into the machinery of nature; *to find* what divine power it is
that skilfully rules this terrestrial abode; where the moon
rises, where it wanes, whence it fills its horns, and comes to
the full every month; whence winds are frequent on the main;
what the East wind courts[1] with its blasts, and whence the
clouds are perpetually supplied with water: whether a day is to
come which shall uproot the foundations of the world; why
the purple bow drinks the rain-water; or why the summit of
Perrhæbian Pindus trembled, and the sun's disc and its
horses were in mourning:[2] why Boötes is slow in turning his
oxen, and bringing round his wain; why the group of the
Pleiads gives a confused light; why the deep main passes not
its assigned boundaries; or why the year is divided into four
parts: whether beneath the earth gods rule, and giants are
tortured: if Tisiphone's head rages with black serpent-wreath;
whether Alcmæon is tortured by Furies,[3] or Phineus[4] is starving; whether Cerberus guards the entrance to Hades with
triple jaws; whether nine acres are a scanty lying-room for
Tityus: whether a fabulous belief prevail among the wretched
nations, and there can be nothing to fear beyond the funeral
pyre.[5]   Let me live at the end of my life after this manner:
do you who find more pleasure in arms, carry home the standards lost by Crassus.

ELEGY VI.[6] [iii. 6. K.]

A DIALOGUE BETWEEN LYGDAMUS AND PROPERTIUS.

PROPERTIUS.

"TELL me truly, Lygdamus, what you know of my girl, that
so you may be released from the yoke of your mistress.   Do

[1] *The East wind courts.*]   See Beaumont and Fletcher, *Maid's Tragedy:* "Rather believe the wind *Courts* but the pregnant sails, when the
strong cordage cracks."
[2] *Mourning.*]   A solar eclipse is thus poetically described.
[3] *Alcmæon tortured.*]   For murdering his mother Eriphyle.
[4] *Phineus.*]   The son of Agenor.   He was, for cruelty to his sons, exposed to the Harpies, who stole half his food and soiled the rest, render-
ing it unfit to eat.
[5] *A fabulous belief.*]   As the Epicurean philosophy asserts.
[6] *Elegy VI.*]   Cynthia and Propertius had had a quarrel: the poet
asks Lygdamus, her servant, how she had been behaving since, and calls
upon him to act as a mediator.

you think to elate me with a false joy, and deceive me, by telling me what you think I wish to believe? *You will do so at your peril.* Every messenger ought to be free from disguise, more especially ought a slave, who has the fear of punishment before him, to tell the truth. If you remember anything, then, tell it me from the beginning: I will drink it in with eager ears. Have you seen her weep thus with hair in disorder? Did showers of tears ever stream from her eyes? Have you seen her neglect her looking-glass, Lygdamus, though her bed were luxuriously prepared? Has she been without jewels decking her snow-white hands? Have you seen her dress hanging over her arms in sorrow? Her dressing-case lying shut at the foot of her bed? Was the house sorrowful, and did the servants ply their tasks in melancholy mood, and did she spin in the midst of them? Did she press the wool to her eyes to dry them, and did she tell in sorrowful accents of her quarrel with me?"

LYGDAMUS.

"Lygdamus," she asked, "was this the reward that was promised me in your presence? He dares not, I suppose, break a promise made before a slave. He has the heart to leave me, wretched woman that I am, without any fault of mine,[1] and to say that he has a mistress that can be nowhere equalled. He is delighted at my pining, in solitude, on my empty couch: if he likes, Lygdamus, let him dance for joy at my death. She has not conquered me by graces, but by spells, the wretch! he is drawn away to her by means of a wheel[2] whirled by many a thread. It is a philtre gathered from a bloated bramble-toad, and picked snakes' bones, that are enticing him, and owl-feathers found among ruined tombs: a wreath of wool, too, is, ere this, put round the image of the doomed man. If my dreams, Lygdamus, prelude not what is false, mark my words, he will fall at my feet, late indeed, but he will fall, and I shall be revenged. The spider[3] shall spin her flimsy web in their bed; and may Venus herself remain asleep when they would wake her at night.

---

[1] This verse is, probably, corrupt.   [2] See on iii. 20, 35.
[3] Cf. Hom. *Odyss.* xvi. 34.

PROPERTIUS.

But if my mistress was earnest in this her complaint, run back, Lygdamus, by the way that you came, and carry to her what I tell you with many tears, that her lover may have been angry but has not wronged her. Say, too, that I have been racked with torments like herself, and that for twelve days I have been pure. And if, after so great a quarrel, I be happily restored to agreement with her, you shall be free, Lygdamus, through my instrumentality.

ELEGY VII.[1] [iii. 7. K.]

Thou, money, art then the cause of an anxious life to us: it is owing to thee that we tread the path to death before our time. Thou affordest cruel food to the faults of men: from thee spring the seeds of care. Thou sinkest Pætus thrice and four times in the mad sea, while spreading his sails towards Pharian harbours. For while in pursuit of thee he fell, luckless one, in the prime of life, and is tossing on the waves, a new banquet for the fish of a foreign sea: and his mother cannot commit him with due rites to the kindly earth, nor bury him among the bodies of his kin: but now the sea-birds are perching on thy body; now thou hast the whole Carpathian sea for a grave. O ill-omened Aquilo, terror of the ravished Orithyia, what great booty did his corpse yield thee? or what pleasure, Neptune, dost thou take in ship-wreck? That vessel had on board god-fearing men. Why tell how few thy years, Pætus? Why, when tossing on the water, is the name of thy dear mother on thy lips? The billows have no gods. For all the ropes that moored thee to the cliffs in the stormy night were chafed and gave way. There are shores that testify to Agamemnon's anxiety, where the melancholy death of Argynnus[2] by drowning gives a bad repute to the waters. On the loss of this youth the son of Atreus

---

[1] *Elegy VII.*] A beautiful poem on the death of a young friend named Pætus, who was drowned in a voyage to Egypt undertaken for some mercantile purpose.

[2] *Argynnus.*] Paley reads, *Qua notat Argynni pœna natantis aquas.* Argynnus, according to *Athen.* xiii. 603, was a beautiful youth beloved by Agamemnon, who caused his death by pursuing him to the banks of the Cephisus. Propertius, however, appears to have followed a different

would not let the fleet start, for which delay Iphigenia was sacrificed. Restore, *ye waves,* his body to earth, and now that the water has taken his life, cover Pætus of thy own accord, O worthless sand. As often as the sailor passes his tomb, let him say, " Thou canst serve as a warning even to the bold."

Go: build curved ships, the causes of death: a death of that sort is hurried on by human hands. The earth was too little: we have added the water to our instruments of death. By art have we increased the roads to misery provided for us by Fortune. Can an anchor hold you, whom your own home could not hold ? What, say you, does that man deserve who finds his native land too little ? All your preparations are at the mercy of the winds: not a single ship grows old: even the harbour breaks its faith. With malicious design did Nature spread out the sea to the avaricious: scarcely one of your attempts can succeed. The rocks of Caphareus[1] destroyed the triumphant fleet, when Greece was ship-wrecked and dashed on the mighty main. Ulysses, whose usual skill availed him not on the sea, wept the loss, by degrees, of all his companions. But if *Pætus* were now contentedly ploughing his ancestral fields with the oxen, and had thought that what I am now saying had any weight in it, he would be living, a welcome guest, under his own roof-tree, poor, but on land, where a man can have no cause for sorrow. On land Pætus was not obliged to hear the roaring of the storm, nor to hurt his delicate hands with the hard rope, but could lie, in his chamber of cedar[2] or Orician terebinth, with his head supported on a downy pillow of various colours.

version of the legend, according to which Argynnus perished at sea, and in the same spot where Pætus was lost.

[1] *The rocks of Caphareus.*] Caphareus (*Capo D'Oro*) was the S. E. promontory of *Eubœa,* off which the Grecian fleet was wrecked on its return from Troy.

[2] *Cedar.*] *Thyio.* This word is an adjective from θύα or θυία, which is generally supposed to have been a kind of cedar; but it is more probably a species of arbor vitæ, the *Thuja articulata* of Linnæus, a native of the mountains of the N. W. of Africa, and the timber of which exhales a fragrant odour. The terebinth or turpentine-tree is of large size and stately growth, and is not uncommon in Palestine and many of the Greek islands. It is not one of the coniferæ, but bears a fruit like a small cherry. Sir Charles Fellowes (*Travels in Asia Minor*) compares it with our ash. Our word *turpentine* is a corruption of *terebinthine.—Paley.*

While he struggled for life, the surge tore off his nails by the roots, and as he gasped wretchedly for breath, he swallowed the hateful water; merciless night saw him clinging to a small plank: so many causes united that Pætus might die. Weeping, he uttered these his last sad words, when the black water was closing his dying mouth: "Ye gods, in whose power are the Ægean waves, ye winds, and every wave that is pressing down my head, whither are ye sweeping me, in the prime of youth? The hands that I brought on to your waves were innocent.[1] Luckless that I am, I shall be dashed on to the sharp rocks of the Alcyons: the god of the azure main has grasped his trident[2] against me. May the waves, at all events, throw me on the Italian coast: this will be enough for me, if I do but come to my mother's hands." While saying this, the wave caught him in an eddy and drew him down: these were Pætus' last words, and such was his end. O ye hundred daughters of father Nereus, and thou, Thetis, who hast known a mother's grief, you should have placed your arms under his exhausted chin; he would not have weighed down your hands. But thou, blustering Aquilo, shalt never see my sails: I must be buried, after having lived a quiet life, at my mistress' door.

ELEGY VIII.[3] [iii. 8. K.]

I was delighted with our quarrel last evening, and all the revilings of your frantic tongue. Why, furious with wine, do you upset the table, and throw full flagons at me with raging hand? But be bold enough, *if you will*, to pull my hair, and scratch my face with your pretty fingers! Threaten to thrust a torch in my face and burn my eyes out, and tear my dress open, and bare my breast! In so doing you give me proofs of genuine affection, for unless violently in love, no woman feels offended. A woman that bandies abuse with passionate

---

[1] *Innocent.*] This is most probably the meaning of *longas.* The ancients thought that perjury was often punished by the loss or mutilation of a limb. Cf. Ov. *Am.* iii. 3, 2, Quam *longos* habuit nondum jurata *capillos.* Tam longos postquam numina læsit, habet. See also Horace's beautiful ode to Neæra: Ulla si juris tibi pejerati, &c.

[2] *Grasped his trident.*] See Hom. *Odyss.* v. 291.

[3] *Elegy VIII.*] He assures Cynthia that her violence in a recent quarrel has not estranged him from her; indeed, that he likes it rather than otherwise.

tongue, and throws herself at the feet of mighty Venus, or
surrounds herself, when walking, with troops of attendants, or
rushes down the middle of the road like a frantic Bacchante,
or is timid and often frightened by startling dreams, or is
made miserable by a female portrait;—by such excitement, I
can interpret her feelings truly; I have learnt that those
traits are often found in true love. An attachment that is
not moved by insult, is not trusty. May my enemies meet with
an easy-tempered mistress ! Let my fellows that have not
been bitten, see the wounds on my neck : let the black marks
show that I have held my mistress in my arms. In love I
like either to feel pain or to hear it expressed ; to see either
my own tears or yours, *Cynthia*, when you speak silently
with your knitted brows, or write with your finger what you
cannot say. I hate to have my sleep interrupted by no sighs :
I would always fain be in love with an angry girl. Paris was
more violently enamoured when, amidst fighting with the
Greeks, he could give delight to his mistress, the daughter of
Tyndarus. While the Greeks are conquering, while foreign
Hector continues to resist, he wages mighty wars in Helen's
arms. I shall always be quarrelling, either with you, or with
rivals for you : I like not any peace where you are concerned.
Thank heaven that there is no other as handsome as yourself :
you would suffer, if there were : now you may lawfully be
proud. As to you who have been trying to seduce my mistress, may you have a father-in-law for ever, and a mother
always in your house ! If you have had any opportunity of
stealing a night from me, she has granted it to you from
anger against me, not from good will to you.

ELEGY IX.[1] [iii. 9. K.]

MÆCENAS,[2] knight descended from Etruscan kings, content
to keep within the limits of your fortune, why would you send

---

[1] *Elegy IX.*] In a strain of ingenious compliment to Mæcenas, Propertius alleges his patron's example as a justification of his own unwillingness to enter on the more ambitious flights of heroic poetry. In this
he says he copies his patron's judicious reserve ; for the latter contented
himself with his hereditary rank as Eques, though the highest honours of
the state were within his reach.

[2] *Mæcenas.*] C. Cilnius Mæcenas, prime-minister and favourite of
Augustus, patron of Virgil, Horace, Varius, Propertius, Tucca, and other

me into so vast a field of authorship ? Big sails suit not my
bark. It is disgraceful to take upon one's head a burden beyond what one can bear, and, finding oneself overpowered, to
bend the knee and yield. Every thing is not equally suited
to everybody, nor is fame gained if you are attached to
any yoke-fellow.[1] Lysippus[2] excels in making life-like statues :
Calamis[3] signalizes himself, you observe, by equestrian statuary. Apelles,[4] by his picture of Venus, takes the highest
place ; Parrhasius[5] asserts his position by cabinet-paintings.
Groups on a large scale are Mentor's[6] contributions to art :
but the acanthus of Mys[7] creeps on its tiny way. The Jupiter of Phidias[8] shows himself gracefully in the ivory statue :
the marble wrought with skill peculiar to himself, claims Prax-
itiles.[9] With some, victory always runs in company in the
races at Elis : for others, glory was born for their swiftness of
foot. One is made for peace : an other, adapted for a military
life : each one follows the principles peculiar to his nature.

celebrities, was descended from the *Lucumones* of Etruria. (Hor. *Od.* i. 1 ;
Sat. i. 6, 1 seq.)

[1] *Nor is fame,* &c.] *Fama nec ex æquo ducitur ulla jugo.*—*Paley.*

[2] *Lysippus.*] A famous statuary of Sicyon, B. c. 350 ; patronized by
Alexander the Great : his works are described as "perfectly life-like in
all but breath and motion." (Nicephorus ap. Boisson. *Anecd.* iii. 357.)

[3] *Calamis.*] He lived about 450, B. c. : he was skilled in embossing.
His style is described by Cicero (*Brut.* 18, § 70 : cf. Quintil. xii. 10) as
dura.

[4] *Apelles.*] A native of Cos, or, according to others, of Colophon,
flourished 350, B. c., and painted the Venus Anadyomene either from
Campaspe, a concubine of Alexander, or Phryne. (See on ii. 6, 3.)

[5] *Parrhasius*] was a native of Ephesus, lived B. c. 400.

[6] See on i. 14, 2.

[7] *Mys.*] A toreutic artist who lived B. c. 444. The meaning is, "the
workmanship of Mys is minute : " the *acanthus* would be represented as
enfolding the cup. Cf. Virg. Ecl. iii. 45, Molli circum est ansas com-
plexus acantho. Theocr. i. 29.

[8] *Phidias.*] The great sculptor of Athens, died 432, B. c. His chief
works were the *Athena Promachus, Athena* χρυσελεφαντίνη, and the
Jupiter at Olympia, in the *Altis* or sacred grove. This statue is described
in Pausanias (v. 12).

[9] *Praxiteles.*] *Propria vindicat arte lapis.* Praxiteles, B. c. 364 (?),
was a sculptor of the later Attic school, as contrasted with that of Phidias : his great work was the statue of Venus, (called the Cnidian Venus
from its having been bought by the people of Cnidus,) modelled from
Phryne.

I have adopted your rule of life, Mæcenas, and I am forced to surpass your example. Whereas you, honoured Roman, can wield the lordly axe, and lay down the law in the middle of the forum, or face the desperate Median foe, and ornament your house with stands of armour, and whereas Cæsar is ready to supply you with means for action, and resources offer themselves to you so readily at all times;—you refrain, and modestly retreat into the shade; you reef with your own hand your swelling sails. This resolve, believe me, will be matched with those of the great Camilli; you, also, will be in every man's mouth, and will tread closely in the footsteps of Cæsar's renown. Loyalty will be Mæcenas' true trophy.

I cleave not the swelling sea with a large vessel: I lie safe under the shelter of a little stream. I shall not sing in mournful strains of the citadel of Cadmus fallen amid the ashes of civil war, nor the constant engagements with equal slaughter on both sides: I will not tell of the Scæan gates, nor of Pergamos, the citadel of Apollo, nor of the return of the Grecian fleet in the tenth spring, when the wooden horse, made by the art of Pallas, gave victory to the Greeks, and the plough was driven over the Neptunian walls. Enough will it be to have been received with favour as an imitator of Callimachus, and to have sung in strains like thine, O bard of Cos.[1] Let these efforts of mine inspire boys and maidens with love: and let them hail me as a god and pay sacrifice to me. If you set me the example, I will sing of the wars of Jove, and Cœus, and Oromedon threatening heaven from the Phlegræan heights. I will take for my theme the lofty Palatine hill browsed on by Roman cattle, the walls cemented with the blood of Remus, and the royal twins that sucked the dugs of a wild beast: and my genius will take a higher flight at your command. I will tell of triumphs over eastern and western foes; the swift discharge of the Parthian arrows in cunningly-pretended flight, the fort of Pelusium[2] undermined by Roman weapons, and the hand of Antony[3] fatally raised against himself. Do you take the reins; be a kindly favourer to a young beginner;

[1] *Bard of Cos.*] Philetas. Paley reads *Dore*.
[2] *Pelusium.*] A town that commanded one of the principal mouths of the Nile; destroyed by Octavian B. C. 30.
[3] *Antony.*] He committed suicide B. C. 30.

and, when I have started, gently encourage me. You allow me thus much praise, Mæcenas; and it is owing to you that I shall have the credit of having pursued your own course.

ELEGY X.[1] [iii. 10. K.]

I was wondering what the Muses had sent in the morning, as they stood by my couch at the first blush of day. They sent a token of my love's birthday, and thrice sounded notes of joy with their hands. May this day pass without a cloud, may the winds be hushed in the sky, and may the wave softly still its violence on the shore. On no sorrowers will I look to-day: let even Niobe's statue dry her tears. Let the Halcyons forget their sorrows and be silent, and let not his mother[2] passionately lament the loss of Itys. Do thou, my darling, born with happy omens, arise, and pay to the gods that demand thy worship their due tribute of prayer. First shake off sleep by washing with pure water, and curl thy glossy hair with skilful hand. Next put on the dress with which thou didst first captivate the eyes of Propertius, and leave not thy head without a wreath of flowers. And look for the ornaments that set thee off, that thy beauty may endure, and thy reign with me last for ever. Then when thou hast crowned the altars and offered sacrifice of frankincense thereon, and a propitious flame shall have shone all over the house, prepare a banquet and let us spend the night in drinking, and let the marble vase regale the nostrils with essence of saffron. Let the pipe grow hoarse and breathless with playing for us to dance to at night; indulge thy wanton tongue at will; let our festivities drive dull sleep away; and let our merriment smite the public ear in the neighbouring street. Let the cast of the dice tell us whom the fatal boy is grievously tormenting. When we shall have spent the time in quaffing many a cup, and Venus begins her nightly ministry, let us retire to our chamber, and so finish the celebration of the anniversary of thy birth.

[1] *Elegy X.*] A complimentary Elegy to Cynthia on her birthday.
[2] *His mother.*] Itys, the son of Procne, was killed by his own mother, who afterwards became a swallow.

ELEGY XI.[1] [iii. 11. K.]

WHY wonder that a woman sways my life, and deals with me as her thrall?[2] Why charge me with disgraceful want of spirit because I cannot break the yoke and burst my bonds? A sailor predicts the coming of night better than a landsman: a soldier learns, by his wounds, to fear the conflict. That is what I used to boast of in my youthful days gone by: do you, now, learn to fear from my example. It was the Colchian maid that drove the fire-breathing bulls beneath the adamantine yoke, and sowed the seeds of fight in the ground that teemed with armed men,[3] and closed the fierce mouth of the watchful serpent, that the golden fleece might be carried to the house of Æson. The Mæotian Penthesilea,[4] in times gone by, boldly dared to fight with arrows, on horseback, against the Grecian crews: after her golden helmet was taken off and her face was seen, her beauty overcame her conqueror. Omphale, a Lydian maid that had been dipped in the Gygæan lake, was so fair that he who had built columns[5] as tokens of having subdued the world, spun *at her command;*—too soft a task for a hand hard like his. Semiramis built Babylon, the city of the Persians, so that she raised a work strengthened by a brick wall, and two chariots might be driven, in opposite directions, on the walls, without[6] their sides and their axles touching. She also brought the Euphrates into the

[1] *Elegy XI.*] He excuses himself for being so devoted to Cynthia, by instancing great men who have been captivated by female beauty. Having mentioned Antony and Cleopatra, he takes occasion thence to conclude with a splendid panegyric on Augustus.

[2] *Her thrall.*] *Addictum virum:* a phrase derived from the Roman law by which an insolvent debtor was formally made over to his creditor to be sold as a slave *trans Tiberim.*

[3] *The ground that teemed,* &c.] Having killed the dragon that guarded the fleece, Jason sowed his teeth, and there came up armed men who fought with and slew each other.

[4] *Penthesilea,*] queen of the Amazons; she came to the siege of Troy, and was there slain by *Achilles.*

[5] *Columns.*] The *pillars of Hercules,* set up by him at Calpe and Abyla.

[6] *Without,* &c.] For *ne* used *to express* a *consequence* instead of *ut non.* Compare Tac. *Ann.* xiv. 7, Hactenus adito discrimine *ne* auctor dubitaretur. Livy, i. 7, Institutum mansit *ne* extis vescerentur. *Ib.* 46, Forte inciderat *ne* duo violenta ingenia matrimonis jungerentur.

middle of the space where she had built her citadels, and bade
Bactra rise to be the head of her empire. For why need I
accuse heroes and gods? Jupiter disgraces both himself and
his family. Why need I mention that woman who brought
disgrace on our arms, her that submitted to the embraces of her
menials? As the price to be paid by her degenerate husband,
she demanded the walls of Rome, and the subjection of the
senate to her commands. O guilty Alexandria,[1] land most
skilled in treachery, and Memphis, so often blood-stained by
our disasters, where the shore stripped Pompey[2] of his three
triumphs;—no day will ever clear this disgrace from thee, O
Rome:—better hadst thou died on the Phlegræan plain, or
even intrusted thy head to the mercy of thy father-in-law.
The harlot-queen of debauched Canopus, that sole blot *on our
fame* inflicted by the descendants of Philip,[3] aspired, forsooth,
to set up the barking Anubis against our Jupiter; to force
the Tiber to endure the threats of the Nile; to drive out the
Roman war-trumpet with the jingling sistrum;[4] to follow
Liburnian galleys with boats[5] driven by poles; to spread disgraceful musquito-curtains[6] on the Tarpeian rock, and to lay
down the law among the statues and arms of Marius! Of

[1] *Guilty Alexandria.*] Cf. the character given of the Egyptians in
Theoc. xv. 45 seq.

[2] *Pompey.*] He was murdered on the shore, while escaping after the
battle of Pharsalia. His three triumphs were (1) Sept. B. c. 81, on the
conquest of Numidia: (2) Dec. B. c. 71, for his victories in Spain: (3)
Sept. 30, B. c. 61, on the reduction of Syria.

[3] *The descendants of Philip.*] *Cleopatra* was the daughter of *Ptolemy
Auletes*, and through his ancestor *Ptol. Soter*, the son of Arsinöe, a concubine of Philip of Macedon, one of the *sanguis Philippeus*.

[4] *Sistrum.*] From σείειν, *to shake*, was a jingling brazen instrument, in
shape like the frame of a small battledore, with transverse brass rods
passing loosely through holes in the sides. It was used in the rites of
Isis.

[5] *Boats.*] Baris (βάρις) is the Egyptian name for a boat.

[6] *Musquito-curtains.*] It is curious with what wrath the Romans in
the days of Augustus looked upon this innocent convenience, now so commonly used in Italy. It was perhaps as a foreign innovation that it so excited
their anger; yet they took very kindly to other foreign novelties of a far
less excusable kind. See Hor. *Epod.* ix. 16, Interque signa turpe mili-
taria Sol adspicit *conopium*. "Probably," says Paley, "the conopium
which gave such offence was a peculiar sort of tent, and not a mere curtain; still less, as some have thought, used as an Egyptian standard. It
is hardly necessary to add that we derive our word *canopy* from it, which
a recent writer on etymology has deduced from *cannabis*, 'hemp.'"

what use now would be the breaking of the fasces of Tarquinius, whose cruel life stamps on him a name of like import, if a woman had to be endured? Celebrate a triumph, O Rome, and, saved by Augustus, pray for his long life. But thou, *Cleopatra*, wast forced to fly to the wandering streams of the timid Nile: thy hands suffered Roman bonds: I saw thy arms marked by the bite of the holy asp,[1] and the sleep of death stealing secretly over thy limbs. "O Rome," said she, "I was not to be feared by thee, while thou hadst so illustrious a citizen,[2] nor was *Antony*, with his wine-sodden senses." —What! the city seated on seven hills, that rules over all the world, be frightened in war and quail at a woman's threats! At our feet are the spoils of Hannibal, and records of the conquered Syphax,[3] and the crushed glory of Pyrrhus:[4] Curtius[5] gained a monument by filling up the chasm: Decius[6] ended the fight by charging the enemy on horseback: a pathway bears witness to the cutting down of the bridge behind Cocles:[7] there was one to whom a crow gave a surname.[8] These walls the gods built: these walls they keep: as long as Cæsar is safe Rome needs scarcely fear even Jupiter. Where are now the naval exploits of Scipio?[9] where the prowess of Camillus?[10] or thou, O Bosporus,[11] lately taken by Pompey? Apollo will chronicle the defeat on the Leucadian coast: so much of military achievement has a single day taken from the victors.[12] But, sailor, whether making for or leaving harbour, remember Cæsar all over the Ionian Sea.

[1] *I saw.*] That is, he saw her in effigy in the triumphal procession. The asp is called *sacer* from being sacred to Isis.

[2] Augustus.] Cf. Ovid, *Trist.* iv. 4, 13, Ipse pater patriæ, quid enim *civilius* illo?

[3] *Syphax.*] King of Numidia, conquered, B. C. 203, by Scipio Africanus Major.

[4] *Pyrrhus.*] King of Epirus, beaten, B. C. 274, at Beneventum, by Curius Dentatus.

[5] See Livy, vii. 6.

[6] See Livy, viii. 9.   [7] See Livy, ii. 10.

[8] *A crow.*] M. V. Corvus. Liv. vii. 26.

[9] *The naval exploits of Scipio.*] See Livy, xxviii. 45.

[10] *Camillus.*] Renowned for the siege of Veii. Livy, v. 21 seq.

[11] *Bosporus.*] Pompey, in 66 B. C., in prosecution of the third Mithridatic war, took the kingdom of the Cimmerian Bosphorus, whither M. had fled for refuge.

[12] *So much of military achievement,* &c.] That is, one day has eclipsed all their warlike deeds.

ELEGY XII.[1] [iii. 12. K.]

HAD you the heart, Postumus, to leave Galla in tears, and
to march as a soldier with the brave troops of Augustus?
Was the glory of despoiling a Parthian of so much value to
you as to make you disregard the repeated entreaties of your
Galla? If I may say so, may all you misers perish together,
and every one that has preferred military service to a faithful
bed-partner! But you, madman, are content to cover yourself with a cloak, and drink, when weary, the water of Araxes
from a helmet. She will, meanwhile, be pining away at every
vague report, and fearing lest this valour of yours prove fatal
to you; and lest the Parthian archers exult over your
slaughter, and the warrior, cased in iron mail,[2] over the gilded
trappings of your horse; and lest some melancholy relic of
you be brought back to her in an urn. Thus they return
who fall in that service. Thrice and four times blessed are
you, Postumus, in the chaste Galla: with your disposition
you deserved a different wife! What will your loved one do,
when prevented by no fear, and when Rome can teach her
debauchery? But go in peace. Gifts will not influence
Galla, and she will forget your cruelty. For on the day that
the Fates send you back in safety the chaste Galla will hang
upon your neck. Postumus will be a second Ulysses for his
notable wife. The Ithacan's prolonged absence did him no
harm, nor his warfare for ten years; the fight with the Ci-
cones; the capture of Ismarus; the burning, soon afterwards,
of thy face, Polyphemus; the guiles of Circe; the lotus, seducing plant; nor Scylla and Charybdis, agape with alternat-
ing waters; nor the lowing of Lampetie's[3] oxen when on the
spit,—his daughter Lampetie had fed them for Phœbus; nor
his flight from the embrace of the weeping Aeæan maid; his
being afloat so many wintry nights and days; his having
entered the gloomy and silent abodes of the shades; his hav-

---

[1] *Elegy XII.*] Addressed to Postumus, who had joined the Arabian
expedition under Ælius Gallus, and had left his wife, who would seem to
be related to the Gallus of i. 5, and therefore a connexion of the poet's,
to lament his long absence from home.

[2] *Cased in mail.*] Cataphracti (κατὰ, *thoroughly,* φράσσω, *to hedge, protect*) was a name given to men clad in coats of mail. See Tac. *Hist.* i.
79; Livy, xxxvii. 40.

[3] See *Odyss.* xii. 374 seq.

ing gone to the shore of the Sirens, after having stopped the
ears of his crew; nor his having bent again his old bow to the
slaughter of the suitors, and thus set a period to his wanderings. Nor was it for nothing *he escaped all these dangers:*
his wife had continued chaste at home. Aelia Galla excels
Penelope in fidelity.

ELEGY XIII.[1] [iii. 13. K.]

You ask me how it is that avaricious women charge high
for their embraces, and how Wealth, wasted by Venus, complains of its losses. There is indeed a certain and evident
reason for mischief so terrible: luxuries are introduced too
easily. The Indian ant[2] sends gold from hollow mines; the
shell of Venus is brought from the Eastern sea; Tyre, city of
Cadmus, sends cloths of purple dye; and the nomad Arabian
sweetly-scented cinnamon. These arms force even modest
women to surrender, and those who outdo thy disdain, O
daughter of Icarus.[3] A matron walks, clad in whole fortunes
of spendthrifts, and parades before our faces the costly price
of her dishonour. There are no scruples in demanding, none
in yielding; or, if there are, hesitation is removed by gold.
Eastern[4] husbands alone, whom the blushing Aurora dyes
with her horses, have a happy funeral. For, as soon as the
last torch has been applied to the funeral pile, an affectionate
crowd stand around, with dishevelled hair, and strive as to
who shall die, and follow her husband alive: they count it a
disgrace not to be allowed to die. Those that win are burnt,
and give their person to the flames, and lay their scorched
faces on their husband's. Here we have a faithless race of
wives: no woman here is as faithful as Evadne,[5] or as affectionate as Penelope.

---

[1] *Elegy XIII.*] A tirade against the avarice of women, suggested probably by Cynthia's importunity.

[2] *The Indian ant.*] This alludes to the story in Herodotus, iii. 102, of
the gold-dust (ψάμμος χρυσῖτις) being turned up by the ants, which in
those parts are less than a dog but larger than a fox. See Humboldt's
Cosmos.

[3] *Daughter of Icarus.*] Penelope is called κούρη Ἰκαρίοιο, περίφρων
Πηνελοπεία in *Odyss.* xi. 446.

[4] *Eastern husbands.*] This custom is alluded to by Ælian, *Var. Hist.*
vii. 18. See also Cic. *Tusc.* v 27, § 78; Val. Max. ii. 6, 14.

[5] See on i. 15, 21.

Happy in days of yore were the peace-loving rustic youths, whose orchard and harvest were their wealth. The presents that they made were quinces[1] shaken from the boughs, and baskets full of scarlet bramble-berries; and violets plucked with their own hand, shining lilies for the maids to carry in heaps in their baskets, grapes wrapped in their own leaves, and a beauteous bird with plumage of various hues. In those days maids gave secretly, in grots, to woodland men, kisses bought with such courtesies. A fawn's skin used to cover lovers completely, and the grass grew high, forming a natural couch; the pine waved over them and formed a pliant shade; it was no sin to see goddesses naked, and the horned ram, the leader of the flock, brought back, of his own accord, the sheep, after feeding, to the fold of the shepherd-god: and all the gods and goddesses, whose power is in the country, used to speak encouraging words at the sacrifices offered in their honour by you, *O rustics*. "Thou shalt[2] hunt the hare, O stranger, whoever thou art; and if thou lookest for a bird in my domain, call me, Pan, from the rock to join thee, whether thou seekest booty with rod or dog." But now the groves are deserted and sacrifices are abandoned: all follow gold, piety being now conquered. Honesty is driven out by gold: right can be bought by gold: law follows gold, and decency will soon follow it when law is gone. The scorched thresholds bear witness to the sacrilege of Brennus[3] while visiting the Pythian abode of the unshorn god. But Mount Parnassus, shaken from its laurel-bearing summit, sent a fatal shower of snow against the Gallic foes. To thee, O Polydorus,[4] the wicked Polymestor, king of Thrace, showed treacherous hospitality, having stolen thy gold. That thou,

---

[1] Quinces are called *Cydonia* (*poma*) from Cydon or Cydonia (*Khania*) in Crete, where they were indigenous, and whence they were transported into other countries. The fruit was called Κοδύμαλον in the old Cretan dialect. See Pliny, xv. 10.

[2] *Thou shalt*, &c.] Vs. 43—46, are supposed to be words of encouragement from Pan: they are from an Epigram by Leonidas of Tarentum.

[3] See on iii. 23, 13.

[4] *Polydorus.*] Son of Priam. He was sent to Polymestor, with a great treasure, to be educated by him: he killed the boy, and stole the gold, for which his eyes were afterwards put out by the Trojan women under Hecuba. See *Æn.* iii. 49 seq.; Eur. *Hecuba*, passim.

too, O Eriphyla, mightest have gold bracelets on thy arms,
Amphiaraus disappeared with his horses. I will prophesy,
and may I be mistaken in my forebodings to my country :
Rome is cruelly crushing herself by her own prosperity.
What I say is true, but no one believes me : for the Trojan
prophetess in days of yore[1] was doomed never to be believed
when portending the ruin of Pergamus. She alone declared
that Paris was bringing ruin on Phrygia ; she alone, that the
horse was a trick and a snare. Her madness was wholesome
for her country and her sire : her tongue, though set at
nought, was inspired truly by the gods.

ELEGY XIV.[2]   [iii. 14. K.]

O Sparta, we admire the many laws of thy wrestling-school,
but still more the many good fruits of thy maidens' exercise-
ground, forasmuch as the maiden, though naked and wrestling
with men, exercises her body in no disgraceful games : when the
ball,[3] swiftly thrown from the hand, falls not as expected, and
the crooked wire[4] of the hoop rattles as it rolls, and a woman
stands covered with dust at the end of a foot-race, and suffers
bruises in the rough pancratium. Now joyfully she binds the
cœstus on her arms with thongs ; now she poises and whirls
the weighty quoits ; she gallops round the course, girds her
snow-white side with the sword, and covers her virgin head
with the hollow brass helmet. She bathes, too, as a warlike
troop of Amazons bathes, with bare breasts, in the waters of
Thermodon ; at times she courses with dogs of native breed
over the long ridges of Taygetus, her hair covered with hoar-
frost. As when Pollux and Castor exercised on the sands
of Eurotas, the one destined to excel in boxing, the other in

---

[1] *The Trojan prophetess.*] Cassandra.

[2] *Elegy XIV.*] A panegyric on the simple habits of the Spartan women, as contrasted with the Roman.

[3] *When the ball.*] *Quum pila veloces fallit per brachia jactus,* Paley :
veloci jactu, Kuinoel. K. interprets fallit as λανθάνει, *is not seen :* Paley
takes it of a ball falling unsuccessfully, comparing *Odyss.* vi. 116 ; viii.
374.

[4] *The crooked wire.*] This may have resembled the iron rod, curved
at the end, with which iron hoops are bowled now-a-days. Some suppose
trochus to be *a top,* but top-spinning is not a violent exercise.

horsemanship : and Helen is said to have exercised along with them with bare breasts, and not to have blushed at her divine brothers.[1] So it is at this day. The Spartan custom, in accordance with these habits, forbids lovers to retire : one may be with one's mistress in public. There is no need of anxious fear about a maid, nor of shutting her up and closely guarding her. No one has need to dread the severe vengeance of an angry husband. Without sending a messenger you may speak yourself on your own business: you are not repulsed after long waiting. In Sparta Tyrian robes deceive not the mistaken eye ; they never trouble themselves with perfuming their hair. But a maiden of our country walks surrounded with a great crowd of attendants ; nor is it possible to set a finger among them, the road being so thronged. Nor can you find out what look to assume, or how to address her : a lover walks in darkness. But if, O Rome, thou wouldst imitate the customs and exercises of the Laconians, thou wouldst be dearer to me from doing me that kindness.

ELEGY XV.[2] [iii. 15. K.]

So may I, henceforth, know no trouble in love, and never have to pass a sleepless night without you, *as it is true that* when my youthful modesty [3] was covered by the garb of manhood, and I was allowed to tread in the path of love, Lycinna, influenced (ah me !) by no presents, gave my inexperience the first nightly lessons in the love in which she was herself an adept. It is now not much less than three years, during all which time I scarcely remember ten words passing between us. Your love has buried all traces of her, and no woman after you has ever placed sweet chains upon my neck. Dirce,[4]

[1] Helen was the child of Leda by Zeus, as well as Castor and Pollux.

[2] *Elegy XV.*] The poet, while confessing an old liaison with Lycinna, a servant of Cynthia, assures the latter that he has long discontinued it, and warns her, by the fate of Dirce, not to be severe with the girl.

[3] *My youthful modesty, &c.*] *Ut mihi prætextæ pudor est velatus amictu,* is the common reading, and that admitted into his text by Paley, though he inclines in a note to *elatus* in the sense of *set aside,* comparing vs. 9, Cuncta tuus *sepelivit* amor.

[4] *Dirce.*] Antiope was married to, and afterwards repudiated by, her uncle Lycus, king of Thebes; he made *Dirce* his second wife, who, from jealous motives, treated Antiope disgracefully, till at length she made her

H

so cruel upon real grounds of jealousy towards Antiope, the daughter of Nycteus, the former wife of Lycus, shall be a warning to you. Ah! how often did the queen set on fire her rival's fair hair, and fix her cruel nails in her delicate face: how often did she make her a handmaiden, and load her with unfair tasks, and bid her lay her head on the hard ground! Often she suffered her to remain in darkness and filth; often did she deny her, though fasting, the trifling boon of a cup of water. "Jupiter," she cried, "wilt thou never help Antiope in such distress? the harsh chain galls my hands. If thou art a god, it is disgraceful to thee that thy damsel should be in bondage: whom but Jove is Antiope to call upon when a prisoner?" By herself, however, slight though her strength was, she broke with both hands the bonds imposed by the queen. Then, with timid foot, she ran to Cithæron's heights: it was night, and her wretched bed, the ground, was covered with hoar-frost. Often, startled by the roar of the swift flowing Asopus, she fancied that the footsteps of her mistress were following behind her. Then the mother, an outcast from her home, found stern Zethus and Amphion softened by her tears: and like as when the mighty billows hush their fury, when the east wind ceases to struggle with the south, and the shore is at length noiseless, and the lashing of the sand grows faint; so did the young mother faint and bend her knee. But affection, though late, yet showed itself: her sons felt their error: O old man,[1] worthy guardian of the children of Jupiter, thou restorest the mother to the children; and they bound Dirce to the neck of a fierce bull to be dragged along. Antiope, acknowledge the power of Jove: Dirce is dragged for you to exult over, and to be made a mangled corpse. Zethus made the meadows bloody, and victorious Amphion played a pæan on thy rock, O Aracynthus.[2] But do not you trouble Lycinna undeservedly: the torrent of your wrath never knows when to stop. Let no tale about me annoy your ears: you alone, even when burnt on the funeral-pile, may I continue to love.

escape, and informed Amphion and Zethus, her sons by Zeus. Thereupon they slew Dirce and Lycus. Cf. *Odyss.* xi. 260.

[1] *Old man.*] The apostrophe is addressed to an old shepherd, who had educated the youths, and discovered their relationship to their mother.

[2] *Aracynthus,*] was probably a mountain between Attica and Bœotia. Cf. Virg. *Ecl.* ii. 24, Amphion Dircæus in *Actæo* Aracyntho.

ELEGY XVI.[1] [iii. 16. K.]

It was midnight, and a letter came to me from my mistress from Tibur: she bade me come without delay, to where the hill-tops show the two towers, and where Anio's water falls into a wide basin. What am I to do? am I to trust myself to the darkness that now shrouds the earth, and consequently fear a violent attack on my person? But if I put off this order through fear, the sad result will be more cruel to me than a nightly enemy. I once offended, and was cast off for a year: she has no gentle hand for me. But there is no one able to hurt lovers, for they are charmed; one may walk, then, in the middle of Sciron's road.[2] Any lover may walk in the middle of the plains of Scythia: no one will be cruel enough to hurt him. The moon waits on his journey: the stars show him the rough ground: Love goes before with a torch and keeps it bright. Fierce and mad dogs turn aside their mouths though eager to bite: this class of men may walk in safety at all times. Why, what villain will stain himself with the insignificant blood of a lover?—Venus herself accompanies them on their solitary way. But if certain death were to follow any accident that might happen to me, at such a price I would even buy death. She will bring unguents for my funeral, and will sit as a guardian at my grave, and deck my remains with garlands. May the god grant that she lay not my bones in a crowded spot, where the common herd are constantly passing. Thus it is that lovers' tombs are dishonoured after death: may I be laid in a by-path shaded with trees, or may a heap of sand, in a retired place, fence in my body: I like not to have my name in the public road.

[1] *Elegy XVI.*] The poet, having received at midnight a letter from Cynthia bidding him come to her immediately, debates whether to go or not, consoles himself with the reflection that lovers bear a charmed life, and speculates on the consequences of his death.

[2] *Sciron's road.*] The via Scironis, (Σκιρωνὶς ὁδὸς, Hdt. viii. 71,) was between Attica and Megara, and named after Sciron, a notorious robber, who compelled travellers to do him homage by washing his feet, during which operation he kicked them into the sea: he was slain by Theseus. The road is now called *Kaka Scala* (Bad Stairs).

ELEGY XVII.[1] [iii. 17. K.]

Now, O Bacchus, we approach thy altars in humble attitude: give me a fair wind and a smooth sea. Thou canst
quell the arrogance of termagant Venus, and love-cares are
healed by thy wine. By thee lovers are joined, by thee parted: do thou wash out vexation from my mind with wine, O
Bacchus. That thou, also, art not unacquainted with love, is
testified among the constellations by Ariadna, who was carried
up to heaven by thy lynxes. This malady of mine that keeps
its old fire alive in my bones, will be cured either by my
death or thy wine. *I will have recourse to thee;* for a sober
night always racks lovers on their lonely bed, and hope
and fear distract my mind. But if, O Bacchus, sleep pro-
cured by thy gifts come over my heated brow and frame,
with my own hand will I plant vines, and build trellis-work
in a row, and will take care that no wild beasts shall hurt
them. Provided my casks continue to froth with the purple
must, and the fresh grape-juice stains my feet as I tread it
out, I will live all my life long through thee and thy horns,
and will style myself the bard of thy valour. I will tell of
the delivery of thy mother[2] accompanied by Ætnæan fire;
the routing of the Indian forces by the Nysæan crew;[3]
the useless fury of Lycurgus[4] on the newly introduced vine;
the death of Pentheus,[5] delightful to thee, and effected by three
companies; the Tyrrhenian sailors[6] jumping over-board into

[1] *Elegy XVII.*] Propertius declares that he will become a votary of
Bacchus, to see if he can thus drive dull care away.

[2] *The mother*, &c.] See on iii. 20, 27.

[3] *The Indian forces*, &c.] The attendants of Bacchus are called
Nysæi chori from Mount Nysa in Thrace, on which he was nursed. His
expedition to India, undertaken by Hera inflicting madness on him,
lasted three, or, according to some, fifty-two years. He conquered the
Indians, and taught them the cultivation of the vine.

[4] *Lycurgus.*] A king of Thrace, professed foe to Bacchus. He would
have no vines in his country, for which he was made mad, and killed his
wife, his son, and himself.

[5] *Pentheus,*] king of Thebes, another opponent of the worship of Bacchus. He was torn to pieces by his own mother Agave, and two other
Mænads, Ino and Autonoe. See Theocr. xxvi.; Eur. *Bacch.* 1043—1152.

[6] *The Tyrrhenian pirates.*] Bacchus was on board a ship belonging
to Tyrrhenian pirates, who intended to sell him, whereupon he changed

the waves, in the form of crooked dolphins, from the ship that sprouted into vines ; and now through the middle of Naxos there flows a sweet-smelling spring sacred to thee, whence the Naxian people drink thy wine. The Lydian mitre shall surround thy hair, O Bassareus, with the flowing ivy-clusters falling heavily on thy fair neck: thy smooth neck shall flow with sweet-scented oil, and thou shalt sweep thy naked feet with a flowing robe. Dircæan Thebes shall strike the soft tympana in thy honour: the goat-footed Fauns shall play on the open reed: beside thee, the mighty goddess Cybelle, with turretted head, shall clash the hoarse cymbals to Idæan choirs. Before the doors of thy temple the priest shall place a golden bowl, flowing with wine poured out for thy sacrifices. I will chronicle all this in no humble strain, but in such language as peals from Pindar's mouth. Do thou only release me from my cruel slavery, and overcome this troubled head with sleep.

ELEGY XVIII.[1] [iii. 18. K.]

WHERE the lake,[2] shut out from the shady shores of Aver-nus, dashes up to the smoky ponds of the hot water of Baiæ, and where Misenus, the Trojan trumpeter, lies buried on the shore, and the causeway, built by the labour of Hercules, re-echoes with the waves, here, where the cymbals clashed in honour of the god of Thebes, when he was winning mortal cities with his own right hand,—but now, O Baiæ, deeply guilty and hated, what hostile god has set his foot in your water,— here he was laid low, and sank into the Stygian waters, and his spirit is flitting in your lake. Of what use to him were

the mast and oars into serpents, and made the sailors mad, so that they leaped into the sea, where they were turned into dolphins. See Hom. *Hymn.* vii. (ed. Herm.) ; Ovid, *Met.* iii. 582 seq. The expression in vs. 26 is in accordance with the Homeric account.

[1] *Elegy XVIII.*] On the death of M. Cl. Marcellus, the son of Caius Marcellus and Octavia, the sister of Augustus, which event, caused, most probably, by incautious and excessive use of the bath, took place at Baiæ B. C. 23, when he was in his 20th year. He is immortalized in *Æn.* vi. 860 seq. The year before his death he had been curule ædile, and had celebrated games with great splendour (vs. 13—20). For the topography, see on i. 11.

[2] *The lake.*] Paley takes *Pontus* as the Lucrine lake, not as the open sea.

his high birth, his manly worth, or his excellent mother, or his having been a member of Cæsar's family ?[1] Or the awnings lately waving in the crowded theatre, and every thing managed by his mother's hands ?[2] He is dead, and his twentieth year, poor youth, had just begun : so many virtues did his short life enclose in so small a space. Go now, raise your spirits, and picture triumphs to yourself, and let the whole theatre rising together for applause delight you. Excel the tapestry of Attalus, and let every thing be decked with gems at great games celebrated by you : you must give all the *splendour* to the flames. Nevertheless all must come to the grave, highest and lowest alike : the public boat of the grim ferryman must be entered. Though a man be so cautious as to hide himself in brass and iron, yet death drags out his guarded head. Nireus[3] was not exempt for his beauty, nor Achilles for his strength, nor Crœsus for the riches produced by the water of Pactolus. In former times this grief made havoc among the unconscious Greeks, when his second affection cost Atrides dear. But may the ferryman, transporter[4] of the shades of good men, convey thy lifeless body thither by the same way that Claudius,[5] conqueror of the Sicilian land, and *Julius* Cæsar, left the path of men and reached the skies.

ELEGY XIX.[6] [iii. 19. K.]

You are so often reproaching me with my hot passions : believe me, your own sway you more. When you have burst all bonds of decency, you know not how to set a limit to your wild desires. Sooner will fire stop in a burning field of corn, rivers flow back to the fountain-head, the Syrtes afford a

[1] *A member*, &c.] He had been betrothed to Julia, the daughter of Augustus.
[2] *His mother's hands.*] Octavia had conducted the duties of her son as Ædile, when he was unable through illness to attend to them. The theatre of Marcellus was erected by Augustus in the name of his nephew.
[3] *Nireus*,] the son of Charopos and Aglaia : his beauty became proverbial. He is celebrated by Homer (*Iliad* ii. 671).
[4] *Trajicit.*] Paley.
[5] *Claudius.*] Cl. Marcellus, conqueror of Syracuse, в. c. 212.
[6] *Elegy XIX.*] The poet shows by the instances of Pasiphaë, Tyro, Myrrha, Medea, Clytæmnestra, and Scylla, that the passions of women are stronger than those of men.

quiet harbour, and dreadful Malea shelter sailors in a safe retreat, than any one ever stop your career, and check your wanton impulses. She who suffered the disdain of the Cretan
bull,[1] and put on false cow-horns of fir, is a proof of it. The
daughter of Salmoneus,[2] who, burning with love for the Thracian Enipeus, consented to submit entirely to the embraces of
the river-god, is a proof. Myrrha[3] too, who was changed
into the branches of a young tree, and who was secretly enamoured of her old father, was a guilty proof. Why need I
mention the guilt of Medea, when love expiated the mother's
wrath by the murder of her children ? Or that of Clytæmnestra, through whom the whole house of Pelops was disgraced
by adultery at Mycenæ ? Thou also, Scylla,[4] wast bribed by
the beauty of Minos to cut off thy father's kingdom with his
purple lock of hair. This, then, the maid had promised to the
foe as her dower. Love treacherously opened thy gates, O
Nisus. Do you, O maidens, marry more auspiciously: the
damsel was dragged through the sea at the stern of the Cretan's ship. But Minos is not undeservedly made judge in Orcus :
though conqueror, he yet dealt fairly in the case of a foe.

ELEGY XX.[5] [iii. 20. K.]

Do you think that he, whom you have seen depart from
your bed, remembers your beauty now ? Hard was he, who
had the heart to exchange a mistress for gold ! Was the

---

[1] *She who suffered*, &c.] Pasiphaë.

[2] *The daughter of Salmoneus.*] Tyro. See on i. 13, 21.

[3] *Myrrha.*] The daughter of Cinyras, by whom she became mother of
Adonis : there are divers forms of her legend : all, however, agree that
she was changed into a myrrh-tree, from which Adonis came forth on its
being struck by the sword of Cinyras. See Ovid, *Met.* x. 298 seq. : and
for *condita* in vs. 16, ib. ix. 362, Sub eodem cortice *condi.*

[4] *Scylla,*] the daughter of Nisus, king of Megara, whose life and kingdom depended on a lock of purple or golden hair on the top of his head :
this she pulled out and enabled Minos to take the city. Her father was
changed into a sea-eagle ; and she either into a fish or a bird called
Ciris. See *Georg.* i. 404 seq. ; Ovid, *Met.* viii. 6 seq.

[5] *Elegy XX.*] A proposal to Cynthia to become his mistress, and written
therefore, it may be presumed, in or before A. U. C. 726. The name of
Cynthia does not occur in it, probably because Propertius had not yet
conferred that pseudonym on Hostia.

whole of Africa worth your tears? But you, simpleton, keep
dreaming of gods *to avenge you,*—mere imagination! Most
likely he is torturing his heart with another love. You have
brilliant beauty, and accomplishments such as chaste Pallas
loves; and a shining reflection of fame is cast upon you from
your learned ancestor.[1] Your family will be happy, if you
have but a faithful friend: I will be faithful: run, maiden, to
my embrace. And do thou, Phœbus, who drivest thy fires
more widely in summer, abridge the lingering path of light!
The first night *of my happiness* is close at hand: O moon,
make the first night of my embraces longer: we must first
make our agreement, and legal bonds must be duly signed, and
I must draw up a contract on newly entering upon my love-
engagement. Love will set his own seal to the compact: the
whole chaplet of the starry-mantled goddess shall be witnesses. How many hours must I talk away before Venus
prepares so delicious a warfare for me? *Wearisome but necessary delay!* For, when a marriage-contract is not duly
made, no vengeance of the gods ensues upon nightly wrongs,
and caprice will soon undo the ties that caprice formed:
—may our marriage-auspices insure our constancy! On him,
then, that shall have violated altars pledged in attestation of
the contract, and defiled marriage-rites by forming a new attachment, may there fall all the woes that love is wont to
bring, and may he become a subject for trumpet-tongued
scandal; and, though he weep, may his mistress's windows
never be open to him at night: may he always be in love, and
always destitute of the fruits of love.

ELEGY XXI.[2] [iii. 21. K.]

I AM forced to take a great journey to learned Athens, to
get rid of my troublesome love by the length of the way: for

---

[1] *Your learned ancestor.*] See on i. 1, 1.

[2] *Elegy XXI.*] It is altogether uncertain whether the journey to
Athens here spoken of was ever really made, or even really contemplated.
It may have been a mere threat,—a *ruse* to alarm the jealousy of Cynthia.
The argument bears some resemblance to the various passages in the first
book, (I. i. 30; ib. 6 and 15,) where he speaks of travelling as a remedy
for love. Hertzberg is inclined to suspect that the same journey is here
alluded to: but observes, (Quæst. p. 26,) that if he had really made the
tour of Athens and Asia, some allusion to it might have been looked for

my regard for the girl increases by constantly beholding her: Love himself supplies his own most ample aliment. I have tried every possible means of scaring him away: but the god keeps pressing on me from every quarter. But my mistress[1] scarcely ever admits me, or but once after frequent refusals: or, if she comes to me, she sleeps at the edge of the bed. There will be but one help for it: when I have left the country, love will be as far from my mind as Cynthia from my eyes. Now, my friends, launch the bark into the waves; draw lots for your turns at the oar in couples; hoist the lucky canvass to the mast-head: the breeze is now favouring the path of the sailors over the ocean. Ye towers of Rome, and you, my friends, farewell; farewell, too, O damsel, however you feel towards me. Now, then, I shall ride, a guest of the rude Adriatic waves, and be forced to approach in prayer the gods that thunder in concert with the waves. Then, having crossed the Ionian, when my bark shall rest its weary sails in the quiet water in Lechæum,[2] bear me, my feet, over the remainder, speed me on the toilsome way, where the Isthmus keeps off the two seas from the land. Then when the shore, with the harbour of Piræus, receives me, I will climb the long branches of the Thesean road. There will I begin to purify my mind by the study of Plato, or in thy gardens, O learned Epicurus: or I will pursue the study of eloquence, the ringing periods of Demosthenes, and thy witty writings, O smart Menander: or, at all events, I shall find pictures to captivate my eyes, or pieces of workmanship elaborately carved in ivory, or rather, in brass. Either long years, and a great expanse of deep sea between us, will assuage my wounds in a quiet nook; or else I shall die, a natural death, not heart-broken by a discreditable attachment; and the day of my death, come when it may, will be honourable to me.

in the following Elegies. It seems more probable that he was becoming anxious to shake off Cynthia, though he disguises his real feelings. We may perhaps surmise that the poet, who has elsewhere frequently arranged his Elegies in connected couples, purposely placed the present after the preceding, that the commencement of his love might be contrasted with the valediction—for such it virtually is—he has resolved to pronounce.

[1] Dormit *amica* toro.—*Paley*. Most editions have *amicta*.

[2] *Lechæum.*] Now *Balaga*, the Northern harbour of Corinth, on the Sinus Corinthiacus, and connected with the city by walls, twelve stadia in length: the other port, on the Sinus Saronicus, was Cenchrea.

ELEGY XXII.[1] [iii. 22. K.]

TULLUS, you have been so long pleased with cold Cyzicus,[2]
where the isthmus-like strait of the Propontis flows, and Din-
dymus, and the holy statue of Cybelle in the form of a heifer,
and the path taken by the horses of the ravisher[3] Dis.   If
you happen to be pleased with the cities of Helle, the
daughter of Athamas, and are not moved, Tullus, with regret
for me: though you delight to look at Atlas with all the heavens on his shoulders; the head of the daughter of Phorcys[4]
cut off by the hand of Perseus; the stables of Geryon, and
the marks of Hercules and Antæus[5] struggling in the dust,
and the troops of the Hesperides; and though you cleave with
your crew the Colchan Phasis, and go over, in person, the
whole voyage of the ship cut from Pelion,[6] where the un-
travelled pine, lately forced into the form of a ship, floated
through the rock, accompanied by the Argonauts' dove; and
though you sail where may be seen the region of the Lydian
Cayster, and where the river divides its waters into seven
channels:—yet all the wonders of the world yield to the Roman land.   Nature has placed here all the beauties of every
land.   The land is more fitted for war than prone to inflict
injury; O Rome, fame is not ashamed of recording thee.   For
we are as strong in good faith as by the sword: our anger, even
in conquest, can restrain its hands.   In this land thou flowest,
O Tiburtine Anio, and Clitumnus from the Umbrian dells,

---

[1] *Elegy XXII.*] He invites his friend Tullus to come back to Italy
from Cyzicus, where he had voluntarily prolonged his stay, after the
termination of his year of office as legatus to his uncle.

[2] *Cyzicus.*] (*Kyzik*) a noble and picturesque city on the N. W. coast of
Asia, in an island of the same name, separated from the mainland by a
very narrow channel: the city was dedicated to Proserpine, and famed
for its gold coin, giving name to the *Cyzicene stater*, which afterwards
became the *sequiæ*.   See Ovid, *Trist.* i. 10, 29.

[3] *The ravisher.*]   Dis, or *Pluto*, who carried off Proserpine.

[4] *The daughter of Phorcys.*]   *Medusa* was one of the δηναιαὶ κόραι,
[*Æsch.* P. V. 794,] daughters of Phorcys.   Kuinoel takes this of the
Gorgades Insulæ.

[5] *Antæus.*]   A giant and wrestler in Libya, and invincible as long as he
remained in contact with his mother earth.   Hercules discovered the
source of his strength, and accordingly crushed him in the air.

[6] *The ship cut from Pelion.*]   The *Argo:* cf. Catull. *Epith.* Pel. et
Thet. 1.

and thou, O aqueduct of Marcius,[1] work destined to last for
ever. We have the Alban lake, and the Nemorensian springing from a source in connexion with it, and the wholesome
stream[2] drunk by the horse of Pollux. But there are no
horned serpents, with scaly bellies, gliding through the land,
nor does the Italian wave flow with unheard-of monsters.
Here no chains clank on Andromeda,[3] for her mother's fault;
nor dost thou dread to be scared by a banquet in Italy, O
Phœbus;[4] nor has fire blazed forth in his absence, against
the life of any one, a mother[5] compassing destruction for her
own son. Savage Bacchantes do not hunt for Pentheus on
a tree: nor does the substitution of a stag enable ships to sail,
as once with the Greeks: nor has Juno been able to make
crooked horns grow on a rival, or disfigure her face by the
foul shape of a cow: Italy knows not the torturing trees of
Sinis,[6] and the rocks unkindly to Grecian travellers, and the
branches bent for his own destruction. This is your native
land, Tullus, this your most beauteous abode; here you should
seek for honour as becomes your high family; here you have
citizens to whom to exhibit your eloquence; here ample hope
of grandchildren, and of a loving marriage.

ELEGY XXIII.[7] [iii. 23. K.]

So I have lost my learned tablets, and with them so many
precious things have been lost! They had been worn in my

[1] *The aqueduct of Marcius.*] See on iv. 2, 12.
[2] *The wholesome stream.*] The *Lacus Juturnæ* in the Roman forum,
at which Castor and Pollux are said to have watered their horses after the
battle at the Lake Regillus. See Ovid, *Fast.* i. 707, and *Macaulay's
Lays.*   [3] See on i. 3, 4.
[4] *Scared by a banquet.*] The Sun, says the legend, could not look
upon the horrid banquet of Thyestes, at which *Atreus* served up to him
his (Th.) two children.
[5] *A mother,* &c.] This alludes to the story of *Althæa,* who threw on
the fire the fatal log of wood, on which depended the life of her son
Meleager.
[6] *Sinis.*] A robber of the Isthmus of Corinth, who used to kill travellers by tying them to the tops of tall flexible trees, which he had bent to
the ground, and then letting the trees fly upwards: in this way he was
himself killed by Theseus.
[7] *Elegy XXIII.*] The poet, having lost his *tabellæ,* issues the following handbill. The *tabellæ* were thin tablets of wood covered with wax,
and hinged together. They served among other uses for the transmission

hands by such long use as had gained credence for them even
when unsealed. They knew, by this time, how to appease my
female acquaintances, and speak some eloquent words without
me. No golden ornaments had made them dear to me: they
were of common box-wood and cheap wax. Such as they
were, they always remained faithful to me, and won good
effects for me. Perhaps the following message was intrusted
to those tablets: "I am angry at your having been slow in
coming yesterday, you dawdler. Have you seen some one
you think prettier than me? Or are you maliciously composing abuse about me?" Or else she said: "Come to-day,
we will dine together: Love has prepared entertainment for
you for all night:" and all the trifles that a clever girl readily
thinks of, when she names a time for talking and saying soft
nothings in secret. Wretched man that I am! some miser is
entering his accounts in them, and placing them amongst his
heartless ledgers! If any one brings them back to me, he
shall be rewarded with gold. Who would keep bits of wood
for wealth? Go, boy, and quickly fix this notice on some
column, and say that your master lives at the Esquiline hill.

ELEGY XXIV.[1] [iii. 24. K.]

WOMAN, false is that confidence of yours in your beauty,
that was once made too arrogant by my *partial* eyes. It was
my love, Cynthia, that gave you such praise: I am ashamed
of your being celebrated by my verses. Often have I praised
the various charms of your form, so that love feigned you to
be what you are not. And your complexion has often been
compared to the blushing morning, whereas the bloom
on your face has been artificial. What my oldest friends
could not turn me away from, nor a Thessalian witch wash
out even with the mighty ocean, this I will confess, without
being forced by torture or fire, and even if shipwrecked in the
middle of the Ægean main, to have been mere words. I was
erst a victim and constantly being tortured in the cruel furnace
of Venus: once I was bound with my hands behind my back.

of messages by post. For the method of folding and tying these missives
the reader may consult Bekker's *Gallus*, p. 339.

[1] *Elegy XXIV.*] A taunting address to Cynthia, for whom he professes to have had no real attachment.

Now the vessel is wreathed,[1] and come to port, I have passed the Syrtes, I have cast anchor. Now, at length, we are recovering our senses, weary with our long voyage; my wounds have now united and are whole again. O Reason,[2] since thou art a goddess, I dedicate myself as an offering to thy shrine: so many vows of mine had fallen unheeded on the deaf ear of Jove.

ELEGY XXV.[3] [iii. 25. K]

I USED to be a laughing-stock when the tables were set for feasting, and any one who pleased might be facetious about me. I submitted to serve you faithfully for five years: you will often bite your nails and regret my lost allegiance. I am not a whit moved by your tears: I was taken in by that trick: you generally shed tears, Cynthia, with an artful motive. I shall shed tears on leaving Rome, but my sense of wrong will conquer my tears: it is you who will not allow the yoke to be borne in concert. Farewell now to the threshold *that has often* wept at my words *of woe*, and to the door that after all was not broken by my angry hand. But may time press heavy on you, though you strive to conceal your years, and may unwelcome wrinkles come upon your beauty! Then may you desire to pluck out grey hairs by the roots, your mirror, alas, officiously pressing your wrinkles on your notice: may you, in turn, excluded, be forced to suffer cruel disdain, and may you in your old age regret the deeds you have done. These are the curses that my page denounces on you. Learn to fear what will come at last to your beauty.

[1] *The vessel is wreathed.*] See Virg. *Georg.* i. 303, Ceu fessæ quum jam portum tetigere carinæ Puppibus et læti nautæ *posuere coronas.*

[2] *Reason.*] There was a temple to *Mens Bona*, as we find from Ovid, *Fast.* vi. 241, *Mens* quoque numen habet. *Menti* delubra videmus, compared with *Am.* i. 2, 31, *Mens Bona* ducetur manibus post terga retortis. See *Livy*, xxii. 9, where we find that after the defeat, B. C. 216, of C. Flaminius at the Thrasymene Lake, the Sibylline Books were consulted, and, by their advice, *ludi magni* and temples were ordered for Venus Erycina and *Mens.*

[3] *Elegy XXV.*] The subject of this Elegy is closely connected with that of the preceding, and is probably a reply to Cynthia's tears and expostulations on receiving it.

BOOK V.[1]

ELEGY I.[2] [iv. 1. K.]

STRANGER, all the present extent that you see of mighty Rome was, before *the time* of Phrygian Æneas, a grassy mound: and where the Palatine, hallowed by the temple of Naval Phœbus,[3] now stands, the cows of Evander strayed and fed. These temples, now golden, first sprang up in honour of earthenware gods, and a shrine built in no costly manner was no disgrace. The Tarpeian sire, too, used to thunder from a bare rock, and the Tiber met,[4] on its way, our oxen only. The spot to which yonder house of Remus[5] has raised

---

[1] *Book V.*] The Elegies in this Book are of a miscellaneous character and of dates varying between A. U. C. 726 and 738. It is the opinion of Lachmann, in which Hertzberg concurs, that they were not published during the life of the poet, but collected and edited by his friends; and he thinks they are generally in a more rude and imperfect state than the others. However this may be, it is certain that not a few of these posthumous poems are of surpassing beauty, and a very high order of poetical merit. There is a marked difference in style between this Book and the first, especially in the studied use in the first of long words at the end of pentameters.—*Paley.*

[2] *Elegy I.*] This difficult Elegy, as far as vs. 70, is supposed by Hertzberg to have been designed as a prœmium to a book of Roman Fasti, undertaken by the poet, probably in the year of the city 726, and just before his love for Cynthia, in imitation of the Αἴτια of Callimachus. To the same work probably belong El. 2, 4, 9, 10, all of which are among his earliest performances. The latter part of the present Elegy was evidently added after his attachment had commenced, and was meant as a kind of apology for not pursuing the historic style of composition further, but devoting himself to amatory versification. Hence the *hospes* addressed in vs. 1, originally represented an imaginary stranger to whom the poet was pointing out the antiquities of the city; the idea of making him speak in the character of a Babylonian seer seems to have subsequently suggested itself.—*Paley.*

[3] Vs. 3. By *Navalis Phœbus* is meant the *Actius Apollo*, called *Navalis* both from his having a temple, on the promontory of Actium, overlooking the sea, and from the naval victory there gained by Augustus.

[4] Vs. 8. A river is an *advena* to each town that it visits on its course: the meaning is that there was no one there to greet the waters of the Tiber but a few oxen.

[5] *Yonder house of Remus.*] The *domus Remi*, more commonly called

itself by steps, was once the brethren's only hearth, and ample kingdom too. The lofty Curia that is now ornamented by a prætexta-wearing Senate once held rustic sires, men clad in coats of skins. The trumpet used to summon the Quirites, in days of old, to debates: many a time did the original hundred form a Senate in a meadow. The bellying awnings were not hanging over the vaulted theatre: the stage did not smell, as ordinarily now, of saffron. No one busied himself with looking after foreign gods, when the crowd, all eager attention, were trembling at the native rite; *their care then was* to celebrate the Palilia[1] with burnt hay, and to perform such sacrifices as are now renewed *from time to time* with blood from the stump of a horse's tail. Vesta was then poor, and content with *a procession of* crowned asses:[2] lean oxen used to drag the humble sacrifices *to the temple.* Fatted porkers used to purify the narrow streets, and the shepherd offered, to the music of a pipe, the entrails of a sheep. The ploughman, decked with pieces of goat-skin, dealt his leathern blows, from which custom the licentious Fabian Lupercus[3] derives his rites. The inexperienced soldier shone not then in hostile armour: they used to fight naked, and with stakes charred in the fire. Lycmon, with the goat-skin cap, was the first to build a general's tent: and the greater part of Tatius' decisions concerned pastoral matters. Hence came the warlike Titiens, and Ramnes, and the agricultural Luceres; hence Romulus

casa Romuli, was traditionally said to be the veritable abode of the founder of Rome, and as such was repaired and kept up even to the time of the empire. See iii. 7, 20; Ovid, *Fast.* i. 199. It stood on the Palatine Hill. *Quo sustulit* may be simply understood "the spot to which the hut of Romulus raised itself by steps." This passage confirms Mr. Macaulay's conjecture (Pref. to *Lays of Ancient Rome*) that it was removed from its original site near the Circus.—*Paley.*

[1] Vs. 18. The Palilia, or Parilia, (pro *partu* pecorum,) were kept on the 21st of April, in honour of Pales, the divinity of shepherds. The ceremonies consisted in a purification by fire and smoke, the smoke being made from the coagulated blood of a horse's tail, (whence *curtus equus,*) that had been dropped on the altar of Vesta in the preceding October, whence the horse was called *October equus.*

[2] Vs. 21. On the festival of Vesta, (June 9,) a procession took place in her honour, in which an ass, decked with strings of loaves, held a prominent place. See Ovid, *Fast.* vi. 313 seq.

[3] Vs. 26. The priests of Lupercus (*Defender from Wolves*) were called Fabii and Quintilii, from their respective founders, Remus and Romulus.

drove his four white horses in triumph: *he then could do so:* for, when the city was small, Bovillæ was not so close in the suburbs, and Gabii, that is now nothing,[1] had a very great population: powerful Alba, too, named after the omen of a white sow, was in existence, on the road[2] *beyond* Fidenæ, which was then thought a long journey off. The Roman nurseling has nothing ancestral but the name: it is not ashamed at having a she-wolf as the nurturer of its line. O Troy, for better, indeed, hast thou sent hither thy fugitives! with what a happy omen was the Dardan ship[3] wafted! There was already a good omen in the very circumstance that the womb of the wooden horse did not, on being opened, harm that ship when the sire clung trembling to his son's neck, and the fire feared to scorch his affectionate shoulders. Then came the manly Decius, and the stern Brutus,[4] and Venus, in person, brought the arms of Cæsar her son. The land, adopting the conquering arms of newly-rising Troy, happily received thy gods, O Iulus! If the oracular-tripod of the feeble-voiced Sibyl of Avernus pointed out the spot to be purified for Aventine Remus, or if the slowly-fulfilled prophecies of the Trojan priestess,[5] addressed to aged Priam, were true:— " Turn back the horse, O Greeks," *said she:* "your conquest will be fatal to you. The Ilian land will revive, and Jupiter will give power to these ashes." O she-wolf, sent by Mars,[6] best of nurses hast thou proved to our fortunes! how great are the walls that have grown from thy milk! It is the walls that I am trying to describe duly in affectionate strains: woe is me that my speech is but humble! But, nevertheless, every rivulet of song that shall have flowed from my lowly breast

[1] Vs. 34. Cf Hor. *Ep.* i. 11, 7, Gabiis desertior atque Fidenis vicus.

[2] *The road.*] Alba was farther from Rome than Fidenæ, a journey to which was thought long; much more, therefore, would the road to Alba be long.

[3] *The Dardan ship.*] The fleet of Æneas.

[4] Brutus, as consul, (whence *Bruti secures,*) ordered the execution of his sons for conspiring for the restoration of Tarquinius. See Livy, ii. 3 seq.

[5] *The Trojan priestess.*] Cassandra. The conquest of Troy by the Greeks would be fatal to them, because from the ashes of Troy there would come a race, the Romans, by whom they were afterwards conquered.

[6] *Sent by Mars.*] Mars, as the father, by Ilia, of Romulus or Remus, is said to have sent the wolf to save his offspring.

shall entirely serve my country. Let Ennius[1] surround his strains with a roughly made chaplet: Bacchus, give to me leaves from thy own ivy: that Umbria may be proud of and exalt herself in my writings, Umbria, the country of the Roman Callimachus. If any one sees the walls rising from the valleys, let him measure their greatness by my genius.—Give ear, O Rome; I am beginning a work in thy honour: citizens, give favourable omens, and let my enterprise be attended by kindly auspices. I will sing of sacrifices, and holidays, and ancient names of places: to these goals must my steed toil.—

O truant Propertius, why are you imprudently rushing into a description of sacrifices? Alas, your threads are not skilfully arranged on the distaff. You sing against the will of the Graces: Apollo is unfavourable: you demand from your unwilling lyre strains it will have to repent of. I will bring forward certain proofs on certain authority; or else I am a seer that knows not how to show the motion of the stars in a brass orrery.[2] The Babylonian Horos, scion of Archytas, gave me birth, and a family, descended from Conon, gives his to Horos. The gods are my witnesses that I have not disgraced my ancestors, and that in my writings nothing is preferred to truth. Now *the pretenders to my craft* have turned the gods to profit —even Jupiter is misrepresented for gold,—and the hackneyed signs of the obliquely turned sphere, and the lucky constellations of Jove, and that of greedy Mars, and the star of Saturn, fatal to everybody; also what is being portended by Pisces, and the violent constellation of Leo, and by Capricorn that bathes in the western waves. I could say, O Troy, thou shalt fall, and thou, O Trojan Rome, thou shalt rise again; and I could tell of the long entombment to come of the sea and land. I said, when Arria was leading forward her two sons,—she was sending them, against the will of the god, to battle,—that they would not be able to bring back their arms to their own home: two tombs of a surety now attest my faith. Again Lupercus, while covering his horse's wounded face, did not, alas, look out for himself, when his horse fell forward: while Gallus, defending, in battle, the standard committed to his charge, fell down before the blood-stained beak of his own eagle. Doomed were the boys: two deaths were

---

[1] "Let Ennius' poetry be rough and harsh."
[2] *Or else*, &c.] Cf. Ovid, *Fasti*, vi. 269 seq. Cic. *De Div.* ii. 34, § 88.

I

there for the grasping mother: my predictions, then, were
true, though I would fain have had it otherwise. I, too, when
Lucina was protracting the labour pains of Cinara, and the
burden of her womb was long in coming forth, said, Offer to
Juno a prayer for deliverance. She is delivered: my books
were in high credit. Such a prediction as this is not put
forth by the sandy cavern-oracle of Jove in Libya,[1] nor by
the entrails that declare the *will of* the gods as revealed to
them, nor by any one skilled in the moving of a raven's wing,
nor does a departed shade declare such from *a vessel filled*
with magic waters. You must look to the path of the sky,
and its track through the stars, and true oracles must be sought
from the five zones. Calchas shall be a weighty proof of this:
for it was he that loosed from Aulis the ships that were properly fast to the rocks, the averters of mischief:[2] he stained a
sword with the blood of the daughter of Agamemnon, and
Atrides, when he started, had his sails defiled with blood.
But the Greeks returned not. O plundered Troy, repress thy
tears, and look to the bays of Eubœa. Nauplius[3] held up, at
night, avenging lights, and Greece, weighed down by her own
spoils, is wrecked. O victorious son of Oïleus,[4] ravish now
and persist in loving the priestess whom Minerva forbids to
be torn from her robe. So far history. Now I will take a
flight to your stars: begin to listen patiently to new themes
of sorrow. Ancient Umbria, well-known district, gave you
birth,—am I false, or have I hit upon your native place ?—
where cloudy Mevania[5] sends dews upon the hollow plain,
and the waters of the Umbrian stream are warm in summer-
time, and the wall, better known from your genius, rises on
the crest of the towering Asis.[6] You gathered, too, the bones

[1] *Libya.*] The oracle of Jupiter Ammon.
[2] Vs. 110. The rocks are called *pia*.
[3] *Nauplius.*] Nauplius, father of Palamedes, who had been killed by
Ulysses and Diomede, caused beacons to be placed on the most dangerous
part of the Eubœan coast: the sailors, thus misguided, were consequently
shipwrecked. See Eur. *Orest*. 433, and *Schol*. in loc.
[4] *O victorious son.*] Ajax, son of Oïleus, ravished Cassandra in the temple of Minerva, though she clung to the statue of the goddess. *Vestis* is
the πίπλος that was placed on the statue.
[5] *Mevania.*] Mevania (*Bevagna*) was on the confines of Umbria: in vs.
124, Lacus Umber is the river Clitumnus.
[6] *Asis.*] *Asis* is believed to be the name of a mountain, whence the
town of Asisium was so called.

of your father, that should not have been gathered at so early
an age, and you are reduced yourself to a small estate. For
whereas many oxen used to plough your acres, the melancholy
measuring rod [1] has swept away your carefully-kept lands. In
time, when the golden amulet was taken from your young neck,
and the toga of liberty put on before your mother's gods, [2]
then Apollo taught you a little of his own poetry, and forbad
you to thunder forth your eloquence in the jarring forum.
But frame elegies, a tricksome work : make this your camp,
and let the rest of the poet-crowd write after your model.
You will suffer war in Venus' stern campaigns, and will be
a gallant foe to the Loves. For one mistress will render vain
your palms of victory, the produce of all your toil : and
though you may extricate from your chin [3] the firmly-fixed
hook, it will be of no use ; the handle will grasp you with its
knob. At her will you will see light and darkness ; no
tear will fall from your eyes, but at her bidding. A thousand
night watches, and the marking of her threshold, will not help
you : for a woman that has made up her mind to deceive, a
keyhole is enough. Now though your ship be tossing in the
middle of the sea, or you face, unarmed, an enemy in armour,
or the earth shake and gape from its inmost hollows, *fear not:*
be in dread of *nothing but* the ill-omened back of the eight-
footed crab. [4]

ELEGY II. [5] [iv. 2. K.]

WHY wonder at my having so many shapes in one body ?
Listen to the native characteristics of the god Vertumnus. A
Tuscan am I, from the Tuscans I spring, nor am I ashamed of

---

[1] *The measuring rod.*] By which the confiscated lands were assigned,
B. c. 40, to the soldiers of Octavian. See Virg. *Eclog.* i.

[2] *Your mother's gods.*] The Lares are so called, his father being dead.
Cf. Persius, v. 31, *Bullaque succinctis Laribus donata pependit.*

[3] *Your chin, &c.*] Criminals were dragged through the street by a stick
with a hook at one end (of. Juv. x. 66) : at the other end there would
probably be a crooked handle, to prevent its slipping. The meaning
seems to be, " you will no sooner be out of one difficulty than you will be
in another."

[4] *The eight-footed crab.*] The meaning is, that " a woman born under
Cancer will be your ruin : " Cancer is supposed to have been the symbol
of grasping avarice, a prominent trait in Cynthia's character.

[5] *Elegy II.*] The god Vertumnus gives an account of the origin of
his name, and of his various attributes. Cf. Ovid, *Met.* xiv. 641 seq.,
which passage has been imitated by Swift.

having deserted the hearths of Volsinium during war-time.
This crowded neighbourhood pleases me: nor do I rejoice in
a temple of ivory: it is enough to be able to see the Roman
forum. The Tiber once flowed this way, and they say that the
sound of oars was heard on the waters. But since he yielded
so much to his nurselings, I am called the god Vertumnus from
the diverting of the stream. Or, again, because we taste the
first fruit of the declining year, a festival is believed to have
been instituted to Vertumnus. For me first does the clustering grape grow black and change its colour, and the ears of
corn swell with their milky produce. Here you see sweet
cherries, and autumnal plums, and blood-red mulberries on a
summer's day. The grafter here pays his vows by a chaplet
of apple blossom when the unwilling pear-stock has borne
apples. O lying report, you do me wrong. I have another
reason for my name: as regards his own birth, believe a god
only: my nature suits all shapes: change me into any one
that you please; I shall look well. Dress me in robes of Coan
dye; I shall become a yielding maid: who can say that I am
not a man when I put on the toga? Give me a sickle, and
bind my brows with a hay-band; you will swear that grass has
been cut by my hand. Once I bore arms, and, I recollect, got
praised therefor: with a heavy basket on my head, I was a
reaper. I am not disposed for quarrels; but put a wreath on
me, and you will cry out that I have got wine in me. Bind
my head with a turban, I shall steal the shape of Bacchus;
also of Phœbus, if you but give me the quill. Throw nets on
my shoulder, and I am a huntsman: but when I take reeds I
am a Faun deity, skilled in catching feathered game. Vertumnus also adopts the figure of a charioteer, and of one
who nimbly passes his weight from horse to horse. Give
me the means and I will catch fish with a reed: I can also
go as a spruce pedlar with flowing tunics. I can, as a
shepherd, bend me to a staff, or carry roses in baskets in the
middle of the dust *of the circus*. Why need I add what I get
most credit from, the garden-gifts that my hands approve?
The blooming cucumber, and the gourd with swelling belly,
and the cabbage tied with the pliant rush, distinguish me:
and not a flower in the meadow buds without first, as is due,
being placed upon my brow to fade. Because, being but one,
I change myself into every shape, my native tongue gave me

a name from that circumstance : and thou, O Rome, hast given
honour to my fellow Tuscans, whence the Tuscan street has
now its name.[1]   At the time that the leader Lycomedius came
with his band of allies and crushed the power of the fierce
Sabine Tatius, I saw lines tottering, and weapons brought
low, and foe-men disgracefully turning their backs in flight.
But, O father of the gods, grant that, throughout eternity,
the toga-wearing Roman people may pass before my feet.   Six
verses remain : you who are hastening on business I will not
detain : this is the extreme end to my descant.   I once was
a log of maple, hastily hewn with an adze, and, before Numa's
time, a roughly made god in a city that was dear to me.   But,
O Mamurius,[2] graver of my statue in brass, may the Oscan soil
not lie heavily on thy clever hands, thou that hadst skill to
cast me so easily and make me take what form thou wouldst.
Thy work is but one, but honour is not given to the work
under one aspect only.

ELEGY III.[3]   [iv. 3. K.]

THIS message Arethusa sends to her Lycotas, if you can
be mine, since you are so often away from me.   But if any
part be blotted and wanting when you come to read,—the
blotting will have been made by my tears : or if any letter
deceive you by its indistinct form, each that does so will be a
mark of my hand already stiffening in death.   Bactra, among
the repeatedly visited Orientals, has lately seen thee, and the
Neuric[4] foe with horses clad in armour, and the wintry Getæ,
and the Britons with their painted cars, and the scorched Indian, of different hue from us, *dweller* near the Eastern wave.
Is this a husband's faith ?   Was this the way your nights
were pledged to me, when, in innocence, I yielded to your im-

---

[1] *The Tuscan street.*]   Allusion is made to the assistance lent to the
Romans, against the Sabines, by the Tuscans, under Cæles Vibenna, who
gave his name to Mons Cælius.   See Tac. *Ann.* iv. 65.

[2] Mamurius Veturius is said to have been the maker of the eleven an-
cilia after the model of that sent from heaven to Numa.

[3] *Elegy III.*]   This purports to be an Epistle from Arethusa (*Ælia Galla*)
to Lycotas, (*Postumus.*   See iv. 12,) begging him to come home, and describing her solitude.

[4] *Neuricus*, Paley : the Neuri were a tribe in Sarmatia : others read
Noricus. Sericus.

portunity? The ominous torch that was carried before me
when I was brought home drew its dusky light from a half-
extinct funeral pile: I was sprinkled with some Stygian water,
and the fillet was not put straight on my hair: I wedded without a god to accompany me. Alas, my vows that aré hanging
on all the gates are injurious to me: this is the fourth military
cloak that I am weaving to send to you to the war. Death
to him who first cut a stake from the guiltless tree, and made
of bone the hoarse and grating trumpet: more worthy is he
than Ocnus[1] to twist the rope-coil, and to feed for ever thy
hunger, O ass. Tell me, does the coat of mail gall your delicate arms? does the heavy spear chafe your hands unaccustomed to war? I would rather this should hurt you, than
that any girl should print with her teeth marks on your neck
deplorable for me. You are said, too, to be thin in the face:
but I hope that appearance is from regret for me. But, when
evening has brought to me the bitter shades of night, I kiss
all your armour that you have left. Then I grow nervous
because the counterpane slips off the bed, and because the
birds, who herald the light, do not sound their alarm. During
the winter nights I toil at my task to send to you in camp.
I cut the Tyrian wool properly for the shuttle; I try to learn in
what quarter flows the Araxes, the object of your expedition,
and how many miles the Parthian steed can run without
water: I try to learn from the map the countries, as set down,
one after the other, and the nature of their settlement by the
all-wise god; what soil is adhesive from cold, what crumbling
from heat, what wind is favourable for wafting ships to Italy.
One sister alone sits by me, and my nurse, pale with anxiety,
swears, though she knows it to be false, that your delay is
owing to the stormy weather. Happy Hippolyte, with naked
breast she bore arms, and, being a barbarian, covered her delicate head with a helmet. Would that the camp was open
to Roman maids: I would be a faithful attendant on your
campaign: nor would Scythia's mountains keep me back,
when the Father binds the waters into ice under a cold clear
sky.[2] All love is powerful, surpassingly great is love for a

---

[1] *More worthy than Ocnus.*] This alludes to a picture in which Ocnus
was represented as making a rope which a donkey ate as fast as it was
made: a symbol of an extravagant wife wasting her husband's property
as fast as he earned it. See Pausan. *Phocic.* x. 29, § 1.

[2] *A clear sky.*] We read *Aprico,* the correction of Hertzberg, which is

lawful husband: Venus herself waves that torch to make it burn vividly. What care I that there is glowing purple of Phœnician dye in your house, and the sparkling crystal ornaments my hands? Everything is mute and still, and only occasionally, on the kalends, one maid, accustomed to do it often, opens the closet of the Lares. I love to hear the melancholy bark of the lap-dog Glaucis: it alone, as it lies on the bed, claims a part of your prerogative. I deck the chapels with flowers, strew the cross-roads with vervain, and the Sabine herb crackles at the old hearth. If an owl perches on a neighbouring beam and hoots, or if the waning lamp requires to be touched with wine,[1] that day portends death to yearling lambs, and the sacrificers tuck up their dress and busily prepare for fresh perquisites. Value not, I pray, so much, the glory of mounting the breach at Bactra, or wresting from some scented general the standard of linen cloth, when the leaden missiles of the twisted sling are flying, and the crafty archers twang the bow as they ride away. But, the denizens of the Parthian land having been subdued, may a pointless spear, in your hands, follow the triumphant car. Keep faithful to me and your marriage-bed: on that condition only would I have you back. And when I take your arms and offer them at the Capene gate, I will write underneath, "A grateful wife, on her husband's safe return."

ELEGY IV.[2]   [iv. 4. K.]

I WILL speak of the Tarpeian grove, the disgraceful death of Tarpeia, and the capture of the ancient shrine of Jove. There was a grove enclosed within an ivy-clad ravine, with many a tree rustling in concert with the plash of native waters, the shady abode of Sylvanus, whither the sweet pipe

---

approved, but not adopted, by Paley. *Africus*, the old reading, if retained, must be understood to mean as *any* wind.

[1] "If the lamp sputtered, an arrival was expected, and the wine poured out in acknowledgment." *Paley.* Cf. Ovid, *Heroid.* xix. 151 seq.

[2] *Elegy IV.*] The legend of Tarpeia is here told at length. See *Livy*, i. 11. Propertius so far departs from the common version of the story, that instead of attributing Tarpeia's conduct to so sordid and unpoetical a motive as covetousness, he represents her as influenced by a passion for Tatius, the Sabine king. He thus renders her character less despicable; but the conduct of Tatius becomes in proportion more odious.

called the sheep out of the glare to drink. This fountain
Tatius bordered[1] with a fence of maple, and placed his trusty
camp on the crest of the elevation. What was Rome then,
when the trumpeter of the Cures shook with its long-drawn
blast the neighbouring rocks of Jupiter, and the Sabine arms
were grounded in the Roman forum where law is now laid
down for conquered lands? The mountains were a wall:[2]
the war-horse drank from a fount where now is the enclosed
Curia. From this spring Tarpeia drew water for the goddess: an earthenware urn was balanced on her head. And
was one death enough for the wicked girl that wished to deceive thy fire, O Vesta? She saw Tatius exercising on the
sandy plain, and brandishing his flashing arms about his helmet's yellow plumes. She was struck dumb at the king's
beauty and his royal arms, and her urn fell from her careless
hands. Often she made a pretext of ominous appearances in
the guiltless Moon, and said she must dip her hair in the
stream. Often she took silver-white lilies to propitiate the
Nymphs that the spear of Romulus might not hurt the face
of Tatius: and while ascending the Capitol, built among the
clouds, in the early smoke of evening, and returning thence,
she scratched her arms with the rough brambles: and when
she got back from the Tarpeian citadel she wept over her
love-pangs destined not be tolerated by her neighbour Jove:

"O camp-fires, *said she*, and tent of the body-guard of Tatius, and Sabine arms, beauteous to my eyes, oh that I were
sitting a captive in your innermost recesses, could I but look
in captivity on the arms of Tatius. Ye Roman hills, and
thou, O Rome, built on the hills, and Vesta, about to be put
to the blush by my disgrace, farewell. That horse, that horse
shall restore my love to the camp, whose mane Tatius combs,
with his own hands, to the right side. What wonder is it
that Scylla was merciless to her father's hair, and that the
lower part of her fair form was changed into fierce dogs?[3]

[1] *Bordered.*] *Præcingit.* It is manifest that Tatius did not completely
enclose the fountain, since it was still in the possession of the besieged,
but that he merely approached it with his camp lines. Perhaps, as Paley
inclines to think, *hunc fontem* means rather the pond at the bottom of the
hill than the spring-head.

[2] *The mountains were a wall.*] The Tarpeian rock, steep as a wall,
was a natural fortress.

[3] *Changed into fierce dogs.*] Propertius here confounds Scylla, the

what wonder that the horns of her monster brother were betrayed *by Ariadne*, when the mazy way was laid open by following a clue? How great a guilt am I going to lay upon Ausonian maids, I a faithless attendant on the virgin hearth to which I have been chosen! If any one is surprised at the fire of Pallas[1] being extinct, let him pardon me: the altar is drenched with my tears. To-morrow, so says report, fighting will be going on all over the city: do you follow the wet edge of the thorny ravine. The whole way is slippery and treacherous, for it conceals, throughout, the waters that trickle noiselessly in their unseen channel. Oh that I knew the strains of magic verse! this tongue, too, would then have helped you, beautiful Sabine. It is you the embroidered robe becomes, not one whom, born to his mother's disgrace, the hard dug of a fierce she-wolf nursed. Whether I am to be a concubine to you, or bear you children as a queen in your palace, I bring you no mean dower in the betrayal of Rome. If this please you not, carry me off, that the Sabine women be not carried off unavenged, and pay back in turn what you owe them. I can separate the armies that are in battle-array: ye married women, form an alliance through my marriage. Hymen, add thy lays: trumpeter, stop thy fierce blare; trust to me, my embrace shall soften your fatigue in arms. And now the fourth trumpet is heralding the coming of light, and the very stars are sinking into ocean. I will court sleep: I will desire dreams about you. Come to my eyes a kindly shade."

She spoke and dropped her arms in sleep, ignorant, alas, that she had gone to slumber with fresh furies in her heart. For Vesta, trusty guardian of fire brought from Troy, fosters her guilt, and puts more fires into her bones. She rushes forth like as a Thracian Bacchante, with rent robe and bosom bare, speeds along by the swift Thermodon. There was a holiday in the city: the fathers had ordered the Palilia: it was the birthday of the city-walls. It was the shepherds'

---

daughter of Nisus, (lv. 19, 21,) with Scylla the sea-monster. The same mistake has been made by Ovid, *Fast.* iv. 500; *A. A.* i. 331. With vs. 40, cf. *Catull.* ix. 2, Sylla *latrans* infimâ inguinum parti.

[1] *The fire of Pallas.*] The celestial image of Minerva, the Palladium, was kept in the temple of Vesta, and its custody was an equally important duty of the Vestals as the maintenance of the perpetual fire. See Ovid, *Trist.* iii. 1, 29, Hic locus est Vestæ, qui Pallada servat et ignem.

yearly feast, a merry time in the city, when the village dishes reek with delicacies, and the drunken rabble leap with their dirty feet over loose heaps of blazing hay. Romulus ordered the pickets to rest, the trumpet to cease sounding, and all things to be silent in the camp. Tarpeia, thinking this was her time, goes to meet the foe: she makes her compact, and is ready to accompany her confederates. The hill was difficult in ascent, and, as it was a holiday, but negligently guarded: without delay Tatius despatches with his sword the dogs that would have given the alarm. All things combined to lull the garrison to sleep: but Jupiter alone determined to keep awake for thy punishment, *Tarpeia*. She had betrayed her trust at the gate, and her sleeping home, and she asked leave to name a wedding-day at her choice. But Tatius,—for, though a foe, he paid no honour to villany,—said, "Marry at once and ascend the marriage-bed of my kingdom." He spoke, and overwhelmed her by throwing his followers' arms on her. This, O maid, was fit payment for thy services. The mountain has got its name from the commander Tarpeius: O guard,[1] thou hast the reward for thy undeserved fate.

ELEGY V.[2] [iv. 5. K.]

MAY the earth, O procuress, cover your tomb with thorns; may your shade feel thirst,[3] which you so dislike; may your manes not rest with your ashes, and may avenging Cerberus frighten your vile bones by his hungry bark. She had skill to make even obstinate Hippolytus become a votary of Venus, and was always a bird of most fatal omen to a happy bed; she would have forced even Penelope to despise the report of her husband being alive, and marry the wanton Antinous. Should she wish it, the magnet would not be able to attract iron, and the bird would be as cruel as a stepmother to her own nestlings. Moreover, should she bring to the magic trench herbs from the Colline gate,[4] solid places would

---

[1] *O guard.*] *O vigil:* addressed to the father whose *injusta sors* (death by the Sabine captors) is opposed to the deserved fate of the daughter.

[2] *Elegy V.*] A malediction on the memory of an old bawd, Acanthis, who had wished to set Cynthia against him.

[3] Cf. Ovid, *Am.* i. 8, 1 seq.

[4] *The Colline gate,*] near the *Porta Collina,* was the *Campus Sceleratus*

be drenched with running water. She was bold enough to attempt to enchant the moon, and impose conditions on it, and to change her own form and prowl by night as a wolf: in order to be able to deceive anxious husbands by her cunning, she gouged out with her nail the guiltless eyes of ravens: she also consulted owls on my destruction, and against me gathered the hippomanes,[1] droppings of a mare with foal. She used to gloss over the work of infamy by words, accordingly as the seductive crime readily kindled the heart, or by assiduous efforts surmounted the stony path of virtue:

"If, Doryxenium," she would say, "you have a mind for the treasures of the Orient shore, and the shell that proudly glows beneath the Tyrian water, and Euripulus' texture of Coan silk, and tattered fragments of tapestry cut from couches of Attalus, or the productions sent by palm-bearing Thebes, and myrrhine vases baked in Parthian fires, despise honour, trample on the gods, let lies be your ruling principle, and break the laws of ruinous modesty. To pretend that you have a husband pays well. Avail yourself of *all plausible* excuses: the longer the night is put off the more ardent will be your lover's passion. If he chance to ruffle your hair, his anger is a good thing for you: by and by, when he has had to buy his peace, you will be able to keep a tight hand over him. Then, when he has purchased your favours and you have promised him an embrace, take care to pretend, time after time, that it is the feast of Saturn,[2] and that you must keep pure. Let your maid Iole urge that it is April, let Amycle din into his ears that it is your birthday on the Ides of May. He is sitting at your feet, *we will suppose:* do you take a chair, and write something or other. Make him believe that you are writing a billet-doux to another lover of yours: if he is dismayed by this trick, you have him fast. Have always fresh marks of bites about your neck, and let him think you got them in a struggle with another. Do not choose to be ill-treated like fond Medea; she was disdained because she had ventured to make the first proposals; be

where Vestal Virgins who had broken their vows were buried alive: as such it was a good botanical field for witches. *Paley.*

[1] *Hippomanes.*] See this described in Virgil, *Georg.* iii. 281 seq.; *Æn.* iv. 515.

[2] *That it is the feast of Saturn.*] *Puros sideris esse dies.* Literally, that it is the pure day of the planet. The *sidus* may, without much straining, be *Saturnus.* Some read *Isidis*, with which compare iii. 32.

rather the greedy Thais of the clever Menander, when, as a harlot in the play, she takes the fancy of the cunning Getæ.[1] Humour your man; if he court your favour by his singing, strike up, and join your tipsy voice with his. Let your porter be awake for such as come with presents: for such as come empty-handed, let him be deaf and fast asleep against the bar that closes the door. I would not have you dislike a soldier, though not made for love, nor a sailor with horny palm, if he bring money, nor even one of those who have had labels hung round their foreign necks, when they danced in the middle of the forum with chalked feet.[2] Look to the gold, not to the sort of hand that brings it. After listening to poetry, what have you got but words?[3] A man that gives verses without a Coan dress,—let his lyre have no effect on you without money. While your blood is young, and age has brought you no wrinkles, make the best of your time, lest to-morrow snatch something from your mouth. I have seen the rose gardens of scented Pæstum, that seemed likely to live, fall scorched beneath a morning's south wind."

While Acanthis was tampering in this way with my mistress's heart, you might have counted my bones through my skin, I was so thin. But, O Venus, for thy good offices, receive at thy altars the offering of a ring-dove. I have seen a cough gathering in her wrinkled neck, and blood-stained sputa come from between her gapped teeth; I have seen her breathing out her rotten soul in her beggar-father's wrappers. The confined garret was chilly, and there was no fire on the hearth. Her obsequies were a stolen chaplet to tie up the remains of her hair, and a filthy old faded turban, and a dog that, to my sorrow, was too wakeful, when I wanted to undo the bolts noiselessly with my thumb. Let the bawd's tomb have over it an old urn with broken neck, and let thy weight, O wild fig, lie heavy upon it. All ye lovers, pelt the tomb with pieces of stone, and, as ye throw, curse her.

[1] *Geta.*] This was a common Gentile name for a slave, as we speak of *niggers*.

[2] *Chalked feet.*] Foreign slaves imported for sale used to stand in the forum with feet chalked, (cf. *Tibullus,* ii. 2, 59,) with a paper about their necks specifying their age, abilities, country, &c.

[3] There follow here by way of quotation, in some edd., the first two lines from i. 2. These, though, judice Hertzbergio, they are *nervi totius elegiæ,* we venture to omit.

ELEGY VI.[1]   [iv. 6. K.]

THE priest is offering sacrifice:[2] keep a religious silence
during the ceremony, and let a heifer fall stricken before my
altars. Let the Roman tablet vie with the ivy-berries of Philetas, and let the urn of Cyrene[3] contribute its streams. Give
me the soft unguent, and the grateful and honourable frankincense, and thrice let the woollen chaplet be wound about the
altar.   Sprinkle me with water, and let the ivory pipe pour
forth music from Phrygian stores at the altars of fresh turf.
Begone far away, deceits ! Let guile be in another clime :
the pure laurel-leaf is carpeting a new path to the priest. My
Muse, let us tell of the temple of Palatine Apollo : the subject
is worthy of thy favour, Calliope.   It is Cæsar's name that
demands my song ; Jupiter, thyself attend I pray while I sing
of Cæsar. There is a port of Phœbus receding into the Athamanian shores,[4] where a bay encloses the murmuring Ionian
waters, a bay memorable for the naval victory of the descendant of Iulus, at Actium, and that is now of easy passage for
sailors.   Here met the forces of the world : the pine-built
mass rested on the waves, and favourable omens did not
equally attend both.   One fleet was condemned by the Trojan
Quirinus, as were the javelins disgracefully thrown by a
woman's hand. On the other side was the ship of Augustus,
with sails bellying by the good-will of Jupiter, and the standards of his country, by this time skilled in conquering.   At
length Nereus had divided the fleets into two crescents : the
water, as it rippled, shone with the brightness of the armour :
when Phœbus, leaving Delos[5] that stands through dread of

[1] *Elegy VI.*] A eulogy on Augustus for the victory at Actium, in commemoration of which he had remodelled certain ancient games, and appointed them to be celebrated every five years. It was probably on the
occasion of their being held for the fourth time, B. C. 15, that this piece
was written.

[2] *The priest is offering sacrifice.*] The poet represents himself as a
priest about to perform a sacrifice, and hence in the succeeding verses
he borrows metaphors strictly derived from sacrificial usages.

[3] *The urn of Cyrene.*] Alluding to Callimachus of Cyrene.

[4] *The Athamanian shores.*] Athamania was a district in the S. E. of
Epirus. The Ambracian Gulf is meant.

[5] Delos was formerly not fixed, (hence Ovid, *Met.* vi. 332, *erratica*

him,—for it alone was once movable and at the mercy of the
angry south winds,—came and hovered over the poop of Augustus, and shone there, a strange flame, thrice curving like a
torch when held aslant.   He came not with hair waving on
his neck, nor with the unwarlike strain of his ivory lyre, but
with countenance like as when he looked at Agamemnon[1] the
descendant of Pelops, and piled the Dorian camp with greedy
funeral fires: or like as when he crushed the coiled folds of
the serpent Python, whereat the peaceful Muses trembled.
Soon he said:

"Augustus, preserver of the world, descended from long
Alba, known as more powerful than thy Trojan ancestors,
conquer by sea: the land is long ago thine: with thee my
bow fights, and all this burden on my shoulders favours thee.
Release from fear thy country, which now, relying on thy
championship, has set public prayers on thy prow.   If thou
save not her, Romulus, when looking for a site for his walls by
augury, saw not the birds on the Palatine fly past with lucky
omen.   See, they are too venturous with their oars: oh it is
disgraceful for the Latins, with thee at their head, to allow
the queen's fleet to be upon the waves!   Be not afraid at the
fleet having vessels with a hundred oars: the sea bears it
unwillingly.   As to the prows carrying figures that threaten
to hurl stones like the Centaurs, you will find them but hollow
boards and painted scare-crows.   With soldiers the cause they
fight for raises or depresses their strength: if it is not just,
shame makes them drop their arms.   The time is at hand;
begin the fight: I, who have given the time, will lead the
Julian ship with a crown of laurel in my hand."

He spoke, and exhausted the contents of his quiver in
shooting: next to his bow was the spear of Cæsar.   Rome
conquers as Phœbus promised; the woman pays the penalty;
the vanquished queen flies over the Ionian waves.   But father
Cæsar looks on in admiration from the Idalian star: "I am
a god," he says, "and this is a guarantee that he is of my
blood."   Triton advances winding his horn, and all the sea
goddesses applauded round the now free standards.   She

Delos,) till Phœbus secured it: he is called *vindex* from his threat of
reducing to complete instability again if it was not steady.

[1] *Agamemnon.*]   The allusion is to the plague, described by Homer,
(*Iliad* i. 40—50,) as having been sent by Apollo against the Greeks.

made for the Nile, weakly relying on a swift bark, and fortunate in this alone, that she was not destined to die on the day appointed *by the conqueror*. The gods ordered it for the best : *but* what a triumph would one woman have made, in the streets through which Jugurtha was led before ! Actian Apollo hence obtained his monument, because one arrow shot from his bow conquered ten ships.

Of wars I have sung enough : victorious Apollo now calls for the lyre, and puts off his arms for the peaceful dance. Let the guests, clad in white, now enter the sacred grove ; let soft wreaths of roses flow over my neck ; let wine drawn from Falernian presses flow, and let the Cilician saffron-essence thrice lave my hair. Let the Muse stimulate the genius of her poet-votaries as they drink. O Bacchus, thou art wont to be suggestive to thy Phœbus. Let one poet relate that the marshy Sicambri are enslaved ; another sing of Cephean Meroe and its swarthy kingdom. Let another recount that the Parthian has at length acknowledged the yoke of Rome : let him restore the standards of Remus, he will soon have to surrender his own. Or if Augustus spares anything in his eastern victories, may he but leave those conquests for his boys.[1] Crassus, if sensible at all, rejoice among the black sands : we may go over the Euphrates to thy tomb. Thus will I pass the night in drinking and song, till day sheds its beams over my wine.

ELEGY VII.[2] [iv. 7. K.]

THERE are, then, such things as spirits : death does not finish everything, and the lurid shade overcomes and escapes the funeral pile. For Cynthia, who was lately buried where the murmur from the remote causeway falls faintly on the ear, appeared to me to be hovering over my bed, when my sleep was made unsound by thoughts of my love's obsequies, and I bewailed the chilly solitude of my bed. She had the same hair as when carried out to burial, and the same eyes :

---

[1] *His boys.*] Caius and Julius, the sons of his daughter Julia, were adopted by Augustus.

[2] *Elegy VII.*] The ghost of Cynthia appears to Propertius as he is asleep and dreaming of her, and upbraids him with his neglect of her in her last moments, and his indifference to her memory.

her dress was scorched and clung to her side: the fire had
devoured the beryl that she generally wore on her finger, and
the water of Lethe had washed her lips.   She breathed, as in
life, and spoke, but the frail fingers[1] of her hands rattled.

"Traitor," she said, "and one whom no girl can ever hope
to find better, can sleep already have any power over you?
Had you already forgotten, when you fell asleep, our stolen
interviews in the wakeful Subura, and my window worn by
nightly cunning attempts?   How often have I let myself
down to you through it by a rope, sliding hand under hand,
into your arms!   Often have I lain in your embrace in the
thoroughfare, and warmed the pavement with my cloak.   Alas
for our secret bond of affection, the little regarded words of
which were carried away by the south winds that would not
hear.   No one cried out[2] to me when my eyes were sinking:
I should have obtained one more day, had you recalled me.
No watcher[3] sounded on my account on a split reed, and my
head was cut by a broken tile on which it was propped.
Lastly, who saw you bowed down with grief at my funeral?
Who saw your black dress warm with tears?   If you were
ashamed of going beyond the door, you might have ordered
my bier to have been carried more slowly to the pyre.   Why
did you not, ungrateful one, pray yourself for a breeze to blow
on my funeral pile?   Why was not the fire that consumed me
scented with spikenard?   It was even too much trouble for
you to throw cheap hyacinths[4] over me, and to place a
broken vase as a hallowed offering over my tomb.   Let Lygdamus be tortured, let the iron glow for the slave; I felt the
effect, when I drank the deadly wine that had been drug-
ged for me.   But let cunning Nomas lay aside her secret

[1] *But the frail fingers.*]   *At* implies that the words were those of the
living, the hands those of the departed, Cynthia.

[2] *Cried out.*]   *Inclamavit.*   See Paley.

[3] *No watcher.*]   The *custos* watched by the body till carried to the
grave, occasionally sounding a shrill note on a pipe, in case it should be
only in a trance.

[4] *Cheap hyacinths.*]   " The hyacinth here meant is probably our own
familiar and beautiful blue-bell, *agraphis nutans*, which is a native of
every country in Europe.   The eastern (or garden) hyacinth, though wild
in the Levant, could hardly have been *vilis* in Italy; and the Martagon
lily or Turk's cap, which is the ἀ γραπτὰ ὑάκινθος of Theocritus, the
flower ' inscribed with woe,' is still less likely to be meant."—*Paley.*

spitting on her hands : the hot tile will then show that they are
guilty.[1] A creature that was lately seen a common nightly street-
walker, now trails a gold-bedizened petticoat over the ground :
and with unfair baskets[2] exacts the penalty of heavier tasks
from any tongue that says a word about my beauty : and because Petale carried some wreaths to my grave, the old woman
feels the weight of the degrading clog. Lalage, too, is beaten,
and hung up by the hair,[3] for daring to make a request in my
name. With your consent she melted down the gold of my
portrait, and dared to win a dower from my burning funeral-
pile. I do not blame you, Propertius, though you deserve it :
long was my reign in your writings. I swear to you by the
song of the Fates, which no one can unsing,[4] and so may the
three-headed dog bark gently at me, that I retained my attachment to you. If I am deceiving you, may a viper hiss in
my grave, and crouch over my bones. For there is a twofold
abode assigned beyond the melancholy stream, and all the
crowd are ferried one way or the other. One road carries off
the adulterous Clytæmnestra, another branch of it the Cretan woman who horribly imitated a cow in wood. See another company ride in a bark wreathed with flowers, to where
the blessed air freshens Elysian roses, where the jovial rebeck
sounds, and the round cymbals of Cybelle, and the Lydian
lute sounds to the mitred choirs : Andromeda,[5] too, and
Hypermnestra,[6] guileless wives, tell their tale, personages noted
for their history ;—the form complains that her arms are black
from the chains put thereon by her mother, and says that her
hands did not deserve the cold rocks ; Hypermnestra relates

[1] *Spitting on her hand*, &c.] As a kind of magic protection against
harm. It would seem that Nomas had undergone the ordeal before, but
had escaped in consequence of having recourse to this unfair expedient.

[2] *Unfair baskets.*] Compare *Uncle Tom's Cabin*, chap. xxxiii., *I do
the weighing*.

[3] *Hung up by the hair.*] See *Juv.* vi. 490 seq., *Martial* ii. 66, for the
cruelty with which mistresses treated their maids.

[4] *No one can unsing.*] *Nulli revolubile :* literally, " which no one can
untwist," like the thread they spin whilst they sing.

[5] *Andromeda.*] See i. 3, 4.

[6] *Hypermnestra.*] One of the daughters of Danaus. She spared her
husband Lynceus on their wedding-night, when her 49 sisters murdered
their respective partners, the sons of Ægyptus the brother of Danaus,
being forced to do so by their father, who was afraid that his nephews were
conspiring against him. See Horace, *Od.* III. xi. 21—48.

K

that her sisters dared a desperate deed, but that her heart was
not hard enough for such wickedness.   Thus by tears shed
after death, we heal the love-wounds of life : I say nothing
of your many misdeeds and perfidies.   But I now give you a
commission, if perchance your feelings are moved, if the spells
of Doris do not hold you completely.   Let not my nurse Par-
thenie want anything in her trembling old age ; she was easy
with you and never grasping : and let not my pet Latris, who
has her name from her business, hold the mirror to your new
mistress : and all the verses that you have ever made on my
account burn, I beg : cease to have credit on my account.
Keep from my grave the ivy, which is twisting round my soft
bones with its struggling clusters and matted stems.   Where
fertilizing Anio keeps guard over the orchards, and where,
by the favour of Hercules,[1] ivory never grows dingy, there
write an epitaph worthy of me on the middle of a pillar, but
short, so that the traveller may read it as he runs from the
city.   " Here in Tiburtine soil lies the golden Cynthia :[2] thy
bank, O Anio, has gained renown."   And do not despise
dreams that come from the kindly gates[3] of sleep : when
kindly dreams come, they have weight.   By night we roam
abroad : night lets loose the incarcerated shades : even Cerberus quits the door and strays.   Our laws compel us to return by day-break to the Lethæan pools : we are ferried over :
the ferryman counts his freight each time.   Now other women
may own you : in time I shall have you to myself ; you will
be with me, and I will mingle my bones with yours."   After
she had finished making her mournful complaint to me, her
shade eluded my embrace.

---

[1] *Hercules.*]   He was worshipped at Tibur, the air of which, from the
mephitical exhalations of the water, was supposed to preserve the colour
of ivory ; in vs. 82, *pallet* is " grows dull."   Cf. Martial iv. 62 ; viii. 28,
11 ; vii. 13.

[2] *Golden Cynthia.*]   *Aurea* is " excellent."   Cf. *Tibull.* i. 6, 57.   Tua
mater me movet, atque iras *aurea* vincit anus.   Shaksp., *Cymb.*,

   " *Golden* lads and lasses must,
   Like chimney-sweepers, come to dust."

[3] *Kindly gates.*]   The gates of sleep were twofold : 1. ivory ; 2. horn :
from the latter true dreams were said to come.   See *Æn.* vi. 894.

ELEGY VIII.[1] [iv. 8. K.]

LEARN what it was that made the watery Esquiliæ turn out
last night, when the crowd of neighbours came hurrying from
the new park.[2] Lanuvium is, of old, protected by an aged
dragon;—here, where the occasion of an amusement so seldom
occurring is not lost; where is the abrupt descent into a dark
and hallowed cave; where is let down,—maiden, beware of
every such journey,—the honorary tribute to the fasting snake,
when he demands his yearly food, and hisses and twists
deep down in the earth. Maidens, let down for such a rite,
grow pale, when their hand is unprotectedly trusted in the
snake's mouth. He snatches at the delicacies if offered by a
maid, the very baskets tremble in the virgin's hands. If they
are chaste, they return and fall on the necks of their parents,
and the farmers cry "We shall have a fruitful year!" Hither
rode my Cynthia, with her ponies neat and trim: Juno[3]
was the cause, but Venus still more so. O Appian Road,
tell me, I pray, how triumphantly she rode as you saw her
wheels flying over your rough pavement, when a disgraceful
brawl was heard in a vile pot-house: if without me, at all
events not without a stain on my good name. As she sat,
with all eyes upon her, she leaned over the pole, and daringly
drove at full speed over the rough road. I say nothing of
the silk-lined vehicle of the closely-shaved dandy, and his
Molossian dogs with ornaments on their necks: he will one
day be forced to sell himself to coarse diet, when the beard of
which he is now ashamed will get the mastery over his close-
shaved cheeks. As my rights were so often invaded, I determined to shift my camp and change my bed. There lives
a certain Phyllis near Diana's temple on Mount Aventine:
when sober, she is rather dull; when she drinks everything

[1] *Elegy VIII.*] A very lively account of the manner in which the
jilted poet retaliated on Cynthia, and how she caught him in the fact and
took summary vengeance upon him and her rivals.
[2] *The new park.*] Vs. 2. *Agris novis.* Mæcenas had converted a ceme-
tery on the Esquiliæ into a park. The poet (cf. iv. 23, 24) lived in that
neighbourhood, and the people came to ask him what the matter was.
Cf. Hor. *Sat.* i. 8, 14.
[3] *Lanuvium.*] This place was celebrated for the worship of Juno Sos-
pita: Milo, the murderer of Clodius, was dictator there.

in her is agreeable.   There is another, Teïa, who lives near
the Tarpeian groves, a pretty woman, but, when she is tipsy,
one man is not enough for her.   I determined to invite these
and enjoy myself in the evening, and with a new mistress to
steal new delights of love.   A sofa was set for us three in the
quiet shrubbery: do you ask how we sat?   I was between
the two.   Lygdamus was our cupbearer; our goblets were of
glass, as it was summer, and our wine Greek, from Methymnæ.[1]   Thou, O Nile, didst supply us with a flute-player.
Phyllis played the castanets, she was neat and simply dressed,
and good-natured to be pelted with roses.   A dwarf, too, with
limbs shrunk and short, shook the hollow castanets of box in
his deformed hands.   But the flame would not burn steadily,
though the lamps were constantly trimmed, and the table fell
flat off its frame: and when I kept trying to get the Venus
with the lucky dice, the cursed aces always came out.   I was
deaf to their singing, blind to their naked charms: I was, alas,
solely at the gate of Lanuvium; when suddenly the door-posts
shook, and the hinges creaked, and a slight noise was heard at
the entrance of the house: in a moment Cynthia throws back
both the folding doors, with her hair not elaborately decked, but
beautiful in her rage.   The cup fell from my paralysed
hands, my lips blanched, though moistened with wine.   She
flashed lightning from her eyes, and raged as only a woman
can: the sight was as terrible as the taking of a city.   She
angrily dashed her nails into Phyllis' face: Teïa, panic-struck,
cried out to the neighbours to bring water.[2]   Lights were
brought out, which roused the sleeping Romans, and every
path rings with the nightly brawl.   The first wine-shop on
the dark road sheltered my visitors, with hair torn off their
heads, and garments rent.   Cynthia stands exulting amid the
spoils, and, having routed her foes, comes back to me, and,
with ruthless hand, scratches my face, bites my neck and makes
it bloody, and above all strikes at my guilty eyes. When she has
tired her arms with beating me, Lygdamus, hidden near the
hind legs of the sofa, is pulled out, and, on his knees, implores
my genius: Lygdamus, I could do nothing, I was a prisoner as

[1] *Methymnæ.*] In Lesbos.
[2] *To bring water.*] A ludicrous image of the panic produced by Cynthia's irruption. One of the girls screamed " Water! water! " as if the
house was on fire.

well as yourself. At length, with clasped hands, I proposed
an agreement, when at last she allowed me to touch her feet,
and said, "If you wish me to forgive the guilt that you have
committed, listen to the conditions I impose. You will neither
walk, in full dress, in Pompey's portico, nor when sand
strews the noisy forum.[1] Beware of looking up, with your neck
bent obliquely, to the top of the theatre,[2] or of loitering with
your litter open. And in the very first place let Lygdamus,[3]
the origin of all my complaint, be sold, and trail fetters on
both his feet!" Thus she laid down the law. I answered,
"I accept the conditions." She laughed, proud of the imperious rule she had imposed. Then she fumigated every spot
that the strange girls had touched, and washed the threshold
with pure water. She ordered me too to change all my clothes,
and thrice touched my head with sulphur-smoke. Then we
changed the bed-clothes sheet by sheet; I agreed to do what
she wanted, and, now that the bed was harmless, we made up
our quarrel.

ELEGY IX.[4] [iv. 9. K.]

At the time that the son of Amphitryon had driven herds
from thy stalls, O Erythea,[5] he came to the Palatine mountain ridge abounding in cattle, and, weary himself, halted his
weary cattle, where the Velabra were overspread by their own
marshy stream, and the boat-man sailed over waters that have
given place to what is now part of the city. But they remained not safe in the faithless hospitality of Cacus; by
stealing them he profaned the god of hospitality. Cacus lived
hard by, a robber, in a fearful cave, who discharged flames
separately through three mouths. He, to prevent the traces
of his barefaced plunder from being clearly seen, drew the
oxen backwards, by their tails, into the cave, but not without a god seeing it: the heifers gave token of the theft by
lowing, and *Hercules* in anger burst open the stronghold of

[1] *Sand strews*, &c.] The gladiators exhibited in the forum, the scene
of many a dispute at other times.
[2] *The top of the theatre*,] where the women sat apart.
[3] *Lygdamus*, &c.] He had invited her rivals.
[4] *Elegy IX.*] This Elegy contains an account of the building, by Hercules, of the Ara Maxima, and the occasion thereof. Cf. Livy, i. 7.
[5] *Erithyia.*] Geryon kept his herds at Erithea, near Gades.

the monster. Cacus fell, stricken by a blow on his three heads from the Arcadian club. Alcides then said, " Go, my oxen, go, oxen of Hercules, last toilsome trophy of my club, oxen twice sought for, twice won by me, and mark this ground as ox-fields by your long-continued lowing: your pasture-ground shall be the noble forum of Rome.[1] " Thus he spoke, while his mouth and parched palate were racked with thirst, and no teeming earth supplied him with water. Suddenly he hears some girls laughing, in retirement, at a distance, where a grove had grown into a forest with shady circuit, *containing* the secret shrine of the feminine goddess,[2] and the springs used in sacrifices, and the rites profaned with impunity by none. Purple fillets covered the retired abodes ; the timeworn shrine glowed with burning incense ; the poplar, too, ornamented the temple with its masses of foliage, and many a shady bower sheltered the birds as they sang. Hither he rushed, and sweeping the ground with his beard, dry and matted with dust, he poured forth, before the door, words beneath the language of a god: " To you I pray, O ye that are sporting in a sacred grotto in the grove, open your shrine, in hospitality, to weary travellers. I am wandering in want of water, and that, too, about a country of murmuring streams, and as much water as I can hold in the hollow of my hand is enough. Have ye heard of one who has borne the world on his back ? I am he : the rescued earth calls me Alcides. Who has not heard of the bold deeds of the club of Hercules, and of his arrows powerless against no beast that is born, and of the Stygian darkness opened to him only of men ? Receive me: at last this land is open before me, weary one that I am. Though ye were offering a sacrifice to Juno my bitter enemy, even she, stepmother though she is, would not have shut up her water from me. But if any one of you is frightened by my looks, or my lion's skin, and my hair scorched in Libya's sun, I am the same one that performed servile offices in a purple robe, and spun my daily task with the Lydian distaff: my hairy breast has been confined in a soft girdle, and, though my hands are hard, I made a handy girl."

Thus spoke Alcides: and the venerable priestess answered him as follows, having her grey hair bound with a purple fillet:

[1] *The forum.*] The part of Rome afterwards called the *forum boarium.*
[2] *The feminine goddess.*] The Bona Dea.

"Gaze no longer, stranger, and withdraw from the hallowed grove: quickly begone, and fly from our threshold whilst thou canst leave it in safety ! The altar that protects itself in a retired shrine is forbidden to men, and *profanation of it* is punished by a fearful penalty. At a great price[1] did the priest Tiresias gaze on Pallas, while she laved her stalwart limbs, having laid aside the Gorgon-shield. May the gods send thee other fountains : the spring that flows here, out of the way, and with secret approach, is peculiar to maidens !" Thus said the old woman : he pushed with his shoulder the door that hid the fountain from his view, and the closed door was not proof against his assault, angry and thirsty as he was. But after he had fairly drained the stream and quenched his thirst, he laid down severe laws before drying his lips. "This corner of the world," said he, "receives me, in the course of fulfilling my destiny : at length this land is open to me, weary as I am. May this great altar, dedicated by me on the recovery of my flocks, made great by my own hands, never be open to the worship of women, that the thirst of the great Hercules be not unrevenged !" Hail, O holy father, to whom savage Juno is at length kind, consent, propitiously, to be in my poem. This man, since by his hands he had cleansed the world, the Sabine Cures set up in a temple as Holy.

ELEGY X.[2] [iv. 10. K.]

I will now begin to sing the origin of the name of Jupiter Feretrius, and the taking of the three suits of armour from the three chieftains. I am beginning a steep ascent, but glory gives me strength; a crown gathered from an easy ascent pleases me not. Thou, O Romulus, suppliest the first instance of this victory, by returning, laden with the foeman's spoils, what time with thy victorious spear thou felledst Acron[3] of Cœnina, when approaching the gates, and laid low both man and horse. Acron, descended from Hercules, chief from Cœnina's citadel, was once a terror to thy boundaries, O Rome. He dared to look for spoils from the shoulders of Quirinus, and

[1] *At a great price.*] That of blindness.
[2] *Elegy X.*] The derivation of the obscure title Jupiter Feretrius, is here discussed.
[3] *Acron.*] See Livy, i. 10.

gave up his own, still wet with his blood. Romulus saw him
poising his dart before the hollow towers, and, having previously registered a vow, closed with him : Jupiter, to-day shall
this victim, Acron, be offered to thee. He had vowed : and
Acron fell, a spoil for Jupiter. This was the way the father
of the Roman city and valour was used to conquer, he who
bore the cold camp, with the sky for his roof. He was
a horseman and skilled in riding ; a husbandman skilled in
ploughing ; his wolf-skin helmet was crested with a shaggy
horse's tail, and his shield was not ornamented or glittering
with plates of bronze. After him comes Cossus,[1] who killed
the Veientine Tolumnius, when the conquest of Veii was toilsome. Not yet was the sound of war heard beyond the Tiber :
the limit of their booty was Nomentum, and the tripartite
land taken with Cora.[2] O ancient Veii, you, too, were then
a city, and the golden chair of state was placed in your forum.
Now within your walls the pipe of the idle shepherd sounds,
and among your remains fields are mown. By chance the
Veientine chief took up his position over the gate-tower, and
confidently challenged the foe from his own city. So while
the battering-ram was knocking at the wall with its iron
head, where the long penthouse afforded shelter for the work,
Cossus says, "It were better for a brave man to meet his foe on
level ground." Without delay, each is ready on the plain.
The gods helped the arm of the Latin : the severed neck of Tolumnius splashed the Roman horses with blood. Next Claudius
Marcellus repulsed the enemy who had passed into the country
from the Rhine, when the shield of the mighty Belgic hero
Virdumarus was brought back. This man boasted his descent from the god of Rhine himself ; right skilled was he in
hurling the javelin, standing upright in the car. To Claudius
there fell, after cutting off his head, a crooked chain from the
hero clad in striped breeches, while hurling the javelin in the
front rank. Now there are three sets of spoils stored up in
the temple : the origin of the name Feretrius is from each
leader striking[3] down his opponent by a sure blow. Or else

---

[1] *Cossus.*] See Livy, iv. 20.

[2] *Cora.*] Cora (*Cori*) was about 37 miles from Rome, and is mentioned
in *Æn.* vi. 776. Nómentum (*La Mentana*) was among the Sabines, and
afterwards famed for its wine.

[3] *Striking.*] From *ferire*, to strike.

because they carried[1] on their shoulders this armour won from their conquered foe, the proud altar of Jupiter Feretrius has its name.

ELEGY XI.[2]   [iv. 11. K.]

FORBEAR, Paullus, to dwell continually, with tears, on my death : the black gate opens to no prayers. When once dead bodies have entered the infernal domain, egress is barred by inflexible adamant. Though the god of the gloomy hall may hear you, *it will be in vain,* for the shore that cannot hear will drink in your tears. Prayers move the gods above : but when the ferryman has received his toll, the gloomy gate is shut fast upon those who have been committed to the grassy sod. Such was the note of the mournful trumpet, when the unfriendly torch, applied to the foot of the pile, was withdrawing my head from the bier. What availed my marriage with Paullus, the triumphs of my ancestors, or the tokens of my nobility, great though they were ? Did I, a Cornelia though I was, find the Fates less severe ? Lo, I am a weight that may be lifted with five fingers. O darkness of the damned, and ye sluggish pools of water, and every wave that entangles my feet, though before my time, yet came I not here guilty. May the Father, accordingly, lay mild conditions on my shade. Or, if there be an Æacus that sits as judge with an urn before him, may he, if I am found guilty, give the ballot against me, and punish my remains. May his fellows sit by him, and may the stern crew of Eumenides be near the seat of Minos in the listening court. May Sisyphus leave his stone ; may Ixion's wheel be still ; may the deceitful water

---

[1] *Carried.*]   From *ferre,* to bear.
[2] *Elegy XI.*]   This Elegy may fairly be regarded as a masterpiece of the poet's genius. It is a splendid composition, full of pathos and eloquent appeal, and is on the whole worthy of the almost extravagant praises which Barth and Kuinoel have bestowed upon it. It assumes the form of an address from a deceased wife, Cornelia, to her husband, Lucius Æmilius Paullus, who was censor in the year B. C. 22. Cornelia was the daughter of Scribonia, formerly wife of P. Cornelius Scipio, but subsequently married to Augustus. She was divorced by the latter on his marriage with Livia. He appears, indeed, to have left her from her unamiable temper; "Pertæsus," says Suetonius, "ut scribit, morum perversitatem ejus." This is the latest of the poet's extant writings, the date being A. U. C. 738, as appears from vs. 66. *Paley.* See Dict. of Biog. s. v. *Lepidus,* 19.

stop for Tantalus; may Cerberus to-day forbear from mischievously snapping at any shades, and may the chain fall
from the lock, and the door be still. I am pleading[1] for myself. If I am deceiving, may the persecuting urn, the punishment of the sisters,[2] press on my shoulders. If the fame of
ancestral trophies was ever an honour to any one, *I can boast
that* the realms of Africa speak of my Numantine[3] ancestors.
Another class comprises my maternal ancestors, the Libones,[4]
of equal celebrity, and my family, on both sides, is exalted by
its honours. Afterwards, when the maiden's dress had given
way to the marriage-torch, and a new fillet had bound my
hair as a wedded wife, I was joined in wedlock to you, Paullus, doomed to be my only husband: on my tombstone I shall
be read of as having been married to you alone. I call to
witness the ashes of my ancestors, to be adored by thee, O
Rome, below whose epitaphs, thou, O Africa, liest with shorn
hair, and him who crushed Perses,[5] pretending to the courage
of his ancestor Achilles, and thy house, *O Perses*, descended
from Achilles, and that I was not the cause for relaxing the
laws of the Censorship, and that your altars never blushed at
any fault of mine. Cornelia did not prove a disgrace to such
great trophies: nay more, she was a praiseworthy member
even of her noble family. Nor did my life alter; the whole
of it is free from guilt: I lived a model from the marriage to
the funeral-torch. Nature gave me principles inherited from
my birth, so that I could not be better from fear of punishment. Let any jury pass a severe sentence on me: no one
will be disgraced by contact with me. Neither thou, O
Claudia,[6] who didst, after others had failed, move with a rope
Cybelle, model attendant on the goddess with the crest of

---

[1] *I am pleading.*]   This is supposed to be the speech of Cornelia before
the assembled tribunal of Orcus.

[2] *The sisters.*]   The Danaides.

[3] *Numantine.*]   P. Cornelius Scipio Africanus Æmilianus Minor, obtained the agnomen of *Numantinus* from *Numantia* in Spain, which he
took B. C. 133.

[4] We find mention of seven *Scribonii Libones*, after one of whom the
Puteal Libonis was named.

[5] *Him who crushed Perses.*]   L. Æm. Paullus Macedonicus.

[6] *Claudia.*]   She was a Vestal virgin, and accused of incontinence, upon
which, to prove her innocence, she drew, with her own hand, an image of
Cybelle off a shoal in the Tiber, though numbers of men had failed.   See
Ovid, *Fast.* iv. 275 seq.; Livy, xxix. 14; Suet. *Tib.* § 2.

towers :[1] nor thou, *Æmilia*, under whose hands the white cloth kindled the fire, when Vesta claimed the flames intrusted to thee. Nor have I injured thee, my dear mother Scribonia. What, save my early doom, wouldst thou have changed in me ? My praise is sung in my mother's tears and in the city's regrets, and my bones have been protected by the grief of Cæsar. He constantly asserts that a sister worthy of his daughter[2] is no more, and we have seen tears shed by a god.[3] Moreover, I gained the ennobling honours of the garment,[4] and I was not carried off without leaving any children. Thou, Lepidus, and thou, Paullus, wilt assuage my loss now that I am dead ; my eyes were closed in your arms. We also saw our brother[5] attain the double honours of the curule chair, at the time of whose consulship his sister was carried off. My daughter, born a proof of the strictness of thy father's morals, imitate me, and keep to one husband. Do you, *my descendants*, keep up the dignity of the family. The boat is ready for me, not against my will, since so many of mine are left to ennoble my lot. This is the highest glory and triumph for a woman, when report is kind, and praises her after death. Now I commend to you our children, pledges of our common love. This care lives, as it were, branded in my bones. Discharge a mother's duty, O father : all my troop of children will have to be carried on your neck. When you give them kisses, when they weep, add a mother's kisses. The burden of the whole house now begins to be yours. If you must needs grieve, grieve not in their presence : when they come, dry your cheeks, and kiss them with feigned cheerfulness. Let the nights that you wearily spend in thinking of me, Paullus, be enough for you, and the dreams often taken for visions of me : and when you talk in private to my portrait, speak each word as if it was going to answer you. But whether a new marriage-bed be placed opposite the door, and a

[1] *Crest of towers.*] Cybelle is always represented with a *Corona Muralis*.

[2] *His daughter.*] Julia, the daughter of Augustus by Scribonia, would be Cornelia's half-sister.

[3] *A god.*] Julius Cæsar.

[4] *The garment.*] This appears to have been connected with the *Jus Trium Liberorum*, but in what manner is uncertain.

[5] *Our brother.*] P. Cornelius Scipio was consul B. C. 16, with Domitius Ahenobarbus, having previously been ædile and prætor.

suspicious stepmother lie on a couch once mine, acquiesce in and submit to your father's marriage, my boy, his new wife will be captivated by your behaviour. Praise not your mother too much: if compared with a former wife, your stepmother will interpret your free talk as an insult to herself. Or if he respect my memory and remain contented with my shade, and think my ashes worthy of so much attention, learn to mark the very first approach of age, and let there be no way open to make him feel the misery of an unmarried man. May what has been taken from mine be added to your life-time: may Paullus delight in growing old from having my offspring: and it is well: as a mother I never put on mourning: all my company of children followed at my funeral.—I have pleaded my cause. Witnesses, rise, and weep for me, while the grateful earth is paying the tribute to my worth when alive. To some virtues heaven has been opened: may I earn,[1] from my merits, the privilege of being one whose bones are conveyed *into Elysium* in triumph.

[1] *Equis*, Paley: Others read *aquis, avis (ad avos)*, &c.

ELEGIES OF PROPERTIUS.

BOOK I.

ELEGY I. TO TULLUS.

CYNTHIA's insnaring eyes my bondage tied:
  Ah wretch! no loves, till then, had touch'd my breast
Love bent to earth these looks of stedfast pride,
  And on my neck his foot triumphant press'd.

He taught me, then, to loathe the virtuous fair,
  And shameless waste my wild and driftless hours:
Twelve moons this madness lasts; and yet my prayer
  Is breathed in hopeless love to adverse powers.

Minalion, erst, could all adventures brave,
  Till Atalanta's barb'rous heart grew mild:
Love-crazed he trod each drear Parthenian cave,
  And look'd on shaggy beasts in forests wild.

Struck by the branch the monstrous Centaur sway'd,
  Midst shrill Arcadia's rocks he groaning fell;
And thus he tamed the nimble-footed maid:
  Thus love-prayers speed, and acts that merit well.

In me no arts can tardy Love devise;
  His foot can track no more the beaten ways:
Come ye! that draw the moon from charmed skies!
  That bid the hearth in magic orgies blaze!

Come! turn a haughty mistress' marble heart,
　And change her cheek, still paler than my own:
Then will I trust, that stars obey your art,
　And rivers rush, by mutter'd verse alone.

Friends! that too late my sliding feet recall,
　Some antidote to this my frenzy bear:
Bring steel; bring flames and racks: I brave them all:
　But let me freely vent my fierce despair.

Oh snatch me to the world's remotest shore!
　Oh waft me o'er th' immeasurable main!
Where never woman may behold me more,
　Nor trace my way, to sting with her disdain!

Stay ye, to whom the listening god consents;
　Safe in an equal yoke of fondness move;
But Venus all my bitter nights torments:
　No—not a single hour is free from love.

Beware my sufferings: hold the mistress dear
　Whose faith is tried, nor shift th' accustom'd sway:
If to my voice ye bend a slothful ear,
　What pangs shall my remember'd words convey!

ELTON

THE SAME.

FIRST Cynthia's eyes this wretched heart subdued,
　Which ne'er before had sigh'd with am'rous pain;
When Love my unrelenting aspect bow'd,
　And trampled on my neck with proud disdain.

At length the tyrant taught me to detest
　Chaste nymphs, and banish'd reason from my mind:
Nor one whole year has the dire frenzy ceas'd;
　Still Fate forbids my mistress to be kind!

No toils, O Tullus! did Milanion dread,
　When Atalanta's pride he forc'd to yield;
Now to Parthenian caves he raging fled,
　Now bristly monsters daringly beheld.

Struck by the pond'rous club which Hylæus bore,
　Arcadia's rocks could witness each loud groan;

Then braving danger, and the Centaur's power,
  The nimble-footed maid he nobly won.

Thus pray'rs and gen'rous deeds will much avail
  In hopeless flames; yet Love, a tardy friend,
To me no arts, as usual, will reveal,
  No wily ways that to affection tend.

But you, whose spells can draw the toil'd Moon down,
  Whose magic pyres can wailing ghosts appease,
O, let my Cynthia's will your influence own!
  While her wan cheek a hue like mine displays:

Then will I credit that yon starry height,
  That floods, Cytæan incantations rule—
And you, my friends, who warn me when too late,
  O, bring relief, and heal my wounded soul!

Steel and fierce flames with patience I can bear,
  But what rage prompts with freedom let me say;
Waft me through farthest climes, through billows, where
  No prying nymph can track my distant way!

You, to whom Cupid with assenting nod
  Lends a kind ear, whom mutual love delights,
Be happy still! while me the cruel god
  Pursues, and Venus saddens all my nights.

Be warn'd, ye blissful lovers, by my fate;
  And from a nymph that's kind forbear to stray!
Those who reject my counsel, when too late
  Shall think with keen remorse on all I say.   NOTT.

ELEGY II. TO CYNTHIA.

ON HER INORDINATE LOVE OF FINERY.

WHY to walk forth, sweet life, thy tresses braid?
Why in the Coan garb's thin folds array'd?
Why with Orontes' myrrh thy locks imbue?
Thy beauty's price enhance by foreign show?
Why Nature's charms with purchas'd lustre hide,
Nor let thy limbs disclose their genuine pride?
Trust me thy face wants no cosmetic's aid;
Love's naked god abhors the dressing trade:

O, mark what blooms the painted earth displays,
How of themselves best climb the ivy-sprays,
How in lone caves arbutus lovelier grows,
Through untaught channels how the streamlet flows,
How native gems deckt shores spontaneous yield,
And sweeter notes by untamed birds are trill'd!
    Leucippus' daughter, beauteous Phœbe, fired
Young Castor's bosom, with no gauds attired;
And her fair sister Hilaïra too,
As unadorn'd, delighted Pollux' view.
No ostentatious ornaments could boast
Evenus' offspring, on her native coast;
When once the nymph the cause of discord proved
'Twixt Idas, and the god who fondly loved.
Nor Hippodamia, when the stranger's car
In triumph bore away the virgin fair,
By beauties borrow'd from the stores of art,
Subdued to love her Phrygian husband's heart;
No jewels heighten'd her bright face, that show'd
Such tints as in Apelles' pictures glow'd.
These heroines strove not various loves to win,
Enough for them by chastity to shine;
Yet sure in virtue thou canst vie with these;
She wants no charms, who can one lover please.

Since thine is all that Phœbus can inspire,
Thine fond Calliope's Aonian lyre,
Thine the choice gift of pleasing speech, my fair,
Thine all that's Beauty's, all that's Wisdom's care;
'Tis surely thine to gild my life with joy,
But ne'er let odious pomp thy thoughts employ! Nott

ELEGY III.

CYNTHIA FOUND SLEEPING.

As wrapt in slumbers lay the Cretan maid
On the bleak coast, while Theseus' vessel fled;
[As from rude rocks Andromeda unbound,
Slept her first sleep in freedom on the ground;][1]

---

[1] As too the fair Andromeda reposed,
    When first her limbs from the rude cliff were loosed. Nott.

And as the Mænas, with long rites opprest,
Sinks on Apidanus' green marge to rest :
So Cynthia slept, soft breathing, while her arms
Feebly sustain'd her head's reclining charms ;
When to the nymph my reeling steps I bore,
And the boy's midnight torch blazed on before.

Nor yet were all my wand'ring senses fled,
Eager I sought the nymph's soft-printed bed :
And, though my heart a twofold impulse sway'd,
Though Love, though Bacchus, gods by all obey'd,
Bade me attempt her with a soft embrace,
Kiss her ripe lips, and rifle every grace ;
Still I ne'er ventur'd to awake my love,
Lest with her wonted scorn she might reprove ;
But my fond eyes, that from her charms ne'er stray'd,
Those charms in silent ecstasy survey'd :
Not more intent could [Argus scan, I trow,] [1]
Io, unconscious of her budding brow.
Now from my head the chaplet I unbound,
And with the wreath my Cynthia's temples crown'd ;
Now I adjusted, with assiduous care,
The loosen'd plaits of her disorder'd hair ;
Or to her hollow palm, which passive lay,
With am'rous stealth an apple I'd convey.
Such fondness, lavish'd on thy thankless rest,
Seem'd as rejected by thy rising breast :
Oft when I saw thee heave the deep-fetch'd sigh,
Methought some danger it portended nigh ;
That fears unusual did thy dreams invade,
And that some fancied rival forced my maid.

Now through the fronting windows gleam'd the moon,
Whose ling'ring lustre too officious shone ;
The silver radiance oped her slumb'ring eyes,
Then with uplifted head she sweetly cries :

"And dost thou to my bed at length repair,
Debarr'd access to some more fav'rite fair ?
Enfeebled youth, to these fond arms untrue,
Where didst thou waste the night to Cynthia due ?

---

[1]   ——wakeful Argus view. NOTT.

Ah, long, long night! for lo! in yonder skies
Each star's faint beam before the morning flies:
Oh, would heaven grant, unfaithful wretch, 'twere thine
To wear away such tedious nights as mine!
By turns I tried the loom's impurpled toil,
The tuneful lyre, and fain would sleep beguile:
[Sometimes I thought—for prone art thou to stray—][1]
That some new love had caus'd thy long delay;
Till Morpheus waved his glad wings o'er my head;
Thus the fierce torrent of my tears was stay'd." NOTT.

ELEGY IV. TO BASSUS;

PROFESSING UNALTERABLE ATTACHMENT TO CYNTHIA.

TELL me, why thus extol each various maid?
To quit my love would Bassus then persuade?
Why not allow, while this poor life remains,
To hug with transport my accustom'd chains?
Now sweet Antiope of Nyctæan race,
Now bright Hermione the Spartan Grace,
All who adorn this beauty-boasting age,
Thy commendation in their turns engage:
But learn, that Cynthia from the list of fame
Can with her charms erase the fairest name;
[Much less, with meaner beauties matched, shall she,
Judge her who may, come off ingloriously.][1]

But think not, Bassus, 'twas her form alone,
Superior talents my affection won:
Her pure complexion, that no art had stain'd;
The various rare endowments she attain'd;
And the rich joys which well she could impart
Beneath the bed's mute covering, gain'd my heart.
Strive all thou canst our loves to disunite,
And still more strong our mutual faith we'll plight;
Vengeful I'll tell thy arts, my nymph shall rage,
No silent war with thee shall Cynthia wage;

----

[1] Sometimes I wept; then thought, forsook by thee. NOTT.
[2] With meaner beauties then her beauties place,
    And vulgar judges must their worth confess. NOTT.

Urged by thy crimes, she'll treat thee with neglect;
Warn me henceforth thy converse to reject;
[With all our girls she'll bring thee in disgrace;
They'll slam their doors in thy unlucky face;][2]
Her wrathful tears shall on each altar run,
On all that's sacred, on each hallow'd stone:
No loss can Cynthia with less patience bear
Than when Love robs her of what most is dear,
Robs her of me——Thus long may she remain,
Nor ever let her am'rous bard complain! Nott.

ELEGY V. TO GALLUS.

Rival! at length thy odious speech restrain,
And let us each an equal path maintain:
Wouldst thou, rash mortal, tempt the pangs I bear?
Ah, wretch! th' extremes of misery to dare,
Flames yet untried thus madly to explore,
And swallow all Thessalia's pois'nous store.

Cynthia, unlike the varying harlot crew,
With fixt revenge will each offence pursue;
And should she haply grant our bold request,
Oh, with what cares thy peace she would molest!
She'd break thy sleep, thine eyes with tears she'd drown,
To bind the proudest soul is hers alone:
Oft as despis'd thou'lt to my friendship fly,
And thy vain boasts shall vanish with a sigh;
A thrilling horror shall succeed thy tears,
Thy livid cheek betray thy am'rous fears,
Thy falt'ring tongue in vain would speak thy woe,
And where, or what thou art, thou scarce shalt know:
Then learn how hard a bondage is thy doom,
How hard to live an exile from her home;
Then at the love-sick paleness of my face,
At my lank frame, shall all thy wonder cease;
Thy noble lineage thou shalt boast in vain,
Love will thy statued ancestors disdain;
And if in part thou but reveal'st thy flame,
Thy birth with scoffers shall increase thy shame.

---

[1] In female circles she'll thy name traduce,
Till every nymph will banish thee her house. Nott.

To thee shall I deny the ask'd relief,
As yet no med'cine has allay'd my grief;
One fate involves us both; alike distrest,
Our tears we'll mingle on each other's breast.

   To tempt her rigour, Gallus, then forbear;
Cynthia will punish each presumptuous prayer.   NOTT

ELEGY VI. TO TULLUS;

REFUSING AN INVITATION TO TRAVEL.

THINK not I fear to tempt the Adrian sea,
Or plough, my friend, Ægæan waves with thee:
With thee Riphæan heights I'd traverse o'er,
And Æthiopia's farthest lands explore:
But me detains the fond encircling fair,
Her words, her changeful bloom, her ardent prayer;
Now through whole nights my passion she'll upbraid,
Vows there's no gods in heaven, since thus betray'd:
Now she refuses to be mine; and then
Threats all that weeping maids can threat false men.

   And shall I bear one hour that she should mourn?
Perish the wretch, whose flame thus faint could burn!
Can learned Athens yield so much delight,
Can Asia's boasted wealth so charm the sight;
That, when my vessel's launch'd into the main,
Cynthia with keen invectives should complain;
With desperate hands her beauteous face assail,
And piteous tell, how the unfavouring gale
Wafts far away those kisses that are due;
How nought's so hard to bear as love untrue?
Go then, surpass thy uncle's honour'd reign,
Thy lost compatriots' ancient rights regain.

   No am'rous indolence thy temper charm'd,
Thou in thy country's cause wert ever arm'd;
Cupid ne'er taught thee to endure my cares,
Or wish for death to stay thy ceaseless tears:
Th' extremes of fortune since I'm doom'd to prove,
O, let me give my soul a loose to love!
To lasting flames some willing martyrs die,
And midst that number let my relics lie;

Not born for martial toil, or aught that's great,
Beneath Love's banners I enlist my fate.

Shouldst thou Ionia's wanton soil explore,
Or where Pactolus bathes rich Lydia's shore;
Shouldst thou earth's regions tread, or ocean dare,
Or watch that empire trusted to thy care;
Still think, if chance remind thee of thy friend,
That baleful planets on his life attend.   NOTT.

ELEGY VII. TO PONTICUS.

IN VINDICATION OF THE MERITS OF EROTIC POETRY.

WHILE, Ponticus, Cadmean Thebes you sing,
And the dire wars which feuds fraternal bring;
While you, I vow, must share great Homer's praise,
Should the Fates smile propitious on your lays;
My muse with wonted voice of love complains,
And strives to soothe fierce beauty with its strains:
'Tis grief, not genius, bids my numbers flow,
Bids me bewail life's unabating woe:
Such is the race I run; be this my fame,
Hence let my song acquire a deathless name!
Mine is renown, because th' accomplish'd fair
None else could charm, or her proud menace dare:
Neglected lovers, study then my lore,
And gather wisdom from the wrongs I bore!

But if the wanton god should once [lay low
Thy stubborn pride,]¹ with his unerring bow;
(Yet may the am'rous powers, that rule my mind,
Not yet for thee the thread of love unwind!)
Then shall thy camps, then thy seven legions die,
And in the dust for ever silent lie;
Then shalt thou strive to write soft verse in vain,
For Love so late invok'd will thee disdain;
Then, no mean bard, me shalt thou oft admire,
As I to Roman wit's first seat aspire;

¹
                              ——subdue
    Thy untaught heart.   NOTT.

And youths shall say, while o'er my tomb they dwell,
Here sleeps the bard who sang our loves so well.

But let not epic pride disdain my lay,
Such scorn at last Love amply will repay.   NOTT.

ELEGY VIII. TO CYNTHIA.

ON HER PROPOSED DEPARTURE TO ILLYRIA.

ART mad? nor can my cares thy flight beguile?
Am I than cold Illyria's coast more vile?
[Thou lik'st this fellow then so much, thou'lt go
Without me, whatsoever wind may blow.]¹
Canst thou, my Cynthia, hear the roaring deep
Unmoved; and in the hard rough vessel sleep?
Can thy soft feet divide the frosts below?
And canst thou bear unusual drifts of snow?

Oh, double be the winter's rude domain!
Let ling'ring seamen ling'ring stars detain!
On Tyrrhene shores still let thy cable stay,
Nor snatch th' unfriendly blast my prayers away!
Ne'er let my eyes behold these winds subside,
When thy launch'd ship shall cleave the boist'rous tide,
And force me on the desert shore forlorn
With wretched hands to blame thy cruel scorn!
Yet treat me as thou wilt, thou perjur'd maid,
May Galatea still thy passage aid!
And Oricum's calm coast, Ceraunia past
With prosp'rous oars, receive thee safe at last!

No second passion shall my bosom stain;
Still will I haunt thy door, and still complain;
And to each sailor, as he hastens by,
What port now shelters Cynthia? will I cry:
Whether on Atrax', or on Elis' plain,
The nymph abide, she shall be mine again—
Here shall she come!—here, having sworn, she'll stay!
Conquest is mine!—my foes now pine away!

----

¹ Is then this upstart wretch indeed so dear,
   That without me thou any wind wouldst share?   NOTT.

For well I knew, such faithful constant prayer
My mistress' gentle bosom could not bear :
Let carping malice her false joys lay by,
My Cynthia hence desists new paths to try :
She loves me, loves e'en Rome too for my sake ;
And crowns she'd scorn, unless I crowns partake ;
Had rather on some little bed recline,
Content in any manner to be mine,
Than Hippodamia's regal dower obtain,
Or the vast treasures Elis' horses gain :
Though large his gifts, his promises though great,
Her heart, not selfish, courts my humble state :
'Tis not with Eastern shells, or gold, I move ;
'Tis with the soothings of the muse I love.

Nor Phœbus, nor the Nine, a lover shun ;
On these I rest, and Cynthia is my own :
Now sure I tread where highest planets shine,
By night, by day, is peerless Cynthia mine !
No more a rival can supplant my flame,
Hence my white hairs shall lasting glory claim.   NOTT.

ELEGY IX. TO PONTICUS.

ON HIS AMOUR WITH HIS SLAVE GIRL.

I TOLD thee, scoffer, thou shouldst wear Love's chain,
Thy vaunting speech ere long thou shouldst restrain :
Lo ! to the nymph a suppliant wretch art thou ;
And she, so late thy slave, is mistress now :
[I, like Chaonian doves, can augur shrewd
What youths shall languish, by what nymphs subdued.][1]
With grief and tears this skill I've dearly bought ;
Oh, were I free from love, and still untaught !

Say, wretch, what now avails thy epic swell ;
Or of Amphion's lyre-built walls to tell ?
In love, Mimnermus above Homer rose ;
Bland Cupid seeks the strain that sweetly flows :
Go then, aside thy lays disast'rous throw,
And sing what every maid would wish to know !

[1] Sure as Chaonian doves, I can foretell
   What youths shall beauty's powerful influence feel.   NOTT.

[What if no theme were ready to thy hand?
Lack water, blockhead! and in mid-stream stand!]¹
Nor yet thou'rt pale, no real flames you prove;
This the first kindling spark of future love:
Armenian tigers soon thou'lt rather dare,
Or on the wheel Ixion's torture bear,
Than feel the pangs Love's powerful shafts convey,
And a tyrannic nymph's command obey;
For Cupid never lends such flatt'ring wings,
But joy and grief alternately he brings.

By her obedience be not thou misled;
The more she's thine, the more her influence dread:
Think not, when none but her thou joy'st to view,
Liv'st for none else, thou canst thy flame subdue;
Not till the wasted frame our ill declares,
The dire effect of pois'nous love appears:
O shun, whoe'er thou art that read'st my lays,
Shun those officious blandishments that please!
O'er rocks and oaks such blandishments prevail;
Suits then resistance with a wretch so frail?

If shame forbids not, thy fond errors tell;
Oft it relieves, our passion to reveal.   Nott.

ELEGY X. TO GALLUS.

CONGRATULATIONS AND ADVICE.

O blissful night, when [I, who'd seen thy weeping,
Saw thy crown'd love its first glad vigil keeping!
Oh the delicious memory of that night!
Oh source to me of oft-renew'd delight!]¹
'Twas then I saw thee, breathless, speechless, laid;
Entwined, O Gallus! by thy circling maid:
Though scarce my drowsy eyes from sleep refrain'd,
Though their mid sky the red Moon's steeds had gain'd;

¹ What, were thy nymph of hard access? since now
   Thy thirst's unquench'd 'mid waves that freely flow. Nott
²   thy first loves I view'd!
   I, who erst saw each am'rous tear that flow'd:
   O blissful rapture, which that night endears!
   Oft I'll invoke it in my tender prayers.   Nott.

Still from those raptures I could not depart,
Your mutual murmurs breathed such warmth of heart.

But since to me thou hast thy joys declar'd,
Let this thy am'rous confidence reward:
I've learnt not only to conceal thy grief;
My faith, dear friend, can yield still more relief:
'Tis mine the parted pair to reunite,
And ope the door that's shut by beauty's spite;
'Tis mine to heal the lover's recent wound,
And in my counsel no small virtue's found:
'Twas Love, 'twas Cynthia, did my judgment guide;
They taught me what to seek, and what avoid.

Ne'er thwart the nymph, if anger she puts on;
Fastidious speech and tedious silence shun;
Never unkindly what she asks deny,
Nor from thy mind let one fond promise fly:
Wrathful she'll prove, if thou shouldst once disdain;
And if offended, her just wrath maintain:
The more thou'rt humble, and subdued to Love,
The more delicious sweets thou'rt sure to prove.

He with one nymph will live contented most,
Whose captive heart of no free choice can boast. NOTT.

ELEGY XI. TO CYNTHIA.

IN ABSENCE.

IMMERS'D in joys midst Baiæ's gay abode,
Near which extends the Herculean road;
Delighting now Thesprotia to [behold,
And now the waves near great Misenum roll'd;][1]
Say, does the mem'ry of past nights remain?
And dost thou, far removed, thy love maintain?
Does some strange rival, with dissembled flame,
From my fond page blot out my Cynthia's name?
O, wouldst thou rather on the Lucrine tide
Some little skiff with slender paddles guide!

[1] ——survey,
Now great Misenum, wash'd by subject sea. NOTT.

Or shelter'd secret on clear Teuthras' wave,
With pliant arms the yielding waters cleave;
Than, soft reclined upon the tranquil beach,
List to some lover's bland insidious speech:
So the frail beauty, who escapes her spies,
Sins, and forgets love's common deities.

Not but that fame bespeaks thy conduct just;
Yet, such thy state, the lover will mistrust:
O, pardon then, if e'er my erring song
Suspicion breathed !—from fear my guilt has sprung
Dear is thy safety, as a mother's dear!
For life without thee were not worth my care!
Thou, Cynthia! parent, kindred, art to me;
All, all my pleasures are comprised in thee!
If sad, if mirthful, to my friends I seem,
I'll say 'tis Cynthia does my temper frame.

Haste then from Baiæ's dissolute retreat;
With am'rous discord are those shores replete,
Shores that to virtuous nymphs most hostile prove:
Ah, perish Baiæ's stream, that bane of love !   NOTT

ELEGY XII. TO A FRIEND.

ON CYNTHIA'S ABSENCE.

WHY ceaselessly my fancied sloth upbraid,
As still at conscious Rome by love delay'd?
Wide as the Po from Hypanis is spread
The distance that divides her from my bed.
No more with fondling arms she folds me round,
Nor in my ear her dulcet whispers sound.
Once I was dear; nor e'er could lover burn
With such a tender and a true return.
Yes—I was envied—hath some god above
Crush'd me ? or magic herb, that severs love,
Gather'd on Caucasus, bewitch'd my flame?
Nymphs change by distance: I'm no more the same
Oh what a love has fleeted like the wind,
And left no vestige of its trace behind !
Now sad I count the ling'ring nights alone;
And my own ears are startled by my groan.

Happy! the youth who weeps, his mistress nigh;
Love with such tears has mingled ecstasy:
Blest, who, when scorn'd, can change his passing heat;
The pleasures of translated bonds are sweet.
I can no other love; nor hence depart;
For Cynthia, first and last, is mistress of my heart.

                                                      ELTON.

THE SAME.

WHY tax me still with criminal delay,
Because at Rome, at conscious Rome, I stay?
Far distant from these arms is Cynthia now;
Far as from Hypanis, Venetian Po:
To nurse my wonted flame, no more the fair
Folds me, or whispers rapture in mine ear.

There was a time when the dear nymph I charm'd,
No bosoms then such faithful passion warm'd;
But soon to envy were we doom'd a prey,
Some jealous god sure snatch'd our bliss away:
Or the curs'd power of noxious herbs, that grew
On steeps Promethean, broke a love so true:
Changed is my fate, by distance changed the maid!
And, ah, how sudden is affection fled!
Now tedious nights I'm forced to waste alone,
And my own ears I vex with ceaseless moan:
Thrice happy he, who to some present fair
Can weep; for Love enjoys the falling tear!
Or, if neglected, can his flame remove;
For change of bondage gives a gust to love—
Pleas'd with one nymph, from her I'll not depart;
Cynthia first charm'd, and last shall charm my heart!

                                                      NOTT.

ELEGY XIII. TO GALLUS.

IN PRAISE OF HIS MISTRESS.

[LAUGH, as thou'rt wont, to see me sit forlorn,
Left, Gallus, by my truant nymph to mourn;][1]

---

[1] Still, as thou'rt wont, with mirth my woes deride;
    While I forlorn lament a mistress fled.   NOTT.

Yet, faithless youth, I'll not thy taunts return;
No female falsehood may my Gallus mourn!
While nymphs betray'd increase thy am'rous fame,
While fickle still thou rov'st from flame to flame;
Yet for one fair at length thy cheeks grow pale,
And in the first attack thy efforts fail!
One shall avenge full many a slighted maid,
By one the wrongs of thousands be repaid!
One shall each vagrant looser love constrain,
And no new conquest shalt thou strive to gain!
Untaught by fame, unskill'd in prophecy,
I've seen—and canst thou what I saw deny?
Lock'd to her neck, I've seen thee panting laid;
I've seen thy tears; thine arms thrown round the maid;
On her dear lips I've seen thee wish to die;
Nay wish those things, which shame must needs pass by.

Not e'en my presence could your raptures stay,
Such raging passions bore your souls away;
Less fond the god whom Tænarus adores,
When with Enipeus, through Hæmonian shores,
He mixt his waves; and to his fraudful breast
The beauteous daughter of Salmoneus prest:
Less fond Alcides, when from Œta's height
He rose to regions of eternal light,
And first enfolded in his longing arms
Celestial Hebe's ever-blooming charms.
One day!—and thine exceeds all former fires;
No lukewarm flame thy beauteous maid inspires;
[Thy old disdain she lets thee not renew;
No more thou'lt swerve; passion shall keep thee true.]
Nor is it strange that such should be thy love,
When thy bright fair might grace the arms of Jove:
As Leda's self, or Leda's daughter fair,
She with the beauteous three might well compare;
Not Argive heroines with her charms can vie,
Her speech might win the ruler of the sky.

Since doom'd to passion, let thy flame burn on;
Of her thou'rt worthy, and of her alone:

---

[1] She wills; past pride no longer can avail,
No wand'rer thou; her power thy breast shall feel! NOTT.

New is thy love, so prosp'rous may it be!
And let this nymph be every nymph to thee. NOTT.

ELEGY XIV. TO TULLUS.

LOVE PREFERRED TO WEALTH.

Go then, on Tiber's velvet banks recline;
And in Mentorean cups quaff Lesbian wine:
Go view thy rapid wherries cleave the tide,
Or drawn by cords thy barges slowly glide;
View thy tall trees their cultur'd ranges spread,
Like woods that burden'd Caucasus o'ershade:
Yet what are these compar'd with my fond joys?
Love will not yield to all that wealth supplies!
Methinks if e'er with me she spends the night,
Or kindly wastes the day in dear delight;
Beneath my roof Pactolus rolls its stores,
And gems I cull on Erythræan shores:
Then beyond kings my joys proclaim me blest;
May these remain, while life shall warm this breast!
If cross'd in passion, who will riches heed?
When Venus smiles not, then we're poor indeed!
She lays the hero's boasted vigour low,
'Tis Venus melts the hardest heart to woe;
She on Arabian thresholds dares to tread,
Th' empurpled couch, O Tullus! dares invade;
She on his bed can stretch the sighing swain,
Then o'er it spreads the pictur'd silk in vain.—

Propitious prove, thou charmer of the skies!
And thrones I'll scorn, Alcinous' wealth despise! NOTT.

ELEGY XV. TO CYNTHIA.

REPROACHING HER INDIFFERENCE.

OFT has thy frailty, Cynthia, moved my fear:
But this deceit I little thought to bear:
Ah, see what dangers Fortune round me throws!
Yet art thou slow to heed my dreaded woes:
Thy wanton fingers still new-braid thy hair,
Adjust thy person with protracted care;

Still Eastern gems irradiate all thy breast;
So shines some nymph for her new bridegroom drest.

Not thus Calypso, on the desert shore,
Did once her flying Ithacus deplore;
With scatter'd locks for many a day sat she
All mournful, and reproach'd the faithless sea;
Though he was doom'd no more to charm her sight,
She sooth'd her grief with thoughts of past delight.
Alphesibœa, with her brothers' breath,
Fondly avenged her much-loved husband's death;
And love, uxorious love! in her withstood
Those ties by most held dear, the ties of blood!
Not thus when Jason far, far distant sail'd,
Her widow'd bed Hypsipyle bewail'd;
She let no second fires inflame her breast,
But languish'd still for her Hæmonian guest.
Evadne, first mid virtuous Argives placed,
Breathed on her husband's parting pyre her last:
Yet such examples can't thy mind engage,
Like these, to grace the bright historic page!
Cynthia, no more repeat thy perjuries,
Nor rouse the slumb'ring vengeance of the skies!
Too daring wretch! some sad reverse of fate
Shall haply teach thee to lament my state.

Rather may floods glide noiseless to the main,
Or through the year inverted seasons reign;
Than in my breast this passion should decline,
Or thou, whate'er thou art, shouldst not be mine;
Than I should gaze with hatred on those eyes,
Which oft have smiled such pleasing perfidies!
By these thou'st sworn, that if thy faith betray'd
One vow, those hands should tear them from thy head!
And canst thou lift them to yon glorious Sun,
Nor conscious dread those wrongs which thou hast done?
Who forced thy cheeks to wear this varying hue,
Or bade unwilling tears thine eyes bedew?

O witless youths! like me who sadly sigh,
Trust not those blandishments by which I die.　　NOTT.

ELEGY XVI.

THE COMPLAINT OF THE WANTON'S DOOR.

OPEN to splendid triumphs once was I,
No stranger to Tarpeian Chastity;
My threshold, bathed with captives' suppliant tears,
Has gain'd renown from gold-emblazon'd cars;
But vext with drunkards' midnight broils, and beat
By impious hands, I now lament my fate;
With unchaste wreaths I'm hung; and oft is seen
Some torch extinct that speaks th' excluded swain:
My mistress's lewd nights I can't deny;
So known, so drest with bawdy rhymes am I!
Nor will she learn a virtuous name to prize,
Or shun, less vile, this age of luxuries:
While, from a suppliant's plaint more piteous grown,
His long, long vigils I with tears bemoan;
My wakeful frame is ever doom'd to hear
The silver flatt'ry of his tuneful prayer.

"O door, more cruel than thy mistress, why
Do thy mute valves, unkind, access deny?
Wilt thou ne'er open to my am'rous woe;
Or, kindly moved, report each secret vow?
Shall nought at length my ceaseless sorrows charm?
Shall my rude slumbers still thy threshold warm?
E'en waning stars, e'en midnight's hallow'd reign,
And the chill breath of morn regard my pain;
Thou, only thou! untouch'd by human grief,
On silent hinges hung, deniest relief:
O, much I wish, some pervious cleft could bear
My murmur'd accents to her wond'ring ear!
As Ætna's rocks unfeeling were the fair,
Let her with iron or with steel compare;
Yet sure soft pity would bedew her eyes,
And midst her tears she'd heave unbidden sighs.
While some loved youth now folds her with delight,
Pour'd is my moan on the vain blast of night.
O door! thou sole chief cause of all my woe,
Not bribed by all the off'rings I bestow,

Thee with rude phrase my tongue did ne'er ill-treat,
Such phrase as youths, when vext, to doors repeat ;
That I, grown hoarse with frequent wail, should meet
Such long neglect, and nightly range the street !
Oft in choice verse for thee I framed the song,
And to thy steps my warmest kisses clung ;
Turn'd to thy frame, vile thing ! how oft I've stood,
And paid with secret hand each vow I owed."

    These, and such plaints as suit a swain forlorn,
He'll urge, and stun the clam'rous birds of morn :
Thus the still-weeping youth, and lustful dame,
Brand with eternal infamy my frame.   NOTT.

ELEGY XVII. REPININGS AT SEA.

AND justly sure, since from the nymph I fled,
To the lorn halcyons am I doom'd to plead ;
My bark Cassiope regards no more,
Lost are my vows upon the faithless shore !
For absent Cynthia are the blasts combined ;
Hark, how hoarse vengeance murmurs in each wind !
Shall no kind fortune smooth the billowy waste ?
On these mean sands shall my wreckt bones be cast ?
Thy imprecations spare ! for yon black skies,
Yon dangerous shoals, thy vengeance should suffice :
Tearless couldst thou compose my corse, and strain
To thy fond breast the ashes that remain ?
Perish the wretch ! who first upon the sea
Placed barks and sails, and plough'd th' unbidden way !
Ah, sweeter far a mistress to persuade !
(For though hard-hearted, matchless is my maid !)
Than thus to view strange woods surround the shore,
And the Twin-brothers ardently implore ;
Should fate, where dwells the nymph, inter my woes,
And the sad stone mark where her loves repose ;
With her dear tresses sure she'll dress my tomb,
And in my urn bid short-lived roses bloom !
Oft to my latest dust my name address ;
So might the turf my relics lightly press !

And you, ye Nereids, from fair Doris sprung,
Loose the white sails, and come a prosp'rous throng!
If Love from heaven e'er sought your moist abode,
Give stormless shores to one who serves that god!

NOTT.

ELEGY XVIII.

THE LOVER'S SOLILOQUY ON CYNTHIA'S CRUELTY.

LONESOME these glooms, and peaceful to lorn swains;
Along th' unpeopled grove bland Zephyr reigns:
Here may we dare our secret griefs to tell,
For desert rocks those griefs will ne'er reveal.

Whence, O my Cynthia! shall I date thy scorn?
When was it first that Cynthia bade me mourn?
I, who late bore a happy lover's name,
Now see my passion doom'd to fatal shame!
Why treat me thus? what spell subverts thy love?
Say, does some rival nymph thy hatred move?
As to my home no stranger fair has borne
Her steps; so may'st thou, credulous! return:
And though to thee their sting my sorrows owe,
Not so resentful shall my anger flow,
That thou shouldst e'er grow frantic with despair,
And thy swoll'n eyes the recent tear declare.
Say, does neglect my change of love proclaim?
And do no vows breathe forth my am'rous flame?
Witness, thou beech! (if trees make love their care,)
And by Arcadia's god, thou pine! held dear;
How your green shades my song has vocal made,
And CYNTHIA's name your letter'd rinds display'd:
Say, do my cares spring from thy wrongs alone?
Those cares, which only to mute doors are known!
Fearful I wont thy dictates to obey,
Nor loudly murmur'd at thy haughty sway:
For this, ye gelid rocks! ye founts divine!
In these wild haunts is sleepless torment mine;
For this! I'm doom'd, alone to tuneful choirs
To sing whate'er my tender woe inspires.

M

But true, or faithless, be my Cynthia found ;
CYNTHIA's sweet name let woods and hills resound !
NOTT

ELEGY XIX. TO CYNTHIA.

PROFESSIONS OF UNALTERABLE ATTACHMENT.

I FEAR not, Cynthia, through death's gloom to stray,
Nor would the funeral pile's last debt delay ;
But lest thy fondness with my life expire,
Brings dread far greater than the fatal pyre.

Caught were these eyes by no faint spark of love,
For e'en my dust shall ne'er oblivious prove :
The brave Protesilaus, in realms of night,
Could not forget his bosom's sole delight ;
But the Thessalian ghost, to press the dame
With airy grasp, to his loved mansion came.
Yet, in those realms whate'er the change I prove,
Thy faithful shade shall never change in love !
Passions so vast as mine are wafted o'er
The lurid wave, and reach the Stygian shore :
Yes ! to those realms let all the Dardan fair,
Heroines a prize to Argive chiefs, repair ;
Still none to me will look like Cynthia bright ;
And sacred Earth shall deem my judgment right !
To wan old age should fate prolong thy years,
E'en in the shades thy death I'll mourn with tears :
O feel ! while living, all I feel for thee ;
And then content I'll die, whate'er it be.
Ah, Cynthia ! much I fear, lest Love unjust
Teach thee to shun my grave, and spurn my dust ;
Force thee to stay the torrent of thy tears ;
For firmest hearts will yield to ceaseless prayers.

Then let's improve short pleasures while we may,
An age of passion seems but as a day.　　　NOTT.

ELEGY XX. TO GALLUS.

THE DEATH OF HYLAS.

BE warn'd by friendship, which thou long hast tried ;
Nor let my precepts from thy mem'ry slide :

Dire fate attends whoe'er has rashly loved;
Ascanius baleful to the Minyæ proved.

Alike thy Hylas, both in name and face,
To him who boasts Thiodamantean race:
Then, whether coasting on the wood-hung wave,
Whether thy footsteps Anio's waters lave,
Whether thou roam'st the Giant-peopled shore,
Or fliest, a vagrant guest, where torrents pour;
Still of the am'rous Nymphs, fond thefts beware,
Ausonian Dryads too make love their care:
Not to cool rocks or rugged mountains stray;
Nor to enamour'd lakes e'er bend thy way;
Wand'ring to foreign climes, Alcides tried
All these, and wept by cold Ascanius' side.

Once from the Pagasean port, 'tis said,
The Argo sail'd, and far as Phasis fled;
Then o'er the Hellespont the vessel pass'd,
And Mysia's rocky haven reach'd at last:
Here the brave throng the grateful shore o'erspread,
And on the turf with leaves they form'd their bed:
Meanwhile th' unconquer'd hero's boy went on,
To find the scarce stream's secret fount alone;
Zethes and Calais, twins from Boreas sprung,
Pursued him close, and pressing round him hung;
Pois'd by their hands, they bear each kiss supine
Aloft, and snatch by turns the theft divine;
Uprais'd in air, the youth avoids th' embrace,
And in their wings' last shelter hides his face;
Then with a little bough he soon removes
The swift attacks of their insidious loves.
And now Orithyia's sons, of Pandion race,
Foil'd in th' attempt, gave o'er their am'rous chase;
When Hylas onward hasten'd to his doom,
And sought, ah grief! the Hamadryads' home.

Beneath Arganthus' lofty height there stood
A fount, the Thynian Naiads' moist abode;
On the wild trees, that deckt its margin, grew,
Estrang'd to culture, apples fed with dew;

M 2

And lilies in the dank surrounding meads,
'Mid crimson poppies rear'd their silver heads:
To cull these flow'rs with artless fingers went
The boy, unmindful of his first intent;
Then near the painted wave unconscious lay,
And his reflected charms prolong'd his stay;
At length, with hands plung'd in, the wave he sought;
His right arm lab'ring with the vase full fraught:
The Dryad-maids, whom his fair beauties fir'd,
Forsook their choral frolics, and admir'd;
As Hylas fell, beneath the yielding flood
They drew the boy, who wept his rape aloud;
Far off Alcides answer'd as he mourn'd,
And echo from deep founts his name return'd.

Thus warn'd, O Gallus! watch thy love with care;
Nor trust with nymphs a youth like Hylas fair.   NOTT

ELEGY XXI.   THE MURDERED SOLDIER.

THOU! who the battle's common fate hast fled,
Hast by a wound from Tuscan ramparts bled,
Why for my loss roll thy swoll'n eyes in tears?
Because I late partook thy martial cares:
O warrior! let thy pearly sorrows tell
To my lov'd Acca, how her brother fell;
So may thy parents greet thy safe return!
Tell her, how Gallus, who, through dangers borne
Mid Cæsar's armed legions, death defied,
At last by hands of unknown ruffians died:
And learn, O stranger! when loose bones you see
On Tyrrhene heights, those bones belong to me.   NOTT.

ELEGY XXII.   TO TULLUS.

ON THE AUTHOR'S BIRTH-PLACE.

MY race, my nation, fain would Tullus know;
Long friendship sure the question will allow:—
No stranger thou to fam'd Perusia's war,
In which my ruin'd country bore its share;

What time Italia labour'd with her doom,
And discord arm'd the citizens of Rome.
(Etruria! thou chief cause of all my woe;
Ah wretched soil! that basely couldst allow
My kinsman's corse unburied to remain,
Nor let some scanty sod his bones contain.)
Then, bord'ring on this spot of conquer'd earth,
Umbria's rich meadows lie, which gave me birth.   NOTT.

BOOK II.

ELEGY II. ON HIMSELF.

AH! thou, that vaunted'st nought could harm thy breast,
　Art caught: that haughty spirit crouches tame:
Scarce one short month art thou content to rest,
　And lo! another love-book speaks thy shame.

Late I was free; my sleep without a thorn;
　In widow'd bed, and single quiet laid;
I trusted to the peace which Love had sworn,
　But false and hollow was the truce he made.

I sought if fishes on the sands might live,
　Or the wild boar through seas accustom'd stray:
If wakeful studies might abstraction give:
　Love, though deferr'd, is never chased away.

As from his neck the bull shakes fierce the plough,
　But soon bends mildly to the wonted yoke:
Young lovers blustering chafe, but humbled bow,
　And tamely bear each light and heavy stroke.

Inglorious chains Melampus patient took,
　Who stole from Iphiclus his herds away;
Not gain compell'd, but Pero's lovely look:
　Thus in his brother's arms a bride she lay.

'Twas not her face, though fair, that caught my sight
　　Less fair the lily's bell: as Scythian snows
Should blend with Ebro's red their virgin white,
　　Or in pure cream as floats the scatter'd rose:

Not tresses, that enring'd in crisped twine,
　　Flow loose with their accustom'd careless art
Down her smooth marble neck; nor eyes that shine,
　　Torches of passion; load-stars of my heart:

Not that through silken folds of Araby
　　The nymph's fine limbs with lucid motion gleam;
(For no ideal beauties heaves my sigh;
　　Nor airy nothings prompt my amorous dream:)

Not all so charms, as when aside she lays
　　The mantling cup, and glides before my view;
Graceful as Ariadne through the maze
　　Of choral dance with Bacchic revellers flew:

Or when, inspired by Aganippe's stream,
　　O'er Sappho's lyre with sportive touch she strays;
And challenges Corinna's ancient theme,
　　And coldly listens to Erinne's lays.

When first, sweet soul! you saw the light of heaven
　　Did Love with clear, shrill-echoed omen sneeze?
The gods have all thy rare endowments given;
　　The gods have given, nor from thy mother these.

Not these the fruit of merely human birth,
　　Nor ten short moons matured thy every grace;
Thou art the glory of our Roman earth,
　　A bride for Jove, the first of Roman race:

Not always on my mortal couch to lie,
　　A second Helen treads this earthly ball;
What wonder, that our youth in ardour sigh?
　　For her, O Troy! more splendid were thy fall.

I once admired, that for a woman's eyes
　　Round Ilium's ramparts Europe, Asia, strove:
Wise Paris was, and Menelaus wise,
　　Who claim'd, and who refused, the cause of love!

But hers are charms that might Achilles bend,
  Might warm old Priam, and might sanction war;
Hers ancient paintings' breathing forms transcend,
  To all of pictured fame superior far.

To west and east her blooming portrait show,
  Both east and west she shall inflame with love:
Why tarries she in human form below?
  Thy ancient gallantries I pardon, Jove!

Yellow her hair; her shapely hands are long;
  Tall her fine form, and Juno-like she treads:
So Pallas walks Dulichian shrines among,
  While her broad breast the snaky mail o'erspreads.

Such as Ischomache, the heroine-bride,
  When rape of wine-flushed Centaurs dared her charms:
Such virgin Brimo, nothing loth, beside
  Bebœis' fountain sank in Hermes' arms.

Yield, goddesses! whom erst the shepherd saw
  Disrobe your limbs in Ida's mountain-glade:
May never age its lines transforming draw,
  Though hers the lustres of the Sibyl maid.   ELTON.

ELEGY V.   TO CYNTHIA.

THEN wide through Rome—and is it, Cynthia, true?
  Thy name is blown; thy wanton actions fly:
Look'd I for this!—this, traitress! thou shalt rue;
  The northern wind shall teach me constancy.

One, whom thy sex's treachery less inspires,
  I'll seek; who from my song will covet fame;
Whose shamelessness will not insult my fires;
  Whose nimble tongue shall scandalize thy name.

Oh long beloved! too late thy tears will flow!
  Now fresh my fury; let me now depart;
When anger cools, alas! too well I know,
  Love will resume its influence o'er my heart.

Not so the north-wind turns Carpathian tides,
  Nor blackening clouds the veering south obey ;
As, at a word, the lover soothed subsides ;
  Loose, then, th' unequal yoke, while yet we may.

And thou, not wholly from compunction free,
  Wilt somewhat grieve ; but only on the night
When thy late lover first is missed by thee ;
  All ills of love become by patience light.

But oh ! by Juno's dear, protecting name,
  Harm not thyself, nor give these passions rein ;
Not the horn'd bull, alone, will wrongs inflame ;
  E'en the mild sheep, if injured, turns again.

I will not from thy perjured bosom tear
  The vest away ; thy bolted chamber storm ;
Pluck with infuriate grasp thy braided hair,
  Nor with hard nails thy tender cheeks deform :

Thus let the rustic churl his anger show ;
  To such these base revenges I resign ;
For whom no garlands of the Muses grow,
  Round whose rude brow no ivy tendrils twine :

But I will write—what thou wouldst blot in vain ;
  Of Cynthia—Cynthia, beautiful and frail ;
Fame's busy murmurs thou may'st still disdain,
  Yet this my verse shall dye thy cheek with pale !
                                             ELTON

ELEGY VI.   TO CYNTHIA.

NOT such Corinthian Lais' sighing train,
Before whose gates all prostrate Greece had lain ;
Not such a crowd Menander's Thais drew,
Whose charms th' Athenian people joy'd to woo ;
Nor she, who could the Theban towers rebuild,
When hosts of suitors had their coffers fill'd.
Nay—by false kinsmen are thy lips carest ;
By sanction'd, simulated kisses prest.
The forms of youths and beauteous gods, that rise
Around thy pictured roof, offend mine eyes.

The tender lisping babe, by thee carest
Within its cradle, wounds my jealous breast.
I fear thy mother's kiss, thy sister dread;
Suspect the virgin partner of her bed:
All wakes my spleen, a very coward grown:
Forgive the fears that spring from thee alone.
Wretched in jealous terror, to my eyes
Beneath each female robe a lover lies.
Blest was Admetus' spouse, and blest the dame
Who shared Ulysses' couch in modest fame:
Oh! ever happy shall the fair-one prove,
Who by her husband's threshold bounds her love.
Ah! why should Modesty's pure fane ascend?
Why at her shrine the blushing maiden bend?
If, when she weds, her passions spurn control;
If the bold matron sates her wishful soul?
The hand, that first in naked colours traced
Groups of loose loves, on walls that once were chaste:
And full exposed, broad burning on the light,
The shapes and postures that abash the sight;
Made artless minds in crime's refinements wise,
And flash'd enlightening vice on virgin eyes.
Woe to the wretch! who thus insidious wove
Mute rapture's veil o'er wrath and tears of love!
Not thus the roofs were deck'd in olden time,
Nor the stain'd walls were painted with a crime:
Then, for some cause, the desert fanes of Rome
Wave with rank grass, while spiders veil the dome.
What guards, O Cynthia! shall thy path confine?
What threshold bound that wilful foot of thine?
Weak is constraint, if women loth obey,
And she is safe, who, blushing, fears to stray.   ELTON

ELEGY IX.   ON A RIVAL.

TWICE ten long years Penelope was woo'd,
Yet chaste remain'd, by countless lovers sued:
With fictious woof her wedlock could delay,
And rent by night the threads she wove by day:

Hopeless Ulysses to behold again,
Yet, tarrying, saw her youthful beauties wane.
Briseis' arms the dead Achilles press'd,
With frantic hand she smote her snowy breast,
Mourning her bleeding lord ; and, though a slave,
Wash'd his stain'd corse in Simois' shallower wave :
Soil'd her fair locks, and in her slender hold
Cull'd from the pile those bones of giant mould.
No sire, no blue-hair'd mother of the sea,
Nor widow'd Deidamia mourn'd for thee.
Then her true sons did Grecia's glory wield,
When modest love could bless the tented field.
Thou not a single night alone canst stay :
No—shameless woman ! not a single day.
Now thy gay laugh 'midst circling goblets flies ;
Myself, perchance, thy raillery's sacrifice.
E'en him thou seek'st, who late forsook thy charms :
Then, may the gods consign him to thy arms !
But, when in tears we stood around thy bed ;
When Styx had nigh o'erwhelm'd thy sinking head
When my fond vows were silent breathed for thee,
Where then, perfidious ! where and what was he ?
Wouldst thou for me thus fondly breathe the prayer
Did I to farthest Ind the standard bear ;
Or in mid-ocean were my galley placed,
A lonely speck amidst the watery waste ?
Yes—words and smooth deceits are thine at will :
This task is easy to a woman still.
Not Afric's sands so fluctuate to the blast,
Or quivering leaves on wintry gales are cast ;
As passion's gust bids woman's promise fly,
Be rage the cause, or be it levity.
Since 'tis thy pleasure, I no more contend :
Ye cruel loves ! yet keener arrows bend ;
Right-aiming at my heart, dissolve my life ;
My blood the palm of this your glorious strife.
And must thou thus, Propertius ! in the bloom
Of opening youth descend into the tomb ?
Must thou then die ? yes, die—that she may view
Thy corse with smiles ; thy fleeting ghost pursue

With her tormenting scorn; disturb thee dead;
Leap on thy pyre, and on thy ashes tread.
What? did not Hæmon on his bloody glaive
Fall, by Antigone's untimely grave;
And mix his ashes in the maiden's urn,
Nor would, without her, to his Thebes return?
Thou shalt not 'scape; yes, thou my death shalt feel:
Our mingled blood shall trickle from the steel.
Yes—though thy death to ages brand my name,
That death shall reach thee, and I brave the shame.
Witness the stars! the dews of morning's hour!
The stealthy door, which open'd to thy bower:
That nought in life more precious was to me,
And still I love thee: yes, in spite of thee!
No other nymph shall on my couch recline;
Alone and loveless, since no longer thine.
Ah! if my life some virtuous years have known,
May he thy arms enfold be turn'd to stone!
Not with more horrid zest and thirst of blood,
Thebes' princes fought, while near their mother stood,
Than I, if Cynthia's presence fired the strife,
Would yield my ówn to snatch my rival's life.   ELTON.

BOOK III.

ELEGY II.   TO CYNTHIA.

BE praised by others, or unknown remain:
Who sings thy praise will sow a barren plain.
The funeral couch, that last, that gloomy day,
Shall bear those offerings, with thyself, away.
The traveller o'er thy slighted bones shall tread,
With heedless foot, unconscious of the dead;
Nor, lingering at thy nameless grave, declare,
"This heap of dust was an accomplished fair."   ELTON.

ELEGY III.   EFFIGY OF LOVE.

HAD he not hands of rare device, whoe'er
    First painted Love in figure of a boy?
He saw what thoughtless beings lovers were,
    Who blessings lose, whilst lightest cares employ.

Nor added he those airy wings in vain,
    And bade through human hearts the godhead fly;
For we are tost upon a wavering main;
    Our gale, inconstant, veers around the sky.

Nor, without cause, he grasps those barbed darts,
    The Cretan quiver o'er his shoulder cast;
Ere we suspect a foe, he strikes our hearts;
    And those inflicted wounds for ever last.

In me are fix'd those arrows, in my breast;
    But sure his wings are shorn, the boy remains;
For never takes he flight, nor knows he rest;
    Still, still I feel him warring through my veins.

In these scorch'd vitals dost thou joy to dwell?
    Oh shame! to others let thy arrows flee;
Let veins untouch'd with all thy venom swell;
    Not me thou torturest, but the shade of me.

Destroy me—who shall then describe the fair?
    This my light Muse to thee high glory brings:
When the nymph's tapering fingers, flowing hair,
    And eyes of jet, and gliding feet she sings.   ELTON

PART OF ELEGY IV.   ON HIS POETRY.

FEWER the Persic darts in Susa's bands
    Than in my breast those arrows sheath'd by Love:
He not to scorn the tender Muse commands,
    And bids my dwelling be th' Ascræan grove.

Not that Pierian oaks may seek my lyre,
    Nor savage beasts from vales Ismarian throng;
But that my Cynthia may the strain admire,
    And I than Linus rise more famed in song.

Not an engaging form so charms mine eye ;
   Not so the fair one's noble lineage moves ;
As on th' accomplish'd nymph's soft breast to lie,
   And read what she with chasten'd ear approves.

Be this my lot, and henceforth I despise
   The mingled babblings of the vulgar throng :
What are to me e'en Jove's dread enmities,
   If she appeased relent, and love my song ?   Elton.

PART OF ELEGY IV. TO CYNTHIA.

Then, soon as night o'ershades my dying eyes,
   Hear my last charge : let no procession trail
Its lengthen'd pomp, to grace my obsequies,
   No trump with empty moan my fate bewail.

Let not the ivory stand my bier sustain,
   Nor on embroider'd vests my corse recline ;
Nor odour-breathing censers crowd the train :
   The poor man's mean solemnities be mine.

Enough of state—enough, if of my verse
   Three slender rolls be borne with pious care :
No greater gift, attendant on my hearse,
   Can soothe the breast of hell's imperial fair.

But thou, slow-following, beat thy naked breast,
   Nor weary faint with calling on the dead :
Be thy last kisses to my cold lips prest,
   While alabaster vases unguents shed.

When flames the pyre, and I am embers made,
   My relics to an earthen shell convey :
Then plant a laurel, which the tomb may shade,
   Where my quench'd ashes rest, and grave the lay :

" What here a heap of shapeless ashes lies,
   Was once the faithful slave of Love alone : "
Then shall my sepulchre renown'd arise
   As the betroth'd Achilles' blood-stain'd stone.

And thou, whene'er thou yieldest thus to fate,
   Oh dear one! seek the memorable way
Already trod; the mindful stones await
   Thy second coming, and for thee they stay.

Meantime, whilst life endures, oh, warn'd beware
   Lest thou the buried lover shouldst despise:
Some conscious spark e'en mould'ring ashes share:
   The senseless clay is touch'd by injuries.

Ah! would some kinder Fate, while yet I lay
   In cradled sleep, had bid me breathe my last!
What boots the breath of our precarious day!
   Nestor is dead, his three long ages past.

On Ilium's rampart had the Phrygian spear
   Abridged his age, and sent a swifter doom:
He ne'er had seen his son's untimely bier,
   Nor cried, "O death! why art thou slow to come?"

Thou thy lost friend shalt many a time deplore;
   And love may ever last for those who die:
Witness Adonis, when the ruthless boar
   Smote in th' Idalian brake his snowy thigh:

'Tis said, that Venus wept her lover lost,
   Trod the dank soil, and spread her streaming hair:
Thou too in vain wouldst call upon my ghost:
   These moulder'd bones are dumb to thy despair.

                                  ELTON

ELEGY VII. ON VENAL INFIDELITY.

THE Prætor from Illyria comes again;
Thy spoil and prey; my torment and my bane:
Could not Ceraunian rocks his bark have wreck'd?
What gifts, O Neptune! had thy altars deck'd!
Now is thy table fill'd; thy midnight door
Left soft ajar; but ah! for me no more.
Yes—now, if wise, the inviting harvest reap;
Fleece with no sparing hand the silly sheep:
Then, when his gifts run dry, command him sail
To new Illyrias with a prosperous gale.

No wreaths, no fasces draw my Cynthia's gaze;
But evermore her lover's purse she weighs.
Aid, Venus! aid my anguish! quick—dispense
Th' unnerving plagues of blasted impotence!
Then barter'd gifts can now a mistress move?
For gifts, O Jupiter! she pines in love.
For lucid gems she sends me o'er the main,
And bids me seek in Tyre the purple grain:
Oh that in Rome no lords of wealth we saw;
That e'en the palace-roof were thatch'd with straw!
No venal mistress then would melt to gold:
Beneath one roof the bride would then grow old.
Not that seven nights, while I apart recline,
Thy snowy arms round that vile reptile twine:
Not, bear me witness, am I wroth with thee:
I curse the fair's proverbial levity.
A stranger tracks the traces of my kiss,
And, sudden blest, usurps my throne of bliss.
Ah; Eriphyle's bitter gifts survey!
On Jason's bride see fiery torments prey!
Can then no wrongs forbid my tears to flow,
Nor I the vice forsake, that feel the woe?
Whole days have fled; nor longer Mars's field,
The theatre, the Muse, delight can yield:
Shame! where is now thy blush? but ah! I fear
That a disgraceful passion cannot hear.
Look on the chief, who late with treason's host
Raised empty uproar on the Actian coast:
Love ignominious turn'd his flying prores,
And drove him to the world's remotest shores:
Augustus' brow a double glory wreaths:
The hand that conquer'd now the falchion sheaths.
Oh! may those robes, those emeralds which he gave,
Be snatch'd by storms through air or o'er the wave:
Those chrysolites, that gleam with yellow light,
Be turn'd to earth and water in thy sight!
Not always Jove when perjur'd lovers swear
Complacent laughs, nor deaf rejects the prayer.
Heard'st thou yon roll of thunder, muttering deep?
Saw'st thou from ether's vault the lightnings leap?

No Pleiads—no Orion's clouds are here;
Nor casual falls the fiery atmosphere.
On nymphs forsworn wrath lightens from above,
For e'en the god has wept, betray'd in love.
Is Sidon's crimson garment still thy care?
But tremble, false one! at the darken'd air!   ELTON

ELEGY X. TO CYNTHIA,

WHEN IN THE COUNTRY.

THOUGH, with unwilling eyes, from Rome I see
    Thy mourn'd departure, my regretted love!
Yet I rejoice that, e'en remote from me,
    Thy feet the solitary woodlands rove.

In the chaste fields no soft seducer sighs
    With blandishments, that force thee to thy shame;
No wanton brawls before thy windows rise;
    Nor scared thy sleep with those that call thy name.

Thou art in solitude—and all around
    Lone hills, and herds, and humble cots appear;
No theatres can here thy virtue wound,
    No fanes, the cause of sin, corrupt thee here.

Thou shalt behold the steers the furrows turn;
    The curv'd knife, dexterous, prune the foliaged vine
Thy grains of incense in rude chapel burn,
    And see the goat fall at a rustic shrine;

Or, with bare leg, the rural dance essay,
    But safe from each strange lover's prying sight:
And I will seek the chase: alternate pay
    To Venus vows, and join Diana's rite.

Chide the bold hound; in woodland covert lie,
    And hang the antler'd spoil on pine-tree boughs;
But no huge lion in his lair defy,
    Nor savage boar, with nimble onset, rouse.

My prowess be to seize the timid hare,
  Or from my reedy quiver pierce the bird;
Nigh where Clitumnus winds his waters fair
  Through arching trees, and laves the snow-white herd.

Whate'er thy sports, remember, sweetest soul!
  A few short days will bring me to thy side;
For not the lonely woods, the rills that roll
  Down mossy crags in smooth, meandering tide,

Can so divert the jealousy of fear,
  But that I name thee by some fancied name,
While earnest in thy praise; lest they, that hear,
  Should seek thee absent, and seduce to shame. ELTON.

ELEGY XV. DEFENCE OF INCONSTANCY.

"FRAMEST thou excuse, who art a tale to all?
Whose Cynthia long is read at every stall?"
These words might damp a deaf man's brow, and move
A candid blush for mean and nameless love.
But did my Cynthia breathe a melting sigh,
I were not called the head of levity:
Nor broad town-scandal should traduce my fame:
Then would I speak, though branded thus by name.
Wonder not thou that meaner nymphs invite:
They less defame me: are the causes light?
She'll now a fan of peacock's plumes demand;
And now a crystal ball to cool her hand:
Tease me to death for ivory dice, and pray
For glittering baubles of the sacred way.
Ah! let me die if I regard the cost:
A jilting fair one's mockery stings me most.
Was this the favour to transport my heart?
Thou feel'st no blush, thus charming as thou art:
Scarce two short nights in tender joys are sped,
And I am call'd intruder on thy bed.
Yet wouldst thou praise my person; read my lay:
Has this thy love then flown so swift away?
The race of genius may my rival run:
But let him learn from me to love but one.
What! he forsooth will Lerna's snake enfold;
Snatch from th' Hesperian dragon fruits of gold;

N

Drain poisonous juice ; or shipwreck'd gulp the sea ;
And from no miseries shrink, for sake of thee ?
Ah ! would, my life ! these tasks were proved in me !
Then should we find this gallant, now so proud,
Skulk his mean head among the coward crowd.
Let the vain braggart vaunt his puff'd success ;
One short year shall divorce your tenderness.
No Sibyl's years, Herculean toils, avail,
Nor that last gloomy day to make my fondness fail.
Yes—thou shalt cull my bones, which tears bedew :
"Propertius ! these were thine: ah tried and true !
Ah me ! most true ! though not through noble veins
Flow'd thy rich blood, nor ample thy domains."
Yes—I will all endure : all wrongs are slight :
A beauteous woman makes the burden light.
Many for thee, I well believe, have sigh'd ;
But few of men in constancy are tried.
Brief time for Ariadne Theseus burn'd :
Demophoön from his Phillis ingrate turn'd :
In Jason's bark the sea Medea braved,
Yet, lone abandon'd, cursed the man she saved :
Hard too the woman's heart, whose feign'd desire
For many lovers fans the ready fire.
Not to the suitors, vain of noble race,
Not to the wealthy, yield thy bribed embrace :
Of these scarce one would shed a tear for thee,
Or near thy urn be found, as I shall be.
Yet rather thou for me, grant, heaven ! the prayer,
Smite on thy naked breast, and strew thy streaming hair.
                                                        ELTON

ELEGY XVII.   ON HIS JEALOUSY OF A RIVAL.

OH lovely torment ! for my anguish born,
Since oft excluded from thy door in scorn :
Come to these arms ; my verse renown can give ;
Here thou the fairest of thy sex shalt live :
Let not my boast Catullus' ear offend ;
Let gentle Calvus too his pardon lend.
The veteran, gray with service, quits the field ;
Their necks no more the age-worn oxen yield ;

On the waste sands their mouldering barks remain,
And the cleft shield hangs idle in the fane.
Were it not better crouch, a tyrant's slave,
And in thy brazen bulls, Perillus! rave:
At Gorgon's visage stiffen into stone,
Or under Caucasus' keen vultures groan.
Still I persist: lo! rust can steel decay,
And gentle droppings wear the flint away.
Love to the marble threshold clings, nor feels
The wearing stone; though threaten'd, patient kneels;
Though wrong'd, pleads guilt; implores the foot that
    spurns;
And, loth returning, yet, when call'd, returns.
And thou, full-flush'd with bliss! be taught from me,
Fond rival! woman's light inconstancy.
In the mid-storm who pays his thanks to heaven,
When oft, in port, the floating wreck is driven?
Who claims the prize, ere seven times round the goal,
With grazing wheel, the kindling chariot roll?
In love's fair sky fallacious breezes blow,
And heavy comes the storm, when threatening slow.
E'en though she love thee, be thy joy supprest,
And lock the secret in thy silent breast.
The boastings of successful passion prove,
I know not how, injurious oft in love.
Go once, for many times that she invites;
Short is the bliss, which prying envy blights.
Oh, if the ages past could votaries find,
And if our nymphs were of that ancient kind,
What now thou art, should I, unrivall'd, be;
The time's corruption hath supplanted me.
Not from this age my nature takes its hue;
Each has his path, and I my own pursue.
But thou, whose courtship thus promiscuous roves,
How must thine eyes be tortured by thy loves!
Thou seest the skin with lunar clearness white,
Thou seest the brown of tint, and both delight;
Charm'd by the shape through Grecian robes display'd,
By vestures ravish'd of the Roman maid.
Be russet garments, or the purple, worn,
By both alike thy tender breast is torn,

One only nymph might well employ thy dreams ;
One nymph variety of torment seems. ELTON.

ELEGY XIX. THE LOVER.

MORTALS ! ye fain would search, with curious eyes,
    Death's hovering hour, and ever-varied way ;
Scan with Phœnician art the starlight skies,
    And, kind or adverse, read each planet's ray.

Britons our fleets, and Parths our legions, fear,
    Yet still blind perils haunt the earth and main ;
Anxious ye rue the tumult thickening near,
    When Mars joins havoc on the dubious plain.

Ye dread, lest flames your crashing roofs devour,
    Or livid poison lurk within your bowl :
The lover only knows his fated hour ;
    Nor blasts, nor arms, give terror to his soul.

Though now on reedy Styx the oar he ply,
    Ev'n now, the murky sail of Hell survey ;
Let her he loves recall him with a sigh,
    He shall retrace that unpermitted way. ELTON.

ELEGY XXI. TO CYNTHIA.

As yesternight, my life ! I roam'd the street,
Flush'd with the grape, no slave to guide my feet,
A tiny multitude of boys drew near ;
I could not count them for my wildering fear.
Some torches shook ; some brandish'd darts in air
Some rattled chains ; their rosy limbs were bare.
Till one, more petulant in mischief, cried,
"Seize, bind him ! he is known to us, and tried :
'Tis he, mark'd out by an offended fair."
Instant my neck was noosed in knotted snare :
One shouts to drag me forth ; another cries,
"Wretch ! if he doubts that we are gods, he dies.
For thee, all undeserving as thou art,
She wakeful counts the hours, that slow depart :
And still expectant sighs ; while some strange fair
Attracts thee to her door : we know not where.

Fond fool! when, disentangled from her head
Her nightly turban's purple fillet's spread,
As, drooping with moist sleep, she lifts her eyes,
Such odours from her locks dishevelled rise,
As ne'er Arabia's breathing balms diffuse;
For Love's own hands extract those essenced dews.
But spare him, brothers! the repentant youth
Gives his free promise now of amorous truth:
And see, we reach th' appointed house," he said:
Then my stript mantle o'er my shoulders spread,
And led me in: "Go now: no longer roam:
But learn from this to pass thy nights at home." ELTON.

BOOK IV.

ELEGY I. PREDICTION OF POETIC IMMORTALITY.

SPRITE of Callimachus! and thou blest shade,
  Coan Philetas! I your grove would tread:
Me, Love's vow'd priest, have Grecia's choirs obey'd,
  From their pure fount in Latian's orgies led.

Say, Spirits! what inspiring grotto gave
  Alike to both that subtly tender strain?
Which foot auspicious enter'd first the cave,
  Or from what spring ye drank your flowing vein?

Who lists, may din with arms Apollo's ear:
  Smooth let the numbers glide, whose fame on high
Lifts me from earth: behold my Muse appear!
  And on wreath'd coursers pass in triumph by!

With me the little Loves the car ascend;
  My chariot-wheels a throng of bards pursues;
Why, with loose reins, in idle strife contend?
  Narrow the course which Heaven assigns the Muse.

Full many, Rome, shall bid thy annals shine,
    And Asian Bactra rise thy empire's bound;
Mine are the lays of peace, and flowers are mine
    Gather'd on Helicon's untrodden ground.

Maids of the sacred fount! with no harsh crown,
    But with soft garland wreathe your poet's head!
Those honours, which th' invidious crowd disown,
    While yet I live, shall doubly grace me dead.

Whate'er the silent tomb has veil'd in shade
    Shines more august through venerable fame;
Time has the merits of the dead display'd,
    And rescued from the dust a glorious name.

Who, else, would know, that e'er Troy-towers had bow'd
    To the pine-steed? that e'er Achilles strove
With grappling rivers? that round Ida flow'd
    The stream of Simois, cradling infant Jove?

If Hector's blood dyed thrice the wheel-track'd plain?
    Polydamas, Deiphobus, once fell,
Or Helenus was number'd with the slain?
    Scarce his own soil could of her Paris tell.

Shrunk were thy record, Troy! whose captured wall
    Felt twice th' Ætæan god's resistless rage:
Nor he, the bard that register'd thy fall,
    Had left his growing song to every age.

Me too shall Rome, among her last, revere;
    But that far day shall on my ashes rise;
No stone a worthless sepulchre shall rear,
    The mean memorial where a poet lies.

So may the Lycian god my vows approve!
    Now let my verse its wonted sphere regain;
That, touch'd with sympathies of joy and love,
    The melting nymph may listen to my strain.

'Tis sung that Orpheus, with his Thracian tones,
    Stay'd the wild herd, and stay'd the troubled flood;
Moved by Amphion's lute Cythæron's stones
    Leap'd into form, and Thebes aspiring stood.

Beneath rude Ætna's crag, O Polypheme!
   On the smooth deep did Galatea rein
Her horses, dropping with the briny stream,
   And wind their course to catch thy floating strain.

Then, if the god of verse, the god of wine,
   Look down propitious, and with smiles approve;
What wonder, if the fair's applause be mine,
   If thronging virgins list the lays of love?

Though no green marble, from Tænarian mines,
   Swells in the columns that my roof uphold;
No ceiling's arch with burnish'd ivory shines,
   And intersecting beams that blaze with gold;

My orchards vie not with Phæacian groves,
   Through my carved grot no Marcian fountains play;
With me the Muse in breathless dances roves;
   Nymphs haunt my dwelling; readers love my lay.

Oh fortunate, fair maid! whoe'er thou art,
   That, in my gentle song, shalt honour'd be!
This to each charm shall lasting bloom impart;
   Each tender verse a monument of thee!

The sumptuous pyramids, that stately rise
   Among the stars, the Mausolean tomb,
Th' Olympic fane, expanded like the skies—
   Not these can scape th' irrevocable doom.

The force of rushing rains, or wasting flame,
   The weight of years may bow their glories down;
But Genius wins an undecaying name,
   Through ages strong, and deathless in renown. ELTON.

ELEGY III. THE DREAM OF PROPERTIUS.

METHOUGHT I lay by Pegasus' fresh fount,
On pleasant Helicon's umbrageous mount:
The feats, O Alba! of thy storied kings
Already trembled on my murmuring strings:
Vent'rous I stoop'd that mightier stream to sip,
Whence father Ennius slaked his thirsty lip;

The Curian and Horatian spears he sung;
Th' Æmilian bark with regal trophies hung;
Fabius' slow conquests; Cannæ's fatal plain;
And heaven by pious offerings turn'd again:
Rome's gods that forth the Punic spoiler drove,
And the shrill bird that saved the fane of Jove.

When, from a laurel by Castalia's wave,
Propt on his golden harp before a cave,
Apollo saw: he fix'd his glance, and cried,
" What wouldst thou, madman! with so vast a tide?
Who bade thee thus heroic numbers claim?
Not hence, Propertius! hope the wreath of fame.
Rather with slender track thy chariot lead
To print the verdure of the velvet mead:
While careless on the couch thy page is thrown,
Where she, that waits a lover, sighs alone.
Why quit the ring that bounds thy lay's renown?
Or weigh the pinnace of thy genius down?
One oar the sea and one the sand should sweep:
Be safe, for stormiest rolls the midmost deep."

Then with his ivory quill he show'd a seat,
And path of springing moss, by foot unbeat:
Studding the grot, stones green with lichens clung;
And timbrels from the rock's worn vault were hung:
Silenus old with clay-form'd Muses stood;
And piping Pan from his Arcadian wood:
My darling doves, light-hovering round their queen.
Dipp'd their red beaks in rills from Hippocrene.
The sculptured Sisters, ranged on either side,
In various tasks their yielding fingers plied:
This culls for Bacchic spears the ivy sprays;
That tunes the stringed lyre, and sets the lays:
Another's hands the braided garland bind
With roses, white and red, alternate twined.
One, rising from the group, drew near to me,
Her air, methought. bespoke Calliope:

" Let snow-plumed swans for ever waft thy car,
Nor steeds strong-thundering whirl thee to the war.
Blow not the dismal trumpet's hoarse alarms,
Nor stern beset th' Aonian bowers with arms:

Bid not the Marian banners flout the sky;
From Rome's firm shock the broken Teutons fly;
Or barb'rous Rhine along his wailing flood
Roll heaps of Suevian slain, and blush with blood.
Sing thou the lovers that, with garlands crown'd,
Another's doors with amorous siege surround;
Sing of the torches glaring through the night,
And riot-ensigns of inebriate flight;
To him the secrets of thy lore impart,
Who aims to dupe a rigid keeper's art;
And teach him, by the magic of a lay,
Through bars and bolts to lure the nymph away."

She said: and on my brow the waters threw,
Drawn from the fountain, whence Philetas drew.
ELTON.

ELEGY V.   PRAISE OF A LIFE OF EASE.

LOVE is the god of peace: we lovers know
But love's hard combats, and a mistress-foe:
Not gold's devouring want my soul has curst;
Not from a jewell'd cup I slake my thirst;
I plough not wide Campania's mellow'd soil,
Nor for thy brass in ships, O Corinth! toil.
Ah! hapless clay that erst Prometheus press'd,
Moulding a rash and unforeseeing breast:
The skill, that knit the frame, o'erlook'd the heart;
An upright reasoning soul escaped his art.
Now tost by winds we roam the troubled flood,
Link foe to foe, and restless pant for blood.
Fool! not on Acheron thy wealth shall float,
All naked drifting in th' infernal boat.
The conqueror with the captive skims the tide,
And chain'd Jugurtha sits at Marius' side:
Robed Crœsus shares the tatter'd Irus' doom,
And owns that death the best, which soon shall come.
Me in youth's flower could Helicon entrance,
My hands with Muses link'd in mazy dance:
Me has it charm'd to bathe my soul in wine,
And vernal roses round my temples twine:

When irksome age hath stolen on love's delight,
And strewn my sable locks with sprinkled white:
Then may it please to search in Nature's ways,
And learn what god the world's vast fabric sways;
How dawns the rising east and fades again;
How the round moon repairs her crescent wane;
How winds the salt sea sweep, and th' eastern blast
The billows warps, and clouds their ceaseless waters cast.
Whether a day shall come, when headlong hurl'd
Shall fall the tottering pillars of the world;
Why drinks the purpling bow the rainy cloud;
Why Pindus' summits reel, in earthquake bow'd;
Why shines the sun's wheel'd orb with umber'd light,
His golden coursers pall'd in mourning night;
Why turns Boötes slow his starry wain,
Why sparkling throng the Pleiads' cluster'd train;
Why bounded roll the deepening ocean's tides;
Why the full year in parted seasons glides;
If under earth gods judge, and giants rave;
Tisiphone's fierce ringlets snaky wave;
Furies Alcmæon scourge, and Phineas hungering crave;
Thirst burn in streams, wheels whirl, rocks backward leap
Or hell's dark mouth three-headed Cerberus keep:
If Tityos' straiten'd limbs nine acres press;
Or fables mock man's credulous wretchedness
Through long tradition's age: nor terror's strife
Survive the pyre:—be such my close of life.
Go ye who list, the Parthian overcome,
Bring Crassus' wrested standards back to Rome.   ELTON

ELEGY X.   THE BIRTH-DAY OF CYNTHIA.

I MARVELL'D what the smiling Muses led,
While blush'd the rising sun, beside my bed.
My fair one's birth-day shone; and, standing round,
Thrice with clapp'd hands they gave the signal sound.
May this day cloudless pass, winds breathe no more;
And raging waves roll smoothly to the shore.
Let no sad looks on this blest day appear;
Ev'n Niobe suppress the marble tear:

The Halcyon's bills lay now their moans aside,
Nor on her son devour'd let Progne chide.
And, dear one! thou, in light-wing'd moments born,
Rise, pray the heavens for blessings on thy morn.
Disperse the dews of sleep with waters fair,
With parting fingers sleek thy glossy hair;
The robe, that first allured Propertius' eyes,
Assume, nor for thy brow the flower despise.
Pray that those powerful beauties ne'er may fade,
And still my neck may bow, by Cynthia sway'd.
When smoke of purifying incense streams
From the wreath'd altar, and its broadening gleams
Fill all the gilt saloon with happy light,
Arrange the board; let goblets speed the night.
From box of yellow agate sweet dispense
The liquid nard moist breathing on the sense:
Let the sigh'd flute sob hoarse in midnight dance;
Thy wit in libertine gay sallies glance;
From jocund feast unwelcome sleep retreat,
And ringing echo din the neighbouring street.
Let the dice rattle and the throw denote
Whom that wing'd boy with heaviest pinions smote.
When many an hour has flow'd in bumpers by,
Let Venus lend her nightly ministry:
Let us the yearly solemn love-rites pay,
And crown the pleasures of thy natal-day.   ELTON.

THE SATYRICON

OF

TITUS PETRONIUS ARBITER

THE SATYRICON

OF

TITUS PETRONIUS ARBITER.

CHAPTER I.

ENCOLPIUS HARANGUES ON THE CORRUPTION OF ELOQUENCE.—THE THEME
IS TAKEN UP BY AGAMEMNON.—POETICAL ESSAY ON THE EDUCATION OF
THE ORATOR.—ENCOLPIUS AND ASCYLTOS INVEIGLED TO A BROTHEL.—
THEIR ADVENTURES THERE.—THEIR QUARREL AND RECONCILIATION.

[It is so long since I promised to relate my adventures to you that I
am resolved to fulfil my engagement to-day, now that we are happily met
not only to talk of matters of learning, but also to season our merry conversation with pleasant tales.

Fabricius Veiento [1] has already discoursed ably on the abuses of religion,
and exposed the fraudulent mania of pretended inspiration with which priests
impudently expound mysteries of which they often know nothing; but]
are not our declaimers possessed with another kind of fury,
who cry out : These wounds I received in defence of the public liberty ; This eye was lost in your service ! Give me some
helpful hand to lead me to my children ; for my severed
hams [2] can no longer support me.

---

[1] *Fabricius Veiento.*] Tacitus mentions him as the author of a tremendous satire against the priests of his day, in which he described the
method of getting up those divine frenzies with which they pretended
to be visited in the performance of the sacred offices. The same historian speaks also of another satire against the senators for their corruption in selling justice. For writing this satire Veiento was banished by
Nero.

[2] *Severed hams.*] Hannibal is said to have hamstrung several of his

Even this might be endured if it served to lead young beginners into the way to true eloquence ; whereas now all they gain by this exaggeration of matter and this empty noise of words, is, that when they enter the forum they think themselves transported into another world.   And in my opinion, the reason why young people are made such blockheads in the schools, is, that they neither hear nor see any of those things which belong to the common usage of life, but only pirates standing on the shore with chains ; tyrants issuing edicts wherein they command sons to cut off their fathers' heads ; oracles delivered in time of pestilence, ordering that three or more virgins be immolated ; fine honey pellets of words, and everything so said and done is as if it were all spice and garnish.

It is no more possible for those who are brought up in this way to display correct taste, than for those who live in a kitchen not to smell of grease.   Under your favour, let me take the liberty of saying, that you rhetoricians, before all others, have ruined eloquence ; for by tickling the ear with an idle jingle of words, you have contrived that the substance of the discourse should become enervated and lifeless.

Young people were not yet confined to the practice of composing declamations when Sophocles or Euripides found fit terms in which to express themselves.   No misty pedant had yet spoiled the intellects of youth, when Pindar and the nine Lyric poets shrank from attempting the Homeric strain.   And not to speak of the poets only, I certainly do not find that either Plato or Demosthenes practised this sort of exercise. A noble, and, if I may be allowed the expression, a chaste style, is not bedizened or turgid, but is exalted by its own natural beauty.

It is not long since this windy and extravagant flux of words passed over to Athens from Asia, and like some pestilent constellation, blasted the aspiring minds of youth, and at once corrupted and stifled all true eloquence.

Who since that time came up to the height of Thucydides ? Who reached the fame of Hyperides ?   Nay, there has not appeared a single poem of wholesome complexion, but all of them, as if fed upon the same garbage, have been unable to

Roman prisoners after the battle of Cannæ.—*His pernas succidit iniqua superbia Pœni.* ENNIUS.

reach the period of old age. Painting also shared the same
fate after the Egyptians had the audacity to invent a com-
pendious method for the cultivation of that great art.

[I was declaiming one day to this effect, when Agamemnon came up
to us, and curiously scrutinizing a person to whom the audience were
lending so attentive an ear,] he would not allow me to declaim
longer in the portico than he himself had sweated in the
school. "Young man," said he, "since you express yourself
in no commonplace terms, and what is rarely seen, you are a
lover of good sense, I will not hold back from you the secrets
of our art. With respect to these exercises in the schools, the
fault by no means lies with the masters, who are forced to be
mad with madmen; for unless they taught what their scholars
approved, they would be left, as Cicero says, to keep school
by themselves. Just as subtle flatterers, who scheme for invitations to the tables of the rich, study nothing more than what
they think may be most agreeable to their hearers (for they
can never compass their wishes unless they cajole the ear);
so a master of eloquence, unless fisherman-like he first baits
his hook with what he knows the fish will bite at, may wait
long enough on the rocks without catching anything.

"How stands the matter then? It is the parents deserve
reprehension, who will not allow their children to enjoy the
advantage of strict method in their studies. For, in the first
place, they devote their hopes, like everything else, to ambition;
and then, in their haste to arrive at their wishes, they hurry
young men into the forum before they have yet digested
what they have read, and thrust mere boys upon the profession of eloquence, than which they themselves confess there is
nothing more arduous. But if they would suffer them to pass
through a regular gradation of studies, so that they might be
rendered docile by earnest reading; that their minds might be
fashioned by the precepts of wisdom; that they might correct
the faults of their own compositions with unsparing rigour; that
they might long hear what they were inclined to imitate, and
not be enraptured with such things as please boys; then would
eloquence re-appear as of old in all the grandeur and weight of
its majesty. But now boys trifle in the schools, young men are
laughed at in the forum, and what is more shameful than both,
no one will confess in his age the false bent he contracted in his
school-boy days. But that you may not suppose I entirely

o

condemn those impromptu effusions which are thrown off in Lucilius's easy manner,[1] I will myself give you my thoughts in verse.

> Whoso would be an orator, and own
> The mighty powers born of true art alone,
> Must prize the ancient discipline, and be
> A liegeman true to pale Frugality:
> Not with prone front in regal mansions wait;
> Not fawn for invitations on the great;
> Nor quench in wine his mental fire; nor waste
> His time on stage shows, and corrupt his taste;
> But whether to Tritonia's letter'd halls [2]
> The Muses lead his steps, or to the walls
> Founded by Spartan colonists, [3] or where
> The Syren's soul haunts the voluptuous air, [4]
> Let Poesy his early years engage,
> And Homer's fount his happy thirst assuage.
> To bolder efforts he will rise, when fraught
> With all the lore the wise Athenian taught, [5]

[1] *Lucilius's easy manner.*] Lucilius was an early Roman, noted for his rapidity in composition, so that, as Horace says, he could dash off a couple of hundred lines while standing on one leg.

[2] *Tritonia's letter'd halls.*] Athens. Tritonia was one of the names of Pallas, the tutelary goddess of that city.

[3] *Founded by Spartan colonists.*] Tarentum. It happened about the year 700 B. C., that the whole manhood of Sparta was engaged abroad in a perilous war with the Messenians, and being apprehensive lest their death or their prolonged absence from home should deprive their country of a new generation of warriors, they sent back the youngest men in their camp to prevent that calamity by making mothers of all the Lacedæmonian maidens. The children thus begotten were called Parthenians (from παρθενος, a virgin). When the Spartans returned home victorious, they did not take very kindly to these Parthenians, who therefore emigrated under the leadership of Phalantus, and established themselves in Calabria, where they rebuilt the old city of Tarentum. Hence Horace, speaking of that city, says,

> regnata petam Laconi
> Rura Phalanto.

[4] *The Syren's soul*, &c.] Naples, otherwise Parthenopeia, so called from Parthenope, one of the Syrens, who was buried there.

[5] *The wise Athenian.*] Socrates.

And dare to shake the mighty spear and shield
Which great Demosthenes was wont to wield.
Then to new sounds let him attune his ear,
And Grecian sense in Roman accents hear.
Nor only in the forum will he find
Fit occupation for his studious mind ;
With books he 'll feed its vigour, with the lines
Through which the poet's fervid genius shines,
Heroic tales of war, and words of fire,
That flash'd from Tully in his patriot ire.

This do : then, Orator, pour forth amain
The mighty flood-burst of thy teeming brain.

My attention being fixed on the speaker, I did not perceive
that Ascyltos had given me the slip ; and I was still borne
along by the tide of rhetoric, when a great crowd of scholars
filled the portico, just come, as it appeared, from an extemporaneous declamation of some one or other who had taken
exceptions to Agamemnon's discourse. So whilst the lads
were ridiculing the sentiments and condemning the arrangement of the whole harangue, I took the opportunity to withdraw, and set off running in quest of Ascyltos. But I did
not well know the way, nor where our inn was situated ; so
that whatever road I took I found myself coming back to the
spot I had left. At last, tired with running, and bathed in
perspiration, I accosted an old woman who sold herbs : "Pray,
mother, said I, do you happen to know where I lodge ?" Delighted with the humorous absurdity of the question, "Why
not ?" she replied ; and getting up, went on before me. I
thought her a witch ; but presently, when we had come into a
by-place, the old woman threw back her hood, and said,
"Here is where you should live."

While I was protesting that I did not know the house, I
saw some persons walking stealthily about between cells with
bills on them,[1] and among naked harlots. Too late then

---

[1] *Cells with bills on them.*] In the Roman brothels the name of each
prostitute and her price were posted on the door of her room. Hence
Juvenal, speaking of Messalina, who had borrowed the chamber of the
famous Lycisca, says *Titulum mentita Lysiscæ.* The form of one of

I discovered that I had been brought to a brothel; so cursing the old woman's treachery, I covered my head, and
ran through the midst of the brothel to the opposite end;
when behold, just at the outlet whom should I meet but Ascyltos, tired and half dead like myself; you would have
thought he had been brought there by the same old woman.
Saluting him therefore with a smile, I asked what he was
doing in such a disgraceful place. "If you but knew what
has happened to me," he replied, wiping the sweat from his
face with his hands.

What is the matter? said I.

He answered with a faint voice, "As I was wandering all
over the town, unable to find our inn, a respectable looking
man came up to me and very civilly offered to show me my
way. He led me through some very dark and intricate lanes
till we came to this place, ...[1] where, had I not been the
stronger, it would have been all over with me."

[While Ascyltos was relating his adventure to me, up came his respectable man, accompanied by a woman by no means bad looking, and addressing himself to Ascyltos, begged him to walk in, assuring him he had
nothing to fear.[2] The woman on her part was very pressing with me to
accompany her. We followed the pair, therefore, who led us along between ranges of bills, and we saw several persons of both sexes demean-
ing themselves,] so that they all appeared to me to have drunk
satyrion.[3] . . . . . [Ascyltos was again assailed, but] unit-

these *tituli* is preserved in the history of Apollonius Tirius. It is rather
curious:

    QUICUMQUE TARSIAM DEFLORAVERIT MEDIAM LIBRAM DABIT
    POSTEA POPULO PATEBIT AD SINGULOS SOLIDOS.

The Italian translator of Petronius informs us that this custom still exists
in his country.

  [1] In hunc me locum perduxit, prolatoque pecullo cœpit rogare stuprum.
Jam pro cella meretrix assem exegerat; jam ille mihi injecerat manum,
&c.]—There is a double meaning in the word *peculium;* in its primitive
sense, it is a man's stock of money, all he has got; metaphorically, it is
synonymous with *mentula.* Homines bene vasatos et *majoris peculii.*
Lamprid. in Vita Heliogab.

  [2] Certiorem faciens nil timendum; sed cum patiens esse nollet saltem
agens foret.

  [3] Ut conspicimur, nos cynædica petulantia allicere conati sunt: sta-
timque unus alte succinctus invadit Ascylton, et super eum, grabato pro-
stratum, molere conatus est.]—Satyrion was a generic name among the
Greeks for aphrodinars of all kinds [Plin. xxvi. 63]. *Satirione* is the

ing our forces we made nothing of the troublesome fellow. [Ascyltos ran out of doors and made off, leaving me to shift for myself; but finding me too strong for them they left me alone.

After I had run almost all over the city,] I saw as if through a fog Giton standing at the corner of a street, [on the threshold of our inn,] and hurrying up to him, I asked what my favourite had provided for our dinner, whereupon the boy sat down on the bed, and wiped away his flowing tears with his thumb. Exceedingly surprised at the boy's distress, I asked him what was the matter; but I could get nothing out of him for a long time, nor until I had mingled threats with entreaties. At last he said, " That brother or comrade of yours came in here a little before you, and wanted to force me; and when I cried out he drew a sword and said, If you are a Lucretia you have found a Tarquin."

On hearing this I cried out to Ascyltos, putting my fists before his eyes, What do you say to this, you Ganymede, whose very breath is impure ?

Ascyltos affected indignation, and imitating my gesture with more force, he bawled out still louder, " Will you hold your tongue, you obscene gladiator, you that escaped from the amphitheatre,[1] [to which you were sent for murdering your host.] Hold your tongue, you night-pad, who even when you were in vigour never lay with a decent woman. Did not I serve you formerly in the orchard as this boy does now in the inn ?"

Why did you steal away, said I, from Agamemnon's harangue ?

" And what would you have had me do, you booby, when I was dying of hunger ? Stop and listen to fine phrases, as much to the purpose as the jingling of broken glass, or interpretations of dreams ? By Hercules, it is you that are much worse than I, you that flattered a poet for sake of a supper." Our most unseemly brawling now gave place to

name of a love potion known in Italy. See *Clizia*, a comedy by Machiavelli.

[1] *Escaped from the amphitheatre.*] The original is, *Quem de ruina arena* dimisit, which expression alludes to those *Pegmata amphitheatralia* described by Seneca, Ep. 91. They were large boarded machines, so contrived as to lift up or let down at pleasure. On these were placed condemned criminals, who either fought together after the manner of gladiators; or, the machine flying open on a sudden, they fell among wild beasts, or fires put there to consume them.

hearty laughter, and we began to talk more quietly of other things.

But the recollection of the late injury coming fresh upon me again, Ascyltos, said I, I find we shall never agree together; let us therefore divide our little common stock, and let each of us make shift separately to mend his own fortunes. You are a scholar and so am I; but that I may be no hinderance to your projects, I will turn my thoughts to something else; otherwise we shall have a thousand contentions every day, and become the talk of the whole town.

Ascyltos made no objection. "As we have to-day accepted an invitation to supper," said he, " as men of letters, we must not lose our night; but to-morrow, since you wish it, I will look out for myself another lodging, and another bed-fellow."

It is never too soon, said I, to do what one has a mind to. It was the ardour of my desires that made me wish to hurry on this separation, for I had long wished to rid myself of an irksome observer, that I might resume my old intercourse with Giton.

[Offended at my importunity, Ascyltos dashed out of the room without saying a word. So sudden an exit foreboded something unpleasant; for I was well aware of the violence of his temper and of his passion for Giton. I therefore went after him, both to observe his designs and to prevent them; but losing sight of him, I was a long while in pursuit of him to no purpose.]

After I had searched the whole city, I returned to my room, where I made myself happy.[1] Meanwhile Ascyltos stole to the door, and violently bursting it open, he clapped his hands and made the room ring with his laughter . . . . "What were you doing, my most sanctified brother?" he cried. . . . . Nor was he content with words only, but untying the thong that bound his wallet, he whipt me with all his might, mingling sarcasms with the stripes he laid on—" This is the way you divide stock with your comrade! Don't think to do so!"

---

[1] In cellulam redii, osculisque tandem bona fide exactis, alligo arctissimis complexibus puerum, fruorque votis usque ad invidiam felicibus. Nec adhuc quidem omnia erant facta, cum Ascyltos furtim se foribus admovit, discussisque fortissime claustris, invenit me cum fratre ludentem: risu itaque plausuque cellulam implevit, opertumque amiculo evolvit. Et quid agebas, inquit, frater sanctissime? Quid vesticontubernium facis?

[The suddenness of the thing compelled me to take his abuse and his blows in silence: I therefore treated the matter as a joke, and therein I did wisely, for otherwise I must have had a fight with my comrade. My counterfeit mirth calmed his passion, and even made him smile. "Look you, Encolpius," said he, "you are so buried in your pleasures, you never reflect that our money is gone, and that what things we have left are of no value. There is nothing to be got in the town in summer-time; we shall have better luck in the country; let us go visit our friends."

CHAPTER II.

ENCOLPIUS, ASCYLTOS, AND GITON AT THE COUNTRY HOUSE OF LYCURGUS —PROMISCUOUS INTRIGUES BETWEEN LYCAS, ENCOLPIUS, GITON, TRYPHÆNA, AND DORIS — ENCOLPIUS AND GITON PLUNDER A STRANDED VESSEL—LYCURGUS LOCKS THEM UP—WITH THE HELP OF ASCYLTOS THEY ROB HIM AND ESCAPE—THEY STEAL A CLOAK AND A BAG OF GOLD AT AN INN—AND WITH DIFFICULTY GET SAFE BACK TO NAPLES.

NECESSITY compelled me to approve of his advice and smother my resentment. So loading Giton with our baggage, we left the city, and went to the country house of Lycurgus, a Roman knight. In consequence of his old fraternity with Ascyltos, he received us handsomely, and the company we found there made our entertainment still more agreeable. Above all, Tryphæna was there, a very beautiful woman, who had come with Lycas, the master of a ship and owner of lands in the neighbourhood of the sea.

No tongue can tell the delights we enjoyed in this charming place, though Lycurgus kept a frugal table. You must know that we all paired together as lovers without delay. The beautiful Tryphæna took my fancy, and readily inclined to my wishes. But hardly had I enjoyed her favours when Lycas, enraged at my having filched his pleasures from him, insisted that I should indemnify him. The lady had been an old flame of his; so he pleasantly proposed that I should make good his loss in person. He pressed me hotly, but as Tryphæna had my heart, my ears were shut against Lycas. Refusal made him keener; he followed me wherever I went, and getting into my chamber at night, when he found entreaties of no avail he would have forced me; but I made such an outcry that I raised the whole house, and, with the help of Lycurgus, I was saved from his violence.

Finding at last that Lycurgus's house was not convenient for his designs, he tried to entice me to his own; and when I rejected his invitation he made use of Triphæna's influence over me; and she the rather persuaded me to comply with Lycas's wishes, as she hoped to be under less restraint at his house. I did therefore as my charmer desired; but Lycurgus had renewed his old intimacy with Ascyltos, and would not suffer him to go; accordingly we agreed that he should stay with Lycurgus, and we should go with Lycas. Moreover we resolved that each of us should make booty as occasion served, for the common stock.

Incredibly delighted at my consent, Lycas hastened our departure, and forthwith, bidding our friends farewell, we arrived on the same day at his house.

Lycas had so artfully arranged it, that he sat next me on the journey, and Triphæna next to Giton; and this he had contrived on account of the notorious inconstancy of that woman. Nor was he mistaken in his aim, for she immediately became enamoured of the boy, and I easily perceived it. Lycas too did all he could to make me take accurate note of it. For this reason I treated him with more complaisance, whereat he was overjoyed, feeling assured that the infidelity of my mistress would make me despise her, and that in consequence of my resentment against Triphæna I should be more disposed to treat him favourably.

Such was the posture of affairs while we were at Lycas's. Triphæna was desperately in love with Giton; Giton doted upon her; I cared little for the sight of either of them; and Lycas, studying to please me, found me every day some new diversion; in all which his wife Doris, a fine woman, strove to surpass him, and that too with such grace that she soon expelled Triphæna from my heart. My eyes told Doris of my love, and Doris responded with voluptuous glances; so that this mute language, anticipating the office of the tongue, furtively expressed the mutual inclination we both conceived at the same moment.

It was the knowledge I had of the jealous temper of Lycas that kept me silent; and passion itself gave his wife a quick insight into his designs with regard to me. Tho first time we had an opportunity of talking together, she told me what she had discovered, and I candidly confessed the fact, and told her how harshly I had always repulsed his overtures. But she, like a very discreet woman, said, " We must use our wits," and following her advice, I found that giving way to the one was the means of obtaining possession of the other.

Meanwhile Triphæna, leaving Giton, whom she had used up, to recruit his strength, would fain have returned to me; but meeting with a bad reception, her love changed into furious hatred; and as she followed me with unceasing pertinacity, she detected my intrigue with both the husband and the wife. She cared nothing for his wantonness with me, as she lost nothing by it; but she fell foul of Doris's furtive amour, and denounced it to Lycas, whose jealousy being stronger than love, ran all to revenge; but Doris, having been put on her guard by Tryphæna's maid, abstained from any more clandestine meetings.

As soon as I was aware of all this, cursing Tryphæna's treachery and the ingratitude of Lycas, I resolved to abscond, and Fortune favoured my design; for a ship consecrated to Isis,[1] and richly laden, had the day before run upon the rocks.

I talked over the matter with Giton, and found him as willing as myself to be gone; for Tryphæna now manifestly neglected him after having exhausted his strength. Very early next morning, therefore, we set off to the sea-side, and got on board the vessel without any difficulty, because we were known to Lycas's servants who had charge of her; but as they followed us out of respect wherever we went, so that we had no opportunity to filch anything, I managed to slip away, leaving Giton with them, and got into the stern, where stood the image of Isis. This I stripped of a rich mantle and a silver sistrum,[2] and having picked up other good booties in the master's cabin, I let myself down by a rope, unseen by any but Giton, who also quitted his companions and sneaked after me.

As soon as he came up I showed him the plunder, and we both resolved to make what haste we could to Ascyltos, but were not able to reach the house of Lycurgus until the next day. Then I told Ascyltos briefly about the robbery, and our amorous misadventures. He advised us to engage Lycurgus in our favour, by acquainting him that the new persecutions I had suffered from Lycas had been the cause of our sudden and secret change of quarters. We followed his advice, and Lycurgus, when he heard our story, swore that he would for ever protect us against our enemies.

Our flight was not perceived until Tryphæna and Doris were out of bed; for we made it a practice, like assiduous gallants, to attend their

---

[1] *A ship consecrated to Isis.*] Among the ancients navigation was suspended during the winter months, and was re-opened with great ceremony on the festival day of Isis, in March, by a ship which was specially dedicated to the goddess. For an account of the proceedings on that occasion, see The Golden Ass of Apuleius, book xi.

[2] *A silver sistrum.*] This was a metallic instrument appropriate to the worship of Isis. It was in shape like a battledore, but with a shorter handle, and had four transverse rods of metal inserted in holes on the frame, and playing freely in them, so as to make a jingling noise when the instrument was shaken.

morning toilette. When therefore we were found missing, contrary to custom, Lycas sent out messengers to look for us, and particularly to the sea-coast, whence he received word that we had been to the wreck; but nothing was said about the theft, which was not yet known, for the stern was to seaward, and the master had not yet returned to the wreck.

At last our flight being known for certain, Lycas was greatly vexed, and vented his fury on Doris, whom he accused of having caused our departure. I will say nothing of the hard words and the blows he gave her, not knowing the details; it is enough to say, that Tryphæna, who had been the originator of all this disturbance, persuaded Lycas to go in quest of us to Lycurgus's, as the place where in all likelihood we had taken refuge; and she chose to accompany him, that she might load us with abuse as she thought we deserved.

Next day they set out and arrived at the mansion. We were not in; for Lycurgus had taken us to a feast in honour of Hercules, which was held in a little town in the neighbourhood. But having heard we were there, they followed in all haste, and met us in the portico of the temple. We were greatly confounded at the sight of them: Lycas vehemently complained of our flight to Lycurgus, but was received with such a contracted brow and so haughty air, that taking courage, I loudly cried shame upon his lewd attempts against me, both in the house of Lycurgus and in his own; and Tryphæna, who endeavoured to stop my mouth, had her share of the infamy, for I exposed her vile conduct to the crowd that had gathered to hear the brawl; and in token of the truth of what I stated, I showed them poor exhausted Giton, and myself, who had been brought to death's door by the lasciviousness of that harlot.

The shouts of laughter that burst from the crowd put our enemies so out of countenance that they went off in the dumps, pondering how they might be revenged. Seeing that we had prepossessed Lycurgus in our favour, they determined to wait for him at his own house, in order to disabuse his mind.

The solemnities ended too late for us to return that day to the mansion, and Lycurgus having taken us to a farm of his which lay midway thither, left us still sleeping there next morning when he went home to despatch some business. He found Lycas and Tryphæna waiting for him, and they talked so wheedlingly to him that they prevailed upon him to give us up into their hands. Lycurgus, naturally barbarous and faithless, began to contrive which way to betray us, and sent Lycas to get some help, whilst he himself went to the farm to have us secured.

Thither he came, and accosted us on entering with such a countenance as Lycas might have shown; then wringing his hands, he upbraided us with the lie we had told of Lycas, and ordered us to be locked up in the room in which we lay, after turning out Ascyltos, whom he would not hear speak a word in our defence. He then put us under watch and ward until his return, and went off to his mansion, taking Ascyltos with him.

Ascyltos on the road tried in vain to mollify Lycurgus, but neither entreaties, nor caresses, nor tears could move him. It therefore came into our comrade's head to set us free by other means; and coming to an open rupture with Lycurgus, he was so much the freer to execute his project.[1]

As soon as all the household were fast asleep, Ascyltos took our baggage on his shoulders, and passing through a breach he had previously remarked in the wall, he arrived by day-break at the farm, and meeting no one to stop him, he stepped in and came to our room, which our guards had taken care to make fast. But he had no difficulty in breaking it open, the bolt being of wood he forced it aside with a piece of iron, and woke us with the fall of the lock; for we were snoring in spite of our ill fortune.

Our guards had so overwatched themselves that they had fallen into a deep sleep, which was the reason that we alone were wakened by the breaking of the door. Ascyltos having come in, told us briefly what he had done for us. There was no need of more words. While we were carefully putting on our clothes it came into my head to kill our keepers and plunder the farm-house. I imparted the idea to Ascyltos, who approved of the pillage, but put us in the way of effecting our wishes without bloodshed; for being well acquainted with every corner of the house, he took us to the store closet, the lock of which he picked, and there helping ourselves to the best, we got off while it was yet early in the morning, and avoiding the main roads, we did not halt until we thought ourselves safe from pursuit.

Then Ascyltos, having taken breath, expatiated on the delight he had felt in robbing that most miserly Lycurgus, of whose stinginess he had good reason to complain, for he had been paid nothing for his services, and he had been kept upon short and dry commons: for Lycurgus was so sordid, that notwithstanding his immense wealth, he denied himself the common necessaries of life.]

Unhappy Tantalus, with plenty curst,
'Mid fruits for hunger faints, 'mid streams for thirst:
The miser's emblem! who of all possess'd,
Yet fears to taste, in blessings most unbless'd.

---

[1] Et certe, Lycurgi contumeliam succensus, dormire cum eo noluit, sicque, quod animo conceperat, facilius executus est.

[Ascyltos was for entering Naples that same day; but said I, it would be imprudent to go to a place, where in all probability we shall be sought after. Let us therefore absent ourselves for a while and ramble about; we have wherewithal to make ourselves comfortable. The advice was approved, and we set out for a hamlet embellished with charming lodges, where several of our acquaintance were enjoying the pleasures of the season. But we had scarcely got half way, when the rain coming down upon us in bucketfuls compelled us to run for shelter to the nearest village, where entering an inn, we found many other persons who had also turned in there to escape the storm. The throng prevented our being observed, and as it gave us the opportunity of prying here and there to see what we might filch, Ascyltos picked up from the ground, unobserved by any one, a little bag in which he found several pieces of gold. We were overjoyed at this fortunate beginning; but fearing lest some one should reclaim the money, we stole out at the back door. There we saw a servant saddling horses, and he left them just at that moment and went back into the house as if to fetch something he had forgotten. As soon as he was gone, I saw a very handsome mantle[1] fastened to a saddle. I undid the straps, secured the mantle, and we made off with it under the cover of some outhouses into a neighbouring wood.

Having sat ourselves down in the heart of the wood, where we thought ourselves more out of danger, we began to contrive how we should hide our gold, so that we might neither be found with that evidence of our theft upon us, nor be robbed of it ourselves. At last we determined to sew it up in the lining of an old thread-bare tunic, which I then threw over my shoulders, committing the care of the cloak to Ascyltos, and we prepared to start for the city by cross-ways. But as we were quitting the wood we heard somebody say on our left, "They shall not escape us; they entered the wood; let us separate and beat about, that we may be the surer of catching them."

---

[1] *A very handsome mantle.*] Pallium. The English word *cloak*, though commonly adopted as the proper translation of pallium, palliolum, or palla, conveys no accurate conception of the form, material, or use of that which those terms denoted. The article designated by them was always a rectangular piece of cloth, exactly, or at least nearly, square. It was used in the very form in which it was taken from the loom, without any aid from the tailor, except to repair the injuries it sustained by time. Such a piece of cloth might of course be used in a variety of ways: as a blanket, a carpet, a curtain, a horse-cloth, &c. When it served as a garment, it might be wrapped round the whole person, or put on like a Spanish cloak, or a Scotch plaid; or it might be fastened with a brooch over the right shoulder, leaving the right arm free, as represented in the admired statue of Phocion preserved in the Vatican.

We were struck with such consternation at these words, that Ascyltos and Giton darted off through the thickets towards the city; while I turned back in such a hurry that, without my perceiving it, the precious tunic fell off from my shoulders. At last being quite tired and unable to go any farther, I stretched myself at the foot of a tree, and there I first discovered my loss. The pang I felt gave me new strength. I started up again to search for the treasure, and beat about for a long time to no purpose, till, spent with toil and vexation, I plunged into the thickest parts of the forest, and stayed there at least four hours. Weary at last of that frightful solitude, I sought my way out; but as I went forward I fell in with a countryman. Then indeed I had need of all my assurance, and it did not fail me. Going boldly up to him, I asked my way to the city, complaining that I had been for a long time lost in the wood. Pitying my appearance, for I was deadly pale, and all over dirt, he asked me if I had seen any one in the wood? No one, said I. Then he very civilly led me into the highway, where he met two of his friends, who told him they had beat the wood through and through, but had found nothing but a tunic which they showed him.

I had not the impudence to claim it, as may readily be supposed, though I well knew its value. Afflicted more than ever, and mourning over my lost treasure, my weakness increased, I slackened my pace, and fell into the rear of the countrymen, who took no more notice of me.

It was late therefore when I reached the city, and entering the inn I found Ascyltos stretched on a bed half dead. I threw myself upon another, and was not able to utter a single word. Uneasy at not seeing the tunic left in my care, he hastily asked what had become of it. But I had not strength enough to reply, and only let my drooping eyes hint to him that for which I had no words. At length recovering little by little, I plainly told him my misfortune; but he thought I was joking; and though the shower of tears I shed might have been taken as confirmation of my oaths, he was manifestly incredulous, and could not be persuaded but that I had a mind to cheat him. Giton, who was standing by, was as much distressed as myself; the boy's sadness increased mine; but what distracted me most was the search that was made after us. I spoke of this to Ascyltos, but he made light of it, because he had got happily out of the scrape for the present. Moreover, he felt assured that we were out of all danger, since we were neither known nor had been seen by anybody as yet. We thought proper to pretend that we were unwell, that we might have a pretext for keeping to our room so much the longer. But as our money fell short, necessity compelled us to go abroad sooner than we had intended, and sell some of our things.]

CHAPTER III.

THE ADVENTURE IN THE MARKET FOR STOLEN GOODS—INTRUSION UPON
THE MYSTERIES OF PRIAPUS—THE THREE FRIENDS ARE VISITED BY
QUARTILLA.

It was growing dark when we arrived at the forum, where
we saw a great quantity of things for sale, of no extraordinary
value it is true, but such as had need of being hawked about
under cover of the dark, as they had not been too honestly
come by. As we too had brought our stolen mantle with us,
we began to use our opportunity, and flourish the skirt of it in
a corner, to see if perchance the splendour of the garment
might tempt some purchaser.

We had not waited long before a countryman, whom I
thought I had seen before, came up to us with a little woman
in his company, and began to inspect the mantle with great attention; whilst on the other hand Ascyltos cast his eyes on the
countryman's shoulders, and was suddenly struck dumb with
astonishment.   Neither indeed could I myself look on the
man without some commotion of mind, for he seemed to be
the same who had found our tunic in the wood ; and so he
really was. But Ascyltos, doubting whether he should trust
his own eyes, and that he might do nothing rashly, first went
up to the man as a buyer, took the tunic off his shoulders, and
began to scrutinize it minutely. Oh wonderful caprice of fortune! The countryman had not yet had the curiosity to examine the seams, and he even offered it for sale with contemptuous indifference as a beggarly thing.

As soon as Ascyltos saw that the money we had hidden in
the lining was untouched, and that the seller was a person of
no consequence, he took me aside, and said : " Do you know,
brother, that the treasure I was lamenting is come back to us ?
There is our tunic to all appearance still full of gold pieces.
What shall we do then, or how shall we get our own again ?"

My spirits being greatly raised, not only because I had caught
sight again of our booty, but also because Fortune had cleared
me from a very ugly suspicion, I was by no means for going
about the bush, but straightway bringing an action against
the fellow, so that if he refused to give up what did not be-

long to him to the right owner, he should be compelled to do so by law. Ascyltos, on the other hand, was afraid of the law. "Who," said he, "knows us in this place, or will give any credit to what we say? I am decidedly for buying it, though we know it to be our own, and recovering the treasure with a little money, rather 'than embroil ourselves in an uncertain suit.

"What worth are laws where gold alone is strong,
 Where to be poor is to be in the wrong?
 Cynics themselves, heroes in abstinence,
 Like now and then to sell their eloquence.
 Justice is marketable ware, you buy it,
 And have your right confirmed by judge's fiat."

But all the money we had was only two small pieces, with which we intended to buy some pulse. Lest, therefore, the prey should escape us in the mean time, we agreed to sell the mantle at a lower price, that the advantage we got by the one might make amends for what we lost by the other.

Accordingly we spread out our merchandise, when the woman, who stood muffled by the countryman, having closely observed some marks upon it, seized it with both hands, and cried out with all her might, Thieves, thieves!

We were very much disconcerted by this occurrence, but that we might not appear to admit our guilt if we did nothing, we laid hold of the dirty, tattered tunic, and as spitefully bawled out that it was ours, and that they had robbed us of it. But our case was in no wise like theirs; and the crowd that gathered upon the outcry, made fun of us and our claim, and naturally enough, because the other asserted their right to a rich mantle, and we to an old rag scarce worth a good patch. But Ascyltos cleverly put a stop to the laughter, when, after silence had been obtained, he cried out, "Every one, we see, likes his own best. Give us our tunic, and let them take the mantle."

The countryman and the woman were very well satisfied with the exchange; but certain lawyers, who were in fact a sort of night-prowlers, having a mind to turn the mantle to their own profit, importunately required that both mantle and tunic should be left in their hands, and that the cause should

come before the judge on the morrow; for it was not alone
the ownership of things in question that should be inquired
into, but quite another matter, namely, a strong suspicion of
robbery on both sides.

At last the opinion of the by-standers was in favour of the
sequestration, when a fellow with a bald pate, and a most
pimply face, a sort of touter for the lawyers,[1] laid hold of the
mantle, declaring that he would be security it should be forth-
coming at the time of trial. But it was manifest he had no
other intention than that, having once got it into his knavish
hands, he might smuggle it away, as it was not likely we
would ever come to own it for fear of the consequences. For
our part we were quite as willing as he, and chance befriended
both of us : for the countryman, disgusted at our insisting on
the formal surrender of an old rag, threw the tunic at Ascyltos's head, discharging us of all claims except as to the mantle,
which he required to be secured as the only subject of litiga-
tion. Having therefore recovered our treasure, as we thought,
we hurried away to our inn, and having bolted our door, we
made ourselves merry at the acuteness both of the mob and
of our accusers, who had with so much cleverness and circumspection given us back our money.

[While we were ripping the tunic and taking out the gold, we over-
heard some one asking the innkeeper, what kind of people those were
that had just now come in.   Being startled at the question, I went down,
after the inquirer was gone, to see what was the matter, and learned
that a Prætor's lictor, whose office it was to see that the names of all
strangers were entered in the public registers, had seen a couple enter
the inn, whose names he had not yet taken down, and therefore inquired
of what country they were, and what was their way of living.

The innkeeper told me this in so off-hand a manner as to make me
suspect we were not safe there; so for fear of being taken up, we thought
it best to go out for the present, and not return again till late at night,
but leave the care of our supper to Giton's management.

Our intention being to keep out of the main streets, we made for that
quarter of the city in which we were likely to meet least company; and

---

[1] *A sort of touter for the lawyers.*]   Qui solebat aliquando et ad causas
agere.   The advocate and orator was said agere causas; but agere *ad*
causas was to exercise functions analogous to those of the modern attor-
ney.   The word *aliquando* implies that the person here spoken of was
not a regular practitioner.

there in a by-place we saw two handsome matronly-looking[1] women, and followed them softly to a small temple, which they entered, and whence we heard an odd humming noise, as though it were voices issuing from the interior of a cave. Curiosity impelled us to go in after them; and we saw a great number of women like Bacchants, each holding a lusty emblem of Priapus in her hand. More we were not allowed to see, for no sooner were they aware of our presence than they set up such a shout, as made the roof of the temple[2] shake again, and rushed at us to seize us; but we took to our heels, and ran as fast as we could to our inn.]

We had scarcely despatched the supper which Giton had provided for us, when we were startled by an unusually loud knocking at the door. We turned pale, and asked who was there? "Open the door and you will see," was the answer. While we were talking the bolt dropped off, the door flew open, and a woman with her head veiled came in, the very same who a little before had been with the countryman in the market. "What," said she, "did you think to make a fool of me? I am the servant of Quartilla, whose service at the shrine you disturbed. She is just at hand, and desires to speak with you. Do not be alarmed. She neither denounces your fault, nor wishes to punish it; nay, she rather wonders what god has brought such well-bred youths into her neighbourhood."

We remained silent and knew not what to think of all this, when in came the mistress herself attended by a young girl,

[1] *Matronly-looking women.*] Mulieres stolatas : literally women dressed in stoles. The stola was the characteristic dress of the Roman matrons, as the toga was of the Roman men. Hence the meretrices were not allowed to wear it, but only a dark-coloured toga, and accordingly Horace (Sat. i. 2, 63) speaks of the matrona in contradistinction to the togata. The stola was worn over the tunic, came as low as the ankles or feet, and was fastened round the body by a girdle, leaving broad folds above the breast. The tunic did not reach much below the knee; but the essential difference between the tunic and stola seems to have been, that the latter had always an instita or flounce sewed to the bottom and reaching to the instep.

[2] *The roof of the temple.*] Templi camera. The place in question was called some lines back sacellum, a word which is not synonymous with templum, but means a sacred enclosure, surrounded by a fence or wall, and containing an altar, sometimes also a statue of the god to whom it was dedicated. Festus expressly states that a sacellum never had a roof. If that assertion is correct, it follows either that Petronius blundered strangely in the use of two very common words, or that the passage before us, which belongs to the so-called Belgrade discovery, is not genuine.

and sitting down on my bed, fell a weeping for some time. Still we said not a word, but stood watching in astonishment this extraordinary display of factitious sorrow. When the big shower was over, she turned back her hood, displayed a stern countenance, and wringing her hands till the joints cracked, "What impudence," she said, "is this? Where learned you these shams, and that slight of hand you have lately been beholden to? In good faith I am sorry for you; for no one ever beheld with impunity what it was unlawful for him to look upon; and truly our part of the world has in it so many present deities, that you may more easily meet with a god than a man. But do not think I am come with any vindictive purpose; I am rather affected with compassion for your youth than angry at the affront you have put upon me; for I still think it was in pure ignorance you committed a sacrilegious crime.

"Last night I was seized with such a perilous shaking fit that I was afraid I had got a tertian ague; wherefore in my sleep I prayed for a cure, and I was commanded to go in search of you, that you might allay the violence of my disorder by the contrivance indicated to me. But it is not the cure I am so much concerned about; the thought that anguishes me to death is, lest in youthful levity you declare what you saw in the temple of Priapus, and disclose the mysteries of the gods among the vulgar. I therefore stretch forth my suppliant hands to your knees, and beg and beseech you not to make a jest and a mock of our nocturnal rites, nor to divulge things which have been kept secret for so many years, and which are not thoroughly known to every one even among our mystics."

After this deprecatory harangue, she burst again into tears, and sobbing violently threw herself on her face upon my bed. Thereupon, moved at the same time by pity and fear, I bade her take courage, and assured her that we would never open our lips about those holy mysteries, and that moreover, if her god had indicated any other means of curing her fever, we would second the intentions of divine providence at any risk to ourselves.

Cheering up at this promise of mine, the woman fell to kissing me thick and three-fold, and passing from tears to laughter, she combed back some hairs that hung over my cheeks with her fingers. "I make a truce with you," she said, "and withdraw my plaint against you. But had you not complied with respect to that cure I required at your hands, I had plenty of persons in readiness for to-morrow, who would have avenged my honour and the affront you put upon me.

> "Contempt is loathsome; glorious 'tis to sway
> Obedient minds; I love to have my way.
> The wise themselves will oft resent an ill;
> But they are victors most who spare to kill."

Then clapping her hands together, she suddenly broke out into such a violent fit of laughter that she alarmed us; so did the woman who had come in first; so did the girl who accompanied Quartilla; while we, who saw no cause for so sudden a change, stood amazed, and stared now upon each other, and now upon the women.

At last Quartilla said, I have given orders that no mortal be permitted to come into this inn to-day, that I may receive from you the remedy for my ague without interruption.

Ascyltos was somewhat astounded at this declaration, and as for me, I turned colder than a Gallic winter, and had not power to utter a word. But I ceased to fear much when I considered the strength of the party; for they were but three women, quite too weak to effect anything against us, who, if we had nothing more of man about us, had at least the advantage of being of the manly sex. We were all well prepared for the event; and I had so contrived the couples, that if it came to a fray, I was to grapple with Quartilla, Ascyltos with her woman, and Giton with the girl.

[While I was thus contriving the matter, Quartilla came up to me that I might cure her of her ague; but finding herself disappointed, she flew out in a passion, and returning soon after, she had us seized by some unknown persons, and forcibly conveyed into a magnificent palace.]

CHAPTER IV.

LEWD ORGIES IN QUARTILLA'S HOUSE—NUPTIALS OF GITON AND PANNYCHIS.

Now indeed our courage quite failed us, and nothing but certain death stared us miserably in the face. So I said to Quartilla, If you intend to do your worst by us, madam, pray despatch us quickly, for we have not done anything so heinous as to deserve that we should be racked to death. Thereupon the maid-servant, whose name was Psyche, spread a carpet on the floor, and tried to put me on my mettle; but it was lost labour; I was as cold as a thousand deaths could make me.[1] Ascyltos had muffled his head in his mantle, as having had a warning that it was a dangerous thing to meddle with other people's secrets. Meanwhile Psyche drew out two ribbons from her bosom, and bound my hands with one of them and my feet with the other.

[Finding myself thus manacled and fettered, This is not the way, said I, to enable me to cure your mistress's ague. "I know that," she answered, "but I have other and surer medicaments at hand:" saying which she handed me a cup full of satyrion, and so merrily did she run on in praise of its wonderful virtues, that she induced me to drink up almost the whole of it; but because Ascyltos had lately slighted her advances, she threw what was left of it upon his back without his perceiving it.]

"What!" said Ascyltos, when this pleasant chat was over, "am I not worthy to get a sup?" Psyche, betrayed by my laughter, clapped her hands and cried, "I have given it you, my lad; you have drunk up the whole potion to your own share."

"Is it so?" said Quartilla, shaking her sides with not ungraceful laughter. "Has Encolpius drunk up all the satyrion we had?" At last not even Giton could abstain from laughing, especially when the little girl had thrown her arms round his neck, and given him a multitude of kisses, to which he showed no repugnance.

We would fain have cried out, but there was no one to help us in our distress; moreover Psyche pricked my cheeks with

[1] Sollicitavit inguina mea mille jam mortibus frigida.

her hair-pin whenever I seemed disposed to invoke the aid of the public, whilst the little girl persecuted Ascyltos with a sponge which she had dipped in satyrion. Lastly, in came an obscene buffoon, dressed in a myrtle-coloured robe, with a belt round his middle, who at one time nearly worried the life out of us;[1] until Quartilla, holding her whalebone wand in her hand, and with her robe tucked up, made a sign to give us quarter. Then each of us took a most solemn oath that so horrible a secret should die with us.

After this a great number of wrestlers came in, and rubbed us all over with stimulating oil, until, being somewhat recruited after our fatigues, we put on dinner dresses, and were shown into the next room, where three couches were laid, and all the other appurtenances of a repast in the most sumptuous style. We took our places as we were invited; the banquet opened with a marvellous first course, and we were abundantly treated with Falernian wine. Several other courses having followed, when we began to nod, "What?" said Quartilla, "do you think of sleeping, when you know that this whole live-long night is due to the worship of Priapus?"

Ascyltos, however, being unable to keep awake after all he had undergone, Psyche, whom he had so cruelly scorned, smeared all his face with lampblack, as he lay unconscious, and charcoaled his lips and his shoulders.

I too, being worn out by the persecutions I had suffered, had just begun as it were to sip the sweets of repose; all the household too, within doors and without, had done the same; some lay up and down at our feet, some leaned against a wall, and some lay head to head fast asleep on the threshold. The oil in the lamps having burnt low, they gave a weak and glimmering light, when two Syrian slaves crept into the banquet room to steal a jar of wine. But while they were scuffling among the dinner utensils and snatching the jar one from the other, it broke in two, and threw down the table with all the plate upon it; at the same time also a cup falling from some height on Psyche's bed as she lay asleep, cut her head open.

---

[1] Ultimo cinœdus supervenit myrthea subornatus gausapina, cinguloque succinctus, modo extortis nos clunibus cecidit, modo basiis olidissimis inquinavit.

Starting up at the blow she screamed aloud, thereby discovering the thieves, and waking some of the drunkards. The Syrians seeing themselves caught in the fact, threw themselves down beside one of the couches, and began to snore as if they had been a long while asleep.

The butler having by this time woke up, put more oil into the dying lamps, and the attendants having rubbed their eyes returned to their business, when in came a woman who played on the cymbals,[1] and roused us all with her tinkling. The banquet was therefore renewed, and Quartilla again challenged us to drink; whilst the cymbal-player put still more animation into the revellers.

Presently appeared an obscene rascal, the most witless of all buffoons, and one quite worthy of that house, who, clapping his hands together, spouted the following verses :

> All who love uncurb'd delight,
> Delian eunuchs,[2] young or old,
> Hither wing your sportive flight,
> Here your wanton arts unfold.[3]

Having done with his poetry, he smeared my lips with loathsome kisses; then getting on the couch he brayed and kneaded me with all his might.[4] Streams of sweat mingled with paint as thick as gum poured down his forehead and face, the wrinkles of which were so stuffed with plaster as to look like

---

[1] *A woman who played on the cymbals.*] The cymbal was a very ancient instrument, being used in the worship of Cybele, Bacchus, Juno, and all the earlier deities of the Grecian and Roman mythology. It probably came from the East. Among the Jews it appears to have been in common use. Several kinds of cymbals are represented on ancient monuments. The most usual form was that of two hollow half globes, either with transverse handles, or with cylindrical stems running off from their convexities.

[2] *Delian eunuchs.*] The inhabitants of the island of Delos were very expert in the practice of castration; and it appears from Cicero (*pro Cornelio*) that they carried on an extensive export trade in eunuchs.

[3] Huc huc convenite nunc spatalocinædi,
Pede tendite, cursum addite, convolate planta,
Femore facili, clune agili, et manu procace,
Molles, veteres, Deliaci manu recisi.

[4] Mox et super lectum venit, atque omni vi detexit recusantes. Super inguina mea diu multumque frustra moluit.

a naked wall washed by rain. I could no longer restrain my tears, but vexed beyond endurance, I beseech you, madam, I cried, is this the embasicete you promised I should have?

"O the witty man," she exclaimed, gently clapping her hands; "how clever you are! Do you not know that a fellow of this kind is called an embasicete?"[1]

Thereupon, that my comrade might not fare better than myself, said I to her, But I put it to your conscience, shall Ascyltos alone keep holiday here?

"Is it so?" said she. "Let Ascyltos have his share too." At the word my incubus quitted me for my companion, and nearly pounded him to a jelly.[2] Giton stood laughing all the while as if his sides would split. Quartilla took notice of him, and asked with much curiosity whose boy he was. When I told her he was my favourite. "Why then," said she, "has he not kissed me?" And calling him to her she began to kiss him; then putting her hand under his robe, and taking hold of what he hardly knew the use of, "This," said she, "will be well enough by way of a whet for me to-morrow; for to-day I am not inclined to put the beggar over the gentleman."[3]

As she said this, Psyche went up to her laughing, and whispered something in her ear. "Right, right," said Quartilla, "that was well thought of. Why should not our Pannychis lose her maidenhead? There can never be a finer opportunity." Immediately there was brought in a pretty little girl, apparently not more than seven years old, the same that had accompanied Quartilla to our inn. All present applauded the proposal, and in compliance with their eager demands the nuptial proceedings began.

---

[1] *Do you not know, &c.*] Quid tu non intellexeras cinœdum embasicœtam vocari? The joke consists in the double meaning of the word *embasicœtas*, which is properly a cup on getting into bed, (εμβασις κοιτης,) what we call familiarly "a nightcap," but may also signify one who mounts upon a bed, one who *perambulabit omnium cubilia*, as Catullus says.

[2] Ab hac voce equum cinœdus mutavit, transituque ad comitem meum facto, clunibus, eum basiisque distrivit.

[3] *Put the beggar over the gentleman.*] Post asellum diaria non sumo: literally, I will not partake of ordinary fare after choice fish. Here again there is a play of words. Asellus (jackass) was the name of a fish greatly esteemed by Roman epicures; it was also a common term for designating a *homo bene vasatus, asini instar.*

I was quite amazed, and protested that an innocent lad like
Giton was incapable of playing a part in such an obscene exhibition, and that Pannychis was not of an age to endure
what a bride must submit to.

" Why," said Quartilla, " is she younger than I was when
I began ?   May my Juno confound me,[1] if I can remember
that I ever was a maid ; for when I was a child I played
with boys of my own age, and afterwards with bigger and
bigger ones as my years increased, until I reached my present age.   Hence, I believe, comes the proverb, She will bear
him a bull who bore him a calf."[2]

Lest, therefore, Giton should run a great hazard in my
absence, I also got up to assist at the wedding.

Psyche had already covered the girl's head with the nuptial
veil ;[3] the embasicete led the way with a torch ; a long train
of drunken women followed, clapping their hands, having previously strewed the nuptial couch.   Then Quartilla, fired by
the wanton spectacle, caught hold of Giton, and dragged him
into the bed-chamber ; but indeed the boy was not loth to go,
nor did the girl seem frightened at the name of matrimony.
As soon then as they were in bed, and the door shut on them,
we stole softly to it, and first of all Quartilla put her eye to a
slit made on purpose, and watched their childish dalliance
with libidinous curiosity.   She also drew me gently to her to
share her enjoyment of the scene ; and as our faces met, she

[1] *May my Juno confound me.*]   The Juno here appealed to is to be
understood as the feminine of Genius.   The latter was the tutelary god
assigned to every man at his birth, a divine soul, as it were, attached to
his mortal existence ; the corresponding deity peculiar to the other sex
was called the Juno of this or that woman.—Burns, who was certainly not
a reader of Petronius, puts into the mouth of one of his Jolly Beggars an
avowal exactly like Quartilla's :

> I once was a maid, but I cannot tell when,
> And all my delight is in proper young men.
> Some one of a troop of dragoons was my daddie ;
> No wonder I'm fond of a sodger laddie.

[2] *She will bear him a bull,* &c.]   An allusion to the feat performed by
Milo of Crotona, who carried a two-year-old bull a furlong at the Olympic
games, and then killed him with his fist.   He had begun by carrying the
animal when it was a calf, and had continued the practice daily up to the
time of his grand exhibition.

[3] *The nuptial veil.*]   The *flammeum*, which was of a bright saffron or
flame colour, designed to conceal the blushes of the bride.   The torch
was an invariable accompaniment of the marriage procession.

every now and then snatched an open-mouthed kiss, as if by
stealth, when she was not occupied in peeping.[1]

[1] In the year 1800, there was published at Strasburg a pretended fragment of Petronius, said to have been found in the abbey of St. Gall, and
purporting to supply what was wanting in the text of the previous editions
at this place.   It was one of the ablest literary forgeries ever perpetrated.
So well was the style of the original imitated as to deceive all the critics,
until the hoax was confessed by its author, a Spaniard named Marchena.
His pamphlet being now very rare, we will gratify the reader's curiosity
by a reprint of the supposititious text.

FRAGMENTUM PETRONII.

Hæc dum fiunt, ingenti sono fores repente perstrepunt, omnibusque,
quid tam inopinus sonitus esset, mirantibus, militem, ex excubiis noc-
turnis unum, districto gladio, adolescentorumque turba stipatum, con-
spicimus.   Trucibus ille oculis ac Thrasonico gestu omnia circumspici-
ebat; tandem Quartillam intuens: Quid id est, inquit, mulier impudis-
sima?   Falsis me pollicitationibus ludis, nocteque promissa fraudas? At
non impune feres, tuque amatorque iste tuus me esse hominem intel-
ligetis.

Dicto audientes militis comites me Quartillamque adligant, os ori,
pectori pectus, femur denique femori applicantes, nec sine magno risu.
Embasicœtas autem, jussu militis, olidi oris fœdissimis osculis totum me
miserum conspurcabat; quæ nec effugere, nec ullo modo vitare valebam.
Constupravit tandem et gaudium integrum hausit.   Interim satyrico,
quod paulo ante ebiberam, omnes in venerem nervos intendente, Quartillam valenter permolere cœpi, nec illa, libidine accensa, ludo gravabatur.
Solvebantur in risum juvenes, jocosa scena permoti; namque a turpis-
simo cinædo subactus, ingratiis ac pene inscius, quam creberrime cevebam
quum Quartilla crissaret.

Pannychis interea, utpote nec veneri matura, clamorem intendit,
milesque ad repentinam lamentationem animum advertit.   Devirgini-
batur enim tenerrima puella, victorque Giton haud incruenta spolia re-
tulerat.   Quo spectaculo miles permotus impetum vi facit; arctissimis-
que amplexibus nunc Pannychida, nunc Gitona, nunc simul ambos per-
stringebat.   Effusa in fletum virgo ætati ut parceret, obsecrabatur; sed
nihil preces proficiebant, furebatque miles in venerem immaturam.
Operuit ergo Pannychis caput, quidquid fata portenderent passura.

Tunc vero anus, illa ipsa quæ dudum me domicilium quærentem luse-
rat, velut a cœlo demissa miseræ Pannychidi auxilio fuit.   Magnis illa
clamoribus domum intrat, vicum proximum pererrare, prædones autu-
mat; frustra cives Quiritium fidem implorare, nec vigilum excubias, aut
somno sopitas, aut commessationibus intentas, præsto esse.   Hic miles

[I was so tired of Quartilla's fulsomeness that I thought of making my escape. I communicated my design to Ascyltos, who was well pleased with it, for he wanted to be rid of Psyche's importunity. The thing might easily have been done, had not Giton been shut up in the chamber; for we were resolved to take him with us, and not leave him at the mercy of those lustful strumpets. While we were anxiously pondering the matter, Pannychis fell out of bed, dragging Giton after her. He was not hurt, but the girl having slightly bruised her head, set up such a squalling, that Quartilla rushed in a fright into the room, leaving us free to escape; and without losing a moment we flew to our inn, where] jumping at once into bed, we passed the rest of the night without fear.

[When we went abroad the next day we fell in with two of the fellows who had carried us off by Quartilla's orders. The moment Ascyltos set eyes on them, he briskly attacked one of them, and having disabled him, came to my aid against the other, who defended himself so vigorously, that he wounded us both, though but slightly, and got off himself unhurt.]

CHAPTER V.

TRIMALCHIO'S BANQUET—THE PRELIMINARIES—TRIMALCHIO'S HOUSE—
THE STEWARD AND THE DELINQUENT SLAVE—THE GUSTATIO OR FIRST
COURSE.

It was now the third day, specified in the invitation we had received to Trimalchio's free banquet;[1] but as we had re-

---

graviter commotus, præcipitanter se ex Quartillæ domo abduxit; eum insecuti comites Pannychida impendente periculo, nos omnes metu liberarunt.

[1] *Free banquet.*] Libera cœna: the meaning of the phrase has been purposely left as undetermined in the translation as it is in the original. It has been variously interpreted, as signifying, 1. a banquet at which there was no *magister* or chairman; 2. one in which the guests were to be without restraint, a free and easy entertainment; 3. or to which persons of all sorts were to be admitted; 4. in which the company was to consist chiefly of freed-men; 5. or at which slaves were to receive their freedom; 6. or at which even slaves were to be free for the nonce as guests. The phrase is applicable in any one of these senses to the narrative which follows.

ceived some wounds, we thought it more advisable to abscond than to remain where we were. Therefore [we hurried to our inn, went to bed, and as our wounds were trifling, we dressed them with wine and oil.

One of our rogues however had been left on the ground, and we were afraid of a discovery.] While then we were anxiously pondering how to get out of this scrape, we were startled by the sudden entrance of Agamemnon's servant. "What," said he, "do you not know who gives an entertainment to-day? It is Trimalchio,[1] a most sumptuous man; he has a time-piece[2] in his banqueting-room, and a trumpeter on purpose to let him know from time to time how much of his span of life has gone by." So we dressed in haste, forgetting all our troubles, and told Giton, who had hitherto very willingly acted the part of a servant, to follow us to the bath.

[1] *Trimalchio.*] A name of Greek etymology, signifying trebly voluptuous.

[2] *A time-piece.*] The Greeks and Romans measured the lapse of time either by the length or the position of the sun's shadow, as ascertained by a gnomon or by a sun-dial, or by the flow of water. The instrument commonly used for the latter purpose was called a clepsydra, and was analogous in principle to our modern hour-glasses, only it was filled with water instead of sand. It seems at first to have been used only for measuring the length of time during which persons were allowed to speak in the courts of justice, and not to have been made of any transparent material, but of bronze or brass, so that it could not be seen in the clepsydra itself what quantity of water had escaped. Such an instrument was not, properly speaking, a horologium; but smaller ones made of glass were used very early in families for the purposes of ordinary life, and for dividing the day into twelve equal parts. These, however, did not show the time quite correctly all the year round; first, because the water ran out faster or slower according to variations of temperature; and secondly, because the length of the hours varied in different seasons of the year. Recourse was had to many contrivances for remedying these defects; but all such improvements on the old clepsydra were excelled by the ingenious invention of Ctesibius, a celebrated mathematician of Alexandria (about 135 B. C.). It was called a hydraulic horologe, and is described by Vitruvius (ix. 9). Water was made to drop upon wheels, which were thereby turned. Their regular movement was communicated to a small statue, which gradually rising pointed with a little stick to the hours marked on a pillar which was attached to the mechanism. It indicated the hours regularly throughout the year, but still required to be often attended to and regulated. This complicated and costly kind of horologe is no doubt the one spoken of in the text. It seems never to have come into general use, and was probably found only in the houses of very wealthy people. See Smith's Dict. Gr. and Rom. Antiq., art. *Horologium.*

We meanwhile, dressed in banqueting costume, began to stray about, or rather to amuse ourselves as we loitered near the groups of ball-players; and there we observed a bald-pated man, in a russet tunic, at play among a group of long-haired boys.[1] But our attention was not so much attracted by the boys, though they were well worth our notice, as by the master of the house himself, who was playing in sandals,[2] with green balls. He never touched one again after it had fallen to the ground ; but a servant stood near with a bag full of balls, with which he supplied the players.

We also remarked other curious things. There were two eunuchs standing opposite each other, one of whom held a silver urinal, and the other counted the balls ; not those which the players were tossing to and fro, but those which fell on the ground.[3]

Whilst we were admiring these refinements, Menelaus came up to us and said, " This is the person with whom you are to dine ;[4] and indeed what you now see is the prelude to your entertainment."

He was yet speaking, when Trimalchio, like a very magnificent man as he was, snapped his fingers, at which sign the eunuch held the urinal to him as he played ; then calling for water to wash his hands, he just dipped his fingers into it and dried them on the boy's hair.

It would have taken too long to note every particular ; so we entered the bath, and from the sweating room we passed

[1] *Long-haired boys.*] To wear the hair long was, in the male sex, a token of the vilest depravity. St. Ambrose quotes a proverb to this effect: Nullus comatus qui non idem cinædus.

[2] *Playing in sandals.*] *Soleatus :* this was one of Trimalchio's endless eccentricities. Among the better classes the use of the solea or sandal was confined to the house or the bath. According to Aulus Gellius, it was indecorous to appear in public in such foot-gear.

[3] *Counted the balls, not those which,* &c.] There were several kinds of ball play in use among the Romans, most of which seem to have consisted in various modes of throwing and catching. The most favourite game was the *trigon,* or pila trigonalis, which was played by three persons standing in the form of a triangle. Another, as represented in a painting in the baths of Titus, in which four players are engaged in throwing and catching six balls.

[4] *You are to dine.*] Literally, you are to plant your elbow, which is equivalent to the slang phrase, to put one's feet under a man's mahogany. The Romans reclined at meals, resting on their left elbows, with their heads to the table, their feet pointing from it.

at once all reeking into the chilling room.[1]   As for Trimalchio, after being sluiced with perfumes he was rubbed dry, not with towels, but with blankets of the softest and finest wool.   Meanwhile three bath doctors[2] were drinking Falernian in his presence ; and as they brawled and spilled a good deal, Trimalchio told them it was the same wine he drank himself. Then they wrapped him in a scarlet mohair mantle,[3] and put him into a litter, preceded by four richly bedizened footmen and a wheeled chair,[4] in which sat his favourite, a withered, blear-eyed eunuch, uglier than his master.   As Trimalchio was borne along, a musician walked beside him with two very small flutes, and bending forward as if to whisper in his ear, he kept playing all the way.   Satiated with wonder, we followed, and arrived with Agamemnon at the gate, on one of the pillars of which hung a tablet with this inscription :

ANY SLAVE
WHO SHALL GO OUT OF DOORS WITHOUT HIS MASTER'S LEAVE,
SHALL RECEIVE
ONE HUNDRED LASHES.

At the entrance stood the porter dressed in green, with a cherry-coloured sash, and engaged in picking peas in a silver dish ; and over the door, in a golden cage, hung a particoloured magpie, who saluted the company as they entered. But while I was staring open-mouthed at all I saw before, I

---

[1] *The sweating room*, &c.] The Roman baths were like those which are in use at this day all over the East, and contained several chambers, in some of which the bather was exposed to vapour of moderate temperature, (*tepidarium*,) or very hot, (*calidarium*,) and in others (*frigidarium*) he was dashed with cold water.

[2] *Bath doctors*.] Iatraliptæ. This was a class of men superior to the aliptæ, or anointers, who were merely bath attendants; the iatraliptæ, on the other hand, professed to be physicians, as their name implies; but they were generally quacks, who had promoted themselves from the lower grade of their calling, like some of the self-dubbed doctors of our own day, who began their career as bath-men at some of the water-cure establishments.

[3] *A mohair mantle*.] Gausapa : this was a kind of thick cloth with very long wool on one side.

[4] *A wheeled chair*.] Cheiramaxio : this has been erroneously translated sedan chair, the Latin name for which is sella gestatoria. The cheiramaxium corresponded to our invalid chair, for it went on wheels, and was moved by men instead of animals.

had liked to have fallen backwards and broken my legs.   For
to the left as we entered, not far from the porter's lodge, an
enormous chained dog was painted on the wall, with an inscription over it in capital letters : BEWARE OF THE DOG.[1]
My companions laughed heartily; but my fright was soon
over, and I continued to examine all the frescoes on the wall.
There was a market of slaves with labels hung from their
necks ; and Trimalchio himself, with long hair, a caduceus in
his hand, and led by Minerva, was making his entry into
Rome.   In another place was shown how he had learned to
keep accounts, and how he had come to be made steward;
and the painter, like an exact man, had been careful to explain
everything by legends.   At the end of the portico Mercury
was lifting up the hero by the chin, and placing him aloft on
a tribunal.   Fortune stood by with her cornucopia, and the
three Fates spinning a golden thread.

I noticed also in the portico a troop of running footmen exercising under the directions of a master.   I saw besides, a
large *console* in a corner, and in it a shrine, in which were
deposited lares of silver, a marble Venus, and a golden casket,
no small one either, in which they told us were preserved the
first shavings of Trimalchio's beard.[2]

I asked the hall-keeper[3] what were the paintings in the
middle of the portico.   The Iliad and Odyssey, he replied,
and the combats of gladiators given under Lænas.

We had no time to examine further, being now arrived at

---

[1] *Beware the dog.*]   A similar painting and inscription have been found
among the ruins at Pompeii.

[2] *The first shavings of Trimalchio's beard.*]   Many commentators see in
this trait a pointed allusion to the fact recorded by Suetonius, that Nero put
up his first beard in a gold box set with pearls and dedicated to Jupiter
Capitolinus.   But this is a groundless assumption; for the practice of
dedicating the first-fruits of the manly chin to some god was common to
all the Romans from the time when the custom of shaving was first introduced among them.   Nor was Nero the only Roman who enclosed the
offering in so costly a case.   Statius, for instance, (*Praf ad Silv.* iii.,)
mentions a person who sent his hair as an offering to Æsculapius Per-
gamenus, and requested Statius to write some dedicatory verses on the
occasion.   He sent the hair with a box set with precious stones (cum
gemmata pyxide) and a mirror.

[3] *The hall-keeper.*]   Atriensem.   This was one of the principal domestics whose business it was to take care of the atrium and its valuable contents.

the banqueting hall, at the entrance of which sat the steward receiving accounts. But what struck me most was to see the door-posts adorned with rods and axes, resting as it were on the brazen prow of a ship, whereon was inscribed,

TO GAIUS POMPEIUS TRIMALCHIO
AN AUGUSTAL SEVIR,[1]
CINNAMUS HIS STEWARD.

Below this inscription a lamp with two branches was suspended from the ceiling, and two tablets were fixed, one on either side of the door: one of these, if I remember rightly, bore this inscription,

ON THE THIRTIETH AND THIRTY-FIRST DAY OF DECEMBER
OUR PATRON GAIUS SUPS ABROAD.

On the other was represented the course of the moon and the seven stars; and what days were lucky, what unlucky, with an embossed stud to distinguish the one from the other.

When we had seen enough of these fine things we were about to enter the banqueting room, when one of the servants, placed there for the purpose, cried out, RIGHT FOOT FOREMOST![2] Truly we were somewhat fluttered lest any of us should transgress the rule; however, just as we were all stepping out together in proper order, a stripped slave threw himself at our feet, entreating us to intercede for him, and save him from punishment; his fault was no great one; it was

---

[1] *An augustal sevir.*] The Augustales were an order of priests in the municipia, whose duty it was to attend to the religious rites belonging to the Lares and Penates, which Augustus put up in places where two or more ways met. The Augustales were selected from the libertini, and in most municipia they formed a kind of corporation, of which the first six in importance had the title of seviri. The office, which was called augustalitas, was looked upon as honourable, and was much sought after by the more wealthy libertini; and it appears that the decuriones in the municipia were accustomed to sell the dignity, since special mention is made of instances in which it was conferred gratuitously, in consideration of benefits conferred on the town.

[2] *Right foot foremost.*] The Romans were most solicitous to avoid the ill omen of passing through a door with the left foot in advance. For this reason Vitruvius (iii. 4) lays it down as a rule, that the steps leading into a temple should always be of an uneven number, because the worshipper, after placing his right foot on the bottom step, would then place the same foot on the threshold also.

only that some of the steward's clothes, hardly worth ten sesterces, had been stolen from him at the bath.[1]

Facing about, therefore, still right foot foremost, we went up to the steward, who was counting gold in his office, and besought him to pardon the slave. Looking up haughtily he replied, "It is not so much the loss which frets me, as the negligence of the rascal. He has lost me the garments I used to wear at table, which a client of mine presented me with on my birth-day. They were of the right Tyrian dye, I assure you, though but once dipped. However, I forgive the offender at your request."

Deeply sensible of this great favour, we went back to the banqueting room, where we were met by the same slave for whom we had interceded, who astonished us with a multitude of kisses and thanks for our kindness. "In fine," said he, "you shall presently know whom you have obliged. The master's favourite wine is the servant's thanks-offering."

At last we took our places. Egyptian boys poured snow-water on our hands; after them came others, who with great dexterity picked our toe-nails;[2] nor were they silent during this unpleasant office, but sang all the while. I had a mind to try if all the household were vocalists, and therefore called for wine : up came a boy on the instant and handed it to me with the same falsetto trilling: call for what you would it was always the same; so that you would rather have taken them for a company of pantomimists than the servants of a man of good station.

A magnificent first course[3] was served up, for we were all reclined except Trimalchio, for whom, after a new fashion, the

---

[1] *Stolen from him at the bath.*] Passages abound in the classics showing that the public baths were greatly infested with thieves, who made booty of the bathers' clothes.

[2] *Picked our toe-nails.*] It was usual to lie barefoot at table. When a man went out to dinner he walked in shoes (calceus), taking with him slippers (soccus) or sandals (solea), which he put on when he entered the house. Before reclining at table these were taken away by a servant.

[3] *A magnificent first course.*] This was the *promulsis* or *antecœna*, here called *gustatio ;* it was usually made up of all sorts of things which were deemed provocative of appetite. Eggs too were so indispensable to the first course, that they almost gave a name to it (*ab ovo usque ad mala*). In the present instance we find the promulsis served up in a sort of epergne called a promulsidary.

chief place[1] was reserved. On the promulsidary stood an ass in Corinthian metal, with two panniers containing olives, white on one side, black on the other; and flanked by two silver dishes,[2] on the borders of which was engraved Trimalchio's name with the weight of metal in each. There were also little salvers in the shape of bridges, on which were laid dormice[3] strewed over with honey and poppy seed; and smoking-hot sausages on a silver gridiron, beneath which [by way of black and live coals] lay damsons and pomegranate grains.

We were in the midst of these dainties when Trimalchio himself was ushered in with a flourish of music, and was bolstered up on his couch with a number of little pillows, which set some indiscreet persons among us a-laughing. And well they might, for his shaven pate poked out of a scarlet mantle, which loaded his neck, and over the mantle he had put a napkin adorned with a laticlave,[4] with fringes that hung on

[1] *The chief place.*] A triclinium consisted of three beds, or couches, ranged along three sides of a quadrilateral table, and each bed accommodated three persons. The three beds, and the several places on each, were distinguished as upper, middle, and lower, (*summus, medius, imus,*) and differed much in point of rank. The middle couch was the most honourable, then the *summus*, which was to the left of the medius, and last the *imus*, which was to the right. The *lectus*, or couch, had a railing along at one end, where lay a cushion; the rest of the places were separated by pillows. On this railing the person lay with his left arm, so that the *imus* would have had the railing next to the *medius*, whilst that of the *summus* would have been at the extreme end opposite. The most honourable place was that next to the railing, then the centre, and lastly the lowest one. But to this rule the *medius* was an exception; for on that the lowest place was first in rank, and also the seat of honour of the whole triclinium, and always left for the most important person; hence it was often called *consularis*. The host took the adjoining place, the uppermost on the *lectus imus*, in order to be as near as possible to the most distinguished guest. See Bekker's Gallus.

[2] *Flanked by two silver dishes.*] Tegebant asellum duæ lancis, i. e. latus aselli claudebant. So Statius,

    Hunc tegit Iasiusque pater, plaudusque Pheroneus.—*Heins.*

[3] *Dormice.*] These little animals are still in good repute among modern Italian epicures.

[4] *A napkin adorned with a laticlave.*] The laticlave, *clavus latus*, was a broad purple band extending down the front of the tunic, and was a distinctive badge of the senatorial order. Those who were entitled to it, would, if vain men, have their napkins adorned with it. See Martial, iv. 46, 17, Lato variata mappa clavo. Trimalchio could not have displayed his vulgar arrogance more strikingly than by the assumption of the laticlave, to which he had no more right than a retired butler has to sport a ducal coronet.

Q

either side. He had also a large gilded ring on the little
finger of his left hand, and on the last joint of the finger next
it a smaller ring that seemed of pure gold, but starred with
steel.[1]   And to let us see that these were not the whole of his
bravery, he stripped his right arm, which was adorned with a
golden bracelet, and an ivory circle fastened with a glistening
plate of gold.

Picking his teeth with a silver pin, " My friends," said he,
" I had no mind to come yet to table; but lest my absence
should keep you waiting, I deprived myself of my amusement.
You will allow me however to finish my game."

A boy followed him with a draught-board of juniper wood
and crystal dice; and I noticed one surpassing piece of
luxury, for instead of black and white pieces he had medals of
silver and gold.

Meantime, whilst he was sweeping off his adversary's pieces,
and we were still engaged with the first course, a machine was
handed in with a basket on it, in which sat a hen carved of
wood, her wings lying round and hollowed as if she was
brooding.   The musicians struck up, and two servants began
immediately to search the straw under the hen, and drawing
forth some peafowl's eggs distributed them among the guests.

At this Trimalchio turned towards us and said, " My
friends, I gave orders that this hen should be set upon peafowl's eggs, but, by Hercules, I am afraid they are half
hatched.   However, we will try if they are yet eatable."

We took our spoons, each of which weighed at least half
a pound, and began to break our paste eggs.   For my part I
had like to have thrown mine away, for it seemed to me to
have a chicken in it; but hearing an old guest say, " There
must be something good in this," I continued my search, and
found a fine fat beccafico surrounded with yolk of egg, sea-
soned with pepper.

Trimalchio having now left off his play had been helped
to everything on the table, and announced in a loud voice
that if any one wished for more honeyed wine he might have
it.   The signal was given by the music, and the first course
was removed by a company of singers; but a dish falling in

---

[1] *Pure gold starred with steel.*]   Freedmen and plebeians were not allowed to wear rings of pure gold, for these were one of the distinguishing
marks of the equestrian order.

the hurry, a servant took it up, which Trimalchio observing, boxed his ears and ordered him to throw it down again; and presently came the groom of the chambers with his broom, and swept away the silver dish with the rest of the litter.

He was followed immediately by two long-haired Ethiopians, with small leather bottles, such as are used for sprinkling the arena of the amphitheatre; and they poured wine on our hands,[1] for no one offered us water.

The master of the house, having been complimented on this piece of elegance, cried out, "Man is a lover of fair play." Then the old fellow gave orders that every man should have his own table; and, continued he, "We shall be less incommoded by heat when we are no longer crowded upon by these stinking servants."

At the same time there were brought in glass jars, close stopped with plaster, and with labels round their necks on which was written,

OPIMIAN FALERNIAN A HUNDRED YEARS OLD.[2]

Whilst we were reading the labels, Trimalchio ejaculated, "O dear! O dear! to think that wine should be longer-lived than we poor manikins. Well, since it is so let us e'en drink till we can hold no more. There's life in wine. This is genuine Opimian, you may take my word for it. I did not put so

---

[1] *Poured wine on our hands.*] The Romans, it must be remembered, ate without forks; hence the necessity for ablutions during meals; and these, we observe, were practised in the same manner as among eastern nations at the present day: the water—or in this instance the wine—was poured over the hands, a basin no doubt being placed on the floor to catch it as it fell from them.

[2] *Opimian Falernian.*] The vintage under the consulate of Opimius was singularly excellent both in quantity and quality. That epoch was to the Romans what "the year of the comet" is to connoisseurs in Burgundy. The addition, "a hundred years old," is a characteristic absurdity, just as if one should talk in the year 1854 of Comet Port ten years old. Opimius was consul A. U. C. 633. Trimalchio's wine, if genuine Opimian, must have been at least 160 or 170 years old. It is also to be noticed that the jars were of glass, and this involves another anachronism, for such vessels were not in use in the time of Opimius. "The lagenæ and amphoræ were generally of clay thinly pitched. Later they were made of glass, upon which only perhaps the labels were hung, as the name was written on the earthen vessels themselves, and frequently became obliterated through age, which was a recommendation. Martial, xiii. 120.—*Bekker's Gallus.*

good on my table yesterday, and I had much more respectable
men than you to dine with me."

So we drank our wine, and mightily extolled all the fine
things set before us; when in came a servant with a silver
skeleton, so artfully put together that its joints and backbone
turned every way. Having cast it a few times on the table,
and made it assume various postures, Trimalchio cried out,

> Vain as vanity are we !
> Swift life's transient flames decay !
> What this is, we soon shall be ;
> Then be merry whilst you may.

CHAPTER VI.

TRIMALCHIO'S BANQUET CONTINUED—THE SECOND COURSE—CONVERSA-
TION ABOUT TRIMALCHIO AND SOME OF HIS GUESTS—TRIMALCHIO DIS-
COURSES ON ASTROLOGY—HE MAKES A FREEDMAN AND A PUN.

THE applause we gave him was followed by the second
course, which certainly did not come up to our expectation ;
yet the novelty of the thing drew every one's eyes upon it.
It was a large circular tray with the twelve signs of the zodiac
round it, upon every one of which the arranger[1] had put an
appropriate dish : on Aries ram's-head pies ; on Taurus a piece
of roast beef ; on Gemini kidneys and lamb's fry ; on Cancer a
crown;[2] on Leo African figs;[3] on Virgo a young sow's haslet;[4]
on Libra a pair of scales, in one of which were tarts,[5] in the

----

[1] *The arranger.*] Structor: an attendant,
qui fercula docte
Componat.   *Juven.* Sat. vii.
It was his business to arrange the dishes on the ferculum or tray.

[2] *On Cancer a crown.*] Because, as Trimalchio explains further on,
he was born under that constellation.

[3] *On Leo African figs.*] Because lions abounded in Africa.

[4] *A young sow's haslet.*] Among the most favourite dishes of the ancients were the womb, *vulva*, and the dugs, *sumen*, of a virgin sow :
hence there is no dish so frequently mentioned, from Plautus down to
the latest period.

[5] *Tarts*] Striblita, a word derived from στρεβλειν, to twist like a

other cheese-cakes; on Scorpio a little sea-fish of the same name; on Sagittarius a hare; on Capricorn a lobster; on Aquarius a goose; on Pisces two mullets; and in the middle there was a green turf, on which lay a honeycomb.

Meanwhile an Egyptian slave carried bread in a silver portable oven, singing at the same time in a very delicate voice a song in praise of wine flavoured with laserpitium.[1] But as we looked rather blank at the coarse fare before us, Trimalchio cried out, "Pray, gentlemen, fall to: you see your dinner."[2]

As he spoke, four fellows came dancing in to the sound of music, and took off the upper part of the tray; which being done, we saw beneath on a second tray crammed fowls, a sow's paps, and in the middle a hare fitted with wings to resemble Pegasus. We also remarked four figures of Marsyas standing at the several corners, and spouting a highly-seasoned sauce[3] on some fish that swam in a very Euripus.[4]

We all joined in the admiring exclamations begun by the

rope. The English word tart was originally *tort*, from the Latin *tortus*, (twisted,) the distinctive feature of things so called being the well-known lattice-work of strips of pastry twisted like ropes.

[1] *Singing at the same time*, &c.] We read, Tenerrima voce de laserpitiario vino canticum extorquet. Laser, Laserpitium, or Gilphion, was a plant in the highest esteem among the ancients, but which the moderns have been unable to identify. It appears that it grew only in Libya, about Cyrene, on the coins of which state it was figured. At first its exportation was wholly prohibited; but this law was afterwards repealed, and the gum of the laser used to sell in Rome for its weight in silver. It was preserved with other precious commodities in the town treasuries. When Julius Cæsar plundered the treasury of Rome after the flight of Pompey, he carried off from it fifteen hundred pounds' weight of laserpitium.

[2] *You see your dinner.*] The text is doubtful. Many copies have, Hoc est jus cœnæ, instead of which Goesius reads, with much probability, Hoc est hujus cœnæ. Burmann understands the passage in the same sense. Trimalchio intended a surprise for his guests; and by and by we shall find him forcibly exclaiming, Putatis me contentum illa cœna, quam in theca repositorii videratis?

[3] *A highly-seasoned sauce.*] Garum piperatum. This highly-prized sauce was extracted from the entrails of fish macerated in sea-water until they began to putrify. Pliny calls it an "exquisite liquor." Seneca, a "precious sanies." It probably was to the ancients what caviare is to us.

[4] *Euripus.*] The proper name of the straits which separated the island of Eubœa from the mainland: it was applied to all kinds of artificial reservoirs of water, such as fish-ponds, and here by a jocular exaggeration to the hollow part of the *repositorium*, in which the fish swam in sauce.

domestics, and merrily fell to at what each liked best. "Cut!"
said Trimalchio, who was not less delighted than ourselves
with a device of the sort; and forth stepped the carver[1] and
began to cut up the meat, keeping time with the music, and
with such antic gestures, you would have thought he was
exerting himself to the sound of a hydraulic organ[2] to win
a chariot race.

Trimalchio nevertheless went on calling out, Cut, from time
to time, in a low voice. Hearing the word so often repeated,
I fancied there must be some joke connected with it, and
therefore ventured to ask the guest who sat next above me
what it meant. As he had often been present at these fool-
eries he replied, "Do you see that servant who is carving:
his name is Cut; and therefore as often as Trimalchio cries
Cut, he both calls and commands."

Not being able to eat any more, I turned to the same person
to satisfy my curiosity in other particulars; and after leading
the way with some pleasantries, What woman is that, said I,
who is bustling about the room?

"She is Trimalchio's wife," he replied, "her name is Fortunata, she counts her money by the bushel. As for what she
was a little while ago, saving your favour, you would have
been loth to take bread out of her hand; but now, no one

---

[1] *The carver.*] Sometimes the *structor* carved; but it was more usual
to have a slave expressly for that office, who was styled *scissor*, carptor,
or diribitor. His art consisted not only in carving in a skilful manner,
but also in performing the operation in a rhythmical manner, with regular
dancing movements.

[2] *A hydraulic organ.*] It is not the least curious fact in the history of
invitations, that the origin of our modern church organs may be distinctly
traced back to so simple an instrument as the Pandean pipes. The ingenious Ctesibius of Alexandria, the inventor of the hydraulic organ,
evidently took the idea from that primitive contrivance. He employed
one or more rows of pipes of very large size, gradually diminishing in
length from one end of the row to the other, and furnished with sliders,
which were moved by keys and levers, so as to open and shut the mouths
of the pipes. A supply was obtained without intermission by bellows,
which were kept in action by the pressure of water. The hydraulic organ continued in use so late as the ninth century of our era. It was an
instrument well adapted to gratify the Roman people in the splendid entertainments provided for them by the emperors and other opulent persons. Nero was very curious about organs, both in regard to their musical
effect and their mechanism. A representation of one occurs on a con-
torniate medal of that emperor.

knows why or wherefore, she has got into heaven, as it were, and is Trimalchio's factotum: in short, if she says it is midnight at high noon he will believe her. He cannot tell his riches, he is so excessively wealthy; but this high-born lady has an eye to everything, and when you least think to meet her she is at your elbow. She drinks little, she is sober and a good adviser; but she has an ugly tongue, and chatters like a magpie in bed. If she likes a body she likes him, and if she dislikes him she dislikes him in good earnest.

"As for Trimalchio, he has as much land as a kite can fly over; he has heaps upon heaps of money.[1] There is more silver lying in his porter's lodge than another man's whole estate is worth. And as for his slaves, wheugh! by Hercules, I do not believe one-tenth of them know their own master, and they stand in such awe of him that he could make every dolt of them creep into a gimlet-hole.[2] You must not imagine that he buys anything; he has all within himself, wool, chalk, pepper, nay, if you have a mind for hen's milk you 'll get it. At first, I grant you, his wool was none of the best, for which reason he bought rams at Tarentum to improve his breed; he had bees fetched from Athens, that he might have Attic honey home-made; and that at the same time the native bees might be bettered by a cross with the Greek. It was only the other day he wrote to India for mushroom-seed; and he has not a single mule but was got by a wild ass. You see all these beds? There is not one of them but is wadded with the finest purple or scarlet wool. Oh what a happy man he is!

"And don't turn up your nose at any of his fellow-freedmen, mind you. They are very snug fellows. You see that one at the end there to the right?[3] He is worth this moment his eight hundred thousand. Yet he began the world with nothing; it is not long since he used to carry wood on his back. They do say, but I don't know how true it may be, I only speak

---

[1] *Heaps upon heaps of money.*] Nummorum nummos. Perhaps this may mean, His money breeds without end; he makes interest upon interest.

[2] *Into a gimlet-hole.*] In rutæ folium, literally, into a leaf of rue. This plant has figured among all nations as an inauspicious emblem.

[3] *At the end there to the right.*] Imus in imo.

from hearsay, that he snatched off an Incubo's hat,[1] and so found a treasure. For my part, I envy no man; if any god has stood his friend, well and good. He can still take a box on the ear for all that;[2] he knows which side his bread is buttered, and lately set up this bill :

C. POMPEIUS DIOGENES
WILL LET THE GARRET FROM THE KALENDS OF JULY,[3]
HAVING HIMSELF BOUGHT THE HOUSE.

"But what think you of him you see in the freedman's place?[4] How well off he was once! I don't upbraid him. He saw his money increase tenfold, but he went wrong at last. I don't suppose he has a hair on his head that is not mortgaged; though, by Hercules, it was not his fault, for there is not a better man living, but his rascally freedmen's, who choused him out of all. Let me tell you, when the pot no longer boils, and a man's fortune declines, farewell friends. And what was the handsome occupation he followed that you see him where he is ? Why he was an undertaker. He used to keep a table like a king's—boars fed on Carian figs,[5] huge

---

[1] *An Incubo's hat.*] A popular superstition not peculiar to any age or country. It prevails in many places to this day. The Irish Leprechaun is nearly allied to the Incubo.

[2] *He can still take a box on the ear.*] Est tamen sub alapa : though he is a freedman he can submit to his patron's petulant humour. Or the phrase may mean, as Burmann suggests : though ostensibly a freedman, he is not yet fully emancipated. Several conditions were requisite to raise a slave to the status of a Civis Romanus ; if any of these were wanting, he became a Latinus, and in some cases only a Dediticius.

[3] *The Kalends of July.*] The usual period for changing lodgings, though perhaps not the only one.—*Bekker's Gallus.*

[4] *The freedman's place.*] A freedman at his master's table would of course take the lowest place, and that, we have seen, was already occupied. Scheffer conjectures that the place here indicated is that of the emperor's freedman, namely, the place of honour, which in Rome was called *consularis.* The imperial freedmen were persons of great importance in the provinces to which they were often sent on special missions. Scheffer's conjecture is ingenious, but it labours under this difficulty, that Trimalchio himself occupied the consular place. By and by, to increase our perplexity, we shall find a new comer, Habinnas, assuming the Prætor's place, which of course would be the same as that of the Consul, though it is not hinted that Trimalchio rose to let him take it, nor is it consistent with his character that he should have done so.

[5] *Boars fed on Carian figs.*] The common reading is, apros gausapa-

pies, wild-fowl, stags—his cooks and pastry-cooks spilled more wine under the table than another man has in his cellar: it was more a dream of fancy than the life of a mortal man. Even when his affairs had grown shaky, lest his creditors should think he was done up, he posted this notice:

JULIUS PROCULUS
WILL SELL BY AUCTION
HIS SUPERFLUOUS MOVEABLES."

Trimalchio interrupted this pleasant chat; for the course had been removed, and as the company, now warm with wine, were beginning to engage in general conversation, he leaned on his elbow and said, "Pray commend this wine by your drinking; you must make your fish swim again. Do you imagine I can be content with such a supper as you saw just now boxed up as it were in a tray? Is Ulysses no better known?[1] Eh, what say you? Even at table we must remember our philology.

"Peace to the bones of my good patron! It was his pleasure to make me a man among men.[2] Nothing can come across me that is new to me, just as it was with him, whereof this tray supplies practical proof.[3]

"This heaven in which dwell twelve gods turns itself into as many different figures. Sometimes it becomes Aries, (the Ram,) so that whoever is born under that sign has many flocks and much wool, a hard head into the bargain, a shameless front, and a sharp horn. Most of your schoolmen and wranglers are born under this sign."

We praised our astrologer's wit, and he went on again.

"Next the whole heaven becomes Taurus, (the Bull,) and then are born stubborn fellows, and neatherds, and such as

tos, which may mean incrusted with pastry made to resemble a shaggy cloth. We adopt the conjectural emendation of Heinsius, apros gaunea pastos.

[1] *Is Ulysses no better known?*]   A quotation from the Æneid, ii. 44; Sic notus Ulysses?

[2] *A man among men.*]   Hominem inter homines, that is to say, a man in the highest sense of the word, in which slaves were not included, free man among free men, and accomplished moreover with liberal arts.

[3] *Just as it was with him*, &c.]   Locus prodigiose corruptus. *Heins.* Locus desperatus ac varie tentatus. *Burm.* The MSS. have Fericulusta mel habuit praxin, the simplest intelligible modification of which is, Fericula ista mei habent praxin.

fill their own bellies. Under Gemini are born those that run
in couples, yoke-fellows, wenchers,[1] and those who keep fair
with both sides.[2] I myself was born under Cancer, (the Crab,)
wherefore I stand on many feet, and have great possessions
both by sea and land ; for Cancer suits one element as well as
the other. And this is why I put nothing just now on that
sign, that I might not eclipse my own nativity. Under Leo,
(the Lion,) are born devourers[3] and men of might; under
Virgo, (the Virgin,) women, runaways, and jail-birds ; under
Libra, (the Balance,) butchers, druggists, and all retail dealers ; under Scorpio, (the Scorpion,) poisoners, and cut-
throats ; under Sagittarius, (the Archer,) squinting people,[4]
who make believe to look at the cabbage, and steal the bacon ;
under Capricorn, labourers whose skins turn to horn through
hard usage ; under Aquarius, (the Waterman,) tavern-keepers,[5]
and fellows with heads like pumpkins ;[6] under Pisces, (the
Fishes,) sauce-makers, and rhetoricians. Thus the world
runs round like a mill, and always to our misfortune somehow
or other, whether we come into or quit it. As for the turf
you see in the middle, and the honeycomb upon it, there is a
reason for that too ; for our mother earth is in the middle, as
round as an egg, and contains all good things in herself, like
a honeycomb."

O the wise man ! we all cried out with our hands uplifted
to the ceiling, and swore that neither Hipparchus nor Aratus
was to be compared to him. Presently servants came in, and
spread tapestry before the couches,[7] on which were depicted

---

[1] *Wenchers.*]   *Colei,* i. e. benevasati.

[2] *Those who keep fair with both sides.*] Qui utrosque parietes linunt.
This is the Greek proverb δύο τοίχους ἀλείφουσι, nearly equivalent to,
They run with the hare and hunt with the hounds. All the English and
French translators have erroneously ascribed to it an obscene meaning.

[3] *Devourers.*] Cataphagæ. The Greek word, and the Latin *comedere,*
have a meaning hardly implied in any English phrase, but which is
exactly expressed in the French phrase, *manger son bien.*

[4] *Squinting people.*] Because archers shut one eye when they take
aim.

[5] *Tavern-keepers.*] A sly hit at their practice of watering their wine.

[6] *Fellows with heads like pumpkins.*] Cucurbitæ ; properly cucumbers. The French call a noodle, *un cornichon,* probably in allusion to
the presumed constitution of his brains. Cucumbers require much
watering ; hence their relation to Aquarius.

[7] *Spread tapestry before the couches.*] Toralia proposuerunt toris.

nets, men in ambush with hunting poles, and all the apparatus of the chase. We were at a loss to imagine what new scene this promised, when on a sudden we heard a great cry without, and in rushed a pack of Spartan hounds, and ran round the table. These were followed by a great tray on which was laid a wild boar of the largest size, with a cap on its head, while from its tusks hung two baskets made of palm leaves, the one full of Syrian, the other of Theban dates ; and about it lay little sweetmeat pigs as if at suck, to signify that a sow was placed before us ; and these were presents to be taken home with them by the guests.

The servant who came to cut up the boar was not that Cut who had carved the fowl, but a big bearded fellow, with leg bands, and a frieze cape,[1] who, drawing his hunting knife, made a great gash in the beast's side, out of which flew a flock of fieldfares.[2] Fowlers stood ready with reeds,[3] and caught them in a moment as they fluttered about the room. Then Trimalchio ordered every man his bird, and added, "Now see what choice acorns this wild pig devoured."[4] Thereupon

Bekker adduces this passage in disproof of the common notion that the *toralia* were the same as the *stragula* (coverlets). It is plain that the slaves could not spread covers over the couches whilst the guests lay on them.

[1] *A frieze cape.*] Alicula polymita. The alicula was a short garment, so called, says Velius Longus, quod alas nobis injecta contineat. The adjective πολύμιτος means thick and stout, woven of *many threads*, its opposite being λεπτόμιτος or ψιλόμιτος.

[2] *The side of the beast, out of which*, &c.] This was what they called a Trojan boar, in allusion to the Trojan horse. Sometimes the belly of the boar contained a fawn, the fawn a hare, the hare a partridge, and the partridge a nightingale.

[3] *Fowlers stood ready with reeds.*] The method of catching birds here alluded to, and more fully detailed in a subsequent chapter, was very ingenious. The fowler was furnished with a series of reeds which could be fastened one to the other like the joints of a fishing-rod, so that without alarming the bird he could reach it with the end of the first reed, which was tipped with birdlime. Valerius Flaccus (vi. 26) speaks of this practice in the following lines :

> Qualem populeæ fidentem nexibus umbræ
> Si quis avem summi deducat ab aëre rami,
> Ante manu tacita, cui plurima crevit arundo,
> Illa dolis viscoque super correpta sequaci
> Implorat ramos, atque irrita concitat alas.

[4] *What choice acorns*, &c.] The common reading is, Etiam videte quam porcus ille sylvaticus totam comederit glandem. It is strange that

the servants took the baskets that hung on the tusks, and distributed both kinds of dates equally to the company.

Meanwhile, thinking over the matter to myself, I made a thousand conjectures as to why the boar had been brought in with a cap on its head. After cogitating for a long while to no purpose, I ventured to apply for a solution of the difficulty to the same person who had already explained other things to me. "Why," said he, "your servant could explain that to you; it is no riddle; the thing is quite clear. This boar escaped from yesterday's dinner, where he was presented at the last course and dismissed by the guests, and so he now returns to table as a freedman." I cursed my own stupidity, and asked no more questions, lest it should seem that I had never before dined among people of fashion.

While we were talking there came in a handsome boy crowned with vine leaves and ivy, who sometimes called himself Bromius, then Lyæus, and sometimes again Evous;[1] he had a little basket of grapes in his hand which he carried round to the company, and he recited in a shrill voice some poems of his master's composition; whereat Trimalchio turned to him and said, "Dionysus, BE THOU LIBER." The boy at once took the cap off the boar's head and put it on his own,[2] and Trimalchio exclaimed, "You will not deny that I have a Liber Pater."[3] We all applauded the witticism, and kissed the young freedman over and over again as he went round us.

---

any editor should have hesitated to adopt Munker's conjectural emendation of *lotam* (that is, lautam, like coda, cauda, copo, caupo) for totam.

[1] *Bromius, Lyæus, Evous,* &c.] All names of Bacchus, or Dionysus. When Trimalchio says to the boy, Liber esto, he gives him his freedom with a pun, for the adjective *liber* means *free*.

[2] *The boy took the cap,* &c.] The felt cap was the emblem of liberty among the Romans. When a slave obtained his freedom, he had his head shaved, and wore instead of his hair an undyed pileus or scull-cap. This change of attire took place in the temple of Feronia, who was the goddess of freedmen. The figure of Liberty on some of the coins of Antoninus Pius, struck A. D. 145, holds this cap in the right hand.

[3] *I have a Liber Pater.*] This pun is untranslatable. You see, says Trimalchio, I have a *Father Liber* among my dependants: otherwise, You must admit I am a gentleman born (ingenuus) since I have a *free father*.

CHAPTER VII.

TRIMALCHIO S BANQUET CONTINUED—THE SECOND COURSE—TABLE-TALK.

TRIMALCHIO got up from table to go to the close stool, and we, being left free by the absence of the monarch,[1] began to indulge in a little table-talk. One of the guests having called for a cup of wine, broke forth thus:

"O day, you are nothing; before you can turn round, it is night. Therefore one cannot do better than go straightway from bed to board. What very cold weather we have had; the bath has scarcely warmed me; but good liquor is your best clothier. I have drunk brimmers and I'm quite fuddled; the wine has got into my head."

Seleucus then struck in: "I don't bathe every day," he said; "your daily bather is no better than a fuller. Water has teeth, and dissolves away one's heart day by day; but when I have lined my stomach with a cup of mulled wine, I bid the cold go be hanged. Indeed I could not bathe to-day, for I have been to a funeral. Poor Chrysanthus has breathed his last; such a nice fellow he was! It seems to me as though I heard him calling me to him but a moment ago. I could fancy I was talking with him even now. Heigho! We are mere blown bladders on two legs; less than flies; they are good for something, and we are no better than bubbles. May be you'll say he did not live low enough? Not a drop of water or a crumb of bread went down his throat for five days; but he died for all that. He was killed by too many doctors, or rather his time was come, for the doctor is good for nothing but as a satisfaction to the mind. However, he was handsomely carried out on the bed he used to lie on, covered with good blankets. The lamentation was very fine, (he manumitted some slaves before he died,) although his wife did not cry as if she cared for him. How would it have been if he had not behaved so well to her? But woman is a sort of kite; a man ought never to waste the least kindness on one of the sex; it

---

[1] *Being left free by the absence of the monarch.*] Nos libertatem sino tyranno nacti.

is all the same as throwing it into a well; and old love is as bad as a jail to them."

Here Phileros interrupted him without ceremony, exclaiming, "Let us talk of the living: he had what was due to him; he lived well and so he died; then what has he to complain of? He began the world with nothing, and to his dying day he would have picked a farthing out of a dunghill with his teeth; therefore he throve all he could, like a honeycomb. By Hercules, I believe he died worth a hundred thousand solidi, and all in ready money. But I will tell you the truth of the matter, that I will, for I have eaten dog's tongue. He had a foul mouth and a rough tongue, and was the very living image of discord. His brother was a fine fellow, a friend to his friend, as free as the day, and kept a plentiful table. At first his own cake was all dough,[1] but his first vintage set him up again, for he sold his wine just for what he would; but what chiefly kept up his chin was an inheritance out of which he stole more than came to him by rights. After all, what does this log do but fall out with his brother, and leave his fortune to some vagabond scum of the earth.[2] He flees far that flees his own kith and kin. But he was led by the ears by a parcel of tittle-tattle servants. A man never can do well that is too ready to believe all he is told, especially a man in business. It is a true saying, however, which he was an instance of all his life-time: *Happy is he that has, not he that ought to have.* He was visibly one of Fortune's sons: lead turned to gold in his hand; and where's the wonder when all things run upon wheels just as you 'd have them? How many years do you think he buried with him? Seventy odd; but he was as tough as horn; he carried his years well, and was as black as a crow. I knew him when he was a young chap no better than he ought to be; and he was a lecher to the last; by Hercules, I don't believe he let a living thing alone in his house down to the very dog. A great wencher he was surely;

---

[1] *His own cake was all dough,*] Malam parram pilavit; literally, "he plucked a bad (unlucky) jay," a proverbial expression, in some degree analogous to our own phrase, "I have a crow to pluck with you." The jay or the magpie (parra) was a bird of ill omen. See Hor. iii. Ode 27,

             Impios parræ recinentis omen
             Ducat.

[2] *Scum of the earth.*] Terræ filius.

nothing came amiss to him: [1] not that I blame him; that is the only advantage he carried out of the world with him." [2]

Here Phileros made an end, and Ganymede began: " You talk of what concerns neither heaven nor earth; meantime no one thinks of the dearness of provisions, or asks where the pinch lies. By Hercules, I could not get a mouthful of bread to-day; for why? the drought continues; it is a twelve-month since I have had a bellyful. Bad luck to these Ædiles; they and the bakers are all in a string together, *Claw me, and I'll claw thee;* and so poor folks are starved; for your rich rascals wag their jaws all the year. O if we had those bully-boys that I found here when I came over first from Asia. Living was living in those days; it was like being in the heart of Sicily for plenty, and they banged those vampires of Ædiles about in such style that Jupiter was their friend no longer. There was Safinius, I remember him well: he lived near the old triumphal arch when I was a boy; he was a peppercorn, not a man; [3] he made the ground smoke under him wherever he went; but he was a downright honest man, no shuffler, a friend to his friend, and one with whom you might have safely played mora in the dark. [4] And then in the court-house! How he pounded them up [5] one and all! He did not talk in figures, but gave everything its right name, as if he was calling the muster-roll. His voice swelled in the forum like a trumpet, without his ever sweating or spitting. I believe indeed he had something of the Asiatic in his blood. And what a civil man he was, returning our salutes, and call-ing us all by name, as if he had been one of us! Accordingly

[1] *Nothing came amiss to him.*] Omnis Minervæ homo: a proverbial expression applied to a man of very versatile talents, one who was skilled in every art. The phrase also admits of a second meaning, such as is here implied, *omnis Minervæ* being equivalent to *omnis virginis.*

[2] *That is the only advantage,* &c.] There is an epigram to the same effect in the Tusculan Questions, book v.

> Hoc habeo, quæ edi, quæque exsaturata libido
> Hausit; at illa jacent multa et præclara relicta.

[3] *A peppercorn, not a man.*] A common form of expression among the Neapolitans to this day : *è tutto pepe.*

[4] *Played mora in the dark.*] This game, at which the populace of modern Italy play incessantly, consists in guessing instantly the number of fingers suddenly held up by one of the two players.

[5] *He pounded them up.*] Vel pilo pertractabat. Some read Velut pilas tractabat—he made nothing of them.

provisions were as cheap as dirt in his time. A halfpenny loaf was more than two men could eat at a meal, but now it is not as big as a bullock's eye. Heigho! things are getting worse and worse every day; our colony is growing down like a calf's tail, as why should it not? since we have an Ædile not worth three figs, who values more the getting of a penny than the lives of us all put together. He may well be jolly at home, for he gets more money in one day than another man's whole fortune comes to. I know where he took a thousand gold denars; but if we were not geldings[1] he would not hold his head so high. But now-o-days the people are lions at home, foxes abroad. For my part I have already eaten up my duds, and if this scarcity continues I must sell my bits of houses. For what is to become of us if neither gods nor men take pity on the colony? Let me never be happy but I think all this proceeds from the deities! for nobody now believes heaven to be heaven; or keeps a fast, or cares a straw for Jupiter; but all shut their eyes, and only trouble their heads about what they are worth. Time was when our matrons, with pure minds and dishevelled hair, went veiled and barefoot up the hill to beseech Jupiter for rain, and presently it rained by pitcherfuls, then or never, and every one rejoiced; but now we think no more of the gods than of mice.[2] Therefore their feet are tied from helping us, and because we are irreligious the fields lie barren."

"Better words!" cries Echion, a freedman who was well to do. "The worse luck now the better next time," as the clown said when he lost his brindled hog. What happens not to-day may happen to-morrow; so life passes. By Hercules, it cannot be said that our country would be more fruitful if there were better men in it; though we suffer at present it is no fault of hers; we ought not to be too nice; the sky is equally distant everywhere, and if you were in another place you would say that hogs ran about here ready cooked. Let me tell you we shall have an excellent gladiator show these holidays, none of your common sort,[3] but most of them freedmen.

---

[1] *If we were not geldings.*] Si nos coleos haberemus.
[2] *We think no more of the gods than of mice.*] The text is doubtful here. Heinsius proposes to read, Et omnes rodebant, avidi tanquam mures. "And everybody fell a picking up his grub, as busy as mice."
[3] *None of your common sort.*] Familia non lanistitia. The gang of

Our patron, Titus, has a large soul and a hot head; it will be a right up and down fight.[1] I think I should know him, seeing I am of his household. He is not the sort to give quarter; he will put sharp swords into their hands, and no way of backing out, till the arena is turned into regular shambles in sight of the spectators. And he has the means to do it, for his father has just left him thirty millions of sesterces; he may squander four hundred thousand and never feel the loss of it, and his name will be up to eternity. He has already got some ponies, a woman that fights from the Gaulish chariot, and Glyco's steward that was caught diverting his mistress. You will see what a row there will be among the people between the cuckolds and the cuckold-makers. Glyco, you see, the rich hunks, condemned the steward to the wild beasts; and what was that but to publish his own shame? How was the servant to blame who was forced to do what he did? It was she deserved, the strumpet,[2] to be tossed by the bull more than he; but he that can't come at the ass, must thrash at the pack-saddle. And how could Glyco expect that the daughter of Hermogenes should ever come to good? that sharper who would steal a kite's claws as she flew. A snake does not bring forth a rope. Glyco, Glyco has given up his own family to infamy; and therefore it will be a brand on him as long as he lives, which nothing but hell can obliterate; but every man's follies are his own concern.

"I seem to scent out that Mammea intends to give us a treat with the usual presents; if he does so, I hope he will cut Norbanus quite out of favour; for you must know he will crack on all sails; and in truth, what good has the other ever done us? He gave us a trumpery show of gladiators, such decrepit wretches you might have blown them down; I have seen better men thrown to the beasts by torch-light; you would have taken them for so many dung-hill cocks. One was so heavy-heeled he could scarce budge, another was club-footed, another, who was half-dead beforehand, was put

wretches purchased and kept by each trainer (lanista) to be exhibited as gladiators were called his *familia*.

[1] *It will be a right up and down fight.*] Literally, It will be either this or that: Aut hoc, aut illud, erit.

[2] *The strumpet.*] *Matella*, hoc est vas ad urinandum, et figurative adultera communis pluribus, uti matella convivis.

up as third man in place of one who had his ham-strings cut.
The only one that had some pith in him was a Thracian,[1]
and he only fought as we shouted him on. In fine, they all
got a flogging,[2] they had proved themselves such a lubberly
rabble, mere runaways. 'Yet after all I have given you a
show,' says he to me; And I have applauded it, said I; cast
up the account, and you will see I have given more than I
got. One good turn requites another.

"Your looks, Agamemnon, seem to say, 'What is this bore
driving at?' I talk, because you who can talk won't talk.
You are not one of our sort, and that is why you laugh at
poor folk's talk. We know that your head leaks, it is so full
of learning.[3] But I say, let me persuade you one of these
days to come to the country, and see our little crib. We'll
find something to eat, a chicken, and a few eggs. I warrant
we'll make ourselves cosy, though the weather has been very
unseasonable this year; ay, ay, we'll forage enough to fill our
bellies. My son Cicaro too is growing up to be your scholar;
he repeats four little declamations already, and if he lives you
will have a little servant always at your side; for he has no
sooner a spare moment than he is poring over his book. He
is a clever lad, has good stuff in him, though he is too fond of
birds; that's his weak point. I killed three of his linnets, and
told him a weasel had eaten them, but he soon found other pets;
and he is uncommonly fond of painting. He has already shown
his heels to his Greek, and begins to take very well to his
Latin, though his master humours him too much; nor can he
ever be made to stick to one thing, but comes and asks for
lessons, and then won't learn them. He has another master,
who has not much learning to be sure, but he has plenty of
zeal, and teaches even more than he knows himself. So he
generally comes to our house on holidays, and whatsoever
you give him he is content. I lately bought the boy some
law books, for I want him to have a smack of that science,

[1] *A Thracian.*] That is to say, a gladiator armed like a Thracian with
a round shield and a short sword.
[2] *They all got a flogging.*] Secti sunt : Reiskius makes these words
mean cæsi flagellis ; rightly so, says Antonius, "iis enim terga secari
sæpius dicuntur."
[3] *Your head leaks, it is so full of learning.*] There is a very droll ambiguity in the original : Scimus te præ literis fatuum esse : fatuus means
either one who can speak well, (from *fari*,) or a fool.

for home use, (it has bread in it,) and as for literature, he has been licked enough with that brush already.[1] If he kicks against it, I am resolved to teach him a trade, either a barber's or an auctioneer's, or above all a lawyer's, which nothing but Hell can take from him. Therefore I din into his ears every day, My first-born son, take my word for it, whatever you learn is your own. You see Phileros the advocate; had he not been a scholar he would have starved; it was only the other day he was a costermonger, and carried his wares on his shoulders, and now he is a match for Norbanus himself in riches. Letters are a treasure, and a trade never starves."

Such was the gossip that went about the table, when Trimalchio returned; and having wiped his forehead and washed his hands in perfume, " Pardon me, my friends," he said, after a short pause, " I have been costive for several days, and my physicians were at a loss about it, but a decoction of pomegranate rind, and fir wood steeped in vinegar, have given me ease ; and now I hope my belly may be ashamed if it keep no better order; for sometimes I have such a rumbling about my stomach you'd think an ox was bellowing. And so if any of you have a mind to relieve himself, he need not blush for the matter. We were none of us born solid; and I know no greater torment than keeping in one's wind; it's a necessity Jove himself can't prevent. What are you laughing at, Fortunata? You that so often keep me awake at night. It was never my way to hinder any man at my table from doing what was needful to his ease ; and physicians forbid us to put a restraint upon nature. If something even more serious presses, you will find every requisite outside, water, closestool, and other little matters. Believe me, when these gastric vapours get into the brain, they cause a fluxion in the whole body. I have known many men lost by it, when they were too modest to tell what ailed them."

We thanked him for his considerate and indulgent courtesy, and took sip after sip of wine in order to keep down our laughter. But we little thought that at this stage of our journey we had still, as the saying is, another hill to climb; for the table being uncovered to a flourish of music, three white

---

[1] *Licked enough with that brush.*] Literis satis *inquinatus* est. There is a ludicrous impropriety in the use of *inquinatus* instead of *infectus*, as if the boy was not only tinged with literature, but dirtied into the bargain.

hogs were brought in with bells about their necks and muz-
zled; one of which, the nomenclator[1] told us, was two years
old, another three, and the third full grown. For my part, I
took them for tumblers, and imagined the hogs were to perform some of those surprising feats practised in the ring; but
Trimalchio put an end to our surmises. "Which of these,"
said he, "will you have dressed for supper? Cocks and
pheasants and such bagatelles are jobs for country-bred cooks,
but mine are in the habit of sending a calf boiled whole to
table."

Immediately sending for one of his cooks, he ordered him,
without waiting for our choice, to kill the largest hog; then
raising his voice, "Of what decuria are you?"[2] he asked.

"Of the fortieth," replied the slave.

"Were you bought," said he, "or born in my house?"

"Neither," said the cook, "but left you by Pansa's testament."

"See then that this is expeditiously dressed, or I shall
have you turned down into the decuria of the farm-servants."
And with this cogent admonition away went the cook with
his charge to the kitchen.

Then smoothing the sternness of his countenance, Trimalchio turned to us and asked if we liked our wine. "If not,"
said he, "it shall be changed; but pray commend it by your
drinking.[3] By the bounty of the gods I do not buy it, but
have everything good for the mouth growing on one of my

[1] *The nomenclator.*] The office of the nomenclator is thus described
by Bekker: "In the times of the Republic those who desired to attain
to high offices were obliged to observe many little attentions, not only to
people of distinction, but also towards the common citizens. Their houses
were open to the visits of everybody, and when they were out of doors
they were expected to remember all their names, and say something
agreeable to them. As it was impossible to recall at a moment the name
and circumstances of each one, there were slaves (nomenclatores) whose
duty consisted in remembering the names of those they met, and inform-
ing their master." The use to which Trimalchio put his nomenclator is
characteristic of that vulgar and ostentatious person. The dishes at his
table were so numerous and uncommon, that a special servant was
requisite to make known their names and their several excellencies to
the guests.

[2] *Of what decuria are you?*] An act of pomposity on the part of Trimalchio, to give his guests an idea of the multitude of his slaves.

[3] *Commend it by your drinking.*] So Martial, v. 79, Vinum tu facies
bonum bibendo.

manors which I never saw myself; but they tell me it borders on Terracina and Tarentum. I am thinking of adding Sicily to my little possessions, so that when I have a mind to pass over into Africa, I may sail by my own coasts.

"But pray tell me, Agamemnon, what subject was it you declaimed on to-day? For though I do not plead myself, yet I have learned the rules for composing an oration. Don't imagine that I have disdained literature; I have three libraries, one Greek, the others Latin. Tell me therefore, if you love me, the argument of your declamation."

Agamemnon began. "A poor man and a rich were at enmity" . . . .

"What is a poor man?" said Trimalchio, cutting him short.

"Good, very good indeed," said Agamemnon, and then he began to unfold I know not what controversy. When he had done, Trimalchio decided the question off-hand in these terms: "If the fact is so, it admits of no controversy; if it is not so, there's an end of the matter."

This dilemma having been hailed with applause, he continued: "Pray, my dear friend Agamemnon, do you happen to remember the twelve labours of Hercules, or the story of Ulysses, how the Cyclops put his thumb out of joint with a switch. I used to read these things in Homer when I was a boy. And the Sibyl, you know! I saw her myself at Cumæ with my own eyes, hanging in a jar; and when the boys asked her, 'What would you, Sibyl,' she answered, 'I would die.'"

CHAPTER VIII.

TRIMALCHIO'S BANQUET CONTINUED—THE BOAR A LA TROYENNE—TRIMALCHIO TALKS LEARNEDLY AND WITTILY ON SUNDRY THINGS, CORINTHIAN BRASS, MALLEABLE GLASS, SILVER VESSELS, &c.—PROPOSES DANCING—HIS DOMESTIC ANNALS—THE TUMBLERS—TRIMALCHIO'S ACCIDENT AND MAGNANIMITY—HE TALKS POETRY—AND PHILOSOPHY—THE LOTTERY.

HE was still running on when a very large hog was brought to table. We all wondered at the expedition which had been used, swearing a capon would not have been dressed in the time ; and what increased our surprise was, that the hog appeared to be much larger than the boar which had been served up previously. "What," cried Trimalchio, looking closely at it, "are his guts not taken out ? No, by Hercules, they are not. Call the cook, call the cook !"

The cook being brought before us, hung down his head, and excused himself, saying he had forgot. "Forgot !" cried Trimalchio, "why the fellow talks as if it was only a pinch of pepper, or cummin omitted. Strip him."

In a moment the poor cook was stripped and standing between two tormentors. We all interceded for him, saying, such mistakes will happen occasionally ; forgive him this time, but if ever he offends again, not one of us will say a good word for him. For my part I felt mercilessly indignant against him, and could not help whispering to Agamemnon, "This must certainly be a most careless rascal. Forget to bowel a hog ! By Hercules, I would not have forgiven him if he had served me so in the dressing of a fish."

Trimalchio seemed to think differently, for returning a pleasant look, "Come," said he, "you with the short memory, let us see if you can bowel him before us."

Then the cook, having put on his tunic again, took his knife, and with a trembling hand slashed the hog on both sides of the belly, and the apertures enlarging under the weight that pressed them, out tumbled a load of puddings and sausages. All the servants set up a spontaneous shout, and cried Felicity to Gaius. The cook too was presented with wine, a silver crown,[1] and a drinking cup on a Corinthian salver, which Agamemnon narrowly viewing, "I am the only person," said Trimalchio, "who has the true Corinthian vessels."

I was expecting that, with his usual arrogance, he would tell us they were brought him from Corinth ; but he gave the matter a better turn. "Perhaps," said he, "you will ask how it is that I alone have the true Corinthian ? Because the brazier I buy them of is named Corinthus, and what's Corinthian but that which is made by Corinthus ? But lest you should think me an ignoramus, I must tell you I know very well the origin of Corinthian vessels.

---

[1] *A silver crown.*] Such crowns, as Pliny informs us, xxi. 2, were made of leaf gold or silver in the form of wreaths.

" When Troy was taken, Hannibal, a cunning fellow and a great plunderer, heaped together all the statues of bronze, gold, and silver, and setting fire to the pile, melted these miscellaneous metals into one; and of this mass the smiths made little plates, and basins, and statuettes; so that your Corinthian is neither this nor that metal in particular, but all together. Excuse my saying so, but I like glass cups better; others are of a different opinion; but were they not so brittle, I should prefer them to gold. Now they are of trifling value.

" There was once, however, a workman who made a glass phial that did not break. So he was admitted to present it to Cæsar, and afterwards he took it back out of the emperor's hands, and threw it on the ground. Cæsar was in the greatest possible alarm; but the other picked up the phial, and behold it was dinted just like a bronze vessel. Then he took out a little hammer from his bosom, and easily and neatly repaired the phial. This being done, he thought he was already in Jove's heaven, particularly when the emperor said to him, ' Does anybody but yourself know how to make this kind of glass? Just think.' On his replying in the negative, Cæsar ordered him to be beheaded, because, in fact, if the secret had become known, we should think no more of gold than of dirt.[1]

---

[1] *There was once, however*, &c.] Instead of the text from which this paragraph is translated, some editions give the story as told by John of Salisbury, who says he takes it from the Trimalchio of Petronius, but evidently presents it in a new dress, as follows:

" There was once an artist who made glass vessels of such toughness that you could no more break them than gold or silver. This man having made a cup of the finest crystal, and such as he thought no one worthy to possess but Cæsar, got admission with his present. Its beauty and the skill of the workman were highly commended, and the gift was graciously accepted. Presently, that he might change the admiration of the beholders into astonishment, and ingratiate himself still more with the emperor, the man took the cup out of Cæsar's hand, and dashed it to the ground with such vehemence as not the most solid and tenacious metal could have borne uninjured. Cæsar was no less astonished than alarmed; but the other, picking up the cup, which was not broken, but only dinted, as if the substance of bronze had put on the appearance of glass. Then he took a hammer out of his bosom, and very dexterously repaired the dint, hammering it out as if it were a bronze vessel. And now he thought

"For my part, I am passionately fond of silver; and have several cups of the capacity of an urn, more or less, on which is to be seen how Cassandra killed her sons,[1] and the dead boys appear so natural, you would take them to be real. I have a large goblet left by Romulus to my patron, on which is represented Dædalus shutting up Niobe in the Trojan horse.[2] Also I have the fights of Hermeros and of Petronas on cups; all massive; for you must know I would not sell my judgment in these things for any money."

Here he was interrupted by the fall of a cup which a servant let slip out of his hands. Trimalchio looked over his shoulder at him and said, "Go and kill yourself instantly, for you are careless." The slave hung his lip and implored pardon. "What is the use of your beseeching me," said Trimalchio, "as though I was very hard upon you? I only require you to secure yourself from being careless in future." But at last he forgave him at our entreaty; whereupon the pardoned slave ran round the table and cried, "Out of doors with the water, in with the wine!" We all took the jest, but more especially Agamemnon, who very well knew in what way to earn another invitation.

he was in Jove's heaven, having, as he imagined, got the friendship of Cæsar and the admiration of all the world; but it turned out quite contrary to his expectation; for Cæsar asked him if any one besides himself knew how to make glass malleable, and on his answering in the negative, immediately ordered his head to be struck off; because, if this art should become known, gold and silver would be as cheap as dirt."

This strange story is told still more circumstantially by Dion Cassius, (lvii. 21,) and is alluded to by Pliny, (H. N. xxxvi. 66,) with an expression of doubt however as to its truth.

The common practice of using the word "brass" as equivalent to χαλκός, or æs, is very erroneous. Brass, which is a compound of copper and zinc, was unknown to the Greeks and Romans. Their bronze was primitively a composition of copper and tin only. With the progress of the arts finer kinds were introduced, consisting in part of silver or gold. Such were the Corinthian, Delian, and Æginetan bronzes. Every one knows the legend so blunderingly told by Trimalchio: it is enough to say, that some of the artists who are said to have wrought in Corinthian brass lived long before the burning of Corinth by Mummius, about 146 B. C.

[1] Cassandra killed her sons.] He confounds Cassandra with Medea.

[2] Dædalus shutting up Niobe in the Trojan horse.] A lively but not quite exact allusion to the legend of Pasiphae, whom Dædalus enclosed in the figure of a cow, to enable her to indulge her monstrous passion for the bull.

Trimalchio meanwhile, hearing himself commended, drank on all the merrier, and being nearly tipsy, " Will none of you," said he, " invite my Fortunata to dance ? I assure you she is capital at the *cordax*,[1] no one better." Then putting his hands to his forehead he began to imitate Syrus the comedian, all the servants singing out together, By Jove, well done ! well done, by Jove ! He would also have stepped out and danced, had not Fortunata whispered in his ear and told him, I suppose, that such low diversions were unbecoming a man of his station. But his humour was most ridiculously unequal ; for sometimes Fortunata, and sometimes his inclination, got the better, and he would certainly have danced, had he not been prevented by the entrance of his historiographer, who read aloud, as if he were reciting the public records of Rome :[2]

" On the seventh of the Calends of July, on Trimalchio's manor at Cuma, were born thirty boys and forty girls. Five hundred thousand bushels of wheat were carried from the threshing-floor to the granary ; and in his stalls were five hundred oxen who bore the yoke.

" The same day Mithridates, one of his slaves, was crucified for cursing the genius of our patron, Gaius.

" The same day were brought back into the treasury a hundred thousand sesterces, for which no proper investment could be found.

" The same day a fire broke out in Pompey's Gardens, which began in the night, in the house of Nasta, the bailiff.

" Eh, what ? " cries Trimalchio, " when were Pompey's Gardens bought for me ?

" Last year," replied the historiographer, " and therefore they have not yet been brought to account."

Upon this Trimalchio flew into a rage ; " And whatever lands shall be purchased for me in future," said he, " if I hear nothing of them within six months, let them never be carried to my account."

---

[1] *The cordax.*] A lascivious dance of so gross a character that it was seldom performed except before drunken spectators. It is described by Meursius in his Orchestra, art. Κόρδαξ.

[2] *The public records of Rome.*] The Acta Diurna, a kind of gazette, published daily at Rome under the authority of the government. It contained an account of the proceedings of the public assemblies, of the law courts, of the punishment of offenders, and a list of births, marriages, deaths. &c.

Then were read the orders of his ædiles, and the wills of his foresters, who with great eulogiums made Trimalchio their heir. The names of his bailiffs were also recited; how his cursitor had repudiated his freedwoman for having caught her in bed with the bath-keeper; how his chamberlain had been banished to Baiæ; his steward indicted; and judgment given in the dispute between his grooms of the chamber.

At last the acrobats came in; and a most dreary buffoon holding up a ladder, ordered his boy to hop upon every round of it singing, up to the top, and then to tumble through red-hot hoops of iron, holding an amphora in his mouth. Trimalchio was the only one who liked this diversion; he said it was an ungrateful service, and added: "There are only two things under heaven which I greatly admire, acrobats and fighting quails; for as to all other creatures and shows, they are mere trash. I bought a company of comedians; but I rather chose to have them act farces,[1] and ordered my leader of the orchestra to play none but Latin airs."

Trimalchio was thus coming out in great force, when suddenly the boy tumbled down upon him, whereat the whole household gave a great shriek; as did also the guests, not out of any concern for such a beast, whose neck they could willingly have seen broke, but for fear the feast should have a tragic end, and they should be compelled to lament for a death.

As for Trimalchio, he fetched a deep groan, and leaned to one side as if his arm was hurt, whilst his physicians[2] flocked round him, and Fortunata among the foremost, with her hair streaming loose, a cup in her hand, and howling out that she was a wretched, unhappy woman.

Meanwhile the boy who had fallen upon him, crept round embracing our knees, and beseeching us to procure his pardon;

---

[1] *To act farces.*] Atellam facere: probably to show his good breeding, and how well versed he, a foreigner, was in the peculiarities of Roman life. The Atellan plays were an entertainment proper to Italy, and derive their name from Atella, a town of the Osci, in Campania. They appear to have been a union of high comedy and its parody, and were distinguished from the mimes by the absence of low buffoonery and ribaldry, being remarkable for a refined humour, such as could be understood and appreciated by educated people.

[2] *His physicians.*] These, as well as the *iatraliptæ* mentioned before, were slaves or freedmen, as usual in most large households.

which put me into a state of uneasy curiosity, for I imagined our intercession might lead to some theatrical surprise. The cook who had forgotten to bowel the hog was not yet out of my mind. I therefore ran my eyes all round the room, expecting every moment to see the wall open and some self-moved machine step out of it; the more so when I saw a slave soundly beaten for having wrapped his master's bruised arm in white flannel instead of using purple-coloured. I was not far astray in my surmises; for instead of the boy's punishment, out came a decree from Trimalchio's lips, giving the offender his freedom, that it might not be said a man of such consequence had been made black and blue by a slave.

We all applauded the generosity of the act, and fell into a moralizing strain of talk on the precarious nature of human affairs. " You are right," said Trimalchio; " nor must an accident like this be allowed to pass without an impromptu." He called immediately for tablets, and without much racking his brains, read to us the following lines :

> " Things fall out crosswise very oft,
> When least we think it; for aloft
> Sits Fortune, ruling our affairs ;
> So let us drink and drown our cares."

This epigram gave rise to a conversation about poets, and for a long while the highest encomiums were bestowed on Morsinus the tragic writer,[1] until Trimalchio turning to Agamemnon said, " Pray, master, what think you is the difference between Cicero and Publius?[2] In my opinion the former was the more eloquent of the two, the latter the more genteel. What, for instance, can be better said than this?

> Degenerate Rome grows weak through luxury ;
> To please her appetite cramm'd peacocks die ;
> For her their plumed Assyrian gold they spread ;
> Capons and guinea-fowls for her are fed ;
> The stork itself, dear, kindly, long-legg'd thing,
> Shunner of winter, herald of the spring,

---

[1] *Morsinus the tragic writer.*] A poet so insufferably bad as to have given occasion to a proverbial saying quoted by Erasmus in his *Adag. tit. Absurda :* Si quis vel verbum e Morsino exscripserit.

[2] *Publius.*] Publius Syrus, the celebrated mime.

Castanet-playing bird, poor foreign guest,
Now in the cruel cauldron makes its nest.
Why have the Indian pearls such valued charms?
To deck the wife for some adulterer's arms?
Why prize you the carbuncle's mineral fire,
Or green pellucid emeralds so desire,
Unless to star your wanton females' pride?
Virtue's the only jewel for a bride.
Should wives to all the world their beauties bare,
Clad in gauze mists, in robes of textured air?

"But what think you now," he continued, "is the most difficult calling, next to that of letters? I think it is the physician's, or the money-changer's; the physician's, because he knows what we poor bodies have got in our very insides, and when the fever-fit will come upon us (though by the way I hate them like poison, for they are always physicking me); and the money-changer's, because he can spy out a piece of bronze through the silver that plates it.

"Of dumb brutes the ox and the sheep are the most laborious; to oxen we are indebted for the bread we eat, and to sheep for the wool that makes us so fine. Only think what a shame it is that any one should eat mutton and wear a tunic! As for bees, I take them to be divine creatures, for they spit up honey, though people do say they fetch it from Jove. That is why they sting too, for there is no sweet without its sour."

He was cutting the philosophers out of their business in this way, when lottery tickets[1] were handed about in a cup, and a servant, whose office it was, read aloud the names of the presents annexed to each. *Humbug Silver!*[2] A gammon was

---

[1] *Lottery tickets.*] It was customary among the Romans to make presents to their guests at their grand entertainments, and these were often distributed by means of a whimsical kind of lottery, in which there were no blanks, but the prizes were very oddly assorted, and designated by the most far-fetched and puzzling titles. Augustus Cæsar, who was a great lover of fun, used to make such lotteries in the Saturnalia for his courtiers; some of his tickets turned up prizes of great value; others conferred upon the holders " cilicia, et spongias, et rutabula, et forcipes, atque alia id genus titulis obscuris et ambiguis." (Suet. in Vita Aug.)

[2] *Humbug silver.*] Literally, wicked silver. Argentum sceleratum.

produced, on which stood cruets of that metal. *A Pillow!*[1]
Forth came a scrag of mutton. *Whey and Contumely!*[2] which
signified wild strawberries and a bowl with an apple. *Pears
and Peaches !*[3] The drawer received a whip and a knife.
Sparrows and a Fly-trap ![4] To this were allotted raisins and
Attic honey. *Dinner dress and Walking dress!*[5] A piece of
meat and tablets. *Canal and Foot-measure!*[6] (A hare and
sandals.) *A Lamprey and a Letter!*[7] (a mouse tied to a frog
and a bundle of beet-root,) excited shouts of laughter. There
were a thousand other things of the same sort which have
now escaped my memory.

CHAPTER IX.

TRIMALCHIO'S BANQUET CONTINUED—ASCYLTOS PROVOKES THE ANGER
OF A GUEST, WHO RAILS AT HIM AND GITON—THE HOMERISTS—A
CALF BOILED WHOLE—PERFUMES—FRUITS AND SWEETMEATS—HOMAGE
TO THE LARES AND TO THE MASTER OF THE HOUSE—HISTORY OF A
WERWOLF—TRIMALCHIO'S TALE OF WITCHCRAFT—THE MINION AND
THE DOGS.

ASCYLTOS became quite intemperate in his mirth ; nothing
escaped his mockery ; he threw his arms up in the air, and

The joke, such as it is, consists in making sceleratum mean legged, from
σκελος.

[1] *A pillow.*] Cervical, from cervix, the neck.

[2] *Whey and Contumely.*] Serisapia et Contumelia ; the latter word is
resolved into *contus* (bowl) and μῆλον (apple). The rest has baffled all
attempts to unriddle it.

[3] *Pears and Peaches.*] The whip is for the pears, *porri,* because it hits
some way off, *porro !* Persica (peaches) stands for a crooked knife, like
the Persian acinaces.

[4] *Sparrows and a Fly-trap.*] Sparrows, *passeres :* raisins, uva *passa.*
" Honey and fly-trap " explains itself.

[5] *Dinner dress and Walking dress.*] Otherwise, Things pertaining to
dinner and to the *Forum,* or to use out of doors (*foras*) : cœnatoria et
forensia.

[6] *Canal and Foot-measure.*] The hare is *canalis,* because it is caught
by the dog, *canis :* a sandal is *pedalis,* a thing worn on the foot.

[7] *A Lamprey and a Letter.*] *Mus* (a mouse) and *rana* (a frog) tied together make *muræna* (a lamprey). The letter represented by a bundle
of beet-root is the Greek Beta.

laughed till the tears rolled down his cheeks. One of Trimalchio's freedmen, the same who sat next above me, seeing this, flew into a rage. "What are you laughing at, you sheep?" he cried. Is my master's entertainment not to your worshipful taste? You are a richer man belike, and fare better every day. So help me the guardian deities of this place, but if I was next him I would give him a box on the ear:[1] a pretty sprig to laugh at others; a nobody knows who, a night sneaker, that is not worth the very water he makes. Why if I only made mine round about him, he'd be done for; he'd never get out of it. By Hercules, I am not easily heated, but worms are bred in tender flesh. He laughs: what has he got to laugh at? Did your father buy a new-dropped lamb for the wool? Are you a Roman knight? And I am the son of a king. Why then, you'll say, have you been in servitude? Because I went into it to please myself, and had rather be a Roman citizen than a tributary king; and now I hope to live and thrive so as to be no man's jest. I am my own man now as good as another, and I a'n't ashamed to show my face. I owe no man a brass farthing, and never had a summons in my life. No one can come up to me in the forum, and say, Pay me what you owe me. I have bought lands, have put by some ingots, feed twenty bellies besides dogs; and have purchased my bed-fellow's freedom, that no man should wipe his hands on her hair. I paid a thousand gold denars to redeem her. I was made a sevir gratis, and hope to die in such wise that I need not blush in my grave. But are you in such a hurry that you cannot look behind you? Can you spy a louse on another man, and not a tick on yourself? Do you find us ridiculous though nobody else does? There's your preceptor, your elder, he does not see anything amiss in us; but you, you brat with the milk in your nose, that can't say boh to a goose, you pipkin, you strip of soaked leather, more limber but none the better, are you richer than we are? Dine twice and sup twice in a day.[2] For my part, I value my credit more than treasures. In a word, where's the man ever dunned me

---

[1] *I would give him a box on the ear.*] Heinsius and Antonius read, *balatu interdixissem*, I would put a stop to his baaing. He had previously called Ascyltos a sheep.

[2] *Dine twice and sup twice.*] This is the French proverb: Si tu es riche, mangez deux miches.

twice? I served forty years, yet no one knows whether I was slave or free. I was a long-haired boy when I came to this colony; the basilica was not yet built. I took pains however to please my master, a man of out and out splendoriferous dignity;[1] the parings of his nails are worth more than your whole body. I had enemies in his house that would fain have tripped me up, but, thanks to my genius, I escaped them all. I tell you for sure and certain, it is as easy to be born of free parents as to make the way I have done.[2] What are you gaping at, like a buck goat in a field of vetches?"

At this last phrase Gito, who was standing at my feet, could no longer hold in his laughter, which burst out uproariously, and thereby drew down upon himself a torrent of abuse from Ascyltos's antagonist.—"And you too, you curl-pated magpie, you laugh, do you? O the Saturnalia! Is this the month of December, pray? When did you count down your twentieth?[3] What do you mean, you gibbet carrion, you crow's meat? I will find some way to put you in Jupiter's bad books, you and that fellow that does not teach you better manners. As I hope to have my fill of bread, it is for my fellow freedman's sake I keep quiet; otherwise I would have settled accounts with you out of hand. All is not right on one side or the other, either with us or with those untaught barbarians that don't keep a tighter hand over you; but it is a true saying, Like master like man. I can hardly contain myself, and I am hot by nature; give me but a mess of peas porridge,[4] and I don't care twopence for my own mother. Never mind, I'll catch you in the street, you mouse, you mushroom.[5] May I never budge if I don't drive your master into

[1] *Splendoriferous dignity.*] If this is not English, neither is *malisto et dignitoso* Latin.

[2] *I tell you for sure,* &c.] Or according to another reading, That was doing bravely in earnest; for to be born a gentleman is as easy as " come here."

[3] *When did you count down your twentieth?*] That means, when were you made free? Every slave who was emancipated had to pay to the state a tax of five per cent. on his own market value.

[4] *Give me but a mess of peas porridge,* &c.] Some read cicereius, cum cœpi. The cicer, says Pliny, parches the ground in which it grows. The meaning then would be, I am one of your vetch sort; when I have once begun, I don't care, &c.

[5] *You mushroom.*] Terræ tuber is elsewhere used by Petronius to signify a puff-ball; possibly it may also mean a truffle, in Italian *tartufo,*

an augur-hole,[1] and you sha'n't escape me, no, by Hercules, not
though you cry for help to Olympian Jove. I won t leave a
hair of those carrotty locks on your poll, and I'll send your
twopenny master flying. Well and good; you'll come under
my tooth; either I don't know myself, or I'll put an end to
your laughing, though you had a beard of gold.[2] I'll set a
witch to work upon you,[3] and upon him that took such fine
care of your education. I never learned geometry, criticism,
and such-like humbug stuff, but I know the lapidary craft,
and can run you over a hundred things as to metal, weight,
and coin. If you have a mind you and I will try it between
us; I'll lay you a wager, you goblin, I'll soon convince you
that your father's money was thrown away upon you, though
I don't know rhetoric. There's no one can baffle me, for I
have a long reach. Shall I tell you which of us skips and
scuttles about and never gains an inch of ground? Which
of us tries to swell himself out all he can and only looks
smaller? You are all in a fidget, as fussy and as scared as a
mouse in a chamber-pot. Therefore hold your tongue, or
don't meddle with your betters, who don't trouble themselves
even to know of your existence; unless mayhap you think I
am taken with those box rings that you stole from your sweetheart. Blessings of Mercury! Let us go into the forum
and borrow money; you shall soon see what credit this iron
has.[4] Aha! is not this a pretty sight?—a fox in a sweat! as
I hope to thrive and die happy, or else may the public vow my
destruction, if I don't hunt you till you are forced to throw
your clothes over your head.[5] A pretty sight, I say again, and
so is he that teaches you such behaviour, a muff he is,[6] not a

a word which the Italian translator of Petronius tells us is still used as a
term of contempt in Naples.

[1] *Into an augur-hole.*] Literally, into a leaf of rue.

[2] *Though you had a beard of gold.*] The statues of the chief gods were
sometimes thus adorned.

[3] *I'll set a witch to work upon you.*] Or, according to another reading,
I'll bring the curse of Minerva upon you.

[4] *What credit this iron has.*] Meaning the iron ring which served him
for a seal: in other words, You will see what moneyed men think of my
seal at the foot of a bond.

[5] *Till you are forced to throw your clothes over your head.*] That is,
to turn up the skirt of your robe as high as possible, that your legs may
be free to run the faster.

[6] *A muff he is.*] All the manuscripts have mufrius, non magister.

master. When I went to school, the master used to say to us, 'You must not forget your manners; salute those you meet, without loitering and looking here or there; don't insult your elders, or amuse yourselves with counting the shops.' Not one of my school-fellows ever came to be worth twopence. That I am what you see me is the fruits of my own cleverness, for which I thank the gods."

Ascyltos had begun to retort the abuse, when Trimalchio, who was charmed with his freedman's eloquence, interposed, saying, "Come, come, no more scurrility; let us rather talk fair and softly; and you, Hermeros, spare the young man: his blood is in a ferment; do you be more reasonable:

'The vanquish'd in such strife is victor still.'

"When you yourself were such another capon, *Coco! Coco!*[1] you were not so stomachful as you are now. Let us therefore make better use of our time, and be jolly till the Homerists come in."

The troop presently entered, rattling their spears and shields. Trimalchio himself sat up on his couch, and whilst the Homerists were carrying on a dialogue in the usual pompous manner, he read aloud from a Latin book. Presently, during an interval of silence, he said, "Do you know what is the story they are acting?

"Diomede and Ganymede were two brothers, and Helen was their sister. Agamemnon carried her off, and palmed a hind on Diana in her stead. So Homer tells us how the Trojans and Tarentines fought together; but Agamemnon conquered, and married his daughter Iphigenia to Achilles, whereupon Ajax went mad, and will presently explain the argument to you."

When Trimalchio had done speaking, the Homerists gave a great shout, and a boiled calf was brought in on a huge dish, with a helmet on its head, amid a great bustle of servants running to and fro. Ajax followed with his drawn sword, and brandishing it like a madman, slashed right and left at the calf, picked up the pieces on the point of his blade, and presented them to the astonished guests.

What *mufrius* may mean no one can tell, except that it is the reverse of complimentary. Various conjectural emendations have been proposed, but none of them satisfactory.

[1] *Coco! Coco!*] Obscœniter: alludit ad gallinas patientes coitum.

We had not much time to admire a device so finely conceived and executed; for on a sudden the ceiling began to
crack, and the whole room trembled. I jumped up in great
alarm, fearing some tumbler might fall on my head; and the
rest of the company looked up in no less astonishment to see
what new wonder was sent down to us from the sky. And
behold you, in a moment the beams of the ceiling opened,
and from the dome above descended a great circle, hung all
round with golden crowns, and alabaster pots filled with perfumes. Being invited to help ourselves to these presents, we
cast our eyes down on the table, which was already covered
with a fresh service of sweetmeats, among which stood an
image of Priapus in pastry, supporting on his ample bosom
apples of all sorts, and clusters of grapes in the usual
way.

We eagerly laid hands on this magnificent dessert, when a
new and unexpected diversion rekindled our mirth; for there
was not a cake or a fruit but was filled with a saffron liquid,
which it spirted over us upon the slightest pressure. Conceiving therefore that there was something sacred in these
cates so religiously perfumed, we all rose up and cried out,
Prosperity to Augustus, the father of his country! But seeing
that some continued, even after this act of reverence, to help
themselves to fruit, we also filled our napkins, myself especially, who thought I could never load Gito's bosom sufficiently.

Meanwhile there came in three slaves dressed in white,
two of whom placed on the table the family Lares with their
bullæ,[1] whilst the third, carrying round a goblet of wine, cried
out, Be propitious, gods! He told us that one of them was
called Cerdo, another Felicio, and the third Lucro.[2] Then
came the bust of Trimalchio, and all the rest having kissed it,
we were ashamed not to follow their example.

---

[1] *Their bullæ.*] The bulla was an ornament, so called from its resemblance in form to a bubble floating on water. It was hung round the
necks of children of both sexes; for those of high birth it was made of
circular plates of gold; children of inferior rank wore only a piece of
leather. The bulla was laid aside at the age of adolescence, along with
the prætexta, and was usually dedicated to the Lares. It was no doubt
intended to serve not only as an ornament, but also as a preservative against
fascination, or the "evil eye." They make breast-pins of peculiar forms
in modern Italy, which are warranted to neutralize that dreaded influence.

[2] *Cerdo, Felicio, Lucro.*] That is to say, Business, Luck, and Gain.

After this, when we had all interchanged good wishes for mind and body,[1] Trimalchio turned to Niceros and said, "You used to be a pleasant table companion; how is it you are so dull to-day, and never utter a word? Do me the pleasure, I entreat you, to tell us one of your adventures."

Charmed by his friend's affability, Niceros replied, "May all good fortune slip away from me, if I am not ready to swoon for joy at your prosperity! Here goes for merriment therefore, and nothing else! though I am afraid these schoolmen will laugh at me. Well, let them. I will tell my story for all that. What shall I be the poorer for any man's laughter? Better my tale be laughed at than myself."

Thus having said . . . .
He began his story.

"When I was in service we lived in a narrow street, in the same house which is now Gavilla's. There, as the gods would have it, I fell in love with the wife of Terentius the tavernkeeper; you knew Melissa the Tarentine, a lovely kissingpiece![2] Yet it was not, by Hercules, in a carnal way, or for venery, that I cultivated her acquaintance, but rather because she was so good-natured. If I asked her a favour she never refused it; if she made a penny I had the half of it; I put all my savings into her keeping, and she never cheated me. Her husband happening to die when they were in the country, I cudgelled my brains how to get to her by hook or by crook, as was but right, for friends are best known in time of trouble.

"Luckily my master had gone to Capua to sell some old clothes. I seized the opportunity, and persuaded our guest to bear me company about five miles out of town; for he was a soldier, and as bold as death. We set out about cock-crow. and the moon shone bright as day, when coming amongst some monuments my man began to converse with the stars, whilst I jogged on singing and counting them. Presently I looked back after him, and saw him strip naked and lay his clothes by the side of the road. My heart was in my mouth in an instant, I stood like a corpse; when what does he do but make water all round his clothes, and in a crack he was

---

[1] *Interchanged good wishes for mind and body.*] A customary ceremony among the ancients at the end of a repast, like the "tak for måd" and the hand-shaking of the Swedes and Norwegians.

[2] *A lovely kissing-piece.*] Pulcherrimum basioballum.

turned into a wolf.   Don't think I'm joking; I would not tell
you a lie for the finest fortune in the world.

"But to go on with my story—after he was turned into a
wolf, he set up a howl and made straight for the woods.   At
first I did not know whether I was on my head or my heels;
but at last going to take up his clothes, I found them turned
into stone.   If ever a man had like to die of fright, it was I.
However I drew my sword, and hewed away at the ghosts
like mad,[1] until I arrived at my sweetheart's country-house.
When I entered her doors, I was all but at the last gasp; the
sweat streamed from my fork,[2] my eyes were set, and I never
expected to get over it.   My Melissa began to wonder why
I walked so late.   'Had you come a little sooner,' she said,
'you might at least have lent us a hand; for a wolf broke into
the farm and has butchered all our cattle; but though he got
off it was no laughing matter for him, for a servant of ours
ran him through the neck with a pike.'

"Hearing this I could not close an eye; but as soon as it
was daylight I ran home like a pedlar that has been eased of
his pack.   Coming by the place where the clothes had been
turned into stone, I saw nothing but a pool of blood; and
when I got home, I found my soldier lying in bed, like an ox
in a stall, and a surgeon dressing his neck.   I saw at once he
was a fellow that could change his skin,[3] and never after could
I eat bread with him, no, not if you would have killed me.
Those who would have taken a different view of the case are
welcome to their opinion; if I tell you a lie, may your genii
confound me!"

The whole company were sunk in speechless wonder.   "I
don't doubt the truth of the story," said Trimalchio; "if
there be faith in man, my hair stands on end! because I

---

[1] *Hewed away at the ghosts like mad.*]   Mataiotatos umbras cecidi.

[2] *Sweat streamed from my fork.*]   Per bifureum.   Burmann is quite
at fault here.   He supposes that *bifureum* means in this place the branch-
ing of the jaws.   Sweating jaws are not pathognomonic of fear, but sweat
from the *nates* and *perinæum* is eminently so.

[3] *A fellow that could change his skin.*]   Versipellis was the peculiar
designation of such a person.   In the middle ages he was called a were-
wolf, (i. e. man-wolf,) or in French *loupgarou*, which means the same
thing.   There was, according to Euanthes, an Arcadian legend that each
member of a certain family was changed into a wolf for nine years, and
after that period again regained his natural shape.

know that Niceros is not in the habit of telling idle tales; on the contrary, he is a trustworthy man, and not at all a bouncer. And by the same token I'll tell you myself a horrible occurrence, as extraordinary as an ass upon the tiles.

"When I was yet a long-haired stripling, (for from a boy I led a Chian life,) Iphis, my master's minion, died. By Hercules! he was a pearl, a paragon, and complete in all points. But whilst his poor mother was lamenting him, and several of us condoling with her, on a sudden the witches began their hubbub, so that you would have taken them for a pack of hounds hunting a hare. We had at that time a Cappadocian in the house, a tall daring fellow, who would have made bold to dethrone thundering Jupiter. This man, wrapping his mantle carefully round his left arm, sprang fearlessly out of doors, and as it might be here (no harm to what I touch!)[1] ran a woman clean through. We heard a groan, but the witches—I won't tell you a lie—we did not see. Back came our champion and threw himself on a bed, but as black and blue all over as if he had been flogged with whips, for it seems some ill hand had touched him. We shut the door, and went on with our mourning; but the mother, embracing her son, and touching him, found nothing but a mawkin; it had neither heart, entrails, nor anything else; for the witches had carried off the boy, and left a wad of straw in his room. What think you now? They are deep ones surely, those hags, they fly by night, and turn everything topsy-turvy. As for our tall fellow, after what happened then, he never came to his own colour again, but died a few days afterwards raving mad."

We all looked amazed, as not doubting what he said, and kissing the table[2] began to entreat the night-hags to keep to their own business and let us alone as we returned from the entertainment. By this time the lamps seemed to me to burn double, and the whole room to turn round, when Trimalchio exclaimed, "I call on you, Plocrimus; have you no story to

---

[1] *No harm to what I touch.*] We are to suppose him illustrating his narration by making a feigned thrust at the nearest guest.

[2] *Kissing the table.*] The table here supplied the place of the altar, as in Ovid, *Amor.* i. 4, 27. A similar superstitious usage was that of touching the ground with the hand at mention of the *inferi*. Plaut. *Most.* ii. 2. 37.

tell? nothing to divert us with? you that used to be so amusing, and to recite such capital dialogues interspersed with songs? Heigho! sweet toothsome things,[1] where are ye?"

"Ah!" said the other, "my racing days are over since I've grown gouty; but when I was young I almost sung myself into a consumption. Then indeed for dancing, for monopolylogues, for all the waggery of a barber's shop, where was there my fellow except Apelles?" So saying, and clapping his hand to his mouth, he sputtered out I know not what horrid gibberish, which he said was Greek. Trimalchio moreover imitated the trumpets, and then turned to his minion, whom he called Crœsus. This was a blear-eyed boy with filthy teeth, who was amusing himself with a little black bitch disgustingly fat; he swathed her in a green scarf, set half a loaf for her on the couch, and when she refused to eat he crammed her with it. This put Trimalchio in mind to send for Scylax, the guard of his house and family; and straightway there was brought in a huge dog with a chain round its neck, which in obedience to a kick from the porter lay down before the table. Trimalchio threw him a piece of white bread, saying, "There's no one in this house of mine loves me better than this dog!" The boy was enraged to hear Scylax so lavishly commended, and setting down his bitch, cheered her on to the combat. Scylax, as might be expected of a dog of his kind, filled the room with a tremendous barking, and nearly shook Crœsus's little Jewel to pieces; nor was this the end of the scuffle; for a candelabrum being overthrown on the table, broke all the crystal vessels, and splashed some of the guests with scalding oil.

Trimalchio, not to seem concerned at the damage, kissed the boy and bade him get on his back. In an instant he was riding cock-horse, and slapping his master's shoulders with the flat of his hand, cried out, laughing, "Horns! Horns! how many horns are here?"[2] After having been made a

---

[1] *Sweet toothsome things, where are ye?*] Abistis dulces carycæ: "καρύχη est intritum ex variis condimentis delicatis compositum." Reines. The last French translator (Nisard's collection) renders the passage thus: "Hélas! vous voilà parties, douces friandises de nos desserts."

[2] *Horns! Horns!* &c.] Bucco, bucco, quot sunt hic? Heinsius understands this of a game still played by children. One of the players has his eyes bandaged, and the others require him to guess the number of fingers they touch him with. Some editors read Bucca, (cheek,)

horse of for a while, Trimalchio ordered a very large vessel to be filled with wine and given to the slaves that sat at our feet; but on this condition, he added, "Whoever refuses his share shall have it poured on his head. Business by day, but now's the time for fun."

CHAPTER X.

TRIMALCHIO'S BANQUET CONCLUDED — ARRIVAL OF A NEW AND DISTINGUISHED GUEST — HIS ACCOUNT OF THE DINNER HE HAS COME FROM — HIS WIFE AND FORTUNATA EXHIBIT THEIR FINERY — HABINNAS'S FAVOURITE SLAVE ENTERTAINS THE COMPANY — THE EPIDIPNION — TRIMALCHIO INVITES HIS SLAVES TO JOIN THE PARTY — HIS DIRECTIONS FOR HIS MONUMENT — HE READS HIS WILL — THE BATH AFTER DINNER — ENCOLPIUS AND ASCYLTOS ATTEMPT TO STEAL OFF, AND FALL INTO THE FOUNTAIN — THEY JOIN THE BATHERS — QUARREL BETWEEN TRIMALCHIO AND FORTUNATA — TRIMALCHIO RELATES HIS OWN HISTORY — AND REHEARSES HIS FUNERAL — THE WATCH THINK THE HOUSE ON FIRE AND BREAK IN — THE THREE FRIENDS ESCAPE IN THE CONFUSION.

AFTER this display of philanthropy, there came in a course of delicacies, the bare remembrance of which, if you will believe me, makes my stomach heave. For there were set before us crammed fowls instead of thrushes, one for each guest, and chaperonned goose-eggs.[1] Trimalchio urged us very pressingly to eat, and assured us the fowls were boned.

At this moment a lictor knocked at the door of the banquet room, and in came a new guest robed in white,[2] with a large train at his heels. Struck by such an appearance of state, and imagining it was the Prætor, I tried to rise and set my naked feet on the ground; but Agamemnon laughed at my

which may be equivalent to trumpeter, or crier. See Juvenal, iii. 35. Bucco is a contemptuous expression, as it were "guess, booby." See Plautus in Bacchid. v. sc. 1, Stulti, stolidi, fatui, fungi, bardi, blenni, buccones.

[1] *Chaperonned goose-eggs.*] That is, having a cap on them, which was formed by making an opening in one end of the raw egg, and mixing flour with the albumen which issued from it during the cooking.

[2] *Robed in white.*] The dresses worn at table were usually coloured; but this new guest, as we shall presently see, had come straight from a funeral banquet, and on all such occasions nothing but white was worn.

trepidation: "Sit still, you booby," he said, "this is Habinnas the Sevir; he is a mason, and excels, it seems, in making monuments."

Reassured by these words, I resumed my place, and watched with great admiration the entrance of Habinnas. He was already drunk and leaned on his wife's shoulder; his head was loaded with garlands, and his forehead so smeared with perfumes, that they trickled into his eyes. He took the Prætor's place,[1] and called immediately for wine and hot water.

Delighted to see his friend thus jovially disposed, Trimalchio himself called for a larger goblet, and asked him how he had been entertained?

"We had everything," replied the other, "except your company; for my inclination was here; though, by Hercules, all went off well. Scissa gave a novendial feast[2] for his servant Misellus, whom he enfranchised after he was dead.[3] I believe he will share a good round sum with the collectors of the twentieths,[4] for they estimate the property of the defunct at fifty thousand; and indeed everything was very pleasant, though we had to pour half our wine on the dead bones."[5]

"But what had you for dinner?" said Trimalchio.

"I'll tell you if I can," replied the other, "but I have such a memory that sometimes I forget my own name. However, for the first course we had a hog crowned with a pudding, and garnished with fritters and giblets, capitally dressed; and there was endive,[6] and bread of whole meal, which I like better than white, for it makes a man strong, and when I do my jobs afterwards, I am not forced to cry.[7]

---

[1] *The Prætor's place.*] That is, the place of honour, that which would be filled by the Prætor, the governor of the province, if he were present.

[2] *A novendial feast.*] It was usual to perform a sacrifice and hold a feast on the ninth day after a funeral; they were thence called novendial.

[3] *Enfranchised after he was dead.*] To entitle the corpse to honourable burial, such as was bestowed only on freemen.

[4] *The collectors of the twentieths.*] The officers who received the duty payable by a slave on his emancipation.

[5] *Pour half our wine on the dead bones.*] This was the regular custom in the novendial. The banquet appears to have been generally held in or near the tomb. Among the tombs at Pompeii there is a funeral triclinium for the celebration of these feasts.

[6] *Endive.*] Instead of *certe betam* we read with Reinesius *cicerbitam*.

[7] *I am not forced to cry.*] The laxative properties of brown bread are well known.

For the next course we had excellent cold tarts with Spanish honey poured warm over them; so I ate no small share of the tarts, and smeared myself well with the honey. All round these chick peas and lupines, nuts in plenty, and an apple a-piece; I however brought away two, and here they are tied up in my napkin; for if I carry home nothing to my favourite slave I get abuse. Ha! true; my wife reminds me we had on a side table a piece of bear's ham, and Scintilla having eat a morsel of it without knowing what it was, had like to throw her heart up. I, on the contrary, ate more than a pound of it, for it tasted quite like boar; and said I, if bears eat a man, with how much more reason may men eat bears? Finally we had cream cheese, grape jelly,[1] a snail a-piece, chitterlings, livers in patépans, chaperonned eggs, turnips and mustard, and, peace be with Palamedes! a dish of kidney beans;[2] there was also handed round a wooden bowl full of salted olives, whence some of the party unfairly helped themselves to fist-fuls; as for the ham, we sent it away. But tell me, Gaius, pray why is not Fortunata at table?"

"Why? You know her," said Trimalchio; "until she has got all her plate together, and distributed our leavings among the servants, not so much as a drop of water passes her lips."

"But if she does not take her place, I'm off," returned Habinnas; and he was getting up accordingly, when at a signal from their master all the servants called out Fortunata! four times and more. In she came then, her robe kilted up with a green girdle, so as to display beneath it her cherry-coloured tunic, her corded buskins, and her gold-laced slippers. Then wiping her hands on the handkerchief she wore round her neck, she placed herself on the couch on which Scintilla, the wife of Habinnas, reclined, and kissed her while the other clapped her hands. "And have I the happiness to see you?" she exclaimed. Ere long they became so very sociable that

[1] *Grape jelly.*] Sapam. This was sweet must thickened by boiling till two-thirds had evaporated.

[2] *A dish of kidney beans.*] This is a most obscure passage. We read, with Antonius, catillum conchiclatum, that is, refertum conchiclis, these being a kind of beans which were cooked in their pods. We confess however that we cannot tell why the mention of such a dish should have called forth the exclamation, Pax, Palamedes! Reinesius reads catillum congelatum per pelamides, a dish jellied with tunny fry.

Fortunata took off her enormous bracelets[1] to show them to the admiring Scintilla; and at last she even undid her buskins and her hair net, which she assured her friend was of the purest gold.

Trimalchio observed these proceedings, and desired all the things to be brought to him. "See," he said, "this woman's finery! This is the way we poor fools are ruined. Six pounds and a half this bracelet should weigh; and nevertheless I have myself a bracelet that weighs ten pounds, and which I have had made out of Mercury's thousandths."[2] And that he might not be thought a liar he sent for scales and had them weighed by us all round. Nor was Scintilla less ostentatious; for taking off a gold box that hung from her neck, and which she called her luck-case, she drew out of it two pendants, and presented them in her turn to Fortunata's inspection. "Thanks to my husband's liberality," she said, "no woman has finer."

"Ay," said Habinnas, "you bothered my life out[3] to make me buy you those glass beans. Most assuredly, if I had a daughter, I would cut off her ears. If there were no women we should have everything as cheap as dirt; but as it is, we must p— hot and drink cold."[4]

---

[1] *Took off her enormous bracelets.*] Otherwise, Took her bracelets off her coarse arms.

[2] *Mercury's thousandths.*] Two different explanations have been given of this phrase. The lowest rate of interest was that which amounted to one thousandth part of the capital per month, being equivalent to a rate of $1\frac{1}{5}$ per cent. per annum. Trimalchio's statement may be tantamount to saying that he had at least ten thousand pounds' weight of gold lent out at interest. Burmann and Antonius think rather that Trimalchio had vowed the tenth part of the profit of some speculation to Mercury the patron of traffic, but had afterwards cheated the god, and made himself a bracelet out of the consecrated thousandth. In either case his intention was to impress his guests with an idea of his enormous wealth.

[3] *You bothered my life out.*] Excatarissasti, a word coined by the semi-Greek Habinnas from ἐκκαταράσσειν. Various other readings have been proposed, among the rest excatharizasti, from καθαρίξειν, to purge, which the last French translator has rendered "Tu m'as tourmenté comme un remède."

[4] *We must p— hot and drink cold.*] Meaning, we must spend a great deal on these women and get very little for our money. The ungallant proverb is taken from the trade of the fullers, to whom the urine they used for cleansing cloth was more valuable than the cold water they drank.

Meanwhile the two women, though piqued, kept laughing to themselves, and interchanging tipsy kisses ; the one extolling the notable management of the lady of the house ; the other complaining of her husband's minions and his unthrift. While they were thus hugging each other, Habinnas got up softly, caught hold of Fortunata's outstretched legs, and upset her on the couch. Ah ! ah ! she screamed out, as her tunic slipped back above her knees. Then quickly re-arranging her drapery, she threw herself on Scintilla's bosom, and hid with her handkerchief a face made uglier by its blushes.

After a little interval, Trimalchio called for the dessert. The servants removed all the first tables, brought in others, then strewed the floor with saw-dust tinged with crocus and vermilion, and (what I had never seen before) with specular stone beaten to powder.[1] This being done, Trimalchio said to us, " I could be content with what is here provided, for here you have your second tables ;[2] however," (turning to a servant,) " if you have anything in the way of dessert, bring it in."

Meanwhile an Egyptian boy that served us with hot water began to imitate the nightingale, Trimalchio crying out from time to time, " Change !"[3] Then came another interlude. A slave who was sitting at the feet of Habinnas, by desire, I believe, of his master, suddenly bawled out

> " Meanwhile Æneas cuts his watery way,
> Fixed on his voyage."[4]

A harsher sound never grated my ears ; for besides the fellow's barbarous pronunciation and false quantities, he mingled the whole with scraps of Atellan farces, so that for the first

---

[1] *Specular stone.*] This was probably talc or mica. Burmann remarks that this passage has a decisive bearing on the question which has been mooted respecting the age to which the author of the Satyrion belonged, for Seneca writes (Epist. lx.) that this use of specular stone was an invention of his own day.

[2] *You have your second tables.*] This is one of Trimalchio's bad jokes. The dessert was called mensæ secundæ, the second table.

[3] *Change !*] That is, Change the strain. Trimalchio admired the performance, and desired the boy to vary his modulations as the nightingale does.

[4] *Meanwhile,* &c.] This is the beginning of the fifth book of the Æneid.

time in my life I was disgusted even with Virgil. Want of
breath compelling him at last to desist, Habinnas exclaimed,
" And the chap has never had any teaching ! Only I sent him
sometimes to hear the mountebanks, and that 's the way he
picked it up ; and so he has not his match whether for imitating the muleteers or the mountebanks. The scamp is pro-
digiously clever. He is a shoemaker, a cook, a confectioner,
a perfect Jack-of-all-trades. He has two faults, however, but
for which he would be worth any money : he is circumcised,
and he snores. As for his squinting, I don't mind that ;
Venus does the same.[1] That 's why his tongue is never still ;
always wide awake. I paid three hundred denars for him."

Here he was interrupted by Scintilla : "Nay, but you don't
mention all the rascal's bad qualities," she said. "He is a
pimp,[2] but I 'll take care he shall have a brand."

Trimalchio laughed and said, " There he shows himself a
true Cappadocian ;[3] he does not cheat himself of anything ;
and, by Hercules, I don't blame him, for no one would mention the fact with honour in his funeral oration. None of your
jealousy, Scintilla ! I know you women believe me. So may
you have me safe and sound, as I used to fence with Mammea
herself, my master's wife, till he suspected it, and therefore
sent me to be bailiff in the country.[4] But peace, tongue ! and
I 'll give you a cake."

Taking all this for laudation, the rascally slave pulled out
an earthenware lamp from his bosom, and for half an hour or
more imitated the sound of the trumpet, whilst Habinnas accompanied him, pressing down his lower lip with his fingers.
Finally he stepped into the middle of the room, and one while
brandishing split reeds he parodied a dance ; at another, with
a frock, and a whip in his hand, he acted the muleteer, till

---

[1] *Venus does the same.*] She was *pœta*, she had a slight cast in her eye.
Hence it was a customary politeness to compare a squinting woman to
Venus. Thus Ovid, Art. Am. ii. 659,

Si qua straba est, Veneri similis ; si rava, Minervæ.

[2] *A pimp.*] Agaga :—and of course served his master in that capacity.

[3] *A Cappadocian.*] It was a very popular adage : τρία κάππα κάκιρα,
three CC stand for superlative rascals, viz. Cappadocians, Cretans, Ci-
licians.

[4] *Sent me to be bailiff in the country.*] The office of the *villicus* was
one of trust, but it was inferior to that of the *dispensator* which Trimalchio had filled in the town house.

Habinnas calling him, kissed him, gave him a cup of wine, and said, " Well done, Massa, I will give you a pair of shoes."

We should never have seen the last of these insufferable stupidities, but for the arrival of the last course, consisting, in the first place, of thrushes in pastry, stuffed with raisins and nuts. Then came quinces stuck over with prickles to resemble sea-urchins. All this would have been tolerable but for another dish, so monstrously revolting, that we would rather have perished of hunger than have touched it. At first we took it for a fat goose surrounded by fish and fowl of all sorts, until Trimalchio said, " Everything you see there is made out of one body."

I, being a man of great sagacity, immediately guessed what it might be, and whispered Agamemnon, " I shall be much surprised if all this is not made out of excrements, or at least of mud ; I have seen such a fictitious banquet at Rome during the Saturnalia."

I had scarce done speaking when Trimalchio resumed : " So may I grow bigger in fortune, not in body, as my cook has made all this out of a hog. A more valuable fellow it would be impossible to find. Only say the word, he will make you a fish out of the belly ; a wood-pigeon out of the lard ; a turtle-dove out of the gammon, and a hen out of the shoulder ; and therefore he has received a very fine name, a conception of my own, for we call him Dædalus ; and because he is a good fellow, I brought him from Rome a present of knives of Noric steel." [1]   And immediately he had the knives brought in, turned them over and admired them, and was even so obliging as to allow us to try their edges on our cheeks.

Just then in rushed two servants who seemed as if they had quarrelled at the fountain ; at any rate they had pitchers still hanging from yokes on their shoulders. When Trimalchio gave his decision upon the point in dispute, neither would abide by his sentence, but each broke the other's pitcher with a stick. Amazed at the insolence of the drunken varlets, we stared with all our eyes at the combat, and saw oysters and scallops falling from the broken pitchers ; and these were gathered up by a servant and carried round in a charger to the guests.

[1] *Noric steel.*]   Norica was the ancient name of the Black Forest in Bavaria.

These elegant devices were matched by the ingenious cook,
who brought in snails upon a silver gridiron, singing all the
while in a cracked and horribly unpleasant voice. I am ashamed
to relate what followed, it was such an unheard-of luxury.
Long-haired boys brought in a rich perfume in a silver basin,
with which they anointed our feet, having first bound them
and our thighs and ancles with garlands of flowers. They
also perfumed the wine vessels with the same ointment, and
poured some of it melted into the lamps.

Fortunata had by this time taken it into her head to dance,
and Scintilla was making more noise with her hands than
with her tongue, when Trimalchio said, "I give you leave to
come to the table, Philargyrus, and you, Carrio, though you are
a champion of the green,[1] and bid your bed-fellow, Minophila,
do the same."

In short, we were almost thrust off our couches, such was
the throng of servants that suddenly invaded the room; and
who should be placed above me but the ingenious cook who
had made a goose out of a pig, all stinking of pickle and
sauces? Nor was it enough for him to recline at table, but
he must immediately begin to imitate Ephesus the tragedian;
after which he offered his master a bet that at the next chariot-
races the green would win.

"My friends," cried Trimalchio, delighted at this challenge,
"slaves too are men; they have sucked the same milk as we,
though an ill fate has borne them down; however, without
prejudice to myself, mine shall soon drink the water of the
free. In a word, I enfranchise them all by my last will and
testament.

"To Philargyrus I leave moreover a farm and his bed-

---

[1] *A champion of the green.*] The drivers of the racing chariots in the
Circus were divided into four companies, each distinguished by a different
colour, to represent the four seasons of the year, and called a *factio* :
thus *factio prasina*, the green, represented the spring ; *factio russata*, red,
the summer ; *factio veneta*, azure, the autumn ; and *facto alba*, or *albata*,
white, the winter. The enthusiasm of the Romans for the chariot-races
of the Circus exceeded all bounds. Lists of the horses, with their names
and colours, and those of the drivers, were handed about, and heavy bets
made on each faction ; and sometimes the contests between two parties
broke out into open violence and bloody quarrels, until at last the disputes
which originated in the Circus had nearly cost the emperor Justinian his
crown.

fellow ; to Carrio a block of houses,[1] a twentieth,[2] and a bed
and bedding complete. As for my dear Fortunata, I make
her my residuary legatee, and commend her to all my friends ;
and all this I publicly declare, to the end that my family may
love me as well now as they will when I am dead."

All the servants were loud in their expressions of gratitude
to so good a master, when Trimalchio, no longer in the sportive mood, called for the copy of his will, and read it aloud
from beginning to end, amid the sighs and sobs of the whole
household. Then turning to Habinnas, "Tell me, my dear
friend," he said, "are you building my monument as I directed? I earnestly entreat that at the feet of my statue you
represent my little bitch, with garlands, and boxes of perfumes, and all the fights of Petronas,[3] that with your good
help I may live after I am dead. Be sure too that it have a
hundred feet frontage, and a depth of two hundred;[4] for I
desire that there be all sorts of fruit trees round my ashes,
and vines in abundance ; since it is a great mistake to adorn
houses for the living, and to bestow no care on those in
which we must dwell so long. Therefore, above all things,
I will have this inscription :

THIS MONUMENT SHALL NOT DESCEND TO MY HEIR.

"Moreover, I will take care to provide by my will that my
mortal remains receive no insult ; for I will appoint one of
my freedmen custodian of my tomb, that the rabble may not
come and drop their wax about it. I beg too that you will
carve me ships under full sail,[5] and myself in my senatorial
robes sitting on the tribunal, with five gold rings[6] on my fingers,
and throwing money out of a bag among the people ; for you

[1] *A block of houses.*] Insulam. This was properly a detached house ;
an insula, however, generally contained several separate houses, or at
least separate apartments or shops, which were let to different families.

[2] *A twentieth.*] That is to say, the amount of the tax he would have
to pay on obtaining his freedom. Thus among ourselves bequests to servants are usually made clear of legacy duty.

[3] *All the fights of Petronas.*] Probably a gladiator belonging to him.

[4] *A hundred feet frontage,* &c.] Enormous dimensions for a monument. Few extant measure more than twenty feet in any direction.

[5] *Ships under full sail.*] Emblems of prosperity.

[6] *Five gold rings.*] Nothing less would content him than a gold ring
on each finger, though as a freedman he was not entitled to wear even
one.

know I gave a public banquet and two gold denars to every
guest. Let there be shown, if it so please you, a banqueting-
hall; and let all the people be seen enjoying themselves to
their hearts' content. On my right hand place my Fortunata's
statue, holding a dove, and leading a little bitch[1] in a string;
also my Cicaro; also some large jars, close stopped, that the
wine may not run out; but you may sculpture one of them
as broken, and a boy crying over it; in the middle a horologe,
that whoever wants to see what time of day it is, must, will
he, nill he, read my name. As for the epitaph, examine this
carefully, and see if you think it will do:

> C. POMPEIUS TRIMALCHIO, ANOTHER MÆCENAS,
> RESTS HERE.
> THE RANK OF SEVIR WAS DECREED TO HIM IN HIS ABSENCE.
> THOUGH HE MIGHT HAVE BEEN IN ALL THE DECURIÆ OF
> ROME,
> YET HE WOULD NOT.
> PIOUS, BRAVE, LOYAL,
> HE RAISED HIMSELF FROM LITTLE,
> LEFT BEHIND HIM THIRTY MILLIONS OF SESTERCES, YET
> NEVER
> HEARD A PHILOSOPHER.
> MAYEST THOU PROSPER TOO.

When he had read this, Trimalchio began to shed a deluge
of tears; Fortunata wept; Habinnas wept; in fine, all the
servants, as if they had been invited to a funeral, filled the
room with their lamentations. Nay, even I myself was beginning to cry, when Trimalchio exclaimed, "Since, then, we
know we must die, why do we not make the most of life? If
you'd be happy, let us fling ourselves into the bath. I will
take upon myself to say none of you will repent it, for it is as
hot as an oven."

"Surely, surely," said Habinnas, "of one day to make two,[2]

---

[1] *Holding a dove, and leading a little bitch.*] Emblems of conjugal
love and fidelity.

[2] *Of one day to make two.*] Among the Romans the bath was taken
so regularly before the principal meal, the cœna, that bathing came to be
considered as a preparation for eating. Hence Habinnas approves so
heartily the proposal of a second bath, as inferring of course a second
banquet. The practice of bathing after dinner was noted as a mark of
intemperance: thus Apuleius says in his Apology, "I say that Crassus

I desire nothing better !" and getting up barefoot he followed Trimalchio, who led the way in great glee.

"What say you?" said I, turning to Ascyltos, " as for me, if I see the bath, I shall faint at once."

" Let us assent," he replied, " and make our escape in the bustle when they are going to the bath."

I agreed. Giton led the way through the portico and we reached the door, where a chained dog received us with such a terrible barking, that Ascyltos fell into the tank.[1] I too, who was drunk, and who had been frightened by a painted dog, in trying to help him, fell in myself; we were rescued, however, by the porter, who quieted the dog, pulled us out, and laid us shivering on the dry ground. Giton had found out a very clever way to ransom himself from the dog, by throwing everything we had given him from the dinner to the barking brute, whose rage was stilled by this diversion. But when, shaking with cold, we asked the porter to let us out, " You are mistaken," he said, "if you suppose you can go out the same way you came in. No guest is ever let out at the same gate ; they come in at one and go out at another."

What could we do in this unfortunate dilemma, prisoners in this new kind of labyrinth, and now brought to such a pass as even to wish for the bath ? We therefore desired the porter to show us the way to it; and throwing off our clothes, which Giton spread to dry in the porch, we entered the bath, which was narrow and like a cooling cistern. Trimalchio stood upright in it, and not even there could he abstain from his filthy boasting ; for nothing, he said, was more agreeable than to bathe without a crowd, and that the place had once been a bake-house. Lassitude compelled him at last to sit down, and tempted by the resonance of the bath-room, he opened his drunken mouth, turned it up to the ceiling, and began to murder the songs of Menecrates, as we were told by those who understood his jargon.

has been snoring drunk this long while, or that he is taking a second bath and sweating off his wine, that he may be ready for a second drinking bout after dinner."

[1] *The tank.*] The centre of the atrium was usually open to the sky. The cavity of the roof was called *compluvium*, and the corresponding part of the floor, which received the rain-water in a quadrangular basin, was called the *impluvium*. Sometimes the basin received also the water of a fountain.

Some of the guests were running round the margin holding
hands, giggling, and making a great uproar; others were
trying to pick up a ring from the floor with their hands tied
behind them, or kneeling down to bend back and kiss their
toes.   Whilst they were diverting themselves in this way, we
descended into a hot bath prepared for Trimalchio, after which,
having got rid of the fumes of our wine, we were conducted
into another saloon, where Fortunata had set out a splendid
repast in her own way.   Over our heads hung lustres with
little figures of fishermen in bronze; the tables were of massive silver, the cups of gilded pottery; and before us was a
wine-bag, pouring out its contents in a stream.

"My friends," said Trimalchio, "this day a slave of mine
has cut his first beard. He is a notable and thrifty lad, barring mischance.[1]   So let us moisten our clay, and make revel
till daylight."

The words were hardly uttered when a cock crew, to the
great discomfiture of Trimalchio, who immediately ordered
wine to be thrown under the table, and the lamps to be
sprinkled with it; besides which he shifted a ring to his right
hand, and said, "It is not for nothing this trumpeter has
sounded; for either there is sure to be a fire, or somebody
will die in the neighbourhood. Far from us be the omen!
And so whoever brings me this prophet of evil shall have a
present."

In a twinkling a cock was brought in, and Trimalchio
ordering him to fricasseed, he was torn up and put into a stew-
pan, by that most accomplished cook who a little before had
manufactured fowls and fish; and whilst Dædalus was making
the water boil, Fortunata pounded pepper in a boxwood
mortar.

Having despatched this delicate dish, Trimalchio said to
the servants, "What, have not you supped yet? Be off and
let others take your places;" whereupon, in came another set
of servants, the outgoers crying, Farewell, Gaius! the in-
comers, Hail, Gaius! And here our mirth began to be disturbed; for a good-looking boy coming in with the last set of
attendants, Trimalchio laid hold of him, and kissed him over

---

[1] *Barring mischance.*] Præfiscine. In praising any one, the superstitious Romans used this word parenthetically, by way of deprecating
the ill luck attendant on such language.

and over again. Fortunata, that she might be even with her husband, and assert her lawful rights, began to load him with abuse, calling him a lump of dirt, an infamous man, that would not set bounds to his lechery; and she wound up by saying he was a dog.

Confounded and enraged at this attack, Trimalchio flung his cup at the head of Fortunata, who squalled as if her eye was knocked out, and clapped her trembling hands to her face. Scintilla too was all dismay, and sheltered her distressed friend in her bosom; and at the same time a servant officiously applied a pitcher full of cold water to her cheek, over which she leaned moaning and weeping.

"What!" cried Trimalchio, "could not this strumpet let me be? Though I took her from the kneading-trough, and made her an honest woman; but now she swells like a frog, and beslavers her own bosom, the faggot! But so it is, one who is born in a garret does not dream of a palace. So help me my Genius! I will take the conceit out of this trolloping Cassandra. When I was not worth twopence, I might have married a fortune of ten millions of sesterces. You know it's no lie. It was no longer ago than yesterday that Agatho the perfumer took me aside, and says he to me, "I advise you not to let your race die out;" but I, who wished to act like a good-natured man, and not to seem changeable, I have stuck a thorn in my own foot.[1] Never mind: I'll warrant I'll make you wish you could dig me up with your nails; and that you may know this moment what you have done for yourself—Habinnas! I forbid you to put her statue on my tomb, that I may have none of her wrangling when I am dead; nay, that she may know I can plague her, I will not have her kiss my corpse."

After this thunder-clap Habinnas began to entreat him to forget his anger. "There is none of us," said he, "but does amiss; we are not gods, but men." Scintilla spoke to the same purpose amidst her tears, and besought him by his Genius, and calling him Gaius, to be pacified.

Trimalchio could no longer refrain from tears. "I beseech you, Habinnas," said he, "as you hope to enjoy what you have got, if I have done any harm, spit in my face. I kissed

---

[1] *I have stuck a thorn*, &c.] Literally, I have driven the adze into my own leg.

the boy it is true, not for his beauty, but because he is a hopeful, thrifty lad. He can say ten declamations by heart, reads his book at sight, has saved the price of his freedom out of his daily rations, and has got him out of his own money a little box-stool and two drinking cups. Does he not deserve that I should prize him like the apple of my eye? But Fortunata will not have it so. That's your game, is it, bandy-legs? Take my advice, make much of what you have got, you she-kite! Don't provoke me, sweetheart; or may be I'll let you see whose head is hardest. You know me; what I have once made up my mind to is as fixed as a tenpenny nail.—But let us think of the living.

"I entreat you, my friends, be merry. I myself was once as you are, but by my own merit I have come to be what you see me. It is the heart that makes the man, all the rest is but stuff. I buy well, I sell well; others will tell you a different story; but as for me, I am ready to burst with prosperity. What, crying still, you grunter? Wait a bit, and I will give you something to cry for in earnest.

"But as I was saying, it was my thrift and steadiness made me the man I am. When I came from Asia I was no bigger than this candlestick. I used to measure myself by it every day; and that I might the sooner have a beard under my nose, I used to rub my lips with the lamp oil. However, I served my master's pleasure for fourteen years (it's no dishonour to obey one's master) and satisfied my mistress at the same time. You know what I mean. I say no more, for I am not one of the boasting sort."

"At last, as the gods would have it, I found myself master in the house, and trust me, I began to live after my own fancy. To make a long story short, my master made me co-heir with Cæsar, and I came in for a senator's fortune. But no one ever has enough, and I had a desire to turn merchant. Not to detain you long, I built five ships, freighted them with wine, (it was worth its weight in gold then,) and sent them to Rome. Just as if I had bid them do it on purpose, they were wrecked, every one of them. It's a fact, and no story: in one day Neptune swallowed me thirty millions of sesterces. You fancy I lost courage? No, by Hercules! this loss only sharpened my appetite. I went to work as though nothing had happened, and built other ships, larger, better, and more fortunate, so that everybody said I was a man of pluck. A great ship, you know, has great strength.[1] Again I shipped wine, bacon, beans, Capuan perfumery, and slaves. Fortunata behaved like a wife on this occasion; for she sold all her jewels and all her clothes, and put a hundred gold pieces into my hand; this was the leaven of my little fortune. What the gods will is soon done; by one trip I cleared a round ten millions of sesterces. I immediately redeemed all the lands that had been my patron's; built a house; bought cattle to sell again; everything throve under my hand like a honey-comb. After I came to have more wealth than my whole country is worth, hands off! I withdrew from commerce, and began to lend money on usury to freedmen. And being quite unwilling to continue my business, I was dissuaded[2] from doing so by an astrologer who had chanced to come to our colony, a little Greek, Serapa by name, a man who was in the counsels of the gods. He told me lots of things I had clean forgotten, and laid them all before me as past as thread to needle; he knew my very inside, and could all but have told me what I had had for dinner the day before. You would have thought he had lived with me all his life.

"I say, Habinnas, you were present, I think, when he said, 'You have made use of all that wealth of yours to put a mis-tress over you; you are not very lucky in friends; no one ever repays your kindness; you have vast estates; you are fostering a viper under your wing.' And why should I not tell you that he made known to me I have still thirty years, four months, and two days of life before me; and that, more-over, I shall have another estate left me shortly?

"This was what my stars foretold me; and if I have the luck to extend my lands to Apulia, I shall have made pretty good way in this world. Meanwhile, by the favour of Mer-cury, I have built me this house; it was a mere cottage, as you know, and now it is a temple. It has four dining-rooms,

---

[1] *A great ship has great strength.*] Magna navis magnam fortitudinem habet. This is said jocularly, the phrase having another meaning besides that we have given it, namely, To build a great ship implies great bold-ness.

[2] *I was dissuaded.*] Some editors have proposed an alteration of the text here, because of the absurdity of dissuading a man from what he has no mind to; but it is by the practice of such absurdities that chartalans thrive.

twenty bed-chambers, two marble porticoes, a store-room on
the upper story, a chamber in which I sleep myself, a sitting-
room for this viper,[1] a capital porter's lodge, and accommoda-
tion for a hundred guests. In short, whenever Scaurus comes
this way, he will lodge nowhere else, though his father has a
house by the sea-side. I have many other conveniences too,
which I will show you presently. Take my word for it, *Have
a penny, worth a penny; Have something, you'll be thought
something;* and so your friend, who was once a frog, is now
a king.

"And now, Stichus, fetch me the furniture in which I intend to be carried out; bring also the perfume, and a taste of
the wine in which I desire that my bones be washed."

Without delay Stichus brought in a white coverlet and a
prætexta,[2] and bade us handle them and see if they were made
of good wool. "Take care, Stichus," said Trimalchio, smiling, "that neither mice nor moths get at them; or else I'll
burn you alive. I mean to be buried in all my glory, that
the whole people may give me their benedictions."

Then he opened a pot of spikenard, and rubbed us all with
it, saying, "I hope it will delight me as much when I am
dead as it does now that I am alive." Then ordering the wine
vessels to be filled, "Imagine," said he, "that you are invited
to my funeral feast."

The whole affair was becoming supremely disgusting, when
Trimalchio, now beastly drunk, bethought him of a new interlude; for ordering in horn-blowers, he stretched himself
out as if he was lying in state, with many pillows under him,
saying, "Now make believe I am dead, and say something
handsome on the occasion."

The horn-blowers sounded as at a funeral; in particular
one servant of the undertaker, who seemed the most respectable man in the room, made such a noise that he roused the
whole neighbourhood. The watchmen of the district, thinking that Trimalchio's house was on fire, suddenly broke open
the door, and rushed in with water and axes in their usual

---

[1] *A sitting-room for this viper.*] Viperæ hujus sessorium. Wesseling
explains *sessorium* as the room in which Fortunata sat with her female
domestics, and he illustrates the passage before us by the following extract from Vitruvius, lib. vi. Archit. 9, In his locis constituuntur introrsus
oeci magni, in quibus matris familiarum cum lanificis habent sessionem.

[2] *A prætexta.*] A toga with a broad purple border, worn by magistrates.

tumultuous manner; and we, availing ourselves of so favourable an opportunity, gave Agamemnon the slip, and fled as
from a real conflagration.

CHAPTER XI.

THE REVELLERS RETURN TO THE INN—GITON QUITS ENCOLPIUS FOR ASCYL-
TOS—THE LATTER VOWS VENGEANCE—BUT TAMELY SURRENDERS HIS
SWORD TO A BOLD ROGUE—TURNING INTO A PICTURE-GALLERY, HE
MAKES ACQUAINTANCE WITH EUMOLPUS, WHO DIVERTS HIS MELANCHOLY
WITH MERRY TALES, REFLECTIONS ON THE DECLINE OF THE ARTS, AND
EXTEMPORIZED VERSES—THE POET IS PELTED WITH STONES.

WE had no torch to show us the way, and the silence of the
night, which was now in the middle of its course, left us no
hope of meeting any one with a light. To this was added the
effects of the wine we had drunk, and our ignorance of the
way, which was intricate even by daylight. After having
stumbled about then for nearly an hour, over heaps of gravel
and broken projecting stones, that made our feet bleed, we
were at last relieved by Giton's ingenious precaution. For
he being afraid, the day before, of missing the way even
by sunshine, had marked all the posts and pillars with chalk;
and the white lines, shining distinctly through the pitchy
darkness of the night, enabled us to find our way. Nor were
we less perplexed when we came to our inn, for the old
woman of the house had swilled so long with her customers,
that you might have set her on the fire without her feeling it;
and perhaps we should have passed the night in the street,
but for the timely arrival of one of Trimalchio's men, with a
train of ten waggons. Without wasting time in trying to
make himself heard, he broke in the door of the inn, and gave
us an entrance through the same breach.

[Hurrying to my room, cum fratre lectum petii, et opipare epulatus,
ardensque tentigine, me totum voluptatibus ingurgitavi.]

Who can the charms of that blest night declare!
How soft, ye gods, our warm embraces were!

We clung, we glowed, losing ourselves in bliss,
And interchanged our souls in every kiss.
Farewell for ever, mortal cares! since I,
Thus tasting death, found it so sweet to die.

But I have little reason to boast of my happiness. For
when my arms, unnerved by wine, could no longer retain
their hold, Ascyltos, the contriver of all iniquity, stole the
boy from me in the dark, and conveyed him to his own bed ;
where, in violation of all justice, volutatus liberius cum fratre
non suo ... indormivit alienis amplexibus, Giton not perceiving the fraud, or feigning to be unconscious of it. When
I awoke I felt all over the bed, and finding it robbed of delight,
by all that is faithful in love! I was half inclined to stab
them both and make their sleep eternal. At last, adopting a
less violent course, I awoke Giton with a beating, and looking
sternly on Ascyltos, "Villain," said I, "since you have broken
the bonds of honour and our common friendship, pack up
your things forthwith, and go find some other place to be the
scene of your infamous misdeeds."

He made no objection to this, but when we had divided
our plunder with scrupulous exactness, "Now then," said he,
"let us divide the boy." I thought this was a parting jest ;
but drawing his sword with a parricidal hand, he cried, "You
shall not engross this prey ; I must have my share, though I
cut it off with this sword ; it is all the same to me." Thereupon I also drew, and wrapping my mantle round my left
arm, put myself into a fighting attitude.

Woebegone at our deplorable fury, the boy threw himself
between us, and embracing our knees with tears implored us
not to renew the tragedy of the Theban brothers in a pitiful
tavern, nor mutually pollute with blood the sanctity of so
dear a friendship. "If there must be murder," he said, "here
I bare my throat ; strike here ; bury your swords here. It
is I who must die, since I have broken the sacred tie of
friendship."

We sheathed our swords at these entreaties. Ascyltos
spoke first, and said, "I will put an end to this difference.
Let Giton follow whichever of us he pleases ; only let him be
perfectly free to make his choice."

Presuming that my long intimacy with the boy had bound him to me as by ties of blood, I was so far from fearing the proposal, that I caught at it with great eagerness, and committed the question to the judge's decision; but the word had no sooner passed my lips than Giton, without a moment's deliberation, or so much as a hesitating look, jumped up and declared in favour of Ascyltos.

Thunderstruck at this sentence, and unarmed as I was, I threw myself on the bed, and would have laid desperate hands on myself, had I not grudged my enemy such a triumph. Ascyltos exultingly went away with his prize, and left me forlorn in a strange place, me who a little before had been his dear comrade, and the partner of all his adventures.

Friendship's a name whose shifting value rates

For just so much as present use dictates.

While Fortune stays, our friends how staunch and true!

When she departs, farewell the faithless crew!

So on the stage, with nice mimetic art,

This plays a lover's, that a father's part;

But when at last the comic scenes are o'er,

The masks are dropp'd; the actor feigns no more;

Each to his natural inclination turns;

The father dotes not, nor the lover burns.

I did not long indulge my grief; but fearing that, among the rest of my misfortunes, Menelaus, the sub-professor, should find me left alone in the inn, I packed up my things, and with a heavy heart went and hired a lonely lodging near the sea. There shutting myself up for three days, whilst the thought of my solitude and humiliation haunted my mind, I beat my breast and poured out ejaculations broken by sobs and groans: "Why has no earthquake swallowed me? Why has not the sea, which spares not even the guiltless, ingulfed me? I have fled from justice, I have escaped from the arena, I have slain my host, that among the other titles of my shame I should find myself a beggar and a vagabond, left forlorn in a paltry inn in a Greek city.[1] And who was it that reduced

[1] *A Greek city.*] Naples, one of the chief cities of that part of Italy which was colonized by Greeks, and hence called Magna Græcia.

me to this desolation? A youth defiled by all kinds of lewdness; one who by his own confession deserves banishment; who gained his freedom by his prostitution; who was raffled for; and who hired himself out as a girl to those who knew him to be a man. And what is the other? O ye gods! one who put on a woman's habit in lieu of the virile toga; who was bent from his cradle on not being of his own sex; who served as a prostitute in a slave's prison; and who, after having embezzled[1] what belonged to another, and given himself up to the vilest profligacy, forswore our old friendship, and, oh infamy! like a common strumpet, sacrificed everything for a single night. Now the lovers lie locked in each other's arms whole nights together; and perhaps in the intervals of their lustful pleasure they make sport of my loneliness; but they shall not do so with impunity; for I am not a man, and a freeman, or I will wash out the insult they have cast upon me in their blood."

Thus saying I buckled on my sword; and lest want of strength should defeat my warlike purpose, I recruited my vigour with copious food; then sallied out, and stalked like a madman about all the porticoes. But whilst with a haggard and ferocious countenance I breathed nothing but blood and havoc, often clapping my hand to the hilt of my sword, I was observed by a soldier, if such indeed he was, and not some thievish vagabond or cut-throat. "Hallo! comrade," said he, "of what legion are you, and who is your centurion?" I named both centurion and legion with perfect intrepidity in lying. "But hark you," said he, "do the soldiers in your division wear Greek shoes?"[2] And then, as my face and my agitation betrayed the imposture, he ordered me to lay down my arms,[3] and take care I did not get into trouble.

---

[1] *Having embezzled*, &c.] Qui postquam conturbavit, et libidinis suæ solum vertit. Slaves who embezzled their masters' money were said *conturbare*; but the word is here used figuratively. *Solum*, locus qui aratur; etiam pro αἰδοίῳ. Sic *arvum* quoque et *sulcus* dicuntur muliebria, ut e contra vomer virilia. ERHARD.

[2] *Greek shoes*.] Phæcasiati milites ambulant? The common soldiers in the Roman armies invariably wore the *caliga*, a stout sandal with thick soles, studded with hob-nails. Appian mentions the phæcasium as worn by the priests of Athens and Alexandria.

[3] *Ordered me to lay down my arms*.] The laws of Rome prohibited civilians, under heavy penalties, from wearing arms in public.

Thus despoiled and left without the means of vengeance, I retraced my steps to my lodging, my desperate resolution gradually faded away, and I began to thank the robber for his audacity.

[Still I found it no easy task to conquer the love of revenge; and after having wasted half the night in anxiety, I rose at dawn, and visited all the public porticoes, in hopes of beguiling my wounded feelings.] I entered a picture-gallery full of admirable specimens of various styles of art. There I saw the hand of Zeuxis not yet vanquished by the injuries of time; and examined, not without awe, some sketches by Protogenes, which vied in truth with Nature's self. With adoration too I beheld the Monochroms,[1] as the Greeks call them, of Apelles; for the outlines of the figures were traced with such exquisite and life-like precision, that you would have thought the very souls were portrayed. Here was the eagle bearing the divine cupbearer to heaven; there the beauteous Hylas struggling with a lascivious Naiad; elsewhere Apollo execrated his own homicidal hand, and adorned his unstrung lyre with the newly-created flower.[2]

Surrounded by these painted lovers I cried out as though I were alone, "Does love then spare not even the gods? Jupiter could not satisfy his choice in heaven; but when he came to play the gallant on earth, at least he wronged no one. The nymph that ravished Hylas would have stifled her passion, had she believed that Hercules would have come to prohibit it. Apollo recalled the shade of his boy into a flower; and all these legends of the gods speak of love enjoyed without a rival. But I have taken for my friend and inmate a traitor more cruel than Lycurgus."[3]

While I was thus complaining to the air, there entered the gallery a white-headed man, with a worn countenance, and

[1] *Monochroms.*] Pictures in chiaroscuro, of a single colour, generally vermilion, red lead, or red ochre.
[2] *The newly-created flower.*] The Hyacinth. The beautiful youth of that name was killed by a quoit thrown by Apollo, and made to swerve by jealous Zephyr.
[3] *Lycurgus.*] Some commentators suppose that the Lycurgus here mentioned is the same whose villa was plundered by the three rogues; others, with more reason, think that Encolpius uses a common proverbial expression, referring to that king of Thrace who used to feed his horses on human flesh.

an air that seemed to promise something extraordinary. His
dress however was anything but handsome, so that it was
easy to perceive he was one of that class of literati to whom
the rich are usually no friends. "I," said he, "am a poet,[1]
and, as I hope, of no mean genius, if indeed any faith is to be
put in these crowns, which partial favour too often bestows on
dunces. Why then, you will say, are you so badly dressed?
For that very reason: the love of high art never yet led any
one to opulence.

> Great gains repay the merchant's risk and toil;
> The soldier's belt is fill'd with golden spoil;
> On Tyrian beds the flatterer carouses;
> And ladies for their favourites rob their spouses.
> Learning alone, in rags, takes barren pain,
> And starving asks the Muses' aid in vain.

"Undoubtedly it is so. In the first place, whoever professes himself an enemy to every vice, and is strict in following the path of rectitude, incurs odium for the singularity of
his principles (for who can approve of habits the reverse of
his own?); and then those who have no thought but how to
heap up wealth, cannot bear that in the opinion of the world
there should be anything better than what they themselves
possess. Therefore are men of letters exposed in every possible way to the scoffs of fortune, that they may appear of
less worth than money-bags."

"I know not how it is that penury is talent's sister,"
[I said with a sigh.

"It is with good reason," he replied, "you deplore the fate of men of
letters."

"That is not the reason of my sighs," I returned; "I have a different
and far heavier cause for sorrow." And in accordance with the natural
propensity of mankind to pour one's private griefs into another's ears, I
told him of my misfortune, and above all portrayed the perfidy of
Ascyltos in the blackest colours, ejaculating amidst a world of sighs,]
"Would that my enemy was not so guilty of my enforced con-
tinence! that there might be some hope of softening him!

---

[1] *I am a poet.*] Compare Hor. Sat. ii. 9, Noris nos, inquit, docti
sumus.

But he is a veteran in villany ; no pimp is a match for him in rascality."

Moved by my frankness, the old man began to console me ; and that he might divert my melancholy, he related to me an amorous adventure that had happened to himself.

"When I went to Asia," he said, "as a stipendiary in the Quæstor's suite, I lodged in a house at Pergamus, which I found very much to my taste, not only on account of the neatness of the apartments, but still more for the great beauty of my host's son ; and this was the method I devised that I might not be suspected by the father as a seducer. Whenever any mention happened to be made at table of the abuse of handsome boys, I affected such keen indignation, I protested with such an air of austere morality against the violence done to my ears by such obscene discourse, that the mother especially looked upon me as one of the seven sages. Already then I began to conduct the youth to the gymnasium ; it was I who had the regulation of his studies, who acted as his monitor, and took care above all that no one should enter the house who might debauch him.

"It happened once that we lay down to sleep in the dining-room (for it was a holiday ; the school had closed early ; and our prolonged festivity had made us too lazy to retire to our chamber). About midnight I perceived that my pupil was awake ; so with a timid voice I murmured this prayer : 'O sovereign Venus, if I may steal a kiss from this boy, and he not know it, I will make him a present to-morrow of a pair of turtle doves.'

"Hearing the price offered for the favour, he began to snore, and I, approaching the pretended sleeper, stole two or three kisses. Content with this beginning, I rose early in the morning, brought him, as he expected, a choice pair of turtles, and so acquitted myself of my vow.

"The next night, finding the same opportunity, I changed my petition : 'If I may pass my wanton hand over this boy,' I said, 'and he not perceive it, I will give him for his silence a pair of most pugnacious fighting cocks.' At this promise the lad moved towards me of his own accord, and was afraid, I verily believe, lest he should find me asleep. However, I quieted his uneasiness on that score, totoque corpore citra

summam voluptatem me ingurgitavi.   Then when daylight
came, I made him happy with what I had promised him.

" The third night, being again free to venture, I leaned
over his wakeful ear and said : 'Immortal gods, si ego huic
dormienti abstulero coïtum plenum et optabilem, in return for
this felicity I will to-morrow give the boy a fine horse, a cross
between the Asturian and the Macedonian breed.'   Never
had the lad slept more soundly.   Itaque primum implevi lac-
tentibus papillis manus, mox basio inhæsi, deinde in unum
omnia vota conjunxi.   Next morning he remained sitting in
his room, expecting my present as usual.   It is much easier,
you know, to buy turtle doves and fighting cocks than an
Asturian horse ; and besides, I was afraid lest so considerable
a present should render the motives of my liberality suspected.
So after walking about for some hours, I returned to my lodgings, and gave the boy nothing but a kiss.   He looked about
him on all sides, then throwing his arms round my neck, ' I
say, master,' said he, ' where is the Asturian ?'

" Though by this breach of faith I had cut myself off from
the access I had contrived, I ventured upon another attempt.
After the lapse of a few days, a similar chance having created
for us just such another opportunity, I began, as soon as I
heard the father snoring, to beg the lad to be reconciled to me,
that is to say, ut pateretur satisfieri sibi, et cetera quæ libido
distenta dictat.   But he was downright angry, and gave me
no other answer than this : ' Go to sleep, or I will call my
father.'

" But there is nothing, be it ever so difficult, that cannot be
achieved by perseverance.   Dum dicit, Patrem excitabo, ir-
repsi tamen, et male repugnanti gaudium extorsi.   At ille
non indelectatus nequitia mea, after long complaining that he
was cheated, and made a fool of, and exposed before his school-
fellows, to whom he had boasted of my costly gift : Videris
tamen, inquit, non ero tui similis.   Si quid vis, fac iterum.
Ego vero, deposita omni offensa, cum puero in gratiam redii,
ususque beneficio ejus, in somnum delapsus sum.   Sed non
fuit contentus iteratione ephebus plenæ maturitatis, et annis
ad patiendum gestientibus.   Itaque excitavit me sopitum, et,
Numquid vis ? inquit.   Et non plane jam molestum erat
munus.   Utcunque igitur, inter anhelitus sudoresque tritus,

quod voluerat, accepit, rursusque in somnum decidi, gaudio
lassus. Interposita minus hora, pungere me manu cœpit et
dicere: Quare non facimus? Then indeed, incensed beyond
measure at being so often disturbed, I retorted his own words:
'Go to sleep, or I will call your father.'"

My depressed spirits were raised by this merry tale, and I
began to question my new acquaintance, who was more a con-
noisseur than I, as to the ages of the pictures, and the subjects
of some which I did not understand. I asked him too what
was the cause of that prevailing supineness which had suffered
the finest of the arts to perish, among the rest painting, of
which not a vestige remained.

"Greed of money," said he, "has produced this revolution.
In primitive times, when simple worth was still esteemed, the
liberal arts flourished, and the greatest subject of emulation
among men was how to hinder anything that could profit
future ages from lying long in oblivion. Then it was that
Democritus extracted the virtues of all herbs, and spent his
whole life in experiments in order that no property of plant
or mineral might escape him. Eudoxus grew old on the summit of a lofty mountain, that he might observe the motion of
the stars; and Chrysippus thrice purged his brain with hel-
lebore, that it might be the more lucid and inventive.

"But let us turn to statuary. Lysippus was so intent on
finishing one figure that he perished for want of food, and
Myron, who almost embodied the souls of men and brutes in
bronze, could not find an heir.[1] But we, engrossed in wine
and women, have not the courage to master the arts already
discovered; depreciators of antiquity, vice is the only thing
we learn and teach. What is become of Dialectics? of
Astronomy? of Philosophy, whose oracles were so much consulted? Who, I say, ever enters a temple and puts up a vow,
that he may attain to eloquence? Who does so that he approach the fountain of philosophy? No one even prays for
sound health; but before ever they touch the threshold of the
Capitol, one promises an offering, if he buries a rich relation;
another, if he digs up a treasure; another, if he lives to be
worth his thirty millions of sesterces. The senate itself, that
preceptor of all that is good and righteous, is in the habit of

[1] *Could not find an heir.*] He died so poor that no one would ad-
minister his effects.

voting a thousand marks of gold to the god of the Capitol ;
and to relieve cupidity from all scruples, it bargains even with
Jupiter for his favours. Do not wonder then, if painting is
decayed, since in all eyes, both gods' and men's, a lump of
gold is more a beautiful thing than ever was produced by
those crazy Greeks, Apelles and Phidias.

"But I see you are absorbed in that picture which represents the capture of Troy:[1] I will therefore endeavour to
expound the subject to you in verse.

> Now the last summer of ten circling years
> Saw leaguered Troy a prey to doubts and fears ;
> Saw wavering faith in Calchas merged almost
> In gloomy fear, among the Grecian host :
> When toppling down from Ida's verdant crest
> Whole forests roll'd, so Delius gave behest ;[2]
> And deftly join'd, a mountain mass of wood,
> In semblance of a horse before us stood.
> His monstrous sides a dreadful cavern boast,
> An ample den, capacious of a host,
> Within which horrid gloom, by fate inspired,
> And by a ten years' thirst of vengeance fired,
> Deep lay concealed, intent on endless fame,
> The pride and glory of the Argive name.

[1] *The capture of Troy.*] The verses that follow are a bombastic imitation of part of the second book of Virgil's Æneid, a mere jumble of poetic
phraseology, without poetry. The faults of the copy have been contrasted
with the elegance of the original by Lessing in his Laocoon (P. i. p. 54) ;
and Jacob Tollius in his commentary on Longinus has elaborately criti-
cised the poem before us, and vituperated its author. Therein he only
proved himself to be a blundering pedant, for the faults that offended him
were intentional. Fancy how such a learned owl might hoot at Pope
for his "Verses by a Person of Quality," or at Shakspeare for his absurd interlude of Bottom and his company ! Petronius holds up to
ridicule, in the person of Eumolpus, the versifying mania which prevailed
in his day, and he puts into the mouth of his *improvisatore* just such lines
as a fluent man, with a memory well stored with the commonplaces of
poetic diction, might be supposed to throw off extempore.

[2] *So Delius gave behest.*] In the hurry of extemporaneous composition
Eumolpus attributes to Apollo, (Delius,) the friend of the Trojans, the
device of their enemy, Minerva.

O my poor country! credulous we dream'd
A thousand ships dispers'd, our land redeem'd;
For so the legend on the horse implied,
So ran the tale when Sinon foully lied;
This was the hope that lured us to our harm;
This gave the traitor's words their deadly charm.

Through the free gates, rev'lling in their release,
The Trojans rush to hail the pledge of peace.
So tremulous their joy, it seems like grief,
And floods of tears give their full hearts relief.
Fear check'd them soon; for wildly hurrying on
With streaming hair, behold Laocoon,
The priest of Neptune! Through the wondering crowd
He burst his fateful way with outcries loud;
His javelin at the horse he flung, but foil'd
By destiny, the weapon back recoil'd.
The baffled sacrilege the Trojans awed,
Their faith confirming in the Grecian fraud.
Yet his collected strength once more he tried,
And hid his axe within the monster's side;
The imprison'd youth in hollow murmurs groan,
And the wood breathes an anguish not its own.
In vain! Captive they went to capture Troy,
And win by fraud what force could ne'er destroy.

To other prodigies now turn your eyes,
Where Tenedos's beetling cliffs arise,
And the pent wave, swelling against the steep,
Lash'd into spray, curls back upon the deep.
As in the silent night far o'er the main
Is heard the plash, where the vex'd waves complain,
As urging to its speed their flying fleet,
The rowers' sturdy arms their strokes repeat,

u

Ev'n thus two serpents, rolling coil on coil,
Come sweeping o'er the straits to Ilium's soil;
With crests erect they o'er blue Neptune ride,
Like lofty ships, and lash the surge aside;
The deep resounds;[1] like flamy gold aspire
Their burnish'd scales; their eyes the ocean fire;
Tremble the waves their direful hiss to hear,
And all the mute spectators freeze with fear.
Behold, Laocoon's two sons are there
In sacred garb, with fillet-circled hair;
Round these the serpents wind their sinuous train;
Each rears his little hands, but rears in vain;
His brother, not himself, to aid he tries,
And wounded with fraternal anguish dies.
Their sire, too weak to hinder, shares their fate;
Gorged with destruction, and with death elate,
The monsters pull him down; the priest expires,
A quivering victim, by his altars' fires.
Thus wretched Troy, to certain fate ordain'd,
First lost her gods,[2] by sacrilege profaned.

Now Phœbe, in her noon of glory bright,
Led with full orb the lesser fires of night,
When on poor Troy, by sleep and wine betray'd,
The imprison'd Greeks their fatal sally made;
Impatient as some brave Thessalian steed,
Just from the galling yoke of bondage freed,

---

[1] *The deep resounds, &c.*] Part of this description of the serpents, as given in the translation of Petronius "By Several Hands," (1714,) is so choice a specimen of the unintentional mock-heroic, that we cannot withhold it from the reader:

> Their golden crests with gaudy horror blaze,
> Burn sporting fish, and gods marine amaze.
> Affrighted Neptune shuns the odd surprize,
> And to the beach and ouzie harbour flies.

[2] *First lost her gods.*] The tutelary gods of any place were always supposed to leave it before its destruction.

He snuffs the air, and shakes his generous mane,
Enjoys the race, and paws the trembling plain.
Their glittering swords unsheath'd, they grasp their
    shields,
And seize the victory thoughtless Ilium yields.
This stabs the wretch in drunken slumbers fast,
And makes the dream of luxury his last,
Whilst others at the altars kindle brands,
And Troy's own gods arm her destroyers' hands.

Some of the people who were walking in the gallery, pelted Eumolpus with stones in return for his recitation; but he, who was no stranger to that kind of applause, covered his head, and fled out of the temple.[1] I was afraid they would take me too for a poet, so I followed the fugitive to the sea-shore, where coming to a halt as soon as we were out of reach of shot, "I beseech you," said I, "what do you mean by this cursed disease of yours? I have not been two hours in your company, and in that time you have talked oftener like a rapt poet than an ordinary mortal. No wonder people pelt you; I myself must fill my pocket with stones, that I may bleed you in the head whenever I find you going off in a fit."

He shook his ears and replied, "O my lad, it is not to-day I got my first taste of this sort of thing; why, when I enter the theatre to recite a piece, such is the reception with which I am usually greeted by the audience. However, with you at least, that we may not quarrel all day long, I will keep my hand out of this dish."

"Well," said I, "if you abjure your delirium for this day, you shall dine with me." Then I gave directions to the portress at my lodgings to prepare our little repast [and we went at once to the baths].

---

[1] *Fled out of the temple.*] Of which the portico contained the picture gallery.

CHAPTER XII.

[At the baths] I saw Giton with towels and scrapers in
his hand, leaning against the wall, and looking vexed and
confused. It was plain he did the office of a servant with
no good-will. While I was gazing intently upon him, he
turned towards me with a face radiant with joy, and said,
" Have pity on me, brother! I can speak freely now that
there are no weapons to fear. Save me from this barbarous
ruffian, and punish your repentant judge as severely as you
please. It will be a sufficient consolation to me in my wretchedness to perish by your decree."

I bade him stifle his lamentations, lest any one should discover our designs, and leaving Eumolpus to himself, (he was
reciting verses in the bath,) I hurried Giton away by a dark
and dirty passage, and flew with him to my lodging, where
clapping to the door, I fell on his neck and kissed away the
tears that bathed his face. It was some time before either of
us could speak, for the boy was almost strangled with his
sighs. " Oh shameful weakness!" I exclaimed. " Though
you forsook me I love you still; the deep wound inflicted on
my heart has not left so much as a scar behind. What can
you say in excuse for your perfidy? Did I deserve such an
outrage?"

Finding that he was still loved, he began to brighten up:

At once to love and chide is labour vain,
An effort Hercules could scarce sustain:

By Love all jarring passions are subdued,
All discord temper'd to his sovereign mood.[1]

"And yet," I continued, "I did not leave the choice of whom you should love to the decision of a third person; but all is forgiven and forgotten, if your repentance is sincere."

As I spoke thus, my words were mingled with sighs and tears. Giton wiped my face with his mantle and replied, "I beseech you, Encolpius, let me appeal to your own recollection: was it I that forsook you, or you that gave me up? I confess indeed, and I plead it as my excuse, that when I saw you both with weapons drawn, I cast myself for safety on the stronger of the two." I kissed the bosom so full of prudence, and throwing my arms round his neck, I pressed him closely to my own, to show him that he was fully restored to favour, and that my affection for him was revived in full force.

It was now quite dark, and the woman had prepared the repast I had ordered, when Eumolpus knocked at our door. I called out, "How many of you are there?" and peeping through a chink in the door, examined narrowly whether Ascyltos was not with him; but seeing that my guest was alone, I let him in. Eumolpus threw himself on my couch, and seeing Giton in attendance, he nodded and said, "A charming Ganymede, truly: we must enjoy ourselves to-day."

I was not at all pleased with so keen a beginning, and was afraid I had opened my door to another Ascyltos. Eumolpus went on in the same strain, and when the boy had helped him to wine, "I would rather have you," he said, "than all I saw in the bath." Then emptying his cup at one draught, he vowed he had never been more annoyed in his life. "When I was in the bath," said he, "I had like to be beaten for offering to recite some verses to the persons who were seated round the basin; and after I was turned out, just as at the theatre, I ran about looking for you in every corner of the building,

---

[1] Accusare et amare tempore uno
    Ipsi vix fuit Herculi ferendum.
    Dividias mentis conficit omnis amor.

This is one of the poetical fragments to which the editors of Petronius have not been able to assign a place in the Satyricon. It seems to us to fit not unaptly here.

and shouting, Encolpius! Encolpius! as loud as I could bawl.
In another place a naked young man who had lost his clothes
was roaring with no less clamorous indignation for Giton.
As for me, some of the attendants, who took me for a madman,
mimicked me in the most insolent manner; whilst round the
young man there gathered a great throng, who clapped their
hands and gazed upon him with the most respectful admiration. The fact was, he showed such an enormous development of virility that you would have thought the man was
but an appendage to a part of himself.[1] Oh the indefatigable
athlete! I warrant he'd begin to-day and not leave off till the
day after to-morrow. Accordingly he soon found relief, for
some Roman knight or another, a great reprobate they said,
threw his own mantle over him, and took him home with himself, in hopes, I suppose, to engross so great a prize; whilst I
could not so much as obtain my clothes from the keeper, if I
had not produced some one to vouch for me. So much more
profitable is it to improve the body than the mind."[2]

Whilst Eumolpus was telling his story, I often changed
countenance, being glad or sorry as my enemy met with good
or bad fortune. Affecting however not to be acquainted with
the subject of the adventure, I said nothing about it, but only
recited our bill of fare to Eumolpus. [I had hardly finished when
our little repast came in—plain homely food, but substantial, which our
famishing poet greedily devoured, whilst he thus extolled its simplicity:]

> Whate'er can nature's genuine wants relieve,
> The indulgent gods with kind profusion give.
> Wild herbs, and berries from the thorny spray,
> Suffice the pangs of hunger to allay.
> What fool would thirst beside a stream, or stand
> In the cold blast, with a good fire at hand?
> The marriage bed we guard with laws severe,
> Yet the chaste bride indulges without fear.

[1] *Showed such an enormous development, &c.*] Habebat enim inguinum
pondus tam grande, ut ipsum hominem laciniam fascini crederes.
[2] *To improve the body, &c.*] Tanto magis impedit inguina quam ingenia
fricare.

Boon nature every needful thing bestows ;
But pride's insatiate lust no limit knows.[1]

[When he had completely gorged himself he began to moralize, and to
inveigh against those who despise common things and like nothing but
what is rare, to whom] everything seems vile that is easily pro-
curable, and whose perverted minds delight in difficulties—

I would not what I wish at once obtain ;
The conquest that's too facile I disdain.
The Phasian bird[2] from Colchos' distant shore,
And Afric fowl, are viands I adore ;
For these are costly things, unlike the goose,
Or painted duck, dainties for vulgar use.
Give me the scare on coasts remotest caught,
Or choicer fish from keel-ploughed Syrtis, bought
With lives of shipwrecked men.   The mullet's grown
Heavy in all ways.[3]   Each man to his own
Prefers his neighbour's wife.   The well-bred nose
Delights in cinnamon, and scorns the rose.

[1] Omnia quæ miseras possunt finire querelas
   In promptu voluit candidus esse Deus.
Vile olus, et duris hærentia mora rubetis,
   Pugnantis stomachi composuere famem.
Flumine vicino stultus sitit, et riget Euro,
   Cum calidus tepido consonat igne rogus
Lex armata sedet circum fera limina nuptæ,
   Nil metuit licito fusa puella toro.
Quod satiare potest, dives natura ministrat,
   Quod docet infrenis gloria fine caret.

[2] *The Phasian bird.*]   The pheasant (Phasianus Colchicus) derives its
name and origin from the region of the Phasis, whence, according to
Greek tradition, it was brought by the Argonauts.

[3] *The mullet's grown heavy in all ways.*]   Mullets of two pounds
weight were common and little esteemed; but their value increased with
their weight to an almost incredible amount.   Horace (Sat. ii. 2) says to
a gourmand : You extol with infatuation a mullet of three pounds weight.
One which weighed six pounds was sold for eight thousand sesterces in
the reign of Claudius.   Mullus jam gravis est, says Eumolpus, using the
word gravis in a double sense, his full meaning being, The mullet is now
commonly a heavy fish, and therefore no longer acceptable.

> Rare things are excellent; a taste polite
> For nothing cares unless 'tis recondite.

"Is this your promise," said I, "that you would not make another verse to-day? If you have any conscience, at least spare us who never pelted you. If any one of those who are drinking under this roof scent you out for a poet, he will raise the whole neighbourhood, and we shall be inevitably involved in the same misfortune. Have some compassion on us, and think of the picture gallery and the bath." Giton, who was gentleness itself, chided me for talking in this way, saying it was ill done in me to jeer at an older man, that I forgot my duty as a host, and spoiled all the grace of the entertainment by inviting a guest to my table only to insult him. Many other things too he said, full of good sense and propriety, which well became so handsome a speaker.

"Happy the mother that bore you!" cried Eumolpus. "Go on and prosper! How rare it is to see so much beauty united with so much discretion! Think not therefore that so many noble words have been uttered in vain; you have secured an ardent admirer. Your praises shall fill my verse. I will be your instructor, your guardian; I will go with you everywhere, even unbidden; nor can Encolpius take it amiss, since he loves another."

It was lucky for Eumolpus that the soldier had robbed me of my sword; for otherwise the wrath I had stored up against Ascyltos would have wreaked itself in the poet's blood. Giton perceived the storm rising, and prudently avoided the outburst of my indignation by going out as if to make water. His absence having somewhat abated the heat of my resentment, "Eumolpus," I said, "I would rather endure your verses than hear you express your sentiments in that fashion. I am very passionate, and you are very lewd: such being our dispositions, you may judge how little we are likely to agree together. Suppose then that I am raving mad; humour my frenzy, and begone this moment."

Confounded by this explosion, Eumolpus did not stay to inquire the cause of my anger, but at once quitted the room, pulled the door to after him, locked me in when I least expected it, and taking the key with him, went off in quest of Giton.

Finding myself thus entrapped, I resolved to hang myself, and having fastened my belt to the bed pole which stood by the wall, I was putting the noose round my neck, when the door opened, Eumolpus came in along with Giton, and hindered the fatal catastrophe. Giton's passionate grief swelled into rage; uttering a loud cry he seized me with both hands and threw me on the bed. "You deceive yourself, Encolpius," he said, "if you think to die before me. I was beforehand with you; I sought for a sword in Ascyltos's lodging. Had I not found you I would have thrown myself down a precipice; and that you may know that death is not long absent from those who seek it, behold in your turn the tragedy you had designed for my eyes."

So saying, he snatched a razor from Eumolpus's hired attendant, and drawing it three or four times across his throat, he fell down at our feet. I shrieked with horror, and falling like him on the floor, sought death by the same weapon. But neither did Giton show the least trace of a wound, nor did I feel any pain; for the razor had no edge, being one of those instruments which are made blunt on purpose to prepare barber's apprentices to handle a sharper; for which reason the servant from whom it was snatched had felt no alarm, nor had Eumolpus offered any impediment to this farcical suicide.[1]

In the midst of this love comedy the landlord brought in the remainder of the dinner, and seeing us sprawling so unbecomingly, "Hallo, are you drunk?" said he, "or runaways? or both? Who turned up that bed against the wall? What is the meaning of these underhand preparations? You meant, by Hercules, to be off to-night, and escape paying the hire of the room; but you shan't get off so easily. I will let you know that you are not in the house of a lone widow, but of M. Manicius."

"Do you threaten?" cried Eumolpus, giving him a hearty slap on the face. The landlord, whose courage had been warmed up by the numerous cups he had drained with his guests, threw an earthen jug at his assailant's head, cut it

---

[1] *Farcical suicide.*] To complete the details of this scene, we may presume that Eumolpus's servant coming in with his master, and seeing a man in the act of hanging himself, hastily took out his razor case to cut him down, and that Giton, seeing him do this, seized one of the razors, but luckily a blunt one.

open, and rushed out of the room. Incensed at this insult,
Eumolpus seized a wooden candlestick, pursued the fugitive,
and revenged his bloody brow with a shower of blows. The
whole house was in an uproar, and all the tipplers thronged to
see the fray. Now was my time to retaliate; I seized the
opportunity, locked Eumolpus out, and serving him as he had
served me, found myself without a rival, and free to dispose
of my chamber and my night as I pleased. Meanwhile
Eumolpus was assailed by all the scullions and helpers in the
house. One, making a javelin of a spit taken with the meat
hissing hot from the fire, took aim at his eyes; another,
snatching up a flesh-hook, put himself into a fighting attitude;
but worse than all, a blear-eyed old woman in a filthy apron,
and mounted upon two wooden shoes, not fellows, dragged a
great mastiff in by the chain, and set him at Eumolpus, who
with his wooden candlestick defended himself valiantly against
all his assailants.

We saw the whole scene through a hole that had been made
a little before by wrenching off the handle of the door, and
I wished Eumolpus joy of his drubbing. But Giton, always
compassionate, was for opening the door and succouring the
distressed poet. My anger being still hot, I could not hold
my hand, and gave the soft-hearted boy a smart fillip on the
ear. He sat down crying on the bed; while I, applying now
one eye, now the other, to the hole in the door, inwardly commended Eumolpus's assailants, and banqueted on the sight before me. Presently Bargates, the agent of the estate,[1] who
had been called off from his dinner, was carried into the midst
of the brawl by two chair-porters, for he had the gout. After
furiously haranguing for a long while in a very extraordinary
voice against drunkards and run-away tenants, he cast his
eyes on Eumolpus and exclaimed, "Oh! is it you, best of
poets? and these rascally slaves don't hold their hands and
vanish with all speed?" [Then bending towards Eumolpus's

---

[1] *The agent of the estate.*] Procurator insulæ. This was not a magistrate, as most commentators and translators have supposed, but a person
appointed by the proprietor of the insula, or block of houses, to collect the
rents of the tenants, and to look after the property. So far from being a
magistrate, Bargates was either a slave or a freedman, as appears from
the word *contubernalis*, (not *uxor*,) by which he designates his better
half.

ear, he said in a half-whisper,] "My bed-fellow gives herself airs with me; so if you love me, blackguard her in verse, and make her ashamed of herself."

Whilst Eumolpus was talking privately with Bargates, a crier, accompanied by a public slave and a considerable crowd, entered the inn, and shaking a torch that gave out more smoke than light, made proclamation as follows:

"Went astray a little while ago at the public bath, a youth about sixteen years of age; curly-headed; a minion by calling; handsome featured; Giton by name. Whoever will bring him back, or give information where he may be found, shall receive a thousand sesterces."

Not far from the crier stood Ascyltos in a party-coloured tunic, holding out the description and the promised reward on a silver platter. I ordered Giton to creep quickly under the bed, and fasten his hands and feet in the cords that supported the mattress; so that stretching himself at full length beneath, as Ulysses of old clung to the ram's belly, he might escape the hands of the searchers. Giton obeyed at once, and in an instant fixed his hands in the cords so cleverly, that Ulysses was surpassed by his imitator. In order to leave no room for suspicion, I covered the bed with clothes, and made an impression upon it like that of a single person of my own stature. Meanwhile Ascyltos, who had gone round all the rooms with the poursuivant, came to mine, where he was the more hopeful of success from finding the door so carefully fastened. The public slave then inserted his axe between the valves of the door, and undid the bolt.

I threw myself at the feet of Ascyltos, imploring him by the memory of our friendship and our companionship in misfortune, that at least he would let me see Giton; and to give the more colour to my feigned prayers, "I know, Ascyltos," said I, "that you are come to seek my life; else why have you brought these axes? Glut your wrath then; here is my neck; shed that blood you come to spill under pretence of a search."

Ascyltos repudiated the odious imputation, and said he was only looking for his deserter; he sought no man's death, no suppliant's; least of all that of one whom since our fatal quarrel he still held most dear.

Meanwhile the public slave was not idle; but snatching a

cane out of the innkeeper's hands he thrust it under the bed, and poked it even into every crack in the wall. Giton shrank out of the way of the stick, and holding his breath for fear, kept his face in contact with the bugs.

[The two inquisitors had hardly left the room] when in rushed Eumolpus, (for the broken doors could keep no one out,) shouting in great excitement, "The thousand sesterces are mine; I will run after the crier, denounce you as you richly deserve, and put Giton into his hands."

Finding him in earnest, I embraced his knees, entreating him not to kill the dying. "You would have reason for your anger," I said, "if when you denounced Giton you could produce him. But he has escaped among the crowd, and I have no idea which way he is gone. In the name of heaven, Eumolpus, bring back the boy and restore him — ay, even to Ascyltos."

Just as I had worked him into a belief in my assertions, Giton, whose pent-up breath half choked him, sneezed three times one after the other, so that the bed shook. Eumolpus faced about at the sound, and cried, "Jove keep you, Giton!" Then throwing off the bedding he saw our Ulysses, whom even the hungry Cyclops might have spared. Presently turning to me, "What's all this, you thief?" he said. "You could not bring yourself to speak the truth even when found out? In short, if some divinity who rules over human affairs had not forced the boy to discover the place where he was hanging, I should have wandered to no purpose from one tavern to another."

Then Giton, who could wheedle much better than I, dipping a cobweb in oil, staunched the wound that had been made in his forehead; exchanged his little mantle for the poet's torn robe; then seeing him somewhat softened, embraced him, and kissed his bruises by way of making them well again. "Dearest father," he said, "we are in your keeping. If you love your Giton, save him, oh please do. Oh that the raging fire would consume me alone! Oh that the stormy sea would overwhelm me! For I am the subject and the cause of all these unhappy occurrences. My death would reconcile two enemies."

[Touched by our misfortunes, and particularly by Giton's blandishments, Eumolpus said to us, "You are certainly very foolish, both of you.

With talents enough to make your fortunes, yet you lead a life of misery, and every day run your heads into new torments.] My plan of life has always been to spend every day as if I were never to see another, [that is to say, without care. If you will follow my example, avoid everything that may disturb your repose. Ascyltos persecutes you here; put yourselves out of his reach, and accompany me in a voyage I am about to make to foreign countries. I shall probably sail to-night in a vessel in which I have engaged a berth; I am well known on board, and we shall be well received.]

> Linger in this unkindly land no more;
> Away, brave youth! a foreign world explore.
> Yield not to adverse Fortune; better days
> And loftier things await thee. Seek the blaze
> Of orient Phœbus, or the climes that last
> Receive his fading light; the icy blast
> That curdles Ister; or the sunny plain
> Water'd by placid Nile. Descend amain
> Into some new arena, and in thee
> Let other lands anew Ulysses see.[1]

[This advice seemed to me very good, for it tended to free me from all annoyance on the part of Ascyltos, and offered me the prospect of a happier life. Overcome by Eumolpus's generosity, I was heartily sorry for the insult I had lately offered him, and repented of my jealousy which had caused him so many vexations.] Bathed in tears, I begged and implored him to receive me too again into favour; telling that it was not in the power of lovers to control the fury of jealousy; but that for the future I would endeavour to say or do nothing that could give him offence; only I hoped that he, a professor of such excellent arts, would banish all irritation from his mind, so that not a trace of it should remain. The snow lies long, I said, on rude and uncultivated ground, but where the soil has been disciplined and cleansed by the plough the

---

[1] Linque tuos sedes, alienaque littora quære,
O juvenis! major rerum tibi nascitur ordo.
Ne succumbe malis: te noverit ultimus Ister,
Te Boreas gelidus, securaque regna Canopi,
Quique renascentem Phœbum, cernuntque cadentem.
Major in externas Ithacus descendat arenas.

light flake dissolves in a moment.   So it is with anger in the
human breast, it abides long in uncultivated minds, and melts
away in those of the enlightened.

"To prove the truth of what you say," replied Eumolpus,
"my anger expires with this kiss.   So pack up your things
in the name of good luck, and either follow me, or go on
before me if you choose."

He had not done speaking when the door was thrown open
with a bang, and a rough-bearded sailor stood before us.
"What keeps you, Eumolpus?" he said.   "Don't you see it is
near daylight?"

We started up without more delay; Eumolpus woke his
servant, who had long since fallen asleep, and hurried him off
with his baggage, whilst Giton and I packed up all we had;
and after paying our adorations to the stars we went on board.

CHAPTER XIII.

ENCOLPIUS AND GITON FIND THEMSELVES ON BOARD LYCAS'S VESSEL—
THEY DISCUSS VARIOUS PLANS FOR ESCAPING WITH EUMOLPUS—THEY
SHAVE THEIR HEADS AND EYEBROWS, AND ARE SEEN IN THE ILL-
OMENED ACT BY A PASSENGER—LYCAS AND TRYPHÆNA DREAM THAT
THE TWO FUGITIVES ARE ON BOARD—A POEM ON THE VANITY OF
DREAMS—ENCOLPIUS AND GITON DISCOVERED, AND SENTENCED TO BE
FLOGGED—EUMOLPUS PLEADS FOR THEM—LYCAS REPLIES—A GE-
NERAL FIGHT—A TRUCE PROPOSED BY TRYPHÆNA—THE TREATY OF
PEACE—JOYOUS BANQUET—AMUSEMENTS IN A CALM—EUMOLPUS
CRACKS JOKES IN PROSE AND VERSE ON THE SHAVED—AND TELLS
THE TALE OF THE EPHESIAN MATRON.

[WE placed ourselves in a retired spot near the poop, and as it was not
yet day, Eumolpus fell asleep; but neither Giton nor I could get a wink.
I was filled with anxiety when I reflected that I had made a comrade of
Eumolpus, a more formidable rival than Ascyltos. Reason, however, coming to my aid, "To be sure," said I,] "it is an untoward thing that
the boy is so charming in the eyes of Eumolpus; but then,
are not all the most excellent productions of nature common
to all mankind? The sun shines on all; and the moon with
her countless train of stars lights even wild beasts to their

forage. What can be more beautiful than water? Yet it flows for public use. And shall love alone be a thing to be filched, rather than a prize to be openly won? Nay, I care only to possess such things as all the world may covet. A single rival, and he an old man, ought not to make me very uneasy; even if he should attempt to take any liberty, he will lose his labour for want of breath."

Having cheated my jealousy with this assurance, I muffled my head in my mantle, and tried to persuade myself I was asleep. But on a sudden, as if Fortune was resolved to upset my composure, I heard some one on deck dolefully ejaculating, "He has fooled me then!" My heart fluttered, for it was a man's voice, and one, I was afraid, I knew too well. Nor was this all, for a woman, who appeared to be exasperated to the highest pitch of indignation, cried out, "If some god would put Giton into my hands, what a fine reception I would give the vagabond!"

Stunned by these unexpected words, we both turned pale as death; for myself especially, it seemed as though some horrid nightmare were stifling me in a shroud; it was a long while before I could recover the power of utterance; when plucking Eumolpus by the skirt with trembling hands as he was dropping off to sleep, "Upon your faith, father, I said, whose ship is this? And what passengers has he on board? Can you tell me?"

He was in a pet at being roused out of his sleep. "So this was why you were pleased," said he, "to make us occupy the most retired berth under the deck, that you might not suffer us to rest? What will you be the better for it if I tell you that Lycas a Tarentine commands this ship, and that he is carrying the vagabond Tryphæna to Tarentum?"

I shook from head to foot at this thunder-stroke, and baring my throat, ejaculated, "Now indeed, Fortune, thou hast wholly vanquished me." And as for Giton, he had fallen on my breast and lay in a swoon. At last a profuse sweat having relieved us both, I clasped Eumolpus's knees and cried, "Take pity on two dying wretches; I beseech you, in the name of what we both love, lend us your aid. Death impends over us, and unless you render it, perhaps it will be a good thing for us."

Overwhelmed by the odious imputation implied in my

words,[1] Eumolpus swore by all the gods and goddesses that he did not know what had happened; that he had never harboured a thought of mischief; but that in perfect innocence and good faith he had brought us on board a ship in which he himself had long engaged a passage. "But what hostile designs have you to fear? What Hannibal have we on board? Lycas the Tarentine, a very well-behaved man, owner not only of this ship, which he commands in person, but also of several estates in land, and of a commercial establishment, has freighted his vessel with merchandise for exportation. This is the Cyclops, the arch-pirate, to whom we owe the price of our passage; and besides him there is Tryphæna, one of the most beautiful women in the world, who sails about for her amusement."

"These are the very persons we fly from," said Giton; and then he gave the astonished and agitated Eumolpus a short account of the reasons of their malice and our imminent danger.

He was so confounded that he knew not what to advise, but called on us to speak our minds. "Fancy," said he, "that we have got into the Cyclops' den; we must cast about for some means of escape from it, unless we prefer to throw ourselves into the sea and thus be quit of all danger."

"Well," said Giton, "prevail on the pilot to run the vessel into some port, for a reward of course, and tell him that your brother suffers so much from sea-sickness that he is at the point of death. You may colour this story with tears and a woeful countenance, so that the pilot shall be moved to pity and grant your request."

"It could not be done," replied Eumolpus; "for large ships are not worked into harbour without difficulty, nor will it appear likely that my brother should be so desperately ill all at once; add to this, that Lycas may think himself bound in civility to visit his sick passenger. Consider how very convenient it would be to have this captain, whom you want to shun, come of his own accord to see you. But suppose that the ship could be turned out of the course it is now running under full sail, and that Lycas should omit visiting his sick, how shall we get out without being seen by everybody? With

---

[1] *Overwhelmed by the odious imputation, &c.*]   Inundatus hac invidia. Encolpius seemed to think, though he did not say so, that Eumolpus had purposely entrapped him.

our heads muffled, or bare? If muffled, who will not be forward to lend a hand to sick persons? If bare, what else would it be than to betray ourselves?"

"Why not rather make a bold stroke?" said I. "Slip down by a rope into the boat, cut the painter, and leave the rest to Fortune? I do not desire Eumolpus to share this danger; for why should we involve an innocent person in other men's perils? I shall be content if chance favours our descent into the boat."

"Not a bad notion," said Eumolpus, "if there was any way to put it in practice: but how could your movements fail to be seen by everybody, especially by the pilot, who day and night watches even the motion of the stars? There might possibly be a chance of eluding him whilst he slept for a moment, if we could leave the ship by another way, but we must slip down by the poop, by the helm itself, since the hawser of the boat is made fast there. Besides this, I am surprised it did not occur to you, Encolpius, that there is a sailor on duty both night and day in the boat, and that you cannot get rid of him without cutting his throat or throwing him overboard. Whether this is practicable, ask your own courage. As for my accompanying you, I shrink from no danger which offers the least hope of safety; but to throw away life as a possession of no value, is what I believe you yourselves think unreasonable. Hear how you like my proposal: I will sew you up in two skins, and cord you up among my clothes as part of my baggage, leaving of course holes through which you may breathe and eat. This being done, I will bawl out that my slaves, fearing a greater punishment, leaped by night into the sea; and as soon as we come into any port, I will carry you on shore as baggage without exciting any suspicion."

"Very like, indeed," said I; "you will pack us up as if we were solid, and never troubled with evacuations; never sneeze or snore; or as if this sort of stratagem had once succeeded so well with me.[1] But suppose we could endure this bondage for a day, what if it continue longer? What is to become of us if a calm or a tempest prolong it? Even clothes that are too long packed up cut in the folds, and papers tied

---

[1] *This sort of stratagem, &c.*] An allusion apparently to some adventure narrated in a part of the Satyricon now lost.

in bundles become illegible. Do you suppose that we who
are young and unused to hardship, can bear to be swathed
and bound like statues? We must seek another method of
escape; listen then to what I have hit on: Eumolpus, as a
man of letters, of course carries ink about him; let us then
black ourselves from top to toe. Then in the disguise of
Ethiopian slaves we shall be at your orders, merry and safe
from the fear of punishment, and by our change of colour we
shall deceive our enemies?"

"Why not circumcise us?" interrupted Giton, "that we
may seem Jews; or bore our ears to imitate Arabians; or
whitewash our faces, that Gaul might mistake us for her own
children? As if colour alone could change the whole aspect!
As if there needed not a multitude of things to combine in
order to complete the delusion! Grant that our daubed faces
would keep their colour; suppose no chance sprinkling of
water should wash it off, and that the ink should not stick to
our clothes, which often happens even when no gum is added,
yet tell me, how are we to give ourselves horribly swollen
lips? to curl and crisp our hair with tongs? to scar our foreheads? to bow our shins? to bring our ankles down to the
ground? to give an outlandish figure to our beards? An
artificial colour only dirties the skin, but does not change the
person. Take my advice; let us adopt the remedy of the
desperate, cover our heads in our garments, and jump into
the sea."

"Forbid it, gods and men!" cried Eumolpus, "that you
should end your lives in so ignominious a manner. Rather
do as I tell you: my servant, as you are aware from the
adventure of the razor, is a barber; let him immediately shave
you both, not only your heads, but your eyebrows[1] too. Next
I will mark your foreheads with an inscription skilfully laid
on, so that you may appear as branded slaves. Thus these
marks will both divert the suspicions of those who are looking
for you, and conceal your countenances under the mask of
punishment."

This stratagem was executed without delay. Stealing to
the side of the vessel, we committed our heads and eyebrows

---

[1] *Your eyebrows.*] The object being to make it appear that Encolpius
and Giton were slaves under punishment, the shaving of the eyebrows is
proposed as a signal mark of ignominy.

to the barber's hands; after which Eumolpus covered our
whole foreheads with great letters, and liberally marked our
faces with the known marks of fugitives.[1] It happened however that one of the sea-sick passengers, who was emptying
his stomach over the ship's side, perceived by moonlight our
barber engaged in this unseasonable occupation, and cursing
the omen, which seemed a last vow before shipwreck, rushed
back to his berth. Pretending not to hear the imprecations
of the sea-sick man, we returned to our former melancholy
musings, and observing a circumspect silence, passed the remainder of the night in a restless manner.

[Next morning, as soon as Eumolpus knew that Tryphæna was out of
bed, he entered Lycas's cabin, when after a conversation about the prosperous voyage portended by the fine weather, Lycas turned to Tryphæna
and said:] "Priapus appeared to me in my sleep and said,
'Know that Encolpius, whom you are in quest of, has been
brought by me on board your ship.'"

Tryphæna started: "One would suppose we had slept together," she said; "for I too had a dream, in which appeared
to me that image of Neptune which I marked at Baiæ, and
said, 'You will find Giton on board of Lycas's ship.'"

"Hence you may perceive," observed Eumolpus, "what
a divine man is Epicurus, who so ingeniously ridiculed these
sports of fancy."

> When in a dream presented to our view
> Those airy forms appear so like the true,
> No prescient shrine, no god the vision sends,
> But every breast its own delusion lends.
> For when soft sleep the body wraps in ease,
> And from the inactive mass the fancy frees,
> What most by day affects, at night returns:
> Thus he who shakes proud states, and cities burns,
> Sees showers of darts, forced lines, disorder'd wings,
> Blood-reeking fields, and deaths of vanquish'd kings;

[1] *The known mark of fugitives.*] Known of course to the ancients. At
present it is doubtful whether this mark was a single F or more. Thieves
were branded or tattooed (*stigmata, stigmosi*) with the full word *Fur*,
whence they were jocularly called "men of three letters," equivalent to
men of three names, i. e. of gentle birth. Slaves had but one name.

He that by day litigious knots untied,
And charm'd the drowsy bench to either side,
By night a crowd of cringing clients sees,
Smiles on the fools, and kindly takes their fees ;
The miser hides his wealth, new treasure finds ;
Through echoing woods his horn the huntsman winds ;
The sailor's dream wild scenes of wreck describes ;
The whore writes billets-doux ; the adultress bribes ;
Hounds in full cry, in sleep, the hare pursue ;
And hapless wretches their old griefs renew.

But Lycas, having expiated Tryphæna's dream,[1] said, "What hinders us from searching the ship, that we may not seem to slight the divine admonition ?"

Upon this, one Hesus, the passenger who had unfortunately discovered our secret doings in the night, cried out, "Who are those persons who were shaved last night by moonshine ? By Jupiter, it is an abominable example ; for, as I am told, it is not lawful for any mortal either to pare his nails, or cut off his hair, on shipboard, unless when the wind is wroth with the waves."

Lycas flew into a rage on hearing this. "Is it so?" said he ; "has any one cut off his hair in this ship, and in a calm night too ? Bring forward the offenders this moment, that I may know with whose blood to purge the vessel."

"It was I commanded it," said Eumolpus ; "and moreover I did so for luck' sake, as I was to be on board the same ship; the rascals had long shaggy hair, which I ordered to be shaved off that I might not seem to make a jail of the ship, and also that the marks with which they are branded might be conspicuous to everybody, when they were no longer shaded by the hair. Among other crimes they have committed, they have squandered my money on a doxy who served them both, and from whom I took them away last night, all reeking with wine and perfumes. In short, they still smell of the debauch they gave themselves at my expense."

Hereupon, as an expiation due to the tutelary god of the

---

[1] *Expiated Tryphæna's dream.*] Washing or aspersion with wine or pure water formed a principal part of this religious ceremony.

vessel, it was ordered that each of us should receive forty stripes. Without more delay the sailors fell furiously upon us with ropes, and sought to appease their patron with our vile blood. I endured three stripes with Spartan heroism; but Giton, at the very first taste of the rope, set up such an outcry that the well-known voice struck fully on Tryphæna's ears; nor was she the only one whom it startled, for all her maids, hearing a voice that was so familiar to them, ran to the spot where he was getting his flogging. Already his marvellous beauty had disarmed the sailors and mutely deprecated their cruelty, when Tryphæna's women all cried out together: "It is Giton! it is Giton! Hold your barbarous hands! Help, mistress! it is Giton!"

Tryphæna turned a willing ear to these cries, and flew to Giton's side. Lycas, who knew me perfectly well, ran up also, as if he had heard my voice, and looked neither at my hands nor my face, but casting his eyes lower down, put his hands on me and said, "Good day, Encolpius!" Let it be no longer a wonder that the nurse of Ulysses recognised after a lapse of twenty years the scar that identified him, since this very knowing man, in spite of the defacement of all the lineaments of my visage and figure, lighted so shrewdly upon the single token that betrayed his fugitive. Meanwhile Tryphæna, deceived by our trick, and thinking the slavish inscriptions on our foreheads were real, burst into tears, and asked in a low voice: Into what slaves' prison could these runagates have fallen, or what hands could be so cruel as to inflict such a punishment? Some disgrace they had certainly deserved, the runaways, who had made such an odious return for her favours.

Stamping with passion, Lycas cried out, "O you simple woman, to believe that these letters were shaped by the branding iron! Would that their foreheads were indelibly marked with these signs of infamy! our satisfaction would be complete; but now we have a farce played off upon us, and are mocked with a sham inscription."

Tryphæna was disposed to compassion, seeing that all was not lost for her pleasures; but Lycas, in whose mind still rankled the thought of his wife's seduction, and of the insults heaped upon him in the portico of Hercules, vehemently exclaimed, with a face convulsed with anger, "I suppose you are convinced, Tryphæna, that the immortal gods preside over human affairs, since they have not only brought our enemies unwittingly on board our vessel, but have also revealed it to us by dreams which agree in every particular. Judge then how expedient it would be to pardon those whom the gods themselves have brought to punishment. For my part, I am not naturally cruel; but am afraid, should I spare them, that the vengeance would fall on my own head."

This superstitious argument made a convert of Tryphæna; she said she would no longer oppose our punishment; she would even take part in that most just retribution; for she had been not less flagrantly outraged than Lycas, her chaste reputation having been traduced in the midst of a mob.

From servile fear the fancied gods first came;
When the fork'd lightnings with impetuous flame
Levell'd proud walls, and lofty Athos fired,
Religious horror every breast inspired.
Lustrations next were paid the radiant Sun,
And changeful Cynthia heavenly honours won.
Hence idol crowds the timorous world o'erflow'd,
And not one month but had its patron god.
By such an impotence of mind betray'd,
The swain to Ceres autumn honours paid;
Bacchus was crown'd with clusters of the vine,
And from the sheep-cot Pales grew divine;
Neptune was set to rule the ocean's tide,
And Pallas o'er the olive to preside.
Whoever had an object to attain,
Of public interest or private gain,
Subjects and rulers vied in self-deceit,
Invented gods, and swell'd the pious cheat.[1]

[1] Primus in orbe deos fecit timor : ardua cœlo
Fulmina cum caderent, discussaque mœnia flammis,
Atque ictu flagaret Athos : Mox Phœbus ad ortus,
Lustrata dejectus humo ; Lunæque senectus,
Et reparatus honos. Hinc signa effusa per orbem,
Et permutatis disjunctus mensibus annus

[Lycas finding Tryphæna as eager for revenge as himself, ordered our punishment to be renewed; whereupon Eumolpus endeavoured to mollify him by the following harangue :

"These unfortunates, on whose destruction you are resolved, implore your compassion, Lycas, and] have requested me, as a person not unknown to you, to undertake the office of mediator, and make them friends again with those who once held them most dear. You may perhaps imagine that these young men have fallen into the trap unawares ; but how can that be, since it is always the first care of every one who embarks on shipboard, to inquire the name of him to whose care he commits his safety? Relent then ; be assuaged by the satisfaction you have received, and suffer freemen to proceed to their destination without injury. Even the most implacable masters suspend their rancour, when their slaves return in penitence, and we spare enemies who surrender at discretion. What more would you have then? What can you desire? Prostrate before your eyes lie these suppliant youths, men of birth and breeding, and what is more than all, once your intimate friends. By Hercules ! had they embezzled your money, or treacherously broken faith with you, yet might your resentment be satiated by the state to which you see them reduced. Slavery, behold ! is written on their foreheads, and these faces of freemen wear spontaneously the legal stamp of ignominy."

Here Lycas interrupted the deprecatory harangue : "Do not confuse the question," he said, "but speak to each particular distinctly." And first of all, if they came hither of their own accord, why did they cut off their hair ? He who disguises himself intends to delude, not to give satisfaction. In the next place, if it was their design to have themselves restored to favour, through your intercession, why have you taken all possible pains to conceal your clients ? Hence it is manifest that the culprits have fallen unawares into the trap, and that

> Projecit vitium hoc; atque error jussit inanis
> Agricolas primos Cereri dare messis honores;
> Palmitibus plenis Bacchum vincire ; Palemque
> Pastorum gaudere manu. Natat obrutus, omni
> Neptunus demersus aqua ; Pallasque palæstras
> Vindicat. Et voti reus, et qui condidit urbem
> Jam sibi quisque deos avido certamine fingit.

you only hunt for subterfuges to withdraw them from the effects of our resentment.

"As to your invidious dinning in our ears that they are men of birth and breeding, take care that you do not damage your cause by a groundless confidence. What should the injured do when the guilty run blindly to their punishment? But they were our friends forsooth! So much the more do they deserve chastisement, for he who assails strangers is a robber, but he who assails his friends is little better than a parricide."

Eumolpus met this damnatory reasoning by saying, "I am aware that nothing weighs more heavily against these unfortunate young men than the fact that they cut off their hair at midnight, whence you conclude that their coming on board this ship was accidental, not voluntary. Fain would I hope that my explanation may appear to you as plain and candid as the act itself was innocently done. They designed before they embarked to ease their heads of that troublesome and useless burden, but the sudden springing up of the wind compelled them to postpone the operation; nor did they suppose that it mattered at all where they performed it, for they were not aware either of the omen or of the custom of mariners."

"To what purpose, as suppliants, did they shave their heads?" retorted Lycas: "Unless you mean to tell me that bald people are usually objects of peculiar pity. But what is the use of inquiring after the truth through an interpreter? What have you to say for yourself, ruffian? What salamander has stripped off your eyebrows? To what god have you dedicated your hair? Answer, scapegoat."

I remained stupidly silent, terrified by the fear of punishment; unable to say a word, the case was so plain against me; confused by my ugliness, with my head ignobly despoiled, and my brows as bare as my head, so that I could neither say nor do anything handsomely. But when my face, already bathed with tears, was wiped with a wet sponge, and the dissolved ink overspread my whole face, and obscured all my features in a sooty cloud, his anger turned to hatred. Seeing this, Eumolpus protested he would not suffer any one to disgrace freemen contrary to right and law, and he met the menaces of our persecutors not only with words but with strength of hand. His servant also stood by him, and one or two sea-sick passengers, who served rather to encourage than to increase our force. Thereupon, so far from asking any mercy for myself, I shook my fists in Tryphæna's face, and proclaimed in a loud and decided tone that I would use them against her, if she did not keep off from Giton, the reprobate woman that she was, the only person in the ship that deserved a flogging.

Lycas was doubly incensed by my impudence, and indignant that I abandoned my own cause to defend that of another. Nor was Tryphæna less enraged at the affront, so that the whole ship was divided into two parties. On one side the barber servant distributed among us the implements of his trade, with one of which he himself was armed ; and on the other Tryphæna's attendants advanced to the combat with their bare nails for weapons ; nor was any lack of war-cries in their array. The pilot alone was neutral, and declared that he would quit the helm, unless there was an end to this furious uproar about a couple of lecherous blackguards. The combat continued to rage nevertheless, our adversaries fighting for revenge, we for life. Many fell on both sides, though not killed ; many retired wounded and bleeding, as from a pitched battle ; nor yet did the wrath of either party show any signs of abatement.

Then the most valorous Giton, clapping a razor to that part of him Tryphæna most admired, threatened to cut off the cause of all our misfortunes ; but Tryphæna forbade the perpetration of so monstrous a deed, and loudly granted him quarter. On my part I frequently applied a razor to my throat, but with no more intention to kill myself than Giton had to execute what he threatened ; but he enacted the tragic scene more boldly than I, because he knew that he held in his hand the same razor with which he had before cut his throat.

Each party still keeping the field, and the pilot, perceiving it was likely to be no common fight, with difficulty brought it about that Tryphæna should officiate as a herald and effect a truce ; whereupon mutual faith being pledged according to ancient usage, she snatched an olive branch from the image of the tutelary deity, and boldly advanced to parley.

What rage, she cries, invades soft peace with arms?
What crime of ours provokes these rude alarms?
We've here no Paris, no Atridan bride,
Nor with fraternal gore Medea dyed:
'Tis slighted love inspires this feud, and craves
For blood amidst the homicidal waves.
One death's enough! Your stormy rage forbear,
Nor show the seas a more tempestuous war.

Tryphæna having delivered this effusion in clamorous agitation, a pause ensued, and the pacific appeal was followed by a cessation of hostilities. Our captain, Eumolpus, seized the opportunity of a return to better feelings, and after sharply rating Lycas, put his seal to a treaty of peace, the tenour of which was as follows :

" You, Tryphæna, promise from the bottom of your heart never to complain of any injury you have received from Giton; nor to upbraid, or punish, or seek in anywise to molest him for anything he may have done before this day; also that you will neither hug, nor kiss, nor solicit him to any further pleasure against his will, under the immediate forfeiture of a hundred denars for every such offence.

" Item: you, Lycas, promise from the bottom of your heart that you will not annoy Encolpius with a contumelious word or look, nor inquire where he sleeps at night; or if you do, that you shall immediately forfeit two hundred denars for every such offence."

The terms of the convention being thus agreed on, we laid down our arms; and lest any rancour should remain notwithstanding our oath, it was resolved that we should efface all that was past by mutual embraces. Exhorted by the general voice, our swelling resentments subsided, and a banquet, brought forth with emulous alacrity,[1] put the stamp of good cheer to our reconciliation. The whole ship resounded with songs, and a sudden calm having stopped her course, one

---

[1] *A banquet, brought forth with emulous alacrity.*] Epulæ qui, *ad certamen* prolatæ: i. e. *certatim* prolatæ. The English and French translators have misconstrued the passage, making *ad certamen* mean " to the field of battle."

amused himself with harpooning the fish which leaped above water, while another, covering his hooks with alluring baits, drew up the floundering prey. Sea-birds too came and perched upon the yard, and these a skilful fowler touched with his jointed reeds. Glued to the limed rods, they were brought down into our hands; their down fluttered in the air, whilst their larger feathers were tossed about on the foam of the waves.

Already Lycas had begun to reinstate me in his good graces, and Tryphæna sprinkled Giton with the last drops in her cup, when Eumolpus, who by this time was warmed with wine, took it into his head to crack jokes on people who were crop-headed and stigmatized; at last, having exhausted his insipid witticisms, he returned to his versifying humour, and delivered a little elegy on the loss of our hair.

> Beauty's chief ornament, your hair, is lost;
> That vernal grace has felt untimely frost;
> Your naked temples mourn their ravish'd shade,
> Waste as a stubble-field your pate is laid.
> Fallacious gods! how swiftly fades our bloom!
> The gifts you first bestow, you first resume.
> Unhappy youth! Less brightly glister
> The locks of Phœbus or his sister,
> Than yours of late; but in their stead
> What see we now? A naked head,
> Polish'd as brass, a sorry sight!
> Like a great puff-ball, round and white!
> A coward now, the girls you shun,
> And from their gamesome laughter run.
> Impending death you well may fear,
> Not without warning he draws near;
> In part you have already perish'd;
> They're Pluto's now, those locks you cherish'd.[1]

[1] *They're Pluto's now, those locks you cherish'd.*] The ancients believe that Proserpine cut off a lock from the head of the dying, and that death could not take place until that preliminary had been fulfilled. Hence Virgil's Dido found it so hard to die. (Æneid iv. 698.)

He would have treated us, I believe, to more of this sort of stuff, or worse; but one of Tryphæna's women took Giton below, and dressed him up in her mistress's false hair. She also took eyebrows out of a little box,[1] and skilfully retracing the form of the lost lineaments, completely restored his beauty. Tryphæna recognised the real Giton, and then it was that, transported even to tears, she kissed him with all her heart. For my part, although I was glad to see the boy restored to his former beauty, yet I hid my face as much as possible, and felt that I must be uncommonly disfigured, since even Lycas did not deign to bestow a word upon me. But these sad thoughts were relieved by the same maid, who, taking me aside, adorned me with a no less elegant head of hair; nay, as it was of a yellow hue, it very much improved my appearance.

After this, Eumolpus, the advocate of the distressed, and the mediator of the existing concord, that our mirth might not flag for want of pleasant talk, launched out into sarcasms upon the levity of women; their alacrity to fall in love; their readiness to forget even their sons for their lovers; averring that there was no woman so chaste but might be wrought into the very fury of an illegitimate passion; that he would not advert to ancient tragedies or to famous examples of former ages, but would relate to us a thing that occurred within his own memory, if we desired to hear it. Accordingly, all eyes and ears being fixed upon him, he began as follows.

The Story of the Ephesian Matron.

There was at Ephesus a certain matron in such high repute for her chastity, that the women even of the neighbouring countries used to come to see her as a marvel. When her husband was carried to the grave, she was not content to follow the corpse, after the common custom, with dishevelled hair, and beating her bosom in presence of all beholders; but followed the defunct even into his last home, and when his corpse was laid in the hypogeum,[2] in the Greek manner, she made

---

[1] *She also took eyebrows out of a little box.*] Not false eyebrows made of hair, which there seems no reason to suppose were known to the Greeks or Romans, but the black powder used for adorning the eyebrows and eyelashes in the manner universally practised by Eastern women to this day.

[2] *The hypogeum.*] That is to say, a cavern, or vault, under ground.

herself its guardian, and wept over it night and day. Thus afflicting herself, and compassing her own death by starvation, neither her parents nor her relations could dissuade her from her purpose; finally, the magistrates failed in the same attempt, and all Ephesus bewailed the exemplary and incomparable woman, who was now dragging through the fifth day without food.

A faithful handmaid sat with the sorrowing woman, mingled her tears with those of her mistress, and as often as occasion required, trimmed a lamp that burned in the tomb. Nothing else was talked of throughout the city, and all ranks of men confessed that never had there been seen before such a shining instance of chastity and affection.

It happened just then that the governor of the province ordered certain robbers to be affixed to crosses near the dismal cave where the matron was weeping over her lately interred husband. The following night, the sentinel who watched the crosses lest the bodies should be stolen for burial, seeing a light glimmering among the tombs, and hearing the groans of some one in sorrow, was led by a curiosity common to mankind to see who or what it might be. He went down therefore into the tomb, where seeing a very beautiful woman, he stood amazed at first as though he beheld some unearthly apparition; but presently observing the corpse, the lady's tears, and her face lacerated by her nails, he rightly concluded that she could not endure the yearning sense of her recent loss. Upon this he went back, fetched his humble meal into the tomb, and began to exhort her to desist from superfluous sorrow, and from rending her bosom with unavailing sobs; telling her that death was a necessary exit, that the grave was a home for all, and repeating all those arguments which are employed to soothe an anguished soul. But she, shocked by such unlooked-for attempts to console her, began to beat her breasts with double vehemence, and to tear her hair and to strew it on the dead body.

The soldier, however, did not give way, but with the same exhortations endeavoured to prevail on her to take some nourishment, till at last the maid, seduced, I make no doubt, by

The Greeks either buried or burned their dead. Both practices prevailed in all ages; but modern writers are greatly divided in opinion as to which of the two was the more usual.

the scent of the wine, confessed her defeat by holding out her
hand to the charitable solicitor, and after refreshing herself
with food and drink, began herself to combat the obstinacy
of her mistress.   "What good will it do you," she said, "to
starve yourself in this way; to bury yourself alive, and resign your breath before the Fates demand it?

"'Think you such things give pleasure to the dead?'[1]

"Will you come back to life?   Will you cast off this prejudice of our sex, and enjoy the good things of this world
whilst you may?   The very corpse that lies before you ought
to warn you to make the most of life."

No one ever listens reluctantly when he is pressed to take
food or to live. The lady, exhausted by an abstinence of several
days, suffered her obstinacy to be overcome, and satisfied her
hunger with no less avidity than the maid who had been the
first to yield.   You know to what temptations mortal flesh is
exposed after a hearty meal: the very same arguments the
soldier had used to combat her despair, he now employed
against her chastity.   The young man, so thought this virtuous dame, was neither ill-looking nor deficient in address,
and the maid spoke in his behalf:

Why with a pleasing passion will you fight,
Nor ever call to mind your past delight?

In a word, the lady observed the same abstinence in this
respect as in the other, and the gallant soldier was a second
time successful in his persuasions. They passed not only that
first nuptial together, but the next night, and the night after
that, the doors of the tomb being of course carefully closed,
so that if any one, friend or stranger, should come thither, he
would conclude that this most virtuous of wives had expired
on the body of her husband. Meanwhile the soldier, delighted
with the beauty of his mistress and with the mystery of his
amour, bought for her all the good things his means could
procure, and as soon as night came, carried them into the tomb.

In the mean time the relations of one of the malefactors,
observing the remissness of the guard, carried off the body in
the night and buried it.   Next day, when the circumvented

---

[1] *Think you such things give pleasure to the dead?*]   These are Anna's
words to her sister Dido. Æn.

soldier saw one of the crosses without a body, dismayed at the fatal consequences to himself, he hastened to acquaint his mistress with what had happened ; telling her he would not await the sentence of the judge ; his own sword should do justice upon his negligence ; would she only afford him sepulture, and join the lover to the husband in that fatal place ?

" Nay," replied the no less compassionate than chaste matron, " the gods forbid that I should have before my eyes at the same time the dead bodies of two men who were most dear to me ! I will rather hang up the dead than be the death of the living." And in accordance with these sentiments, she orders the corpse of her husband to be taken out of its coffin and fixed to the vacant cross. The soldier availed himself of the expedient suggested by the discreet lady ; and next day every one wondered how it was that the dead man had found his way to the cross.

> Give your bark to the winds, not your heart to the fair ;
> Less perfidious are they than the winds and the sea.
> They are all of them naught : if a good one was e'er,
> How a bad thing came good is a riddle to me.[1]

[1] Crede ratem ventis, animum ne crede puellis ;
     Namque est feminea tutior unda fide.
   Femina nulla bona est ; vel, si bona contigit ulla,
     Nescio quo fato res mala facta bona est.

This celebrated story of the Ephesian Matron is one of those Milesian Fables which have gone the round of the world. A story nearly the same exists, under the title of The Widow who was Comforted, in the Seven Wise Masters, which is one of the oldest collections of oriental tales. There however the levity of the widow is aggravated by the circumstance, that the husband had died in consequence of alarm at a danger to which his wife had been exposed, and that she consented to mutilate his body, in order to give it a perfect resemblance to that of the malefactor which had been taken down from the cross. This story of female levity has frequently been imitated, and is found in the new fables attributed to Phædrus, in the tales of Musæus, in Brantôme, La Fontaine, &c. It is the Fabliau de la Femme qui se fist putain sur la fosse de son mari. It is a common story in China, and is included in the collection of *Contes Chinois* translated by Abel Remusat : but the most singular place for the introduction of such a tale was the Rule and Exercise of Holy Dying by Jeremy Taylor, where it forms part of the fifth chapter, entitled, Of the Contingencies of Death and Treating our Dead.

CHAPTER XIV.

TRYPHÆNA AND LYCAS RENEW THEIR LASCIVIOUS IMPORTUNITIES IN VIO-
LATION OF THE TREATY—LYCAS IS SWEPT OVERBOARD IN A STORM—
THE SHIP IS WRECKED—EUMOLPUS'S POETIC RAPTURE IN THE CRISIS OF
PERIL—REFLECTIONS OF ENCOLPIUS ON DISCOVERING THE DEAD BODY
OF LYCAS—THE THREE FRIENDS TRAVEL TOWARDS CROTONA—MANNERS
AND CUSTOMS OF CROTONA—SWINDLING PROJECT—INSOLENCE OF CORAX
—EUMOLPUS'S HINTS ON THE COMPOSITION OF AN EPIC POEM.

THE sailors laughed heartily at this story, and Tryphæna,
blushing not a little, laid her face amorously on Giton's neck.
Lycas did not laugh, but shaking his head with an indignant
air, " If the governor," said he, " had been a just man, he would
have had the husband's body carried back to the tomb, and
the woman hung on the cross." No doubt the wrong done
to his bed recurred to his mind, and the pillage of his ship in
the wanton cruise. But the terms of the treaty forbade him
to complain, and the mirth that possessed us all left no opportunity for anger. Meanwhile Tryphæna, seated on Giton's
lap, sometimes covered his bosom with kisses, sometimes
amused herself with adjusting his artificial hair so as to set
off his face to the best advantage.

I was so out of humour and impatient of this new league,
that I could neither eat nor drink, but sat looking grimly
askance on the pair. Every kiss the wanton gave him, every
meretricious blandishment she employed, cut me to the heart ;
and I know not whether I was more angry with the boy for
robbing me of my mistress, or with my mistress for debauch-
ing the boy. Both were most offensive to my eyes, and worse
than my late captivity. To complete my misery, neither
Tryphæna spoke to me as an intimate acquaintance and a
once favoured lover, nor did Giton so much as drink to me or
vouchsafe me a syllable upon the most indifferent subject.
He was afraid, I believe, in the first moments of her returning favour, to re-open a scarcely closed wound. Tears of spite
fell upon my bosom, and the groans I tried to stifle almost
choked me.

The vulture tearing at the bosom's core,
Mangling the living vitals day and night,

Is not the bird of legendary lore,
But rankling jealousy and fell despite.[1]

[Lycas perceived, notwithstanding my vexation, how well my yellow wig became me, and being inflamed afresh,] began to solicit me, not with the imperiousness of a master, but as a friend who asks a favour. [At last meeting with a decisive repulse, his love turned to fury, and he endeavoured to extort by violence what he could not win by entreaty; but Tryphæna suddenly bolting in, prevented his design, whereupon he hurried off in confusion.

The lustful Tryphæna asked me what was the meaning of all this? and compelled me to explain. Fired by the relation, and mindful of our old amours, she offered to renew them; but I was sick of all this debauchery, and met her advances coldly. Then throwing her arms round me in a rage of lust, she hugged me so tightly that she forced me to cry out. In rushes one of her maids, and believing I would have forced from her mistress the favour I refused her, she dragged us asunder. Incensed to the highest degree by her disappointment, Tryphæna abused and threatened me, and then hurried off to exasperate Lycas still more against me, and to join him in pursuit of revenge.

You must know I was formerly a favourite with this waiting-woman of Tryphæna's, when I carried on a correspondence with her mistress, for which reason she was extremely nettled at catching me with her, and sobbed most bitterly. I pressed her to tell me the reason, and after a little resistance] she burst out: "If you have a drop of good blood in your veins, you will value her no more than a common prostitute. If you are a man, you will not go near such a filthy whore."

This incident not a little perplexed me; but what I chiefly feared was lest Eumolpus should come to the knowledge of my adventure, and that in the versifying mania he should take it into his head to revenge my quarrel in a satire: [for his fiery zeal would certainly have exposed me to ridicule, and that was a thing I greatly dreaded.

Whilst I was contriving how to prevent his suspicion, Eumolpus himself came to me, already acquainted with what had happened; for Tryphæna had communicated her grief to Giton, and sought to be indemnified

---

[1] Qui vultur jecor intimum pererrat,
Et pectus trahit, intimasque fibras,
Non est quem lepidi vocant poetæ,
Sed cordis mala, livor atque luctus.

at his cost for the affront I had offered her; whereat Eumolpus was greatly incensed, the more so because these wanton importunities were an open breach of the treaty.

As soon as the old man saw me he bemoaned my hard fortune, and desired to know the whole affair from myself; so finding him already informed, I frankly told him of Lycas's lewd attempt, and the lascivious assault of Tryphæna. When I had finished,] Eumolpus swore a solemn oath [that he would signally avenge me, and that the gods were too just to suffer so many crimes to go unpunished.]

Whilst we were thus discoursing, the sea grew rough, and the face of day was obscured by thick clouds gathering from every point. The mariners hurried to and fro to their work as fast as fear could make them, and took in the sails. But the wind veered continually, and the helmsman knew not which way to steer. Sometimes we were driven towards Sicily; very often the north wind, which prevails on the coasts of Italy, drove the ship hither and thither at its mercy; and what was more dangerous than all the squalls was a sudden darkness, so thick, that the steersman could not even see to the end of the prow. The tempest being now at its height, Lycas held out his suppliant hands to me in great agitation, saying, " Succour us, Encolpius, in our peril, I mean, restore that divine robe and the sistrum to the vessel. By all you hold sacred, have pity on us, you who are usually so good-natured." While he was thus vociferating a gust of wind swept him into the sea; the raging billows whirled him round for a moment, and then ingulfed him.

Tryphæna was snatched from certain death by the fidelity of her servants, who saved her with the greater part of her goods in the ship's boat.

For my part, locking Giton in my arms, I wept aloud and cried, " At least we deserved this of the gods, that they should unite us in death, but cruel Fortune will not permit it; for see, the waves are just about to overset the vessel; see, the angry deep will soon sever our loving embraces. Therefore if you ever truly loved, Giton, kiss me while you may, and let us snatch this last joy from impending fate."

When I had thus said, Giton threw off his vest, and creeping under my tunic, protruded his head to kiss me; and that the malicious waves might not tear us asunder, he girt us together with his girdle. " If we have no other hope," he said, "at least we shall thus be the longer united in death; or if death will be so merciful as to cast us on the same shore, either the next person who passes that way will in common humanity heap a few stones over us, or at least, in spite of the angry waves, the unconscious sand will cover our remains." I submitted to that last bond, and arranged as on my death-bed, I awaited the fatal moment which I no longer feared.

Meanwhile the storm accomplishes the decrees of fate and sweeps away all the rigging of the vessel. Neither mast nor rudder was left, nor a rope, nor an oar, but a shapeless mass of logs as it were drifted with the billows. Some fishermen hastily put to sea in their small craft in hopes of plunder, but seeing some persons in the wreck who were capable of defending their own, they changed their aggressive purposes into offers of aid.

Just then we heard a strange noise that came from below the master's cabin, and sounded like the howlings of a wild beast that wanted to get out. Following the noise, we found Eumolpus seated, in the act of covering a great sheet of parchment with verses. We were astonished how a man so near death could amuse himself with poetry, and notwithstanding his cries to the contrary, we hauled him out of his hole, and told him to leave off his fooling; but he was vexed at being interrupted, and cried, "Let me alone till I finish this sentence; the poem is just travailing towards its completion." I laid violent hands on the madman, and made Giton come and help me to drag the bellowing poet ashore. This task being accomplished, not without difficulty, we took shelter with sad hearts in a fisherman's hut, where after refreshing ourselves as best we might with some of our provisions which the salt water had spoiled, we passed a most wretched night.

Next day, as we were deliberating which way we should direct our steps, I suddenly descried a human body which the waves were floating with a gentle rolling motion to the shore. Saddened by the sight, I stopped and gazed with moist eyes on the perfidious element. "And this man, perhaps," I exclaimed, "is expected in some corner of the world by a wife all unconscious of her loss; by a son who knows not that there has been a storm; perhaps he has left behind a father whom he kissed as he departed. These are the designs

of mortals! Such is the issue of their great projects! See
how the man rides the waves!"

I was thus deploring an unknown victim, as I thought,
when the waves turned the face to the shore. It was quite
unaltered, and I recognised him who so lately had made me
tremble, the implacable Lycas, cast as it were beneath my feet.
I could refrain from tears no longer; again and again I smote
my breast, exclaiming, "Where now is your wrath? Where
now your despotism? There you lie, a prey to fishes and wild
beasts; and you, who but a little while ago so loudly vaunted
the might of your dominion, have not even a plank out of
the wreck of your great vessel. Go now, mortals, puff yourselves up with grand anticipations; go, crafty ones, lay plans
a thousand years long for the disposal of that wealth you have
won by fraud. It was but yesterday this lifeless thing cast
up the net amount of his fortune; he even fixed in his imagination the very day on which he was to see his country
again. O all ye gods! how far he lies from his point of destination! But it is not the sea alone that keeps its promises
in this sort: the warrior is betrayed by his arms; another, in
the act of paying his offerings to the gods, is buried under
the ruin of his penates; a third falls from his chariot, and
suddenly breathes his last; one is choked by gluttony, another
dies of abstinence. Do but calculate rightly, and it is plain
there is shipwreck everywhere.—But the man whom the sea
devours does not obtain burial.—Why, what matters it how
his perishable carcase is consumed, whether by fire, water, or
time? Whatever you do, all these means tend to the same
result.—But wild beasts will tear the body.—Will the fire
deal with it more gently? fire, which we think the most cruel
punishment we can inflict on our slaves in our anger. What
folly is it then to be thus anxious that nothing of us remain unburied, since, whether we will or not, destiny provides for this."

And Lycas too lay on the blazing pile, which had been
reared by the hands of his enemies; whilst Eumolpus, who
was busy about the dead man's epitaph, fixed his eyes on
vacancy in search of ideas, [*and muttered from time to time
some verses, of which I remember only these:*]

Not in the hollow'd rock or marble dome
    We laid thy victim, ruthless Destiny!

Five feet of earth compose the narrow home
That holds his noble dust eternally.[1]

Having freely discharged this charitable office, we continued
our proposed journey, and soon arrived, all bathed in sweat,
at the summit of a mountain, where we saw at no great distance a large town seated on a steep hill. We did not know
what place it was, until a countryman informed us it was
Crotona, a very ancient city, and once the most flourishing in
Italy. We then inquired with much interest what sort of
people inhabited this famous place, and what kind of commerce they chiefly maintained since their impoverishment by
so many wars.

" Good strangers," replied the man, " if you are merchants,
change your plans and choose some other way of living. But
if you are men of a more polite stamp, who can lie stoutly
and without end, you are in the right road to fortune. For
in Crotona learning is in no esteem ; eloquence finds no ac-
ceptance ; nor can temperance and morality meet with commendation, much less lead to profit ; but all the men you see
in that city, know for certain that they belong to one or other
of two classes ; for they either hunt or are hunted for legacies.
No one there rears children ; for whoever has natural heirs is
not admitted to any public shows or entertainments, is excluded from all social privileges, and herds obscurely with
the dregs of the people. On the contrary, those who have
never married, and have no near kindred, are advanced to the
highest honours ; they are the only brave, the only fit to command, and in short the only virtuous. You will see," he
added, " a city like those fields in the time of a pestilence in
which there are only torn carcases, and crows tearing them."

Eumolpus, who was more knowing than we, reflected upon
this new kind of policy, and confessed it was a way to wealth
which did not displease him. I took this to be a jocular extravagance on the part of the old poet, until he added, " Oh
that I had a more ample outfit, that is to say, a more fashion-
able dress, to give probability to the imposture. By Hercules,

---

[1]   Ineluctabile fatum.
At non exciso defossa est marmore petra.
Quinque pedum fabricata domus, qua nobile corpus
Exiguo requievit humo.

I would carry scrip no more, but conduct you straightway to great opulence."

I promised he should have what he required, if he were satisfied with the garment which served as an auxiliary in my plundering enterprises, and with the spoil we had taken from the villa of Lycurgus. As for cash for present use, the Mother of the gods would in conscience provide that. "Well then," said Eumolpus, "what stops us? Let us arrange our drama. Make me the master, if you like the business."

No one ever condemned a project that cost him nothing. Therefore, for the better concealment of our roguery, we took a solemn oath to Eumolpus that we would suffer for him, fire, prison, stripes, steel, and death, and whatsoever else he commanded. Thus like true gladiators we devoted ourselves, body and soul, to the will of our master.

After the ceremony of our oath, assuming the character of slaves, we saluted our new master, and were instructed to give out that Eumolpus had lately lost his son, a youth of great hopes and extraordinary eloquence; and that for this reason the unhappy old man had left his country, that the daily visits of his son's dependants and companions, and the sight of his tomb, might not continually renew his sorrow; that this affliction had been followed by a recent shipwreck, in which he had lost upwards of two millions of sesterces; but that he was not so much concerned about the loss of his money, as that he found himself in a position so inconsistent with his dignity, for want of a proper retinue of servants; moreover that he had thirty millions of sesterces, lands and securities, in Africa, and as many slaves dispersed about Numidia as would be enough even to take Carthage.

Agreeably with this scheme we advised Eumolpus to cough a great deal; to seem at all events weak at his stomach; to affect disgust at everything he ate before company; to talk of nothing but silver and gold, of farms that deceived his expectations, and of the perpetual barrenness of land. Also that he should affect to be busy every day with his accounts; that he should be perpetually altering his will in everybody's favour; and that, to complete the farce, whenever he called any of us he should mistake our names, so as to make it plain that the master still remembers the servants he has left behind him.

Matters thus settled, after prayers to the gods for success, we set forward. But Giton could not support his unusual burthen, and Corax, Eumolpus's servant, grumbling at his work, often rested his load, cursed those who went too fast, and declared he would either throw down his bundles or run away with them. "What," cried he, "do you take me for a beast of burthen, or a ship to carry marble? I hired myself out to do a man's work, not a horse's. I am a freeman no less than you, though my father left me poor." And not content with bad language, he lifted up one leg from time to time, and filled the road with an abominable noise and stench. Giton laughed at his insolence, and followed every explosion with an imitative sound from his lips.

"Young men," Eumolpus suddenly exclaimed, " how many have been deceived in thinking they had a vocation for poetry! For as soon as any one can make a verse stand upon its feet, or clothe a thought in dainty words, he forthwith conceits that he has scaled Helicon. Hence it is that so many, tired of forensic labours, retreat to the calm delights of poetry, as to an easier harbour, imagining that it is a less difficult task to compose a poem than an argumentative harangue tricked out with sparkling sentences. But a mind of some elevation likes not this vanity; nor can the mind conceive or bring forth a true poetic birth unless it be inundated with a great flood of learning. You must avoid in your choice of words everything that savours of what I call lowness, and use expressions above the vulgar reach.

'I hate, and bid avaunt! the vulgar herd.'

"You must also take care not to deform the work with sentiments that stand out from the body of it like excrescences; let them rather be interwoven with its texture, and shine with the same colour. Homer is an example of this, and the Greek Lyrics, our own Roman Virgil, and the happy correctness of Horace.[1] As for the rest, they were either ignorant of the true path to poetry, or afraid to tread it. There is that grand subject, our civil wars : whoever attempts it, unless he be fully accomplished in literature, will sink under the task. For the thing to be done is not to comprise a series of facts in

---

[1] *The happy correctness of Horace.*] A Latinism, which the translator ventures to think allowable for the sake of its terseness.

verse;[1] an historian can much better execute such a narrative;
but the free spirit must be hurried along through mazy in-
volutions, divine interventions, marvellous machinery, and
elaborate conceptions; so that we may recognise rather the
inspired frenzy of the poet, than the scrupulous veracity of
the narrator of attested facts; take for example, if you please,
this rapid effusion, though it has not yet received the last
hand.

POEM ON THE CIVIL WARS.

Now had Rome triumph'd o'er the subject globe
From sun to sun, as far as earth extends
Or ocean rolls; unsated yet her greed.
With plunder fraught her vessels swept the seas,
And if a corner of the earth was found
Pregnant with gold, war to that land of gold!
War to accumulate the fatal cause
Of civil war.   All homely joys were scorn'd,
All facile pleasures pall'd.   The soldier learn'd
To prize the Assyrian purple, and the gem
That vies in lustre with the sea-shell's dye.
Numidia and the distant Seres sent
New kinds of fleeces,[2] and Arabia's shrubs[3]

---

[1] *To comprise a series of facts in verse.*]   It scarcely admits of doubt
that Petronius points his criticism especially against Lucan, whose Pharsalia is composed, according to Quintilian, rather in the style of history
than of poetry. Servius (in his commentary on the first book of the
Æneid) says the same thing of Lucan: In numero poetarum esse non
meruit, quia historiam composuisse videtur, non poema. The reader will
observe that the following poem on the Civil Wars is not an improvisa-
tion, like the Capture of Troy previously recited by Eumolpus, but an
elaborate composition, in which the author has put out all his strength,
in accordance with the critical canons he has propounded in the passage
before us.

[2] *New kinds of fleeces.*]   Several commentators have been under the
impression that Numidia supplied the Romans with nothing but marble. Antonius, however, quotes a passage from Pliny (lib. v. c. 1) to
the following effect: The roots of Mount Atlas are full of forests of an
unknown kind of tree, covered with a fine down, from which, with the
help of art, garments can be made like those woven of silk (e bombyce).

[3] *Arabia's shrubs.*]   Pliny (lib. ii. c. 11) speaks of the cotton plant

Were of their down despoil'd.   Lo ! other scenes
Of blood and havoc, desecrating peace :
The Mauric wilds are track'd, the utmost verge
Of Ammon ransack'd, lest for carnage fail
The precious ravager, and that o'er sea
Borne in his gilded cage, the tiger may
Lap human gore amidst the applause of Rome.
I blush to tell of the nefarious art
From Persia borrow'd ; how with impious steel
Was lopp'd the germ of manhood, that the change
Which should accompany progressive years
Might be delay'd, and, thwarted in her course,
Nature might fail to recognise herself.
Each had his minion, loved its mincing gait,
Its snaky locks, its wantonness of dress,
And odious ambiguity of sex.
Lo ! more profusion : citron tables [1] brought

as the growth of Arabia, and elsewhere (xix. 1) as indigenous in that part of Upper Egypt which adjoins Arabia. It is thus mentioned by Virgil, (Georg. ii. 120,) Quid nemora Æthiopum, molli canentia lana ?

[1] *Citron tables.*] In no articles of furniture, says Bekker, (Gallus, p. 21, n.,) was greater expense incurred than in the tables ; indeed the extravagance in this particular would be scarcely credible, did not the most trustworthy writers give us express information about it. The *orbes* especially cost immense sums of money : by this word *orbis* is not to be understood always round tables, but massive slabs or plates of wood, cut off the stem in its whole diameter. For this purpose the wood of the citrus was preferred above all others, by which we must not understand the citron tree, but the Thuya cypressoides, Θυΐα, Θύον, as is evident from Pliny, xii. 16, who expressly distinguishes it from the regular *citrus*. This tree was found especially in Mauritania, (hence *secti Atlantide sylva orbes,* Luc. x. 144 ; Mart. xiv. 89,) and was of such magnitude as the citron tree never attained to. Pliny, c. 15, mentions plates nearly four feet in diameter, which were cut off the trunk of the thickness of nearly half a foot. Unlike other tables, they were not provided with several feet, but rested on an ivory column, and were thence termed *Monopodia,* Liv. xxxix. 6 ; Mart. ii. 43, 9. The price of such tables was enormous. Pliny relates that Cicero himself had paid for one, that was then still extant, 1,000,000 sesterces, [between £8000 and £9000,] and he mentions even more extraordinary cases. The most costly specimens were those cut off near the root, not only because the tree was broadest there, but on account of the wood being dappled and speckled. Pliny mentions *tigrinæ,*

From Africa, enrich'd with golden stains ;
Whole troops of slaves, bright purple tapestry,
Making their owners beggars.   Round the board
So mischievously precious, drown'd in wine,
Lie the imbruted revellers ; his arms
The soldier leaves to rust,[1] and banqueting
Consumes the wealth wrung from a plunder'd world.
Ingenious too is gluttony ; the scare,
Caught in Sicilian seas, is brought alive
To Roman tables ; from the Lucrine shore
The oyster comes to give the feast its zest,
More appetising for its cost ; the banks of Phasis,
Mourning their ravish'd birds, resound alone
To the winds piping through the trees forlorn.

Nor less the frenzy in the Campus, where
The bought Quirites, brawling, turn'd their votes
To lucre ; venal was the people's choice,
Venal the senate ; by the chink of gold
Men won their favour.   Age itself had lost
Its ancient dower of freedom ; lawful rule
Was merged in interest, and, undone by gold,
Rome's majesty was trampled in the mire.
Cato was spurn'd and spat on ; more abash'd
Was he who gain'd the people's suffrage, shamed
Ev'n by his victory that from Cato's hand
Wrested the fasces.   O disgrace to Rome !
O downfal of her virtues ! It was not

pantherinæ undatim crispæ, pavonum caudæ oculos imitantes, apiatæ mensæ.
These tables, however, were too dear, and not large enough to use at
meals, although they did sometimes serve for this purpose.   Mart. ix. 60,
9.   Hence larger ones of common wood were made, and veneered with
the wood of the citrus, and, according to Pliny, even Tiberius used such
an one ; xvi. 42, 48.

[1] *His arms the soldier leaves to rust.*]   The common reading, *correptis
armis*, hardly makes sense.   Burmann suggests *contemtis*, which we
adopt.

One man alone they spurn'd, but with that one
Their liberty and glory.   So lost Rome,
Sold by herself, became a helpless prey.

Immersed moreover in a double slough
On either hand, of usury and debt,
The whole republic lay.   No man could call
His house, nay, nor his very self, his own ;
So like a creeping pestilence debt wrought
The tortured vitals of the social frame.
Wretched and desperate, now they rush'd to arms,
That rapine might repair the ruins made
By luxury.   He safely dares whom want
Secures from loss.   Could aught else wake up Rome,
As wallowing in the mire entranced she lay,
But fire, and sword, and the fierce lust of war ?
Three mighty chiefs had Fortune raised, all whom
The fell Erinnys brought in various ways
To bloody death.   Crassus in Parthia fell ;
Great Pompey perish'd on the Libyan shore ;
And thankless Rome saw greater Julius bleed.
As though one soil too narrow were to hold
Their mighty dust, world-wide apart they lie.
Of Glory's service such the recompense.

Between the Siren's city and the fields
Of great Dicarchis[1] yawns a gulf profound,
Through which Cocytus rolls its sulphurous flood
Poisoning the upper air.   Within the reek
Of its hot surge no lusty autumn crowns
The year with gladness ; verdure never decks
The blasted sod ; nor vernal choristers
With jocund turbulence of melody
Make the green copses vocal ; all around

[1] *The Siren's city—Dicarchis.*]   That is, between Naples (Parthenope)
and Puteoli.

Blank desolation reigns, rocks piled on rocks,
Ragged and black, on which the cypress casts
A darker horror.   'Twas amid these scenes
The monarch of the shades put forth his head,
With funeral fires and hoary ashes crown'd,
And to swift fleeting Fortune spoke these words :

" O swayer of things human and divine,
Fortune, who never on that power dost look
Complacently, that too securely stands,
Thou who delight'st in new things, and but giv'st
Thy favours to resume them, dost thou not
Begin to weary of Rome's ponderous weight,
And long to let her tottering grandeur fall ?
Her manhood sickens of its very might,
And the stupendous fabric ill sustains,
Its valour rear'd.   Behold o'er all the land
The lavish waste of spoil, the mad excess
Of sumptuous luxury.   They build in gold,
Their mansions flout the stars.   Seas into land,
Land into sea, are turn'd ; they break the laws
Of Nature, and invert her order.   Lo !
Me too they threaten, and invade my realms,
Tearing from out the bowels of the earth
Whole mountain masses, scooping caverns deep,
That groan and threaten ruin, till the ghosts
Begin to hope for day.   Come therefore, Fortune,
Change thy mild aspect for grim looks of war ;
Fire every Roman breast with civil rage,
And people with more dead my ghostly realms.
My lips have not enjoy'd a plenteous draught
Of human blood, nor my Tisiphone
Slaked her hot thirst, since Sylla's reeking blade
Made fat the crimson'd earth, and harvests sprang
Exuberant from fields manured with gore."

He spoke, and stretching forth his hand to clasp
The goddess' hand, rent the firm earth in twain.
Fortune replied : "O sire, by all beneath
The upper world obey'd, if truth to speak
Be not forbidden, I shall have my wish.
For know that in my breast, as in thine own,
Wrath fiercely burns.   All I have done for Rome
With loathing I repent.   Let that same god [1]
Pull down her towering might, who piled it up
So arrogantly high.   My purpose holds
To arm her sons against her, and with blood
To pamper their profusion.   I descry
Philippi's mutual carnage, corpses heap'd
On the Thessalian plain, and funeral piles
Innumerous blazing on Iberia's shore.
The clash of arms smites on my ears ; I see
The Libyan camp, thine, Nilus, the sea-fight
At Actium, and the barks in panic flight
Shunning Apollo's shafts. [2]   Throw open wide
The gates of greedy hell, give free access
To thy new subjects.   Charon's boat will be
Too scanty for the ghostly multitudes,
That throng the dismal banks ; the ferryman
Will need a fleet.   Revel, Tisiphone,
In the huge havoc ; lick the gaping wounds,
And glut thyself with blood.   The mangled world
Is hurrying headlong to the Stygian shades."

Scarce had she ended ere fork'd lightnings flash'd
From the rent clouds, and thunder peal'd.   Down sank
The king of shades, and hid within the earth,

---

[1] *That same god.*]   Namely, Mars.
[2] *Apollo's shafts.*]   It was a point of faith much insisted on by Augustus and the poets of his court, that Apollo fought in person on his side at the battle of Actium.   See Propertius, book v. elegy vi.

Aghast with terror at his brother's bolts.
Straightway with portents dire the gods announced
The coming devastation ; the Sun veil'd
His blood-red face in hideous fogs, as though
Already he beheld the butchery ;
Nor less abhorring on such deeds to shine,
The Moon her full orb quench'd.   Mountain tops riv'n
Down thunder'd ; and wide-straying rivers left
Their channels dry.   Hosts battled in the heavens,
And clarions peal'd their death-calls 'mid the stars ;
Whilst Ætna, with unusual fires devour'd,
Fulmined against the sky.   Among the tombs
And bones unsepulchred, with horrid shrieks,
Terrific phantoms wander'd ; meteors flamed,
Led by a blazing comet, and red Jove
In showers of blood descended.

                                        Soon the gods
Resolved these portents ; for on vengeance bent,
Impatient of delay, Cæsar withdrew
His arms from Gaul, and rush'd to civil war.
Amid the Alps, where, by the Grecian god
First trodden, lower sink the rocks, and yield
Passage for foot of man, there is a place
Sacred to Hercules ; there winter dwells
Perpetual, lock'd in frozen snow, whereon
The sky appears to rest ; meridian suns
Avail not, nor the genial breath of spring,
To thaw those adamantine piles of ice,
Whose giant shoulders might support the world.
Here Cæsar with his joyful legions climb'd ;
Here camp'd ; and from the lofty pinnacle
Surveying all Hesperia's fertile plains,
With hands and voice uplifted thus exclaim'd :

"Almighty Jove, and thou Saturnian land,
Gladden'd so oft by my victorious arms,
Bear witness both with what unwillingness
I enter on this war, compell'd by wrongs
Too keen to bear, prohibited my home,
Whilst I with native gore purpled the Rhine,
And drove back from the Alps the threatening Gaul,
Prepared once more to storm our Capitol.
For Germans quell'd, exile is my reward ;
And fifty victories o'er my country's foes
Make me a manifest traitor. Who are they
Whom glory so affrights, at whose behest
War is begun ? Base hireling tools of faction,
Unworthy of my Rome, whom she, methinks,
Not with impunity adopts ; this arm
To dastards yields not tamely. Victors, on !
On in your wrath, my valiant men ! and plead
Your cause with your good swords. Our crime's the same,
One common danger waits us. Not alone
I conquer'd ; you who shared the toil must share
The recompense. Since therefore punishment
Is for our trophies the appointed meed,
And we with all our victories have earn'd
Nought but defilement, let the die be cast,[1]
Judge, Fortune, how it falls. Onward to war,
And try your strength upon these challengers.
My course is fix'd. 'Mid such a gallant host
Not all the world can vanquish me in arms."

He spoke : the Delphic bird, on pinions swift
Descending from the sky, glad omens gave ;
Forth from the awful forest on the left

---

[1] *Let the die be cast.*] "The die is cast !" said Cæsar as he crossed
e Rubicon. Eatur, inquit, quo deorum ostenta, et inimicorum iniquitas
cat. Jacta est alea, inquit. Sueton. Jul. 32.

Unwonted voices came, and flashing fire;
And Phœbus, in surpassing plenitude
Of glory crown'd, unveil'd his golden orb.
Fired by these omens, Cæsar bade advance
His standards, he himself the first
To dare the perilous path.   Passive as yet
Its gelid horrors lay; but when the feet
Of men and horse the icy fetters thaw'd,
The melted snow adown the mountain stream'd;
But soon again, as if by Fate's command,
Arrested in their fall, the floods stood fast,
Whilst o'er the treacherous path men, horses, arms
Were roll'd in piteous heaps; fierce whirlwinds lash'd
The broken ranks, and from the storm-swept clouds
Down pour'd their ponderous freight; massive and thick
The pelting hail crash'd on their arms, as though
A frozen sea were falling.   Heaven and earth,
Merged indiscriminate in ice and snow,
Were vanquish'd; but not vanquish'd was the soul
Of dauntless Cæsar; leaning on his spear,
Onward he strode across the horrid waste
With steps unswerving.   So strode Hercules
From the Caucasian summit, or grim Jove
From high Olympus, in his wrathful might,
Descending to the Giants' overthrow.

Rumour meanwhile, with speed by terror urged,
Flew to Mount Palatine, and scatter'd thence
These tidings of dismay: "A hostile fleet
Is riding on the main,[1] and vengeful legions,
With German conquests flush'd, surmount the Alps."
Nought hovers now before the frighted eyes

---

[1] *A hostile fleet is riding on the main.*]   Here Rumour lied as usual
for history tells that Cæsar was unable to pursue his retreating foes be
yond Brundusium for want of ships.

Of Rome's inhabitants but fire and sword,
And all the hideous ills that civil war
Brings in its train. Doubt and perplexity
Rack every bosom; one his flight pursues
By land, another to the sea commits
His safety, for the sea, he thinks, is still
His country. Fear, bold through its own excess,
Would try the chance of arms: fear wings the speed
Of those that fly. Thus variously impell'd,
The panic-stricken people, woeful sight!
Forsook the city; vanquish'd by a breath
Of rumour, the Quirites left behind
Their sorrowing homes; one leads his children forth
With trembling hand; his household gods another
Hides in his bosom, from his threshold turns,
And hurls his curses at the absent foe.
Here the fond husband to his bosom press'd
His sobbing wife; there pious sons bore off
Their aged parents, and nor felt their load,
Nor fear'd but for their venerable charge.
Others, insensate, all their precious store
Bore with them, to increase the victor's spoils.
And (as upon the tempest-tumbled deep,
When unavailing are the seamen's toils,
The master's skill, some lash the ponderous pine,
Others look out for some safe bay with shores
Unvex'd by storms) there were those who thought
Only of swiftest flight, abandoning
To Fortune's keeping all that they possess'd.

But wherefore dwell upon these lesser griefs?
Great Pompey fled, with both the consuls fled,
Pompey, Hydaspes' and proud Pontus' scourge,
The rock to pirates fatal, thrice whom Jove
Had wondering seen in the triumphal car.

z

That mighty chief who gave the Euxine laws,
And whom the Bosphorus obey'd with awe,
O dastardy ! forsook the imperial name,
And Fortune joy'd in the great champion's flight.

From Rome's affrighted denizens to heaven's
The sad contagion spread; the gods themselves
Join'd in the universal rout, forsook
The desecrated earth, and turn'd their backs
On the doom'd race of men.   First gentle Peace
Beating her arms, her olive wreath pull'd down
To hide her drooping brow, fled from the world,
And sought the realms of Pluto; [1] with her went
Meek Faith, and Justice with dishevell'd hair,
And weeping Concord with her mantle torn.
But joyous, through the yawning mouth of hell,
Swarm'd up its evil choir; Erinnys loathed,
Rampant Bellona, and Megæra arm'd
With blazing brands, blood-thirsty Treachery,
And Murder, and the lurid phantom Death.
Among them Fury, from his fetters freed,
Lifts high his gory head; a blood-stain'd casque
Hides his gash'd visage; on his left arm hangs
His batter'd shield, with darts innumerous
Bristling all over; [2] and his right hand wields
A flaming torch to set the world on fire.

The gods again descended to the earth,
Leaving heaven tenantless; for all the court
Of Jove, inclining either way, took part

[1] *Sought the realms of Pluto.*] She went of course to the Elysian
fields, the only place of refuge left her, for war raged in heaven as well
as on earth.

[2] *With darts innumerous bristling.*] That is, with darts shot into it in
fight. Appian relates that Cæsar's shield had two hundred missiles stuck
into it in a battle in Spain, and that Minutius, one of his officers, received
one hundred and thirty in the same way at the battle of Dyrrachium.

With the contending mortals.   First Dione
Champion'd her Cæsar's cause; her Pallas join'd,
And Mars terrific with his brandish'd spear;
Whilst in espousal of great Pompey's part
Cynthia, with Phœbus, and Cyllene's son,
And his own model, great Alcides, join'd.

The clarions peal'd to arms: in upper air
Her Stygean head, with ragged locks defiled,
Discord uplifted.   Clotted gore stood thick
Upon her face; her livid eyes dropp'd brine;
Foul-rusted were her brazen teeth; her tongue
Swelter'd with venom; hissing serpents writhed
About her cheeks; ragged and rent her garb;
And flames danced madly in her restless hand.
From black Cocytus' pit emerged, she stalk'd
Up to the crest of lofty Apennine,
Whence as she gazed o'er all the lands and seas,
And legions deluging the earth with war,
Thus into words her joyful fury broke:

"Now rush, ye nations, rush in burning hate
To arms, and ply the devastating torch
In populous cities.   Woe to those who hide!
Vengeance shall find them out.   Let not a hand
Hold back from the dread work, woman's, nor boy's,
Nor tottering elder's; let earth quake and groan,
And roofs crash down upon their inmates' heads.
Do thou, Marcellus, the decree[1] uphold;
Stir up the people, Curio;[2] Lentulus,[3]

---

[1] *The decree.*]   The decree of the Senate, passed at the instance of
the Consul Marcellus, by which Cæsar was deprived of his government
of Gaul, and commanded to lay down his arms, under pain of being declared an enemy to the republic.
[2] *Curio.*]   Tribune of the People, a partisan of Cæsar.
[3] *Lentulus.*]   Colleague of Marcellus in the consulship.

Be sure thou slack not in thy martial zeal.
Why dost thou tarry, Cæsar? Why so slow
To burst the gates of Rome, lay low her walls,
And seize her treasures? If thou canst not, Pompey,
Hold out in Rome, to Epidamnum hie,
And soak Thessalian fields with human gore."

'Twas done on earth as Discord gave command.

CHAPTER XV.

EUMOLPUS DUPES THE CROTONIANS, AND LIVES SUMPTUOUSLY AT THEIR
EXPENSE—ENCOLPIUS, WHO HAS ASSUMED THE NAME OF POLYÆNOS,
RECEIVES A MESSAGE FROM AN AMOROUS LADY—FIRST INTERVIEW BE-
TWEEN CIRCE AND POLYÆNOS—THE LADY'S CHARMS—THE LOVER'S
IMPOTENCE—CIRCE'S LETTER TO POLYÆNOS—HIS REPLY—PROSELENOS
THE SORCERESS PREPARES HIM FOR A SECOND TRIAL—IT TAKES PLACE,
AND HE IS AGAIN DISCOMFITED—HE IS IGNOMINIOUSLY CHASTISED BY
ORDER OF CIRCE—HIS OBJURGATION OF THE DELINQUENT MEMBER.

EUMOLPUS having thus copiously exhaled his bile,[1] we at
last arrived at Crotona, where we refreshed ourselves at a
paltry inn. On the following day, as we were in search of a
dwelling of richer appearance, we fell in with a pack of legacy
hunters, who inquired what manner of men we were, and
whence we came. According then to the plan prearranged
between us, we answered both questions with bouncing
volubility, and were heard with entire belief. Instantly
they almost fought for the honour of throwing their fortunes
at Eumolpus's feet, and all emulously courted his favour by
dint of presents.

Things having gone on in this way for a long while at
Crotona, Eumolpus forgot, in the intoxication of prosperity, his
former abject fortune to such a degree, that he boasted to his
followers that no one could resist his credit and influence, and

---

[1] *Exhaled his bile.*] That is to say, exhaled his poetic frenzy, the bile
being, according to the humoral pathology, the prime seat of insanity of
all kinds.

that if they committed any offence in the town they were sure of impunity through the protection of his friends. I however, though I revelled and fattened daily more and more on no end of good things, and thought that ill Fortune had withdrawn her watchful eyes from me, yet often reflected both on my present state and its origin. "What," said I, "if some cunning legacy hunter should send for information to Africa, and discover our imposture? What if Eumolpus's servant, surfeited with his present enjoyment, should give a hint to his companions, and maliciously betray our whole intrigue? We should have to take flight again, fall back upon that penury we have so lately overcome, and be beggars once more. O all ye gods, how unhappy are lawless lovers! Always expecting the punishment they deserve."

[Full of these reflections, I left the house in a very melancholy mood, to revive my spirits with fresh air; but had hardly entered the public walk when a girl by no means uncomely met me, and calling Polyænos, the feigned name I had borne since my metamorphosis, told me her mistress desired to speak with me.

"You are mistaken," I answered in surprise. "I am a servant and a stranger, and not worthy of that honour."

"My message," said she, "is to yourself, but] because you know your power of pleasing, you hold your head high, and sell your favours instead of bestowing them. To what purpose else those combed and wavy locks, that face so smoothed with cosmetics, and the provoking languish of those glances? To what purpose that studied gait, and those steps that never deviate from their regular measure, but to show off your person that you may make your market of it? Look at me: I am not skilled in augury, nor do I concern myself with star-gazing like the astrologers, yet I can spell a man by his physiognomy, and as soon as I saw you I read your thoughts. So if you sell what I ask for, a purchaser is ready; or if you bestow it, which is more genteel, let me be under an obligation to you. As for your confessing that you are a servant and of low condition, that only inflames the desires of her who is burning for you; for there are women who are hot after dregs, whose fancy is only roused at the sight of a slave, or a running footman with his gown tucked up. Others dote upon a gladiator, or a dusty muleteer, or a player who parades his graces on the stage. My mistress is one of this sort; her glances shoot

clear over the fourteen rows of benches [1] from the orchestra up
to the rabble at the top of the amphitheatre, in search of the
object of her predilection."

Filled with delight by this flattering declaration, Pray tell
me, said I, this person that loves me,—is it yourself?

The girl laughed a good deal at this awkward speech : "Don't
be so conceited," she said ; "no slave ever got over me that
way yet, and the gods forbid that I should throw away my
embraces on the gallows.[2] If ladies like to kiss the marks of
the whip, that is their own affair ; for my part, though I am
but a servant, I never put up with anything below a knight."

How strangely tastes vary, as fancy disposes !
There are some gather thorns, some better like roses.[3]

I was astonished at such an inequality of tastes, and
reckoned it a marvellous phenomenon, that the maid should
have the pride of the mistress, and the mistress the humble
inclinations of the maid. After many other pleasantries I
asked the girl to bring her lady into the grove of planes ; she
readily assented, and tucking up her skirts, tripped into a
laurel thicket that adjoined the walk. After a short absence
she brought out her lady from her concealment, and placed by
my side a form more perfect than sculptor ever fashioned.
No words can express her charms, and whatever I say will
be unworthy of them. Her hair, which curled naturally, fell
all over her shoulders ; her forehead was very small, and she
wore her hair turned back ; her eyebrows, the fine curve of
which extended to the spring of the cheek, almost met at the
other end ; her eyes were brighter than stars on a moonless
night ; her nose was a little aquiline, and her little mouth
was like that which Praxiteles attributed to Diana. Then
her chin, her neck, her hands, her white feet confined by the
slender bands of her gold-embroidered sandals, would have

---

[1] *The fourteen benches.*] Appropriated to persons of senatorial and
knightly degree.

[2] *Throw away my embraces on the gallows.*] Literally, on the cross :
i. e. that I should embrace one who is liable at any moment to suffer the
punishment of the cross.

[3] Invenias quod quisque velit. Non omnibus unum est
Quod placet : hic spinas colligit, ille rosas.

eclipsed Parian marble. It was then for the first time that
Doris sank to nothing in the esteem of her old admirer.

> Why, a mute fable 'mongst the heavenly powers,
> Reclin'st thou, Jove, in thy Olympian bowers?
> Now, now assume the bull's majestic pride;
> Now thy white locks in whiter plumage hide;
> Here's the true Danaë; touch but this bright frame,
> 'Twill melt thine own in passion's subtle flame.

She was delighted, and smiled so sweetly, that she seemed
like the full moon breaking from a cloud: then, accompanying
her words with an expressive movement of the fingers, she
said, "If you do not disdain a woman of rank, who has only
known your sex within this year, I present you, young man,
with a sister. I know you have a brother, for I thought it
worth while to inquire; but what hinders you from adopting
a sister too? I lay the same claim to your caresses: only
deign when you please to try how you like my kisses."

"Rather," I replied, "let me entreat you by your charming
self, do not disdain to admit an alien among your adorers; you
will find him truly devout if you permit him to worship you:
and that you may not suppose I approach this temple of Love
without an offering, I sacrifice my brother to you."

"Oh very likely," said she, "you will sacrifice to me him
whom you cannot live without; on whose lips your life hangs;
whom you love as I would have you love me." As she spoke
this, there was such a fascination in her voice, the air thrilled
with so sweet a sound, you would have thought the tones of
the Siren choir floated on the breeze. In an ecstasy of admiration, my eyes filled as it seemed with a light more lus-
trous than all the effulgence of heaven, I desired to know the
name of my goddess.

"What!" she said, "has not my maid told you that my
name is Circe? I am not indeed the daughter of the Sun;
nor could my mother stop the revolution of the heavens at
her pleasure; yet I shall have something to thank my stars
for if our fates unite us. Ah, yes! the mysterious purpose
of some god is acting upon us, I know not how. It is not
without cause that Circe loves Polyænos;[1] there is a sympa-

---

[1] *Circe loves Polyænos.*] She alludes to the amour between Circe, the

thy between these two names. Be happy then if you will.
You have no need to fear any prying eyes; your brother is
far from us."

So saying, Circe folded me in her arms more soft than
down, and pulled me with her as she sank upon the flowery
turf.

> On lofty Ida, when imperial Jove
> Indulged in Juno's arms his lawful love,
> His parent Earth her balmy odours threw
> Around the raptured god : the violet blue,
> The blushing rose, the fragrant rosmarine,
> And snowy lilies laughing through the green.
> Such was the couch on which my Venus lay,
> And smiling on our secret love, the day
> Was bright like her, and shone profusely gay.

Locked in each other's arms on the grassy couch, we dallied
with a thousand kisses, preluding a more vigorous joy. [But
a sudden weakness of my nerves disappointed Circe, and reddening with
anger at the affront,] "What is the meaning of this ?" she cried.
"Are my kisses revolting ? Is my breath offensive ? Do I
betray my neglect of cleanliness by any repulsive odour ? If
there is nothing of the sort, are you afraid of Giton ?"

Flushed with shame by her reproaches, if I had any vigour
remaining, I lost it then ; my whole frame seemed unstrung.
"Forbear, my queen, I beseech you," said I, "to aggravate
my distress. I am bewitched."

[Too much enraged to be appeased by so trivial an excuse, Circe
turned from me with contempt, and said to her maid,] "Tell me,
Chrysis, but tell me true, is there anything disgusting about
me ? Anything sluttish in my attire ? Does any natural de-
fect sully my beauty ? Do not deceive your mistress : there
must be something amiss with me."

Chrysis was dumb. Circe snatched a mirror out of her
hand, and after trying all the looks and smiles that quiver
over the face when lovers fondle, she shook out her rumpled

daughter of Apollo, and Ulysses, whom the Sirens call Polyænos in the
twelfth book of Homer's Odyssey.

robe, and flung into a neighbouring temple of Venus. And there was I, a convicted culprit, shuddering like one who has seen some horrible vision, and asking myself whether the happiness of which I was cheated was a reality or a dream.

> So when a dream our sleeping sense beguiles,
> And the earth opening shows us hoarded piles,
> With greedy hands we clutch the prize, we fill
> Our bursting vest, while down our cheeks distil
> Cold drops of sweat, as with a sickening fear
> We hark to fancied spoilers drawing near.
> But when the dear illusion fades away,
> And blank reality returns with day,
> That which we ne'er possess'd as lost we mourn,
> And for imaginary blessings burn.

[My misfortune actually appeared to me a dream, or rather a fascination, and I was so long unnerved that I had no power to rise. But at length the oppression of my spirits abating a little, and my strength reviving by degrees, I returned home, where feigning illness I went to bed. A little after, Giton, hearing I was ill, entered the room in great concern. To make him easy, I told him I had only lain down to repose myself, with a great deal of other chat, but not a word of my adventure, because I dreaded his resentment; and to avoid all suspicion, eum lateri applicans meo, amoris specimen præbere tentavi: sed anhelitus sudoresque fuerunt irriti. He got up in a passion, and upbraiding my inconstancy, told me he had for some time clearly perceived that I expended all my vigour elsewhere.

"Nay, brother, said I, my love for you has always been the same; but now reason prevails over passion."]

"And therefore," said he, "I thank you for the Socratic disinterestedness with which you love me. Alcibiades never left his master's bed with more innocence than I yours."

"Believe me, brother," I replied, "I no longer know or feel myself to be a man. That part of me is dead and buried in which I was once an Achilles."

[Giton perceiving that I was really unmanned, and] fearing if he was found there it might occasion scandal, hurried off and withdrew to an inner apartment. [He was scarcely gone when] Chrysis entered the room, and delivered me her mistress's tablets,[1] in which these words were written:

CIRCE TO POLYÆNUS, GREETING.

"If I were lascivious I should complain of having been disappointed; but on the contrary, I am thankful for your weakness; owing to it I have dallied the longer with the image of pleasure. I wish to know, however, how you do, and whether you got home on your own legs; because physicians declare that without nerves a man cannot walk. Mark my words, young man; beware of paralysis. I never saw a patient in such danger. On my honour, you are in part a dead man. If the same lethargy befall your legs and arms, you may send for the undertaker. But come: though I have received such a flagrant affront, I will not grudge you a remedy for your miserable condition. If you wish to be well, ask leave of Giton; you will recover your vigour if you sleep alone for three nights. As for myself, I am not afraid but that I shall find some one who will think me not without charms. Neither my mirror nor report flatters me falsely.

Farewell, if you can."

When Chrysis saw that I had read the whole of this bitter epistle, " Such accidents as yours are of common occurrence," she said, " especially in this city, where there are women who can bring down the moon from the sky. However, your affair shall be looked to and set to rights; only return a tender answer to my mistress, and appease her in the handsomest manner you can; for to tell you the truth, since the moment you affronted her she has been beside herself."

I willingly complied with the girl's advice, and wrote the following reply:

POLYÆNOS TO CIRCE, GREETING.

"I confess, madam, that I have often offended, for I am a man, and still young; but never before this day was I so capitally delinquent. You have, I say, the confession of the

---

[1] *Tablets.*] Letters were sometimes written on papyrus, (*charta*,) but more frequently on *tabellæ*, thin tablets of wood coated with wax and hinged together. The writing was formed with a *stylus*, and the tablets were bound round with a thread and sealed.

criminal. Whatever you inflict, I have deserved. I have
played the part of a traitor, committed homicide, violated a
temple. Devise a punishment for all these crimes. Is it
your pleasure I should die? I come to you with my sword.
Will stripes content you? I run to cast myself naked at the
feet of my mistress. Only remember it was not myself, but
my implements that failed. The soldier was ready to engage,
but wanted arms. Who robbed me of them, I know not.
Perhaps my imagination outran my tardy body; perhaps in
the excess of my desire I too soon expended my sensibility.
I know not what ailed me. You bid me beware of paralysis;
as if a worse could befall me than that which deprived me of
the power of possessing you. The sum and substance however of my excuse is this: I will give you satisfaction if you
will grant me an opportunity to repair my fault. Farewell."

Having dismissed Chrysis with these fair promises, I took
special care of my culpable body; and abstaining from the
bath, I contented myself with a slight friction. I adopted a
more stimulating diet, such as onions and raw oysters; I also
took a little wine. I then took a short walk before lying down,
and slept alone; for I was so anxious to make my peace that
I durst not run any risk.

Finding myself fresh in body and mind when I rose next
morning, I hastened to the grove of planes; and though I
looked upon the place as ominous, I waited there for my guide
Chrysis. Having taken a turn or two, I sat down in the
same spot as on the preceding day, when Chrysis appeared,
accompanied by a little old woman. After she had saluted me,
" Well, my squeamish sir," she said, "does your stomach begin
to come to you a little?" Then the old woman took out of her
bosom a hank of various colours, and bound it round my neck;
after which, mixing spittle and dust into a paste, she dipped
her middle finger into it, and in spite of my resistance marked
my forehead with it.

> There's hope whilst life! Priapus, hear our prayer;
> Renerve our strength, and steel our arms to dare.

Having chanted these verses, she made me spit thrice, and
thrice put into my bosom little stones, which she had wrapped

in purple, after muttering a charm over them. Then she began to test my virile condition manually. Quicker than speech the nerves responded to the appeal, and filled the old woman's hand with a huge erection. Skipping for joy, she turned to Chrysis, " See here, my dear," she cried, " see here ; I have started the hare for others to course."

[This done, the old woman returned me to Chrysis, who was overjoyed at the recovery of her mistress's treasure, and hastening to her, led me into a most delightful sequestered spot, which nature had prodigally adorned.]

> The plane diffused its bowering verdure wide,
> With nodding pines which to the zephyrs sigh'd ;
> Daphnes with berries crown'd their boughs inwove,
> And the soft cypress ever whispering love.
> Foaming 'mid these a gleesome brooklet stray'd,
> Chiding the pebbles over which it play'd.
> 'Twas love's elysium ! There in tenderest strains
> Aëdon mourn'd, there Progne told her pains.

Circe lay with her garments loose, her marble neck pressing a golden cushion, and fanned the air with a flowering branch of myrtle. When she saw me she crimsoned a little, at the thought, no doubt, of the affront of the preceding day. When we were left alone, she made me sit down beside her, then laid the branch on my eyes, and emboldened thereby, as if a wall had been raised between us, " Well, paralytic," she said, " are you come entire to-day ?"

" Will you rather ask than try ?" I answered ; and throwing myself into her arms without waiting to be invited, I satiated myself with kisses. The charms of her fair body summoned me of themselves to pleasure. Our lips encountered in many a sonorous kiss ; our hands locked together played all kinds of amorous freaks ; and now our bodies embraced as if our souls too had grown together ; [but in the midst of these delicious prolusions, a sudden collapse again deprived me of the highest bliss.]

Exasperated by two such flagrant affronts, the lady flew to revenge, summoned her chamberlains, and ordered them to warm my shoulders. Nor was she content with this cruel treatment, but calling all the drudging wenches, and the mean-est of the house servants, she bade them spit upon me. I clapped my hands to my eyes, and without making any sup-plications, (for I well knew what I deserved,) I was driven out of doors with blows and volleys of spittle. Proselenos was also kicked out, Chrysis beaten, and the whole house was in dismay, every one whispering and asking what had put their mistress so out of humour. This was a sort of com-pensation for what I had endured, and it cheered me up some-what. I skilfully concealed the marks of the blows, lest I should grieve Giton, or make Eumolpus merry with my mis-fortune. I pretended to be unwell, (it was the only thing I could do to hide my shame,) and went to bed, where I turned the whole fire of my wrath against the author of all my dis-asters.

Thrice in my hand I grasp'd a trenchant blade;
Thrice from the bloody deed I shrank dismay'd;
Nor could I now exact the vengeance due,
For cold as ice the snivelling coward flew
Beyond my reach, and struck with panic dread,
Behind a thousand wrinkles hid his head.
But though the rascal baulk'd my first design,
Yet words more sharp than razors still were mine.

Raising myself then on my elbow, I addressed the sullen im-potent nearly in these terms : " What canst thou say for thy-self, thou shame to gods and men ? For in fact it is forbidden even to name thee among serious things. Have I deserved this of thee, to be dragged down from the heaven of my joys to the region of the damned ? To have a scandal fixed on the prime and vigour of my years, and to be reduced to the fee-bleness of extreme old age ? Give me, I beseech thee, some slight evidence of thy vitality." Thus I vented my wrath :

But still his gaze he bent upon the ground,
Nor at my words more raised his guilty head
Than poppies drooping in the noontide heat.[1]

---

[1] *But still his gaze*, &c.] These lines are a parody of a passage in the Æneid.

However, when I had finished this ignoble chiding, I began
to repent of what I had said, and inwardly blushed at having
so far forgot my self-respect as to hold discourse with that
part of the body which men of gravity do not even condescend
to notice.   But then, after rubbing my forehead awhile,
What harm have I done, thought I, in giving such a natural
discharge to my resentment? Is it not usual to confound our
bellies, our throats, or our heads when they ache? Did not
Ulysses quarrel with his heart? And do not our tragedians
rail at their eyes, as if they imagined they could hear them?
The gouty abuse their feet or their hands, the blear-eyed their
eyes; and those who have often hurt their toes, vent all their
ill-humour on their feet.

> Why those knit brows, ye Catos of the age?
> Can plain simplicity provoke your rage?
> Outspoken truth becomes a writer well;
> What Romans do, a Roman tongue may tell.
> Who is a stranger to the joys of Venus?
> Is dallying in bed a crime so heinous?
> Wise Father Epicurus tells us, love
> Is all the heaven the gods possess above.

There is nothing falser than the stupid prejudices of the
world, nor anything sillier than affected gravity.

CHAPTER XVI.

POLYÆNOS PRAYS IN VERSE TO PRIAPUS—PROSELENOS BEATS HIM FOR
HAVING IMPLICATED HER IN HIS OWN DISGRACE—ŒNOTHEA, THE
PRIESTESS OF PRIAPUS, PROMISES TO CURE HIM, AND VAUNTS HER
SUPERNATURAL POWER—PREPARATIONS FOR THE MYSTIC RITES—
POETICAL DESCRIPTION OF THE PRIESTESS'S DWELLING—POLYÆNOS
KILLS THE SACRED GOOSE—ŒNOTHEA'S LAMENTATIONS AND THREATS
ON THE OCCASION—POLYÆNOS APPEASES HER—THE GOOSE IS EATEN
—ŒNOTHEA APPLIES BRISK STIMULANTS—THE PATIENT JUMPS UP
AND ESCAPES.

AFTER this declamation I called Giton to me and said,
"Tell me, brother, but tell me honestly, did Ascyltos offer

violence to you that night he stole you from me, or did he behave with modesty and reserve?" The boy touched his eyes, and swore solemnly that Ascyltos had done him no violence. [In truth, I was so overwhelmed by my misfortunes that I was sometimes beside myself, and knew not what I said. But why, thought I, recall things to mind, the remembrance of which can only make me uneasy? After this, I applied all my attention to the recovery of my lost vigour. I resolved even to devote myself to the gods, and accordingly I went to implore the aid of Priapus.] Happen what might, I feigned a hopeful countenance, and kneeling at the door of the temple, I thus implored the deity in verse :

O thou, beloved of nymphs, of Bacchus graced,
Whom o'er the groves the fair Dione placed ;
Thee Lesbos, blooming Thasos thee adores,
And soft Hypæpa on the Lydian shores.
Joy of the Dryads, Bacchus' champion, grant
Relief to me, thy trembling suppliant.
I kneel not here with guilty hands, bloodstain'd ;
No temples of the gods have I profaned ;
Helpless and poor, alas ! I fell to shame
In part alone, I was not all to blame.
Want pleads its own excuse, thy vengeance cease,
Absolve my indigence, and grant me peace.
And when kind fortune shall my wishes bless,
Rich offerings shall my grateful thanks express ;
A full-horned goat, the pride of all his breed,
And a young pig, shall on thy altars bleed ;
The bowl with new-born Bacchus shall be crown'd,
And reeling youths shall hymn the mystic round.

Whilst I was thus at my devotion, and sedulously intent on my purpose, an old woman with her hair in disorder and hideously dressed in black, entered the shrine, laid hold on me, and dragged me, all trembling, out of the vestibule. "What witches," she said, " have devoured your manhood? What filth, or what carcase, have you trod upon in the streets by night? You could not so much as acquit yourself to the boy, but flabby and faint, you laboured and sweated, like a

jaded horse up-hill, and all for nothing. And not content
with your own delinquency, you have brought down the
anger of the gods upon me; and do you think I will not
make you smart for it?"

Thus saying, she led me without resistance into the
priestess's chamber, threw me on the bed, and snatching a
cane from behind the door, belaboured me. I did not utter
a word, and had not the cane split at the first stroke, and
diminished the force of her blows, she would perhaps have
broken my arms or my head. I groaned piteously, especially
when she began to tease me with attempts to arouse my vigour; and bursting into a flood of tears, hid my face with my
right arm, and leaned upon the pillow. The old woman too
wept no less bitterly, and sitting down on the other side of
the bed, began with a shaky voice to complain that she
had lived too long. At last the priestess came in. "What
brings you here into my room," she said, "as melancholy as
as if you were at a funeral? And that too on a holiday,
when sorrow itself should laugh."

"O Œnothea," replied the other, "this young man you
see here was born under an evil star; he can't dispose of his
goods to either woman or boy. You never saw so unfortunate
a man; he has no more pith in him than a bit of wet leather.
In short, you may guess what he is, who could rise from
Circe's bed without having tasted pleasure."

Upon this Œnothea sat down between us, and nodding her
head awhile, "I am the only one," said she, "that knows
how to cure that malady; and that you may not suppose I
don't know what I am about, I ask to have the young man
sleep one night with me, and see if I don't make that same
as stiff as horn!"

> Through the wide world all things obey my power;
> My voice can wither every vernal flower;
> Can pour from desert rocks a Nile-like tide,
> And make the tumult of the waves subside.
> The Zephyrs breathless fall before my feet;
> And headlong torrents, when I bid, retreat.
> I quench the tiger's rage, the dragon's fire:
> Slight efforts these; still greater feats admire.

The Moon descends my magic verse to hear,
And Sol his chariot backward rolls in fear.
Such power have charms ! By charms the Colchian maid
The fiery bulls subdued ; by charms betray'd,
Ulysses' comrades into brutes most vile
Saw themselves changed in Circe's fatal isle.
Proteus assumes what shape soe'er he please ;
And I, imbued in equal mysteries,
Can plant proud Ida's forest in the deep,
And make strange fountains on its summit weep.

I shuddered with affright to hear her profess such marvellous things, and began to look very earnestly at old Proselenos. "Come then, Œnothea," she cried, "set about your potent work." Then carefully washing her hands, she lay down on the bed, and kissed me again and again.

Œnothea placed an old table on the middle of the altar, filled it with live coals, and then patched up with pitch another damaged antiquity, a wooden bowl. Her next act was to replace in the smoky wall a nail which she had pulled out in reaching down the bowl. Then putting on a square mantle, she set a great kettle on the fire, and with a fork drew out of her cupboard a cloth containing her provision of beans and an old piece of a pig's cheek, with the marks of a thousand cuts upon it. She untied the cloth, shook out part of the beans on the table, and ordered me to strip them speedily. I obeyed, and separated the grains from their filthy pods with a careful hand; but she, chiding my slowness, snatched them from me, and cleverly stripping off the pods with her teeth, spat them out on the floor like dead flies. The ingenuity of poverty is wonderful, and there is a knack in everything. [The priestess appeared so great a lover of this virtue, that it was eminent in everything about her, and her dwelling in particular was a very shrine of poverty.]

Here shone no ivory roofs inlaid with gold,
No marble floor press'd the deluded mould ;
But banded sheafs of empty Ceres, laid
On hurdled boughs, the humble covering made.

2 A

Here earthen mugs in homely order stood,
And there a pitcher from the limpid flood ;
With baskets, earthen mugs of rude design,
And an old cask crusted with lees of wine.
The walls were stubbled mud, heap'd up in haste,
O'er which the reed and bulrush droop'd, disgraced.
Within the hut a smoky pole was slung
From side to side, on which its treasures hung ;
Apples and wither'd savory dangled down,
With grapes disposed in many a rural crown.
In such a cot was Theseus entertain'd,
And Hecale immortal honour gain'd ;
As Battus' son, who sang in happier days,
Records the theme of wonder and of praise.

Œnothea [having shelled the beans] and eaten a morsel or two of the pig's cheek, went to replace the remainder, which was as old as herself, with her fork in the cupboard ; when the rotten stool on which she was mounted broke down under her, and threw her against the altar. The kettle was broken, the fire which had just begun to burn up, was put out; her elbow was burnt by coming in contact with a brand, and her face was grimed all over with the ashes raised by her fall.

I jumped up in a hurry, and set the old woman on her legs, not without laughing at her accident ; and she immediately ran out to fetch fresh fire from the neighbourhood, that nothing might retard the sacrifice. As I then advanced to the door of the lodge, suddenly three holy geese, which as I suppose were accustomed to be fed by the old woman about noon, rushed upon me, and put me in a flurry, besetting me with their nasty rabid cackling. One of them tore my tunic, another untied and dragged at my shoe-strings ; a third, the leader and director of the onslaught, had the audacity to worry my leg with his serrated bill. Thinking it no time to trifle, I pulled off one of the legs of the table, and belaboured the warlike fowl, and not content with a slight blow, I avenged myself by the death of the goose.

Such were the birds Herculean art subdued,
And such the harpies, filthy, poisonous brood,

That on Phinëus' board dropp'd pestilence,
Till the wing'd brothers drove them shrieking thence.
The heavens were startled at their clamorous flight,
And backward seem'd to roll in wild affright.

I left him sprawling; the other two, having picked up the beans that lay scattered over the floor, and having lost their leader as I presume, returned into the temple, when I, exulting in my prey and my vengeance, threw the slaughtered goose behind the bed, washed the slight wound in my leg with vinegar, and for fear of a scolding resolved to be off. I gathered up my clothes and set about my departure, but had not reached the threshold when I saw Œnothea coming back with an earthen pot full of fire. I retreated therefore, and throwing down my clothes, planted myself at the entry, as if I stood there impatiently awaiting her return. She heaped her fire on some broken reeds, put some sticks upon it, and began to excuse herself for staying so long; telling me that her friend would not let her go until she had drained three cups according to custom. "But what have you been doing in my absence?" she said; "and where are the beans?"

Conceiving that I had done a very laudable deed, I gave her a description of the whole battle, and to put an end to her grief, I presented the goose to her as a compensation for her loss.[1] But when the old woman saw its carcase, she set up such an outcry you would have thought the geese were come in again. Bewildered and astonished at being thought criminal upon such novel grounds, I asked her why she was so angry, and why she pitied the goose rather than me.

"You dare to speak, villain?" she cried, clapping her hands. "You know not what an enormous crime you have committed. You have killed the delight of Priapus, a goose, the darling of all matrons. And, to let you know it is no trifle, if the magistrates come to know of it, you will go to the cross. You have polluted with blood my domicile, which was never profaned before this day; and you have done what is enough to

---

[1] *As a compensation for her loss.*] That is to say, the loss of the beans; so Antonius understands the passage. The French translator (Nisard's edition) makes it mean: In order to cut short her grief for the loss of the goose I had killed, I offered to replace it with another.

put it in the power of any one that has a spite against me to turn me out of the priesthood."

> Trembling she spoke, and in her wild despair,
> She tore her cheeks, and pluck'd her silver hair.
> With no dry eyes did she her case deplore ;
> As down the hills the rapid torrents pour
> When Auster with indulgent softness blows,
> Unlocks the streams, and melts the mountain snows ;
> So down her cheeks a flood of sorrow roll'd,
> And sighs and sobs her bosom's anguish told.

"Do not cry and roar," said I, "I beseech you; in place of your goose I will give you an ostrich." But she still sat upon the bed, stunning me with fresh lamentations over the death of her goose. Meanwhile Proselenos came in with the materials for the sacrifice; when seeing the slaughtered goose, and inquiring the cause of her friend's distress, she herself began to cry still more bitterly, and to pity me, as if I had killed my own father, and not a public goose. Tired of this tedious scene, "I beseech you," said I, "might I not purchase expiation for a price, though I were the aggressor, and had even committed homicide? See, here are two gold pieces, with which you may buy both gods and geese."

"Forgive me, young man," said Œnothea, "as soon as she set eyes on them, I am anxious on your account; and that is a proof of affection, not of malice. So we will take care that nobody knows of this matter. Only do you pray to the gods to pardon what you have done."

> Whoe'er has magic gold, secure may sail
> Where'er he please, he's lord of fortune's gale ;
> May in a Danae's arms be blest as Jove,
> And make her father pander to his love.
> He may turn poet, orator, what not ?
> When he harangues, old Cato is forgot.
> A lawyer is he ? All in him behold
> What Servius and what Labeo were of old.

In short, when of the money you're possess'd,
You need but wish: you've Jove within your chest.

Meanwhile the bustling priestess placed a bowl of wine under my hands, made me spread my fingers evenly, and purified them with leeks and parsley; then she threw filberts into the wine, muttering some mystic words, and as they sank or swam, so she drew her prognostics. But I knew well that the blind nuts, which were filled with air, floated on the surface, and those which had full and sound kernels, naturally sank to the bottom. Then she applied herself to the goose, opened its breast, and drawing out a lusty liver, predicted from it my future fortune. Nay, that no vestige of my crime might remain, she cut up the goose, and putting it on a spit, prepared a dainty banquet for the person whom a little before she devoted to death.

Meanwhile draughts of pure wine went merrily round, [and the two old women joyfully devoured the goose they so lately lamented. After this Œnothea, who was half drunk, turned to me and said, "Now we must accomplish our mysteries, in order that you may recover your strength;" and forthwith] she produced an emblem of Priapus, which she smeared with a mixture of oil, ground pepper, and bruised nettle-seeds, and began to insert it by degrees ano meo. The merciless old woman then greased the inside of my thighs with the same composition; next she mixed nasturtium juice with southernwood, and having bathed my foreparts, she took a bunch of green nettles, and gently whipped my belly all over below the navel. Feeling the nettles burn me, I took to my heels; the old women made after me with all their might; and though disordered with wine and lust, they took the same direction and followed me through two or three streets, crying, Stop thief! I escaped, however, but not without making all my toes bloody in my headlong flight.

CHAPTER XVII.

POLYÆNOS SOLILOQUIZES ON HIS MISFORTUNES AND ON CIRCE'S BEAUTY—
CHRYSIS PESTERS HIM WITH HER PASSION—PHILUMENE COMMITS HER
CHILDREN TO THE CARE OF EUMOLPUS—POLYÆNOS EXPOSTULATES WITH
EUMOLPUS—THE LATTER INSERTS AN ODD CLAUSE IN HIS WILL—DIS-
CUSSION ON CANNIBALISM—EUMOLPUS IS DISCOVERED TO BE A CHEAT,
AND IS IMMOLATED BY THE CROTONIANS.

[WHEN I got home, I was so fatigued that I immediately went to bed;
but I could not sleep; for all my misfortunes thronged together on my
mind, and reflecting how incomparably wretched I was, I exclaimed,
" Has not Fortune always persecuted me enough, but that she must needs
call Love to her aid to torment me the more? Wretch that I am!
Fortune and Love now unite their forces for my destruction. Cruel Love
himself has never spared me ; whether I love or am loved, I am tortured.
There is Chrysis now; she dotes on me and never ceases to tease me.
Yes, that] Chrysis who at first loathed your humble condition,
is now bent on following it at the hazard of her life; [for
thus she protested with the most solemn oaths when she discovered to me
the vehemence of her passion. But Circe possesses me wholly: all others
I despise. And indeed who is so charming as she?]

" What was Ariadne or Leda compared to her? What
Helen, or even Venus herself? Paris himself, when he judged
between the rival goddesses, had he seen her sparkling eyes,
would have sacrificed to her both his Helen and the goddesses.
Were I but allowed to kiss that mouth, to press to mine that
heavenly and divine bosom, my bodily powers would perhaps
return ; and those parts would revive which now lie in a
lethargy, cast upon them, I believe, by witchcraft. No scorns
she casts upon me, exhaust my patience: that I have been
beaten is nothing; that I have been kicked out is a joke;
only let me be restored to favour:

> Celestial fires thy star-bright eyes illume ;
> Roses invisible thy neck perfume ;
> More bright than burnish'd gold thy tresses flow ;
> Thy honey'd lips with finest crimson glow ;
> Meand'ring veins sublime thy bosom's white ;
> And every Grace adorns thee for delight.

Each goddess' boasted charms in thine we see,
And vanquish'd Venus yields the prize to thee.

Thy hands are silver, and with amorous pride
The silken threads through thy soft fingers glide;

Thy feet, too lovely e'er to kiss the ground,
From no invidious pebblet fear a wound;

On beds of lilies even you may walk,
Nor with your light step crush one tender stalk.

Let costly gems be meaner beauties' care,
No gauds you need to seem surpassing fair.

Some blemish fancy finds in all we view,
But envy's self can't mend a charm in you.

Could they but hear the magic of your tongue,
Sirens and Muses both would cease their song.

But oh how dangerous the sweet accents prove
When every one wings the keen dart of Love!

A deadly wound is rankling in my heart;
No herbs can cure me, nor the surgeon's art;

Your lips alone my anguish can control,
And still the wild disorders of my soul.

Rack me no longer; let me not be slain,
The victim of your beauty and disdain;

Or if too much this fond request, yet grant
The dying prayer of your poor suppliant,

Embrace me when I'm dead, with pitying arms,
And I shall soon revive to bless your charms.[1]

---

[1] Candida sidereis ardescunt lumina flammis,
 Fundunt colla rosas, et cedit crinibus aurum,
 Mellea purpureum depromunt ora ruborem,
 Lacteaque admixtus sublimat pectora sanguis,
 Ac totus tibi servit honor, formaque dearum
 Fulges, et Venerem cœlesti corpore vincis.
 Argento stat facta manus, digitisque tenellis
 Serica fila trahens, pretioso stamine ludis.
 Planta decens modicos nescit calcare lapillos,
 Et dura lædi scelus est vestigia terra :

[Thus thinking upon the lovely Circe, my imagination became so excited that] I disordered all my bed in the ardour with which I clasped an imaginary Circe. [But being still powerless I lost patience, and began to accuse the cruel divinity that had enchanted me. At last recollecting how many ancient heroes had felt the anger of the gods, I derived some comfort from their misfortunes, and thus broke out;]

> Not I alone immortal wrath have felt;
> Fiercely with others too the gods have dealt.
> Compell'd by Juno and his rigorous fate,
> Alcides bent beneath the starry weight;
> Nor was her rage at impious Pelias vain;
> By sudden war Laomedon was slain;
> Four vengeful gods 'gainst Telephus engaged;
> And angry Neptune 'gainst Ulysses raged.
> I also, or on land, or Nereus' flood,
> By stern Priapus' vengeance am pursued.

[I passed a wretched, anxious night, and as soon as it was day, Giton, who had heard of my coming home to bed, entered my chamber, when, after grievous complaints of my licentious life, he told me that all the household complained loudly of my behaviour, in absenting myself almost entirely from the business of the household, and that the intrigue I was

---

Ipsa tuos cum ferre velis per lilia gressus,
Nulli sternuntur leviori pondere flores.
Guttura nunc aliæ magnis monilibus ornent,
Aut gemmas aptent capiti: tu sola placere
Vel spoliata, potes. Nulli laudabile totum:
In te cuncta probat, si quisquam cernere possit.
Sirenum cantus et dulcia plectra Thaliæ
Ad vocem tacuisse, reor, quæ mella propagas
Dulcia, et in miseros telum jaculares amoris.
Cor grave vulnus alit, nullo sanabile ferro,
Sed tua labra meo sævum de corde dolorem
Depellant, morbumque animæ medicaminis hujus
Cura fuget, nec tanta putres violentia nervos
Dissecet, atque tuæ moriar pro crimine caussæ.
Sed si hoc grande putas, saltem concede precanti,
Ut jam defunctum niveis ambire lacertis
Digneris, vitamque mihi post fata reducas.

pursuing might chance to prove my ruin. Finding he was no stranger to my affairs, I surmised that some one had been to the house to inquire about me; and therefore] I asked Giton whether any one had come in quest of me.

"Not to-day," he replied; "but yesterday there came a very well dressed woman, who after a long conversation, in which she bored me with her inquisitiveness about you, ended by saying that you deserved punishment, and that you would suffer servile chastisement, if the person you had wronged persisted in his complaint." [This news tormented me exceedingly, and I again launched out into invectives against fortune.]

I had not yet ended my ejaculations, when Chrysis came in, and throwing herself upon me, smothered me with kisses, crying out, "At last I have got you, my heart's desire! my love! my delight! Never will you quench this fire of mine, but with my blood."

[I was very much disconcerted by this wantonness, and gave Chrysis all the fair words I could to get rid of her; for I was afraid lest in the excess of her fondness she should make herself heard by Eumolpus, who was so puffed up with his good fortune that he began to behave like a master in earnest; therefore I used every artifice to calm her down, pretended love, whispered soft things, and in short played the part of a lover so cleverly that she believed me one; representing to her how dangerous it would be for us both should she be found in my room, for our master Eumolpus punished even the least offence. On hearing this she left me at once, and in the more haste because she saw Giton returning, who had quitted the room shortly before she came in. She was hardly gone when]

One of our newly-hired servants ran in, and told me that our lord was highly displeased at my two days' absence from duty; and he advised by all means to invent some plausible excuse; for it was scarcely possible that the storm of wrath should subside without a shower of blows.

[Giton saw I was so vexed that he said nothing to me about the woman. He talked only of Eumolpus, and advised me to joke with him rather than put a serious face on the matter. I took the advice, and appeared before the old man with so gay an air, that instead of giving me a stern reception, he began to rally me on the success of my amours, and praised the elegance of my figure and my address which found such favour among the ladies. "It is not unknown to me," he said, "that you are passionately loved by a very beautiful woman. Now this may be of use to us on occasion; therefore, Encolpius, play the lover's part with spirit, whilst I continue to sustain that which I have assumed."

While he was yet speaking, in came] a matron of the first distinction, named Philumene, who had often used her charms with success to fish for legacies, and who now being old and past her bloom, thrust her son and daughter before old men who had no children, and thus continued her old trade through these successors. This woman then came to Eumolpus, to commend her children to his wisdom, and commit herself and her hopes to his goodness; declaring he was the only man in the world to form the minds of young people by the daily inculcation of wholesome precepts; and that in fine she would leave her children in Eumolpus's house that they might learn from his lips, and so acquire the most precious heritage that could be bestowed on youth. Nor was she worse than her word, but leaving a very pretty girl with her brother, a stripling, went out under pretence of going to the temple to perform her devotions.

Eumolpus, who was so continent that even I was a boy in his eyes, lost no time in inviting the girl to sacrifice to Venus Callipyge. But he had told everybody that he was gouty, and crippled in the loins, and if he did not fully keep up the pretence, he ran great risk of ruining the whole drama. Itaque ut constaret mendacio fides, puellam quidem exoravit ut sederet supra commendatam bonitatem, Coraci autem imperavit ut lectum, in quo ipse jacebat, subiret, positisque in pavimento manibus, dominum lumbis suis commoveret. Ille lento parebat imperio, puellæque artificium pari motu remunerabat. Cum ergo res ad effectum spectaret, clara Eumolpus voce exhortabatur Coraca, ut spissaret officium. Sic inter mercenarium amicamque positus senex, veluti oscillatione ludebat. Hoc semel iterumque ingenti risu, etiam suo, Eumolpus fecerat. Itaque ego quoque, ne desidia consuetudinem perderem, dum frater sororis suæ automata per clostellum miratur, accessi tentaturus an pateretur injuriam. Nec se rejiciebat a blanditiis doctissimus puer, sed numen inimicum ibi quoque inveni.

[However, I was not so much concerned at this failure as at those I had suffered before, for soon after my vigour returned, and finding myself in a more efficient condition, I exclaimed,] "It is the celestial gods who have made me entire again!" Mercury, who conveys and

re-conveys souls, has by his bounty restored to me what an
unfriendly hand had deprived me of. Look here ! you see I
am more pleasingly endowed than Protesilaus or any other
hero of yore ? Saying this I lifted up my tunic, and showed
myself to Eumolpus in all my glory. At first he started back
in astonishment, then, the better to convince himself, he felt
with both hands the pledge of the goodness of the gods.

[This great blessing reviving my mirth, we laughed heartily at Philu-
mena's cunning, and at the expertness of her children in their trade,
which would avail them little with us ; for it was plain she had put the
boy and girl into our hands only with the hope of inheriting a fortune.
Reflecting on this sordid method of circumventing childless age, I took
occasion to remark on our own predicament, and I warned Eumolpus
that in biting the biters he might be bitten at last. The least indiscretion
on the part of any of the servants might ruin us.]

> And trust me, every mouth of human mould,
> Much sooner than a secret, fire can hold ;
> For whatsoe'er in secrets you confide,
> Straight flies abroad, exulting far and wide.
> While such additions the proud wonder swell,
> As burthen even Fame herself to tell.
> Thus Midas' ears were whisper'd to the ground ;
> The impatient earth straight quicken'd at the sound,
> And every murmuring reed, with vocal tongue,
> Cried, Midas' ears are as an ass's long.[1]

[All our actions, I cried, must be governed by prudence.]
Socrates, who in the opinion of gods and men was the wisest
of mortals, used to boast that he had never looked into a
tavern, nor allowed himself to be present at any tumultuous

---

[1] Nam citius flammas mortales ore tenebunt,
  Quam secreta tegant. Quidquid dimittis in aula,
  Effluit, et subitis-rumoribus oppida pulsat.
  Nec satis est vulgasse fidem : simulatius exit
  Proditionis opus, famamque onerare laborat.
  Sic commissa verens, avidus reserare minister,
  Fodit humum, regisque patentes prodidit aures.
  Concepit nam terra sonos, calamique loquentes,
  Invenere Midam, qualem narraverat index.

assembly.   So incomparably expedient it is always to take
counsel of wisdom.   What I say is certain; nor are any men
more liable to mischances than those who covet what belongs
to others.   How should vagabonds and swindlers live unless
they were sometimes to shake a purse or a jingling bag of
money in the ears of the crowd by way of bait?   As dumb
fish are taken with something they can eat, so men are not to
be caught by empty hopes, without something solid.   The
ship is not come from Africa, with your money and your
retinue, as you promised.   I perceive that our exhausted for-
tune-hunters begin to stint their liberality, and I am much
mistaken, if Fortune has not already begun to repent of her
favours to us.

[" I have devised a method," said Eumolpus, " which will sorely perplex these fellows;" and taking his tablets out of his scrip, he read his
last testamentary directions, as follows:]

   "All who have legacies bequeathed them by my will, my
" freedmen excepted, receive them on this condition, that they
" cut my body in pieces and eat it in the sight of the people.
" Nor need they be inordinately shocked at this proposal,
" since we know that to this day it is a custom in some coun-
" tries for the dead to be eaten by their relations, for which
" reason the sick are often chided for spoiling their flesh by
" lingering too long.   I put my friends in mind of this, that
" they may not refuse compliance with my last desires, but
" devour my body with the same good will as they wished the
" breath out of it."

[Whilst Eumolpus was reading this first article, some of his most intimate friends entered the room, and seeing the will in his hand, earnestly
entreated he would impart the contents to them.   He complied at once,
and read the document to them from beginning to end.   When they
heard the clause imperatively directing that his body should be eaten,
they were greatly cast down by so extraordinary a provision,] but the
great repute of his wealth blinded the eyes and souls of the
wretches, [and they were so crouching in his presence that they durst
not complain.   One of them, however, named] Gorgias, was ready to
comply, [provided he had not too long to wait.   To this Eumolpus
replied:]

   " I am under no apprehension of a refusal on the part of
your stomach; it will obey orders, if you promise it a profusion
of good things in compensation for a moment's disgust.   It is

only shutting your eyes, and fancying instead of man's flesh you are eating a hundred thousand sesterces. Besides, we shall find some condiment to correct the flavour ; indeed no flesh pleases by itself, but must be altered in some way by art, so as to be reconciled to the repugnant stomach. If you will have examples in point, the Saguntines, when besieged by Hannibal, ate human bodies, yet without the hopes of an inheritance. The Perusians did the same in the extremity of famine, and all they sought from dining in that manner was to escape starvation. When Numantia was taken by Scipio, mothers were found with their children half eaten in their arms. [In fine, since it is only the thought of eating man's flesh that can cause disgust, you will strive with all your might to overcome this repugnance, that you may receive the immense legacies I bequeath you."

Eumolpus delivered these shameless extravagances with so little circumspection, that our legacy hunters began to distrust his promises, and immediately scrutinizing our words and actions more closely, their suspicions grew with their observations, and at last they set us down for vagabonds and swindlers ; and this was confirmed by the arrival of some strangers to whom we happened to be known. Thereupon those whose purses had smarted most for our entertainment, resolved to seize us and take their just revenge. But Chrysis, who was privy to all the intrigues afoot, gave me notice of what the Crotonians intended for us. This so terrified me that I immediately made off with Giton, leaving Eumolpus to his fate ; and a few days afterwards we learned that the Crotonians, enraged at the old rogue's having lived so long and so sumptuously at their expense, had put him to death in the Massilian way. That you may understand what that was, I must tell you that] whenever the Massilians were visited with the pestilence, one or other of the poorest of the people would offer himself as a voluntary victim, on condition of being maintained for a whole year on choice food at the public expense. After this, wreathed with vervain, and dressed in sacred garments, he was led in procession all over the city, loaded with imprecations, that all the public afflictions might devolve bodily upon his head, and so he was thrown headlong from a rock.

THE KISSES

OF

JOHANNES SECUNDUS.

EPIGRAM I.

UPON HIS BOOK OF KISSES.

BECAUSE in this book of mine I sing of kisses in no salacious strain, swarthy Lycinna jeers at my verses; and Ælia, who plies the work of Venus in the streets, calls me "a poet of no penetration." They long, forsooth, to know what I am made of. Leave me alone, lewd ones, I have nothing for you. I sing not for you; my Kisses are not for you. Be they read by the artless maid, the tender youth's betrothed, and by the tender and enamoured youth, not yet mature for the warfare which bounteous Venus exercises in various ways.

> LYCINNA scorns my Kisses; they are chaste,
> Not stout enough for her experienced taste.
> And Ælia calls me " bard with languid strings,"
> She that to Love in streets her off'rings brings.
> Perhaps my utmost strength they seek to know !
> To prove my vigour !—Go ! vile wantons, go !
> My strength, my vigour, long despair to find ;
> For you these Kisses never were design'd ;
> Never for you were these soft measures wrought :
> Read me, ye tender brides of boys untaught ;
> Read me, of brides untaught ye tender boys,
> Yet new to Venus' sweetly-varying joys !   OGLE.

EPIGRAM II. TO THE GRAMMARIANS.

WHY HE WRITES WANTONLY.

Do you ask why I fill all my books with wanton poems?
I do it to repel dull grammarians.   If I sang the warlike exploits of magnanimous Cæsar, or the pious deeds of holy men,
what a load of notes, what corrections of the text, I should
have to endure!   What a torment I should become for little
boys! But now that moist kisses are my theme, and the lusty
blood tingles at my prurient verses, let me be read by the
youth who hopes to please his virgin mistress, by the gentle
girl who longs to please her new-made spouse, and by every
sprightly brother poet who loves voluptuous ease and mirth.
But stand aloof from these frolic joys, ye sour pedants, and
keep off your injurious hands, that no boy, whipped and crying on account of my amorous fancies, may wish the earth to
press hard upon my bones.

You ask why thus I sport in wanton strains;
Why Love, in every verse, luxuriant reigns?
Because I would not have dull pedants cumber
My light effusions with their learned lumber.
If lives of sainted men inspired my lays,
Or if I sang heroic Cæsar's praise,
What notes (oppressive weight!) must I endure;
What comments, obvious readings to obscure;
What tedious stuff conceived by addled brains,
To boys the certain cause of future pains!
But while on Kisses I employ my song,
Kisses, or moist or dry, or short or long;
Me, summon the unmarried youth to aid;
Me, bent on joy, the newly-married maid;
Me, the gay bard, whom lighter studies please,
Wisely indulging in delicious ease.
But from these sports, sour scholiasts, abstain!
These never with unhallow'd hands profane!
Nor turn to grief, what we to mirth design;
Lest, punish'd for some soft perverted line,
Wrong'd innocence, with tears unjustly shed,
Wish the cold earth lie heavy on my head!   OGLE.

KISS I.

WHEN Venus bore off Ascanius in his sleep to the heights of Cythera, she laid him on soft violets, encompassed him with showers of white roses, and bedewed the whole place with liquid odours. Presently she recalled to mind her old passion for Adonis, and the wonted glow stole through her inmost frame. Oh how often did she long to throw her arms round her grandson's neck! Oh how often she said, " Such was Adonis!" But fearing to disturb the boy's calm repose, she printed a thousand kisses on the neighbouring roses. Behold they glow, and a gentle breath issues in a whispering sigh through the lips of yearning Dione. From all the roses she touched, so many new-born kisses returned the goddess multiplied delights. But Cytherea, floating through the clouds with her snow-white swans, began to traverse the globe of the great earth, and in the manner of Triptolemus, scattered kisses over the fruitful soil, and thrice uttered unknown sounds with her mouth. In that way corn first sprang up in the fields for the use of man; in that way sprang the sole remedy for my pains. For ever hail, assuagers of Love's poignant flame, ye humid kisses born of dew-cold roses! Lo! I am the poet by whom your honours shall be sung so long as the summits of the Muses' mountain shall be known, and Love, mindful of the Æneades, and eloquent in the praise of your beloved race, shall speak the tender words of the sons of Romulus.

WHEN young Ascanius, by the Queen of Love,
Was wafted to Cythera's lofty grove;
The slumbering boy upon a couch she laid,
A fragrant couch! of new-blown violets made!
The blissful bower with shadowing roses crown'd,
And balmy-breathing airs diffused around.

Soon, as she watch'd, through all her glowing soul,
Impassion'd thoughts of lost Adonis stole.
How oft, as memory hallow'd all his charms,
She long'd to clasp the sleeper in her arms;
How oft she said, admiring every grace,
" Such was Adonis! such his lovely face!"

2 B

But fearing lest this fond excess of joy
Might break the slumber of the beauteous boy,
On every rose-bud that around him blow'd,
A thousand nectar'd kisses she bestow'd;
And straight each op'ning bud, which late was white,
Blush'd a warm crimson[1] to th' astonish'd sight.
Still in Dione's breast soft wishes rise,
Soft wishes, vented with soft-whisper'd sighs.
Thus, by her lips unnumber'd roses press'd,
Kisses, unfolding in sweet bloom, confess'd;
And, flush'd with rapture at each new-born kiss,
She felt her swelling soul o'erwhelm'd in bliss.

Now round this orb, soft-floating on the air,
The beauteous goddess speeds her radiant car;
As in gay pomp the harness'd cygnets fly,
Their snow-white pinions glitter through the sky:
And like Triptolemus,[2] whose bounteous hand
Strew'd golden plenty o'er the fertile land;
Fair Cytherea, as she flew along,
O'er the vast lap of nature kisses flung;
Pleased from on high she view'd th' enchanted ground,
And from her lips thrice fell a magic sound:
He gave to mortals corn on ev'ry plain,
But she those sweets which mitigate my pain.

Hail then, ye kisses! that can best assuage
The pangs of love, and soften all its rage!
Ye balmy kisses! that from roses sprung;
Roses! on which the lips of Venus hung:

---

[1] *And straight each op'ning bud,* &c.] This metamorphosis reminds
me of one something like it, in Shakspeare, *Midsummer-Night's Dream*:

"Yet mark'd I where the bolt of Cupid fell:
It fell upon a little western flower,
Before milk-white, now purple with Love's wound;
And maidens call it Love in Idleness."

[2] *And like Triptolemus.*] Triptolemus, according to Hyginus, was the
son of Eleusius; or, according to Pausanias, son of Celeus of Eleusis, a
town of Athens. He was bred up from his infancy by Ceres, who fed
him with milk in the day, and covered him with fire at night. She
taught him agriculture, and sent him over the world in a chariot loaded
with corn, to teach mankind that science; when he first instructed
Greece.

Your bard am I; while yet the Aonian shades
Boast their proud verdures, and their flowery glades;
While yet a laurel guards the sacred spring,
My fond, impassion'd muse of you shall sing;
And Love, enraptured with the Latin name,
With that dear race from which your lineage came,
In Latin strains shall celebrate your praise,
And tell your high descent to future days. NOTT.

THE SAME.

WHEN Venus to Cythera's top convey'd
Sleeping Ascanius, 'mongst soft violets laid,
Showers of pale roses on the boy she strew'd,
And with sweet waters all the place bedew'd;
She then her old Adonian fire retains;
The well-known flame steals gently through her veins.
How oft her nephew offer'd she t' embrace!
How often said, "Such my Adonis was!"
But fearing to disturb his soft repose,
Thousands of kisses on the flowers bestows;
The breath, which from her lip the rose receives,
Whispers kind warmth into its glowing leaves;
And from her quick'ning touch new kisses rise,
Whose ripe increase her full joy multiplies:
Then round the earth the goddess, by a pair
Of milk-white swans drawn through the fleeting air,
Sows kisses all the way, and as they fell
On the fat glebe, thrice murmurs a dark spell.
Hence a kind harvest for sick lovers grows;
Hence springs the only cure of all my woes.

Dear kisses! you that scorched hearts renew,
Born of the rose pregnant with sacred dew,
Upon your poet deathless verse distil,
That may endure long as Medusa's hill,
Or whilst Love, mindful still of Rome's dear race,
Shall with his numbers their soft language grace.
STANLEY.

2 B 2

KISS II.

If, as the vine clings amorously to the elm, and the mazy ivy fixes its endless sprays all over the tall oak; if thus, Neæra, thou couldst enring my neck [1] with thy binding arms; if I, Neæra, could thus enfold thy white neck perpetually, and cling to thee in an everlasting kiss; then should no thought of Ceres, or of friendly Bacchus, or of pleasant sleep, tear me, my life, from thy rosy mouth; but when we had spent ourselves with mutual kisses, one boat should carry both lovers to the pallid abode of Pluto. Presently we should be led through fragrant fields and a perpetual spring to the scenes where heroines, mingled with noble heroes, and blessed for ever in the enjoyment of their ancient loves, dance, or sing alternately their songs of joy in the myrtle vale; where the light tremulous shade of the laurel-grove plays upon violets, roses, and yellow blossoms of the narcissus; where tepid zephyrs murmur sweetly for ever, and the earth, uncut by the ploughshare, yields her fruits spontaneously. The whole company of the blessed would rise to give us welcome, and would set us on grassy seats in the foremost place among the Homeric choir; nor would any of the mistresses of Jove be reluctant to yield precedence to thee, nor even Helen, the daughter of Jove.

As round some neighb'ring elm the vine
Its am'rous tendrils loves to twine;
As round the oak, in many a maze,
The ivy flings its gadding sprays;
Couldst thou, Neæra, thus enlace
My neck with clinging close embrace;
If thine with such tenacious hold
My arms, Neæra, could enfold,
And nought could those sweet bonds dissever,
But we cling on and kiss for ever;

[1] *Couldst enring my neck.*] Si queas In mea nexilibus *proserpere* colla lacertis. There is an exquisite beauty in the word *proserpere* (to creep along) which cannot be transferred to any other language. In that one word we have the picture of the creeping plant, and the comparison it suggests.

Then Ceres, Bacchus, sleep, adieu !
Good friends, I'd ask no more of you.
Oh not for these, my love, oh no,
Would I thy vermil lips forego ;
But lost in kisses never ending,
Our lives in mutual bliss expending,
One bark should waft our spirits o'er.
United, to the Stygian shore :
Then, passing through a transient night,
We'd enter soon those fields of light ;
Where, breathing richest odours round,[1]
A spring eternal paints the ground ;
Where heroes, once in valour proved,
And beauteous heroines, once beloved,
Again with mutual passion burn,
Feel all their wonted flames return ;
And now in sportive measures tread
The flowery carpet of the mead ;
Now sing the jocund, tuneful tale,
Alternate in the myrtle vale :
Where ceaseless zephyrs fan the glade,
Soft-murm'ring through the laurel shade ;
Beneath whose waving foliage grow,
The violet sweet of purple glow,
The daffodil that breathes perfume,
And roses of immortal bloom :
Where Earth her gifts spontaneous yields,
Nor ploughshare cuts th' unfurrow'd fields.

Soon as we enter'd these abodes
Of happy souls, of demi-gods,
The blest would all respectful rise,
And view us with admiring eyes ;
Would seat us 'mid th' immortal throng,
Where I, renown'd for tender song,
A poet's and a lover's praise,
At once should claim and gain the bays ;
While thou, enthroned above the rest,
Shouldst shine in Beauty's train confest :

---

[1] *Where, breathing richest odours,* &c.]　This description of Elysium
ems to be imitated from Tibullus, lib. i. Elegy 3.

Nor should the mistresses of Jove
Such partial honours disapprove ;
E'en Helen, though of race divine,
Would to thy charms her rank resign.   NOTT.

THE SAME.

As in a thousand wanton curls the vine
    Doth the loved elm embrace ;
As clasping ivy round the oak doth twine,
    To kiss his leafy face ;

So thou about my neck thy arms shalt fling,
    Joining to mine thy breast ;
So shall my arms about thy fair neck cling,
    My lips on thine imprest.

Ceres nor Bacchus, care of life, nor sleep,
    Shall force me to retire ;
But we at once will on each other's lip
    Our mutual souls expire.

Then hand in hand down to th' Elysian plains
    (Crossing the Stygian lake)
We'll through those fields, where spring eternal reigns
    Our pleasing journey take.

There their fair mistresses the heroes lead,
    And their old loves repeat,
Singing or dancing in a flowery mead,
    With myrtles round beset.

Roses and violets smile beneath a screen
    Of ever-verdant bays ;
And gentle zephyr amorously between
    Their leaves untroubled plays.

There constantly the pregnant earth unplough'd
    Her fruitful store supplies ;
When we come thither, all the happy crowd
    From their green thrones will rise.

There thou in place above Jove's numerous train
    Of mistresses shalt sit ;
Hers Helen, Homer will not his disdain,
    For thee and me to quit.   STANLEY.

KISS III.

"Give me one little kiss," I said, "sweet girl!" You laid your delicious lips on mine, and then, like one who has trod on a snake and starts back in terror, you snatched your mouth away. Light of my eyes, this is not what one should call giving a kiss; it is only giving a piteous craving for a kiss.

> "One little kiss, sweet maid!" I cry[1]—
>   And round my neck your arms you twine!
> Your luscious lips of crimson dye
>   With rapturous haste encounter mine.
>
> But quick those lips my lips forsake,
>   With wanton, tantalizing jest;
> So starts some rustic from the snake
>   Beneath his heedless footstep prest.
>
> Is this to grant the wish'd-for kiss?—
>   Ah! no, my love—'tis but to fire
> The bosom with a transient bliss,
>   Inflaming unallay'd desire.   Nott.

THE SAME.

> A kiss I begg'd, and thou didst join
>   Thy lips to mine;

---

[1] *One little kiss*, &c.] The reader may be pleased to see how this lovely little poem appears in a French dress. Mons. Dorat, in his *Baisers*, (Baiser 2,) entitles it L'Etincelle.

> Donne moi, ma belle maîtresse,
> Donne moi, disois-je, un baiser
> Doux, amoureux, plein de tendresse——
> Tu n'osas me le refuser:
> Mais que mon bonheur fut rapide!
> Ta bouche à peine, souviens-t-en,
> Eut effleuré ma bouche avide,
> Elle s'en détache à l'instant.
> Ainsi s'exhale une étincelle.
> Oui, plus que Tantale agité,
> Je vois comme une Onde infidelle,
> Fuir le bien qui m'est présenté.
> Ton baiser m' échappe, cruelle!
> Le désir seul m'en est resté.

Then, as afraid, snatch'd back their treasure,
    And mock my pleasure;
Again, my dearest! for in this
Thou only gav'st desire, and not a kiss.　　STANLEY.

KISS IV.

It is not kisses Neæra gives, it is nectar, it is fragrant breath-dews, it is nard, and thyme, and cinnamon, and honey such as the bees gather on the brows of Hymettus or in the Attic rose-thickets, and store in osier hives. If many such are given me to devour, I shall soon become immortal and partake of the banquets of the great gods. Be sparing then of such gifts, or become a goddess with me, Neæra. Without you I care not for the tables of the celestials, not though the gods and goddesses would depose Jove, and force me to rule over the sunny realms.

'Tis not a kiss you give, my love!
'Tis richest nectar from above!
A fragrant shower of balmy dews,
Which thy sweet lips alone diffuse!
'Tis every aromatic breeze,
That wafts from Afric's spicy trees;
'Tis honey from the osier hive,
Which chymist bees with care derive
From all the newly-open'd flowers
That bloom in Cecrops' roseate bowers,
Or from the breathing sweets that grow
On famed Hymettus' thymy brow:
But if such kisses you bestow,
If from your lips such raptures flow,
Thus blest, supremely blest by thee,
Ere long I must immortal be;
Must taste on earth those joys that wait
The banquets of celestial state.
Then cease thy bounty, dearest fair!
Such precious gifts, then spare! oh spare!
Or, if I must immortal prove,
Be thou immortal too, my love!

For, should the heavenly powers request
My presence at th' ambrosial feast ;
Nay, should they Jove himself dethrone,
And yield to me his radiant crown ;
I 'd scorn it all, nor would I deign
O'er golden realms of bliss to reign ;
Jove's radiant crown I 'd scorn to wear,
Unless thou might'st such honours share ;
Unless thou too, with equal sway,
Might'st rule with me the realms of day.　Nott.

THE SAME.

'Tis no kiss my fair bestows ;
Nectar 'tis whence new life flows ;
All the sweets which nimble bees
In their osier treasuries
With unequall'd art repose,
In one kiss her lips disclose.
These, if I should many take,
Soon would me immortal make,
Raised to the divine abodes,
And the banquets of the gods.
Be not then too lavish, fair !
But this heavenly treasure spare,
'Less thou 'lt too immortal be ;
For without thy company,
What to me were the abodes,
Or the banquets of the gods ?　Stanley.

KISS V.

When you, Neæra, clasp me in your gentle arms, and hang
upon my shoulder, leaning over me with your whole neck and
bosom, and lascivious face ; when putting your lips to mine,
you bite me and complain of being bitten again ; and dart your
tremulous tongue here and there, and sip with your querulous tongue here and there, breathing on me delicious breath,
dulcet sounding, moist, the sustenance of my poor life, Neæra ;
when you suck away my languid breath, my burning, parched
breath, parched by the heat that rages in my bosom, and ex-

tinguish the flames that consume me, exhausting their heat by
your inhalations; then I exclaim, "Love is the god of gods,
and no god is greater than Love; but if there be any one
greater than Love, you, you alone, Neæra, are in my eyes that
greater one."

WHILE tenderly around me cast
Your arms, Neæra, hold me fast;
And hanging o'er, to view confest,
Your neck, and gently-heaving breast;
Down on my shoulders soft decline
Your beauties more than half divine;
With wand'ring looks that o'er me rove,
And fire the melting soul with love:

While you, Neæra, fondly join
Your little pouting lips with mine;
And frolic bite your am'rous swain,
Complaining soft if bit again;
And sweetly-murm'ring pour along
The trembling accents of your tongue,
Your tongue, now here now there that strays,
Now here now there delighted plays;
That now my humid kisses sips,
Now wanton darts between my lips;
And on my bosom raptured lie,
Venting the gently-whisper'd sigh;
A sigh that kindles warm desires,
And kindly fans life's drooping fires;

[1] *The trembling accents of your tongue*, &c.]   A French writer seems
to have paraphrased these thoughts with no small degree of merit:

Et qu'en ces jeux nos langues fretillardes
S' étreignent mollement ——
Quand je te baise, un gracieux zéphire,
Un petit vent moite et doux qui soupire,
Va mon cœur éventant.   L'ABBE DESPORTES.

Our tongues in humid pleasures roll,
And, 'mid the frolic, blend each soul ——
Whene'er thy lips a kiss impart;
Moist breezes, with voluptuous sighing,
Exhale rich nectar as they 're dying;
Breezes that cool my fever'd heart!   NOTT.

Soft as the zephyr's breezy wing,
And balmy as the breath of spring:

While you, sweet nymph! with am'rous play,
In kisses suck my breath away;
My breath with wasting warmth replete,
Parch'd by my breast's contagious heat;
Till, breathing soft, you pour again
Returning life through every vein;
Thus soothe to rest my passion's rage,
Love's burning fever thus assuage:
Sweet nymph! whose breath can best allay [1]
Those fires that on my bosom prey,
Breath welcome as the cooling gale,
That blows when scorching heats prevail:

Then, more than blest, I fondly swear, [2]
" No power can with Love's power compare!
None in the starry court of Jove
Is greater than the god of Love!
If any can yet greater be,
Yes, my Neæra! yes, 'tis thee!"   NOTT.

---

[1] *Sweet nymph, &c.*] An expression so beautifully, so delicately meta-
phorical, is not to be found in any other writer. Petrarch very frequently
applies the word *gale* to his mistress, for the sake of the *concetti*, so peculiar to Italian poetry; *L'aura*, the gale, signifying also her name, *Laura.*

> L'aura serena, che fra verdi fronde
> Mormorando, à ferir nel volto viemme.   PET. *Sonet.* 103.

Soft gale! that murmurs through the verdant grove,
Plays o'er my face, and playing whispers love.

> L'aura mia sacra al mio stanco riposa
> Spira si spesso.   *Sonet.* 307.

O my sweet gale! gale dear to lost repose,
Breathing so frequent!

But such conceits cannot compare with this one exquisite line of Secundus. NOTT.

[2] *Then, more than blest, &c.*] Thus beautifully again the French imitator:

> Alors je renais, et m' écrie :
> L'Amour soumet la Terre, assujettit les Cieux,
> Les Rois sont à ses pieds, il gouverne les Dieux,
> Il mêle en se jouant des pleurs à l' ambroisie,
> Il est maître absolu : mais Thaïs aujourd'hui
> L'emporte sur les Rois, sur les Dieux, et sur lui.
>   DORAT. *Baiser* 6.

THE SAME.

When thou thy pliant arms dost wreathe
About my neck, and gently breathe
Into my breast that soft sweet air
With which thy soul doth mine repair,
When my faint life thou draw'st away,
My life which scorching flames decay,
O'ercharged, my panting bosom boils,
Whose fever thy kind art beguiles,
And with the breath that did inspire,
Doth mildly fan my glowing fire,
Transported then I cry, above
All other deities is Love!
Or if a deity there be
Greater than Love, 'tis only thee.   Stanley.

KISS VI.

Bargaining for two thousand kisses of the best kind, I gave a thousand and received a thousand. You filled up the number, I own, sweet Neæra, but no number can ever give love its fill. Who praises the field for its numbered ears of corn? Who ever counted the blades of grass in the watered mead? Who ever thanked thee, Bacchus, for a hundred clusters of grapes, or prayed to the rural god for a thousand bees? When kind Jupiter bedews the parched fields, we do not count the drops of falling water. So too when the air is swept by storms, and angry Jupiter has grasped his weapons, he lashes land and main with hail, and cares not how many crops he spoils, or in how many places. Blessings and toils come alike in profusion from heaven; such magnificence becomes the abode of Jove. Since you too are a goddess, fairer than that divinity who rides along the deep in a shell car, why do you constrain me to count your kisses, heavenly gifts! whilst you, hard-hearted girl, do not count my groans? whilst you do not count the tears that have made runnels of ever-flowing water along my cheeks and bosom? If you count tears you may count kisses, otherwise count them not, but give me, vain solace of my woe, countless kisses for countless tears.

Two thousand kisses of the sweetest kind,
'Twas once agreed, our mutual love should bind;
First from my lips a rapturous thousand flow'd,
Then you a thousand in your turn bestow'd;
The promised numbers were fulfill'd, I own,
But love sufficed with numbers ne'er was known!
Who thinks of counting every separate blade
Upon the meadow's verdant robe inlaid?
Who prays for number'd ears of ripening grain,
When lavish Ceres yellows o'er the plain?
Or to a scanty hundred would confine
The clustering grapes, when Bacchus loads the vine?
Who asks the guardian of the honey'd store
To grant a thousand bees, and grant no more?
Or tells the drops, while o'er some thirsty field
The liquid stores are from above distill'd?
When Jove with fury hurls the moulded hail,
And earth and sea destructive storms assail;
Or when he bids, from his tempestuous sky,
The winds unchain'd with wasting horror fly;
The god ne'er heeds what harvests he may spoil,
Nor yet regards each desolated soil:
So, when its blessings bounteous heaven ordains,
It ne'er with sparing hand the good restrains;
Evils in like abundance too it showers;
Well suits profusion with immortal powers!
Then since such gifts with heavenly minds agree,
Shed, goddess-like, your blandishments on me;
And say, Neæra! for that form divine
Speaks thee descended of ethereal line;
Say, goddess! than that goddess lovelier far,
Who roams o'er ocean in her pearly car;
Your kisses, boons celestial, why withhold?
Or why by scanty numbers are they told?
Still you ne'er count, hard-hearted maid! those sighs,
Which in my lab'ring breast incessant rise;
Nor yet those lucid drops of tender woe,
Which down my cheeks in quick succession flow.
Yes, dearest life! your kisses number all;
And number too my sorrowing tears that fall:

Or, if you count not all the tears, my fair !
To count the kisses sure you must forbear.
But let your lips now soothe a lover's pain,
(Yet griefs like mine what soothings shall restrain !)
If tears unnumber'd pity can regard,
Unnumber'd kisses must each tear reward.   NOTT.

THE SAME.

OUR bargain for two thousand kisses made,
A thousand I received, a thousand paid ;
The number I confess thou hast supplied,
But Love with number is not satisfied.
None praise the harvest who can count their ears,
Or sum the blades of grass the meadow wears ;
Who for a hundred clusters Bacchus fees ?
Or sues to Pales for a thousand bees ?
When pious Jove waters the thirsty plain,
We number not the drops of falling rain ;
Or when the troubled air with tempests quakes,
And he displeased, in hand his fear'd arms takes,
At random on the earth he scatters hail,
And fruit or corn securely doth assail ;
Or good or bad, heaven's gifts exceed all sum ;
A majesty that doth Jove's house become.
Wilt thou, dear goddess, then (more bright than she
Who in a shell sail'd through the smiling sea)
Kisses, thy heavenly gifts, strictly confine
To number, yet to count my sighs decline ?
Or sum the drops whose inexhausted spring
Flows from my eyes, my pale cheeks furrowing ?
If thou wilt reckon, reckon both together ;
If both thou number not, ah, number neither.
Give me (to ease the pain my grieved soul bears)
Numberless kisses, for unnumber'd tears.   STANLEY.

KISS VII.

A HUNDRED times a hundred kisses, a thousand times a
hundred kisses, a thousand times a thousand kisses, and as
many thousand thousands as there are drops in the Sicilian

Sea, or stars in heaven, I would bestow without stopping on
those rosy cheeks, those pouting lips, those prattling eyes, O
beautiful Neæra.   But while I am glued to your rosy cheeks,
to your crimson lips, to your prattling eyes, it is not granted
me to behold your lips, nor your rosy cheeks, nor your prattling eyes, nor your gentle smiles; which, like the sun dis-
persing the black clouds from the face of heaven, and shining
in yellow lustre through the clear sky, beams upon me with
golden radiance, and dispels tears from my cheeks, and grief
and sighs from my soul.   Oh what strife there is between my
eyes and my lips!   Could I endure even Jove as a rival, when
my eyes cannot bear the rivalry of my lips?

KISSES told by hundreds o'er,
Thousands told by thousands more,
Millions, countless millions, then,
Told by millions o'er again;
Countless, as the drops that glide
In the ocean's billowy tide;
Countless, as yon orbs of light,
Spangled o'er the vault of night,
I 'll with ceaseless love bestow
On those cheeks of crimson glow,
On those lips so gently swelling,[1]
On those eyes such fond tales telling.

But when circled in thy arms,
As I'm panting o'er thy charms,
O'er thy cheeks of rosy bloom,
O'er thy lips that breathe perfume,
O'er thine eyes so sweetly bright,
Shedding soft expressive light;
Then, nor cheeks of rosy bloom,
Nor thy lips that breathe perfume,

---

[1] *Lips so gently swelling.*]   Turgidulis labris.   These words might
perhaps be best translated by applying Suckling's beautiful description
of a lip:

Her lips were red; and one was thin,
Compared to that was next her chin;
Some bee had stung it newly.

Nor thine eyes' expressive light,
Bless thy lover's envious sight;
Nor that soothing smile, which cheers
All his tender hopes and fears:
For, as radiant Phœbus streams
O'er the globe with placid beams,
Whirling through th' ethereal way
The fiery-axled car of day;
And, from the tempestuous sky,
While the rapid coursers fly,
All the stormy clouds are driven,
Which deform'd the face of heaven:
So, thy golden smile, my fair!
Chases every amorous care;
Dries the torrents of mine eyes;
Calms my fond, tumultuous sighs.

Oh! how emulous the strife
'Twixt my lips and eyes, sweet life!
Of thy charms are these possest,
Those are envious till they're blest:
Think not then that, in my love,
I'll be rivall'd e'en by Jove,
When such jealous conflicts rise
'Twixt my very lips and eyes.   NOTT.

THE SAME.

KISSES a hundred, hundred-fold,
A hundred by a thousand told,
Thousands by thousands number'd o'er,
As many thousand thousand more
As are the drops the seas comprise,
As are the stars that paint the skies,
To this soft cheek, this speaking eye,
This swelling lip will I apply.
But whilst on these my kisses dwell
Close as the cockle clasps her shell,
This swelling lip I cannot spy,
This softer cheek, this speaking eye:
Nor those sweet smiles, which (like the ray
Of Cynthius driving clouds away)

From my swoln eyes dispel all tears,
From my sad heart all jealous fears.
Alas! what discontents arise
Betwixt my emulous lips and eyes!
Can I with patience brook that Jove
Should be a partner in my love,
When my strict eye the rivalship
Disdains to suffer of my lip? STANLEY.

KISS VIII.

WHAT fury impelled you, silly Neæra, thus to assail and wound my tongue with ravening bite? Do you think it nothing that my whole bosom is stuck so full of keen arrows shot by you, unless your teeth wreak their monstrous cruelty on that part with which I so often sang your praises at dawn and set of sun, through livelong days and nights of bitterness? It was this tongue, know you not? unjust one; it was this tongue of mine which extolled in tender verse to the stars and beyond the glowing home of Jove, till heaven was envious, the snaky locks, and sparkling eyes, and milk-white breasts, and dainty neck of pretty Neæra; which called you my life and weal, the blossom of my soul, my love and my joy, my Dione, my dove, my white turtle, till Venus envied the praise it bestowed upon you. Is it indeed for that very reason that you delight, in the insolence of power, to wound that tongue which, you know, lovely one, could never for any injury swell with so much wrath but that bleeding and stammering it would ever descant upon those eyes, those lips, and those wanton teeth that hurt it. Oh arrogant power of beauty!

AH! what ungovern'd rage, declare,
Neæra, too capricious fair!
What unrevenged, unguarded wrong,
Could urge thee thus to wound my tongue?

Perhaps you deem th' afflictive pains
Too trifling, which my heart sustains;
Nor think enough my bosom smarts
With all the sure, destructive darts

2 c

Incessant sped from every charm;
That thus your wanton teeth must harm,[1]
Must harm that little tuneful thing,
Which wont so oft thy praise to sing;
What time the morn has streak'd the skies,
Or evening's faded radiance dies;
Through painful days consuming slow,
Through ling'ring nights of amorous woe.

This tongue, thou know'st, has oft extoll'd
Thy hair in shining ringlets roll'd;
Thine eyes with tender passion bright;
Thy swelling breast of purest white;
Thy taper neck of polish'd grace;
And all the beauties of thy face;
Beyond the lucid orbs above,
Beyond the starry throne of Jove;
Extoll'd them in such lofty lays,
That gods with envy heard the praise.

Oft has it call'd thee every name,
Which boundless rapture taught to frame;
My life! my joy! my soul's desire!
All that my wish could e'er require!
My pretty Venus! and my love!
My gentle turtle! and my dove!
Till Cypria's self with envy heard
Each partial, each endearing word.

Say, beauteous tyrant! dost delight
To wound this tongue in wanton spite?
Because, alas! too well aware,
That every wrong it yet could bear,

---

[1] *That thus your wanton teeth*, &c.]   Dorat (Baiser 11) has thus
beautifully paraphrased this passage:

> Tes dents, ces perles que j' adore,
> D' où s' échappe à mon œil trompé
> Ce sourire développé,
> Transfuge des lèvres de flore;
> Devroient-elles blesser, dis moi,
> Une organe tendre et fidelle,
> Qui t'assure ici de ma foi,
> Et nomma Thais la plus belle?

Ne'er urged it once in angry strain
Of thy unkindness to complain;
But suff'ring patient all its harms,
Still would it sing thy matchless charms;
Sing the soft lustre of thine eye;
Sing thy sweet lips of rosy dye;
Nay, still those guilty teeth 'twould sing,
Whence all its cruel mischiefs spring:
E'en now it lisps in fault'ring lays,
While yet it bleeds, Neæra's praise:[1]
Thus, beauteous tyrant! you control,
Thus sway my fond, enamoured soul! Nott.

KISS IX.

Give me not always a humid kiss, nor murmured endear-
ments and smiles, nor languish always on my neck with your
arms clasped round it. Pleasant things have their limit: the
more sweetly anything affects the mind, the sooner does it
produce satiety and distaste. When I shall ask for thrice
three kisses, withhold seven and give me but two, not long or
humid either of them, but such as chaste Diana gives to her
quiver-bearing brother, or a virgin daughter to her sire; then
trip away, wanton! out of my sight, and hide in the most
secret corner. I will follow and find you out in your lurking-
place, and, flushed with victory, I will throw my masterful
arms round my prey, and bear it off, as the hawk clutches the
feeble dove in its crooked talons. With uplifted hands you
will beseech me to forbear, and hanging from my neck with

---

[1] *While yet it bleeds*, &c.] And again, how impassioned is the strain
of the French poet, Dorat, Baiser 11.

> Crois-tu le contraindre à se taire?
> Non, non, il brave en ce moment
> Tous les maux que tu peux lui faire.
> Viens, renouvelle son tourment:
> Assailli des flèches brûlantes,
> De ces dards perçans du baiser,
> Il veut sur tes lèvres ardentes,
> Il veut encore les aiguiser;
> Et, chargé d' heureuses blessures,
> Doux vestiges de volupté,
> Essayer même aû-lieu d'injures,
> De nouveaux chants à ta beauté.

your arms flung round it, will seek to appease me, silly victim, with seven frolicsome kisses.   You will be disappointed :
in expiation of that offence, I will have seven times seventy
kisses, and I will bind your neck with these arms as with
chains, runaway !   Until, all the forfeit kisses being duly
paid, you shall swear by all your charms that you will often
gladly commit the same fault and incur the same penalty.

> CEASE thy sweet, thy balmy kisses ;
>   Cease thy many-wreathed smiles ;
> Cease thy melting, murmuring blisses ;
>   Cease thy fond, bewitching wiles :
>
> On my bosom soft reclined,
>   Cease to pour thy tender joys ;
> Pleasure's limits are confined,[1]
>   Pleasure oft repeated cloys.
>
> Sparingly your bounty use ;
>   When I ask for kisses nine,
> Seven at least you must refuse,[2]
>   And let only two be mine :
>
> Yet let these be neither long,
>   Nor delicious sweets respire !
> But like those, which virgins young
>   Artless give their aged sire :

[1] *Pleasure's limits are confined.*]   Shakspeare (Romeo and Juliet) expresses the same thought, in the fatherly reproof of the old friar to Romeo.

> These violent delights have violent ends,
> And in their triumph die ; like fire and powder,
> Which, as they meet, consume.   The sweetest honey
> Is loathsome in its own deliciousness,
> And in the taste confounds the appetite.

[2] *Seven at least you must refuse.*]   All amatory poets have dwelt with
delight on these little coquettish cruelties ; thus Horace (lib. ii. Ode 12)
speaks of Licymnia, the mistress of Mecænas :

> Dum flagrantia detorquet ad Oscula
> Cervicem, aut facili sævitiâ negat,
> Quæ poscente magis gaudeat eripi,
>   Interdum rapere occupet.

> While now her bending neck she plies
>   Backward to meet the burning kiss ;
> Then with an easy cruelty denies,
>   And wishes you would snatch, not ask the bliss.   FRANCIS.

Such! as, with a sister's love,
  Beauteous Dian may bestow
On the radiant son of Jove,
  Phœbus of the silver bow.

Tripping light with wanton grace,
  Now my lips disorder'd fly;
And in some retired place
  Hide thee from my searching eye:[1]

Each recess I 'll traverse o'er,
  Where I think thou liest conceal'd;
Every covert I 'll explore,
  Till my wanton's all reveal'd:

Then in sportive, amorous play,
  Victor-like I 'll seize my love;
Seize thee, as the bird of prey
  Pounces on a trembling dove.

Captive then, and sore dismay'd,
  How you 'll fondle, how you 'll plead!
Vainly offering, silly maid,
  Seven sweet kisses, to be freed.

Not so fast, fair runaway!
  Kisses seven times seven be mine!
Chain'd within these arms you stay,
  Till I touch the balmy fine.

Paying then the forfeit due,
  By your much-loved beauties swear,
Faults like these you 'll still pursue,
  Faults which kisses can repair.   NOTT.

---

[1] *Hide thee, &c.*] Cornelius Gallus mentions the same amorous dalliance :

> Erubuit vultus ipsa puella meos,
> Et nunc subridens latebras fugitiva petebat.

At sight of me, deep blush'd the lovely maid,
  Then side-long laugh'd, and flying sought the shade.   DUNKIN.

And such dalliance was equally grateful to Horace (lib. i. Ode 9):

> Nunc et latentis proditor intimo
> Gratus Puellæ risus ab angulo.

The laugh, that from the corner flies,
  The sportive fair one shall betray.   FRANCIS.

THE SAME.

Not always give a melting kiss,
   And smiles with pleasing whispers join'd;
Nor always ecstasied with bliss
   About my neck thy fair arms wind.

The wary lover learns by measure
   To circumscribe his greatest joy;
Lest, what well-husbanded yields pleasure,
   Might by the repetition cloy.

When thrice three kisses I require,
   Give me but two, withhold the other;
Such as cold virgins to their sire,
   Or chaste Diana gives her brother.

Then wantonly snatch back thy lip,
   And smoothly, as sly fishes glide
Through water, giving me the slip,
   Thyself in some dark corner hide.

I'll follow thee with eager haste,
   And having caught, (as hawks their prey,)
In my victorious arm held fast,
   Panting for breath, bear thee away.

Then thy soft arms about me twined,
   Thou shalt use all thy skill to please me,
And offer all that was behind,
   The poor seven kisses, to appease me.

How much mistaken wilt thou be!
   For seven times seven shalt thou pay;
Whilst in my arms I fetter thee,
   Lest thou once more shouldst get away.

Till I at last have made thee swear,
   By all thy beauty and my love,
That thou again the same severe
   Revenge for the same crime wouldst prove.

STANLEY

KISS X.

THE pleasure I derive from kisses is not limited to any particular kind; when you join your moist lips to mine, moist kisses delight me. Nor are dry kisses without their charms; many a time they send a thrilling flush through the frame. Pleasant too it is to lay kisses on wanton eyes, and punish the authors of our pain; or to revel all over a cheek, or a neck, or snowy shoulders, or a snowy bosom, and cover cheek and neck, and white shoulders and bosom, with black marks; or with eager lips to suck a tremulous tongue, and to mingle breath with joined mouths, and transfuse two souls, each into the other's body, whilst Love lies swooning with ecstasy. Welcome to me the kiss, whether short or long, whether with lips that lightly touch or that cling close together, whether you give it me, light of my life, or I give it you. But never give me back such kisses as you receive, but let each vary the delight in different ways. And let whichever of us shall first be at fault for a change of method, hear and obey this sentence with downcast eyes: As many sweet kisses as have been previously given on both sides, so many shall the delinquent give singly to the other, and in as many ways.

IN various kisses various charms I find,
For changeful fancy loves each changeful kind:
Whene'er with mine thy humid lips unite,
Then humid kisses with their sweets delight;
From ardent lips so ardent kisses please,
For glowing transports often spring from these.
What joy! to kiss those eyes that wanton rove,
Then catch the glances of returning love:
Or clinging to the cheek of crimson glow,
The bosom, shoulder, or the neck of snow;
What pleasure! tender passion to assuage;
And see the traces of our amorous rage,[1]

[1] *And see the traces,* &c.] The tender Tibullus (lib. i. Elegy 9) most probably gave Secundus the hint of these voluptuous ideas.

At Venus inveniet Puero succumbere furtim,
Dum tumet, et teneros conserit usque sinus:

On the soft neck, or blooming cheek exprest,
On the white shoulder, or still whiter breast.
'Twixt yielding lips, in every thrilling kiss,
To dart the trembling tongue—what matchless bliss!
Inhaling sweet each other's mingling breath,
While Love lies gasping in the arms of Death!
While soul with soul in ecstasy unites,
Intranced, impassion'd, with the fond delights,
From thee received, or given to thee, my love!
Alike to me those kisses grateful prove;
The kiss that's rapid, or prolong'd with art,
The fierce, the gentle, equal joys impart:
But mark—be all my kisses, beauteous maid!
With diff'rent kisses from thy lips repaid;
Then varying raptures shall from either flow,
As varying kisses either shall bestow:
And let the first, who with an unchanged kiss
Shall cease to thus diversify the bliss,
Observe with looks in meek submission dress'd
That law, by which this forfeiture's express'd:
" As many kisses as each lover gave,
As each might in return again receive;
So many kisses, from the vanquish'd side
The victor claims, so many ways applied."   NOTT.

KISS XI.

SOME say that I practise too luxurious kisses, such as are
unknown to wrinkled fathers. Therefore, my love, when I
clasp your neck with my eager arms, and faint upon your
kisses, let me anxiously inquire what everybody says of me,
though I am hardly in a condition to remember who or where
I am. Lovely Neæra smiled to hear me speak thus, and put-

> Et dare anhelanti pugnantibus uvida linguis
>   Oscula, et in collo figere dente notas.

> But fav'ring Venus, watchful o'er thy joy,
> Shall lay thee secret near th' impassion'd boy;
> His panting bosom shall be prest to thine,
> And his dear lips thy breathless lips shall join;
> With active tongue he'll dart the humid kiss,
> And on thy neck indent his eager bliss.

ting both her snowy arms round my neck, gave me such a voluptuous kiss as never was surpassed by Venus when she toyed with Mars. "What need have you," she said, "to fear the judgment of the censorious? That question belongs to my jurisdiction only."

"Some think my kisses too luxurious told,[1]
Kisses, they say, not known to sires of old:
But, while entranced on thy soft neck I lie,
And o'er thy lips in tender transport die,
Shall I then ask, dear life! perplex'd in vain,
Why rigid cynics censure thus my strain?
Ah no! thy blandishments so rapturous prove,
That every ravish'd sense is lost in love;
Blest with those blandishments, divine I seem,
And all Elysium paints the blissful dream."

Neæra heard—then smiling, instant threw
Around my neck her arm of fairest hue;
And kiss'd me fonder, more voluptuous far,
Than Beauty's queen e'er kiss'd the god of War:
"What! (cries the nymph,) and shall my am'rous bard
Pedantic wisdom's stern decree regard?

[1] *Some think my kisses*, &c.] Dorat's *Kiss* (Baiser 20) on this subject is so beautiful, that I cannot deny it a place here: he calls it La Couronne de Fleurs.

Renversé doucement dans les bras de Thaïs,
 Le front ceint d'un léger núage,
Je lui disois : lorsque tu me souris,
Peut-être sur ma tête il s'élève un orage.
 Que pense-t-on de mes ecrits?
Je dois aimer mes vers, puisqu'ils sont ton ouvrage.
 Occuperai-je les cent voix
 De la vagabonde Déesse?
A ses faveurs pour obtenir des droits,
Suffit-il, ô Thaïs, de sentir la tendresse?
 Thaïs alors sur de récens gazons
Cueille des fleurs, en tresse une couronne.
 Tiens, c'est ainsi que je répons;
 Voilà le prix de tes chansons,
 Et c'est ma main qui te le donne:
Renonce, me dit-elle, à l'orgueil des lauriers;
Laisse ces froids honneurs qu'ici tu te proposes;
 Il faut des couronnes de roses
A qui peignit l'amour, et chanta les baisers.

Thy cause must be at my tribunal tried,
None but Neæra can the point decide." NOTT.

KISS XII.

WHY do you turn away your modest faces, chaste matrons and damsels? My song is not of the amorous intrigues of gods, or monstrous forms of lust; in this book of mine there are no Priapic poems, none which the austere schoolmaster might not read to his innocent pupils. I, a chaste priest of the Aonian choir, sing of simple kisses that have no harm in them. But all the chaste matrons and damsels look petulantly upon me, because I may have heedlessly let slip here and there some naughty word. Get agone, you irksome pack, prudish matrons and damsels! How much chaster is my Neæra, who would rather that her poet's book than himself should be without you know what!

MODEST matrons, maidens, say,
Why thus turn your looks away?
Frolic feats of lawless love,
Of the lustful powers above;
Forms obscene, that shock the sight,
In my verse I ne'er recite;
Verse where nought indecent reigns;
Guiltless are my tender strains;
Such as pedagogues austere
Might with strict decorum hear,
Might, with no licentious speech,
To their youth reproachless teach.
I, chaste votary of the Nine,
Kisses sing of chaste design.
Maids and matrons yet, with rage,
Frown upon my blameless page;
Frown, because some wanton word
Here and there by chance occurr'd;
Or the cheated fancy caught
Some obscure, though harmless thought.
Hence, ye prudish matrons! hence,
Squeamish maids devoid of sense!

And shall these in virtue dare
With my virtuous maid compare?
She, who in the bard will prize
What she'll in his lays despise;
Wantonness with love agrees,
But reserve in verse must please.   NOTT.

KISS XIII.

FAINT and languid from the sweet conflict, I lay, my love, with my arm upon your neck. My breath, all wasted in my parching mouth, could yield my heart no refreshment. Already I had Styx before my eyes, and the sunless realms, and old Charon's lurid boat; when you breathed on my dry lips a deep-fetched moist kiss, a kiss that brought me back from the Stygian vale, and left the old ferryman without a freight. I was wrong: he did not go back with an empty boat, for my shade went with him to the sad regions of the dead. Part of your soul, my life! lives in this body, and upholds my frame; but impatient to return to its original command, it strives fretfully to make its way out by secret issues; and unless you cherish it with your loved breath, it will presently desert my fainting frame. Come then, glue your lips to mine, and let one breath continually animate us both; until, when age shall have wearied but not sated our passionate hearts, one single life shall quit our two bodies.

WITH amorous strife exanimate I lay,
    Around your neck my languid arm I threw,
My trembling heart had just forgot to play,
    Its vital spirit from my bosom flew:

The Stygian lake; the dreary realms below,
    To which the sun a cheering beam denies;
Old Charon's boat, slow-wand'ring to and fro,
    Promiscuous pass'd before my swimming eyes:

When you, Neæra! with your humid breath,
    O'er my parch'd lips the deep-fetch'd kiss bestow'd;
Sudden my fleeting soul return'd from death,
    And freightless hence th' infernal pilot row'd.

Yet soft,—for oh! my erring senses stray ;—
  Not quite unfreighted to the Stygian shore
Old Charon steer'd his lurid bark away,
  My plaintive shade he to the Manes bore.

Then since my soul can here no more remain,
  A part of thine, sweet life! that loss supplies ;
But what this feeble fabric must sustain,
  If of thy soul that part its aid denies!

And much I fear:—for struggling to be free,
  Oft from its new abode it fain would roam ;
Oft seeks, impatient to return to thee,
  Some secret pass to gain its native home :

Unless thy fost'ring breath retards its flight,
  It now prepares to quit this falling frame :
Haste then ; to mine thy clinging lips unite,
  And let one spirit feed each vital flame.

Till, after frequent ecstasies of bliss,
  Mutual, unsating to th' impassion'd heart,
From bodies thus conjoin'd, in one long kiss,
  That single life which nourish'd both shall part.[1]
                                          NOTT.

---

[1] There is a little Epigram in Marullus, (lib. ii.,) which contains the
same thought as this Basium ; it is so neatly and delicately turned, that I
am certain my readers will not be displeased to see it inserted here.

  Suaviolum invitæ rapio dum casta Neæra,
    Imprudens vestris liqui animam in labiis.
  Exanimusque diu, cùm nec per se ipsa rediret,
    Et mora lethalis quantulacumque foret,
  Misi cor quæsitum animam, sed cor quoque blandis
    Captum oculis nunquam deinde mihi rediit.
  Quòd nisi Suaviolo, flammam quoque casta Neæra
    Hausissem, quæ me substinet exanimam,
  lle dies misero mihi crede supremus amanti
    Luxisset, rapui cùm tibi Suaviolum.

  A kiss from chaste Neæra's lips I stole,
  But on those lips, in kissing, left my soul ;
  Incautious youth!—long time the loss I mourn'd,
  And waited long, my soul still ne'er return'd :
  At length, exanimate with slow delay,
  I sent my heart to seek my soul astray ;

THE SAME.

I LAY of life, by thee, my life, bereaved.
About thy neck my arms were loosely weaved.
Supplies of breath my wasted spirits fail,
Nor could relieve my heart with one fresh gale:
Styx now before my eyes appear'd, the dark
Region, and aged Charon's swarthy bark;
When thou upon my lip a kiss imprest
Drawn from the depth of thy enlivening breast;
A kiss, that call'd me from the Stygian lake,
And made the ferryman go empty back.
Ah! I mistook! he went not back alone,
My mournful shade along with him is gone;
Part of thy soul within this body reigns,
And friendly my declining limbs sustains;
Which of return impatient, roves about,
Ransacking every passage to get out;
And if no kindness she from thee receive,
Ev'n now her falling tenement will leave.
Come then, unite thy melting lip to mine,
And let one spirit both our breasts combine,
Till, in an ecstasy of wild desire,
Together both our breasts one life expire. STANLEY.

KISS XIV.

WHY do you offer me your little cherry lip? I do not choose to kiss you, hard-hearted Neæra, harder than hardest marble. Do you expect me to prize your mere kisses so much that for sake of them I should be content to lie so often swelling and raging with unsatisfied desire?[1] Whither are you

But my poor heart, by beauty's power enchain'd,
With my lost soul, and with the nymph remain'd:
Then, oh! unless, to foster this sad frame,
I from Neæra's lips draw vital flame,
That day I kiss'd thee must for ever prove
Wretched to me, the greatest wretch in love! NOTT.

[1] *Swelling and raging*, &c.] Baffled by the extraordinary stiffness he finds in the original, the translator subjoins the Latin:

Tanti istas ego ut osculationes
Imbelles faciam, superba, vestras,

going? Stay, and deprive me not of those eyes or that cherry
lip. I will, I will kiss you, soft-hearted girl, softer than softest down.

> Those tempting lips, of scarlet glow,
>   Why pout with fond, bewitching art?
> For to those lips, Neæra, know,
>   My lips shall not one kiss impart.
>
> Perhaps you'd have me greatly prize,
>   Hard-hearted fair, your precious kiss;
> But learn, proud mortal, I despise
>   Such cold, such unimpassion'd bliss.
>
> Think'st thou I calmly feel the flame,
>   That all my rending bosom fires?
> And patient bear, through all my frame,
>   The pangs of unallay'd desires?
>
> Ah! no;—but turn not thus aside
>   Those tempting lips of scarlet glow;
> Nor yet avert, with angry pride,
>   Those eyes, from whence such raptures flow!
>
> Forgive the past, sweet-natured maid!
>   My kisses, love! are all thy own;
> Then let my lips to thine be laid,
>   To thine, more soft than softest down.   NOTT.

KISS XV.

THE Idalian boy had drawn his bow and was in the act of
shooting at you, fair Neæra, but seeing your forehead, and the
locks that overspread it, your restless, expressive eyes, your
rosy cheeks, and your bosom worthy of his mother, he dropped
the slackened bow from his hesitating hand, and rushing with
boyish impetuosity into your arms, he laid a thousand kisses on
you in a thousand ways, which breathed myrtle and Cyprian

> Ut, nervo toties rigens supino,
> Pertundam tunicas meas, tuasque,
> Et desiderio furens inani,
> Tabescam miser æstuante venâ?

aromas into your inmost bosom, and swore by all the gods and by his mother Venus, that he would never again think of doing you any mischief. Can we wonder then why your kisses are so fragrant, and why your heart is always untouched by gentle love?

Th' Idalian boy, to pierce Neæra's heart,
Had bent his bow, had chose the fatal dart;
But when the child, in wonder lost, survey'd
That brow, o'er which your sunny tresses play'd,
Those cheeks, that blush'd the rose's warmest dye,
That streamy languish of your lucid eye,
That bosom too with matchless beauty bright,
(Scarce Cypria's own could boast so pure a white,)
Though mischief urged him first to wound my fair,
Yet partial fondness urged him now to spare;
But doubting still, he linger'd to decide;
At length resolved, he flung the shaft aside;
Then sudden rush'd impetuous to thy arms,
And hung voluptuous on thy heavenly charms:
There as the boy in wanton folds was laid,
His lips o'er thine in varied kisses play'd;
With every kiss he tried a thousand wiles,
A thousand gestures, and a thousand smiles;
Your inmost breast with Cyprian odours fill'd,
And all the myrtle's luscious scent instill'd:
Lastly, he swore by every power above,
By Venus' self, the potent Queen of Love,
That you, blest nymph, for ever should remain
Exempt from am'rous care, from am'rous pain.
What wonder then such balmy sweets should flow,
In every grateful kiss your lips bestow?
What wonder then, obdurate maid, you prove
Averse to all the tenderness of love?   NOTT.

THE SAME.

Th' Idalian boy his arrow to the head
(Neæra) drew, ready to strike thee dead;
But when thy brow, and on thy brow thy hair,
Thy eyes' quick restless light, thy cheeks more fair,

Breasts whiter than his mother's, he did view,
Away his wavering hand the slack shaft threw:
Then to thy arms with childish joy he skips,
Printing a thousand kisses on thy lips;
Which Cyprian spirits and the myrtle's juice
Into thy bosom gently did infuse;
And by the gods and his fair mother swore,
He never would attempt to hurt thee more.
Wonder we then thy kisses are so sweet?
Or why no love thy cold breast will admit? STANLEY.

KISS XVI.

SWEET girl, sweeter than Diana's silver orb, and lovelier than the golden star of Venus, give me a hundred kisses; give me as many as Lesbia gave and took with her importunate poet; as many as are the graces and the loves that stray about your lips and your rosy cheeks; as the lives and deaths with which your eyes are fraught; as the hopes and fears, the joys mixed with lasting cares, and the sighs of lovers. Give me kisses as many as the darts which the dread hand of the winged god has implanted in my breast, and those which he retains in his golden quiver. Add too caresses, and open words of love, and sweet whispers, not without pleasant laughter, not without pleasant bites; like as Chaonian doves coo and fondle alternately with tremulous billings, when the frosts of winter yield to the first zephyrs. And leaning bewildered on my cheek, roll your swimming eyes to and fro, and bid me sustain your fainting frame in my arms. I will clasp you closely in my arms, press your chilled form to my glowing bosom, and revive you with a long-breathed kiss; till my breath too fails and faints upon those dewy kisses, and I say, Hold me in your arms, or I fall. You will clasp me closely in your arms, my own girl, and will breathe life into me with the dew of a long kiss. Thus, light of my eyes, let us together enjoy the delights of our spring time. Infirm age ere long will bring with it wretched cares, and sickness, and death.

BRIGHT as Venus' golden star,
Fair as Dian's silver car,
Nymph, with every charm replete,
Give me hundred kisses sweet;
Then as many kisses more
O'er my lips profusely pour,
As th' insatiate bard could want,
Or his bounteous Lesbia grant;
As the vagrant Loves that stray
On thy lips' nectareous way;
As the dimpling Graces spread
On thy cheeks' carnation'd bed;
As the deaths thy lovers die;
As the conquests of thine eye,
Or the cares, and fond delights,
Which its changeful beam incites;
As the hopes and fears we prove,
Or th' impassion'd sighs, in love;
As the shafts by Cupid sped,
Shafts by which my heart has bled;
As the countless stores that still
All his golden quiver fill.
Whisper'd plaints, and wanton wiles;
Speeches soft, and soothing smiles;
Teeth-imprinted, tell-tale blisses,
Intermix with all thy kisses.
So, when Zephyr's breezy wing
Wafts the balmy breath of spring,
Turtles thus their loves repeat,
Fondly billing, murm'ring sweet,
While their trembling pinions tell
What delights their bosoms swell.

Kiss me, press me, till you feel
All your raptured senses reel;
Till your eyes, half-closed and dim,
In a dizzy transport swim,
And you murmur faintly, "Grasp me,
Swooning, in your arms oh clasp me."
In my fond sustaining arms
I will hold your drooping charms;

2 D

While the long, life-teeming kiss
Shall recall your soul to bliss ;
And, as thus the vital store
From my humid lips I pour,
Till, exhausted with the play,
All my spirit wastes away ;
Sudden, in my turn, I'll cry,
"Oh! support me, for I die."
To your fost'ring breast you'll hold me,
In your warm embrace enfold me ;
While your breath, in nectar'd gales,
O'er my sinking soul prevails ;
While your kisses sweet impart
Life and rapture to my heart.
   Thus, when youth is in its prime,[1]
Let's enjoy the golden time ;
For, when smiling youth is past,
Age these tender joys shall blast :
Sickness, which our bloom impairs ;
Slow-consuming, painful cares ;
Death, with dire remorseless rage ;
All attend the steps of age.   NOTT.

THE SAME.

THOU than Latona's star more bright,
Fairer than Venus' golden light,
    A hundred kisses pay ;
    Many as Lesbia
Gave and received from her glad lover ;
As are the Graces round thee hover,
    Or Cupids that do skip
    About thy cheek and lip ;

---

[1] *Thus, when youth, &c.*] Horace gives much such advice to his fair
friend, Leuconoë, Ode ii. lib. i. :

        Dum loquimur, fugerit invida
Ætas. Carpe diem, quàm minimùm credula postero.

    Ev'n while we talk in careless ease,
      Our envious minutes wing their flight ;
    Instant the fleeting pleasure seize,
      Nor trust to-morrow's doubtful light.   FRANCIS.

As lives and deaths thy bright eye wears ;
As many hopes, as many fears,
　　Joys interlined with woe,
　　Or sighs from lovers flow ;
As many as the darts, that on
My heart by the wing'd boy are sown ;
　　As many as do lie
　　In his gilt armoury ;
To these kind blandishments, with glad
Whispers, and mirthful dalliance add ;
　　With grateful smiles, that may
　　Our full delight betray ;
As two Chaonian turtles bill,
And the soft air with murmurs fill,
　　When winter's rigid snows
　　Away young Zephyr blows ;
Rest on my cheek in ecstasy,
Ready to close thy dying eye ;
　　And as thou faint'st away
　　Me to uphold thee pray :
My arms about thee I will twine ;
My warm to thy cold bosom join,
　　And call thee back from death,
　　With a long kiss's breath :
Till me like fate of life bereave,
Who in that kiss my spirit leave,
　　And, as I sink away,
　　Thee to uphold me pray :
Thy arms about me thou shalt tie,
Thy warm to my cold breast apply,
　　And summon me from death
　　With a long kiss's breath.
Thus let us, dear, in mutual joy
The florid part of time employ :
　　For age our lives will waste ;
　　Sickness and death make haste.　STANLEY.

KISS XVII.

RED with such a colour as roses display in the purple dawn,
when they have been washed with nightly dews, are the lips

of my mistress in the morning, when bedewed through the
long night with my kisses. A face of snowy brightness en-
circles them, as the white hand of a virgin holds a violet.
So glows the cherry amid the late blossoms, when spring and
summer meet together in the same tree. Woe is me! why
am I constrained to leave your chamber when your kisses are
most burning? Oh keep, at least, lovely girl, this crimson
on your lips till the stillness of night brings me back to you?
But if, meanwhile, another's kisses brush off their bloom, may
they become paler than my cheeks.

> Roses, refresh'd with nightly dew, display
> New beauties blushing to the dawn of day;
> So, by the kisses of a rapturous night,
> Thy vermil lips at morn blush doubly bright;
> And in a face, as exquisitely fair
> As new-fall'n snow, is set that vermil pair;
> Deep-purpled violets thus a deeper glow,
> Held in some virgin's snowy hand, will show;
> And early-ripening cherries thus assume,
> 'Mid the late blossoms, a superior bloom,
> When spring and summer boast united power,
> At once producing both the fruit and flower.
> But why, when most thy kisses fire my heart,
> Why, from th' endearing transport must I part?
> Oh! let that crimson on those lips remain,
> Till evening brings me to thy arms again:
> Yet should those lips ere then some rival bless,
> Some youth whom thou in secret shalt caress;
> Then may they cease for ever to disclose
> That beauteous blush, which emulates the rose!
> Then paler turn than my pale cheek shall prove,
> Whene'er I view this mark of faithless love![1]   Nott.

[1] *Then paler turn*, &c.] i. e. paler than my cheeks shall become at
seeing this evident testimony of infidelity, viz. your lips losing their rosy
colour. The idea of infidelity's being punished by some failure of beauty
is also Horace's, lib. ii. Ode 8:

> Ulla si juris tibi perjerati
> Pœna, Barine, nocuisset unquam:
> Dente si nigro fieres, vel uno
>   Turpior ungui;
> Crederem: &c.

THE SAME.

In such a colour as the morning rose
Doth, water'd with the tears of night, disclose,
The blushing kisses of Neæra shine,
When they the humid print retain of mine;
Round which the beauties of her face beset,
As when some white hand crops a violet;
As flowers with cherries, that together wear
The spring and summer's livery, appear.
Unhappy! why now when thy kind lip warms
My soul, am I constrain'd to quit thy arms?
This crimson treasure, ah! reserve for me,
Till night return and bring me back to thee;
But if mean time they any other seek,
May they become far paler than my cheek.

STANLEY.

KISS XVIII.

When Venus beheld the lips of my girl, encircled by her fair face, it is said she wept and groaned, called together the wanton Loves, and said, " What avails it that with my rosy lips I conquered on Ida, in the shepherd's judgment, Pallas and the sister-spouse of Jove, since this Neæra surpasses me in the judgment of the poet? But go all of you, fall furi-

If ever injured power had shed
The slightest vengeance on thy head;
If but a nail or tooth of thee
Were blacken'd by thy perjury,
Again thy falsehood might deceive,
And I the faithless vow believe. FRANCIS.

And thus Ovid to the same purpose, *Amor*. lib. iii. Eleg. 3 :

Esse deos credamne ?—fidem jurata fefellit,
Et facies illi, quæ fuit ante, manet.
Quam longos habuit, nondum perjura, capillos,
Tam longos, postquam numina læsit, habet.

Can there be gods?—the perjured fair-one swore,
Yet looks as lovely as she look'd before.
Long flow'd the careless tresses of her hair,
While yet she shone as innocent as fair;
Long flow the tresses of the wanton now,
And sport as trophies of her broken vow. DUNKIN.

ously on this poet, and shoot sharply with your twanging bows dire shafts from your full quivers into his soft vitals, through his breast and his gamesome liver. As for her, let her glow with no fire, but, smitten with a leaden arrow, let her inmost veins be cold as ice."

So was it done: I burn in my inmost vitals, and my liver melts with scorching fire. You, with a heart fenced round with rugged icicles, and rocks like those beaten by the stormy wave of the Sicilian or the Adriatic Sea, make sport securely of your distracted lover. Ungrateful girl, it is for praising those ruddy lips that I am smitten.[1] You know not, infatuated as you are, why you hate, nor what the ungoverned anger of the gods and the wrath of Dione can do. Mitigate, sweetheart, your harsh disdain, and adopt a behaviour worthy of that face; and join to mine those honeyed lips which are the cause of my sufferings, that you may suck out a little of my poison from my head, and pine with me, the victim of a mutual flame. But fear not the gods nor Dione; a lovely girl can sway the gods.

WHEN Cytherea first beheld
　　Those lips with ruby lustre bright,
Those lips, which, as they blushing swell'd,
　　Blush'd deeper from th' encircling white;

(So, when some artist's skill inlays
　　Coral 'mid ivory's paler hue,
That height'ning coral soon displays
　　A warmer crimson to the view;)

Then, urged by envy and by hate,
　　Which rising sighs and tears betray'd,
She call'd her wanton Loves,—and straight
　　The wanton Loves her call obey'd:

To whom the queen in plaintive strain:—
　　"Ah! what, my boys, avails it now,
That to these lips the Phrygian swain
　　Decreed the prize on Ida's brow?

---

[1] *I am smitten.*] Ingrata propter ista labra rubra
　　　　　　　Laudata plector.
Nott has mistaken the meaning of this passage.

" That prize for which, elate with pride,
　　The martial maid contentious strove ;
That prize to Juno's self denied,
　　Though sister, though the wife of Jove :

" If, to pervert this swain's decree,
　　A poet's partial judgment dare
His mortal nymph prefer to me,
　　Her lips with lips divine compare !

" Swift then, ye vengeful Cupids, fly
　　With loaded quivers to the bard ;
Let all the pangs ye can supply
　　His matchless insolence reward.

" Go, practise every cruel art
　　Revenge can frame, without delay ;
His bosom pierce with every dart
　　Which Love's soft poison may convey.

" But wound not with such darts the fair,
　　Her breast must ever cold remain ;
Your shafts of lead[1] lodge deeply there,
　　To freeze the current of each vein."

She spoke :—now more than usual fire
　　Consumes apace my melting soul ;
And now, fierce torrents of desire
　　Tumultuous through my bosom roll.

While thou, whose icy heart betrays
　　No more concern than rocks that brave
The fury of Sicilian seas,
　　Or Adria's rudely-dashing wave,

Canst, in unfeeling scorn secure,
　　Mock all thy tortured lover's pain,
Who for fond praise is doom'd t' endure,
　　Ungrateful maid ! thy cold disdain.

Yet why, infatuate, you despise,
　　You know not ;—nor how fierce may prove
Th' ungovern'd anger of the skies,
　　The vengeance of the Queen of Love !

---

[1] *Your shafts of lead.*]　The god of Love was said to have two kinds of
darts ; one of gold, causing love, the other of lead, causing aversion.

Oh put away that cruel scorn,
    Which ill becomes each outward grace ;
Sure, sweetest manners should adorn
    The nymph who boasts so sweet a face.

Then let your lips to mine be prest,
    Those honey'd lips, which cause my care ;
Imbibing from my inmost breast
    The latent poison rankling there.

And, as you thus partake the smart
    Of all my torture,—in your turn
You 'll catch the flame that warms my heart,
    And soon with mutual passion burn.

But fear not thou the powers divine,
    Fear not the potent Queen of Love ;
Beauty, well-guarded maid, like thine,
    Can sway th' imperial souls above.   NOTT

THE SAME.

NEÆRA's lips, (to which adds grace
The ambient whiteness of her face,
As coral berries smiling lie
Within their case of ivory,)
When Venus saw, she wept, and all
Her little Loves did to her call.
" What boots it," cries she, " that on Ide
From Pallas and Jove's sister-bride
My lips the glorious prize did gain,
By judgment of the Phrygian swain,
If now another arbiter
Neæra's may to mine prefer ?
Go, spend upon him every dart,
Empty your quivers on his heart ;
But into hers a frost, that may
Congeal her youthful veins, convey."
This scarce was spoke, but straight I felt
My soul in a soft flame to melt ;
Whilst thy white breast, which far outgoes
In coldness winter's sharpest snows,

In hardness Adria's stubborn rocks,
Thy suffering lover safely mocks.
Ungrateful, for those lips am I
Tormented thus, nor know'st thou why
Thou hat'st, or what effects may rise
From discontented deities:
Remit thy anger, and assume
A smile that may thy cheek become;
Thy lips (of all my misery
The only cause) to mine apply;
And from my scorching bosom draw
A warmth that may thy coldness thaw.
Jove fear not, nor Cythera's hate;
Beauty controls the power of fate.   STANLEY.

KISS XIX.

WHY, ye winged honey-gatherers, do you still sip the white-blossomed thyme, the roses, and the nectareous dew of the vernal violet, or the flower of the anise spreading its scent afar? Come all of you to the lips of my mistress. They exhale all the perfumes of roses and thyme, and the nectareous juice of the vernal violet; thence is the sweet scent of the anise diffused afar; they are moist with the true tears of Narcissus, and with the fragrant blood of Hyacinthus, such as either liquid was when it fell, and mixed with ethereal nectar and pure air, filled the ground with a new birth of changed colour. But do not ungratefully repel me when I sip those honeyed lips as is my right; not yet greedily fill all your cells, lest my mistress's lips be left drained, and I be woefully recompensed for my communicativeness, when I press my thirsty kisses on dry lips. And oh, do not prick that soft lip with your stings; she too shoots out stings as keen from her eyes. Believe me, she will suffer no wound without exacting vengeance. Gather your honey, ye bees, gently and harmlessly.

WHEREFORE, ye bees, so widely do ye fly?
Why gather honey so laboriously
From blossom'd thyme empurpling all the ground?
From the rich anise breathing odours round?

Why sip the vernal violet's nectar'd dew?
Or spoil the fragrant rose of blushing hue?
Fly to the lips, ye wantons, of my fair,
And gather all your balmy treasures there;
Thence catch the fragrance of the blushing rose;
Thence sip that dew which from the violet flows;
Thence the rich odours of the anise steal;
And thence the blossom'd thyme's perfume inhale:
Lips, where those tears in genuine moisture dwell,
That from Narcissus self-enamour'd fell;
Lips deeply tinged with Hyacinthus' blood,
Which, with the tears in one commingled flood,
Impregnating the fertile womb of earth,
First gave the variegated flower its birth;
Soon, by the nectar'd showers that heaven bestow'd,
With fanning gales, the motley offspring blow'd:
For drops of blood, lo, crimson streaks appear,
And streaks uncolour'd, for each lucid tear.

But still, ye bees so favour'd, grateful prove,
Let no unkind refusals pay my love,
If e'er I claim (what sure 's my rightful due)
To share those lips, those honey'd lips, with you:
Nor, in too greedy haste your cells to fill,
Exhaust at once the fragrance they distil,
Lest, when my thirsty kisses fain would sip
Balm that no more bedews Neæra's lip,
Sadly I own, with vain contrition wrung,
I'm justly punish'd for my babbling tongue.

And, oh! wound not those tender lips; her eyes
With darts as poignant as your own surprise;
Nor, as ye sip, inflict the slightest pain,
For unrevenged the wrong will not remain;
But gently gather, from those precious rills,
Th' ambrosial drops each humid lip distils.   Nott

THE SAME.

Ye wing'd confectioners, why thyme and roses,
The sweets the vernal violet discloses,
Why suck ye, or the breath of flowery dill?
Come, at my mistress' lips your soft bags fill.

Thyme, and the scent of roses, they produce,
The vernal violet's nectarean juice;
The blooming dill's sweet breath far off they spread,
They're steep'd in the true tears Narcissus shed,
And bathed in Hyacinthus' fragrant blood,
Such, as when falling in a mixed flood
Of heavenly nectar, whilst the blended shower
Raised from the earth a party-colour'd flower.

But when I come to taste these joys with you,
Do not, ungrateful! drive me from my due,
Nor greedy with your store stretch every hive,
Lest of all sweetness you her lips deprive,
And in her next (insipid) kisses, I
Find the reward of my discovery.
Nor wound her soft lips with your little darts,
Wounds far more deadly her bright eye imparts;
Believe 't, your wrongs will never pass forgot:
Suck honey gently thence, but sting her not.   STANLEY.

EPITHALAMIUM.

THE hour is come with the ordained changes of the heavens, the sweet voluptuous hour; hour for fondlings, mirth, and laughter; hour for sweet dalliance, and sport, and whispers; hour for kisses and for enjoyment equal to that of Jupiter and the great gods; hour than which none happier could be granted by the holy goddess of Gnidos; nor by him who roams the world with his quiver, mingling delicious joys with sorrows, the glittering golden-winged Cupid; nor by the sister-spouse of the great thunderer; nor by the flower-decked dweller on the tuneful rock, Hymen, who snatches blooming maids from their mothers' close embrace, and clasps them in the bridegroom's eager arms. O happy youth! happy maid!

Happy bridegroom! the object of thy ardent desire now rests within thy arms, a maid blessed with heavenly beauty, such as might content great Venus, or Juno, or helmeted Pallas born of Jove's divine brain, should they resolve to go again together to the shady valleys of green Ida; beauty decked with which any one of the three would, by the decision of any judge, victoriously bear back the golden apple to the skies. O happy youth! happy maid!

Happy bride! the object of thy ardent desire, a youth of excelling beauty, soon stretched beside thee in the blissful bed, will clasp thy neck in his arms; the youth who, smitten by those rosy lips, those snowy breasts, that sunny hair, and vanquished by those expressive eyes, has long been devoured by a secret flame, and ever chides the slow-paced sun, and ever invokes the tardy-coming moon. O happy youth! happy maid!

Forbear your wishes, hot bridegroom; cease your sighs and complaints: the sweet time is hurrying on; gentle Venus has heard the prayers of her votaries. Cynthius hides his face, and plunging into the Iberean Sea, makes way for his night-travelling sister; and Hesperus, the leader of the golden host, of all stars that shine the dearest to lovers, lifts his head and glitters in the sky. O happy youth! happy maid!

Soon will the virgin enter the chamber, whence, bridegroom, let her not depart a virgin. Soon the virgin laid between the snowy sheets, and covered with ingenuous blushes, will long for and tremble at your approach. Perhaps too her cheeks will be wet with tears, and she will sigh and lament; but you will come without delay, and put an end to plaints, and sighs, and tears, drying her eyes with your lips, and making a sweet murmuring take the place of her complainings. O happy youth! happy maid!

When then the happy bed receives the fair limbs of the beautiful virgin, (limbs disposed to soft slumber,) and when you too laid in bed, are exalted by blessed Dione above purpled kings and Jove himself, soon stirred with due fervour, you will address yourself to pretty-phrased disputes and tender strife; boldly planting here and there prosperous standards of bloodless war, laying many kisses on her neck, many on her cheeks, more on her lips, more on her eyes. She will resist and will call you "naughty," and say "enough" with a trembling voice, and will stop your froward lips with her hand, and push away your froward hand. O night thrice blest, and more!

Let her resist strenuously; let her resist: the tender loves like to be fed by resistance; resistance will redouble your ardour and give you new vigour for the conflict. Pass your lustful hand nimbly over her white neck, over that breast that vies in hue with ivory, over her smooth thighs and her belly, and the parts which are next to both, and give her as many kisses as there are shining stars in heaven. O four times blessed night!

And fail not to utter phrases of endearment, and all sorts of touching words, and murmurings sweet as those which the leaves utter to the gentle zephyr, or the dove, or the aged swan emits with dying bill; until, overcome by the potent arrows and the secret fire of the winged boy, and growing by degrees less and less coy, she shall lay aside her blushing bashfulness, yielding her neck to your clasping arms, and folding her arms round yours. O four times blessed night!

Then, then you will take delicious kisses, not snatched hastily, but lingering, close, and varied. Then the maid will venture in her turn on similar dalliance, and putting her half-open mouth to yours, which she now allows you to keep unclosed, she will enchant your glowing soul with the rapturous excitement of her fragrant breath. Soon growing bolder, she will utter sweeter words of endearment, will put forth her fingers with more freedom, and will practise more wanton toying. O too, too blest night!

Then stand to your arms; then Venus and Cupid call to arms; then charge and deal pleasing wounds; nimbly wield the spear, whose frequent thrusts are guided by the raging hand not of the sister but the mistress of Mars, of Venus, who always delights in new blood. Let your laborious flanks have no rest, nor your active hips, until panting, exhausted, with languid limbs, both shall be bathed in twofold exudations. O too, too blest night!

Toil thus to the full of your desires, and spend long days and nights in unstinted dalliance, and soon produce sweet children, and children's children in long succession, a little throng to soothe your age, relieve your pains in sickness, cherish you in your infirm years, and lay you in the grave with filial piety. O happy youth! happy maid!

> Lo! the hour with transport fraught,
> Yon revolving heaven has brought;
> Hour, that tenderest smiles employ,
> Blandishments of wanton joy;

Hour, that teems with murmur'd bliss,
Teems with many a frolic kiss,
Teems with dalliance and with play,
All that's mirthful, all that's gay;
Hour that heaven's great sire might prize
And the synod of the skies.
Not the deity who reigns
O'er the happy Gnydian plains,
Could so sweet an hour bestow;
Hour, where pleasures rapturous flow;
Nor the boy of golden wing,
Tempering joy with sorrow's sting,
Cupid, whose resistless dart
Conquers every human heart;
Nor the sister-bride of Jove;
Nor gay Hymen, friend to love,
Who from her fond mother's arms
Tears the maid of blooming charms;
And upon a lover's breast
Lays her closely, warmly prest;
Hymen, sporting with delight
On the tuneful mountain's height,
Braiding with fresh flowers his hair.
Happy youth, and happy fair!

Happy bridegroom! thou shalt prove
All the expected sweets of love.
Now within thy soft embrace
Rests the nymph of matchless grace.
Juno, or the Queen of Love,
Or the maid whom mighty Jove
Brought forth from his brain, in arms,
Could not wish for richer charms,
If the shepherd-judge again
Stood upon the shadowy plain,
In the lap of leafy Ide,
Beauty's contest to decide.
But the swain, beholding thee,
Would reject the beauteous three;
Thine the golden prize declare.
Happy youth, and happy fair!

Happy bride! thou soon shalt know
All that rapture can bestow:
Now the beauteous youth is thine,
Now his arms thy neck entwine;
He who, burnt with latent fire
Languish'd long with fierce desire
For those lips of crimson glow,
For those breasts of virgin snow,
For those tresses sunny bright,
For those eyes that look delight.
Oft he chides the god of day,
Loitering with unwelcome ray;
Oft invokes the queen of night
Soon to beam with amorous light,
Thinks her slow pace mocks his prayer.
Happy youth, and happy fair!

Cease, impatient murmurer, cease;
Be thy fretful heart at peace:
Hither the wish'd moments fly;
Venus hears her votaries' sigh.
Phœbus to his billowy bed
Sinks and hides his radiant head;
Plunging in the western main,
To his sister's placid reign,
Lovely wanderer of the night,
He consigns the realms of light:
And, behold! that beauteous star,
Of heaven's lights most beauteous far
To the soul that feels love's tie,
Glitters in the evening sky,
Hesperus of grateful ray,
Leading on their silent way
Hosts that gild yon fields of air.
Happy youth, and happy fair!

Now the virgin, duly led,
Trembling climbs the genial bed;
Virgin thence no more to rise;
Bridegroom, this be thine emprise.
Now the virgin fair behold,
Whom the snow-white sheets enfold.

Half in hope and half in fear,
Bent thy coming step to hear;
While her mantling cheek o'erspread
Blushes of ingenuous red.
If at intervals should rise
Trickling tears, or plaints, or sighs,
Let not these thy pity move,
Mindful of the rites of love.
Kiss each trickling tear away,
All her plaints, her sighs repay,
Kindly soothe her amorous care.
Happy youth, and happy fair!

When the nuptial bed is blest
With its chaste, its beauteous guest,
And the languors of soft sleep
O'er her frame begin to creep,
Thou, close clinging to her charms,
Rouse each sense with false alarms;
And while this sweet joy you prove,
Favour'd by the Queen of Love,
Nor the regal purple prize,
Nor the empire of the skies.
Now the fervours of thy soul
Shall exert their strong control,
Blandishments of dear delight
Now shall haste the tender fight:
Shower upon her many a kiss,
Preluding the war of bliss;
On her neck of matchless white,
On her cheek of crimson bright,
On her lip of orient dye,
On her languid, streaming eye.
Still she'll each attempt elude,
Often call thy dalliance "rude,"
Oft in trembling accents blame,
Urge full oft her maiden shame;
If your lips should strive to kiss
Her dear lips averse to bliss,
If your hands in wanton play
O'er her lovely limbs should stray;

She those kisses will withstand,
She'll repulse your daring hand,
While soft tremours swell her breast.
O blest night, and more than blest!

Now the unwilling nymph employs
Strife provoking amorous joys,
Strife that nurtures, that improves,
All the little tender loves;
And, in conflict with the maid,
Lends invigorating aid:
Then all o'er that neck so fair
O'er her breast, that may compare
With the ivory's purest white,
Breast that courts the enamour'd sight;
O'er her smooth, her well-turn'd thigh,
O'er the blissful regions nigh,
Far as the secret bower of love,
Let thy hand voluptuous rove:
While sweet kisses of delight,
Countless as the fires of night,
On her lips are fond imprest.
O blest night, night three times blest!

Let sweet speeches, framed with art,
Phrases fond that touch the heart,
Many a gentle murmur'd tale
Soft her listening ear assail;
Soft as zephyrs fan the groves;
Soft as turtles coo their loves;
Soft as swans their dying notes
Warble from their tuneful throats;
Till, half-conquer'd by the fires
Which the wanton god inspires,
Vanquish'd by the thrilling smart
Of his soul-subduing dart,
Less averse the maid shall prove,
Reconciled at length to love,
Shall to raptures half divine,
All her glowing frame resign:
Thou shalt clasp her neck's dear charms,
And by her enamour'd arms

2 E

Thy loved neck too shall be prest.
O blest night, O three times blest!

Then, oh then, thy raptured lip
Shall the tenderest kisses sip,
Kisses varied many a way,
As thy lingering lips shall play;
Then the gamesome maid shall prove
Equal in the sports of love,
Equal dalliance shall return,
And with mutual ardour burn:
Those dear lips that late with thine
She repugnant durst not join,
Shall their proffer'd kisses bring,
And to thine with transport cling;
While her soul in every kiss
Drinks a deeper draught of bliss.
Bolder grown from wanton play,
Now more wanton words she'll say;
Now more free her hands shall rove,
And with more licentious love
Thou, dear youth, shalt be carest.
O blest night, night far too blest!

Cupid beats the brisk alarms,
Venus calls, "To arms, to arms!"
This is now the time to prove
Grateful wounds, the wounds of love
Yes, stern Mars, thy mistress fair,
Not thy sister, guides this war,
Cypria, who delights to see
Newly-bleeding chastity;
She incites the conflict here,
Brandishes love's active spear,
And against the hostile maid
Gives the well-urged weapon aid.
Nor will either nimble foe
The delicious fight forego
Till their wasted vigour flies,
Till each frame all breathless lies,
Till the bliss-excited tide
Down their dewy limbs shall glide,

And the toil demands sweet rest.
O blest night, O far too blest !

Happy pair ! pursue such joy,
Still be love your dear employ,
Through the bliss-protracted day,
Through the night's voluptuous stay.
May a beauteous, lengthening race,
Crown, ere long, your fond embrace ;
Offsprings rise from offsprings fair,
Who shall soothe with duteous care
All their aged parents' pain,
And their faltering limbs sustain ;
And when life's sad scene they leave,
Their cold relics to the grave
Shall with filial sorrow bear.
Happy youth, and happy fair !   Nott.

THE SAME.

The hour is come, with pleasure crown'd,
Borne in eternal order round :
Hour of endearing looks and smiles ;
Hour of voluptuous sports and wiles ;
Hour fraught with fondly-murmuring sighs ;
Hour blest with softly-dying eyes ;
Hour with commingling kisses sweet ;
Hour of transporting bliss replete ;
Hour worthy ev'n of gods above ;
Hour worthy all-commanding Jove ;
For not a fairer-omen'd hour
Could promise the kind Gnidian power ; [1]
Not tender Cupid could bestow,
The boy with silver-splendid bow,
And golden wing ; delicious boy !
That sorrow still allays with joy.
Nor, wont at nuptials to preside,
She,[2] that of Jove is sister-bride !
Nor he,[3] on tuneful summit[4] born,
The god whom flowery wreaths adorn ;

---

[1] Venus.   [2] Juno.   [3] Hymen.   [4] Helicon.

2 E 2

Who blooming beauty tears away,
Bears off by force the charming prey,
From the reluctant mother tears,
To the rapacious lover bears.
Hour long desired! hour long delay'd!
Thrice happy youth! thrice happy maid!

　　Thrice happy youth! supremely blest,
Of every wish in one possest;
To thee the maid of form divine
Comes, seeming loth, but inly thine.
Such form as Juno's self might choose,
Nor yet the martial maid refuse,
(Though that th' ethereal sceptre sways,
And this the shining shield displays,)
Nor yet the Cyprian queen disdain,
Bent to re-seek the Phrygian swain,
And cause of beauty re-decide,
In shady vale of flowering Ide.
How sure to gain the golden prize,
(Though judged by less discerning eyes,)
She, in that matchless form array'd!
Thrice happy youth! thrice happy maid!

　　Thrice happy maid! supremely blest,
Of every wish in one possest;
To thee, on wings of love and truth,
Comes, all-devote, the raptured youth.
Thy bending neck with eager hold,
Thy waist, impatient to enfold.
While, for that hair of easy flow,
While, for that breast of virgin snow,
While, for that lip of rosy dye,
While, for that sweetly-speaking eye,
With silent passion he expires,
And burns with still consuming fires;
Now Phœbus, slow to quit the skies,
Now loit'ring Phœbe, slow to rise,
Persists, alternate, to upbraid.
Thrice happy youth! thrice happy maid!

　　Spare, youth, your vows, vain off'rings spare
Forbear your needless sighs, forbear!

Lo! Time, in ever-varying race,
Brings on at last the wish'd-for space.
Mild Venus, with propitious ears,
The sorrows of her votaries hears.
While Cynthius, down the western steeps,
Low plunges in Iberian deeps;
And quits the ample fields of air,
To his night-wandering sister's care,
Than whom, no light more grateful shines,
To souls which mutual love conjoins.
Not he that leads the stars along,
Brightest of all the glittering throng,
Hesper with golden torch display'd.
Thrice happy youth! thrice happy maid!

See where the maid, all-panting, lies,
(Ah! never more a maid to rise!)
And longs, yet trembles at thy tread;
Her cheeks suffused with decent red;
Expressing half her inward flame!
Half springing from ingenuous shame!
Tears from her eyes, perhaps, may steal,
Her joys the better to conceal;
Then sighs, with grief unreal fraught,
Then follow plaints of wrongs unthought.
But cease not thou with idle fears,
For all her plaints, or sighs, or tears.
Kiss'd be the tears from off her eyes;
With tender murmurs stopp'd her sighs;
With soothings soft her plaints allay'd.
Thrice happy youth! thrice happy maid!

The maid, in decent order placed,
With every bridal honour graced,
Through all her limbs begin to spread
The glowings of the genial bed;
And languid sleep dispose to take,
Did not the youth, more watchful, wake,
And the mild queen of fierce desire,
With warmth not disproportion'd, fire:
Taught hence, nor purpled kings to prize,
Nor scepter'd Jove, that rules the skies.

Soon for soft combats he prepares,
And gentle toils of amorous wars.
Declared, but with no loud alarms;
Begun, but with no dreaded arms;
Kisses! which, wanton as he strays,
He darts a thousand wanton ways,
At mouth or neck, at eyes or cheeks.
Him humbly she full oft bespeaks,
Entreats, " a helpless maid to spare!"
And begs, with trembling voice, "Forbear
Full oft his rudeness loudly blames,
His boundless insolence proclaims.
His lips, with lips averse, withstands,
With hands, restrains his roving hands.
Resistance sweet! delicious fight!
O night! O doubly-happy night!

Contention obstinate succeeds.
The tender Loves contention feeds;
By that redoubled ardour burns;
By that redoubled strength returns.
Now o'er her neck take nimble flight;
Her breast as spotless ivory white;
Her waist of gradual rising charms;
Soft-moulded legs; smooth-polish'd arms:
Search all the tracts, in curious sport,
Conductive to the Cyprian court.
Through all the dark recesses go,
And all the shady coverts know.
To this, unnumber'd kisses join,
Unnumber'd as the stars that shine,
Commingling rays of blended light.
O night! O doubly-happy night!

Then spare no blandishments of love;
Sounds, that with soft'ning flattery move;
Sighs, that with soothing murmur please,
The injured virgin to appease;
Such, as when Zephyr fans the grove,
Or coos the am'rous-billing dove;
Or sings the swan with tuneful breath,
Conscious of near approaching death;

Till, pierced by Cupid's powerful dart,
As by degrees relents her heart,
The virgin, less and less severe,
Quits, by degrees, her stubborn fear;
Now on your arms her neck reclines;
Now with her arms your neck entwines;
As Love's resistless flames incite.
O night! O doubly-happy night!

Sweet kisses shall reward your pains,
Kisses which no rude rapine stains;
From lips on swelling lips that swell;
From lips on dwelling lips that dwell;
That play return with equal play;
That bliss with equal bliss repay;
That vital stores, from either heart,
Imbibing, soul for soul impart;
Till now the maid, adventurous grown,
Attempts new frolics of her own;
Now suffers, strangers to the way,
Her far more daring hands to stray.
Now sports far more salacious seeks,
Now words far more licentious speaks;
Words that past sufferings well requite.
O night! O doubly-happy night!

To arms! to arms! now Cupid sounds.
Now is the time for grateful wounds.
Here Venus waves the nimble spear—
Venus is warlike goddess here.
Here not thy sister, Mars, presides,
Thy mistress in these conflicts prides;
While close engage the struggling foes,
And, restless, breast to breast oppose;
While, eager, this disputes the field,
And that alike disdains to yield;
Till, lo! in breathless transports tost,
Till in resistless raptures lost,
Their limbs with liquid dews distil;
Their hearts with pleasing horrors thrill;
And faint away in wild delight.
O night! O doubly-happy night!

Oh may you oft these sports renew,
And through long days and nights pursue!
With many an early moon begun;
Prolong'd to many a setting sun.
May a fair offspring crown your joys,
Of prattling girls, and smiling boys;
And yet another offspring rise,
Sweet objects to parental eyes,
The cares, assiduous to assuage,
That still solicit querulous age;
Careful your trembling limbs to stay,
That fail with unperceived decay;
Pious, when summon'd hence you go,
The last kind office to bestow;
Office with unfeign'd sorrow paid.
Thrice happy youth! thrice happy maid!

                                        OGLE

PIECES BY VARIOUS AUTHORS.

TO LYDIA.[1]

LYDIA, lovely girl, whose complexion far surpasses milk and lilies, or roses both red and white, or polished Indian ivory; display, fair girl, thy yellow hair, bright as burnished gold; display thy white neck, tapering finely from thy white shoulders; display thy starry eyes, and the black eyebrows arched above them; display thy rosy cheeks, suffused with the rich crimson of Tyre; stretch out thy lips, thy coral lips, give me sweet billing kisses. Thou suckest away part of my ravished soul; those kisses of thine pierce my heart; why dost thou suck my life-blood? Hide thy breasts, hide those twin balls, which begin to swell with compressed milk. Thy opened bosom diffuses aromatic sweets; delights exhale from every part of thee. Hide thy breasts, that rack me with their whiteness, and with the voluptuousness of thy snowy bosom. Cruel girl, dost thou not see that I languish? Wilt thou leave me thus half dead?

> LOVELY Lydia! lovely maid!
> Either rose in thee's display'd;
> Roses of a blushing red
> O'er thy lips and cheeks are shed;
> Roses of a paly hue
> In thy fairer charms we view.
> Now thy braided hair unbind;
> Now, luxuriant, unconfined,

---

[1] *To Lydia.*] This pretty little poem is commonly attributed to Cornelius Gallus, the unfortunate contemporary of Virgil; but the style is that of a much later age.

Let thy wavy tresses flow ;
Tresses bright, of burnish'd glow !
Bare thy iv'ry neck, my fair !
Now thy snowy shoulders bare ;
Bid the vivid lustre rise
In thy passion-streaming eyes ;
See, the lucent meteors gleam !
See, they speak the wishful flame !
And how gracefully above,
Modell'd from the bow of Love,
Are thy arching brows display'd,
Soft'ning in a sable shade !
Let a warmer crimson streak
The velvet of thy downy cheek :
Let thy lips, that breathe perfume,
Deeper purple now assume :
Give me little billing kisses,
Intermixt with murm'ring blisses,
Soft, my love !—my angel, stay !—
Soft !—you suck my breath away ;
Drink the life-drops of my heart ;
Draw my soul from every part :
Scarce my senses can sustain
So much pleasure, so much pain !
Hide thy broad, voluptuous breast !
Hide that balmy heaven of rest !
See, to feast th' enamour'd eyes,
How the snowy hillocks rise !
Parted by the luscious vale,
Whence luxurious sweets exhale :
Nature framed thee but t' inspire
Never-ending, fond desire !
Again, above its envious vest,
See, thy bosom heaves confest !
Hide the rapt'rous, dear delight !
Hide it from my ravish'd sight !
Hide it !—for through all my soul
Tides of madd'ning transport roll :
Venting now th' impassion'd sigh,
See me languish, see me die !

Tear not from me then thy charms!
Snatch, oh, snatch me to thy arms!
With a life-inspiring kiss,
Wake my sinking soul to bliss! NOTT.

THE SAME.

LYDIA! girl of prettiest mien,
And fairest skin, that e'er were seen:
Lilies, cream, thy cheeks disclose;
The ruddy and the milky rose;
Smooth thy limbs as ivory shine,
Burnish'd from the Indic mine.
Oh, sweet girl! those ringlets spread,
Long and loose, from all thy head;
Glistening like gold in yellow light
O'er thy falling shoulders white.
Show, sweet girl! thy starry eyes,
And black-bent brows that arching rise:
Show, sweet girl! thy rose-bloom cheeks,
Which Tyre's vermilion scarlet streaks:
Drop those pouting lips to mine,
Those ripe, those coral lips of thine.
Give me, soft, a velvet kiss,
Dove-like glued in searching bliss:
You suck my breath! O heaven! remove
Your lips—I faint—my sweetest love!
Your kisses—hold! they pierce my heart:
I feel thee in each vital part:
Hold—thou wicked creature! why
Suck my life's blood thus cruelly?
Hide those breasts, that rise and fall,
Those twinn'd apples, round and small;
Full with balmy juices flowing,
Now just budding, heaving, growing;
Breathing from their broaden'd zone
Opening sweets of cinnamon.
Delicacies round thee rise:
Hide those globes—they wound mine eyes
With their white and dazzling glow,
With their luxury of snow!

Cruel ! see you not I languish,
Thrilling with ecstatic anguish ?
Do you leave me ; leave me lying,
Almost fainting, almost dying ?   ELTON.

TO LESBIA.

BY ANDREAS FRANCISCUS LANDESIUS.

WHILST Lesbia (she who stole young Cupid's bow and torch) caresses me with a salacious kiss, and assails and excites me with many a bite, I burn in every fibre of my frame. Not so many are the stars that shine in the cloudless sky, not so many are the flushing clusters of the vine, as are the delights and desires that fill me with pungent bliss.[1] But, my Lesbia, say, dear one, why do you caress me only with a salacious kiss, and assail and excite me with many a bite ? Oh let me hold you on a voluptuous bed, let me hold you in my straining arms, fainting in the fervour of love ! And if you faint in the fervour of love, surely you will welcome such a death.

WHEN beauteous Lesbia fires my melting soul
(She who the torch and bow from Cupid stole)
By many a smile, by many an ardent kiss,
And with her teeth imprints the tell-tale bliss ;
Through all my frame the madding transport glows,
Through every vein the tide of rapture flows.
As many stars as o'er heaven's concave shine,
Or clusters as adorn the fruitful vine ;
So many blandishments, voluptuous joys,
T' inflame my breast, the wily maid employs.
But, dearest Lesbia ! gentle mistress ! say,
Why thus d' ye wound my lips in amorous play ?
With kisses, smiles, and every wanton art,
Why raise the burning fever of my heart ?

---

[1] *Fill me with pungent bliss.*] Accensum exacuunt beatulumque. It is not easy to express the meaning of these words with the brevity aimed at in these prose versions. Lesbia's caresses set him on fire (accensum); they steep him in bliss (beatulum); and they put the sharpest edge to his desires (exacuunt).

Let us, my love! on yon soft couch reclined,
Each other's arms around each other twined,
Yield to the pleasing force of strong desire,
And panting, struggling, both at once expire!
For oh, my Lesbia! sure that death is sweet,
Which lovers in the fond contention meet!   NOTT.

KISS XVI. OF BONEFONIUS.

WHILST I closely press your lips, my girl, and eagerly inhale your fragrant breath, I seem to myself one of the gods,
or something more exalted and blest.   Presently, when you
snatch yourself away, I, who had deemed myself one of the
supernals, or something more exalted and blest, suddenly find
myself cast down to the shades of Orcus, or to some lower
and more dismal depths.

Clasp'd, sweet maid! in thy embrace;
While I view thy smiling face,
And the sweets with rapture sip,
Flowing from thy honey'd lip;
Then I taste, in heavenly state,
All that's happy, all that's great:
But when you forsake my arms,
And displeasure clouds your charms,
Sudden I, who proved so late
All that's happy, all that's great,
Prove the tortures of a ghost,
Wand'ring on the Stygian coast.   NOTT.

THE PASTIME OF VENUS.

ONCE, after elaborate meditation, the Cyprian goddess fabri-
cated kisses with lascivious hand.   She tempered ambrosial
juices with mystic skill, and tinctured her fragrant work with
nectar.   Then she added to it a part of the honey which
roguish Love had stolen, not with impunity, from the hive,
and mixed with it odours shaken from violet leaves, and multitudes of spoils from summer roses.   Also she added allure-

ments, and thousands of prettinesses, and all the joys contained in her own magic girdle. Of these ingredients the goddess composed kisses. Taste fair Chloe's lips, and you find them all there.

> INTENT to frame some new design of bliss,
> The wanton Cyprian queen composed a kiss:
> An ample portion of ambrosial juice
> With mystic skill she temper'd first for use:
> This done, her infant work was well bedew'd
> With choicest nectar; and o'er all she strew'd
> Part of that honey, which sly Cupid stole
> Much to his cost,[1] and blended with the whole;
> Then, that soft scent which from the violet flows,
> She mixt with spoils of many a vernal rose;
> Each gentle blandishment in love we find,
> Each graceful winning gesture next she join'd;
> And all those joys that in her zone abound,
> Made up the kiss, and the rich labour crown'd:
> Considering now what beauteous nymph might prove
> Worthy the gift, and worthy of her love,
> She fixt on Chloe, as her fav'rite maid;
> To whom the goddess sweetly-smiling said,
> "Take this, my fair! to perfect every grace,
> And on thy lips the fragrant blessing place."   NOTT.

[1] *Sly Cupid stole*, &c.]   See the nineteenth Idyllium of Theocritus, to which this alludes.

THE

LOVE EPISTLES

OF

ARISTÆNETUS:

Translated from the Greek into English Metre.

BY

RICHARD BRINSLEY SHERIDAN AND MR. HALHED

" —————— Love refines
The thoughts, and heart enlarges ; hath his seat
In reason, and is judicious."—

MILTON's Paradise Lost. book viii.

PREFACE.

THE critics have not yet decided at what time Aristænetus appeared, or indeed whether or not he ever existed; for, as he is mentioned by no ancient author, it has been conjectured that there never was such a person, and that the name prefixed to the first Epistle was taken by the publisher for that of the writer. This work was never known nor heard of till Sambucus gave it to the world in the year 1566; since which time there have been several editions of it published at Paris, where the book seems to have been held in greater estimation than amongst us. As to the real date of its composition, we have nothing but conjecture to offer. By the twenty-sixth Epistle it should seem that the author lived in the time of the later emperors, when Byzantium was called New Rome: and therein mention is made of the pantomime actor Caramallus, who was contemporary with Sidonius Apollinaris.

These Epistles are certainly terse, elegant, and very poetical, both in language and sentiment; yet, pleasing as they are, they have scarcely any thing original in them, being a cento from the writings of Plato, Lucian, Philostratus, and almost all the ancient Greek authors, whose sentences are most agreeably woven together, and applied to every passion incident to love. This circumstance, though it may lessen our idea of the invention of the author, should not in the least depreciate the performance, as it opens to us a new source of entertainment, in contemplating the taste of the composer in the selection of his sentences, and his ingenuity in the application of them, whilst the authority and reputation of the works from whence these sweets are extracted, adds dignity to the subject on which they are bestowed.

Having said thus much of the original, custom seems to demand some apology for the translation. And, first, it may to some appear a whimsical undertaking to give a metrical translation of a prosaic author; but the English reader, it is to be presumed, will not find any deficiency of poetical thoughts on that account, however the diction may have suffered by passing through unworthy hands; and to such as are acquainted with that elegant luxuriance which characterizes the Greek prose, this point will not need a solution. Nor can it be deemed derogatory from the merit of our own language to affirm, that the superiority of the Greek in this respect is so forcible, that even the most trifling of these Epistles must have suffered considerably both in spirit and simplicity, if committed to the languid formality of an English prosaic translation.

The ingenious Tom Brown has translated, or rather imitated, some select pieces from this collection, but he either totally misconceived the spirit of his author, or was very unequal to the execution of it. He presents you, it is true, with a portrait of the author, and a portrait that has some resemblance to him; but it is painted in a bad attitude, and placed in a disadvantageous light. In the original, the language is neat, though energetic; it is elegant as well as witty. Brown has failed in both; and

2 F

though a strict adherence to these points in a metrical translation may be esteemed difficult, yet it is hoped that the English dress in which Aristænetus is at present offered to the public, will appear to become him more than any he has ever worn in this country.

It were absurd to pretend that this translation is perfectly literal; the very genius of prose and verse forbid it; and the learned reader who shall consult the original, will find many reasons for the impropriety as well as difficulty of following the author's expressions too closely. Some things there were which it was scarce possible to handle in verse, and they are entirely omitted, or paraphrastically imitated; many passages have been softened as indelicate, some suppressed as indecent. But beside these allowable deviations, a still further licence has been taken; for where the subject would admit of it, many new ideas are associated with the original substance, yet so far affecting the author's proper style, that its native simplicity might not be obscured by their introduction. And two or three Epistles there are in this collection which must shelter themselves under the name of Aristænetus, without any other title to his protection than that of adhering to the subject of the several Epistles which they have supplanted. The only apology which can be offered for this, is an avowal that the object of this translation was not so much to bring to light the merit of an undistinguished and almost unknown ancient, as to endeavour to introduce into our language a species of poetry not frequently attempted, and but very seldom with success; that species which has been called the "simplex munditiis" in writing, where the thoughts are spirited and fanciful without quaintness, and the style simple, yet not inelegant. Though the merit of succeeding in this point should not be given to the present attempt, yet it may in some measure become serviceable to the cause, by inciting others of better taste and abilities to endeavour to redeem our language from the imputation of barbarity in this respect.

As to the many different measures which are here introduced, something beside the translator's caprice may be urged in their favour. For by a variation of metre, the style almost necessarily undergoes an alteration; and in general, the particular strain of each Epistle suggested the particular measure in which it is written. Had they been all in one kind of verse, they would have fatigued, they might have disgusted. At present, it is hoped that some analogy will be found between the mode of passion in each Epistle and the versification by which it is expressed; at the same time that a variety of metres, like a variety of prospects on a road, will conduct the reader with greater satisfaction through the whole stage, short though it be.

The digression in the 12th Epistle having been censured as being of an immoral tendency, the writer would gladly have omitted it, had he had an earlier intelligence of the republication of these Epistles: however, he hopes the note annexed to that piece will point out another interpretation. Though from the pen of a lover, a light thought, or hasty expression, can scarcely be deemed out of character; or, in trifles of this kind, be of importance enough to demand a suppression. To a truly virtuous mind the voice of libertinism is the voice of folly; and a vicious one needs no instigator: the former may even be diverted at its extravagance; the latter cannot be injured by its levity.

H(ALHED). S(HERIDAN).

LOVE EPISTLES OF ARISTÆNETUS.

EPISTLE I. LAIS.

ARISTÆNETUS TO PHILOCALUS.[1]

BLEST with a form of heavenly frame,[2]
  Blest with a soul beyond that form,
With more than mortal ought to claim,
  With all that can a mortal warm,
Laïs was from her birth design'd
To charm, yet triumph o'er mankind.
There Nature, lavish of her store,
Gave all she could, and wish'd for more ;
Whilst Venus gazed, her form was such !
Wondering how Nature gave so much ;
Yet added she new charms, for she
  Could add—" A fourth bright grace," she said,
" A fourth, beyond the other three,
  Shall raise my power in this sweet maid."
Then Cupid, to enhance the prize,
  Gave all his little arts could reach :
To dart Love's language from the eyes
  He taught—'twas all was left to teach.

---

[1] There is a studied propriety in the very names of the supposed correspondents in these Epistles ; having in the original this peculiar beauty, that generally one, and often both of them, bear an agreeable allusion to the subject of the several letters to which they are prefixed.

[2] In this letter Aristænetus describes the beauties of his mistress to his friend. This description differs in one circumstance from the usual poetic analysis of beauty, which is this, that (if we except the epithets " ruby," " snowy," &c., which could not well have been avoided) the lady it paints would be really beautiful ; whereas it is generally said, " that a negro would be handsome, compared to woman in poetical dress."

O fairest of the virgin band !
Thou master-piece of Nature's hand !
So like the Cyprian queen, I'd swear
Her image fraught with life were there :
But silent all ; and silent be,
That you may hear her praise from me :
I'll paint my Laïs' form ; nor aid
I ask—for I have seen the maid.

Her cheek with native crimson glows,
But crimson soften'd by the rose :
'Twas Hebe's self bestow'd the hue,
Yet health has added something too :
But if an over-tinge there be,
Impute it to her modesty.
Her lips of deeper red, how thin !
How nicely white the teeth within !
Her nose how taper to the tip !
And slender as her ruby lip :
Her brows in arches proudly rise,
As conscious of her powerful eyes :
Those eyes, majestic-black, display
The lustre of the god of day ;
And by the contrast of the white,
The jetty pupil shines more bright.
There the glad Graces keep their court,
And in the liquid mirror sport.
Her tresses, when no fillets bind,
Wanton luxurious in the wind ;
Like Dian's auburn locks they shone,
But Venus wreath'd them like her own.
Her neck, which well with snow might vie,
Is form'd with nicest symmetry ;
In native elegance secure
     The most obdurate heart to wound ;
But she, to make her conquests sure,
     With sparkling gems bedecks it round :
With gems that, ranged in order due,
Present the fair one's name to view.[1]

---

[1] *With gems*, &c.] This conceit was formerly reckoned a peculiar
elegance in a lady's dress.

Her light-spun robes in every part
Are fashion'd with the nicest art,
T' improve her stature, and to grace
The polish'd limbs which they embrace.
How beautiful she looks when drest!
　But view her freed from this disguise,
Stript of th' unnecessary vest—
　'Tis Beauty's self before your eyes.

　How stately doth my Laïs go!
With studied step, composedly slow;
Superb, as some tall mountain fir,
Whom Zephyr's wing doth slightly stir:
(For surely Beauty is allied
By Nature very near to Pride:)
The groves indeed mild breezes move,
But her the gentler gales of Love.
From her the pencil learns its dye—
The rosy lip, the sparkling eye;
And bids the pictured form assume
Bright Helen's mien, and Hebe's bloom.
But how shall I describe her breast?
　That now first swells with panting throb
To burst the fond embracing vest,
　And emulate her snow-white robe.
So exquisitely soft her limbs!
That not a bone but pliant seems;
As if th' embrace of Love—so warm!
Would quite dissolve her beauteous form.
But when she speaks!—good heavens! e'en now
　Methinks I hear my fav'rite song;
E'en yet with Love's respect I bow
　To all th' enchantment of her tongue.
Her voice most clear, yet 'tis not strong;
Her periods full, though seldom long;
With wit, good-natured wit, endow'd;
Fluent her speech, but never loud.
Witness, ye Loves! witness; for well I know
　To her you 've oft attention given;
Oft pensile flutter'd on your wings of snow
　To waft each dying sound to heaven.

Ah! sure this fair enchantress found
The zone which all the Graces bound:
Not Momus could a blemish find
Or in her person or her mind.—
But why should Beauty's goddess spare
To me this all-accomplish'd fair?
I for her charms did ne'er decide,[1]
As Paris erst on lofty Ide;
I pleased her not in that dispute;
I gave her not the golden fruit:
Then why the Paphian queen so free?
Why grant the precious boon to me?
Venus! what sacrifice, what prayer
   Can show my thanks for such a prize!
—To bless a mortal with a fair,
   Whose charms are worthy of the skies.

She too, like Helen, can inspire
Th' unfeeling heart of age with fire;
Can teach their lazy blood to move,
And light again the torch of love.[2]
"Oh!" cry the old, "that erst such charms
Had bloom'd to bless our youthful arms;
Or that we now were young, to show
How we could love—some years ago!"

Have I not seen th' admiring throng
For hours attending to her song?
Whilst from her eyes such lustre shone,
It added brightness to their own:
Sweet grateful beams of thanks they'd dart,
That show'd the feelings of her heart.
Silent we've sat, with rapt'rous gaze!
Silent—but all our thoughts were praise:
Each turn'd with pleasure to the rest;
And this the prayer that warm'd each breast:

[1] *I for her charms did ne'er decide.*] This alludes to the well-know
contest between Juno, Venus, and Minerva, for the golden apple.
[2] *She too, like Helen, &c.*]
   Οὐ Νέμεσις, Τρῶας καὶ εὐκνημῖας Ἀχαιοὺς
   Τοιῇ δ' ἀμφὶ γυναικὶ πολὺν χρόνον ἄλγεα πάσχειν,
   Αἰνῶς ἀθανάτῃσι θεῇς εἰς ὦπα ἔοικεν.   Hom.

" Thus may that lovely bloom for ever glow,
    Thus may those eyes for ever shine !
Oh may'st thou never feel the scourge of woe !
    Oh never be misfortune thine !
Ne'er may the crazy hand of pining care
    Thy mirth and youthful spirits break !
Never come sickness, or love-cross'd despair,
    To pluck the roses from thy cheek !
But bliss be thine—the cares which love supplies,
    Be all the cares that you shall dread ;
The graceful drop, now glist'ning in your eyes,
    Be all the tears you ever shed."

    But hush'd be now thy am'rous song,
And yield a theme, thy praises wrong :
Just to her charms, thou canst not raise
Thy notes—but must I cease to praise ?
Yes—I will cease—for she 'll inspire
Again the lay, who strung my lyre.
Then fresh I 'll paint the charming maid,
    Content, if she my strain approves ;
Again my lyre shall lend its aid,
    And dwell upon the theme it loves.

EPISTLE II.   THE PLEASING CONSTRAINT.[1]

In a snug little court as I stood t' other day,
And caroll'd the loitering minutes away ;
Came a brace of fair nymphs, with such beautiful faces,
That they yielded in number alone to the Graces :
Disputing they were, and that earnestly too,
When thus they address'd me as nearer they drew :
" So sweet is your voice, and your numbers so sweet,
Such sentiment join'd with such harmony meet ;
Each note which you raise finds its way to our hearts,
Where Cupid engraves it wi' the point of his darts :
But oh ! by these strains, which so deeply can pierce,
Inform us for whom you intended your verse :

---

[1] This sufficiently explains itself. It has no names prefixed to it in
the original, and is very literally translated.

'Tis for her, she affirms—I maintain 'tis for me—
And we often pull caps in asserting our plea."[1]

"Why, ladies," cried I, "you're both handsome, 'tis true,
But cease your dispute, I love neither of you;
My life on another dear creature depends;
Her I hasten to visit:—so kiss and be friends."
"Oh ho!" said they, "now you convince us quite clear,
For no pretty woman lives anywhere here—
That's plainly a sham.   Now, to humour us both,
You shall swear you love neither; so come, take your oath."

I laughing replied, "'Tis tyrannical dealing
To make a man swear, when 'tis plain he's not willing."

"Why, friend, we've long sought thy fair person to seize;
And think you we'll take such excuses as these?
No, 'twas chance brought you hither, and here you shall stay;—
Help, Phædra! to hold, or he'll sure get away."
Thus spoken, to keep me between 'em they tried;
'Twas a pleasing constraint, and I gladly complied.
If I struggled, 'twas to make 'em imprison me more,
And strove—but for shackles more tight than before;
But think not I'll tell how the minutes were spent;
You may think what you please—but they both were content.

EPISTLE III.   THE GARDEN OF PHYLLION.[2]

PHILOPLATANUS TO ANTHOCOME.

BLEST was my lot—ah! sure 'twas bliss, my friend,
The day—by heavens! the live-long day to spend
With Love and my Limona!   Hence! in vain
Would mimic Fancy bring those scenes again;

---

[1] *And we often pull caps*, &c.]   This is almost literally the Greek expression: Καὶ διὰ σὲ φιλονείκως καὶ μέγρι τριχῶν συμπλεκόμεθα πολλάκις ἀλλήλαις.

[2] This is surely a most elegant descriptive pastoral, and hardly inferior to any of Theocritus.   The images are all extremely natural and simple, though the expression is glowing and luxurious: they are selected from a variety of Greek authors, but chiefly from the Phædrus of Plato.— What intersertions there may be, have been before apologized for; but their detection shall be left to the sagacity or inquisition of the reader. The case is the same with the first Epistle, and indeed with most of them.

In vain delighted memory tries to raise
My doubtful song, and aid my will to praise.
In vain !   Nor fancy strikes, nor memory knows,
The little springs from whence those joys arose.
Yet come, coy Fancy, sympathetic maid !
Yes, I will ask, I will implore thy aid :
For I would tell my friend whate'er befell ;
Whate'er I saw, whate'er I did, I 'll tell.
But what I felt—sweet Venus ! there inspire
My lay, or wrap his soul in all thy fire.

Bright rose the morn, and bright remain'd the day;
The mead was spangled with the bloom of May :
We on the bank of a sweet stream were laid,
With blushing rose and lowly violets spread ;
Fast by our side a spreading plane-tree grew,
And waved its head, that shone with morning dew.
The bank acclivous rose, and swell'd above—
The frizzled moss a pillow for my love.
Trees with their ripen'd stores glow'd all around,
The loaded branches bow'd upon the ground ;
Sure the fair virgins of Pomona's train
In those glad orchards hold their fertile reign.
The fruit nectareous, and the scented bloom
Wafted on Zephyr's wing their rich perfume ;
A leaf I bruised—what grateful scents arose ![1]
Ye gods ! what odours did a leaf disclose.
Aloft each elm slow waved its dusky top,
The willing vine embraced the sturdy prop :
And while we stray'd the ripen'd grape to find,
Around our necks the clasping tendrils twined ;
I with a smile would tell th' entangled fair,
I envied e'en the vines a lodging there ;
Then twist them off, and soothe with am'rous play
Her breasts, and kiss each rosy mark away.
Cautious Limona trod—her step was slow—
For much she fear'd the skulking fruits below ;
Cautious—lest haply she, with slipp'ry tread,
Might tinge her snowy feet with vinous red.

[1] *A leaf I bruised*, &c.]   Nothing can be more rural, and at the same
time more forcible, than this image ; where the universal fragrance of the
spot is not expatiated on, but marked at once by this simple specimen.

Around with critic glance we view'd the store,
And oft rejected what we'd praised before;
This would my love accept, and this refuse,
For varied plenty puzzled us to choose.
" Here may the bunches tasteless, immature,
Unheeded learn to blush, and swell secure;
In richer garb yon turgid clusters stand,
And glowing purple tempts the plund'ring hand."
" Then reach 'em down," she said, " for you can reach
And cull, with daintiest hand, the best of each."
Pleased I obey'd, and gave my love—whilst she
Return'd sweet thanks, and pick'd the best for me:
'Twas pleasing sure—yet I refused her suit,
But kiss'd the liberal hand that held the fruit.

Hard by the ever-jovial harvest train
Hail the glad season of Pomona's reign;
With rustic song around her fane they stand,
And lisping children join the choral band:
They busily intent now strive to aid,
Now first they're taught th' hereditary trade:
'Tis theirs to class the fruits in order due,
For pliant rush to search the meadow through;
To mark if chance unbruised a wind-fall drop,
Or teach the infant vine to know its prop.
And haply too some aged sire is there,
To check disputes, and give to each his share;
With feeble voice their little work he cheers,
Smiles at their toil, and half forgets his years.
" Here let the pippin, fretted o'er with gold,
In fost'ring straw defy the winter's cold;
The hardier russet here will safely keep,
And dusky rennet with its crimson cheek;
But mind, my boys, the mellow pear to place
In soft enclosure, with divided space;
And mindful most how lies the purple plum,
Nor soil, with heedless touch, its native bloom."

Intent they listen'd to th' instructing lord;
But most intent to glean their own reward.

Now turn, my loved Limona, turn and view
How changed the scene! how elegantly new!

Mark how yon vintager enjoys his toil ;
Glows with flush red, and Bacchanalian smile :
His slipp'ry sandals burst the luscious vine,
And splash alternate in the new-born wine.
Not far the lab'ring train, whose care supplies
The trodden press, and bids fresh plenty rise.
The teeming boughs that bend beneath their freight,
One busy peasant eases of the weight ;
One climbs to where th' aspiring summits shoot ;
Beneath, a hoary sire receives the fruit.

Pleased we admired the jovial bustling throng,
Blest e'en in toil !—but we admired not long.
For calmer joys we left the busy scene,
And sought the thicket and the stream again ;
For sacred was the fount, and all the grove
Was hallow'd kept, and dedicate to love.
Soon gentle breezes, freshen'd from the wave,
Our temples fann'd, and whisper'd us to lave.
The stream itself seem'd murm'ring at our feet
Sweet invitation from the noon-day heat.
We bathed—and while we swam, so clear it flow'd,
That every limb the crystal mirror show'd.
But my love's bosom oft deceived my eye,
Resembling those fair fruits that glided by ;
For when I thought her swelling breast to clasp,[1]
An apple met my disappointed grasp.
Delightful was the stream itself—I swear,
By those glad nymphs who make the founts their care,
It was delightful :—but more pleasing still,
When sweet Limona sported in the rill :
For her soft blush such sweet reflection gave,
It tinged with rosy hues the pallid wave.
Thus, thus delicious was the murm'ring spring,
Nor less delicious the cool zephyr's wing ;

---

[1] *For when I thought, &c.*] This allusion seems forced : but the ancients had an apple which came from Cydon, a town of Crete, and was
called Cydonian, that, from its size and beautiful colour, might be said
to resemble a woman's breast : and the allusion is frequent in the old
poets. In the eighteenth of these Epistles, too, we meet with the κυδώ-
νιον μῆλον.

Which mild allay'd the sun's meridian power,
And swept the fragrant scent from every flower;
A scent, that feasted my transported sense,
Like that Limona's sweet perfumes dispense:
But still, my love, superior thine, I swear—
At least thy partial lover thinks they are.

Near where we sat, full many a gladd'ning sound,
Beside the rustling breeze, was heard around:
The little grasshopper essay'd its song,
As if 'twould emulate the feather'd throng:
Still lisp'd it uniform—yet now and then
It something chirp'd, and skipp'd upon the green.
Aloft the sprightly warblers fill'd the grove;
Sweet native melody! sweet notes of love!
While nightingales their artless strains essay'd,
The air, methought, felt cooler in the glade:
A thousand feather'd throats the chorus join'd,
And held harmonious converse with mankind.

Still in mine eye the sprightly songsters play,
Sport on the wing, or twitter on the spray;
On foot alternate rest their little limbs,
Or cool their pinions in the gliding streams;
Surprise the worm, or sip the brook aloof,
Or watch the spider weave his subtle woof.—
We the meantime discoursed in whispers low,
Lest haply speech disturb the rural show.

Listen.—Another pleasure I display,
That help'd delightfully the time away.
From distant vales, where bubbles from its source
A crystal rill, they dug a winding course:
See! through the grove a narrow lake extends,
Crosses each plot, to each plantation bends;
And while the fount in new meanders glides,
The forest brightens with refreshing tides.
Towards us they taught the new-born stream to flow,
Towards us it crept irresolute and slow:
Scarce had the infant current trickled by,[1]
When lo! a wondrous fleet attracts our eye:

---

[1] *Scarce had*, &c.] This is an excessively pretty image. The water

Laden with draughts might greet a monarch's tongue,
The mimic navigation swam along.
Hasten, ye ship-like goblets, down the vale,
Your freight a flagon, and a leaf your sail.[1]
Oh may no envious rush thy course impede,
Or floating apple stop thy tide-borne speed.
His mildest breath a gentle zephyr gave;
The little vessels trimly stemm'd the wave:
Their precious merchandise to land they bore,
And one by one resign'd the balmy store.
Stretch but a hand, we boarded them, and quaft
With native luxury the temper'd draught.
For where they loaded the nectareous fleet,
The goblet glow'd with too intense a heat;
Cool'd by degrees in these convivial ships,
With nicest taste it met our thirsty lips.

Thus in delight the flowery path we trod
To Venus sacred, and the rosy god:
Here might we kiss, here Love secure might reign,
And revel free, with all his am'rous train.—
And we did kiss, my friend, and Love was there,
And smooth'd the rustic couch that held my fair.
Like a spring-mead with scented blossoms crown'd,[2]
Her head with choicest wreaths Limona bound:
But Love, sweet Love! his sacred torch so bright
Had fann'd, that, glowing from the rosy light,
A blush (the print of a connubial kiss,
The conscious tattler of consummate bliss)
Still flush'd upon her cheek; and well might show
The choicest wreaths she'd made, how they should glow;

bailiff dug a small water-course, which came by the feet of these people
in the garden; and the stream had scarce passed by them when the
servants sent down several drinking vessels in the shape of ships, which
held warm liquor so nicely tempered, that the coolness of the water which
encompassed it in its passage, was just sufficient to render it palatable
when it arrived at the port of destination.

[1] *Your freight a flagon*, &c.] In the original, this luxurious image
is pursued so far, that the very leaf, which is represented as the sail of
the vessel, is particularized as of a medicinal nature, capable of preventing
any ill effects the wine might produce.

[2] *Like a spring-mead*, &c.] The word λειμων signifies a meadow: and
the author takes occasion to play upon it, by saying, that Limona crowned
herself with these flowers, to look like the meadow in which they grew.

Might every flower with kindred bloom o'erspread,
And tinge the vernal rose with deeper red.

But come, my friend, and share my happy lot:
The bounteous Phyllion owns this blissful spot;
Phyllion, whose gen'rous care to all extends,
And most is blest while he can bless his friends.
Then come, and quickly come; but with thee bring
The nymph, whose praises oft I've heard thee sing—
The blooming Myrtala; she'll not refuse
To tread the solitude her swain shall choose.
Thy sight will all my busy schemes destroy,
I'll dedicate another day to joy,
When social converse shall the scene improve,
And sympathy bestow new charms on love.
Then shall th' accustom'd bank a couch be made;
Once more the nodding plane shall lend its shade;
Once more I'll view Pomona's jovial throng;
Once more the birds shall raise the sprightly song;
Again the little stream be taught to flow;
Again the little fleet its balm bestow;
Again I'll gaze upon Limona's charms,
And sink transported in her quiv'ring arms;
Again my cheek shall glow upon her breast;
Again she'll yield, and I again be blest.

EPISTLE IV. THE EXPERIMENT.[1]

PHILOCHORUS TO POLYÆNUS.

As Hippias t' other day and I
    Walk'd arm and arm, he said,
"That pretty creature dost thou spy,
    Who leans upon her maid?

"She's tall, and has a comely shape,
    And treads well too, I swear:
Come on—by this good light we'll scrape
    Acquaintance with the fair."

[1] In this letter a man describes the excellence of his friend in discovering the particular dispositions of the fair sex.

Good God! cried I, she is not game,
   I'm sure, for you or me:
Do nothing rashly—you're to blame;
   She's modest, you may see.

But he, who knew all womankind,
   Thus answer'd with a sneer:
" You're quite a novice, friend, I find—
   There's nothing modest here.

" A virtuous dame this hour, no doubt,
   Would choose to walk the streets;
Especially so dizen'd out,
   And smile on all she meets.

" Her rings, her bracelets, her perfumes,
   Her wanton actions, prove
The character which she assumes,
   And that her trade is love.

" See now, she fidgets with her vest—
   To settle it, be sure,
And not at all to show her breast,
   Nor wishing to allure.

" Her robe tuck'd up with nicest care—
   But that's to show she's neat;
And though her legs are half-way bare,
   She means to hide her feet.

" But see! she turns to look behind,
   And laughs, I'll take my oath:
Come on—I warrant we shall find
   The damsel nothing loth."

So up he march'd, and made his bow—
   No sooner off his hat,
But, lover-like, he 'gan to vow,
   And soon grew intimate.

But first premised the ways were rough—
   " Madam, for fear of harm,
I beg "—so cleverly enough
   He made her take his arm.

Then—" Fairest, for thy beauty's sake,
   Which long has fired my breast,

Permit me to your maid to make
 A single short request!

" And yet you know what I'd require,
 And wherefore I apply:
Nought unrequited I desire,
 But gold the boon shall buy.

" I'll give, my fairest, what you please—
 You'll not exact, I'm sure:
Then deign, bright charmer, deign to ease
 The torments I endure."

Assent sat smiling in her eyes;
 Her lily hand he seized;
Nor feign'd she very great surprise,
 Nor look'd so much displeased.

She blush'd a little too, methought,
 As though she should refuse—
But women, I've been told, are taught
 To blush whene'er they choose.

Hippias was now quite hand in glove
 With Miss, and firmly bent
To take her to the bower of Love,
 He whisper'd as he went—

" Well, Phil, say now whose judgment's best?
 Was I so very wrong?
You saw, not eagerly I press'd,
 Nor did I press her long.

" But you are ignorant, I see,
 So follow, and improve;
For few, I ween, can teach like me
 The mysteries of Love."

EPISTLE V. THE EXPEDIENT.[1]

ALCIPHRON TO LUCIAN.

T' OTHER day Charidemus a feast did prepare,
 And with all his acquaintances fill'd up the room:

[1] The writer here describes an ingenious device practised by a lady of
gallantry to deceive a suspicious husband.

'Mong the rest, (for you know his tendresse for the fair,)
    Another man's wife he persuaded to come.

The guests were all seated, when in comes our spark,
    Introducing to table a musty old dad,
Whom as soon as the lady had time to remark,
    To another apartment she scuttled like mad.

"Charidemus," said she, "do you know what you've done?
    That old fellow's my husband just now you brought in:
I shall here be discover'd, as sure as a gun,
    By the cloak I pull'd off, and which hangs on a pin.

"But if you can assist me, and privately send
    That cloak to my house, with a dish of your meat,
I've a trick that shall quickly his jealousy end;
    His suspicions I'll 'scape, and his vigilance cheat."

Away then she slipt, and got quick to her house,
    Then sent for a gossip, her help to implore;
And they'd scarce fix'd their plan the old cuckold to chouse,
    When blust'ring and swearing he came to the door.

He cried, while he sought for his poignard to stab her,
    "No more shall you shame me;—your cloak show'd your
        pranks."—
But while he was storming thus, in pops her neighbour,
    The cloak to return to its owner with thanks.

"I'm come to acknowledge your favour," she said,
    "And some prog from the feast have I brought with me
        here:
I knew that at home all the ev'ning you stay'd,
    So was willing to give you a taste of our cheer."

The silly curmudgeon grew meek as a lamb,
    On hearing this story, and seeing the meat;
For pardon he sued from his retrograde dame,
    And bow'd with contrition quite down to her feet

He vow'd that he ne'er would suspect her again,
    If now she'd accept his most humble submission;
And swore Dian herself sent the old woman in,
    To show him the folly of groundless suspicion.

EPISTLE VI. THE CONSOLATION.[1]

HERMOCRATES TO EUPHORION.[2]

Says a girl to her nurse, "I've a tale to unfold,
    Of utmost concern to us both ;
But first you must swear not to blab when you're told."
    —Nurse greedily swallow'd the oath.

"I've lost, my dear mother," the innocent said,
    "What should be a virgin's chief pride."—
I wish you had seen what a face the dame made,
    And heard how she blubber'd and cried.

"Hush, for God's sake," says Miss, in a whispering tone,
    The people will hear you within ;
You have sworn to discover my secret to none,
    Then why such a horrible din ?

"My virtue long all opposition withstood,
    And scorn'd at Love's efforts to flinch ;
It retreated at last—but as slow as it could,
    Disputing the ground inch by inch.

"In vain to my aid did I reason invoke ;
    Young Cupid no reason could quell ;
He'd got root in my heart, and there grew like an oak,
    So I fell—but reluctantly fell.

"Yet surely young Lysias has charms to betray ;
    Too charming, alas, to be true !
But you never heard the soft things he can say—
    Ah ! would I had ne'er heard them too :

"For now that the spoiler has robb'd me of all
    My innocent heart used to prize,
He cruelly mocks at my tears as they fall—
    The tears he has drawn from my eyes."

---

[1] This Epistle describes the distress of a girl who has been debauched, with the consolation of the good old woman her nurse.

[2] The subject of this Epistle does not in the least regard the writer ; who, as in the preceding one, only entertains his correspondent with a little tale, or amusing description. The case is the same with many of the subsequent ones.

" You've play'd a sad game," cries the matron, aghast ;
　　" Besides, you disgrace my grey head :
But since no reflections can alter what 's past,
　　Cheer up—there 's no more to be said.

"Cheer up, child, I say ; why there 's no such great crime ;
　　Sure I too have met with false men :
I 've known what it was to be trick'd in my time ;
　　But I know too—to trick them again.

" But do so no more ; lest, should you be rash,
　　Your apron-strings publish your tricks :
Your father, I hope, has a round sum of cash,
　　And soon on your husband will fix.

" Some innocent swain, (if such innocence be !)
　　Unskill'd in the mysteries of love ;
Whose gallantry ne'er went 'yond Phyllis's knee,
　　Or fast'ning the garter above.

" My humble petition may Jupiter hear,
　　And grant that you quickly may wed."—
" So at present, dear mother, I 've nothing to fear
　　No tale-telling urchin to dread ?"—

" You 're safe, my dear daughter, I fancy, as yet ;
　　And when at the altar you 're tied,
I 'll teach you a method your husband to cheat,
　　For a virgin, as well as a bride."

EPISTLE VII.[1]　THE DISAPPOINTMENT.

CYRTION TO DICTYS.

LATE as upon the rocky strand
　　Alone the death-barb'd bait I threw,
Just as I tow'd a fish to land,
　　Which almost broke my line in two—

Comes a fair maid, whose native bloom
　　The tinct of art excell'd as far,
As the wild fruits of Nature's womb
　　Beyond the hotbed's produce are.

---

[1] *Epistle VII.*]　A disagreeable end to a pleasing rencounter.

This prize is better than my fish,
   Thought I—'tis sure a lucky day.—
" I want to bathe, sir, and I wish
   You'd watch my clothes while I'm away."

" Yes, yes, I eagerly replied,"
   In hopes her naked charms to spy,
" I 'll watch your clothes, and by their side
   My faithful little dog shall lie."

She bow'd, and doff'd her mantle blue;
   Good heavens ! what beauties struck my sight
Thus morn's sweet ruddy skies I view,
   Fresh from the mist of lagging night.

Bright polish'd arms, a neck of snow,
   Through locks of lovely jet were seen;
Which by their blackness seem'd to throw
   An added lustre on her skin.

Two rising globules at her breast,
   Whose swelling throb was such,
They seem'd upheaving to be prest,
   And sued impatient for the touch.

The wind was hush'd, the sea was calm,
   And in she leap'd, and plough'd the tide—
The froth that bubbled as she swam,
   Lost all its whiteness by her side.

But soon the wave's impetuous gush
   Dash'd o'er her form a crimson hue ;
She blush'd—you've seen the rosebud blush
   Beneath its morning coat of dew.

Askance she view'd the watery space,
   Her neck averted from the tide,
As if old Ocean's cold embrace
   Would shock her modest virgin-pride.

Each pressing wave, that seem'd to try
   With am'rous haste her limbs to kiss,
With coy rebuke she patted by ;
   Rebuked—but never could dismiss.

Still as she stemm'd her liquid way,
   Thought I, a Nereid 'tis that laves:

And when she tired, and left her play,
  'Twas Venus rising from the waves.

Then from her oozy bed she sprung,
  And shiv'ring on the bank reclined,
The while her dripping locks she wrung,
  And spread them to the fanning wind.

Quick to present her clothes I rush,
  And towards her stretch my longing arms.
But she repulsed me with a blush—
  A blush that added to her charms.

Rage would have sparkled in her eyes;
  Yet still they twinkled lovely sweet:
As suns in farthest distant skies
  Emit their light without their heat.

Her robe she snatch'd, and round her waist
  The azure mantle instant threw.—
"I'm sorry, sir, I'm in such haste;
  I thank you—but must bid adieu."

I gently press'd her hand;—she frown'd;
  Yet took she not her hand away:
I kiss'd her hand—she turn'd around
  To hide what conscious smiles betray.

At length she broke my rod and net;
  Into the sea my capture toss'd:
Then left me vainly to regret
  The fish I'd caught, and her I lost.

EPISTLE VIII. FROM THE GROOM OF A KNIGHT IN LOVE.[1]

ECHEPOLUS TO MELESIPPUS.

    "OH! the grace, the art to rein
    Fiery coursers round the plain!
    See yon valiant hero ride,
    Skill'd with either hand to guide:

[1] This is an odd subject.—While a gentleman was riding on horse-back his groom, struck with his beauty, was exclaiming that sure so glorious a form could never have been in love. This the master overhears, and informs his groom to the contrary; who writes an account of the transaction to his friend.

See how beautiful and strong !
See how swift he glides away !
Sure fell Cupid's arrowy storm
Ne'er assail'd that blooming form.
No—'tis sure Adonis fair,
All the nymphs' peculiar care."
Speaking thus, the cavalier
Chanced my words to overhear.—
" Hush," said he, " thy words are vain :
Love alone can guide the rein.
Love impels, through me, the steed,
Nerves my arm, and fires my speed :
Quick as lightning though we run,
Still dread Cupid urges on.
Mount yon car, begin thy strain ;
Songs best suit the lover's pain."
I submitted—and from him
Took at once the sudden theme.
" Little reck'd I, hapless lord,
Cupid's shaft thy heart had gored :
If so fair a form as thine
Can with hopeless passion pine,
By the Cyprian queen I swear,
All the Loves fell tyrants are.
Yet be't thine to brave the smart,
Boldly bear the tingling dart :—
Well might they disturb your rest,
Who could pierce their mother's breast." [1]

EPISTLE IX.[2] THE SLIP.

STESICHORUS TO ERATOSTHENES.

A LADY walking in the street
Her lover lately chanced to meet :
But dared not speak when he came nigh,
Nor make a sign, nor wink her eye,

---

[1] *Who could pierce,* &c.] " Et majores tuos irreverenter pulsasti toties,
et ipsam matrem tuam, me inquam ipsam, parricida, denudas quotidie."
APOL. MIL. v.

[2] *Epistle IX.* contains the stratagem of a lady who wanted to speak to
her lover in the presence of her husband and servants.

Lest watchful spouse should see or hear:
And servants too were in the rear.
A plea she sought to stop his walk,
To touch his hand, to hear him talk:
A plea she sought, nor sought in vain;
A lucky scheme inspired her brain.
Just as they met, she feign'd to trip,
And sprain her ancle in the slip.
The lover, ready at his cue,
Suspected what she had in view;
And as he pass'd at little distance,
Officious ran to her assistance.
Contrived her slender waist to seize,
And catch her snowy hand in his.
With unexpected raptures fill'd,
Through all their veins love instant thrill'd:
Their limbs were palsied with delight,
Which seem'd the trembling caused by fright.
Feigning condolence, he drew near,
And spoke his passion in her ear;
While she, to act the real strain,
Affects to writhe and twist with pain:
A well-concerted plan to kiss
The hand her lover touch'd with his:
Then, looking amorously sly,
She put it to her jetty eye;
But rubb'd in vain to force a tear
Might seem the genuine fruits of fear.

EPISTLE X.[1] ACONTIUS AND CYDIPPE.

ERATOCLEA TO DIONYSIS.

Long buffeted by adverse fate,
The victim of Diana's hate,
At last the blest Acontius led
Cydippe to the bridal bed.

[1] *Epistle X.*] This is an epistolary narration of the loves of Acontius
and Cydippe.—Acontius was a youth of the isle of Cea, who going to Delos during the solemnities of Diana, fell in love with Cydippe; and being
inferior to her in wealth and rank, he there practised the deceit which is
the subject of this Epistle. We find the story in Ovid.

Ne'er had been form'd by Nature's care
So lovely, so complete a pair.
And truth to that belief gave rise,[1]
That similarities so nice,
By destiny's impulsive act
Each other mutually attract.
On fair Cydippe Beauty's queen
Had lavish'd all her magazine:
From all her charms the magic cest[2]
Reserved, and freely gave the rest:
That cest, not fit for mortal bodies,
Her own prerogative as goddess;
And but for which distinction, no man
Could know th' immortal from the woman.
In three, like Hesiod, to comprise
The graces sparkling in her eyes,
Were idle; since to count them all,
A thousand were a sum too small.
Nor were his eyes devoid of light,
Bold and yet modest, sweet though bright:
Whilst health and glowing vigour spread
His downy cheek with native red.
Numbers from every quarter ran,
To see this master-piece of man:
Crowds at the Forum might you meet,
—And if he did but cross the street,
Th' applauding train his steps pursued,
And praised and wonder'd as they view'd.
Such was th' accomplish'd youth, whose breast
The fair Cydippe robb'd of rest.
And 'twas but justice that the swain
For whom so many sigh'd in vain,
Should feel how exquisite the smart
That rankles in a lover's heart.—
So Cupid, throwing to the ground
His shafts that tickle while they wound,

---

[1] *And truth*, &c.]

—— ὁμοίον ἄγει θεὸς ὡς τὸν ὁμοίον.

[2] *From all her charms*, &c.] Homer tells us of this magic girdle belonging to Venus, which made the person who wore it the object of universal love, and which Juno once borrowed to deceive Jupiter.

Aim'd at the youth with all his strength
An arrow of a wondrous length :
His aim, alas ! was all too true ;
Quick to its goal the weapon flew.——
But when Acontius felt the blow,
What language can express his woe?
The fair one's heart he vow'd to move,[1]
Or end at once his life and love.
While he who shot so keen a dart,
The god of stratagem and art,
Awed haply by his graceful mien,
Fraught him with wiles the fair to win.
Thus while at Dian's hallow'd fane
Cydippe join'd the maiden train,
Towards her attendant's feet he roll'd
(Inscribed with characters of gold)
An apple of Cydonian stem :
(Love's garden raised the budding gem.)
The girl immediate seized the prize,
Admired its colour and its size :
Much wond'ring from what virgin's zone
So fair a pris'ner could have flown.
" 'Tis sure," said she, " a fruit divine ;
But then, what means this mystic line?
Cydippe, see, just now I found
This apple ; view how large, how round :
See how it shames the rose's bloom,
And smell its exquisite perfume.
And, dearest mistress, tell me, pray,
The meaning which these words convey?"
The blushing fruit Cydippe eyed,
Then read th' inscription on its side.——
" By chaste Diana's sacred head,
I swear I will Acontius wed."
Thus vow'd she at the hallow'd shrine,
Though rashly, though without design ;
And utter'd not, for modest dread,
The last emphatic word, to wed :

The fair one's heart, &c.]
    Aut ego sigæos repetam te conjuge portus,
      Aut ego Tænariâ contegar exul humô. OVID.

Which but to hear, much more to speak,[1]
With blushes paints a virgin's cheek.
"Ah!" cries the half-distracted fair,
"Diana sure has heard me swear:
Yes, favour'd youth, without dispute
She has assented to thy suit."

He the meanwhile from day to day
In ceaseless anguish pined away.
His tears usurp'd the place of sleep;
For shame forbade all day to weep.
Sickly and thin his body grew:
His cheeks had lost their ruddy hue.
Thousand pretences would he feign,
To loiter on the lonely plain;
Striving most eagerly to fly
The keenness of his father's eye.
Oft with the morn's first beam he'd leave
His tear-bathed couch; and to deceive
His friend's concern, some untouch'd book
As studious bent, the lover took:
Then to the grove, the peaceful grove,
Where silence yields full scope to love.
Thus from their hard attention freed,
He wept unsought, yet seem'd to read.
Thither if chance his father drew,
And bared the wand'rer to his view,
Knowledge he thought the stripling's aim,
A laudable desire for fame;
And every sigh his sorrow brought,
The old man construed into thought;
Or if he wept,—as tears would flow,—
He only wept at others' woe.

Still too, when pleasant evening came,
And others sought the frolic game,
Still was his wont to shun the feast,
To feign that angling pleased him best;

---

[1] *Which but to hear, &c.*]
    Nomine conjugii dicto, confusa pudore
      Sensi me totis erubuisse genis.   OVID.

Then busy with his rod and hook,
He sought some solitary brook.
But ye were safe, ye finny brood,
And safely stemm'd your native flood,
Secure around his float to glide,
And dash th' unbaited hook aside.

Yet still 'twas solitude! and he
Must give his solitude a plea:
Besides, the posture pleased, for grief
In humblest postures finds relief:
True love the suppliant's bend will please,
And sorrow unrestrain'd is ease.
His friends, who found he fled the town,
Concluded him a farmer grown;
And call'd him, in derision pleasant,
Laertes, or the new-made peasant.—
But he, sad lover, little made
The vines his care, or plied the spade;
Little he cared how sped the bower,
And little mark'd the drooping flower,
But wand'ring through the bushy brake,
Thus in bewilder'd accents spake:
" Oh! that each pine, and spreading beech,
Were blest with reason and with speech!
So might they evermore declare
Cydippe fairest of the fair.
At least, ye thickets, will I mark
Her lovely name upon your bark.
O dear inspirer of my pain,
Let not thy oath be sworn in vain:
Let not the goddess find that thou
Hast dared to falsify a vow.
With vengeance every crime she threats,
But never perjury forgets.—
Yet, not on thee the fatal meed;
'Tis I, who caused thy crime, should bleed.
On me then, Dian, vent thine ire,
And let her crime with me expire.
But tell me, lofty groves, oh tell,
Ye seats where feather'd warblers dwell.

Can Love your knotty bosoms reach,
And burns the cypress for the beech?
Ah no—ye never feel the smart;
Ne'er Cupid pierced that stubborn heart.
Think ye your worthless leaves, ye trees
His mighty anger could appease?
No—silly woods; his ample fire
Above your branches would aspire;
Upon the very trunk would prey,
And burn your hardest root away."

Meantime, a happier lover's arms
Prepared to clasp Cydippe's charms.
Already had the virgin throng
Attuned their Hymeneal song—
" Strike ye now the golden lyre,
Modulate the vocal choir"—
But hark!—what horrid shrieks arise?
Cydippe faints—Cydippe dies.
The bridal pomp, alas! is fled;
Funereal sounds are heard instead.
Yet soft—she lives—she breathes again,
" Louder raise the nuptial strain."
A second time the fever burns:
A second time her health returns.
Again the marriage torches blaze:
Again Cydippe's bloom decays.
No longer will her sire await
The fourth avenging stroke of Fate;
But of the Pythian shrine demands,
What god opposed the nuptial bands?
Phœbus at once revealed the truth,
The vow, the apple, and the youth.—
Told him, her oath the maid must keep,
Or ne'er would Dian's vengeance sleep.
Then added thus the god, " Whene'er
Acontius gains the blooming fair,
Not silver shall be join'd with lead,
But gold the purest gold shall wed."
So spoke the shrine divinely skill'd—
Cydippe soon her vow fulfill'd:

No clouds of sickness intervene
To darken the delightful scene.—
While striking with directive hand,
A virgin led the choral band;
Attentive to each warbling throat,
She chided each discordant note.
Others their hands applausive beat,
Like cymbals sounding as they meet.

But ill Acontius brook'd their noise—
He sigh'd for more substantial joys.
Ne'er had he seen so long a day:
Night never pass'd so quick away.
The sun had gain'd its summit, ere
Acontius left the rifled fair:
But first her cheek he kiss'd, whilst she
Dissembled sleep through modesty;—
But well her tell-tale blushes spake
The conscious nymph was still awake.
Alone at length, she raised her head,
And blushing view'd the bridal bed;
Then with chaste rapture, hanging o'er
The place Acontius press'd before,
"Protect, ye powers divine," she said,
"Protect the wife, who led the maid;
And oh! be doubly kind to him
Who must be now Cydippe's theme.
And thou, chaste Hymen, who dost guide
The steps of each untainted bride,
Teach me what fits I should be taught,
Nor let me wander e'en in thought.
So may your altars ever burn,
So may each day like this return;
And every night."—Speak, trifler, speak;
Whence virgin blushes on thy cheek?—
"And every night"—she hung her head—
Be crown'd like this.—she would have said.

EPISTLE XI.[1]   THE ARTFUL MAID.

PHILOSTRATUS TO EUAGORAS.

A LADY thus her maid address'd—
"Like you the beauteous youth
On whom I dote, in whom I'm blest?
I charge you tell me truth.

"Or is't my love that paints him fair,
And all my fancy warms?
For lovers oft deceived are,
And prize ideal charms.

"But say, the swain whom I admire,
Do other women praise?
Do they behold him with desire,
Or view with scornful gaze?"

The girl replied, who saw her cue,
Deep learn'd in flattery's lore,
"They all his beauty praise with you,
With you they all adore.

"'Behold,' they cry, 'that form divine
The sculptor's art should trace,
To bid the bust of Hermes shine[2]
With every manly grace.'

"I've heard them praise his arched nose,
And praise his auburn hair,
That spreading o'er his forehead grows,
To make his face more fair.

"I've heard them praise his stature high,
And praise his manly sense;
I've heard them praise!—and sure, thought I,
'Tis Love gives eloquence.

[1] *Epistle XI.*]   A lady inquires whether the man she loved was really beautiful : her maid flatters, and assures her of it.

[2] *To bid the bust*, &c.]   The ancient sculptors used to copy the face of Hermes, or Mercury, from that of Alcibiades, who was reckoned the most beautiful model : "but now," says the maid, "women think your lover superior to him."

" His very dress has merit too,
  Where taste with art agrees :
For though it is not always new,
  It never fails to please.——

"' Blest,' will they say, ' thrice blest the fair
  For whom his heart shall burn : [1]
Who shall a mutual ardour share,
  And all his love return.

"' On her the Graces sure have smiled
  With most propitious eye.'
Thus the whole sex with passion wild
  For the same object sigh."

But while the crafty maid arranged
  His charms in fairest light,
Full oft the lady's colour changed
  With raptures exquisite.

Convinced his grace was not ideal,
  Which all her sex could fire,
For women know that beauty real,
  When all who see, admire.

EPISTLE XII.[2]   THE ENRAPTURED LOVER.

EUHEMERUS TO LEUCIPPUS.

HITHER, ye travellers, who've known
The beauties of the Eastern zone,
  Or those who sparkle in the West :
Hither—oh tell, and truly tell,
That few can equal, none excel,
  The fair who captivates my breast.

---

[1] *Blest*, &c.] Ergo mecastor, pulcher est, inquit mihi,
     Et liberalis.   Vide cæsaries quam decet :
     Ne illæ sunt fortunatœ quæ cum illo, &c.
                                        PLAUTUS MILITE.

[2] *Epistle XII.*] A lover here summons all the judges of beauty to
decide in favour of his mistress. The libertine digression with which it
concludes must be morally interpreted, as meant to show into what extravagance a man may be led by an attachment whose foundation is in
vice.

Survey her in whatever light—
New beauties still engage your sight:
   Nor does a single fault appear.
Momus might search, and search again,
But all his searches would be vain,
   To find occasion for a sneer.

Her height, her shape—'tis all complete;
And e'en remarkable her feet
   For taper size, genteelly slim.—
And little feet, each lover knows,
Impart a striking charm to those
   Who boast no other graceful limb.

But not her beauties only strike—
Her pleasing manners too I like:
   From these new strength my passion gains.
For though her chastity be gone,
She deals deceitfully by none;
   And still some modesty remains.

And still may Pythias make pretence
To something much like innocence,
   Which forges all my chains to last:
Whate'er you give, she turns to praise;
Unlike the harlot's odious ways,
   Who sneers at presents e'er so vast.

We, like two thrushes on a spray,
Together sit, together play;—
   But telling would our pleasures wrong.—
Suffice it, Pythias will oppose
My wanton passion, till it grows
   By opposition doubly strong.[1]

Her neck ambrosial sweets exhales;
Her kisses, like Arabian gales,
   The scent of musky flowers impart.
And I, reclining on her breast,
In slumbers, happy slumbers, rest,
   Rock'd by the beating of her heart!

[1] *Suffice it,* &c.]
   Quæ cum ita pugnaret tanquam quæ vincere nollet,
    Victa est non ægre proditione suâ.   OVID

Oft have I heard the vulgar say,
That absence makes our love decay,
 And friends are friends but while in view:
But absence kindles my desire;
It adds fresh fuel to the fire
 Which keeps my heart for ever true.

And oh! may fate my thanks receive,
In that it forced me not to leave
 The fair in whom my soul is placed.
With truth my case did Homer write; [1]
For every time with new delight
 My oft-repeated joys I taste.

Sure this is joy—true native joy!
Which malice never can destroy,
 Nor holy shackled fools receive.
Free joys! which from ourselves must flow;
Such as free souls alone can know,
 And unchain'd Love alone can give.

But say, ye prudes! ye worthless tribe!
Who swear no gifts could ever bribe
 Your hearts sweet virtue to forsake—
What is this treasure which ye boast?
Ye vaunt because you have not lost
 —What none had charity to take.

Myrina carries on her back
An antidote to Love's attack;
 Yet still at Pythias will she sneer.
And as my love is passing by,
Chrysis distorts her single eye,
 With looks of scorn and virtuous fear.

Philinna scoffs at Pythias too,
 —Yet she is handsome, it is true;
 But then her heart's a heart of steel:
Incapable of all desire,
She ridicules Love's sacred fire,
 And mocks the joys she cannot feel.

---

[1] *With truth*, &c.]
 Ασπάσιον λέκτροιο παλαιον θεσμὸν ἵκοντο. HOM. IL. Ψ.

Yet this is virtue! woman's pride!
From which if once she step aside,
 Her peace, her fame's for ever gone!
—Away; 'tis impious satire says,
That woman's good, and woman's praise,
 Consist in chastity alone.

Can one short hour of native joy
Nature's inherent good destroy?
 And pluck all feeling from within?
Shall shame ne'er strike the base deceiver,
But follow still the poor believer,
 And make all confidence a sin?

Did gentle Pity never move
The heart once led astray by Love?
 Was Poverty ne'er made its care?
Did Gratitude ne'er warm the breast
Where guilty joy was held a guest?
 Was Charity ne'er harbour'd there?

Does coy Sincerity disclaim
The neighb'rhood of a lawless flame?
 Does Truth with fame and fortune fall?
Does every tim'rous virtue fly
With that cold thing, call'd Chastity?
 —And has my Pythias lost them all?

No! no!—In thee, my life, my soul,
I swear I can comprise the whole
 Of all that's good as well as fair:
And though thou'st lost what fools call fame
Though branded with a harlot's name,
 To me thou shalt be doubly dear.

Then whence these fetters for desire?
Who made these laws for Cupid's fire?
 Why is their rigour so uncommon?
Why is this honour-giving plan
So much extoll'd by tyrant man,
 Yet binding only to poor woman?

Search not in Nature for the cause;
Nature disclaims such partial laws;
 'Tis all a creature of th' imagination:

By frozen prudes invented first,
Or hags with ugliness accurst—
  A phantom of our own creation!

Two classes thus, my Pythias, show
Their insolence to scoff at you:
  First, they who've passions given by Nature:
But as the task of fame is hard,
They've blest Deformity to guard
  Grim Virtue in each rugged feature.

And second, they who neither know
What passion means, nor love can do:
  Yet still for abstinence they preach;
Whilst Envy, rankling in the breast,
Inflames them, seeing others blest,
  To curse the joys they cannot reach.

Not but there are—though but a few!
With charms, with love—and virtue too:
  But malice never comes from them!
With charity they judge of all,
They weep to see a woman fall,
  And pity where they most condemn.

If, Pythias, then, thou'st done amiss,
This is thy crime, and only this:
  That Nature gave thee charms to move,
Gave thee a heart to joy inclined,
Gave thee a sympathetic mind,
  And gave a soul attuned to love.

When Malice scoffs, then, Pythias, why
Glistens abash'd thy tearful eye?
  Why glows thy cheek that should be gay?
For though from shame thy sorrows gush,
Though conscious guilt imprints the blush,
  By heavens, thou'rt modester than they.

But let them scoff, and let them sneer—
I heed them not, my love, I swear:
  Nor shall they triumph in thy fall.
I'll kiss away each tear of woe,
Hid by my breast thy cheek shall glow,
  And Love shall make amends for all.

2 H 2

EPISTLE XIII.[1] THE SAGACIOUS DOCTOR.

EUTYCHOBULUS TO ACESTODORUS.

FORTUNE, my friend, I've often thought,
Is weak, if Art assist her not:
So equally all Arts are vain,
If Fortune help them not again:
They've little lustre of their own,
If separate, and view'd alone;
But when together they unite,
They lend each other mutual light.—
But since all symphony seems long
To those impatient for the song,
And lest my apophthegms should fail,
I'll haste to enter on my tale.

Once on a time, (for time has been,
When men thought neither shame nor sin,
To keep, beside their lawful spouses,
A buxom filly in their houses,)
Once on a time then, as I said,
A hopeful youth, well-born, well-bred,
Seized by a flame he could not hinder,
Was scorch'd and roasted to a cinder.
For why, the cause of all his pain
Was, that he fear'd all hope was vain:
—In short, the youth must needs adore
The nymph his father loved before.
" His father's mistress ?"—even so,
And sure 'twas cause enough for woe.
In mere despair he kept his bed,
But feign'd some illness in its stead.

[1] *Epistle XIII.*] This is the story of Antiochus and Seleucus; but related in Aristænetus under different names. Seleucus was one of Alexander's successors in Asia, having Syria for his kingdom : he married Stratonice, daughter to Demetrius, having had, by a former marriage, a son named Antiochus. Stratonice was the most beautiful and accomplished princess of her time ; and unhappily inspired her son-in-law with the most ardent passion. He fell sick, and Seleucus was in the greatest despair, when Erasistratus, one of his physicians, discovered the cause of the prince's malady, and, by his address, prevailed on the king to save his son's life, by resigning to him his wife, though he passionately loved her.

His father, grieved at his condition,
Sends post for an expert physician.
The doctor comes—consults his pulse—
No feverish quickness—no convulse;
Observes his looks, his skin, his eye—
No symptoms there of malady;
—At least of none within the knowledge
Of all the pharmaceutic college.
Long did our Galen wond'ring stand,
Reflecting on the case in hand.—
Thus as he paused, came by the fair,
The cause of all his patient's care.—
   Then his pulse beat quick and high;
   Glow'd his cheek, and roll'd his eye.
Alike his face and arm confest
The conflict lab'ring in his breast.
Thus chance reveal'd the hidden smart,
That baffled all the search of art.
Still paused the doctor to proclaim
The luckily-discover'd flame:
But made a second inquisition,
To satisfy his new suspicion.
From all the chambers, every woman,
Wives, maids, and widows, did he summon;
And one by one he had them led
In order by the patient's bed.
He the meanwhile stood watchful nigh,
And felt his pulse, and mark'd his eye;
(For by the pulse physicians find
The hidden motions of the mind;)
While other girls walk'd by attractive,
The lover's art'ry lay inactive;
But when his charmer pass'd along,
His pulse beat doubly quick and strong.
Now all the malady appear'd;
Now all the doctor's doubts were clear'd;
Who feign'd occasion to depart,
To mix his drugs, consult his art:
He bid the father hope the best,
The lover set his heart at rest,
Then took his fee and went away,
But promised to return next day.

Day came—the family environ
With anxious eagerness our Chiron.
But he repulsed them rough, and cried,
" Ne'er can my remedy be tried."
The father humbly question'd, why
They might not use the remedy?
Th' enraged physician nought would say,
But earnest seem'd to haste away.
Th' afflicted sire more humble yet is,
Doubles his offers, prayers, entreaties—
While he, as if at last compell'd
To speak what better were withheld,
In anger cried, " Your son must perish—
My wife alone his life can cherish—
On her th' adult'rer dotes—and I
My rival's hated sight would fly."
The sire was now alike distrest,
To save his boy, or hurt his guest:
Long struggled he 'twixt love and shame
At last parental love o'ercame.
And now he begs without remorse
His friend to grant this last resource;
Entreats him o'er and o'er t' apply
This hard, but only remedy.
" What, prostitute my wife!" exclaims
The doctor, " pimp for lawless flames?"—
Yet still the father teased and prest;—
" Oh grant a doting sire's request!
The necessary cure permit,
And make my happiness complete."
Thus did the doctor's art and care
The anxious parent's heart prepare;
And found him trying long and often
The term adultery to soften.
—He own'd, " that custom, sure enough,
Had made it sound a little rough:
But then, said he, we ought to trace
The source and causes of the case.
All prejudice let's lay aside,
And taking Nature for our guide,
We'll try with candour to examine
On what pretence this fashion came in."

Then much he talk'd of man's first state,
(A copious subject for debate !)
Of choice and instinct then disputes,
With many parallels to brutes ;
All tending notably to prove
That instinct was the law of Love ;—
In short, that Nature gave us woman,
Like earth and air, to hold in common.
Then learned authors would he quote,
Philosophers of special note,
Who only thought their dames worth feeding,
As long as they held out for breeding ;
And when employ'd in studious courses,
Would let them out, as we do horses.
Last follow'd a facetious query,
To rank the sex *naturæ feræ*.

The doctor, when the speech was closed,
Confess'd he was a little posed.
Then looking impudently grave,
" And how would you," said he, " behave ?
Would you part freely with your wife,
To save a friend's expiring life ?"—
" By Jove, I'd act as I advise,"
The father eagerly replies.—
" Then," cries the doctor, " I have done—
Entreat yourself to save your son.
He loves your girl—can you endure
To work the necessary cure ?
If it were just that I should give
My wife to cause a friend to live,
You surely may bestow with joy
Your mistress, to preserve your boy."
He spoke with sense, he spoke with art :
Conviction touch'd the father's heart :—
" 'Tis hard," he cried, " 'tis passing hard,
To lose what I so much regard !
But when two dread misfortunes press,
'Tis wisdom sure to choose the less."

EPISTLE XIV.[1] THE PROVIDENT SHEPHERDESS.

PHILEMATIUM TO EUMUSUS.

HENCE! hence! ye songsters; hence! ye idle train!
Vain is the song, the pipe's soft warbling vain:
  In me nor joy thy strains inspire,
    Nor passion can thy numbers move;
  The thrills of the resounding lyre
    To me are not the thrills of Love.
For I know well to value gold aright;
I scorn a passion—while its gifts are light.

Puff not your cheeks, fond youths! dismiss the flute;
Hush'd be the harp, the soft guitar be mute:
  Or hie where pensive Echo sits
    Moping the lonely rocks among;
  She'll listen to your chanting fits,
    Applaud, and pay you song for song.
But I know well to value gold aright,
And scorn a passion while its gifts are light.

Do, good Charmides, stop thy tuneful tongue;
And friendly Lycias trust not to thy song.
  There is a sound—and well you know
    That sound I never heard from thee—
  The smallest clink of which, I vow,
    Is sweetest harmony to me.
For I've been taught to value gold aright,
And scorn a passion while its gifts are light.

Why do your vows in tuneful numbers flow?
Why urge the joys I do not wish to know?
  Say, youth, can thy poetic fire
    Make folly pleasant to the ear?
  Can thy soft notes, and soothing lyre,
    Make oaths, and lover's oaths, sincere?
Go! go! I know to value gold aright,
And scorn a passion while its gifts are light.

---

[1] *Epistle XIV.*] This letter is from a girl to her lovers, who courted
her with music instead of money.

Soft is thy note, my friend, I grant 'tis soft;
Sweet is thy lay—but I have heard it oft:
   And will thy piping ne'er disgust,
     When all the novelty is past?
   Your stock will fail—you know it must;
     And sweetest sounds will tire at last.
Then now's the time to value gold aright,
To scorn a passion while its gifts are light.

When the cold hand of age has damp'd thy fire,
Unstrung thy harp, and hush'd th' unheeded lyre;
   Say, will thy tuneless, crazy voice
     Keep chilling penury away?
   Will mem'ry lead us to rejoice
     Because, poor bard, thou once couldst play?
No! no! Then still I'll value gold aright,
And still the lover scorn whose gifts are light.

   Then hence! ye songsters; hence! ye idle train!
Vain is the song, the pipe's soft warbling vain:
No idle triflings captivate this breast;—
Produce your money—I'll excuse the rest.

   Puff not your cheeks, fond youths! dismiss the flute,
Hush'd be the harp, the soft guitar be mute:
Such signs of passion in contempt I hold:—
But there's substantial proof of love—in gold.

   I know you fancy me an easy fool,
Raw, and undisciplined in Venus' school;
A thoughtless victim, whom a song could move,
And each fond lay inspire with throbs of love:
Deluded swains! but vain do ye opine—
Know, the whole science of intrigue is mine.
A dame, experienced in the mystic art,
Taught me to play with ablest skill my part;
Taught me to laugh at songs, and empty strains;
And taught how Cupid shone—in golden chains.
My sister too, and all her am'rous train,
Tutor'd my youth,—nor were their lessons vain.
Full oft her suitors hath she frankly told,
" Your aim is beauty, sirs, and mine is—gold:

Each other's wants let's mutually supply."—
'Twas thus my sister spoke,—and thus speak I.
With her, I laugh at Cupid's batter'd name,
With her, I mock what fools call gen'rous flame
With her, my theme's to value gold aright,
And scorn a passion while its gifts are light.

EPISTLE XV.[1] THE FORCE OF LOVE.

APHRODISIUS TO LYSIMACHUS.

Love, or of force, or of persuasion,
Avails him as best suits th' occasion:
And all, who've felt his tingling dart,
Will own its conquest o'er the heart.
Love can the thirst of blood assuage,
And bid the battle cease to rage;
Quell the rude discord, and compose
To peace the most determined foes.
Vain is the lance, and vain the shield,
And vain the wide embattled field;
Vain the long military train,
And Mars with all his terrors vain.
Cupid his stubborn angry soul
Can with a little shaft control.—
Each champion, who with fury brave
Would stem war's most destructive wave,
Without a stroke, to Love will yield,
And quit at once his useless shield.—
T' insure your credit to my text,
A case in point is here annext.

Two cities of no mean estate,
Miletus this, and Myus that,
Had long in mutual conflicts bled,
While commerce droop'd with languid head
And only while Miletus kept
Diana's feast, the contest slept:
A solemn truce was then allow'd:—
At Dian's shrine each city bow'd.—

[1] *Epistle XV.*] A narrative.

And, till the festive revels cease,
'Twas nought but harmony and peace.
Then gleams the hostile blade again,
And reeking gore manures the plain.
But Venus little could sustain
That Discord should eternal reign;
So closed for ever their dispute:
And thus she found the means to do't.

From Myus to Miletus came
A girl, (Piëria was her name,)
Bright as the morn she was by nature,
And Venus now retouch'd each feature.

Then, at what time the sacred train
Attended at Diana's fane,
The prince of the Miletians came,
And saw the maid, and felt the flame.
And soon the prince his love address'd,
" Speak, charmer, speak thy first request?
Whate'er thy wish, whate'er thy want,
Be't mine to make a double grant."
But thee, fair maid, supreme in mind,
As well as charms, o'er womankind,
No idle choice seduced aside,
No giddy wish, no hurtful pride:
Thee could no costly gem insnare,
No trinket to adorn thy hair:
No Carian slave didst thou request,
No precious chain, no Tyrian vest.
But long didst stand with downcast eye,
As hesitating to reply;
Essaying, but in vain, to speak,
While blushes dyed thy modest cheek.
At last thy falt'ring tongue with fear
Thus utter'd faintly in his ear,
" Prince, to these walls give access free,
At all times, for my friends and me."
Phrygius full well perceived her drift,
Yet nobly ratified his gift.
A peace was soon proclaim'd around,
And mighty Love the treaty bound:

A more sufficient guarantee,
Than any bonds or oaths could be.
And this example well may prove
That nought's so eloquent as Love:
For oft had orators, whose style was
Mellifluent as the seer's of Pylos,[1]
Convened, debated, and return'd,
While still the rage of battle burn'd.
But Cupid's sweeter elocution
Brought matters quick to a conclusion.
And hence the Ionian maids deduce
Th' expression now so much in use,
" May we such noble presents have,
As erst the princely Phrygius gave!
And may our lords as faithful be,
As thine, Piëria, was to thee."

EPISTLE XVI.[2] THE BASHFUL LOVER.

LAMPRIAS TO PHILIPPIDES.

In secret pining thus I sigh'd,
  " Love, thou alone my flame dost know,
Who didst the fatal arrow guide,
  And Venus, who prepared thy bow.

" Not to my friend, to her much less
  Dare I my hopeless flame disclose;
And love conceal'd burns to excess,
  And with redoubled ardour glows.

" Me, Cupid, hast thou robb'd of rest;
  Wound too the maid whose love I seek;
But pierce with lighter shaft her breast,
  Lest grief make wan that blooming cheek."

Sweet did she speak, and sweetly smile,
  When lately I admittance had,
Yet seem'd she so reserved the while,
  The inconsistence made me mad.

---

[1] *Seer of Pylos.*]   Nestor, famous in Homer for his eloquence.
[2] *Epistle XVI.*]   A lover, who long had feared to disclose his passion
at length describes to his friend the circumstances of success.

Her snowy hands, her lovely face,
  I view'd, with admiration fill'd:
Her easy negligence of dress,
  Her bosom, seat of bliss, reveal'd!

Still dared I not my love make known,
  But silently to Cupid pray'd,
" Grant that she first her passion own!"—
  The powerful archer lent his aid.

Sudden she seized my hand—her eyes
  With am'rous elocution speak—
Instant her wonted rigour flies,
  And Love sits dimpling on her cheek.

Intoxicated with desire,
  Her panting neck she did incline;
And kiss'd me with such life and fire,
  I thought her soul would blend with mine.

—Description can no further go,
  T' express our happiness too weak—
But well did half-form'd accents show,
  Our joys were more than we could speak.

EPISTLE XVII.[1] THE HAUGHTY BEAUTY.

XENOPEITHES TO DEMARETUS.

YES, she is cold!—oh! how severely cold!—
  That breast Love's gentle taper ne'er could warm.—
Who could believe a heart of savage mould
  Was e'er enshrined within so bright a form?

Yet not unnoticed in the fields of Love
  Have I sustain'd full many a brisk campaign:
For many a trophy strove,—nor vainly strove,—
  While maids, and wives, and widows own'd my reign.

But now, alas! that idle boast expires;
  And Daphnis wears the laurels I had won.
Now Xenopeithes pines with new desires,
  And all his fame in one defeat is flown.

----

[1] *Epistle XVII.*] From a lover complaining of the pride and insensibility of his mistress.

Yes—she is every way replete with wiles—
　Loves she ?—'tis silence.—Is she loved ?—'tis scorn.
Flattery she hates ; at proffer'd gifts she smiles.—
　As law, must her imperious will be borne.

Laughs she ?—her lips alone that laughter own ;
　No smiling dimples on her cheeks are spread ;
And once I ventured to reprove her frown,
　And told her, "Charms should love inspire, not dread

As well might I have spoken to the air,
　Or to an ass have touch'd the melting lute.
But still—The falling drop the stone will wear,[1]—
　And still I 'll ply my disappointed suit.

With more delusive baits my hook I 'll gild—
　Still on my line the slipp'ry prize shall play.
And 'tis Love's grand distinction not to yield,
　But toil and toil, although he lose the day.

Ten years could vanquish heaven-defended Troy.
　And oh ! do thou, my friend, assist my aim—
(For thou hast felt the all-destructive boy)—
　The same our labours, as our skiff the same.

EPISTLE XVIII.[3] EXCUSES.

CALLICÆTA TO MEIRACIOPHILA.

UNNUMBER'D pleasures are your own,
Who youth and beauty prize alone—
Who seek not riches to excess,
But place them after happiness :
Who from the sighing, am'rous crew
Select alone the lovely few ;

---

[1] *The falling drop*, &c.] An ancient proverb.
　　Nonne vides etiam guttas in saxa cadentes,
　　Humoris longo spatio pertundere saxa. LUCRET. lib. iii.
　　" Hard bodies, which the lightest stroke receive,
　　In length of time will moulder and decay ;
　　And stones with drops of rain are wash'd away."
[2] *The same our labours*, &c.] Another Greek proverb.
　　　　In eâdem es navi.—　　　　CIC. Epist. ii.
[3] *Epistle XVIII.*] A panegyric on a dainty courtesan.

And when a beauteous swain you meet,
His flame with mutual ardour greet ;
But scorn the mean, the sottish hind,
Whose wealth would bribe you to be kind.
You can, like Spartan hounds, discover,
With quickest scent, a worthy lover,
Skilful to beat, to wind, to double,
For game that may reward your trouble.
Then hoary dotards you despise—
'Tis that which proves you truly wise.
Were any wretch, deform'd and old,
To bring inestimable gold,
His treasures vainly were employ'd,
Though great as Tantalus enjoy'd :
Not all his presents could atone
For youth, and health, and vigour flown ;
Haggard with age, and with disease,
You'd loathe his person—scorn his fees.
The mere description shocks one much—
How then th' original to touch ?—
Hence many a cogent cause appears
T' advise equality of years :
For similarity of ages
To similar pursuits engages.
And you draw arguments from truth
In praise of every diff'rent youth.
Say, has your love a little nose ?
How neat, how delicate it shows !—
If aquiline, it arches high,
Oh ! the grand type of majesty !—
If neither large it be, nor small,
'Tis due proportion—best of all !—
A swarthy skin, is manly grace ;—
The fairer youths, a heavenly race ;—
In short, you catch at each pretence,
And torture words to every sense,
For every youthful swain to find
Excuses, why you should be kind :
As drunkards every reason think
May sanction a demand for drink.

"Come—we are young—let's t' other pot "—
"The tankard here, to cheer the old "—
Some drink because " 'tis parching hot,"—
And some, because " 'tis bitter cold."
T' exemplify the love of wine,
I cease to write—the case is mine.

EPISTLE XIX.[1] MERIT RESCUED FROM SHAME.

EUPHRONIUM TO THELXINOE.

SURE Fortune has smiled on Melissa benign,
From the theatre freed, in abundance to shine:
While I, less in favour, am still doom'd to linger
My life on the stage, an unfortunate singer.
Melissa's beginning was poor past expression—
For when she first studied her scenic profession,
Her mother and she in a pitiful cot
Were starving together, and scarce worth a groat;
But soon she eclipsed all the girls of her age,
And her musical talents engaged the whole stage.
At first people sneer'd, to distinguish their taste;
But they soon turn'd to praise, and they envied at last.
Her charms, and her dress, and her musical skill,
Soon gain'd her rich generous lovers at will.
She was splendidly kept,—but was highly afraid
Lest breeding should spoil so important a trade.
(And frequently breeding, to tell you the truth,
Is the worst of destroyers to beauty and youth.)
Among the old gossips she learn'd to divine
Whene'er she conceived, by infallible sign:
So when the case happen'd, she told her old dame,
And to me for advice, as more knowing, they came.
I gave my opinion, and added a drug,
Which demolish'd her fears, expeditious and snug.
But with Charicles when she commenced an affair,
Whose wealth was immense, as his beauty was rare,

---

[1] *Epistle XIX.*] From a girl on the stage to her friend, describing the
good fortune of a young actress of their acquaintance.

She changed her request to the rulers above,
And with fervency pray'd for a pledge of their love.
The gods of Olympus consentingly smiled,
And Lucina's assistance deliver'd the child—[1]
A child with all kinds of perfection endued,
And the father himself in a miniature view'd.
The mother with rapture beheld the young boy,
The little Eutychides, offspring of joy.
For children, the more they are beautiful, move
With greater incitement their parents to love.
While Charicles, blest in an infant so dear,
Determined the fame of its mother to clear:
From her scenic employment he rescued the fair,
His hand, and his heart, and his riches to share:
And the lady forgot, while she gazed on her son,
Both the life she had led, and the risk she had run.
A visit I lately to Pythias paid,
(For she took a new name when she left her old trade,)
She show'd me her jewels, each ring, and each toy;
—And be sure I'd a sight of her sweet little boy:
His cheek I kiss'd sweetly—but tenderly too;
For 'twas soft as the rose, it resembled in hue.—
The lady's so changed,—'tis amazing to see't;
So modest her air, and her look so discreet:
Her hair braided neat, without art or design;
Her ornaments grave; neither flaunty nor fine.
When she walks, 'tis with caution and prudence, they say,
And you'd think by her steps she had ne'er gone astray.
So one of these days, when the time you can spare,
I advise you, Thelxinoë, visit the fair:
But be very exact not Melissa to name her,
'Twould look like an insult intended to shame her:
The word, when I saw her, was at my tongue's end,
But they gave me a jog, and the hint saved your friend.

---

[1] *And Lucina's assistance*, &c.] Both Juno and Diana were worshipped under this name, as goddesses presiding over child-birth.

EPISTLE XX.[1] THE JAILOR TRICKED.

PHYLACIDES TO PHRURION.

LATE an adult'rous youth I seized;
  And "guard him closely," was the charge.
But with his age and figure pleased,
  I kept him prisoner at large.

Unfetter'd through my house he stray'd:
  Thought I, he may reform his life.—
He my compassion well repaid,
  And—gratefully seduced my wife.

The thief, Eurybates,[2] ne'er strain'd
  His wit to so complete a job;
Who first his jailor's pity gain'd,
  Then show'd him how he used to rob.

The brazen pens they wrote withal
  Sharper than needles did he grind:
Then stuck them in the prison wall,
  And fled—but left their wives behind.

Soon as the villany was heard,
  Which robb'd my bosom of its rest,
It first incredible appear'd,
  And then became the public jest.

—The public jest—ah! that wounds deep—
  That I—who live by bolts and chains,
In my own prison could not keep
  The honour of my wife from stains.

---

[1] *Epistle XX.*] From a jailor, whose wife was seduced by a young
man confined in his house for adultery.

[2] *Eurybates.*] A famous robber of Attica, who escaped once from
prison by means of some brazen pens, by which he descended the
walls.

EPISTLE XXI.[1]   CRUEL COMPASSION.

ARISTOMENES TO MYRONIDES.

THE god of the love-darting bow,
　　Whose bliss is man's heart to destroy,
Oft contrives to embitter our woe
　　By a specious resemblance of joy.—

Long—long had Architeles sigh'd
　　The fair Telesippe to gain:
She coolly his passion denied,
　　Yet seem'd somewhat moved at his pain.

At length she consented to hear;
　　But 'twas done with a view to beguile:
For her terms were most harsh and severe,
　　And a frown was as good as her smile.

" You may freely," says she, " touch my breast,
　　And kiss, while a kiss has its charms;
And (provided I am not undrest)
　　Encircle me round in your arms.

" In short, any favour you please,
　　But expect not, nor think of the last:
Lest enraged I revoke my decrees,
　　And your sentence of exile be cast."—

" Be it so," cried the youth, with delight,
　　" Thy pleasure, my fair one, is mine:
Since I'm blest as a prince at your sight,
　　Sure to touch thee, will make me divine.

" But why keep one favour alone,
　　And grant such a number beside?"—
" Because the men value the boon
　　But only so long as denied.

" They seek it with labour and pain;
　　When gain'd, throw it quickly away:
For youth is unsettled and vain,
　　And its choice scarce persists for a day."

---

[1] *Epistle XXI.*]　A whimsical account of a lover and his mistress, who admitted him to every favour but the last.

—Thus pines the poor victim away,
　Forced to nibble and starve on a kiss.
Served worse than e'en eunuchs—for they
　Can never feel torture like this.

EPISTLE XXII.[1]　PRIDE DEJECTED.
LUCIAN TO ALCIPHRON.

LONG Glycera had loved, and still
Charisius loves; but brooking ill
Those supercilious airs of his,
(For pride, you know, his foible is,)
Determined, if she could, at once
Her hopeless passion to renounce.
A wish to love him, caused her hate:
Hatred too strong did love create.
Howe'er, to Doris she applied,
Her maid, her oracle, her guide:
To her all circumstances stated;
And long together they debated:
At length their consultation done,
The confidant went out alone.
She'd walk'd through half a street and better,
When at a turn Charisius met her:
Ask'd how she fared, and how she sped.—
" So, so," she cried, and shook her head.
" Is aught the matter?" said the youth;
" For God's sake, Doris, tell me truth."
Forcing a tear from either eye,
The crafty jade thus answer'd sly:
" My mistress madly dotes upon
That dolt, that idiot, Polemon.
What's worse, and you'll esteem it such,
She hates your company as much."—
" Is't true?" th' astonish'd lover cries.
" Alas! too true," the maid replies:
" I'm sure she beats me black and blue,
If once I dare but mention you."—
'Twas now Charisius plainly proved
He loved her more than he was loved.

---

[1] *Epistle XXII.*]　The address of a cunning maid-servant

(For oft when men neglect the fair,
Whose favours they might freely share,
A rival cleverly thrown in,
Their assiduities may win.)
His haughtiness was now no more;
He begg'd, protested, wept, and swore.
(For beyond bounds is pride dejected,
If once it find itself neglected.)
" Wherein," he cried, " wherein have I
Affronted her unknowingly?
For never purposely, I swear,
Offended I in aught the fair.—
But I 'll go deprecate her ire,
In person my offence inquire.—
Then let my charmer bring her action;
I 'll make her any satisfaction.
Though I have err'd, will no repentance
Induce her to revoke my sentence?"
But Doris hesitated yet,
To make the triumph more complete.
" If on my knees I try to move her,"
Exclaim'd the miserable lover,
" Still must I meet a harsh denial?"—
" Far be 't from me t' oppose the trial,"
Said Doris—" go—entreat her pity;
And still, perhaps, she may admit ye."—
Charisius now, with hope inspired,
(That beauteous youth, so long admired!)
A kind reception flew to meet,
And fell at his beloved's feet.
But Glycera in raptures gazed,
And from his knees the suppliant raised;
Then slily turn'd about to kiss
The hand which had been touch'd by his.
And soon was his forgiveness past,
For Love forbade her rage to last.
The crafty maid stood smiling by
The while, and archly wink'd her eye,
To show, that she alone had wit
To make the haughty swain submit.

EPISTLE XXIII.[1]   THE DOUBLE MISFORTUNE.

MONOCHORUS TO PHILOCUBUS.

How hard is my lot, and my fate how perverse!
Whom two dread misfortunes join forces to curse:
When one is sufficient to plague one's life through,
'Tis the devil indeed to be saddled with two:
And that each is an evil, will scarce be denied,
Though which the severest, is hard to decide.
First, a profligate jilt throws my money away—
Then my happier rivals all beat me at play:
For as soon as the dice and the tables are set,
Love pops in my head—spoils each cast and each bet.
Thus all my antagonists win what they will,
Though much my inferiors in practice and skill:
For disturb'd, I forget how the chances have gone,
And place to their side what I've gain'd on my own.
Then leaving my play for my mistress, I meet
A rebuff more severe than my former defeat:
For my rivals outbid me, enrich'd at my cost,
And give, what the moment before I have lost.
Scorn'd and slighted am I, the while they are carest,
And I lend them the weapon to stab my own breast.—
Thus misfortunes, together when join'd, become worse,
And gain from each other additional force.

EPISTLE XXIV.[2]   CONSTANCY.

MUSARIUM TO HER DEAREST LYSIAS.

My lovers, a detested set,
Last night at my apartments met.—
Long did they sit, and stare, while each
Seem'd to have lost the powers of speech;
Expecting when his neighbour's jaws
Should open in the common cause.
At length the boldest of the gang
Arose, and made a fine harangue.

[1] *Epistle XXIII.*] From a man unfortunate both in play and love.
[2] *Epistle XXIV.*] From a girl to her favoured lover, for whose sake she had dismissed her other admirers.

In which the wordy youth profest
Only t' advise me for the best:
But really meant (I guess'd his theme)
To rival you in my esteem.
" No girl," said he, " who treads the stage,
Like you can all our hearts engage ;
And since your charms surpass them all,
Why should your profits be so small ?
Whereas we gladly would supply you,
But are repulsed and slighted by you,
For Lysias ; who, to say the truth,
Is but a very awkward youth.
Did he remarkably excel us,
We had no reason to be jealous :
And you might feasibly maintain
That beauty pleased you more than gain.
But now you 've not a single plea
For praising him to this degree.
And yet you still remain the same,
And stun us with his odious name ;
So oft repeated, that we seem
To hear it even when we dream.
Can it be passion thus to dote ?
No—'t must some phrensy sure denote.
But all we now desire to hear, is
A faithful answer to our queries.
Can Lysias only touch your breast ?—
Resolve you to dismiss the rest ?—
Speak but the word—and we desist ;
But let us know your mind at least."
Thus the whole evening did they preach
In many a long and fruitless speech.
But 'twould require a day and more
To copy half their nonsense o'er—
Suffice it, all their idle chat
Went in at this ear, out at that.
This, and this only, I replied,
" 'Tis Cupid that my choice did guide :
He bade my heart its feelings own ;
For Lysias live—for him alone."

"Who," cried they, "would that wretch admire,
That antidote to all desire?
What heart for such a clown can pine?"—
"Mine," answer'd I with rapture, "mine."
Then rising, "Fare ye well," I cried,
"But cease my lover to deride.
Your proffer'd treasures I despise,
In Lysias all my transport lies."—
Haste then, loved youth, oh hither haste;
The precious moments do not waste:
Oh bring me but one tender kiss;
With int'rest I'll repay the bliss.
Oh! grant me, Venus, this request,
And send the idol of my breast.—
Come, Lysias, come, and soothe my pangs,
On thee my very being hangs.
E'en while I write time slips away:
Then why this torturing delay?—
Ne'er shall those brutes avail with me—
They're satyrs, when compared with thee.

EPISTLE XXV.[1]　THE SISTERS.

PHILANIS TO PETALA.

As yesterday I went to dine
With Pamphilus, a swain of mine,
I took my sister, little heeding
The net I for myself was spreading;
Though many circumstances led
To prove she'd mischief in her head.
For first her dress in every part
Was studied with the nicest art:
Deck'd out with necklaces and rings,
And twenty other foolish things;
And she had curl'd and bound her hair
With more than ordinary care:
And then, to show her youth the more,
A light, transparent robe she wore—

---

[1] *Epistle XXV.*] From a girl, accusing her sister of seducing her lover's affections.

From head to heel she seem'd t' admire
In raptures all her fine attire:
And often turn'd aside to view
If others gazed with raptures too.—
At dinner, grown more bold and free,
She parted Pamphilus and me;
For veering round unheard, unseen,
She slily drew her chair between.
Then with alluring, am'rous smiles,
And nods, and other wanton wiles,
The unsuspecting youth insnared,
And rivall'd me in his regard.—
Next she affectedly would sip
The liquor that had touch'd his lip.
He, whose whole thoughts to love incline,
And heated with th' enliv'ning wine,
With interest repaid her glances,
And answer'd all her kind advances.
Thus sip they from the goblet's brink
Each other's kisses while they drink;
Which with the sparkling wine combined,
Quick passage to the heart did find.
Then Pamphilus an apple broke,
And at her bosom aim'd the stroke;
While she the fragment kiss'd and press'd,
And hid it wanton in her breast.
But I, be sure, was in amaze,
To see my sister's artful ways:
" These are returns," I said, " quite fit
To me, who nursed you when a chit.
For shame, lay by this envious art;—
Is this to act a sister's part?"
But vain were words, entreaties vain,
The crafty witch secured my swain.—
By heavens, my sister does me wrong;
But oh! she shall not triumph long.
Well Venus knows I'm not in fault—
'Twas she who gave the first assault:
And since our peace her treach'ry broke,
Let me return her stroke for stroke.

She'll quickly feel, and to her cost,
Not all their fire my eyes have lost—
And soon with grief shall she resign
Six of her swains for one of mine.

EPISTLE XXVI.[1] THE PANTOMIME ACTRESS.

SPEUSIPPUS TO PANARETE.

Long had Fame thy praises sung,
Sweetest theme of every tongue:
Long mine ears those graces knew,
Which till now ne'er blest my view.
Now thy charms my bosom fire,
More and more I now admire;
Finding them so far excel
All that Fame had words to tell.
On thy gestures who could gaze,
Nor be lost in wild amaze?
Who unhurt, with bosom cold,
Could thy beauteous form behold?—
'Mong th' immortal race divine,
Venus and Polymnia[2] shine.
They presided at thy birth,
And ordain'd, that thou on earth,
Like th' expressive muse shouldst move,
And inspire, like Venus, love.
Art thou orator or painter?
Which allusion is the quainter?
Words thou canst with skill express;
Things in native colours dress;
While thy animated arm,
Limbs with elocution warm;
Motions just, and nicely true,
Are thy tongue and pencil too.

---

[1] *Epistle XXVI.*] A panegyrical Epistle to a pantomime actress
(ΟΡΧΗΣΤΡΙΔΑ). The celebrated Casaubon, who wrote some critiques
upon this work, points out a peculiar elegance in this Epistle; but it is
to be feared much of it depended on the expressions of the original.—
However, it throws some light on the art of the ancient times.

[2] *Polymnia* particularly presided over gesture.

Thou, thus eloquently mute,
Canst each part, like Proteus, suit:
As the strains, or light or slow,
Bid successive passions flow.

Now with loud-applauding hand
See the rapt spectators stand:
Now you hear th' astonish'd throng
Joining in alternate song:
Now they shake their robes in praise;[1]
Now in speechless wonder gaze:
While in whispers each explains
What thy mimic silence means;
And to show his approbation,
Labours at thy imitation.
Thou with gestures nice, exact,
Dost like Caramallus act:
Him thy all-expressive grace
Doth with true resemblance trace.
Pleased may e'en the wise, the old,
Thy dumb eloquence behold:
Such amusements to attend,
Gravity may well unbend.—
I, on public business bound,
Many cities have gone round;
Either Rome I 've travell'd through,
Both the ancient and the new;
Yet in neither did I see
Aught that might be match'd with thee.—

Such thy charms, and such thy art;
Blest is he who wins thy heart!

EPISTLE XXVII.[2] THE COXCOMB.

CLEARCHUS TO AMYNANDER.

As just beneath a lady's eye
A youth officiously pass'd by,

---

[1] *Now they shake their robes, &c.*] This was a sign of the highest approbation among the ancients.
[2] *Epistle XXVII.*] From a lady, ridiculing the addresses of a self-sufficient lover.

Another lady, standing near,
Jogg'd her, and whisper'd in her ear,
" Yon swain, by Beauty's queen 'tis true,
Walk'd by to be observed by you ;
And really, on examination,
His figure merits observation.
His dress is very neatly laced,
And fashion'd with a pretty taste.
And then observe, his jetty hair
Is buckled with the nicest care
(For Cupid can transform, you know,
The greatest sloven to a beau)."
" That man," said t' other, " I detest,[1]
However shaped, however dress'd,
Who flatters his own charms too much,
And thinks we can't resist the touch.
This made him choose, and this alone,
The name of Philo for his own :
This gave the self-sufficient airs
Which in his haughty brow he bears.
I hate the lover who can dare
To be a rival to the fair :
Who, if she deign to bless his arms,
Thinks he repays her charms for charms.
The man who courts a lady so,
Courts only that the world may know.
But hear me vex my stately swain,
It cannot fail to entertain :—
' A youth there is who frequent tries
With love my bosom to surprise ;
In vain my court he daily haunts,
In vain his idle ditties chaunts ;—
Yet fears not to repeat his song,
Both every day, and all day long :
While I tormented hide my face,
And blush myself for his disgrace.' "

    Thus with insulting words the fair
    Mock'd her desponding lover's care :

----

[1] *That man*, &c.] This is a very lively description of an intriguing
coxcomb ; and perhaps not inapplicable to some modern characters.

And then, to fasten his devotion,
Contrived, with easy, careless motion,
A leg of most enchanting shape
Should from beneath her robe escape.

The poor Adonis heard, and view'd
Just as the lady wish'd he should:
And, "Oh! insulting maid," he cried,
"Continue still my flame to chide:
Not me thy bitter taunts approach,
The god of Love alone they touch:
Nor he, I trust, will bear them long,
But choose an arrow sure and strong;
The shaft thy stubborn heart shall gore,
And thou in turn my love implore."
"That dreadful lot far distant be,"
She cried affectedly, "from me!
Go on, vain youth, persist to please
Your pride with such conceits as these;
And wait till your superior beauty
Compels my love-sick heart to sue t' ye;
And till avenging Cupid draws
His bow, to vanquish in your cause.
Meantime, still haunt my court in vain,
And chaunt, and watch, and chaunt again:
On Love's tempestuous billows tost,
Too weak to keep or quit your post;
Forbidden aught to touch that's mine,
And left with hopeless cares to pine,
And not a kiss your toils repay—
Yet have not strength to get away."

EPISTLE XXVIII.[1]   THE RIVAL FRIENDS.

NICOSTRATUS TO TIMOCRATES.

TYRANT o' the heart! inconstant, faithless boy!
Source of these tears—as once dear source of joy!—
Inhuman trifler! whose delusive smile
Charms to insnare, and soothes but to beguile—

Epistle XXVIII.] From a lover, resigning his mistress to his friend.

Hence! tyrant, I renounce thy sway.—And thou,
False goddess, who prepar'st the stripling's bow,
Whose skill marks out the soft, the yielding heart,
Guides the boy's arm, and barbs the madd'ning dart,
Thou shalt no more my midnight vows receive,
To thee no more the votive fruits I 'll give,
No more for thee the festive altar raise,
Nor ever tune another note of praise.

This I have done.—Witness, each sacred grove!
Where wand'ring lovers sing the maid they love;
Ye awful fanes! to this false goddess raised,
Fanes that have oft with my free incense blazed;
And chiefly thou, sweet solitary bird,
Bear witness to my vows,—for thou hast heard;
And many a night hast braved the dewy wind,
To soothe, with thy soft notes, my pensive mind:
But when the churlish blast has hush'd thy lays,
Have I not fill'd the interval with praise—
With praise still varied to the Cyprian queen,
And sighs, the heart's best tribute, breathed between
Till slumb'ring Echo started from her cave,
Admiring at the late response she gave;
And thou, best warbler of the feather'd throng,
With double sweetness didst renew thy song.
—Nor were ye slow, ye gentle gales of night,
To catch such notes, and stop your silent flight,
Till on your dewy wings, with morrow's rays,
To Cypria's queen ye waft the song of praise.
—In vain! officious gales;—she heeds you not;
My vows are scorn'd, and all my gifts forgot:
A happier rival must her power defend;—
And in that rival I have lost a friend!

Thee then, my friend—if yet a wretch may claim
A last attention by that once dear name—
Thee I address:—the cause you must approve;—
I yield you—what I cannot cease to love.
Be thine the blissful lot, the nymph be thine:—
I yield my love—sure friendship may be mine.
Yet must no thought of me torment thy breast;—
Forget me, if my griefs disturb thy rest,

Whilst still I'll pray that thou may'st never know
The pangs of baffled love, or feel my woe.
But sure to thee, dear charming—fatal maid!
(For me thou'st charm'd, and me thou hast betray'd,)
This last request I need not recommend—
Forget the lover thou, as he the friend.
Bootless such charge! for ne'er did pity move
A heart that mock'd the suit of humble love.—
Yet in some thoughtful hour, if such can be,
Where Love, Timocrates, is join'd with thee,
In some lone pause of joy, when pleasures pall,
And fancy broods o'er joys it can't recall,
Haply a thought of me, (for thou, my friend,
May'st then have taught that stubborn heart to bend,)
A thought of him, whose passion was not weak,
May dash one transient blush upon her cheek;
Haply a tear—(for I shall surely then
Be past all power to raise her scorn again)—
Haply, I say, one self-dried tear may fall:
One tear she'll give,—for whom I yielded all!
Then wanton on thy neck for comfort hang,
And soon forget the momentary pang;
Whilst thy fond arms—Oh down, my jealous soul!
What racking thoughts within my bosom roll!
How busy fancy kindles every vein,
Tears my burst heart, and fires my madd'ning brain.—
Hush'd be the ill-timed storm—for what hast thou,
Poor outcast wretch, to do with passion now?
I will be calm;—'tis Reason's voice commands,
And injured Friendship shakes her recent bands.
I will be calm;—but thou, sweet peace of mind,
That rock'd my pillow to the whistling wind;
Thou flatt'rer, Hope! thyself a cure for sorrow,
Who never show'd'st the wretch a sad to-morrow,
Thou coz'ner, ever whisp'ring at my ear
What vanity was ever pleased to hear—
Whither, ye faithless phantoms, whither flown!
—Alas! these tears bear witness ye are gone.
Return!—In vain the call! ye cannot find
One blissful seat within this sullen mind:

Ye cannot mix with Pride and surly Care;
Ye cannot brood with Envy and Despair.

My life has lost its aim! that fatal fair
Was all its object, all its hope or care;
She was the goal to which my course was bent,
Where every wish, where every thought was sent;
A secret influence darted from her eyes,—
Each look, attraction! and herself the prize.
Concentred there, I lived for her alone,—
To make her glad, and to be blest, was one.

Her I have lost!—and can I blame this poor
Forsaken heart—sad heart that joys no more!
That faintly beats against my aching breast,
Conscious it wants the animating guest:
Then senseless droops, nor yields a sign of pain,
Save the sad sigh it breathes, to search in vain.

Adieu, my friend,—nor blame this sad adieu,—
Though sorrow guides my pen, it blames not you.
Forget me—'tis my prayer; nor seek to know
The fate of him whose portion must be woe,
Till the cold earth outstretch her friendly arms,
And Death convince me that he can have charms.

E'en where I write, with desert views around,
An emblem of my state has sorrow found:
I saw a little stream full briskly glide,
Whilst some near spring renew'd its infant tide;
But when a churlish hand disturb'd its source,
How soon the panting riv'let flagg'd its course!
Awhile it skulk'd sad murm'ring through the grass
Whilst whisp'ring rushes mock'd its lazy pace;
Then sunk its head, by the first hillock's side,
And sought the covert earth, it once supplied.

THE END.

INDEX.

2 к